Fr Ca
emndefull of
pampered, bed.me ~ a genui
saint

MW00571141

EMBRACING SERAFINA

with my best wishes,
cathy, Penny Petrone

PROSE SERIES 56

Guernica Editions Inc. acknowledges support of The Canada
Council for the Arts.
Guernica Editions Inc. acknowledges support from the Ontario
Arts Council.

Canadä

Guernica Editions Inc. acknowledges the financial support of the
Government of Canada through the Book Publishing Industry
Development Program (BPIDP).

PENNY PETRONE

EMBRACING SERAFINA

GUERNICA
TORONTO·BUFFALO·LANCASTER (U.K.)
2000

Copyright © 2000, by Penny Petrone and Guernica Editions Inc.
All rights reserved. The use of any part of this publication,
reproduced, transmitted in any form or by any means, electronic,
mechanical, photocopying, recording or otherwise stored in a
retrieval system, without the prior consent of the publisher is an
infringement of the copyright law.

Antonio D'Alfonso, editor
Guernica Editions Inc.
P.O. Box 117, Station P, Toronto (ON), Canada M5S 2S6
2250 Military Road, Tonawanda, N.Y. 14150-6000 U.S.A.
Gazelle, Falcon House, Queen Square, Lancaster LA1 1RN U.K.

Printed in Canada.

Legal Deposit — First Quarter
National Library of Canada
Library of Congress Catalog Card Number: 99-76609
Canadian Cataloguing in Publication Data
Petrone, Penny
Embracing Serafina
(Prose series ; 56)
Sequel to: Breaking the mould.
ISBN 1-55071-112-1
1. Petrone, Penny. 2. Authors, Canadian (English) — 20th century
— Biography. 3. Italian Canadian — Ontario — Thunder Bay —
Biography. I. Title. II. Title: Breaking the mould. III. Series
FC3099.T48Z49 2000 C818'.5409 C99-901598-2
F1059.5.T44P48 2000

Contents

DEDICATED TO CALABRIA

The Road to Now

In 1995 I published *Breaking the Mould*, my memoir that tells what it was like growing up in Port Arthur, as the daughter of Italian immigrants, pulled in one direction by my parents' insistence on Old World traditions and in the opposite direction by a dominant society that was xenophobic and WASP, a term I did not know then. For all their wisdom, my parents were blissfully unaware of my dilemma. In my desire to fit in and feel more accepted in the mainstream society of the city I was born in, I discarded my Italian name, Serafina, which I abhorred, and called myself Penny. I was seventeen.

By this time I had become thoroughly assimilated and deeply devoted to British traditions, British royalty and the British Empire. I loved the cadences and hypnotic rhythms of Churchill's speeches and admired English courage during the Battle of Britain. Never once did I question the rightness of colonization and my unexamined assimilation. I was English. I loved my new English name, Penny.

And so it was that as Penny Petrone I circled the globe, travelling to seven continents, seven seas, eighty countries and a million miles or more.

I have been told that travel becomes more meaningful in retrospect, after distance and the passage of time have enabled one to reflect upon one's past experience. Now, over four decades after my first trip abroad, I am beginning to examine my life of travel, to confront the reasons for my restlessness.

I did not resolve this question in *Breaking the Mould*. My memoir ended when I was twenty, in my second year of teaching, in a one-room rural school. I had not yet begun my odyssey.

toward 1997

In my Philosophy of Education courses I taught that the ancient Greek philosopher, Socrates, had said that the unexamined life is not worth living. I have also read somewhere that knowledge of self is a lifetime job. It has taken me four years after writing *Breaking the Mould* to reflect on the motives that prompted my lifetime of travel. Looking back, I now realize that I had been pursuing some end, intangible and largely inarticulate, arbitrarily summed up in notions of fun, adventure, romance and learning, and that I was ill-equipped to grasp the deeper motivation which had something to do with what I was trying to discover and at the same time trying to escape. I am finally forced to expose something I have always hidden from myself — the Serafina within the Penny. Paradoxically, the very being I was avoiding was the very being I was trying to find in foreign lands, struggling within and against captivity.

My epiphany took place in 1997 in my mother's home town in Piane Crati in Southern Italy. At a ceremony making me an honourary citizen of the town, I was finally able to exorcise the hatred so deeply rooted in my psyche for my Italian name, Serafina, and to accept my true identity.

Embracing Serafina tells the story of this quest for my true identity, my long journey that enabled Penny to accept Serafina, so long silenced. To embrace my Italianness without shame, to embrace Serafina.

In writing this book, I have come to realize that I am both women, Serafina, the Italian girl I thought I could reject and Penny, the English woman I wanted to become. It has taken me over half a century to recognize this truth: I am both Penny and Serafina.

My lifelong journey began in the Summer of 1952 when three girlfriends and I travelled to Europe. The trip was a newsworthy item that made the society page of the local daily paper, *The News-Chronicle*. Travelling abroad in 1952 was still beyond the wildest dreams of the inhabitants of Port Arthur.

Mass tourism was unheard of. Passenger air travel had not arrived. There were no travel agencies such as we have today. Except for a few financially independent single women high school teachers, it was the rare individual who could travel abroad.

I did not know it at the time, but my Summer trip of 1952 would be the beginning of a life of travel. My first trip to Europe had captivated me completely. It had worked wonders on my wobbly self-esteem. I felt newly liberated, finding the freedom, acceptance and respectability that eluded me in the little town where I was born, but never felt I belonged. My appetite for travel had been awakened. It had so exhilarated me that when I heard, three years later, that Canada's Department of National Defence was looking for teachers for its overseas school system in Europe, I applied immediately!

At the time I was teaching at Hillcrest High School and living at home with my parents. To be a member of an Italian family was never to be simply yourself. Family members were expected to suppress their own individuality within the traditional and confining structure of the family. I needed to get away. When the Port Arthur Public School Board agreed to give me a two-year secondment to teach in Germany, I was ecstatic. I was asserting my own identity. I was escaping the family despite my mother's admonition that the beaten path is the safe path.

I taught in Germany from 1955-1956, and in France from 1956 to 1958, returning home in 1958. During my three years' residence in Europe, I travelled extensively in Western Europe with my teaching colleagues and our male friends in the Services. We were all young and carefree Canadians seeking and finding adventure and romance, new friends and experiences. But for me, it was also something more.

Germany was forever gray, damp and chilly, and I longed for the sun. I spent the Summer of 1956 travelling alone through the sun-drenched countries of the Balkans and the Middle East. It did not occur to me, however, that an unaccompanied female was viewed with suspicion and considered fair game in these countries. I was unaware, too, of the volatile political situation between East and West. Because of my ignorance, the trip had its dangerous encounters. But apart from them, the trip held the same magic I felt when I first set foot in Europe in 1952.

During the summer of 1957 I made pilgrimages to a number of religious shrines including Lourdes, Avila, and Fatima travelling through France, Spain and Portugal. In Spain I saw my first bullfight in Valencia and the famous Running of the Bulls in Pamplona. I flew to England, but did not find the sun which travel folders claimed I could find on the English Riviera. I visited Ireland for the first time and kissed the celebrated Blarney Stone. My summer holidays ended in Scotland where, to my delight, I heard Maria Callas, the tempestuous Metropolitan Opera prima donna.

During the Summer of 1958 I joined the first bus tour from the West that was given permission to travel behind the Iron Curtain. We, in the West, were absolutely terrified of Communism, and I must confess I was really frightened during the whole tour. But I witnessed this dreaded ideology at work, first hand, and although I could admire the zeal of the people I met, for their utopian Bolshevik dream, I was not convinced it was a better political and social system than my own.

When I returned home after my three year stay in Europe, I was interviewed by the media, and a number of articles on my travels appeared in the local newspapers, *The News-Chronicle* in Port Arthur and *The Times-Journal* of Fort William, our twin city. I was swamped with invitations to speak. My talks on the Holy Land and on my trip behind the Iron Curtain were especially popular. My travels were giving me the respectability I craved. I even appeared on local television promoting the advantages of travel in a speech which I gave on an afternoon programme. With my 8 mm Bolex-Paillard movie camera, I had made movies of my trips and they, too, were much in demand.

I had just returned from my three year stint in Europe and less than a year later, I was making plans to go abroad again. The thought of circling the globe tantalized me. Europe was the trendy destination then, and the Far East was still untravelled. In recent years television and motion pictures have brought the region into our very living rooms. We even watched the Vietnam War on television. But it was 1959, years before anyone had heard about the Viet Cong, the Khmer Rouge and the Killing Fields, years, too, before karma, mantra and guru became household words, and before the beatniks and hippies discovered India, Nepal and Afghanistan.

Since the jet plane was now making travel to distant places more convenient, I was sure we could go around the world during my two month summer vacation and be back in time to teach early in September. I mentioned my plans to Miss Rutledge, longtime head of the Commercial Department at Hillcrest, who was nearing retirement. She needed no encouragement; she decided to join me immediately. She was larger than life — a formidable presence in the school whose enormous energy and insistence on excellence intimidated all students.

We had no time to prepare ourselves for the trip. As a result, we harboured no expectations. I wanted my trip to be full of surprises. After all, if you know everything about a place, why go? The wonder engendered by just being in a place is an attraction in itself. We agreed not to nail ourselves to a firm itinerary.

My mother, of course, was not happy. Rooted in her Calabrian psyche was the notion that talking about dangers prevented them, and airing fears dissipated the conditions that caused them. I don't know how many times she repeated the Italian equivalent to "a rolling stone gathers no moss." I don't know how many times she warned me about the dangers and temptations of strangers and the outside world. Without fail, each time I was leaving home, in true Southern Italian fashion, she thought in terms of disaster. Her last words would be, "go away but you won't find me here when you come back." Exasperated, she entrusted me to God's care. Assured in the belief that I would be looked after by Divine Providence, and wholly absorbed in the care of her family, she could return to her daily routines. But I felt guilty. I left her forwarding addresses but she rarely wrote me. Nor did we ever telephone each other. Long

distance telephone communication was practically unheard of in those days.

Looking back, I am surprised that, although my
mother disapproved of my "gadding about" so much,
she put no pressure on me to get married and have
children. I did not have a hope chest which needed to be
filled while I waited for a marriage proposal. In some
ways my mother was ahead of her time. In the 50s,
women's magazines still promoted marriage as the final
goal, and careers for women merely a stop-gap between
a father's home and marriage. As a teacher I had a career
I loved. And with the money I saved, I travelled. Travelling allowed me to see beyond the confines of home and
city. Gradually, through the years, I discovered that I
could take care of myself. After all, I was not raised to
wait for my Prince Charming.

My global odyssey was a culture shock. I wandered
among people and scenes unimaginably removed from
anything I had ever known. My world of western ideas,
traditions and customs had been shattered. Direct contact with civilizations so antithetical to my own made me
admire many of their qualities: their dignity and poise in
the midst of abject poverty; their attitudes towards time
and mortality and suffering; their lack of consumerism
and materialism; their unhurried, small social graces and
conventions; their heroic efforts struggling for their very
survival. Everything was so new, so unrelated to anything I had encountered in my Italian and Roman
Catholic upbringing and British/Canadian education.
For the first time in my life I realized that "Religion is
the base of culture."

My trip had also taught me how unjust, societies can
be. The discrimination against women appalled me. My
own struggles and confusions in my private life suddenly

became minuscule. But I knew I would never be the same again.I now began to question British imperialism and colonization, as well as our arrogant and sanctimonious attitudes of cultural superiority. I had learned, for example, that while Christendom declared the world to be flat, Moslems were teaching geography with the use of globes. I had seen ruins of past empires that testified to complex societies and architectural achievements that had succumbed to the decay of time and conquest.

But I was surprised that foreign countries knew so very little about Canada. It seemed as if we had no national identity. I began to think a lot about what it meant to be a Canadian.

The next year, 1960, I left secondary school teaching to accept a position in the newly opened Lakehead Teachers' College. By this time I was becoming obsessed with the Philosophy of Education. I was interested only in intellectual stimulation and worked hard at excelling in my own teaching and at inspiring my student teachers to be the best, forever quoting Browning to them: "ah, but thy reach should exceed thy grasp,/Or what's a heaven for." I revelled in the joy of teaching and consciously sought to acquire a large repertoire of teaching approaches which would be most engaging and productive for my students. I also subscribed to mastery learning.

My educational philosophy had been deepened and developed by my travel experiences around the world. It was 1960. Like Tennyson's Ulysses, "I [was] a part of all that I [had] met!" I poured my intellectual energies into my English and Philosophy of Education courses, trying to bring the outside world into the cloistered lives of my students. I encouraged them to travel, to learn about other cultures and world views, and to question their own. Many of them did.

I had no patience with administrative political correctness. I expressed my stance with these two lines from Kipling: "Daughter am I in my father's house,/But mistress in my own." When I shut the door to my classroom, I was happiest because then I was free. I chose themes of alienation, social repression and racism for my literature classes.

I encouraged critical thinking. I was now openly questioning British colonialism and saw the connections between Asia's colonials and the disenfranchised Natives of Canada. I began teaching poems like "The Negress," by Audrey Alexandra Brown; "The Half-Breed Girl," by Duncan Campbell Scott and his other poems about Canadian Natives; "The Gipsy Girl," by Ralph Hodgson; and "The Congo," by the African American poet, Vachel Lindsay.

I fostered a love for Canada, Canadian history and Canadian nationalism and I emphasized poems by Earle Birney, E. J. Pratt, and the Confederation poets, Charles G. D. Roberts and Bliss Carman. This was six years before Expo 67, when Canada would be a century old and caught up in the debate about Canadian national identity.

As a teacher of Grades V and VI Social Studies many years ago, I had conformed to the authorized curriculum and focussed only on pirates and buccaneers, swashbuckling sea captains like Sir Francis Drake and John Hawkins who were knighted by a grateful English Queen for their daring raids on Spanish galleons, but I had taught virtually nothing about the indigenous peoples of the New World, the Caribs, Arawaks, Incas, Mayans and Aztecs. In the summer of 1961 I would go to the Caribbean and to South America to learn about these ancient and complex civilizations. I also went seeking the sun because I suffered from chronic respiratory and sinus infections during our long and cold winters.

I had seen the misery and squalor in Asia, but I did not expect them in the New World where I saw illiteracy, malnutrition, high infant mortality, low life expectancy and wealth ordained to a privileged few. I now understood that indigenous America was a product of past colonial history and present capitalist imperialism. I returned to Canada deeply repelled by what I had seen. I wanted to help.

In 1963 Canada's Department of External Aid accepted my application to teach in their Special Commonwealth Africa Aid Programme, assigning me to Bishop Willis Teacher Training College in Iganga, Uganda. Despite my mother's protests and those of friends who kept reminding me of the Mau-Mau horrors and despite my own fears of catching malaria, I was looking forward to my posting. Publishers and friends provided me with a plethora of teaching materials that ranged from jelly pads and tuning forks to picture books.

By 1963, after travelling through the colonial worlds of Asia and South America, I was convinced that colonialism was an unmitigated evil. I left home with messianic dedication and zeal to help the "poor" natives.

It was the most exciting year of my life. I travelled extensively throughout Africa, a world totally unlike any I'd ever known. I delighted in its diversity of mass, contour, colour and animal life. In grade school I had been taught that the big animals lived in the jungle, but to my amazement, I found out that this was not true.

However, it was the African people who intrigued me most. Over the year I became attached to them and realized that they were as contradictory and complex as peoples anywhere. In getting to know them, I grew to love them. I had arrived with my stereotypes, ready to civilize and educate "the pagans" and "the primitive savages." But they educated me instead. I found a new world of ideas, attitudes and ways of behaviour enjoyed by generations of ancestors, and civilizations more developed and stable than I had ever imagined.

After I returned home from Africa, there was a lull in my life of travel. Since Ontario Teachers' Colleges were to be amalgamated into the Universities, I was advised to begin post-graduate study, not in education, but in English Literature, my academic discipline. As a result, my next four summers were spent studying for my M.A. in English. I chose the University of Ottawa because it was the only bilingual university in Ontario, and I wanted to improve my French conversational skills. However, I soon discovered the presence of "two solitudes." I had to give up my idea of perfecting my French there.

I loved academic life. I was always a dedicated and serious student. It was the mid-1960s, and Canadian Literature was still unknown on Canadian University campuses. My American Literature Professor, Dr. O'Neill, used the last two weeks of the course to lecture on "Can Lit." I was mesmerized. Dr. O'Neill was the best teacher I have ever had.

In my seventeenth century British authors class, I met a Ph.D. candidate, Jim (not his real name), who was writing his thesis on Jean-Jacques Rousseau's Natural Man. I was impressed. I soon discovered that he had studied for the priesthood at the Jesuit Seminary, had left and married. His wife had died seven years earlier of breast cancer, leaving him with an eight-year-old daughter. On 1 September 1965, seven weeks after we had met, we married. I was transferred to Ottawa Teachers' College to be with him. But our marriage soon turned into disaster. I wanted a companion; he preferred his drinking buddies. He was dour and laconic. I broke up our marriage after three months. I was consumed with guilt. I felt nothing but despair. How I got through those days of pain, I'll never know. Only through the kindness of good friends, like my teaching colleague, Inez Sunderland, was I able to cope.

In 1965 divorce was still a humiliation. My mother was scandalized. She told me she could no longer walk down the aisle of her church holding her head up high. I was too afraid to tell my Principal. I was anxious for a reconciliation, but a priest who had studied with Jim, to whom I kept going for advice, counselled against it. I even took the bold step of going to visit Jim's former mother-in-law in Montreal for advice. She agreed with the priest.

I loved teaching at Ottawa Teachers' College but an event soon happened which changed the course of my life.

In the summer of 1967, my doctor told me I needed a biopsy to determine whether or not I had breast cancer, but added that I could wait until I finished my summer courses. Immediately after they had ended, I went to the hospital. I woke up to find that my right breast had been removed.

I was sent to the Cancer Clinic in Port Arthur for my radiation treatments. My plans to spend more time at Expo '67 in Montreal after my Summer School ended were shattered. Luckily I had had a day's visit earlier in the year. I can still recall being overwhelmed by Habitat, Moshe Safdie's revolutionary experiment in city living which looked like a mammoth beehive hanging over the harbour, and Buckminster Fuller's radical geodesic dome puffing out over the American Pavilion.

But it was the Canadian Pavilion which was celebrating Canada's Centennial Year which interested me most. If I had been disappointed in the Canadian Pavilion at the Brussel's World Fair nine years earlier, I certainly wasn't now. For the first time, I heard the voices of Canada's Natives. A poem by Duke Redbird, an early red power militant, which was the theme of the pavilion, amazed me. I promised myself that I would return to spend more time here. I didn't make it.

Canada's one hundredth birthday generated an explosion of joy in Ottawa. It was a time for patriotism, American-style. I was no longer a British subject. The impulse to celebrate our history and our achievements had finally arrived. I was Canadian. The French President Charles de Gaulle's cry of *Vive le Québec libre*, uttered from the balcony of Montreal's City Hall during Expo 67, shocked me. I was glad that Prime Minister Lester B. Pearson compelled De Gaulle to leave Canada. Never could I have foreseen the militant French-Canadian nationalism that was brewing.

At the Port Arthur Cancer Clinic, I was given no hope for survival. Cancer in those days was an unspoken word. It was a death sentence, and few people were willing to discuss it. During my cobalt bomb radiation treatments at home, people were so terrified of "catching" it that I had very few visitors. However, my mother cared for me dearly.

As soon as my treatments were over, I returned immediately to Ottawa to finish the 1967-1968 school year. Fortunately, I had the support of very close friends who gave me the will to survive. And I wrote poetry:

> My God, my God
> Why me, why me, me?
> Why this sudden terror
> This tumour malignant
> This wild tissue disorder
> These cells unnatural
> Sinister, lethal
> Death in life.
> Fear ensnared.
> Dreams but shadows.
> Death a spectre
> Despised
> Why, why, why me?

In retrospect, I now wonder why, why, why not me? I hated to leave Ottawa Teachers' College.

When I did in June, the staff presented me with *The Oxford Companion to Canadian History and Literature* by Norah Story. No other gift could have been more fitting. I still have their gift card with thirty-six signatures. I always feel so grateful when I refer to it. And when I recall my wonderful days teaching at Ottawa Teachers' College and the lovely farewell party they gave me, I feel blessed. Not only did I survive, but I also, ironically, eventually contributed to subsequent editions of *The Companion.*

I went home to die. I had received a transfer back to Lakehead Teachers' College. Working was my salvation while I just waited. At a Christmas party, one of the guests, a local doctor, Dr. Schiewe, noticed that I looked depressed and defeated. He told me that I could fight cancer; he was the first person who had ever given me a modicum of hope. That's all the encouragement I needed. I would fight this dreaded disease.

I returned to the business of living with fresh hope and vitality. But I was forever feeling lumps in my left breast. I was afraid. As a last resort, I sought advice at the Mayo Clinic where, in desperation about the options I was given, I chose a prophylactic mastectomy of the left breast.

In a week's time I was back at work. My M.A. studies had to begin all over again at Lakehead University which offered only one M.A. type of thesis: the critical investigation of the extant books printed in the sixteenth century within a framework of the cultural conditions which produced them. It was so work-intensive that it had stopped several graduate English students from continuing. But I agreed to tackle the year 1594 because I felt so privileged to have been accepted. The research necessitated my reading 202 publications, most of them available only on microfilm, and many, hundreds of pages in length. Some had to be read at the libraries of the British Museum, the British and Foreign Bible Society and Westminster Abbey in London, Oxford and Cambridge Universities, Lincoln Cathedral and Edinburgh University.

In 1969 Lakehead Teachers' College was amalgamated into Lakehead University, the first Teachers' College in Ontario to do so. I was advised to get my Ph.D. Since my M.A. thesis dealt with the Elizabethan Age and the Renaissance in England, I decided to concentrate on Shakespeare. During the summer of 1970 I read everything he wrote in order to prepare myself for entry into the Ph.D. programme in English at the University of Alberta. But during a seventeenth century British Literature seminar I made a momentous decision.

There were two young Englishmen from Oxford and Cambridge Universities, on fellowships, taking the course. I was intimidated by their aura of complete self-confidence, their refined accents, and their low and controlled speaking voices. During a discussion the first week of classes on whether or not there was any such thing as Canadian Literature, they told me that Canadians had a colonial mentality, and an inferiority complex. We didn't even know whether a Canadian Literature existed. I knew that Canadian Literature, as a subject, was relatively unknown. By this time I was proud I was Canadian. Except for a two week course on Canadian Literature at the University of Ottawa, and a few Canadian writers I had lectured on, I did not know the history of Canadian Literature.

On the last day that we were allowed to change our courses, I changed my English specialization to Canadian. I took courses in Prairie Fiction by Rudy Wiebe, on Canadian Poetry by Dorothy Livesay and I audited a survey Canadian Literature course by Diane Bessai. I kept my seventeenth century British Literature seminar. In exchange for room and board I was Assistant Dean of Women at Pembina Hall, the Graduate residence for girls.

I loved graduate school. I was so busy studying and working that I hardly knew anything about the terrible events happening in my own country. I didn't have time to stop and think about the murder of Pierre Laporte or Prime Minister Pierre Trudeau and his federal Cabinet invoking the *War Measures Act*, suspending civil liberties in Canada. However, I did take an hour off my precious studies to go hear Réné Levesque speak at the University. He was so charismatic he nearly won my sympathy. But

I was too preoccupied in my studies to give the shocking events in Quebec much thought.

Dorothy Livesay suggested I do my doctoral research on Isabella Valancy Crawford (1850 - 1887), a little known Canadian free-lance writer whose literary reputation had been based on her poetry. I spent several summers trying to locate Crawford's prose in unindexed nineteenth century magazines and stopping at old houses on my route to investigate attics for possible old magazines. A number of her short stories, which I did find, I published in *Selected Stories of Isabella Valancy Crawford* (1975). Two years later in 1977 I published *Fairy Tales of Isabella Valancy Crawford.*

One summer, which is especially dear to me, I spent researching Isabella with Dorothy, driving throughout Crawford country — the Bruce Peninsula and the Kawarthas — in my big Wapmobile, as Bob Bubba, a fellow Ph.D. student, affectionately called my black Meteor Rideau. Dorothy was a wonderful travelling companion: motherly, capricious, sociable, and she had a terrific sense of humour. During our tour I felt really privileged when we stopped to visit Margaret Lawrence in Lakefield and Al Purdy in Ameliasberg. We made a pilgrimage to the grave of Mazo de la Roche in a Clarkson cemetery. And Dorothy showed me where she wanted to be buried.

After a two year residency at the University of Alberta I returned in 1972 to Lakehead University where I had a cross-appointment with the Department of English. I received my Ph.D. in 1977.

In 1969 I had met Frank (not his real name), a University administrator. He was the one whose encouragement and emotional support, while I was studying for my Ph.D. in Edmonton, helped me through the ordeal. Frank was intelligent, astute and a good dancer. He could make me laugh and I fell in love with him gradually. But he could also be moody, defensive and burdened with an ingrained sense of WASP superiority. Our seven-year relationship was turbulent both in our private and public lives.

In 1975 the Faculty of Education at Lakehead University started the Native Teachers' Education Programme. Because of my travels throughout the Third World, I was seeing connections between the oppressed peoples there and the Native peoples of Canada. I felt that what they needed was to have their literature — so long unknown — recognized. I wrote over two hundred letters to museums and historical societies across Canada. Many replied that there was "no such literature." This response did not deter me. From 1975 to 1982 I travelled across Canada to archives, museums and several reservations trying to unearth this forgotten and buried material. It was a labour of love. I even travelled to Australia in 1980 in my sabbatical year, to gain insights into the aboriginal literary tradition there. I also threw my energies into conceiving a course on Native Literature in Canada. At first, only Native students were allowed to take it. As the course became more popular, non-Native students were allowed in it, and eventually the course was transferred to the Department of English where I taught it until I retired. In 1983 *First People, First Voices* was published. Here, available for the first time in a single volume, were selections of a rich Indian/Métis literature from a long history which has no certain beginning, arranged to give historical perspective and continuity.

Several years later I was commissioned by William Toye of the Oxford University Press to write a critical study of the literature of Canada's Native people. In 1990, *Native Literature in Canada: From the Oral Tradition to the Present* was published.

During my research for Canadian Indian/Metis literature, I came across Knud Rasmussen's *Report of the Fifth Thule Expedition 1921-24*. I was entranced. I mentioned this to my editor at the University of Toronto Press. *First People First Voices* had prompted nearly fifty reviews and sold so well that he suggested I do a similar book for Canada's Inuit. The material culture of the Inuit — their stone carvings, art, tapestries and print — was well-known, but their intellectual culture, the wisdom and truth in their stories and songs was not.

My research necessitated my travelling to a number of Canada's Arctic settlements to interview Inuit elders. It also involved my travelling to libraries at Harvard, Yale, and Dartmouth College where the Stefansson papers were located. I was intrigued when Stefansson compared Canada's Inuit to Southern Italians in North Pole dress. Many of the whaling masters who led expeditions to Canada's North came from American cities on the Northeastern Seaboard of the United States. I visited historical societies and museums to search for their diaries and logbooks in such places as Mystic Seaport, Providence, New London, New Bedford, and New Haven. In Groton, Connecticut, I made a pilgrimage to the grave of Tookoolito, an Inuk seamstress and interpreter born near Cumberland Sound in Baffin Island. Of all the Inuit who assisted the white man in the Arctic, Tookoolito and her husband, Ipirvik, were probably the most remarkable. The couple were the companions and mentors to the American explorer, Charles Francis Hall, in his Arctic expeditions. They accompanied him on his lecture tours in the United States to help him raise funds for his expeditions. Their courageous part during Hall's 1871 Polaris expedition is one of the most heroic in the annals of Arctic exploration. Tookoolito was living in the States when she died of tuberculosis on 31 December 1876.

While I was working in the National Archives and the Smithsonian Institute in Washington, I had to visit the Vietnam War Memorial. On 20 September 1986, I stood in awe before the monument. Maya Lin's black granite wedge was a monument of such touching nobility and dignity, a tribute so simple, factual and eloquent that long after I left, it resonated in my heart and head. A ceremony in the Memorial grounds attracted my attention. A small group of Canadian Vietnam veterans joined by about one hundred and fifty American veterans, many in fatigues, were paying tribute to Canada's war dead in Vietnam. I was surprised to see only one Canadian official present. The ceremony was a simple, quiet service of consolation and community. I was moved. When the American bugler sounded "Taps" I couldn't stop tears from welling upon my eyes.

In my search for more Inuit literature I travelled to the Scott-Polar Institute in Cambridge and the Moravian Archives in London. In the British Library in London and in the Liverpool Archives I researched John Ojijatekha Brant-Sero (1867-1914) a Mohawk celebrity, actor, interpreter, and lecturer, from the Six Nations Reserve near Brantford, Ontario. In 1908 he had won third prize at an international beauty show for gentlemen at Folkestone, England. This research led to an article which was later published in the *Dictionary of Canadian Biography*.

In 1988 *Northern Voices: Inuit Writing in English* was published.

My primary research on Native Literature in Canada prompted curiosity from scholars in Europe and as far as away as India and the Soviet Union. One of my essays, "Native Canadian Literature," translated into Chinese, appeared in *Literature in Canada* published by the Inner Mongolia University Press.

It was this interest in Canada's Inuit that prompted me in July of 1995 along with my cabinmate, Joan Frances Chapple, to board the Russian icebreaker, *Alla Tarasova*, in Baffin Island on an east coast environmental voyage of discovery along the shores of Labrador and Atlantic Canada.

The expedition featured the distinguished writer, Farley Mowat, who lectured on the Albans, a race of people whom Mowat believes reached Northern Canada before the Vikings. As an adjunct resource person, I spoke on the literature of the Inuit.

I was delighted when we stopped at Hebron on Labrador's shore, an abandoned Moravian Mission, where I picked up a shard of Moravian blue and white pottery which sits on the window ledge of my den, where it reminds me of the work of the early Arctic missionaries. But there is another event that keeps recurring in my memory. All day, on Shuldham Island in Saglek Bay, we had been admiring a magnificently massive iceberg as it sat, under brilliant sunshine in the calm waters, a scene that would have inspired Lawren Harris to paint. We reflected on its two and one-half year journey from the Greenland ice cap. On our way back to our ship we circumnavigated it at close range in our zodiac. Just as we struck away, we heard a deafening sound. We looked back and watched stupefied as the iceberg exploded, splintered and flipped over. There, before our very eyes we had witnessed the beauty and the awful power of Nature. If we had been any closer, we would have been sucked underneath the freezing waters of the North Atlantic. A sudden fright came over me.

But the Arctic kept luring me. I had become fascinated with the search for the Northwest Passage that had eluded so many Arctic explorers, for so long including Sir John Franklin. From 5 July to 5 August 1996, I was a member of an historic expedition through the fabled Northwest Passage aboard the Russian icebreaker, *Kapitan Dranitsyn*. We sailed the route from Provideniya in Siberia through the Bering Strait, the Chukchi Sea and the Arctic Ocean to Resolute in the high Arctic.

Shipboard seminars dealt with a variety of topics — Ice Recognition, Icebreaker Technology, Arctic Birds, Arctic Plants, Arctic Whales and Arctic Plankton — but no mention was made of the Inuit people and their culture. I brought this oversight to the attention of the Expedition Director who promptly suggested that I give a lecture on the Inuit of Canada. My lecture was entitled, "From the Inuit Point of View."

Herschel Island in the Beaufort Sea, the famous home base for American whalers who practically decimated the bowhead whale in the late 1800s and early1900s; the excellent Chukchi museum in Provideniya; the important archeological site at Ittygran in Siberia; the sightings of polar bears, muskox, seals or caribou; the pilgrimage to Beechey Island where Sir John Franklin and his crew spent the winter of 1845-1846 before they disappeared forever; the fascination with our powerful icebreaker as it battled its way through metres-thick, multi-year, unpredictable sea-ice; the wonderful buffet lunch of caribou sausage, muskox stroganoff, Arctic char and char chowder all thrilled me.

But none could surpass the wondrous sight, when, from our helicopter, I watched a pair of pristine white beluga whales frolicking in the translucent turquoise waters below us. Nor could they compare to the glorious early morning that glowed so full of a soft pure light, when seated in a zodiac in the vicinity of Prince Leopold Island, we glided among ice floes watching kittiwakes, guillemots and fulmars on the ice. Never before in my life had I felt so at one with nature. Never before had I felt so suffused with the beauty and sanctity of God's creation. Like William Blake I was holding "infinity in the palm of my hand and eternity in an hour."

My fascination with the North now encompassed the polar regions of the Southern Hemisphere. In the winter of 1995 I flew to Ushuaia, the world's southernmost city on the Argentinian side of Tierra del Fuego to board the ice-breaker, *Sergei Vavilov* that was sailing to Antarctica, but the ship was impounded by the Argentinian authorities, and the travel agency cancelled the trip. I was terribly disappointed because I knew I would never go back again.

However, we were allowed to stay on board the icebreaker (which was being guarded by Argentinian police) for the weekend to give us an opportunity to explore the area. Strangely enough, it was neither the penguin colonies, nor the scores of sea-lions, surely, the ugliest animals on earth, that we observed on our sea island tour, that fascinated me. It was the bustling modern town of Ushuaia. Finding a town about thirty thousand, the same size of the town I grew up in, at the end of the world shocked me. And seeing the *Alla Tarasova*, the Russian icebreaker I had travelled on during the summer of 1995 docked next to us in the harbour, was another shock. I went on board, and the first person I met was Stefan. We reminisced about our summer trip, recalling his breathtaking escape from drowning in the icy waters of the Arctic that made this brief trip so memorable.

In the summer of 1978, I had travelled to the Republic of China when, after thirty-two years of isolation, it opened its doors to the first non-speciality tourist group. This was one year before the arrival of Coca-Cola, and eleven years before the world watched in horror as Chinese tanks crushed the pro-democracy movement in Tiananmen Square. Twenty years earlier I had visited the workers' paradise in the U.S.S.R. The Western world was still living in fear of a nuclear attack by the U.S.S.R. and Communist China. This time I wanted to see, first hand, how the ideal society was working in China. I saw a country that had successfully revolutionized human beings. I was astounded. Mao Tse-Tung's dictum had worked: "There can be no construction without destruction." I questioned whether or not the end justified the means. At home there was a great deal of interest in my China trip. As a result, I spoke and showed my movies to a large number of associations and university students.

In the Fall of 1990 I was a member of a group from the National Congress of Italian Canadians that was invited to join the National Organization of Italian American women to attend an International Conference of Women of Italian Ancestry in Italy. Geraldine Ferraro, the first Italian American to run for the Vice-Presidency of the United States, headed the American delegation. I had been reluctant to join the group because I had always been embarrassed by my Italianness. But this trip proved to be an important decision in my life. Never before had I met so many intelligent, dynamic, attractive and successful women of Italian descent.

Their personal life stories resembled mine. We shared the difficulties of straddling two worlds, the personal insecurity, and the social and political prejudice and discrimination. I was surprised at the number of personal histories Italian Americans had written, for example, Pietro Di Donato's *Christ in Concrete,* Jerre Mangione's *Mount Allegro* and Helen Barolini's *Umbertina.* What I read was unbelievable. The history of Italian immigrants in that great bastion of freedom and democracy before and during World War II had been even more horrific than in my British dominion from sea to sea.

The women encouraged me to tell my own story. And so it was that on this trip the seeds for *Breaking the Mould* were planted. No Italian Canadian had told his or her story. I felt duty bound to set the record straight. But even after I had written a few tentative chapters, I was nervous. Who would want to read it? It wasn't until I read several working chapters of *Breaking the Mould* at a conference of the youth wing of the National Congress of Italian Canadians, at the University of Toronto, in February, 1992, that I was convinced that I should continue with the work. The young people's enthusiasm for, and identification with, what I had read was amazing. They gave me the incentive I needed to carry on.

After the book was published, I received scores of complimentary letters and telephone calls from readers of diverse background, who had read *Breaking the Mould* and wanted a sequel.

But I continued my travels, still on the run, still adrift in the world.

Two wilderness holidays around Lake Superior —
both of them with my friend Joan Skelton — remain in
my memory. On one, we saw the Agawa pictographs on
the North shore. The other was a hiking safari in Michigan's Huron mountains. To look at the pictographs
which are painted on a rock wall that plunges into the
lake, I had to pick my way cautiously along a sloping and
slippery ridge of rock within Superior's waters. One
false step would have thrown me into the frigid lake. I
was scared. At last I reached the red ochre paintings. But
they were hardly visible, and I was disappointed. However, I took time to trace one with my finger —
Michibizhiw, the great lynx, the feared and revered
underwater manitou of the Ojibwe, who controls the
waters of Gitchigaming (the great lake).

During the safari we had to cross a wide and deep
crevasse on a fallen trunk of a birch. I was petrified. The
guide held my hand. As well, we had to descend a wall
of rock nearly a hundred feet deep to step on a rock
ledge in the lake. Once again, I was frightened. But when
I stood on the ledge, I felt exhilarated. The lake was in
a benign mood, docile and brightly sparkling. As I gazed
at the vista of forest, rock and water I was reminded of
A. J. M. Smith's *The Lonely Land*:

> This is a beauty
> of dissonance,
> this resonance
> of stony strand . . .
> This is the beauty of strength
> broken by strength
> and still strong.

My eye caught a solitary bluebell clinging defiantly to
stubborn rock on the wall, and once again lines from a

poem I had studied long ago came to mind. This time it was Tennyson:

> Flower in the crannied wall
> . . . *if* I could understand
> what you are, root and all, and all in all,
> I should understand what God and man is.

I stood in awe of God's creation.

When I climbed back up to the top of the high cliff, I was ecstatic. My own physical strength and endurance had been tested. I felt rejuvenated and strong. I had always been attracted to the Old World rather than the New, to the urban cultures of distant lands. I was now being drawn to explore my own native land.

But even these trips did not fulfil me completely. I still felt an indiscernible complex of tensions in my personal life. It seemed as if I had three lives. My professional life had brought me success, international recognition, and self-fulfilment. My life of travel had given me adventure, fun, intellectual stimulation, friendship and even romance. In my private life, however, I was still keeping Serafina caged and anonymous. And I still cringed when I heard my Italian name. Beneath the outward show of strength and confidence lurked a vulnerability which even my closest friends were unaware of. On the deepest, most personal level, I still had to resolve my emotional struggle with the Italian and English/Canadian parts of me.

In 1995, Rita Pradissitto gave me a clipping of an item she had read in *Life Magazine* (5 June 1995) which contained a sentence from an official form letter sent during World War II to every British soldier in Italy who asked permission to marry an Italian girl: "Has anybody told you how quickly these Mediterranean women get ugly and old-looking?"

I was astounded. And angry. It was another example of racial discrimination and British arrogance. And suddenly I remembered my own experience with the armed forces in Europe. Hadn't I been the target of the same discrimination? After receiving marriage proposals from two Canadian officers, I was shocked to learn that their WASP parents convinced them that it would be beneath them to marry an "eyetalian."

By 1995, British colonialism and imperialism had become an anathema to me. I no longer harboured nostalgia for the good old days of British colonialism. I was no longer a daughter of the Empire. I was staunchly Canadian in heart and soul.

I had visited Italy many times, each time learning more and more about my Italian heritage, each time feeling less a stranger. In fact, I revelled in the company of Italians. During my 1987 trip when I lectured on Native Literature in Canada at the Universities of Messina, Catania, Bologna and Pisa, I felt at home. But I still had not been able to reconcile Serafina and Penny, my dual identity. It took another visit to Italy for me to sort it out and rescue Serafina.

This happened in the summer of 1997 when I was invited, once again, to give a series of lectures in Italy, and I took the opportunity to spend two weeks in Calabria to visit kinfolk I had never seen before. The visit was an epiphany for me. I enjoyed feeling connected to family, to blood relatives, to a past, to a culture which was my inheritance. Suddenly, for the first time, I knew who I was. And I was at peace. Suddenly, I understood that Penny and Serafina were not mutually exclusive identities. Italy had been the destination and the journey itself, the place and the process acting together as a sort of double catalyst.

It has taken me half a century to realize how well I was colonized, to realize, too, that we cannot escape our origins, however hard we try; in fact, those origins contain all that we later become. I am what inheritance, education, time, travel and work have made of me. I am also much more than that. So are we all.

I am no longer young. I am an old biddy. I live alone. I have outgrown my obsession with good looks. I have shed my contact lenses. I no longer dress to attract men. They no longer pursue me. But I no longer wait for them to call. I am blessed with many women friends I now find more interesting.

I still love to travel, but I take winter holidays now. I don't lie on sun drenched beaches because I can't tolerate the relentless heat of the sun. I still love to dance, but I do not have a dancing partner. However, I have been very fortunate.

My journey has ended. My search for identity is over. My inner scars have healed, but now I worry about my aging body. I cling to my memories. I may still not be able to wear sweatshirts that proclaim such messages as "Kiss me, I'm Italian," "Life is too short not to be Italian," or "Not only am I perfect, I'm Italian too," but I have embraced Serafina. I now celebrate my Italian heritage without shame. I even started a reading group where we discuss Italian literature in translation. And I no longer wince when I hear my Italian name. Well, maybe, not as much.

First Crossings, 1952

On Board the Scythia

On 7 July 1952 Margaret Mary Black, Shirley Matheson, Joan Gray and I left Quebec City on board the *RMS Scythia* bound for Southampton, England. A graduate of McGill University, Shirley was the Physical Education teacher at the Port Arthur Technical and Commercial High School, the Tech, as it was then popularly called (now Hillcrest High School). She was tall and attractive with fair hair and blue eyes. I thought she resembled Lauren Bacall. Originally from Chapleau, Ontario, she began her teaching career the year before at the Tech and boarded at her brother Goldie's home on Dawson Street not far from the school.

Margaret Mary, a tall brunette with creamy white skin, had been teaching Typing and Shorthand at the Tech for several years. She lived with her parents in the West Hotel which her family owned in Fort William. She was one of only two female teachers at the Tech who drove her own car. I admired her quiet composure at all times and her family status in the community.

I recall feeling so honoured whenever she invited me to dinner with her family in her father's hotel. I loved the formal table settings: the immaculately white linen table cloth and napkins, the crystal and bone china and after dinner coffee served in demitasses. At the time, such elegance made a deep impression on me.

When Shirley's neighbour, Joan Gray, heard of our plans to go abroad, she immediately became the fourth member of our group. Twenty-three years old, she was a few years younger than the rest of us. Petite and perky, with large blue eyes and sandy coloured hair, Joan held a coveted secretarial job at the Abitibi Woods Office. She had a steady boyfriend. I recall her dismissing my surprise at her leaving him for the summer with the quip, "All's fair in love and war." Joan's mother disapproved of her going "to run around Europe, especially in Italy, that horrible country." There was no cafeteria and no food dispensing machines where she worked. Joan, ever enterprising, sold sandwiches which she made in order to supplement her trip to Europe.

I was the new teacher at the Tech. I lived at home on North Hill Street, very close to the school. I had come up through the ranks having taught at the elementary level and then at high schools in Chapleau and Parry Sound under permit because I did not have my B.A. After studying for my B.A. through correspondence and summer courses from the University of Western Ontario, I took a year off from teaching to finish my degree at Assumption College in Windsor which was then affiliated with the University of Western Ontario. At the same time, I taught Physical Education for the Sisters of the Holy Name at St. Mary's Academy in exchange for room and board.

I was given a heavy teaching load: several large classes of Grade IX Business Practice, which I disliked; a Grade IX boys' class of English which I taught in the basement's furnace room; Grade XI Economic Geography and Grade XII Economics to an Industrial Arts boys' class. Except for the English course I had no expertise in the other subjects. Looking back I recall how easily I had

38   Embracing Serafina

accepted my heavy load. But I had been taught at home to be respectful, obedient and submissive.

I remember that, rather than have my students merely copy reams of notes, I encouraged creativity. The construction of the St. Lawrence Seaway, which would enable ocean-going vessels to sail to Thunder Bay, had been making newspaper headlines for months.

I encouraged my Grade XII Economics class to think critically about the significance of the project, a dream of both Sir John A. MacDonald and Sir Wilfred Laurier. They created the most wonderful projects from a scale model of the seaway to a huge wall mural. (On 9 July 1959 the Royal yacht, Britannia, with Queen Elizabeth and Prince Philip, sailed slowly along Thunder Bay's harbour officially launching the Seaway to the resounding cheers of the crowd. I was on my round-the-world-trip and missed the historic event.)

The regulation that any teacher who "smokes, uses liquor in any form, frequents pool or public halls, or gets shaved in a barber shop will give good reason to suspect his worth, intentions, integrity and honesty," may no longer have been an official edict. But the *Ontario Education Act* still mandated that teachers have "the highest regard" for "temperance, industry, sobriety, frugality, purity and all other virtues." I had never heard of the *Act*, but I knew we were expected to be beyond reproach. I recall that teachers did avoid smoking or drinking in public. They would either get a non-teacher to buy their beer or liquor or buy it themselves at a Liquor Control Board where they would not be recognized. Joan remembers that she was surprised to see teachers even eating out. I also remember that we were prohibited from leaving the school premises during school hours, and I remember Mr. Rundle, the principal, standing on guard at the entrance to his office while we signed the attendance book each morning.

There was a huge age gap between the older women on staff who were considered "old maids" and ourselves, three young women who "had brought glamour to the school." Their dress was staid while ours was stylish. I was a fashion plate. I loved wearing angora sweaters with a string of pearls, tight straight skirts and high heels. I wore no makeup except lipstick. Makeup was reserved for evening wear. At the Tech, there was a male staff room and another for "females" only. A double standard prevailed: male teachers were put on a higher pay scale than female teachers. And although the restrictions regarding married women teachers had recently been lifted, they were only allowed to teach part time.

As young women we were under pressure sexually. Shirley was popular and usually had a date for Saturday night. I became infatuated with Jim H., a handsome, tall and blonde Physical Education teacher, the "perfect" WASP from Toronto. Even today when I hear "Moonlight in Vermont" which was our song, I become nostalgic. When I didn't have a Saturday night date, which was often, my deep-seated insecurities regarding my appearance and Italianness made me feel desperately inferior. Germaine Greer, Betty Friedan and Gloria Steinhem had not written their books yet. I would never, never, phone a man. In 1952 young women just waited: waited for the telephone to ring, waited to be asked out for a date and waited to be kissed. We weren't feminists then; the term hadn't been invented. We conformed to such sexual and social clichés of the times, as "Diamonds are a girl's best friend," and "If he has the milk, why should he buy the cow." And, of course, the man always picked up the tab.

I enjoyed the company of my two female colleagues. I felt privileged to have been accepted as their friend, and yet I hid my struggles with my identity, too embarrassed to expose them. It was a private battle not to be revealed.

I don't recall my mother trying to stop me from going on this trip (although she would on subsequent travels), probably because she had made arrangements for me to meet kinfolk.

As befitting prim and proper school teachers we wore our travelling uniforms, specially made at Russell Tailors: grey flannel skirts and navy blue blazers, with our university crests on breast pockets. Our accessories included navy blue pumps and matching kid gloves. With our tummies tucked into our two way stretch elastic girdles, our figures appeared sculptured.

We each brought three-piece Samsonite luggage sets which contained our carefully selected wardrobe meticulously layered between sheets of tissue paper: matching sweater sets, day-time and cocktail dresses, several pairs of white gloves and hats, an overcoat, tailor-made slacks, high heel spikes, silk stockings and garter belts, saddle shoes, and bobby socks. Shirley brought a suitcase packed with Kotex.

Our tourist-class stateroom was filled with flowers, cards and telegrams of good wishes from relatives and friends in accordance with shipboard etiquette of the day. On the first night aboard, I wore my beautiful corsage of gardenias, which my sister Rita had sent, on my permapleated sleeveless red silk dress with the narrow rhinestone belt. I loved this dress and wore it whenever I wanted to make a good impression.

For the first time in my life I was crossing the Atlantic Ocean. What an unforgettable experience it was! The *Scythia* presented me with a whole new world of fun. There were so many Canadian, British and American young men aboard, that I was inundated with invitations to dance, to play deck and party games, to high tea, and to sun tan. I was invited to parties hosted by the Purser and the Captain. At one of the Captain's parties, I drank two dry Martinis one after another. The cabin began to spin and spin. After this initial experience, I sipped my drinks slowly. Dry martinis have never since appealed to me.

During the sing songs in the bar and on deck I enjoyed the wonderful camaraderie. We beat out the rhythm to "Little Brown Jug." We swayed to "Moonlight Bay," and "Daisy" and acted to "Old Macdonald had a Farm" and "MacNamara's Band." We belted out "Pack up your troubles" and "Roll out the Barrel." The Canadians sang "Alouette" and the Americans tried to follow us. I was ecstatic. I danced each night until the wee hours in the morning. My companions left me little notes on my bunk bed each night, and the next day they were always anxious to hear the latest news. When I glided to the last dance "Til we meet again," on the night before disembarking, I was heart broken.

I remember that my popularity surprised me. I, the Italian girl, with olive skin and black hair, plagued with a poor self-image, was accepted, even admired. I was short-sighted and had acne. Luckily, I was fitted with contact lenses shortly before I left. They were made of hard glass and covered the entire eye. I could barely tolerate them, but I persevered because they boosted my self-esteem so much. After all, the art of flirtation is dependant upon the eyes. On board ship I received compliment after compliment about my "large beautiful green eyes." And the glorious sun as we crossed the Atlantic baked my pimples and gave me a smooth, rich tan. I loved the way I felt on board, so joyous, exalted and free.

Never before had I been the object of so much male attention. Joan Grey reminds me that I even "stole" the Purser from her.

Never again would "getting there" be so much fun. Never again would I be able to recapture the magic of this transformation. On board ship, the Penny I had invented at age seventeen had finally materialized. If this was what travel could do to my self-esteem, I promised myself that I would embark on a lifetime of travel.

England

On 16 July we landed on *terra firma* in Southampton, England. We travelled tourist class on the boat train to London. I was horrified by the dirty and smelly WCs [washrooms]. And the overall stench on the train made me nauseous.

The new sights from my window soon began to arrest my attention: the row on row of brick tenement houses with their numerous chimney pots and narrow little gardens, the hedgerows overhanging with pink roses, and the velvety green fields. I was finding England's green and pleasant landscape a treat for my senses. I kept thinking to myself, "how thoroughly England is groomed." I was used to the bush and bare rock of the tangled terrain of a Northern Ontario wilderness. England's lush green and open landscape was so different from the wild boreal forest of home.

But it was the city of London, the capital of the British Empire, I was anxious to see. Ever since I was a little primary school girl acting out the game song:

London bridge is falling down,
Falling down, falling down,
London bridge is falling down,
My fair lady.

London had intrigued me.

Ontario's authorized curriculum had stressed British History and Literature. For me, England had become the source of everything I valued: my literary and historical heritage, good manners, correct speech, and the best quality goods. I was proud of Britain's imperial greatness, proud that I was a British subject.

London was the largest city in the world, the world's leading financial and commercial centre, the heart of the mighty British Empire, so huge that the sun never set on it. The excitement of knowing that I was nearing London made me restless. A hundred questions crowded my mind. Where was London Bridge, the Tower of London, Buckingham Palace? Where was Big Ben and Westminster Abbey?

At last we arrived. From our very first hour I was struck by the seeming chaos of London's traffic. It was all going the wrong way. And round and round. I was afraid to cross the streets. And yet I enjoyed the enormous crowds, the hustle and bustle. Never before had I seen such a busy metropolis!

London fascinated me: its magnificent buildings, flower sellers, fruit vendors, and street singers, the black humped-back cabs sitting in the middle of the streets waiting for fares, Englishmen in bowler hats carrying tightly rolled black umbrellas, winding and twisting streets with few right angles or direct lanes, double decker buses, the huge baby prams, crowds of people eating their lunches on deck chairs in the parks, the musty underground called the "tube," the pomp and ceremony of the changing of the guard at Buckingham Place. The huge blazing neon lights in Piccadilly Circus advertising "Bass on Draught," "Taplow's Wines" and "Schnapps Gin and Tonic" made me realize the insularity and intolerance of my home town. Everything was different. Even the streets, which were called mews, or lanes, rows, courts, inns or closes, places and passages. I was an ingenue in love with the capital of my mother country and the mighty British Empire.

There was so much to see and do. We hurried through the British Museum where I found myself enchanted by the Rosetta Stone and the Elgin marbles. We hurried through the National Gallery where I was astounded at the huge array of paintings. To my surprise, I recognized Turner's "The Fighting Téméraire," and Constable's "The Haywain." "The Fighting Téméraire" held my gaze so long that our guide had to drag me away. We hurried through the long halls lined with scores of paintings so quickly that I carried away only a confused mass of superficial impressions. What I learned most was how very little I knew about art appreciation and art history.

I had never before been in an art gallery or a museum. But my appetite was whetted. I discovered that culture exhilarated me. My lifelong passion for the Arts was born. An innate spirit responded to the beauty of the masterpieces, but I was also proud of my colonial heritage.

London had so many cultural activities. The variety was mind-boggling — live theatre, opera, ballet, concerts, exhibitions, festivals. We listened to the Welsh Guards playing hit tunes from *South Pacific* on the steps of St. Paul's Cathedral. At Covent Garden we saw the New York City Ballet. At Drury Lane, we saw Mary Martin in *South Pacific*. When the Italian basso Ezio Pinza sang "Some Enchanted Evening" I caught myself shouting "Bravo, Bravo." We saw Katherine Hepburn in G. B. Shaw's comedy of money and manners, *The Millionairess*. Seeing two Hollywood stars perform was inconceivable, magical. Dressed in saddle shoes and sweaters, we sat in box seats which we were able to get on the spur of the moment to watch Jennette Dowling's *The Young Elizabeth*, an historical drama covering the turbulent years prior to her accession of the throne of England. All things enthralled me: the opera glasses, the individual tea trays, the tea and sweets and ices served at intermission. I watched, with a twinge of envy, young ladies romantically tearing the cellophane off boxes of chocolates which their escorts had given them.

Although I was surprised to find so little damage and so few ruins, London of 1952 was still reeling under a food austerity program. Butter and fresh eggs were unavailable. We were served stale pound cake, and brussels sprouts so often that even today I cannot eat them.

I found English food insipid, but I enjoyed the gracious service and elegant atmosphere of the restaurants: waiters in tails who hovered over us, and violinists who surrounded our table playing romantic tunes. At one restaurant we were mistaken for Americans and refused service until we showed our maple leaf pins. At the Trocadero several American soldiers asked us to dance. They were promptly told to leave the premises. Post-war England was still very correct! The war-time view that "American soldiers were overpaid, oversexed, and over here" was still currently popular.

My literary and historical heritage came to life in Britain. For instance, visiting Stoke Pages to see the yew tree under which Thomas Gray wrote *Elegy in a Country Churchyard* brought back the verse I had memorized in high school:

> Full many a gem of purest ray serene
> The dark unfathomed caves of ocean bear
> Full many a flower is born to blush unseen
> And waste its sweetness in the desert air.

Although the Lake District was supposed to conjure up pleasant associations with the poetry of Wordsworth and Coleridge, which I loved, going round and round thirteen lakes in drizzling rain was monotonous and boring. However, the steep hills and quaint shops of Windemere attracted me.

Scotland

Magnificent, imposing Edinburgh Castle presided over the royal capital. Dignified and elegant, Edinburgh belied its romantic, turbulent and tragic history. My schoolgirl history lessons had taught me about the scandals and murders associated with the lovely and luckless Roman Catholic Mary, Queen of Scots. Where was Lord Darnley's bedroom and the private staircase that led to Mary's bedroom in Holyrood Castle? Where was the room where her Italian private secretary and confidant, Rizzio, was stabbed fifty-seven times? Where was the place where, in 1567, Darnley was blown to bits?

Mary had always been my favourite Queen. I remember how, in my youthful naiveté, I had been appalled when the cold-hearted Protestant Queen, Elizabeth I, had my Mary beheaded. Holyrood Castle was sacred to me. I had to tear myself away.

Where was St. Giles Cathedral where Jenny Geddes threw a stone at John Knox in the pulpit, whose rigid and dour creed set up the Presbyterian system in Scotland? We visited St. Giles but I was not moved.

Other places and names recalled lessons in British History and Literature: Robert Bruce, William Wallace, Sir Walter Scott, David Livingstone, Robert Louis Stevenson. I knew them all.

We took a motor-coach excursion to Loch Lomond. I wrote in my journal: "The day was foggy with a slight drizzle. We observed no living person on either the highroad or the lowroad ."

I used to love to play this song and sing the sad lines:

Oh! ye'll take the high road, and I'll
take the low road,
And I'll be in Scotland afore ye,
But me and my true love we'll
never meet again
On the bonnie, bonnie banks of
Loch Lomond.

Although the excursion was disappointing, I was glad I saw the place enshrining the lover's lament.

We had only three and one-half days in Scotland. I knew I had to return, but I was also excited to reach our next destination, Paris.

France: Paris

Paris epitomized freedom, and the "bohemian life" in a way that London did not. It was the haven for exiled royals. The Duke and Duchess of Windsor lived in Paris; Russian and Polish *emigrés,* and disaffected young Americans whom Gertrude Stein labelled "the lost generation": Ernest Hemingway, Sherwood Anderson, F. Scott Fitzgerald, Ezra Pound, John Dos Possos. African-American performers such as Josephine Baker, Paul Robeson and Duke Ellington were popular. American and European writers and artists chose to live in Paris because here they could create works that were not understood or accepted in their native countries. James Joyce lived in Paris.

Paris symbolized the avant-garde: the new musicians, artists and writers, and the new intellectuals, such as Jean-Paul Sartre, Picasso, Toulouse-Lautrec, Matisse, Cézanne, Madame Curie, and Jean Cocteau.

It was the hedonist capital of Europe with a nightlife of uncensored pleasures and gaiety, celebrated in song: "How you gonna keep 'em down on the farm/After they've seen Paree?"

Its reputation intrigued me; its revolutionary national anthem thrilled me. I could not wait until I set foot on Parisian soil.

We behaved like typical American tourists in Paris for the first time, shocked at the open smelly pissoirs on the streets and mystified by a fixture in hotel bathrooms. Shirley washed her hair in it; Joan washed her feet. And I didn't want to go near it. It wasn't until we got home that we discovered the fixture that had puzzled us was called a "bidet," but we still didn't know what it was for.

We also saw the three treasures that everybody goes to the Louvre to see: the Mona Lisa, Winged Victory and the Venus de Milo.

I had expected to see ruins, but the city had suffered little damage during the Second World War. We dutifully visited the famous landmarks.

After England's terrible food, French cuisine was wonderful. I loved the croissants with gobs of butter and jam, the crêpes Suzettes, the long loaves of fresh crusty bread, and French coffee served as *filtre*, all of which were unknown to us then.

I was dazzled by the glitter and glamour of the salons of the great French couturiers, Balmain, Christian Dior, Chanel, and the lesser boutiques and shops, all of which displayed the jewellery, perfume, furs, hats, gloves and dresses that made the Parisian woman, whether aristocrat or office girl, *chic*. I was surprised at the large number of window displays devoted only to the beautiful clothes for babies and children.

Chanel No. 5 was *de rigueur*. We each bought a bottle. And I bought a bikini for my friend, Laura G., who had asked me to buy her one after she had seen it in a fashion magazine. Only two were left at the Galeries Lafayette, both chocolate brown, a colour I was afraid she would dislike. We had never seen one before and we were shocked. It was so skimpy. Bikini-clad Laura was a smashing hit in Port Arthur.

It was Paris at night, buzzing with light, music and activity that intrigued us. After all, there wasn't much in the way of entertainment in my small port city on the forgotten side of Lake Superior, remote and isolated from the busy and populated areas of Southern Ontario. We saw *Madame Bovary* at the *Opéra Comique* and the ballet *The Dying Swan* at the *de Marigny*. There was an incredible variety of nightclubs, restaurants and side-walk cafés to choose from!

Paris cabaret life was at once tawdry and luxurious, brash, gaudy and gay. It ranged from scandalous, and disgusting, to naughty and wonderful. As a rather puritanical school teacher, much of what I saw shocked me.

For several nightclubs my diary contains only cryptic comments — "short blonde puffing cigarettes, panties' episode, suggestive gyrations, a wild Apache dance" — I was too embarrassed then to fill in the details and the years have obliterated the memory. But I do remember that I had my first sip of champagne in Paris; in fact, we drank champagne every night.

Wherever we went, showgirls dominated the revues: girls and more girls, beautiful, shapely, bare-breasted, flashy, and fleshy, singing, acting and dancing. We watched the strip-tease in amazement. We saw the Can-Can for the first time. I enjoyed the high kicks in wonderful unison, and the lively music. And when the girls displayed their derrières it was naughty Paris, risqué Paris. I have loved Offenbach's music ever since.

Girls were the special feature at the *Folies-Bergère*. I admired their dazzling costumes and the lavishly mounted settings. I was completely mystified, too, by a wonderful fairy scene where footmen bearing lighted candles walked down a flight of stairs into and under a pool of water. It was magic!

Wherever we went, in the parks, under the bridges, in front of churches and museums, along the city's cobblestone streets, we saw couples holding hands in broad daylight and lovers embracing and kissing in public. We had heard about the "French kiss" and wondered if that's what was going on. We had to agree that Paris was truly the fabled home of lovers. We pretended not to notice, however, because such behaviour was definitely inappropriate at home, but I wondered if I would ever be kissed in broad daylight! But no young Frenchman pursued me. I would have to wait until we got to Rome.

Italy: Rome

The moment I set foot in Rome, I was entranced, not as London or Paris had excited me, but for an inexplicable reason I could not articulate at the time. We visited the obligatory tourist sites: the ancient Rome of the Caesars, the Forum and Colosseum, the triumphal arches, the Circus Maximus and the temples.

We visited Roman Christianity, the catacombs and the Appian Way. We walked in the footsteps of St. Peter along the Way and stopped at a little chapel known as *Quo Vadis* where Jesus appeared to St. Peter. We strolled around beautiful piazzas and ate at pavement cafés in the Via Venito, soaking in the sun and beauty.

One afternoon as we were walking about the Piazza di Spagna, around the "Fountain of the Barcaccia" at the foot of the Spanish steps, we stumbled upon the filming of *Roman Holiday* with Gregory Peck. Peck was every girl's heartthrob. We stayed and watched and watched. When I saw Peck entering Bellini's, an elegant shop in Rome's chic shopping district at the corner of the Piazza and Via Condotti, I rushed in just to be able to stand near him and gaze in silence. We each bought kid gloves in the boutique in order to be able to loiter a little longer. It was such a pleasure to be so close to him. Joan asked him if he would take off his glasses. He obliged and asked what State we were from. He thought we were Americans.

Unlike Paris, we were whistled at and pursued by the Roman playboys whose bravado included asking us how old we were and if we were virgins. I can't say that they harassed us because we enjoyed "the chase" and their Latin charm.

Like all tourists in Rome, my three companions and I visited the four main Basilicas, including St. Peter's in Vatican City. Inside the enormous Basilica, despite the hundreds of tourists milling about, a reverential awe filled my being. I silently admired the priceless works of art which man had created *ad majorem Dei gloriam* (to the greater glory of God). I stopped and meditated upon Christ's crucifixion at the Pietà, which has become one of my favourite statues, and marvelled at the genius of Michelangelo, who created it when he was only twenty-five years old. I gazed in wonder at its perfection and kissed the broken legs of my Lord.

One reminiscence claims precedence over all the rest. We visited the Sistine Chapel, which was breathtaking. The entire ceiling was covered with frescoes of Biblical scenes. I had never seen anything so glorious. Michelangelo worked on them for four years. When he painted "The Last Judgment" Michelangelo was an old man and the gigantic task, which took six years to complete, was agonizing work. His body ached; his arms grew numb; his fingers cramped. I lay on my back on a bench to admire the work (there weren't the heavy crowds then) as Michelangelo did when he painted from his high scaffold. I found "The Creation of Man" inspiring. I found "The Last Judgment" stupendous. Christ is the implacable Judge. On His right are the elect; on His left, the sinners. I could not believe my eyes.

A papal audience was the lifelong dream of Catholics throughout the world. I could have conceived of nothing more singular then, than being in the Pope's presence. On 6 August 1952, my three companions and I saw Pope Pius XII at Castel Gandolfo, the summer seat of the Popes. When he appeared on the balcony at 6:00 p.m., thrills of joy went up my spine as the audience standing around me in the courtyard clapped and cheered, and shouts of *Viva il Papa* soared to the heavens. In my diary I wrote: "It was magic. The Holy Father is so unassuming and gracious. He spoke in Italian, French, German, Spanish, Portuguese and English."

For the first time in my life I was meeting my father's family in Italy, his brother Giovanni in Rome, and their sister, Marietta, in Calabria, in Southern Italy.

My uncle had been a career soldier who had fought with distinction in World Wars I and II. When he came to the Hotel Eden where we were staying, accompanied by his two handsome sons, Dino and Gino, I recognized him immediately from his pictures. They received us with an exquisite courtesy, which surprised me. And when he invited us to his home, the courtly formality of his wife Maria impressed me. I recall that the family was intrigued by Shirley and Joan, because they were the first Protestants they had ever met, and Gino and Dino were shocked that the three of us shaved our legs.

Calabria

We had planned that my girlfriends would remain in Rome while I spent a few days in Calabria where my father's sister lived in Aprigliano. My uncle, who was shocked that we four girls were travelling without a chaperone, would not hear of my going to Calabria alone. He insisted on accompanying me even though I didn't want him to. We stayed awake all night on the train to Cosenza, the capital of Calabria in Southern Italy because of a strike which necessitated our changing trains three times. However, the time passed quickly because the train carrying me to my ancestral homeland was filled with American-Italian soldiers going, like me, to visit relatives we had never met.

We arrived in Cosenza at eleven a.m. on 7 August 1952, and hired a taxi for the fourteen kilometre trip to Aprigliano. We drove through the mountain country-side, up narrow, twisting, steep mountain roads, passing ancient olive groves, terraced cultivated slopes, vine-yards clinging to rocky terrraces, and dry beds of torrents that descend steeply from mountain rivers.

This was the place where my parents were born — Magna Graecia — that part of Italy colonized by Greece centuries before the birth of Christ. I recall my mother telling me that in her time there were pockets in Calabria where the people still spoke Greek and that the Calabrese word for handkerchief is the Greek word *maccaturo*.

A loud chorus of *benvenuto, benvenuto* and enthu-siastic hand clapping greeted us as we got out of the taxi. A gun salute was fired to honour my uncle, the town's war hero. Shouts of *L'Americana, L'Americana* filled the air. (No distinction was made between Americans and Canadians.) Out from the excited crowd advanced a woman who introduced herself, *Sono Zia Marietta* (I am Aunt Mary). We embraced, and she kissed me on each cheek.

Zia Marietta was not the short, squat, middle-aged woman I had expected. She was solidly built, of medium stature, erect; she carried herself with dignity. Her hair was severely pushed back in a braided bun; her face was lined; she wore a plain black dress and black stockings.

After the initial formalities, I was led to my father's childhood home. I noticed the grapevine which formed an arbour over the front door (the only detail my father had ever mentioned about his Calabrian home). Inside, I was shocked to see so few comforts. My studies had included little Italian geography and history. I knew my father had been sending money back home ever since he had started to work in Canada. But I had not realized that the region was one of the poorest and least fertile of Italy.

I had arrived in a white eyelet sun dress, white bobby socks and white and brown saddle shoes. I wore no embellishments, no watch, no rings or other jewellery. I did not realize that my plain appearance had been a disappointment to my Aunt and her neighbours until the morning after my arrival when my Aunt inquired whether I "owned" any watches, bracelets or necklaces. My response was an immediate and simple "*Sì, perché?*" (Yes, why?) "Because," she replied, "my neighbours are disappointed in your plain appearance." (In Calabrese culture the importance of neighbours as critics of conduct cannot be underestimated.) She asked me plaintively to put on some jewellery.

American relatives of her neighbour's, who had visited before me, had bedecked themselves in "diamonds" to their ankles. I had committed an unforgivable breach of conduct in a country where *fare una bella figura* (to appear well in the eyes of others) was sacrosanct. Recognizing the gravity of the situation I hurriedly dug into my suitcase and brought out my rhinestone necklace and bracelet. I never took them off.

To my Aunt's relief, I now sparkled like her neighbour's American relatives.

For Italians, food is the symbol of life and is associated with all that is good and nourishing. For breakfast, the morning after my arrival, Zia Marietta offered me a dish of fresh figs which she had picked very early that morning. I refused them. At the time I neither knew what a luxury fresh figs were, nor to what trouble she had gone to pick them. I didn't realize it was a way of showing her love for me. "Just taste one and I'm sure you'll like it," she said. But I steadfastly refused.

I was still at that stage in my life when I considered Calabrese customs inferior, when I was rebelling against my parent's culture. And when I was obsessed with keeping my figure svelte like the Hollywood sex sirens who were my role models.

Since my Italian was fractured and my vocabulary meagre, and my aunt was reserved and laconic, our conversations were limited. She knew many family secrets, but safeguarding them was deeply embedded within the Calabrese psyche. She offered no insights into her thoughts and feelings. I ask myself now, however, whether I was warm enough, tender enough to her. She was unmarried, childless. During my 1997 trip to Calabria I was told that she had spent her whole life toiling on the family's farm tending the horses, goats and sheep and making the Petrone speciality, Cotrone cheese, a hard round cheese made from goat's milk, highly valued in the region. Little did I realize then that I would never see her again. She died fifteen years later of breast cancer. I was more closely connected to her than I realized. In 1967, I too was diagnosed with breast cancer.

When my parents visited Zia Marietta in 1958, she told my mother: "why that girl ate and drank hardly anything. She never even went to the bathroom." I had avoided the outdoor toilet as much as I could.

My father's relatives and I walked a few kilometres down the mountain slope to Piane Crati, my mother's home town, and I saw the house where my mother grew up. It was exactly as she had described it — a large solid stone structure with thick walls across from the town's water pump and the church named in honour of St. Barbara, the patron saint of the town. I was surprised to see Communist graffiti — the hammer and sickle — painted in red on the outside white washed front wall. I also saw the *terreni* where the Sisco family had grown wheat and cultivated potatoes, figs, onions, olives, beans, grapes, and tomatoes. I noticed that farm life was vastly different from that at home. There were no isolated farm houses here. The peasants lived in small towns and went out each day into the surrounding fields to work the land and returned to their homes each evening. Piane Crati, like my father's little town, consisted only of a few streets lined with closely packed stone houses clustered around the church, which I visited in order to see the life-size statue of St. Barbara in a glass display case.

I found the sombre pessimism and the stagnant economy of the region unnerving. I stopped counting the number of marriage proposals I received. It seemed that every young man wanted to come to America.

I met Tommaso, the son of Angelina, my father's sister, who was spreading Communist ideology around the region. I could understand why. There were no industries. Poverty was endemic. I saw oxen ploughing the fields; donkeys and women laden with heavy loads.

The destitution appalled me. I thought, "No wonder this impoverished region sent multitudes of immigrants to the New World." Tommaso was just leaving for Turin where the local priest had found him a job in order to get rid of him. Tommaso interested me and I was sorry that I never got to know him better. I never saw him again.

After three days, I was anxious to leave. My uncle and I left Calabria on Saturday night, 9 August, for Rome. I was unable and unwilling, at the time, to identify with my Calabrese ancestry. I couldn't wait to get back to Rome. There were no seats on the train and once again I stayed awake all night.

Rome

Back in Rome one evening, when Margaret Mary, Shirley, Joan and I were dining at the roof garden of the Hotel Eden where we were staying, our waiter brought us a bottle of wine, courtesy of a Roman gentleman who soon came to our table and introduced himself. Luigi A. was a tall, middle-aged, urban sophisticate with impeccable manners, most unlike the stereotype of the Italian male that circulated in Port Arthur. Although he was polite to my companions, I soon became aware that his attention was directed towards me. When he invited me to see "his" Rome that night in a *carozella* (carriage) I was thrilled. My heart began racing. But I was afraid, too. I expressed my reluctance to leave my girlfriends. But they kept insisting I should accept his offer. I wanted to accept, but I also sought their approval. They knew I would report the details.

Luigi looked like Yves Montand. Why in the world had he selected me? After all, I considered my girlfriends better looking. I couldn't believe my luck. I felt truly honoured.

I can't recall details about the *carozella* ride along the streets of Rome that night. Nor did I expect to see Luigi again. When he invited me to dinner the next evening, I didn't think I had heard him correctly. He was asking me for a "date"? What did I do to deserve this attention? He was unlike any man I had ever met. He was courtly.

The restaurant, *Alfredo all' Augusteo,* in the Piazza Augusto Imperatore, was famous. It was even written up in *Newsweek,* 10 November 1952, with a picture of Clark Gable dining there.

"Only celebrities dine here," I wrote in my diary and added, "The Duke and Duchess of Windsor dined here last night."

Alfredo, the owner, presided over the restaurant, a noisy, genial man with a jaunty moustache, sleek with pomade. Bowing profusely, he extended us a hearty welcome. I noticed that he had addressed my escort as Commendatore Luigi.

While we dined on *fettuccine al burro* (buttered noodles) "the best fettuccine in the world, mixed by the magic hands of Alfredo himself, with the world-renowned golden fork and spoon presented to him by Mary Pickford and Douglas Fairbanks" (as the menu read), Alfredo performed a lively dance to the strains of "Funiculi Funicula."

Although there was so much activity around us, we were completely occupied in each other's opinions on a wide variety of topics. We discussed the abolition of the Italian Monarchy, the Second World War, the negative attitude of the Italian North towards the South, which astounded me, and the attraction of European men towards North American women.

It was a popular European belief that North American girls were uninhibited and independent. They even travelled alone. They could talk on such men's issues as politics, economics and current affairs. They were idealized and courted by foreign men. They were the envy of all the women in the world. Luigi harboured similar sentiments. I replied that not all North American women offered their favours as freely as the stereotypes suggested. He accepted my opinion with grace. I asked him about his title, Commendatore. In his modesty he revealed only that it was an honour bestowed on him (I can't remember now whether it was by the Italian Republic or the Vatican). I asked him no personal questions because I didn't want to know whether he was married or not. If I knew that he was, my moral values would not have allowed me to continue seeing him. It was better that I did not know. Luigi spoke no English; I spoke my fractured Italian which was Italo-Canadese. But he kept assuring me that he understood everything I said. We were so absorbed in conversation that the waiter hovered about us several times to ask us what we would like for dessert.

The dessert was served with fanfare. All lights were extinguished and the flambé was carried in with flickering blue sparklers. Photographs were snapped. I felt like a movie star.

The time to say goodnight came too soon. I was leaving Rome in two days. Luigi invited me to spend the next day at his villa in Fregene, a summer resort by the sea. I was apprehensive but he had behaved like the perfect gentleman. In fact, there was a spiritual quality about him which appealed to me. He was not the stereo-

typical Italian playboy nor the proverbial hot-blooded
Latin lover. He was the quintessential gentleman.

The next day Luigi sent his chauffeur to my hotel to
take me to his villa. He had also invited a couple to be
our chaperones in order to make me feel more comfortable. I had a glorious day. We meandered through the
tall pines and along paths covered with brown needles.
We bowled on a huge lawn. The villa, built three years
previously, was "out of this world," with the most modern kitchen I had ever seen, deluxe contour chairs,
triangular tables and shiny marble floors. Outside, several miniature doll houses fitted with modern wash
basins and electricity were scattered throughout the
woods, just in case the lady desired to refresh herself.

A butler in white gloves, with fine flourish, served a
superb dinner on shiny silver, the whitest linen and
modern, flamboyant china on a patio that overlooked a
sandy beach and the Mediterranean. We ate a late supper
served on another patio. I was wide-eyed with the surprise of a working-class Canadian girl.

Luigi tried to persuade me to accompany him to his
mountain retreat. But I was too afraid he might try
something, although he had never given me any provo-
cation that had made me suspicious. Nevertheless, I
wasn't taking any chances. Sex outside marriage was
taboo.

Luigi drove all of us to the train station. He pecked
me on the cheek and wished me, *Tante belle cose*. And
we waved each other out of sight.

He wrote faithfully for a year, even sending me a
subscription to an independent weekly *di critica* called
"La Via." I still have the 1 November 1952 issue in
which a whole page is devoted to *La Poesia nella Divina*

Commedia. And of the several letters he wrote I still have a letter dated *Roma, 29 Decembre* 1952:

> . . . Nei poche giorni della nostra conoscenza, ho riportato di Lei una impressione molto amabile, perché I Suoi sentimenti non avevano nulla di artificioso e cosi pure le Sue parole . . . la semplicità è il dono piu grande che una persona possa possedere.

> [We were acquainted only a few days. But during that time you created an endearing impression on me because of your lack of pretension and artificiality that simplicity which is the greatest gift a person can possess.]

As I read these lines today, I wonder how I could have been so insensitive as not to have carried on a correspondence. But I had wanted an Englishman, a Canadian or an American, not an Italian. I never looked up Luigi in my later travels.

"Rome held me in captivity," I wrote in my 1952 diary. Its antiquity had impressed me; its beauty had overwhelmed my senses; its Catholicism had uplifted my soul.

I threw a coin in the Trevi Fountain and I knew I would return.

Florence

Margaret Mary, Shirley, Joan and I travelled to Florence by motorcoach via Perugia and Assisi. I don't know why the haystacks that I kept seeing en route, beautifully yellow and in a variety of shapes were so appealing to me.

We stayed two days exploring Florence by *carrozella* and on foot. Since we had so little time we concentrated on the Duomo, the Piazza della Signoria, and the Pitti and Uffizi art galleries. And we shopped and shopped! On our guided tour of the Pitti we passed through room after room after room hanging with rows of paintings, halls and salons draped and decorated with priceless tapestries, portraits, sculptures, friezes and frescoes. It was mind-boggling. I decided that on subsequent visits I would go without a guide to admire only a few selected masterpieces, like Raphael's "La Madonna della Seggia," painted in 1515, which depicts a nicely plump Madonna clutching a very chubby and alert baby close to her breast; and Murillo's "Madonna and Child," a beautiful, pensive Madonna supporting the lovely baby standing on her lap.

Besides the stupendous Pitti, we toured another fabulous art gallery, the Uffizi, which contained one of the richest collections of art treasures in the world. A guide took us on a quick march throughout the gallery. When I got home, my lack of recall appalled me. I determined once again to concentrate on a few masterpieces which I liked. Two, of course, were Botticelli's "The Birth of Venus" and "La Primavera." Another was Filippo Lippi's "Madonna and Child," a print of which hangs in my bedroom. I was also attracted to "Eve," a painting by Luca Cranach, the Elder. The painting depicts a tall, slender, naked red head with a small, sweet face holding an apple in her right hand and looking at a serpent above her.

We scoured the illuminated shops of goldsmiths, silversmiths and Florence's best jewellery firms, which lined both sides of the Ponte Vecchio, in a relentless search for the best prices. I stocked up on a year's supply of gifts: sterling silver spoons, leather wallets, key chains and lipstick cases, linens, lizard handbags, mosaic brooches and crosses, inlaid wood, marble sculptures, silver filigree earrings, and gold charms.

Venice

I gasped in disbelief when I saw Venice. "The folksong I taught so many times is true," I announced to my companions:

> If you should go to Venice
> You would find a magic town;
> The streets are flowing rivers
> Where the boats glide up and down;
> A gondola stops at the doorway,
> and the boatman sings a song,
> He'll paddle his boat thro' the water,
> You may ride the whole day long.

The gondoliers were wearing their traditional straw hats and blue and white striped shirts. Standing aft in their glossy, black beaked gondolas and singing the Neapolitan love songs "O sole mio" and "Santa Lucia," they enthralled us. It was so romantic. We admired their skill as they silently sliced the waters and glided beneath Gothic and Baroque palaces with lacy arches and wrought iron balconies with pots of geraniums. When they manoeuvred our gondola under the Rialto Bridge, a name I recognized from having taught Shakespeare's *Merchant of Venice,* my excitement was boundless.

From our hotel, the Royal Danieli, with gondolas and boat landing stages just in front of it, we loved to watch the traffic on the Grand Canal, truly the world's most spectacular thoroughfare. It was always crowded with different kinds of boats: the diesel-run vaporettos and *motoscafos* (motorboats) and the sleek launches and scows piled high with vegetables, fruit, fish, meat and other goods. I even saw a gilt ornamented gondola draped in black and gold carrying a casket. The trash that was floating about and the bad smell did not bother me.

We spent two full days in Venice and we did the usual things that tourists do. We sunbathed on the famous Lido Beach. Each day we sauntered the entire length of Piazza San Marco through swooping flocks of pigeons. It was so huge, that when we sat at any one of the four outdoor cafés, four different bands, each playing a different style of music from classical to Dixieland, did not interfere with one another. "Unbelievable," says my diary. We visited the Basilica of St. Mark, a masterpiece of Venetian-Byzantine architecture built in 830 to shelter the tomb of St. Mark. We admired the 1000 year old gem studded gold altar, the geometric floor marbles and mosaics, the bronze doors, and the five Moorish domes of the Basilica. We admired the frescoed ceilings decorated with solid gold in the magnificent Ducal Palace and filed through the Bridge of Sighs to the fifteenth century prison to look at the dark, dank cells where prisoners condemned to death were kept. The British poet, Thomas Hood's "The Bridge of Sighs" came to my mind:

> One more Unfortunate,
> Weary of breath
> Rashly importunate,
> Gone to her death!
> Take her up tenderly,
> Lift her with care;
> Fashioned so slenderly,
> Young, and so fair!

We spent most of our time cruising the canals. Since you couldn't drive in Venice — there are no roads and no cars — we actually believed that we couldn't get from place to place on foot. The water had bewitched us.

I got terribly sick in Venice and my friends summoned a doctor who prescribed suppositories. I didn't even know what they were.

Switzerland

Our summer tour of 1952 was to include Switzerland, Belgium and Holland. But it rained steadily for three days in Switzerland. And so we decided to shorten our visit, not go to Belgium and Holland, but return to Paris and spend more time there. How we missed the glorious Italian sun! The only event in Switzerland I remember today was our visit to the twelfth century water fortress, Château de Chillon, immortalized by Lord Byron.

I had studied Lord Byron's *The Prisoner of Chillon* and became fascinated with François Bonnevard, a leader in Geneva's revolt against the Duke of Savoy whom Byron makes a Promethean figure, defying tyranny and resolutely suffering for noble principles. Bonnevard spent six years chained most of the time to a pillar in the Chillon dungeon. The dungeon was damp and dank when we visited. And as I gazed out of the narrow window I could hear the lapping water as Bonnnevard did. To our surprise, we saw Byron's name carved on the pillar.

My first trip abroad had infinitely enriched my life. It had fed my intellectual curiosity by introducing me to the historic monuments and treasures of western civilization in Europe's greatest museums, art galleries and cities. It gave me days full of summer sun. It gave me male attention and acceptance. It gave me the first meeting with my kinfolk. I may have been disturbed by the poverty I found in the South of Italy, but Italian achievements in art, sculpture, architecture, literature, philosophy, science, and music had exhilarated me. If I was beginning to question why the Italians in the New World were so maligned and misunderstood, I was so thoroughly colonized that I was still British in my admiration of English culture. And my Italianness still embarrassed me. Nevertheless, I would never be the same again.

But best of all, it was a fun trip. For the first time in my life I felt truly free. And my three girlfriends and I have remained close ever since. We still love to get together and reminisce about our wonderful trip. I also remember my youthful exuberance and think of the trip as the most seminal event of my life. I was, from that point on, determined to see the world.

THE OLD WORLD, 1955-1958

Germany, 1955-1956

In 1955 I was fortunate enough to be hired by Canada's Department of National Defence for its overseas school system in Europe. These schools were organized in the spring of 1954 to provide educational facilities for dependants of Canadian NATO forces stationed in Europe.

On 20 August 1955, along with dozens of teachers from across Canada, I walked up the gangway of the "Homeric" docked in Quebec City to a trumpet fanfare and the strains of "Oh Marie" and "Roll out the Barrel" played by the ship's orchestra on the dock. Everyone was in a festive mood. Then suddenly it poured rain and the gangway was raised. I remained on deck to wave goodbye to my friends on the dock who had come to see me off.

The Canadian Government was sending us off in style, in first class. The Italian crew was attentive and I have never felt so pampered. In my diary I wrote that the meals were "scrumptious." I also noted that the teachers were "starchy" and "affected." The six day Atlantic crossing could not compare to the magic of my first. But I did win first prize in the ballroom waltz contest.

After two days in London, we were escorted by train to the port of Harwich where we boarded the "Amsterdam" for The Hook in Holland. At The Hook we boarded a military train for Soest, in northern Germany, in the highly industrialized Ruhr area.

Soest was the railroad station for the Headquarters of the First Canadian Brigade. (The Federal Republic of Germany after the war was divided into three zones of occupation: the British in the north, the American in the south and the French in between.)

What a wonderful welcome we received! The Canadian Army's big brass — colonels and majors each carrying a swagger stick — met us. Cameras flashed. Buses were waiting. Luggage was taken care of. The Army's efficiency impressed me. I was excited and full of joy looking forward to my new teaching position.

Some of the teachers left immediately for Army bases in Werl and in Hemer, located within a twenty-five mile radius of Army Headquarters near Soest. Those of us who were staying in Soest boarded buses which took us to the Red Patch Club where we were briefed about life on an Army base, and assigned accommodation.

Women teachers were assigned to Permanent Married Quarters through a lottery system. I didn't pull an "X," which would entitle me to one, but Kathy Kerr who did, asked me to share her quarters. A few teachers chose to live "on the economy." Single male teachers were housed at Fort Chambly.

In the Army Schools we were classified as Captains; in the Air Force Schools as Flight-Lieutenants; we were associate members of the Officers' Mess. Our home school boards paid us our regular salaries, but they were reimbursed by the Department of National Defence. We were "on loan" for a period of two years.

Four of us, Lillian Lyons and Kathy Kerr (British Columbia) and Ann Stech (Manitoba) and I settled into a two bedroom apartment above the Dependants'

Clinic. It was fully furnished with everything from an umbrella stand to a sleeve presser. There was also a small contingent of Belgian military who had their own barracks in the Soest area, and several girls stayed at the "Club Belaac," which was kept as an Officer's Club for visiting Belgian officers. As Ruth Ratz LeBlanc (Ottawa) remembers:

To offset costs some rooms were rented to the Canadian Military and to teachers who had no other accommodation. It was run like an Officers' Mess — all cleaning was done for us, our beds were made daily and changed weekly. Each room had a washbasin, bed, wardrobe, a table/desk with upright chair and an easy chair. (No visitors of the opposite sex were allowed in rooms.) We could get meals in the dining room from a menu, paid for with Belgian Military francs. Breakfast cost about twenty-five francs (about fifty cents Canadian). Dinners were delicious with white linen and silver — and also very cheap.

In March 1956, the Club Belaac was returned to the German owner who closed it for renovations. And Ruth had to move. She remembers:

I found a room nearby in a house with a landlady who didn't trust any non-German! I recall being quite ill with flu (bedrooms were freezing cold and very damp and we used electric heaters when there). Leo [a Canadian officer, and future husband] came into town one evening and since I couldn't go out I spent the evening sleeping while Leo read and waited for transport back to Fort Henry which normally left Soest about eleven p.m. The next day my landlady practically threatened me with eviction — she didn't want a reputation for running a house of ill-repute! I guess she took the silence for the worst of all scenarios.

Classes didn't begin until 5 September, giving us an opportunity to explore our new surroundings. I took full advantage of the time sightseeing and learning the history of the old town. I walked everywhere: along its narrow cobblestone alleys and winding streets and on the ancient town walls with its watch towers, moat and arrow slots. I was fascinated by everything I saw: the old timbered houses, the onion-shaped church spires, the duck pond, the wrought-iron gates, men in lederhosen and plus fours with reinforced seats, postmen on bicycles, cleaning women carrying their pails and mops bicycling to work, the chimney sweeps, little trees decorated with colourful streamers to placate the Gods of the Forest on the roof top of new houses under construction, the storks and their huge nests on top of chimneys, the honey wagons or horse drawn tanks carrying away waste and the thirteenth century Pilgrim Haus built to provide rest for the pilgrims on their way to the Crusades. I was surprised by the fact that Napoleon had stayed there on his way to Moscow.

I noticed that vegetation thrived. (The fertility of the Soest plain is proverbial.) Never had I seen so much greenness, verdant gardens, lush green meadows and flowers, breathtaking in their profusion. And trees and trees, not the birch and spruce and balsam which I recognize, but trees like the sycamore, beech, linden, and plane tree, which did not grow in my part of the world. The old churches and public buildings glowed a strange green in the sunlight (because they were built of stones rich in glauconite taken from the hills south of the town). The greenness of everything — even the thick moss covering the stones — astonished me.

Each Saturday morning, Kathy and I walked to the market square located in the shadow of the walls of the

cathedral of St. Petroclus where farmers from the surrounding fertile countryside set up their outdoor flower,
vegetable and fruit stalls as they did centuries ago. To my
surprise, we were forbidden to touch any vegetables or
fruit. But the string shopping bags, the antique balance
scales (using the metric system which was at first confus-
ing), the cone-shaped paper bags, the butter in huge
tubs, and the faggots of wood were fascinating. In contrast to this old world charm, the store windows
displayed an unerring modern taste in colour and design. I particularly admired and purchased for myself a
brass watering can; two Hummel figures, "The Happy
Wanderer" and "The Schoolboy;" a Rosenthal "Madonna," and a set of lead crystal for twelve in the
"Nuremberg" pattern.

The Germans had just finished constructing the
senior school where I would be teaching. I had never
seen such a modern and grand school. The windows
were tall and wide. Full-length drapes could be drawn to
conserve heat. Rooms and doors were each painted a
different colour. There was a magnificent central staircase. Halls were very wide and each floor had a spacious
rotunda. There were rubber edges on the stairs. Each
room had a sink and a paper dispenser. Desks had hooks
for school bags. There was even a beautiful stained glass
window in the atrium. And swarms of janitors! I was
impressed.

In all my years of teaching I had never seen so many
supplies. There was a wide assortment of books. Books
and books and more books. There were books on Teaching Methodology which I was sure that no teacher
would read. Textbooks and most other supplies were
ordered from the Department of Education of Ontario.
The Canadian Government was most generous. The

sliding chalkboards were impressive: when closed, the single board had a writing surface approximately six feet wide. But when the board's two shutter-like arms opened from the centre they provided another twelve feet of writing surface. But I used the chalkboard a lot, and even when opened the space was not enough for me. However, the chalkboards did have a feature I liked. A slight pressure on the chalk rail moved the board up or down thus simplifying writing near the extreme top and bottom rims.

And yet, there were few storage facilities and no library. Nothing was hooked up in the science Laboratory. There was no gymnasium. I taught physical education on the first floor rotunda. I recall being regularly observed by German teachers. Only a month after classes had started, on October 7, the National Film Board televised my physical education class.

The official grand opening of the High School took place on 14 October. Brigadier Anderson and Mr. H. R. Low (Director of Education, Department of National Defence, Ottawa) presided. I played the piano for "God Save the Queen."

We followed the Ontario Ministry of Education's curricula and textbooks. This made it difficult to adapt the curriculum to the needs of pupils from ten provincial educational systems. We were chosen because we were experienced, and told that we might not necessarily teach in our own specialties. But we all pitched in and adapted. I taught subjects which I had never taught before, Gr. IX Mathematics, Gr. IX and X French. I also taught Gr. IX-XIII Physical Education as well as a night school class of soldiers who were upgrading their academic qualifications to Gr. VIII. I remember being frequently inspected in class by the handsome Education Officer who kept his swagger stick under his arm.

The Germany I knew was the country at war. When I first arrived I was too mistrustful and afraid to get close to the German people. But gradually I made German friends and started to learn their language. I still have my work book filled with words, phrases and idiomatic expressions which I wrote down as I heard them and committed to memory. I loved the language and I took great delight in conversing in it. I also enjoyed reciting snippets of German poetry like the lines from Heinrich Heine's "Lorelei," *Ich weiss nicht, was soll is bedeuten, dass ich so traurig bin . . .* (I know not why I am so sad). I loved repeating such words as *purzelbaum* (somersault) and *Umleitung* (detour). Since *Umleitung* signs were everywhere; I said the word again and again. A young German, whom I dated for a while, presented me with a wood cut print he had made of St. Sylvester's Shooters which now hangs on the entrance wall of my home.

Having come from an isolated small town in the wilds of Northern Ontario I found the cities and towns of Germany alive with culture: art exhibitions, film festivals, opera and stage plays. Even when the shops in Soest were empty and the concert hall had no roof, Soest's string quartet continued to perform.

In Hanover I sat through Mozart's "Requiem Mass." There was no intermission. But during the lengthy performance there was absolute silence. The Germans loved their Opera. The number of teenagers who attended and understood it was amazing. They even knew the scores. Audiences responded to an exceptionally fine aria rendition with thunderous applause.

The large number of public festivities shocked me. It seemed as if a weekend didn't go by that the Germans couldn't find a reason to celebrate. There were the children's festivals, the Festival of the Cows, *Oktoberfest*, *Fasching*, and other religious feasts to celebrate. Even small villages would be decorated. There were parades, marching bands, streets closed to traffic, midways, street dancing parties, crowds linking arms and singing. I had never seen anything like it at home, and was not prepared for the rowdy carousing capacity of the Germans. War-time movies had depicted a dour and hard people . No wonder I was shocked at their carefree merrymaking. I joined in the *Gemütlichkeit* of as many celebrations as I could.

Autumn wine festivals (*Oktoberfest*) which break out in every town and village along the Rhine and Mosel Rivers were particularly noteworthy. A group of us attended the Rhine in Flames illuminations which bathed the river in fire from St. Goar on one bank to St. Goarshausen on the other where the Lorelei used to wreck the Rhine boats. It was truly a most spectacular sight. The town glowed at night from the flood-lit castles along the river and the red flares along its streets and the lit candles in the windows of the town. When the fireworks burst into the dark sky, the sight was a Disney fantasy.

Fasching

Fasching was a time of spontaneous hilarity celebrated in the Catholic Rhineland and Bavaria. For three days before Ash Wednesday and the fasting and penitential season of Lent, Germans go on a celebratory spree known as *Fasching*. Eat, drink, and be merry is the rule of the day. (Unfaithfulness during *Fasching* cannot be used as grounds for divorce.)

In Köln on 17 February 1957, we watched the
annual Rose Monday parade (the climax to *Fasching*)
from an alcove window we rented to see the passing
parade. The theme of the parade was travel. Scores of
floats, huge and small, depicted travel in all its aspects.
There were yachts, space suits, sports cars, rowboats,
carriages, covered wagons and live camels. There was
the Leaning Tower of Pisa and people sunbathing on
palm lined beaches and skiing. One even showed the
Russian Sputnik, and the American "Explorer" swooping past the peace angel and shouting "meet us at Mars."

For the Karneval (as *Fasching* is called in Köln),
Prince Walter III rode on top of a stack of luggage
bearing labels from a multitude of holiday retreats. He
was throwing out chocolate bars, bottles of eau de
cologne, flower bouquets and boxes of candy to the
spectators who lined the streets.

After the parade, the streets, which were closed to
traffic, were teeming with young and old making merry.
Kids in cowboy outfits brandished toy pistols, old men
guzzled from liquor bottles, young clowns juggled balloons and little brass bands played familiar German
melodies, "Oh, mein Papa," "Eidleweiss," "Du kanst
nicht treu sein," and "Die Fröhliche Wanderer." Noise
and revelry filled the air.

If I was horrified at war's incredible destruction that
I saw in German cities, I marvelled at the even more
incredible reconstruction that peace had brought. At
war's end, the German economy had come to a standstill. No trains ran. For two years no school was open.
Nobody who had belonged to the Nazi party could get
a job. There was widespread unemployment and poverty. Chaos reigned. Fortunately, the U.S. sponsored
Marshall Plan brought about the rebuilding of West

Germany. New industries prospered. Even though a wide variety of consumer goods had become available and the standard of living had rapidly improved, there were still many shortages. Ruth LeBlanc remembers that her Orlon sweaters were stolen from the Belaac Club laundry room and that nylon stockings and perfume were difficult to buy.

A massive building program was taking place. And the economy was booming. The Germans worked. They worked overtime. Hard work. Worked under the burden of rebuilding — shovelling, wrecking, breaking — to rise from the ashes of war. I saw cranes, bulldozers, cement mixers, heavy trucks, concrete blocks, brick and mortar everywhere.

Everywhere, a feverish hurry. To fill up empty spaces, to fit into gaping holes, to repair and duplicate faithfully the original architecture and style. More than one million dwellings were built in the first three years of the Adenauer government. Not with the skyscrapers of America, but with new solid buildings, functional and beautiful in their practical simplicity that were transforming the old bomb-flattened places like Cologne and Kassel, Dusseldorf, Essen, Munster, Hamburg, Frankfort, Bonn and Munich into remarkably prosperous and modern cities.

It was in Berlin, the capital of the mighty Third Reich, heavily damaged by American and British bombers and Russian shells, where I was struck dumb. Berlin had been the seat of Hitler's Nazi Empire, to be sure, but now in 1955 it had become two cities — West Berlin in the American sector and East Berlin in the Soviet Zone of Occupation. (In August 1961, the East Germans built a wall through the middle of Berlin. In 1989, the twenty-eight-year-old wall was removed. In 1990 Germany was reunited.)

The contrast was staggering. Block-long sections of the eastern sector were still empty wastelands. The task of reconstruction was monumental. Ten years after the end of the war, there was still widespread desolation and devastation. Bullet holes still scarred crumbling facades.

In West Berlin, I was still seeing trucks gathering heaps of rubble to take to the rubble mountains on the outskirts of the city to create ski slopes and pleasure parks. Only one bombed-out building was deliberately left standing, the fire blackened shell of the Kaiser Wilhelm Memorial Church whose jagged contours loomed above the Kurfuerstendamm. This once fashionable street was now regaining its former elegance and sophistication as Berlin's Fifth Avenue with its luxury boutiques, shops, restaurants, bars, and outdoor cafés. West Berlin was recovering its gaiety, glitz and prosperity. Its lively nightlife, which had always been famous, if not notorious, once again offered the most incredible variety of night clubs. For me the most fantastic was the Balhaus Risi which featured telephones and pneumatic message tubes (like those in Matthews Dry Good Store at home) to connect each of the 200 tables in the cavernous ballroom. I was surprised and thrilled when several American servicemen used the tubes to ask me to dance. The floor shows were spectacular, especially the water-show with coloured lights on undulating fountains. The Balhaus Risi was definitely a fun place where we flirted and danced, oblivious to the cigarette smoke which encircled our heads.

The Bradenburg Gate, built in the eighteenth century, the pride of old Berlin, large, white and pretentiously imperial, once the symbol of the triumph of a nation united, was the entrance to its now divided part, East Berlin. Twice I toured this other side: once, in the Fall of 1955 with a group of teachers from Soest, and then three years later with a group of tourists from the British Isles. Both times I experienced mixed feelings of sadness, curiosity and fear such as I had not felt in the city's western half. Here in the other half of the divided city — secretive, and dormantly menacing — was the enemy.

Heaps of rubble and broken fragments of wall were all that we could see of what were once the finest palaces, churches, embassies, museums, libraries and great hotels that lined both sides of Unter den Linden, whose name means "under the linden trees," once Berlin's most famous boulevard and one of Europe's most beautiful streets. Berlin's once elegant embassy district was littered with large chunks of rusty iron, bits of broken glass, and bricks, charred and gutted ruins. Hitler's chancellery was a wasteland of concrete lumps and weeds. I stood where Unter den Linden meets Otto-Grotewohl Strasse (formerly Wilhelm Strasse) on the spot where his bunker was now only a heap of rubble, all that was left of an idea in which Berlin and the Third Reich itself were consumed. There was no marker, no commemorative plaque. It was a scene of stupendous dereliction, of wide deserted streets, and silent squares, of torn shells rising up starkly skeletal, of large empty spaces overgrown with weeds and wild straggling bushes.

East Berlin was assuming the character of a Russian City. Stalin Allee, formerly Frankfurter Allee, was the showplace of Russian reconstruction and design. The Soviets built a mile long housing project in the Russian formal architectural style. Although my fellow travellers murmured admiration for the buildings, most of which flaunted gigantic portraits of Marx, Engels and Lenin, and massive red and white banners, I found them, although stately, grossly unimaginative. I preferred the diverse individuality of the new creations in West Berlin.

The visit to East Berlin which is rivetted in my memory was when Ruth Barber (Toronto) and I decided to go there on our own in the Fall of 1955. We both felt uneasy, but bravely we boarded the S Bahn that would take us into the city. We got off at Alexanderplatz from where we walked to a large state operated department store which the Communists called HO (Handels-Organization). Here rationed food and goods could be bought at inflated prices without coupons. In a city where a worker averaged $100 a month, HO charged twelve dollars for a pound of coffee and three dollars for a pound of butter.

The windows of East Berlin reflected the drabness of the few listless people who passed us by. They were poorly dressed. A general air of gloom permeated the place. There were no colours, no neon. There were virtually no automobiles. I heard no laughter. The grey overcast sky of late afternoon did not help the drab despair. We were frightened and we were sad. An hour's sortie into this muted grey desolation was enough. We couldn't wait to scramble aboard the S. Bahn which rattled much too slowly for us along its elevated iron structure.

We could only breathe easily when we reached West Berlin and its hustle and bustle, its blazing neon lights and its post-war euphoria.

*

Never before had I experienced such a fun-packed social life as in Soest. I couldn't believe my popularity. Telephones were a rare commodity in those days in Germany and I was the only teacher lucky to get one.

I always looked forward to the formal dances at the base. But none could compare to my first, the rotation ball of 30 September 1955. I was dazzled by the colourful full dress uniforms worn by the officers of the corps and by different calvary and infantry regiments, each with its own distinctive uniform. I could not identify the uniforms. All I saw was a kaleidoscope of brilliant colour: tunics of scarlet, blue and green; heavy gold braiding; stripes on shoulders and down the outside seam of trousers, wide, narrow and double of silver, white or scarlet; crimson sashes; gilt buckles and buttons; and gold chain. The colourful sight was a visual feast. With their dashing good looks, impeccable manners, and badges of rank and service, every officer was a Canadian hero.

This, of course, was the glamorous side of the military. Although much later I taught the poems of Wilfred Owen, Siegfried Sassoon and Randall Jarrell, which focus on the horrors of war rather than on its seductiveness, I was, then, mesmerized by the military's ceremonial aspects.

Dancing was my magnificent obsession. But at these formal balls, I enjoyed sitting out a dance or two, to admire the beauty and chivalry before me, to watch the military protocol coupled with the pageantry and exuberance of the dance.

Several times a week, there was a dance at the Club Belaac which had a statue of St. Barbara in one corner. How I enjoyed being there! The dance floor was smooth. The orchestra was good. And there was always a crowd of military men, both Canadian and Belgian, eager to dance. I still remember Bobby Calmeyn, a young Belgian officer I dated for several months who fascinated me with his enormously polite manners. He showered me with flowers, but I preferred the company of Canadian and British officers.

Most of them were very good dancers, who would turn and spin me out in space, and bring me back in, so smoothly that I could lose myself in the pure joy of the dance. We waltzed, quick stepped, tangoed and rhumbaed, fox trotted and polkaed. We jived and jitterbugged. I was spun, flipped and twirled. I responded to the music and found it easy to follow my partners' leads. Whether the band played "Now is the Hour" (my father's favourite waltz) or "Begin the Beguine," "Besame Mucho," "Hernando's Hideaway," "Don't Fence Me In," or "Sentimental Journey," each dance was our own. When I was asked to dance "Goodnight Sweetheart," which was always the last dance of the night, I knew it signified a special relationship.

I wore my contact lenses. I believed in the saying popular at the time, that "boys don't make passes at girls who wear glasses." As a result, when I could not tolerate my contact lenses, I still refused to wear my glasses and depended on friends to tell me who was present so that I could decide whether to make myself visible or take refuge in the ladies' room. I had brought a beautiful wardrobe including special dresses made for dancing. A German woman who came regularly once complimented me on my outfits. She could describe each one. I never sat out a dance. I felt so fortunate. Port Arthur was never like this. There was no Serafina here. I was Penny to everyone I met.

Besides the dances, which delighted me, there were other military functions which I found fascinating. I enjoyed the parades. At a special tattoo celebrating Canada Day (1956) at the Rote Erde stadium in Dortmund, the precision drills, the massed band and drums, the marches, and the playing of "O Canada" sent chills up my spine. I was so proud to be Canadian.

Presentation to the Duke of Edinburgh

On 17 October 1955 the Duke of Edinburgh, the Honourary Colonel-in-Chief of the Royal Canadian Regiment, arrived by helicopter at Fort York to present colours to his regiment. An officer of the Regiment had invited me to the ceremonies. I was excited because the Royals have always intrigued me. As a Canadian and a British subject I followed with avid interest the headlines about the young handsome Prince Consort. I would be meeting him!

The day was cold and bleak with fog and hail. I wore my lovely black woollen dress with white cuffs, black patent leather pumps and matching gloves, my grey fur jacket, red velvet hat and black leather purse. I wanted to look elegantly classic.

My escort brought me to a room that was crowded with officers' wives, all waiting to be presented to the Duke. I was the only single lady present. Not one wife spoke to me, but their icy glares spoke volumes. The priggish snobbery of officers' wives was legendary. I wished I had not come. A photographer took a group picture.

The next thing I knew I was being introduced to Prince Philip. He looked bored. I curtsied. He looked straight ahead and said nothing. I was disappointed. But his aide-de-camp, General Browning, Daphne du Maurier's husband, smiled; I think he said something. I reconciled my disappointment by concluding that the Prince wasn't as handsome or as tall as I had imagined.

The official ceremony was convened with the great pomp and circumstance I associated with the military. The precision of the drill movements was impressive, the drum flourishes, bugle calls and quick marches enjoyable. I was proud when "The Maple Leaf Forever" and "The British Grenadiers" were played.

During the luncheon, the band of the Royal Canadian Regiment played regimental marches, Boieldieu's "The Caliph of Bagdad," Strauss's "Roses from the South," "Deep River," "Blue Tail Fly," the "Londonderry Air" and American folk tunes under the direction of Captain J. Purcell. What a fitting surname, I mused.

An uneasy silence prevailed while we feasted on Sherry Consommé, Roast Danish Duck, Parsleyed Potatoes, Minted Green Peas, Asparagus, Hot Rolls, Canadian Apple Pie with Ice Cream, and Coffee. Guests shifted about uncomfortably in their chairs and cast furtive glances about. I could hear the clinking of cutlery against china. But once the Duke left, chattering started. And when the head table left, everyone relaxed over crème de cassis liqueur.

A formal dance in the evening concluded the day's festivities. I wore my sleeveless white chiffon over a full skirt of white tulle, and over the elbow, white kid gloves, silver pumps with matching clutch purse and a rhinestone tiara in my hair. As I floated to the sensual rhythm of "Secret Love" and swirled to the syncopated beat of "Night and Day," I soon forgot the afternoon's disappointment. The last entry of the day in my diary reads, "Imagine, Brigadier Anderson knew my name!"

*

The Christmas season in Germany and France, which begins with Advent, is a festive one. Cities, towns and even small villages are festooned with bright lights and animated Christmas decorations. I had never seen such glitter, and it was years before it arrived in Thunder Bay. In fact, the Advent wreath and calendar did not arrive until years later too.

To see the German Christmas spirit at its best, we visited the Christ Kindl Market in Nuremburg in early December. Thousands of gold leaf angels in all sizes and shapes were for sale. As well as a whole variety of things associated with Christmas, such as trees, toys, and candles. The smells of Christmas, of ginger and marzipan and spices, filled the cool air, as did the strains of Christmas carols. There was nothing like this in my home town. I was fascinated.

Santa Claus, to my surprise, was not known here. The great day for children was not Christmas Day but 6 December, the feast of St. Nicholas. On St. Nicholas Eve, St. Nicholas, wearing a bishop's robe, mitre and white gloves, accompanied by Black Peter, who came with a sack on his shoulder and a birch rod in his hand, made his annual call on children who left a polished shoe in front of their bedrooms. If they had been good, their shoe was filled with candies, toys and holiday treats; if bad, a cluster of twigs.

Christmas Vacation 1955 in Bavaria

Barbara Dickson, a petite and most cheerful primary schoolteacher from Winnipeg, and I left by train for

Bavaria to spend our 1955 Christmas holidays, our first Christmas away from home.

We arrived at Heidelberg at four in the morning and decided to stay the day and the following night. I loved the academic ambience of the city: the university (Germany's oldest), the student prisons, and the student inns, Roter Ochse and Zum Seppl where we heard about the mad-cap escapades of the fraternity students. Heidelberg Castle, destroyed, not by World War II bombs, but by the Orleans Wars of Succession (1689-1693) was another of our favourite haunts.

At Vater Rheim in the Castle, we met two American medical students who were studying in Basle, Switzerland. We danced the night away in the spirit of Perkeo, the dwarf who emptied the famous Heidelberg Tun, the world's largest wine barrel, that has a stairway built up one side leading to a dance floor. Heidelberg has made Perkeo its symbol, the symbol of abundance, fertility and the joyousness of life.

It was raining when we arrived in Garmisch-Partenkirchen in the Bavarian Alps. And it rained most of the time we were on holiday, but we didn't let that spoil our spirits. Hundreds of American servicemen were on leave, all, like us, in search of holiday fun. American Army-run resort leave centres were in Garmisch and Berchtesgaden, and Munich was a major American base, so there was a large selection of tours available to American service personnel. We were lucky to be included.

Skiing was a popular sport. And the Zugspitze, Germany's highest mountain, was the only place that had snow. Ever since my sister broke her leg skiing at Mount Baldy in Port Arthur, I have been reluctant to ski. But one of the American soldiers on ski patrol, who pursued me, encouraged me to try it again. We ascended

9,722 feet by cog train and cable car, and I kept my eyes closed during the ascent. Once we reached the top, I was so entranced by the beauty of the vista before me that I just stood awestruck at the majestic snow-capped Alpine peaks of three countries — Austria, Italy and Switzerland — silhouetted against the brilliant sun. I would have been content just admiring the white wonderland around me, but my friends insisted I put on skiis. Dressed in American issue white parka, ski pants, goggles, skiis and mittens, I took lessons from my ski patroller. But I was just too scared to enjoy it very much. I preferred sipping chocolate at 8,695 feet in the Schneefernerhaus and listening to World War II anecdotes about members of the German and American high command.

Barbara and I spent our days taking sightseeing tours of the Bavarian countryside and Austria, visiting Oberammergau, Eagle's Nest, Hitler's favourite mountain retreat, high on the slopes of Obersalzberg; and Salzburg, the birthplace of Wolfgang Amadeus Mozart.

Our night-life was unbelievable. We danced the nights away to American hit-parade tunes and German songs like *Du gefallst mir* and *Immer Wieder Du*. It wasn't surprising for the dance band to launch into a Chopin polonaise or even a Bach fugue; everyone listened. The German bands were fantastic, playing anything from Bach, boogie and mambo, to Dixieland jazz and Negro spirituals. In Garmisch we went to the Casa Carioca, unique among night clubs in Europe. Tiered like the Roman coliseum, it boasted a dance floor that doubled for an ice rink. The ice review *Home Town U.S.A.* was ravishingly beautiful in sets and skating stars. Despite the glitz, I still preferred places like Madl Bar, a small and cosy German night club that was warm and intimate and had live music. I remember hearing the Third Man theme played on the zither as I have never heard it before, by a woman who had lost both her legs skiing in the mountains. Our German meals were hearty and the portions were generous: Weinerschnitzel à la Holstein (veal cutlet with a fried egg on top), potatoes, beans, beets, and peas, and always my favourite dessert, apple streudel. Instead of beer I drank *gluwein* (hot wine).

Although Munich was 40 per cent destroyed during World War II, the city did not show its open war scars blatantly. I did not feel that choking nausea that I felt in Berlin, Cologne or Essen. Its citizens — typically Bavarian — had recaptured their joie-de-vivre with amazing alacrity. Beer flowed bountifully in the huge grey clay beer steins unique to the Hofbrauhaus, a fabulous night club three stories high, and probably the most famous eating place in Munich.

The Hofbrauhaus was a rowdy, fun-filled place. There was whistling, shouting, loud music, laughter, and a buzz of sounds as guests called for round after round of beer.

We sat at a boisterous, long, wooden table where Germans and tourists alike pounded their feet and rhythmically clapped hands while a brass band played such foot-stomping melodies like "In München steht ein Hofbräuhaus" and "Der Fröhliche Wanderer." Everyone joined in the chorus at the top of their voices to "Oh mein Papa," "Lili Marleen" and "Auf Wiederseh'n." "Gesundheit" and "Gemütlichkeit" reigned. "Ein prosit" was king.

And if an inebriated German became obnoxious, a bouncer just showed him to the door. Nowhere in the world could there be another Hofbrauhaus.

I made sure we got to Midnight Mass at Sheridan Barracks. It wasn't as moving as Midnight Mass back home with choir, nativity scene, lights, and scores of poinsettia plants. But it was familiar and I felt at home. On a rainy Christmas Day we dined on traditional turkey and cranberry sauce, roast potatoes, mince pie, flaming plum pudding decorated with holly, candies, nuts and fruit. And we danced the night away.

We spent New Year's Eve in Berchtesgaden in order to attend the St. Sylvester's Tanz at Hotel Vier Jahreszeiten, a former summer residence of the Kings of Bavaria. The dance was a family affair with mother, father and kids all included. The punch, a hot toddy of red wine, cinnamon, sugar and lemon, called St. Sylvester's, was delicious. But one of my thoughtful American soldiers splurged on Pomeroy Champagne to celebrate.

As the twelfth stroke of the clock resounded from the cathedral, we heard mighty cannon shots at regular short intervals echoing through the mountains. "Christmas shooters" they were called, an old custom of the Berchtesguden region to drive out the old year and salute the new.

On 3 January, Barbara and I left Munich on the train for Soest. I shall never forget my Christmas in Bavaria, my first in Europe, and the American soldiers who had made it so memorable. My diary said it all: "Soest is so far north."

Easter in Italy, 1956

I took a motor trip to Italy for Easter vacation with Isabel Ward from Ottawa, a tall, statuesque redhead who had served in Canada's air force during World War II.

From Soest we drove on the busy German autobahn. It was exciting compared to the mostly quiet, two-lane Trans-Canada Highway: gigantic billboards flashed emergency telephone numbers and car and trucks whizzed by. I had never seen anything like it. When we reached Zurich, we put the car on the train to Como. On the other side of the Gotthard Pass, workmen were shovelling huge banks of snow.

It was Good Friday when we arrived at Lake Como. The harbour was decorated with coloured lanterns and huge crosses for the Good Friday procession which, for the first time in many years, was being held. Balconies on the procession route were draped with red bunting. I was surprised at the large number of the faithful marching slowly and chanting as the procession wound its way to the Lake where priests blessed the waters. Ladies in very high heels were even marching. "It was a touching demonstration of a people's faith," I wrote in my diary.

Milan

Italy, of course, was the place to be for Holy Week. En route to Milan we stopped at a number of decorated villages to visit churches. I was always moved by the piety I observed. We stayed in Milan chiefly to see Leonardo da Vinci's "The Last Supper" and its famous opera house, La Scala. To my surprise, "The Last Supper" was a fresco painted on the wall of Cenacolo Vinciano, the Dominican friars' refectory next to the Renaissance church, Santa Maria delle Grazie. On 16 August 1943 allied bombs had completely destroyed the roof and one wall of the refectory, but the fresco miraculously survived. My diary reads, "How faded it is." La

Scala was smaller than I had pictured it to be. But I loved
its six graceful banks of loges. The interior, bathed in a
dim pink light, projected a cozy feeling. Although it had
been completely renovated since its destruction by Allied bombs in 1943, I noticed Benito Mussolini's name
still above the stage. We saw the opera *La figlia di Jorio*
by Ildebrando Pizzetti (1880-1968) based on the tragedy
by Gabriele D'Annunzio (1863-1938). It was a new
opera first performed in Naples on 4 December 1954.
Set in Italy's Abruzzi region, it tells of the sacrifice which
Mila, the prostitute daughter of Jorio, an old sorcerer,
makes in order to save her true love. The plot was trite,
but the singing, especially that of the chorus, was engaging. Isabel and I were sorry that we missed Maria Callas
who appeared the following week.

Three other landmarks in Milan attracted my interest: the Duomo, the Galleria Vittorio Emanuele and the
Cimiterio Monumentale. The Duomo, Milan's Cathedral, the largest Gothic structure in Italy, was awesome.
It was a fantastic mass of white marble with 135 spires
soaring skywards, the beautiful *Madonnina* 350 feet
high, and surmounting the spires were 2,245 statues that
adorned the exterior. In front of the cathedral was the
huge vari-coloured pavement of the Piazza del Duomo.
Here began the Galleria Vittorio Emanuele, a huge glass-
domed, mosaic-floored shopping arcade with cafés,
bars, bookshops, and restaurants. I had never before
seen anything like it. The elegance and sophistication of
the fashionable Milanese women dazzled me. "Enclosed
shopping malls! Exactly what Canadians need to protect
us from our cold and ice," I remarked to Isabel. There
were no mausoleums in our local cemeteries until a few
years ago and they are ugly, plain, concrete box-like
structures, nothing like Milan's unbelievable Cimiterio

Monumentale. The entrance's facade had shining bands of alternating black and white marble; and the most ostentatious mausoleums in the shapes of pyramids, glass houses, and chapels, adorned with obelisks, gigantic urns and huge statues, all making their dramatic statements. Some may call them artistic monuments to human vanity; for others, the mausoleums offered refuge for the body, the temple of the Holy Spirit. As my mother always reminded me, "Italians remember and honour their dead."

I remembered that it was here in Milan at a service station in the Piazzale Loreto where Italian partisans strung Mussolini and his mistress, Claretta Petacci, heads downward.

We were told that we had to see the Certosa (Charterhouse) of Pavia, one of the world's famous monasteries. It was out of our way, but we decided to go. We found it closed. We had to settle for Easter Sunday Mass at a small unassuming chapel nearby because we wanted to be in Genoa in time for lunch. Genoa, Christopher Columbus's birthplace! We didn't look for any monuments erected in his honour and remained just to have lunch at a quaint little restaurant, *Il pesce d'oro* which specialized in fish. The drive along the Ligurian coast was a joyous surprise. As we ascended and descended corkscrew roads and negotiated the hairpin turns of the high coastal mountains, the magnificent panorama of mountains and sea was stupendous. Known as the Italian Riviera, the Ligurian coast boasted such resort towns as Santa Margherita, Portofino, and Rapallo, popular then with the rich and famous. Blocks of new stucco apartments hugging the cliffs overlooking the Mediterranean Sea were painted in pastel shades of pink, turquoise, green and yellow, each with its own balcony brimming over with red geraniums. The Italians were celebrating Easter Sunday. The streets were alive with beautifully dressed children and scores of small Vespas, carrying glamorous girls in high heels sitting side saddle and even families of four.

We spent Easter Sunday night at the Palazzo di San Giorgio in the quaint little fishing town of La Spezia, an important naval base. Authors such as Dante, Petrarch, Shelley, Byron and D. H. Lawrence had lingered here or had written about the picturesque town.

From La Spezia we passed Lerici where Shelley sailed for Livorno on 1 July 1822, to visit friends. On the voyage back he was drowned on 8 July in a storm off Viareggio. We drove through Carrara, known all over the world for the marble that Michelangelo favoured, into Pisa, where we threaded our way through narrow, twisting alleys to the Leaning Tower. What the Eiffel Tower is to France, and the Statue of Liberty to the United States, the Leaning Tower of Pisa is to Italy. Isabel and I were both awestruck as we gazed and admired it, fifteen feet out of the perpendicular. And I thought of Galileo, who stood on it, to test his theory of gravity. We were surprised to see so many bombed-out buildings; half of Pisa had been destroyed during World War II.

From Pisa we drove to Rome where we took a USO tour that took us to the famous landmarks. The highlight of this visit was seeing Pope Pius XII being carried on his elevated throne down the main aisle of St. Peter's through an enthusiastic, jam-packed crowd, who cheered like screaming fans at a World Cup soccer game. But when His Holiness began to speak, I could have heard a pin drop. That evening we went to the Rome Opera House to hear *I Vespri Siciliani*. It was opening night. I was dazzled by Rome's sophisticated women in mink and ermine and diamonds, but it was the *bravos* from the gallery that delighted me.

A different world met our gaze as we drove from Rome to Naples: there were donkey carts, oxen, mules, peasant women with paniers of brush and fodder or water jugs balanced on heads, flocks of sheep and goats, wooden yokes, fast motor scooters, orange and lemon trees, umbrella pines, shrubs and little chapels in caves and mountain sides. The number of World War II scarred mountain villages shocked me. Allied forces fought some of their fiercest battles of World War II in and around Naples in 1944. Northeast of Naples, Cassino crumbled to charred pieces under Allied air and artillery bombardments in vicious street by street and house by flaming house fighting.

High above the town was the ancient monastery founded by St. Benedict in 529 A.D. that made Cassino famous. The Americans erroneously believed that the Monastery served as a German army observation point. They deliberately released nearly six hundred tons of bombs on the Abbey and its grounds. The Monastery crashed to the ground in utter ruin. Luckily its historic treasures — thousands of priceless manuscripts, books and documents that comprised one of the greatest medieval collections in the world — had been removed to Rome for safekeeping. We drove up the winding road to the 1,703 foot high Monte Cassino hill. The row upon row upon row of white crosses left me numb.

We stayed at the Hotel Patria in Naples but did not explore the city. Instead, we took a tour to Capri. We were then taken by boat to the Blue Grotto and later transferred into a rowboat and paddled into the Grotto, where we had to duck because the entrance was barely three feet high. It was a dull rainy day, but the water was a beautiful aquamarine colour like laundry blueing. We were told that Tiberius, who spent the last eleven years of his reign on Capri, swam in the grotto.

Although we were afraid to drive ourselves, the taxi driver of an ancient Fiat whom we hired was so daring on the narrow twisting roads to Anacapri that we might have been less terrified if we had driven ourselves. After the exhausting drive we were finally able to relax when we saw the villa which belonged to Dr. Axel Munthe whose novel *The Story of San Michele* contributed much to Capri's international fame.

It was raining when we arrived in Pompeii, a name that was familiar to me since childhood because of my mother's devotion to the Madonna di Pompeii. We walked along the straight streets worn into deep ruts by heavy Roman carts. We entered large squares and temples and shops with their jars and counters. We visited the ruins of the Forum, the spacious amphitheatre, patrician homes, public baths and commercial districts recalling day to day life when Rome was at the height of her power. We gazed at graffiti and inscriptions on walls, lecherous caricatures, obscene words of abuse and tender phrases. Women were not allowed into bordello rooms showing the most lecherous scenes. We admired the mosaic friezes illustrating scenes from Greek mythology on the walls of wealthy homes. The best preserved were at the Temple of Apollo, where we marvelled at a mosaic of drinking doves, and another of a cat in the act of seizing a bird. The colours, even in the open air, retained their brilliance; the colour known as "Pompeiian red" has never been duplicated. We noticed ovens, flour mills and sacrificial altars. But it was the statue of the dancing Fawn that captured my imagination and where I lingered longest.

We saw what life must have been like in the city when it was suddenly extinguished in 79 A.D. by the eruption of Mt. Vesuvius. Patricians, tradesmen, freedmen and slaves, were all buried under the downpour of lava, mud and burning ashes thirty-six feet deep. The bodies of some of the victims could be seen in one of the rooms performing the work they were doing at the moment of the eruption. Some had an expression of fear, their hands trying to protect their faces; a few embraced in their last hopeless attempt to shelter one another.

From Pompeii we drove north passing lemon and orange groves. We passed Padua, Bologna and Florence. At Bolzano we encountered snow and trees with pink blossoms sprayed blue. It was a beautiful sight.

We took the Brenner Pass and the Innsbruck route, passing through Tyrol's mountains, picturesque villages, each with a cluster of wooden homes around a church, and isolated little farmhouses perched on green mountain terraces, consisting of a chestnut brown upper storey of wood which often juts beyond the lower storey to provide protection for neatly piled stove wood. The sights and sounds were wonderful: jagged snow-capped peaks, the tinkling of cowbells from mountainside pastures, window boxes brimming with red and pink geraniums, and wayside shrines. But it was the abundance of wood which impressed me. In Italy it was one smooth stuccoed block after another; here in the Tyrol it was one wooden chalet after another. We stopped at Innsbruck to admire its unique setting. The steep sheer sides of the Alps made an impressive backdrop for the green domes and red roofs of the Baroque town tucked beneath.

From Innsbruck we drove to the quaintly picturesque town of Mittenwald where we stopped to admire
the attractive painted facades of a number of homes,
grouped, as was usual in these mountains, around a
magnificent belfry. I entered a beautiful white and
gilded, ornate church, Maria in Weiss, and found the
holy water frozen in the fount.

*

I had spent a wonderful year in Soest. But I felt that
French rather than German would be more useful to me
in Canada. As a result, I had requested a transfer and was
assigned to #2 Fighter Wing at Gros-Tenquin in the
province of Lorraine in France. But I was sad when I left.

Before going to Gros-Tenquin, I had decided on a
trip that would take me to Vienna and then through
Yugoslavia, Greece, Turkey, Lebanon, Syria, Jerusalem,
Egypt and Sicily for my summer holidays. I was searching for sunshine, fun and culture.

I was travelling alone because I had been unable to
find a female companion who wanted to travel so far for
so long. If I had known that a foreign woman travelling
alone in those countries was suspect, that female taboos
made travelling alone embarrassing and dangerous, I
probably would not have gone.

Summer Vacation, 1956 to the Balkans
and Middle East

Austria: Vienna

Summer 1956 was the first summer that Vienna was free
of the occupation and border restrictions imposed by
the Russians. It had survived Nazi annexation during
World War II, Russian liberation, and the four power
occupation by Great Britain, France, the United States
and Russia. Once the centre of a vast empire that
stretched across Central Europe from the borders of
Germany almost to the Black Sea, Vienna had defiantly
wiped away the traces of its war ruins.

On 3 July 1956, naively and a bit apprehensively, I
started on my trip. It never occurred to me that a young
woman travelling by herself was suspect. But I was
determined to take advantage of my stay in Europe to
explore the Balkans and the exotic Middle East. When I
arrived on the train from Soest at the Westbahnhof, I
knew at once that I was going to like this capital city.

But an unfortunate incident soon marred my visit. I
tried to cash a bank draft for $1,500.00 Canadian which
had been sent to me by my bank manager in Port Arthur.
The signatures on the bank draft, however, did not
match the authorized ones. I was refused payment. I
pleaded, but to no avail. It was a late Friday afternoon
and so I rushed to the Canadian Embassy for help. I told
them I had no money for the weekend. But they refused
to help me telling me to wait until Monday when I
should go to the central bank.

I must have walked miles my first weekend in Vienna, entering any historical building that had no
entrance fees, waiting for Monday morning. My hotel

was a small, modest one. The landing and stairs had automatic light switches that allowed only a minute's worth of electricity before turning off. For three nights I groped in the dark to find my room. On Monday I went to the central bank and reported my predicament. After a long distance phone call to my bank manager which I had to pay for, I received my money. I was so nervous that when I went to convert some of my money into Austrian currency, I first went to the wrong wicket. When I finally found the right wicket, I discovered, to my horror, that my purse was missing. I dashed to the first wicket and there, to my relief, my purse was sitting on the counter where I must have left it.

I treated myself and booked into the luxury hotel, the Sacher. Having gone without food for two days I was hungry. I also treated myself to the world-renowned Damel's, founded in 1786. I gorged on its specialty cakes, chocolates and apple strudel heaped with mounds of *sahne* (whipped cream). Even today, my mouth salivates when I remember.

I also treated myself to a performance of the world-famous Lipizzaners at the Spanish Riding School founded by Prince Eugene of Savoy, Austrian hero of the wars with the Turks, who retook Belgrade from the Sultan's forces. I was entranced by the marvellous skill and precision which the horses displayed in their musical riding exercises, and was left speechless with the ballet sequence known as the School Quadrille which ended the programme.

Even though the proud and glorious empire of the Hapsburgs had collapsed decades ago, their legacy remained in the well-known landmarks of Hapsburg Vienna that still dominated the city. My first landmark was beautiful and sprawling Schönbrunn Palace built on the edge of the Wienerwald and surrounded by formal gardens, fountains and monuments, the favourite summer residence of the eighteenth century Empress Maria Theresa.

I also visited St. Stefan's Cathedral, a Gothic masterpiece rivalling any Gothic cathedral I have visited in Italy or Spain or France. Its south tower, known to the Viennese affectionately as the *Seiffl*, the third highest spire in Europe after Ulm and Cologne, still dominates Vienna's skyline. It was my constant landmark during my walking tours of the inner city, as was the musical Anker Clock with its famous midday parade of historical figures.

On each visit to the cathedral, I invariably gravitated towards the stone pulpit and the delicacy of its spun-sugar decoration, a Gothic masterpiece of incomparable beauty carved around 1510. On the parapet are the four Latin fathers of the church, St. Augustine, St. Gregory, St. Jerome and St. Ambrose, each given an individual satiric personality. Lizards and toads, symbols of good and evil, crawl along the balustrade. From below the pulpit steps, the sculptor, Anton Pilgram, leans out of a half-open window surveying his handiwork.

Vienna's great and long musical tradition lured me. I had always associated Vienna with its pre-war elegance and charm, Strauss waltzes and operettas. I had skated to the "Vienna Woods" and waltzed to the "Blue Danube." I had seen Mozart's *Cosi Fan Tutte* and Lehar's *Die Lustige Witwe* (The Merry Widow). I had played the classical composers — Haydn, Mozart, Beethoven, Schubert and Brahms — all of whom had lived and worked in Vienna.

Vienna did not forget them. She remembered them with memorial rooms and monuments and statues: Mozart rising above a swirl of cherubs; a seated

Beethoven, looking like a great Titan surrounded by allegorical allusions to the Ninth Symphony; Brahms listening to music's muse; Schubert sitting meditating, with pencil in hand and scorebook on his lap; and Johann Strauss, Junior, coaxing sweet music from his violin.

But Vienna's musical life in the summer of '56 was meagre. To my utter disappointment, the Burgtheatre and the state Opera House (one of the finest opera houses in the world) were "*geschlossen*" (closed). All I could do was admire their magnificent architecture. However, I was able to see a performance of "Kiss me Kate" performed in German at the Volkstheatre. I was not impressed. It was too slapstick.

A number of years later I was fortunate enough to hear Montserrat Caballé in *La Traviata* at the State Opera. After standing in a queue for four hours on the day of the performance, I was able to get standing room tickets for twenty-five cents. Although it was tiring to stand throughout the entire performance, shifting my balance and trying to support myself by holding on to a bar in front of me, I had a wonderful view of the stage. At intermission I was able to wander about and admire the building which was bombed during an air raid on 12 March 1945, and then rebuilt after the war: the dazzling gold and white of its interior, the sparkling crystal of the chandeliers, the statuary and the paintings. But best of all I enjoyed watching the Viennese men and women in glamorous evening dress pass down the grand staircase.

The Vienna woods which Beethoven loved are an obligatory tourist haunt. An Australian girl and I took the tour. It was the first warm day of the summer and the Viennese were out on picnics among the beech, chestnut, birch and fir trees of the Prater. In Grinzing, a suburb on the slopes at the edge of the Vienna woods, a traditional bunch of evergreen twigs hung above the entrance to each tavern to tell us that the new wine was for sale. In one that we entered, a quartet which included a zither, an accordion and a violin was playing Strauss waltzes.

From these woods I caught my first glimpse of the Danube River below us. Our guide kept calling our attention to its "beautiful" blueness. But, for the world of me, all I could see was a ribbon of dull brown.

While we were on this tour, we passed the Karl Marx Hof, a massive apartment building containing over 1,000 flats which stretches for more than half a mile. Built in 1930, it was a showpiece of the socialist government. This information piqued my curiosity regarding the Communist situation in Vienna. My Australian friend who worked in the Embassy in Vienna told me there were still many Viennese who were Communists. I saw a number of monuments commemorating the Russian occupation: the Russian War Memorial, the cemetery, and the "Red Monster" all of which I found unattractive. As part of the agreement between the Allies and the Soviets, the streets and bridges that were once part of the Russian occupied zone had to preserve their Russian names.

Yugoslavia

I boarded the Tauern Express from Vienna to Rijeka (Fiume), Yugoslavia's largest port, on my way to the seaside resort of Dubrovnik on Yugoslavia's Adriatic coast. The scenery from my train window was spectacular. As we ascended lofty forested mountain slopes on serpentine railroad tracks, cutting through tunnels at close intervals, I thrilled to see the imposing grandeur of hills, the depth of valleys, and the fresh, lush green grass of the meadows.

Once in Yugoslavia, a railroad attendant, standing rigidly at attention with a red flag under his arm, met us at every little station. There was no diner and I wasn't able to get dinars (Yugoslavia's currency). But in my compartment was a very slender, tall, refined-looking woman and her son, who fed and loaned me money. She told me, in excellent German, that she was divorced and worked as an x-ray technician in Zagreb and that her father had died in a German concentration camp. She didn't have to tell me they had been people of wealth. But now she had to be very careful with the little money she earned. Tito's Communist police state was an anethma to her. (It is interesting to note that as long as Marshall Tito was in power, his strong leadership held the country united into a working federation of six republics. When he died in 1980, however, ancient ethnic animosities surfaced. In 1990 the Communist party finally relinquished power, and in 1991, the country began to splinter; Serbian ethnic cleansing raged, and the republics declared their independence. In 1999, NATO conducted an air war against Slobodan Milosevic whose human rights abuse in the former Yugoslavia resulted in a decade of misery and carnage.)

It was six a.m. when we arrived at Rijeka. Since no taxis were in sight, I hired a porter and his trundle cart. We walked to Pretnik, the official Yugoslavian travel agency where I bought dinars and repaid my friend who made sure I was safely on board the *Ragusa*, the Queen of the Adriatic, to Dubrovnik. The ferry was packed with Yugoslavs going to the various offshore islands. On board I met two Canadian girls, one of whom, Mary

Vargo, taught on the same staff as Hilda Smith in British Columbia. The bleak and rugged mountains of the Dalmatian coast were beautiful and the voyage was relaxing.

The pier at Dubrovnik was like a dock anywhere else. But the walled town looked like a medieval picture book. I hired a taxi to take me to a hotel on the beach. The driver suggested the Hotel Excelsior. I knew I was going to like it as soon as I saw it. From my hotel window I could see the beautiful Adriatic Sea as well as one of the grey towers and part of the mighty wall of the inner city.

I remained on the sun-drenched beach from morning to night. Getting a perfect tan during the days of summer was an obsession with me. My role models were the beautifully tanned rich and famous who summered at the famous international beaches. Besides, the hot sun of summer served to hide the horrible acne on my face. I was fiercely determined to burn the pesky pimples away. We weren't told then how extremely dangerous the sun can be. In fact, we spread sun tan oil on our bodies to attract the sun even more and get a darker tan.

After the eight weeks of continuous rain I had endured in Soest, I was very happy to see sunny days. Even though the heat was scorching, I endured it patiently because I badly wanted a tan. However, I was too persistent and acquired a severe sunburn, which, according to a local doctor on the beach, required medical attention. But I was too frightened to go to a hospital. Instead, night after night I endured the pain of burned skin, and I just kept slathering Noxzema on my sunburnt back. After Soest's horribly inclement weather, I was determined not to complain about the golden sun which broiled me for five days. One of the two large jars of Noxzema which I had brought had broken, and the distinctive smell of Noxzema permeated my hotel room. To this day I love the smell.

It was easy to strike up conversations with the bathers on the beach. I had a wonderful time with Dorothy Thomas and her mother and nephew from Belgrade who took me to a number of cultural events that were being staged as part of a summer festival for an International Student Camp nearby. I shall never forget the setting in Dubrovnik's medieval towers and ramparts for Shakespeare's *Othello* and *Hamlet*. And even though I couldn't understand a word being spoken, I was thoroughly entertained. For my last night we went to Labyrinth, a night club tucked in the wall of the inner city with the water lapping underneath, for a concert of National Dances in which Serbs, Macedonians, and Croats, in colourful, distinctive, finely embroidered peasant costumes danced gay folk dances with dramatic and energetic abandon. I especially enjoyed the lively sabre dance.

I was behind the Iron Curtain. Very few people today can imagine the fear of Communism that was instilled in us living in the West. We were petrified. When I decided to go to Yugoslavia I promised myself and my friends that I would be extremely cautious. I would trust no one. A young well-dressed Yugoslavian, a member of the Communist party who held a good job with General Motors in Belgrade, kept pursuing me. I was so afraid that he was an informer that I kept dodging him until the very day I left Dubrovnik. Whenever he managed to have a conversation with me he attacked the Yugoslav aristocracy and the Americans. I reminded him that the Americans were giving Yugoslavia millions of dollars in foreign aid. I'll never forget his sarcastic response: "We want trade, not aid."

My hotel felt like a safe haven. Here I could forget I was in a Communist country. Most of the guests were either English or American. Although the hotel looked more like a first-class international summer resort, the electricity or the water or the lift would often break down, but the hotel management worked hard to please their guests. Only on a few occasions was I reminded that this was the land of the hammer and sickle. I discovered that everyone at the hotel had a customs declaration. I had remembered completing one at the border but never having been given one. And so I was told to go to the customs office. A small, lean, grey-haired man with a kindly face greeted me. We managed to understand each other after attempting Italian and German. He took me up several flights of stairs to "the chief" as he called him, a stocky, handsome man about forty-five. I explained my predicament in German. He told me I would have to bring my bags, camera and money to him for inspection. As politely as I could, I explained that it would be extremely inconvenient to bring my bags. He finally settled for my camera and money. He was surprised I returned so quickly. This time he was much more friendly. In fact he took a benevolent attitude. But I was suspicious of his intentions. As soon as I received the completed required forms I thanked him politely and left immediately, anxious to get away fast and far, very fast and very far. And yet, despite this fearful occurrence, and despite my sunburn and my attempts to evade my young Yugoslav suitor, I hated to leave Dubrovnik.

But it was time to go. I wanted to visit Sarajevo to see the spot where Archduke Franz Ferdinand of Austria, heir to the Hapsburg throne, was assassinated in 1914, touching off World War I. To see the spot was even more imperative to me because I had seen Belvedere Castle in Vienna, the Archduke's home from which he left to start on his fatal trip. I flew JAT, the local airline, to Sarajevo. We took two hours to reach the Dubrovnik airport. To my surprise the runways were dirt, and parked on the tarmac was an old airplane which I was told was an American DC4. I was afraid to get on board and more frightened when a policeman insisted on taking my passport. However, I was assured, in perfect English, by a Yugoslav university student who had attended the International Student Camp at Dubrovnik that my passport would be returned once we boarded the plane. It's impossible to move, let alone procure a hotel room without one's passport, so I felt that my concern was justified.

On board the American DC4 my fears mounted because we were given oxygen masks to wear. It was the only time in my life when I flew an entire trip wearing an oxygen mask. I was afraid I was going to die. However, to my relief, we landed in Sarajevo safely and my passport was returned.

On the way from the airport at Sarajevo to the city, our bus was stopped for half an hour because Egypt's Nasser was passing by. The road was lined with small, scattered groups of adults and children waving the Egyptian and Yugoslavian flags.

There were no taxis at the JAT office in Sarajevo. Once again I had to hire a porter to carry my luggage to the Hotel D'Europe that had been recommended to me at Dubrovnik.

My student friend took me on a walking tour of the city. I asked to see the exact spot of the assassination. On a building at the corner is a commemorative plaque and on the pavement below are the footprints marking the spot where the young Bosnian radical who shot Ferdinand through the heart stood. I was surprised to learn that when the Archduke's wife bent forward to hold her husband, a second shot killed her immediately. My history book never mentioned her death. I stood at the corner of the assassination spot and couldn't help contemplate the twists of fate when my student informant told me that no one had informed Ferdinand's chauffeur that his route had been changed in order to avoid the very corner where Ferdinand was killed.

Sarajevo, capital of Bosnia-Herzegovina, was a complete shock to me. Bosnia-Herzegovina was the republic that most absorbed five hundred years of Ottoman rule. I did not expect this Islamic influence, which is clearly apparent in the numerous mosques, the tall minarets, the oriental houses, the bazaar, and the people's dress and way of life. I spent a day walking alone about the older parts of the city which contain the relics of its Turkish past. I visited the Begova Dzamija Mosque, one of the largest mosques in the Balkans, and was impressed by its cleanliness, its bareness and the soft carpets beneath my bare feet. I saw Moslem women in their traditional *chalwars*, the loose baggy trousers draped at the ankles. Many of them carried babies (I didn't see one baby carriage or stroller). I saw herdsmen and shepherds in their brimless hats of brown curly fleece and sheepskin jackets, driving their large flocks of sheep and goats. I found the poverty and filth depressing: dilapidated little wooden oriental houses, remnants of the Turkish feudal period; and barefoot, brown men dressed in rags which were, in turn, covered with patches.

While I was photographing these scenes, a policeman suddenly appeared out of nowhere and sternly scolded me. He prohibited me from taking any more pictures of the Moslems or risk going to the police station. This sudden turn of events frightened me. Neither the beauty of the Begova Dzamija mosque nor the coolness of its shady and tranquil courtyard could tempt me to stay in Sarajevo any longer. I made arrangements to leave the next morning by plane for Belgrade.

I had no hotel reservation. As a result, I taxied from one hotel to another trying to find accommodation without any success. Belgrade, capital of Yugoslavia and of the republic of Serbia, was suffering from a severe housing shortage. Finally, I remembered that Dorothy Thomas in Dubrovnik had asked me to look up a Miss Avery, World Traveller and Lecturer, at the Palace Hotel. By this time I was frantic. After I explained my predicament over the hotel desk telephone, she kindly told me to tell the hotel clerk that she was willing to have a cot put in her room. Her "yes" was like manna from heaven.

Miss Avery was one of the most interesting people I have ever met. She had just returned from Moscow, and I sat up all night enraptured by the stories which she told me while she was standing on her head doing her yoga exercises.

The next morning, Miss Avery took me on a walking tour of Belgrade. She liked the city. She loved the people. She had taken pictures the day before in the market, and some of the people she had photographed stopped and talked to her. She kept telling me, "they are just starting, just beginning to become mechanized, modernized and westernized. You just wait and watch."

But Belgrade did not impress me. I found it dull and drab with no character. Tito's picture, ranging through a whole roster of sizes, was exhibited in every shop window. At night, the dimly lit main streets were jammed with pedestrians jostling one another to watch a small public outdoor T.V. (Belgrade had been devastated in World War II, first, by German bombs, and then by American. Today, it is the target of NATO's bombs because of Slobodan Milosevic's ethnic cleansing campaign in Kosovo.)

I found Belgrade's shops filled with goods of mediocre quality. Prices were exorbitantly high. Clothing was so expensive that it had to be bought on credit. A university professor who bought a pair of pajamas for 11,000 dinars (thirty-six dollars US) had to purchase them on the instalment plan. It took him eleven months to pay. I saw very few cars. Most were black and state owned, driven by the communist elite.

After a day's stay in Belgrade, I felt I had had enough. I boarded the Orient-Simplon Express for Athens. Although Yugoslavia's fields of golden wheat were beautiful, I saw no modern machinery. The two young Germans in my compartment and I breathed a sigh of relief when we finally crossed the border.

Greece

My first glimpse of Greece was a shock. Barren mountains gave the landscape a desolate and forbidding appearance. I found it difficult to imagine that this was the cradle of western civilization, the birthplace of our cultural and philosophical traditions. On the long and tedious rail trip through Greece to Athens I thought about the Greeks of antiquity, of Aristotle, and Plato. And Socrates, who chose to die by drinking hemlock, Hippocrates, Euclid, Pythagoras, and Ptolemy, whose geocentric cosmic order was still recognized in the sixteenth century despite Copernicus's new heliocentric theory. Somehow the barren countryside had not lived up to its fertile historical past.

After the long overnight train journey from Belgrade, I arrived in Athens tired, sticky, hungry and emotionally let down. I decided to treat myself to a first class hotel. Luckily the Gran Bretagne had vacancies. Its elegant ambience was just what I needed.

The next day I left on a two-day guided bus tour of the Argolis region in the Peloponnese peninsula. And what a rewarding experience it was. Although I had studied the Greek philosophers at University, I had substituted my Grade VIII piano for Grade XI Ancient History at high school, and I had studied neither the history, art and architecture of Greece nor Greek mythology. I had not read *The Iliad* or *The Odyssey*. This trip revealed how woefully ignorant I was of Greek culture.

A group of five cultured young American students who were on the trip, however, soon became my teachers. I was starved for knowledge. I became their eager disciple, devouring all they taught me. C. Dudley Brown and his friend George were especially patient and taught me to recognize the three architectural orders: the simplicity of the Doric column (sixth century B.C.), the fluted Ionic (fifth century B.C.), and the ornate Corinthian (fourth century B.C.). They taught me about dentils, coffered ceilings, egg and dart moulding, lentils, and pedestals, until I was soon able to identify them myself. Although I could identify architectural features, appreciate the beauty of the art and sculptures, and admire the skill of the masters who created such beauty, I knew I could never achieve the intensity of their love of antiquity. They had come as pilgrims. I had come as a tourist.

At Daphni I saw my first laurel tree. According to legend, it was once the nymph Daphne who was changed into a tree in order to escape from the god Apollo. Here too in a magnificently restored eleventh century monastery-church I saw the celebrated mosaics depicting Byzantine salvation history. When the accusing eyes and raised eyebrows of God, whose huge head filled the dome, stared down at me, I immediately asked Him for forgiveness and said a good Act of Contrition for my sins.

At Mycenae, believed to be the home of the Greek King Agamemnon, we stood dumbfounded before the vast walls called Cyclopean by the ancient Greeks because they believed that the massive stones in the walls could have been lifted only by the Cyclopes, one-eyed giants with super-human strength. Massive Cyclopean walls are preserved almost intact at Tiryns nearby. I must confess I couldn't totally share George and Dudley's utter fascination when they saw the Lion's Gate with two lionesses carved in relief above the massive lintel block of stone, which is the entrance into the fortified city of Mycenae. Thirty miles south from Mycenae in Argos, however, I did stand in awe of the huge ancient theatre with a seating capacity of 20,000, the largest in the Greek world when it was built in the fourth century B.C..

My interest was also piqued when we visited Epidaurus, the first health resort in history, where Aesculapius cured the sick. The 2300-year-old amphitheatre set amid pine trees and olive groves took my breath away. To demonstrate the amphitheatre's perfect acoustics, our guide asked in a low voice, "can you hear me?" On top of the fifty-five tiers of crescent stone seats we heard him from below as if he were standing beside us.

Corinth was the once luxurious city of celebrated courtesans where the Apostle Paul preached in the hope of reforming the city's decadent inhabitants. But I was more interested in the narrow and deep Corinth Canal, its straight rock sides rising sheer two hundred feet above the water below, which saves seven or eight hours on the journey around the Peloponnesian Peninsula. Its crossing is tricky, however, because there is a leeway of only two metres on both sides.

My introduction to ancient Greece ended too soon. The tour returned to Athens. My American friends had been wonderful teachers. Their excitement was infectious. I was falling under the spell of ancient Greece. They generously agreed to be my teachers in Athens.

The first place they took me to was the Acropolis. I was immediately enthralled by the Parthenon, the home of Athena, the Goddess of wisdom and valour, the protectress of Athens. Day and night we climbed the steep and slippery hill of the Acropolis to stand in awe of her royal dwelling. Only seventeen fluted outer Doric columns along each side, and eight at each end remain. And yet in the temple's bareness, I fell under its pristine spell. At dawn, and in the sunlight, under fantastically blue skies, its amber grandeur enthralled me. But it was best by moonlight, when its honey-coloured marble columns absorbed the light from the moon and the darkness from the night that the temple cast is unearthly magic.

When I visited the Parthenon again thirty years later, I was appalled at the deterioration. Air pollution had turned the beautiful honey-coloured pillars that I remembered so fondly into an ugly grey. The Parthenon

was roped off. Scaffolding hid much of the ancient
marble columns. I could not sit on ruins nor wander
about the rubble that strews the ground.

There was one other building on the Acropolis
which attracted my attention. This was the well-preserved porch on the Erechtheum whose roof is
supported by the Caryatids, six columns sculpted in the
shape of women, two metres high. The maidens are
beautiful to look at, even though they are not the original ones.

The originals, as well as other pieces from the
Parthenon, were taken by the Earl of Elgin (1766-1841)
and sold to the British government who placed them in
the British Museum in 1816. My American friends and
I felt that the Elgin Marbles, as the originals were called,
should be restored to the Parthenon. Thirty years later I
was told that the originals (except one) had been returned, but were housed within the Acropolis Museum
because of the pollution.

At night, the Acropolis dominates the Athens skyline and offers a breathtaking view of Athens. Each night
we would just sit amid the ruins admiring the beauty of
the Parthenon and of Athens. The refreshing breezes
were a welcome relief after the scorching summer sun.
Below the ramparts of the Acropolis itself are ancient
Roman theatres and the Agora; the historic marketplace
where Socrates and Plato once held court.

We returned to the National Archeological Museum
several times in order to make sure we had seen all the
exhibits that my American friends knew were there. I
was amazed at the number and variety of beautiful
treasures. I had never seen anything like them before. I
stood in wonder at it all. There was so much gold: gold
ritual vessels, gold goblets, gold diadems, gold masks,

gold scales, gold jewellery, a gold rattle, gold cups. There was so much bronze. There were fragments of friezes and murals. There were ancient objects of alabaster and ivory, marble, amber, amethyst and crystal. There were collections of coins, vases and clay tablets. The collections boggled my mind. Here, before me, was the material proof of ancient and rich civilizations. I felt humbled as I stood in reverential meditation.

But there is more to Athens than ancient ruins and museums. George and Dudley introduced me to the Plaka, below the ramparts of the Acropolis, with its narrow streets, tavernas, and its typical Greek dining and dancing places. Because I was accustomed to the garlic and olive oil in Italian food, I liked Greek food. The Greeks can do wonders with eggplant. Wherever I could, I would order moussaka, an eggplant casserole dish with a cheese topping. It was delicious, as were the dolmades, vine leaves stuffed with rice or meat and served hot with egg-lemon sauce. George and Dudley drank Retsina,a Greek wine, and ouzo,a Greek liqueur, both of which are said to cut the oil in food. I liked neither. Nor could I drink the Greek coffee which I found too strong.

One evening we went to a delightful taverna where we had shish kabob as I had never tasted it before. Then we went to an open air nightclub which could accommodate thousands. Here we heard six Greek soloists sing popular Greek tunes. We saw a skillful oriental dancer who had once danced for King Farouk of Egypt. Her dancing was beautiful, but the Greeks received it with an indifference which surprised me. They did, however, display their enthusiasm for a Mexican quartet of guitar players. We drank lemonade and water by the bucket.

I loved the outdoor life of the Mediterranean world. I loved to sit in Athens' sidewalk cafés in the sparkling sun or in the warmth of a summer evening. And since they are the haunt of tourists, you're sure to meet someone you know. I wasn't surprised when I met Martha LaSalle (Soest) at a sidewalk café. Although it was less of a strain to sit by myself, it was fun to try out my German, French or Italian with other tourists.

I loved to sit at Zonar's, Athens' famous sidewalk café, just to watch the people go by. I also liked to gaze at the house across the street, where Heinrich Schliemann, the celebrated German archeologist who excavated Troy, Tiryns and Mycenae, had lived with his young Greek wife. It was at Zonar's where I first tasted the mouth-watering baklava, filo-dough pastry soaked in honey and filled with chopped nuts. After this introduction, wherever I dined in Greece, I had baklava for dessert. I could never get my fill of it.

I liked to watch the changing of the guards ceremony by the extremely tall Evzones, the highly trained fighting men of the Presidential guard. Dressed in short pleated skirts, white stockings, black pom-pomed clogs and pony-tail tasselled hats, they guard the Tomb of the Unknown Soldier and the Royal Palace.

Since my American friends were leaving Athens, I decided to continue my tour of the Middle East and then return to Greece.

On my return flight from Cairo to Athens, my seat companion was a charming Italian engineer, Freddie, whose assistant Guglio met him at the airport. I hadn't made any hotel reservations, but Freddie told me the Y would be a good place for me to stay because I could do my laundry there.

Freddie wanted to be in charge of my return stay in Greece, but I told him that I was supposed to meet other friends. Nevertheless, he asked me out for dinner and I convinced him it would be more fun if we could make up a party. That night Freddie and Guglio took me and two American school teachers, whom I had met in Cairo, out for dinner at Glyfada, a wonderful beach resort near Athens. Here I had the best sea food I have ever tasted. We first inspected the fish in the kitchen. The men chose and we then dined out of doors at a table on the edge of a pier. It was wonderful.

We spent the next few days under sunny skies at the beaches near Athens swimming and sun bathing on the warm sands. The Aegean was the bluest blue. At the Theatre of Dionysus (fourth century B.C.) we paid twenty-five cents to listen to the Athens State Symphony Orchestra. I shall never forget *Brahms Symphony #1 Opus 68* as we sat among the scattered ruins with the stars above us and Greece's warm breeze around us. We also saw an outdoor performance of *A Midsummer's Night Dream* in Greek in the National Garden. The ballet was beautiful, and Puck especially impish.

It was time to return to more historical sites. George and Dudley, who had also returned to Athens from the Middle East, suggested we go to Delphi, the ancient sanctuary of the god Apollo, about one hundred miles from Athens.

On our way we noticed the harsh living conditions in the mountain villages. Flocks of sheep and goats were grazing on mountain slopes. Village women dressed in black were draining water from wells. Donkeys and mules were pulling wooden carts and wagons. Much of Greece is too hilly, and the soil too poor for cultivation, but olive trees do well even on the poorest land. We saw grove after grove; some were gnarled and split and looking very old. The landscape was a sea of beautiful silvery-green olive-tree foliage.

Except for a few pitiful columns, nothing remains of the Temple of Apollo located in a dramatic setting on the slopes of Mt. Parnassus. I was disappointed. But we walked amid the ruins, and George pointed out the great mountain wall of Mount Parnassus. We did not linger. There was too much to see in The Archeological Museum of Delphi.

The moment I beheld him I fell in love with the bronze statue of the charioteer of Delphi created in 476 B.C.. I feasted my eyes on the splendours of his youth: his perfectly rounded, beardless head; his curls; his aquiline nose; his full lips and sturdy neck. His wide open eyes and pupils of onyx held me in their power. Who was the artist who had created such extraordinary power and beauty? As he gazed impassively before him, I could not take my eyes away from him. I don't know how long I stood there in utter fascination. George had to tear me away from him. I promised myself that I would return. And return I did, thirty years later. I spent an hour standing before him, walking past and around, to the side and behind, admiring to the fullest his youthful beauty.

In modern Delphi we stopped at a souvenir shop that had a poster of the charioteer displayed in a window. I was so rhapsodic in my admiration that the owner of the shop gave the poster to me, refusing to be paid. When I got home I had it framed. It hangs in my living room where he continues to delight my eye.

I had studied Lord Byron's poetry at University, and knew that the club-footed, politically liberal poet had died, at the age of thirty-six, fighting with the Greek freedom-fighters against the Turks. George and I recited the well-known lines from *The Corsair:*

> The mountains look on Marathon
> And Marathon looks on the sea;
> And musing there an hour alone
> I dream'd that Greece might still be free . . .

We saw Byron's signature carved on a marble column at Cape Sounion, and our fingers traced the deeply-cut letters.

Cape Sounion is a magnificent rocky promontory high above the coast. From this promontory, with the blue Aegean below us, we could see Salamis, the scene of the naval battle where the Greeks destroyed the Persian fleet under Xerxes in 480 B.C.. Other lines from Byron came back to us: "The Isles of Greece, the isles of Greece!/Where burning Sappho lived and sung."

But I knew I didn't have time to see them. Thirty years later, I visited Crete and Santorini, and learned about Knossos, the centre of the 3000 B.C. Minoan civilization.

I was sad to be leaving Greece, and George and Dudley, who had taught me so much, and Freddy, who had shown me that there was more to Athens than museums and ruins, but the uneasy political situation bothered me. The Cyprus issue was making headlines. Greece was actively seeking union with Cypress, a British possession since 1878. The Papagos government wanted a plebiscite on the union question. But Great Britain was opposed. Turkey insisted that if the British withdrew from Cypress, the island should be given to Turkey. Three Cypriots had been hung in Cyprus by the British and a bitter feeling of indignation against England ran through all of Greece. There were several youth demonstrations with squads of police patrolling the streets. A group of enraged adolescents tore down the sign of one of the more frequented Athenian restaurants, The Picadilly, and in its place erected the sign "Cyprus." In the *Athens News*, an English daily, I read editorials that were blatantly anti-English. In the airport, as I was leaving, I noticed a bulletin board covered with pictures of atrocities that the British had committed in Cypress. The issue was not solved until 1960 when Cypress was granted its independence.

Turkey: Istanbul

Istanbul is the only city in the world that straddles two continents, situated as it is along the Bosphorus, a narrow strait linking the Sea of Marmora to the Black Sea. Known through different ages as Istanbul, Constantinople and Byzantium, it was as Byzantium that it had intrigued me. In my mind the word had conjured images of mystery and intrigue.

Once again I had difficulty finding a hotel room, but finally, thanks to a handsome, wealthy Turk who was my seat-mate on the flight, I was comfortably settled in Istanbul's newest hotel, the Divan.

After the sweltering heat of Athens, I welcomed Istanbul's cool breezes. On the afternoon of my arrival I took a tour to Istanbul on the Asian shore of the Bosphorus, facing the entrance to the Golden Horn. The narrow, crooked, cobblestone streets, flanked by old wooden houses with projecting upper storeys, and windows covered in wooden lattice work caught my interest. As did the enormous Selimiye Barracks, a military establishment, where Florence Nightingale had tended the Crimean wounded. Nearby was the largest

Muslim cemetery in Asia. Among the cypress trees were ancient tombstones, many of them crowned with turbans or tarbushes (fezzes) signifying a male laid to rest.

The tour was worthwhile because it clarified the waterway system that has fascinated me ever since I learned as a young student that Byron had swum the Dardanelles, a word whose musical resonance I still love.

We crossed the Galata bridge, which spans the Golden Horn, an inlet on the European side of the Bosphorus. Because there is no bridge over the Bosphorus, our bus boarded a ferry and in ten minutes we crossed the Bosphorus which joins the Black Sea and the Sea of Marmora and divides Turkey in Asia from Turkey in Europe. I shall not easily forget the cool breezes, and the countless minarets piercing the sky.

The silhouette of the Blue Mosque was unforgettable. It is an architectural wonder. Priceless blue tiles adorn the interior. I remember standing in utter amazement as I gazed and gazed at its ornate and intricate beauty, a sublime symbol of man's creative genius.

Before praying, a Muslim must purify himself with a symbolic wash. After using the water from the pools in the mosque courtyard, he then removes his shoes and enters one of the open niches provided around the walls of the courtyard. The men are separated from the women. I had to remove my shoes or slip large cloth slippers over them. I chose the latter. As in all mosques, the Blue Mosque had no pictures, no paintings, no statues, no chairs, no pews, no images. There were a few inscriptions in Arabic, notably, "There's no God but Allah. Mohammed is the messenger of Allah." The floor was beautifully carpeted. I saw men sleeping and squatting, and a group of young boys, sitting cross-legged in front of the 88,000 word Koran, which lay on a low wooden bookstand that rests on the carpet. They were reciting in a sing-song fashion, swaying the upper body forward and backward as they committed the words to memory.

The slender and graceful minarets overawed me. I invariably stopped to listen to and admire the melodious chant of the *muezzin* who climbs them five times a day calling the faithful to prayer with the phrase, "There is no God but Allah."

Our group was forced to wait half an hour before we were allowed entry to St. Sophia's Church because the President of Pakistan and his entourage, were inside. When they appeared outside, I'll never know why a few of us were picked to shake his hand and take his picture, in the midst of the sleek Cadillacs, the smart, good-looking Turkish policemen and soldiers, and a number of beautiful ladies in their pastel silk saris.

For 900 years St. Sophia's Church, built by Justinian between 532 and 537 A.D., was Christendom's greatest church, glittering with mosaics and art treasurers. When it was completed, Justinian beheld his masterpiece of architecture and declared, "Solomon, I have outdone thee." After 1453, when Constantinople fell to the Ottoman Turks, the building was used as a mosque. In 1935 it became a museum.

We also visited the Topkapi Museum, the historic residence of the Ottoman Emperors. The palace's grandiose facade and exquisite interior mesmerized me. But there were just too many wonders to see. We contented ourselves with the First Court, which housed its huge East Asian porcelain collection, and the Treasury, where I was dazzled by the glitter of diamonds, gold, emeralds, and jade.

I hired a taxi which picked up every fare it could find in spite of my protests, and after delivering them, finally got me to the covered Oriental Bazaar, the Kapali Carsisi, one of the oldest trading centres of the world, a city within a city. Along both sides of its narrow crooked streets are booths, open-fronted shops and small cubbyholes that look like little boxes. 3,500 shops offered an endless array of wares: beaten copperware, tapestries, oriental rugs, pottery, ivory, leather work, ancient Turkish daggers, silver, flintlock guns with mother of pearl handles, gold jewellery, hookahs, tooled brass plates and much much more. Wherever I stopped, I was offered a cup of hot mint tea! I was told I had to bargain here. But I wasn't good at it. I was too impatient. I paid fifty dollars (a lot of money in 1956) for a wide, silver belt with a gorgeously elaborate buckle. It turned out not to be silver at all.

I found Istanbul's street life fascinating: wandering vendors peddling sweet soft drinks in canteens of shiny brass; street sellers barbecuing ears of corn on makeshift grills; Turks, doubled over, carrying the most unbelievably heavy loads on their backs; and Turks smoking a hubble-bubble pipe. I saw Muslim women, draped in yards of black robing, with kohl-lined eyes peering out of a small opening around the face, walking so gracefully; and men donned in *galabieh* robes and *kaffiyahs* on their heads.

My wealthy plane acquaintance — a dashing, debonair sophisticate — showed me Istanbul's night life. The oriental floor shows were fabulous. But it was a real American cowboy act, complete with guns and knives, that fascinated the Turks. When he took me to the terrace of the Hilton Hotel overlooking the Bosphorus, the white Leander Tower, set on a tiny island some 200 yards from the coast of Asia, was illuminated. The lights twinkled from Asia Minor. A full moon shone overhead. The waters of the Bosphorus shimmered silver in the moonlight. The scene was breathtaking!

But my Turk was becoming too romantically inclined. On the second night he pleaded with me, that since I wouldn't DO it, he would be content with a look at my nipples only.

I laughed, "What on earth for?"

"Just to see whether they are pink or red" was his reply.

I held firm. I thought he was nuts. Today, I would be considered extremely naive. But dating patterns in the 1950s were fundamentally different. We flirted, cuddled and snuggled, petted and necked, kissed and smooched, but we never did anything below the neck. Only bad girls DID it. Good girls saved themselves for marriage. I was a good Catholic girl.

I left Istanbul the next day, flying Pan American to Beirut.

Whom did I see while I was waiting in the Pan American office but George and Dudley in the American Express across the street? I rushed to greet them.

The romantic narrative of the beautiful Helen, "the face that launched a thousand ships" and the huge wooden Trojan horse in *The Iliad* had so intrigued me that I promised myself to visit Troy one day. I finally saw the ancient city on a tour I took of Eastern Europe and the Balkans in 1981. The Troy I saw — rows of trenches with piles of earth and stone and a ridiculous gigantic, hollow wooden recreation of the Trojan horse — did not impress me. Nor did the guide's long-winded spiel about Heinrich Schliemann's excavations in the 1870s. I had never been on a tour that had disappointed me so much.

However, there was one redeeming event. When we visited the Anzac Monument at Lone Pine Cemetery, a hauntingly beautiful site with its rows of pines and cypress trees bearing the names of Australian and New Zealand troops killed during the disastrous Gallipoli campaign of 1915, a memorial service was in progress. Once again, as in the World War I and II cemeteries in France, I saw row upon row of white crosses and meditated on man's inhumanity to man.

Lebanon

I experienced my first encounter with officious immigration officials at the Lebanese border, and only after a two-hour deliberation was I allowed to enter Beirut. After this unpleasant experience I decided to stay at a luxury hotel. Luckily, the Riviera overlooking the Mediterranean was not full.

That night while I was dining in the hotel's elegant dining room, my waiter brought me a bottle of wine telling me that a gentleman at another table had sent it. I didn't want to accept it, but the waiter insisted that it was perfectly "in order." After a short interval, my waiter returned and asked me if I would mind if the gentleman joined me at my table.

The gentleman was a tall, well-built, blonde German in the oil business who spoke good English. We chatted busily. I enjoyed his company. He complemented me on my beautiful tan and told me I was an attractive young woman with my beautiful green eyes and good figure. I was flattered by his attention. He seemed such a proper gentleman with the best of manners.

We decided to take a walk along the seashore in front of the hotel. While we strolled, we could hear the waves breaking in white foam as they spent themselves against the concrete wall. I loved the sound they made. I loved the fresh cool night air. I felt so free, so appreciative of God's handiwork.

My date suggested he show me Beirut's night life. I told him that if there was dancing, I would love to go. Dancing is my magnificent obsession. Beirut's nightspots could rival those of any dynamic metropolis from chic clubs to dark discotheques, roof-top bars and glittering cabarets. In one, we watched belly dancers perform their sinuous serpentine movements, but we were soon bored. We settled on a nightclub that had quite a large dance floor.

Peter proved to be a very good dancer. The band, in white dinner jackets, played novelty numbers such as "Aba Daba Honeymoon," "Don't Fence Me In," "How Much is that Doggie in the Window," as well as haunting romantic ballads like "It's Magic," "Secret Love," and "Till I Waltz Again with You." A chanteuse with a deep, lush voice sang "Lili Marlene" and "Some Enchanted Evening," stirring in me pleasant past memories. We had so much fun. The hours flew by and before I realized it, it was one a.m. I insisted that it was time for me to get back to the hotel.

I was unaware that he had directed the taxi driver to an apartment building rather than my hotel. When I queried him, he explained that he wanted to show me the new flat he was having built. When we got inside I noticed that it was furnished. He immediately threw me on a bed and made passes at me. I rebelled, kicking and telling him that I wasn't that kind of girl. I accused him of getting me there under false pretenses. He did not reply. But he realized it was useless to continue. He slapped my face. I was truly scared. He told me he was ordering a taxi to take me back to the hotel. In the taxi I kept wondering whether I had provoked his sexual advances. Echoes of my religious upbringing resounded in my ear: "Woman moves man to sin." I did not see myself as a coquette. I assumed, in my 1950s innocence, that all young men had honourable intentions. What he did had truly shocked me.

The next morning I hired a taxi to take me to Baalbeck in the Bekaa Valley fifty-three miles from Beirut. As I kept climbing and climbing up the perilous mountain roads, I saw vast herds of sheep and goats, Arab refugee camps, black goathair tents and summer resorts 5,000 feet above sea level, all of this while enjoying wonderful glimpses of the sea. I was fascinated by the scores of heavily laden camels that filed past me, so proud and impassive, yet so supercilious.

We finally reached the Bekaa, the base plain between the Lebanon and Antilebanon mountains. The valley was wide and deep and green, rich with orchards and vineyards. Suddenly I caught a glimpse of the Amar complex of temples at Baalbek. I gazed dumbfounded.

When I got close to them, my guide pointed out the ruins of two Roman temples, the Temple of Jupiter and the Temple of Bacchus. Only six columns (sixty-five feet high and eight feet in diameter) of the original enormous fifty-four columns surrounding the shrine of Jupiter had survived. The colour of honey, they stand majestic and erect, crowned by Corinthian capitals, splendid in their proportions.

A few steps away from the Temple of Jupiter was the Temple of Bacchus, the best preserved, and richly ornamented with figures of Mars, Diana, drawing an arrow

from her quiver, a Winged Victory, Vulcan and his hammer, as well as Bacchus wearing clusters of grapes
around his head. The sculpted egg and dart pattern,
wheat and poppies, cupids with bows and arrows riding
on dolphins or dragons, and a broad band of interlacing
vine in which figures of cupids and fauns frolicked also
held my attention. I could only stand and admire the vast
magnitude of their dimensions, the richness of their
ornamentation and the beauty of their architecture.

The third temple, the small Temple of Venus, was
exquisite in its original circular design. Totally different
from the other two, round instead of rectangular, facing
north instead of east, it was truly a dainty jewel.

Lines that I had memorized long ago came to my
mind: "Rome is all the world/And everything is Rome."
How could I not admire this mighty civilization whose
human genius created such masterpieces? It seemed
strange to see workmen constructing a stage amidst the
ruins for a concert the Hamburg Symphony Orchestra
was going to give that very evening. It would have been
breathtaking beneath a full moon.

I returned to Beirut under the spell of Baalbek.

Beirut was a prosperous modern city. I saw large
American cars and Coca-Cola, good wide highways and
Lebanese in modern western dress. But I recognized the
ambience of France in the broad boulevards and sidewalk cafés.

It wasn't until one Sunday morning, when I stood at
the corner of a main square, that I saw the other side.
The fountain was thick with squatted humanity, lying on
the steps, on the sidewalk, crouched against walls. I had
to pick my way around and over them. I saw them, too,
in the bazaar section amidst all the old clothes lying on

the ground for sale. And I then realized that Beirut had its poverty and its squalor.

On the day I was leaving Beirut I was sitting in the hotel lobby when two very tall and dignified Arab sheiks in long flowing robes of the finest silk strode by. I commented on their elegance and grace to my Moslem friend, who informed me they were Arab princes. They exuded a sweet scent.

Later the same day at the Beirut airport, I saw one of the Arab princes whom I had seen in my hotel lobby. I was excited and wanted to take his picture. My Moslem friend informed me that I would have to obtain the Prince's permission. And so he asked one of the Prince's two secretaries who replied, "The Prince of Jedah of Saudi Arabia consents." I was thrilled. I had a pleasant chat with the prince who seemed about thirty years old. He spoke, as he said, "a little English."

When I visited Lebanon in 1956 the country was prosperous. It had successfully blended traditional Arabic and Western influences, mainly French and American, to reach a high level of economic and cultural achievement. Before the civil war of 1970 Beirut, its capital, was the leading financial capital of the Middle East. However, the combined legacies of the Civil War in the 1970s between Christians and Muslims, leftists and rightists, Lebanese nationalists and Palestinians, the Israeli invasion of 1982 and the factional fighting since that time have virtually destroyed the country. Only recently is it gradually recovering from near ruin.

Syria

I struck across the Syrian desert in a hired car to take me from Beirut to Damascus, the capital of Syria, believed by Moslems to sit on the site of the original Garden of Eden. According to tradition, when Mohammed, the prophet, saw the city, he refused to enter because he did not wish to anticipate Paradise. It is the world's oldest continuously inhabited settlement, fabled to have sprung from an oasis in the desert. (Since its independence in 1946, the country has been racked by the Arab-Israeli conflict.)

At the border, officialdom was difficult. I had no Syrian pounds to pay for the visa.

"But I'm going only for the day. And I'll change my traveller's cheques at a bazaar," I remonstrated. Finally, the official agreed to extend me credit until my return crossing.

In Damascus, I told my dragoman (interpreter), that I wanted to walk around the streets alone, stopping wherever I wanted to watch the Levantine world go by. (In many Moslem countries a woman alone on the streets was assumed to be a prostitute.) Of course I did not know this.

Damascus was a babble of sound and a whirl of colour: black-coated and black-veiled Moslem women; coiffured ladies in Western dress with painted lips and finger nails; dashing sheiks in beautiful white loose, beltless robes; countrymen in black baggy trousers with tight fitting leggings to the calves; brown-cloaked Iraqi peasant women with foreheads circled in gold coins; veiled Moslem women with only the eyes uncovered; shepherds in rags; and Arabs in western jackets, trousers, and blood-coloured fezzes or gold and white turbans.

I noticed that I was the only Westerner in the crowds, a stranger in a strange land. I was a bit frightened, especially since I felt hostility toward me whenever I attempted to photograph the Moslems.

I visited the eighth century Umayyed Mosque, one of Islam's holiest shrines, because it contained the tomb of the mighty Saladin who had captured Jerusalem. No fanatic Moslem, he broke down in tears at the sight of the bereaved Crusader women after he captured Jerusalem, and sent a horse to the dismounted Richard at the height of the Battle of Jaffa. Saladin died at the age of fifty-six in 1193, a few months after he had concluded a three-year truce with the Crusaders under Richard the Lion Heart, giving only his handshake as guarantee. I knew I had to read Sir Walter Scott's *The Talisman* where Saladin, magnanimous, chivalrous and loyal, figures prominently.

The space and silence of the great Mosque impressed me. But I was especially fascinated by its magnificent carpeted floor and cool interior, a startling contrast to the noise and confusion outside. And yet what surprised my western eyes was the informality: the faithful were leaning against pillars, sleeping, reclining, and feeling "at home."

I have always found the courtyards of mosques beautiful. This one was no exception. There were jasmine and orange trees. Above the courtyard wall I saw the dome of the tomb of Saladin, where he lies in an ugly and ornate sarcophagus.

My dragoman and I drove to the Christian quarter to see the House of Ananias where Saul was converted to Christianity. We walked along the Biblical Street Called Straight (*Acts*, Chapter 9) where Saul of Tarsus regained his sight 2,000 years ago. Small boys clustered around me trying to prevent me from filming. My dragoman escorted me down a flight of stairs to the small chapel below. There were only a few pews and several candles were burning. I was also shown the prison window from which St. Paul escaped in a basket.

The covered Suq al Hamidiyah bazaar was not unlike the bazaar I had visited in Istanbul. As in Istanbul, merchants cried out the merits of their wares. I was dazzled by the wealth of merchandise: the finest brocades and silks which shone on both sides with intricate and lustrous patterns, copper and brass damascened in silver or gold, furniture inlaid with mother-of-pearl, rugs, mosaics, ivory, old arms, and fabled Damascus blades. The air was pungent with the scents of spices and perfume. I neither had the time to haggle, nor the will-power not to buy. I went on a shopping spree.

On my return trip to Beirut, while I was crossing the Syrian desert and listening to the car radio, I was shocked to hear that the Italian ship, the *Andrea Doria,* had just sunk in New York harbour. It was 26 July 1956.

Jordan, the Holy Land 1956

I flew from Beirut to Jerusalem. In the small airport several Moslem pilgrims from Arabia, dressed in their native costumes — the women seated cross-legged on the floor — were waiting for their plane to Mecca. The Jordanian Tourist Police were most courteous as they processed me through the formalities. A Palestinian whom I had met on the plane insisted on accompanying me to the Casa Nova, a pension operated by the Franciscan nuns where I had booked a reservation.

Casa Nova was located in the old walled-city where cars cannot ascend the narrow, crooked, cobble-stoned step-streets. My Palestinian escort and I walked from the Jaffa Gate to the hotel. Restless to make a good spiritual retreat and determined that I would allow nothing to jeopardize it, I was certain that in this religious pension I would find solitude and separation from worldly distractions.

A young nun led me to a sparsely furnished, quiet room, a perfect base for my spiritual pilgrimage. I unpacked and was looking forward to a long night's rest in order to get a fresh start early the next morning.

A knock at the door revealed a nun who had come to escort me to the refectory. She seated me, to my shock, next to a young man. I had erroneously assumed that only women guests were allowed in the pension.

I soon learned that the young man was a Royal Air Force officer on leave from his base in Cypress. After a week's visit to the holy places, he was ready to see Jerusalem's night life. He invited me to go dancing. At first I refused, explaining that it was my first night in Jerusalem and I wanted to prepare myself for my spiritual retreat. I was tempted, of course, because I loved to dance. But I was not going to budge. I had come to pray and meditate.

I decided to wear my pink sheath and my white gloves and shoes. We walked to the Orient House, a hotel with an outdoor dancing terrace outside the old walls of Jerusalem. He danced beautifully. We glided across the floor in perfect harmony to the rhythms of a dance band that played the latest western hit tunes like the "Tennessee Waltz," "You Belong to Me" and "Strangers in the Night."

It was nearly midnight when we walked out into the lovely moonlit night to return to our hospice. We discovered, to my horror, that the Damascus gate to the inner city was closed. We stood there in stunned silence, not knowing what to do. Suddenly, out of the hushed stillness of the warm air and the blackness of the night, a figure stepped out from nowhere. He was a slim and agile Jordanian soldier wearing his ammunition belt and gun and a *khaffiyeh* (a red and white checkered cloth head covering, held in place by a round black rope). He politely informed us that the gate closed at 9:30 p.m. as a security measure. We would have to walk around the wall and enter the walled city by Herod's Gate. My Air Force officer assured me that he had not known about the curfew. He seemed so sincere that I believed him. I had experienced my first contact with the uneasy tension which exists in Jordan.

We followed the soldier's instructions. It was going to be a long walk. I removed my high heels and started to walk barefoot in silence. I bade farewell to my airman at the hospice door.

The next morning I began my retreat in earnest. In a private car with a guide and an American school teacher, I visited places familiar and sacred to me since childhood: the Mount of Olives; the Garden of Gethsemane, where there are still eight olive trees said to be 2,000 years old; the place of the Ascension; the house of Mary and Martha; the tombs of Lazarus, and of the Blessed Virgin Mary; Bethlehem; the Church of the Nativity; the Shepherd's Field and the Via Dolorosa. As we drove along the gentle rolling Judean hills, bleached and bare, with tall slender cypresses breaking the whiteness, I couldn't believe that I was in the land that felt the footsteps of my Lord, that I had actually "seen" the retreat where Our Saviour had passed His last hours on the night before he was crucified.

Along the Jericho road, at the spot where the Good Samaritan helped a "certain man" I took a picture. A soldier at a military post accused me of photographing him. After he gave me a lecture about what I could, and could not photograph, we were allowed to continue. We stopped at the pool of Bethesda where the women, as in Biblical times, were filling their large water pots.

We followed the Jordan River, and the deep tropical Jordan Valley, with its luxuriant vegetation, was a treat after the barren, stony countryside that we passed. Finally, we came to the Dead Sea in the Negev desert area, the lowest spot on earth. I don't know what I expected, but I was surprised. The Dead Sea was beautiful with its blue waters sparkling in the sun and the distant mountains of Moab etched against the sky. We waded in. I tried to float but couldn't. I tasted the most bitter, salty water.

We entered the shrine of the Visitation. This shrine, towering above the cypress trees, commemorates the meeting of Mary and Elizabeth, the mother of John the Baptist. St. Luke narrates how Mary, informed by the Angel Gabriel of the birth of John, went to see Elizabeth and greeted her pregnant cousin with the *Magnificat*, my favourite prayer of all prayers.

There was no one at the revered Old Wailing Wall, all that remains of Herod's temple, where Jews have gathered together for centuries to lament the destruction of Jerusalem and the diaspora. I saw only a few notes stuck into the tiny spaces between the rocks.

We stopped at the Church of St. Anne where Our Lady was born, and the Chapel of the Flagellation where we saw the very stones marked by the games which the Roman soldiers used to play.

A Moslem gentleman invited me, one evening, to Emmaus, first, to see the house of Cleophas where our Lord supped after His resurrection, and afterwards to dinner. We saw the house, but could not have dinner. In fact, we were advised to make a hurried exit because of a 6:30 curfew, since Emmaus is so close to the Israeli border. I was frightened because we were stopped on the twelve kilometre highway several times at military barriers. Along the way I also saw fleets of military vehicles on the white dusty roads slipping in and out of the barren hills and camp after camp of Arab refugees on the scorched and barren mountainsides who were fed and maintained by the United Nations. I breathed lightly only when we finally reached St. Stephen's Gate.

This incident was another example of the uneasy tension that hung over Jordan because of the animosity between Jordan and Israel which has resulted in frequent border violations, armed raids and frontier clashes. (Jordan would lose Jerusalem in the Arab-Israeli seven-day war in 1967.) I could not really appreciate the complexity of relations between Jews and Arabs in the Middle East in 1956. My Arab guides were so convincing that I favoured their side more often than not. And besides, the twenty-one year old bachelor King Hussein I of Jordan was handsome, even though he was so short. (He died on 7 February 1999)

The mixture of religions and cultures in the Holy Land confused me. I knew that Jerusalem had suffered a galaxy of conquerors and rulers: Crusaders, Romans, Turks, and Arabs; that it had been oppressed from both the tyranny of infidels and foreign inertia. (As recently as this decade it has suffered the ravages of war. Even today it enjoys no peace.)

But I had always associated the Holy Land with Christendom. I did not realize it was also home to other religious sects. The vast majority of its people were Palestinian Moslems from the West and East banks of the Jordan River; the rest are a mix of Arab and Bedouin

Muslim tribes, Arab Christians, and Circassians who have fled Czarist Russia.

The Mosque of Omar, also known as the Dome of the Rock, is second only to Mecca in terms of religious significance because it commemorates the Ascension of Mohammed to Heaven on the back of a winged steed over the very spot where Abraham was about to sacrifice his only son. With its gold plated dome, glittering in the sun, dazzling me, I thought it was one of the most beautiful structures I had ever seen. The artistic ingenuity of this Arabian marvel simply left me speechless.

The Church of the Holy Sepulchre, too, is sacred to four Orthodox denominations as well as the Latin. Ethiopian Orthodox monks and nuns, moreover, live on the roof of the church to press their claim to a portion of the sanctuary below, which they can trace back to a gift Solomon made to the Queen of Sheba. At the entrance to the Church, which was built by the Crusaders in the eleventh century, I was shocked to find a Moslem doorkeeper lying on an elevated wooden divan spread with rugs and cushions. Over eight hundred years ago, Saladin entrusted the locking up of the church to the family of the Moslem doorkeeper. Most of the shrines in Jerusalem suffer from this divided ownership, and it is amazing how each church holds to its rights with ferocious tenacity.

The heat inside the hospice was unbearable. And so I liked wandering along the narrow and winding terraced stone streets in the early evenings. Invariably, I would be stopped by a patrol, stealthily creeping about in the ominous silence, who would tell me that I should not be out. Despite my nervousness, I kept going to the Church of the Holy Sepulchre, and the Via Dolorosa which bore the last footsteps of my Lord.

The holy place I cherished most was Christ's tomb. It is a tiny cell lined with marble inside the Church of the Holy Sepulchre. A slab of white marble, three feet high, covers the rock on which Our Lord was placed after the Crucifixion. Day after day I was drawn irresistibly back to kneel down before the sepulchre which I touched and kissed again and again, lost in prayer, pleading to my God for pardon of my sins. The silence of the tomb, in striking contrast to the din outside, was profound. Never before or since have I experienced such absolute bliss. I visited the tomb time after time, each time, wanting to stay longer. But since there was room for only one person, I had to consider others who were waiting their turn. Unfortunately, the Church of the Holy Sepulchre was so dark, noisy and cluttered with scaffolding and construction equipment inside that I found it difficult to pray. The one time I tried I was distracted by a pontifical high mass being sung in one area while, in another, a Greek orthodox service was in progress. As a result, I would just sit for hours reciting my rosary in the blistering heat of the day on the stone bench in front of the Church. Although crowds of pilgrims were milling about, I felt strangely detached from the world. My vigil of contemplation and prayer in the sanctuary where Jesus died to redeem and save us was one of the sweetest consolations and one of the dearest among many, many memories of the Holy Land which have remained with me forever.

I had observed a way of life that had changed little in thousands of years: the tall, statuesque tattooed women wearing their long beautifully embroidered dresses and carrying their water pots on their shoulders to the pool of Bethesda; and the shepherds, in the flowing Bedouin head veil, herding their flocks of sheep and black goats; and the camels filing past. I felt sorry for the heavily laden donkeys patiently resigned to their state trotting slowly by. I could hear them saying the words from G. K. Chesterton's wonderful little poem:

> . . . I also had my hour;
> One far fierce hour and sweet:
> There was a shout about my ears,
> And palms before my feet.

Jerusalem's street life, too, was full of exotic sights: the money-changers of the bazaar, with its narrow, covered, and crowded lanes; the small dark shops that were completely open to the streets selling large black figs, with a few, large, shiny leaves attached; clusters of dates and grapes, and mouth-watering pastries; while whole carcasses of meat hanging from rafters, were exposed to the mosquitoes and flies, and Greek square-bearded priests, wearing black cassocks, and high round, rimless black hats strode through throngs of people like ancient kings.

Shopkeepers stood out in front of their shops calling prospective customers to come inside. I made purchase after purchase: Maltese crosses, rosaries of olive wood, cards with olive wood crosses and spear-shaped olive "leaves from the Garden of Gethsemane," cards with "flowers from the Holy Land," holy medals, and a Bible with a mother-of-pearl cover. At each shop I was offered a cup of thick, black coffee which I would politely decline because I knew it would be too strong. A verse from Masefield's "Cargoes" often came to mind:

> Quinquereme of Nineveh from distant Ophir
> Rowing home to haven in sunny Palestine
> With a cargo of ivory,

And apes and peacocks,
Sandalwood, cedarwood and sweet white wine.

But it wasn't the exotic sights, it was the spiritual retreat
I made in the land I longed to see all my life that had
brought me ineffable joy and given me the strength of
faith that I cherish to this day.

Egypt, 1956

From Jerusalem I flew Air Jordan to Cairo, the capital
of Egypt. On board there was a group of Arab teachers,
several of whom spoke excellent English, going to Cairo
as guests of the Egyptian Government. I remember how
excited they were when we crossed the Suez Canal.

When we landed, the handsome Director of Public
Relations to the Minister of Education met us. He gave
a speech of welcome and invited me, who was the only
foreigner on board, to join the group. A lone woman
traveller was, after all, a curiosity.

We had dinner in a delightful restaurant on the Nile.
Illuminated Cairo, with its River, its lighted bridges, and
its beautiful Corniche impressed me. My friend was very
well educated and interesting. He had nothing but praise
for the Nasser government. He told me how nationali-
zation helped the majority of Egyptians and how much
construction of roads, bridges, houses and sugar factories had taken place since the Revolution.

He asked me again to be part of the group and live
with them at the University. I refused graciously and told
him that I would join them on a few of the tours. He
wasn't completely satisfied, but he consented. I felt I had
to be cautious.

I wanted to stay at Shepheard's, a famous hotel, but there was no vacancy. And so I checked in at the Gezireh Palace Hotel for two nights and then moved to Shepheard's.

The next day, alone, I walked around the centre of the one thousand year old city built on the banks of the Nile River. "Egypt is the gift of the Nile," said Herodotus, a Greek traveller and historian who visited Egypt in the fifth century B.C. Today, it still is, as in the past. It is the longest river in the world at 4,160 miles in length, with its ultimate source in Lake Victoria in the south of Uganda where I would be teaching in seven years. Egypt would be only desert if it weren't for this most precious natural resource. Most of the country's population lives along its banks and its deltaic mouth.

As I walked along the Corniche, which borders the Nile, admiring the ribbon of green with its beautiful date palms on both sides of this miracle, I saw little boys fishing and taking baths, women washing clothes, and scores of boats, barges, skiffs and sailboats plying up and down its waters.

I was appalled by the poverty I saw and the seemingly lackadaisical attitude of the swarms of poor humanity lying on the grass, on benches, and on pavement. Beggars were squatted on their haunches, asking for *baksheesh*. Women were suckling their babes and whole families were sitting cross-legged on the grass under the shade of a tree, or in the shadow of a wall in the heat of the day. Everyone looked so desperately poor. No one seemed to be working. No one seemed to be going anywhere.

In the afternoon in a private car with a very charming Australian, whose nephew worked in the Australian Embassy in Cairo, we drove to see the pyramids of

Gizeh. They are only three of many, but they are the most famous, and since they are only seven miles from Cairo, they are the most accessible.

The colossal Pyramid of Cheops was the first we saw. We gazed, enraptured. The greatest of all, one of the seven wonders of the ancient world, it was built about 2690 B.C. Heroditus says that 100,000 men worked for three months in each year for twenty years to complete it. Originally sheathed in polished marble, it was a remarkable engineering achievement in its massive size and accuracy of construction. Our dragoman told us that the joinings of the stone are so perfect that neither a hair nor a needle can be forced between them.

I immediately recognized the Sphinx, with the body of the lion symbolizing strength, and the head of a human, wisdom, from the pictures I had seen of it in my Geography book. I knew him well. Since we could not enter its tomb, I just stood dumbfounded at its colossal size, oblivious to the hot sands of the desert on my feet and the heat of the sun blazing down on me out of the cloudless sky. As it gazed out over the world, despite its smashed nose, broken body, missing beard, and the inscrutable smile of its imperious face, it still asserted its power and majesty against the heavens.

It was sunset by the time we had to leave. My new Australian acquaintance and I both felt we couldn't part, bonded as we were, from the awesome sight before us. He invited me to a dinner party his nephew was hosting that night. I had to accept.

The Director of Public Relations had not forgotten me. The next day he called on me to join the group on its tour of the Citadel, King Farouk's Palace, the Mohammed Ali Mosque and the National Museum.

After passing dark, narrow, and winding laneways, broken only by dark openings to cellars or dark little courtyards — a labyrinth of jumbled buildings so typical of the old Cairo — we reached Saladin's twelfth century Citadel. The Egyptian flag was waving over it. The group took pictures.

Dominating Islamic Cairo, the lofty Citadel was begun in 1178 and since then, has been continually expanded and modified. From this promontory we had a panoramic view of the City. The Citadel encloses the Mosque of Mohammed Ali, which is also known as the Alabaster Mosque; the columns, walls and courtyard are all made of alabaster.

The Arab teachers took many pictures inside the Mosque. I couldn't help feel what few differences there were between them and us. They were enthusiastic and eager. They laughed and sang in the bus. They got thirsty and hungry. They were friendly and most kind.

We visited King Farouk's palace where I was amused to learn that the palace clock stopped at the exact minute that the King, deposed in 1952, escaped from the palace.

The Egyptian National Museum must be the world's unrivalled storehouse of pharaonic treasures. And what sumptuous treasures they are! The mummy collection surpassed any that I had seen before. The marvellous artifacts taken from the tomb of Tutankhamen, the boy king (unearthed in 1922), were the most stupendous of all: alabaster lamps and vases and stools; gold carvings, gold chests, gold thrones, gold boats, and chariots, and a coffin made from 2500 pounds of pure gold; dazzling rings, bracelets, and earrings. But the most stupendous treasure was Tutankhamen's famous

yellow gold death mask. Unfortunately, the museum was
a dark and cluttered maze.

That evening one of the group, Wadi Zaki Pyoubi,
who could trace his ancestry to the famous Saladin, the
Turk from Damascus, invited me to see Cairo by night.
We went to Casino Abdine, once King Farouk's private
pleasure haunt on the palace grounds. I noticed Wadi
was especially restless, glancing periodically at a female
member of his group seated at another table. He told me
he was planning "to ask her hand in marriage." He had
asked his friend to take her out "to pave the way for his
proposal." He didn't know her yet but there were three
weeks left in the tour for him to propose. He told me his
mother and sister had been looking for a suitable wife
for him in Jerusalem, but no one was found to suit their
tastes. He thought he had found one now. I asked him
why he hadn't asked her out, after all, how would he
know whether he loved her or not. According to Moslem custom a man doesn't court the girl he intends to
marry. "Love will come after marriage," he told me.
"There are many difficulties," he added. "I earn only
thirty dinars a month (eighty dollars). I will need one
hundred dinars (240 dollars) for the wedding ceremony,
and I will have to pay 200 dinars to the bride's parents."
In Jordan a bride holds a fixed price, although the girl
can raise the price and the groom can bargain. He kept
asking me what I thought of her. I told him that I
thought she was very attractive.

I was danced off my feet. The Arab girls would not
dance (although they could) with their escorts because
they were afraid their parents would find out. So I had
the honour. The music was good. The floor show of
oriental dancing superb. I thoroughly enjoyed myself.

Colonel Gamal Abdel Nasser had seized the Suez Canal a few months earlier and forced the British to withdraw their last troops. This was the first time Egypt was free of British control since 1882. Angered by this move, Britain and France would join with Israel in attacking Egypt. I felt an atmosphere of uneasiness and tension in Cairo's air. Egyptian soldiers were everywhere in sight. There were several youth demonstrations. Patrols with rifles guarded embassies. In front of the American Embassy there were mounted sentries. My own Canadian Embassy warned me not to be curious if I saw two or three people gathered together and to walk only in open spaces. They counselled me to inform them of my activities. Everywhere I felt an uneasy tension. A huge picture of Nasser straddled the main street. A picture of an Egyptian soldier with firearms and a torch straddled another street. The political situation made me refuse further offers of hospitality from the group.

The next morning I left to visit Memphis and Sakkara in a private car with a French teenager whose government warned all French citizens who didn't have to be in Egypt to leave. During the one and one-half hour trip from Shepheard's Hotel I saw mud villages with rows of small mud brick boxes. I can't forget the people living in the mud huts right on the water's edge along the sloping banks of the Nile. They seemed to be part of the Nile. As we drove I marvelled at the luxuriant green vegetation, and the tall date palms. But the dry sands of the barren desert provided a stark contrast to the verdant plain that traced the shores of the Nile.

At Memphis, the first capital of Egypt, we marvelled at the colossal black granite statue of Ramsses II, the Pharaoh usually identified as the oppressor of the Isra-

elites. I found the name Ramsses II inscribed on the
shoulders, breast, girdle and bracelet. Unfortunately, the
ancient capital had vanished among the date palms, but
the *fellaheen* were farming the rich land along the banks
as their ancestors did 5,000 years ago.

At Sakkara, the burial ground of the pharaohs, we
looked at the Step Pyramid of Zoser, the first pyramid
to be constructed in Egypt and the oldest stone building
in the world.

A visit to Cairo would not be complete without
having seen Musky, its grand bazaar. I went with my
dragoman. As in Istanbul and Damascus, Musky overwhelmed the senses. There was a plethora of glowing
gems and wares: brass and copper hand-tooled platters,
leather bags, gold jewellery, exotic perfumes and spices,
onyx eggs, handwoven wool and silk carpets, inlaid
furniture, camel saddles, papyrus paintings, hand-
carved wooden and ivory objects. This time my
dragoman helped me negotiate prices. I bought a beautiful alabaster vase and several others of brass. I also
bought a Queen Nefertite (wearing her unique crown)
sterling silver spoon for my collection. I thought it
prudent to leave for Greece because the political situation in Egypt was continuing to deteriorate. (Egypt
would lose Sinai and Gaza in the Arab-Israeli War of
1967.) Although I was still woefully ignorant about the
past history of this ancient civilization, I had seen a few
of the great monuments that attested to its achievements.

Sicily

I boarded the *Olympia* at Piraeus for Messina in Sicily.
On the ship I met Irene Rigg, who, on learning that I was

going directly to Taormina, invited me to join her and her three companions in their private car. After a gruelling encounter with customs officials at Messina over cigarettes which one of the girls had, we were finally allowed to proceed.

The drive from Messina to Taormina was hectic. It reminded me of the wild drive to Anacapri the previous Easter. We cut through hair-pin curves on two wheels, and scaled lofty mountain heights as beautiful beaches flashed by before we finally screeched into Taormina.

I knew the name since childhood because my mother regularly sent money to *l'orfanatrofio Antoniario Femminile di Taormina*. I never expected the beauty and history that were awaiting me. It was just too good to be true.

Perched 750 feet above the Ionian Sea, Taormina faced the white mass of Mount Etna, Europe's largest volcano. As beautiful as its name, it has lovely beaches, crystal clear waters, blue skies, and unlimited sunshine. It was a photographer's paradise.

Taormina had one of the most lovely parks I have ever seen. Beautifully dressed children — little girls with large colourful bows in their hair — played in huge wooden playhouses, old men sat on benches and mothers sat near the shaded coolness of the fountains. Two Sicilian troubadours sauntered along the paths, singing familiar tunes to the accompaniment of guitars. It was heavenly.

Strolling up and down Taormina's lovely main street, the Corso Umberto, was a ritual in Taormina. I was enchanted by the shrubbery that was sculpted into huge shapes such as teapots and vases.

Stores and boutiques displayed the goods that have made Italians famous: silks, leather goods, jewellery, raffia work, and the famous Taormina embroidery and lace. There were no nickelodeons, no hot dog or French fry odours permeating everything, no streets littered with napkins stained with mustard and ketchup, so typical of the resort towns back home. Instead, one sat down at a sidewalk café, relaxed over a *gelati* or sipped lemonade while a violinist or a live trio played captivating Italian melodies in concert with the fragrance of aromatic herbs of rosemary and laurel.

But Taormina was more than a beautiful sea-side resort for holiday makers. It was initially a Greek city (fourth century), was later Roman, was destroyed and then rebuilt by the Arabs, and was taken over by the Normans in 1079. Historical reminders of its chequered antiquity remained. Arches, columns, doorways, gables, cupolas, towers, and friezes revealed the influences of many invaders and conquerors.

It was sunset when I first saw Taormina's ancient Greek-Roman theatre, much of which has remained intact. It had me spellbound. Its granite columns, brickwork arches, and huge chunks of weathered stone were silhouetted against the dark green of the tall slender cypresses. The crater of Mt. Etna was smouldering in the distance.

I hated to leave Taormina. But I wanted to make a complete circuit of the island. However, I discovered that bus and rail communications from Taormina were not good and I would have to return to Messina to make connections.

When I arrived at Messina I discarded my original idea of a complete tour because Messina was celebrating its greatest feast day of the year on 15 August.

Messina was damaged so much by the earthquake of 1908 that few historical monuments remain. It was a completely rebuilt garden city. I thought it was one of the most charming towns I had ever visited with wide streets, bordered by palm trees, bougainvillea, hibiscus, oleander; many lovely fountains, huge squares, many beautiful parks, and low modern houses. But what won me completely was the incomparable panorama of the hooked harbour. If this view by daylight was breathtaking, by night it was simply not of this world. Myriads of lights twinkled along the two shores; the illuminated statue of the Blessed Virgin, protectress of the city and of sailors, stood out beautifully in its simplicity. I remember admiring this display of light and water, too enraptured to speak. Messina kept its vigil over the legendary two-mile-wide strait which separated it from the mainland, the strait across which Hercules swam, clinging to his sacred bulls, where Ulysses' famous rock and boiling waters — Scylla and Charybdis — lured mariners to their deaths.

The fair of Messina was in progress when I arrived. It incorporated religious, cultural, sporting and recreational events. Operas were held nightly in a huge open-air stadium. I saw *Il Travatore* which ended at one a.m., not unusual in Italy. Small children, too, were invariably present because Italian parents (especially in the south) wouldn't think of going out and leaving them at home.

On 14 August, I saw the procession of the Giants of Messina. *Mata* and *Grifone,* two huge equestrian effigies, swayed through the streets, symbolic representations of the legendary founders of the city.

The next day, on 15 August, *Mezzoagosto*, pontifical high mass was celebrated to honour the Assumption of the Blessed Virgin Mary to Paradise. The cathedral was packed. I couldn't help chuckling to myself when the bells began ringing and I heard several old women in front of me complaining to each other that whoever was ringing the bells didn't know how. Very soon, however, the bells began peeling gloriously, befitting the majestic feast. For dinner, Sicilian families had chicken and watermelon, the only fitting fare for the feast day.

The day's climax was the procession of the Vara. It consisted of one float — a huge stand holding up a pyramid of rotating angels (little girls) — the Madonna triumphant, crowning all, at the apex. The little girl who was the Madonna a few years before had fallen from the top to her death. Since then a doll had been used. Long lines of barefoot men and women who had a special devotion to Mary gripped thick ropes to pull the float. A truck preceded them, watering the streets. The grand finale, a huge, magnificent display of fireworks, (as only the Italians can stage) flashed through the sky.

Three decades later in 1987, with my friend Rita Ubriaco, I made the circle trip around Sicily that I had forfeited in the summer of '56. In a rented Opel, we drove from Messina to Acireale, Syracuse, Agrigento and Palermo.

In the ancient Greek city of Acireale, on Good Friday, we noticed a poster advertising *Il riscatto d' Adamo*, a Passion Play to be performed that evening in the medieval town of Aci San Antonio which was destroyed several times by Etna and then rebuilt. The town was also the seat of one of the last artisans dedicated to preserving the traditional art of constructing the *Carretto Siciliano* (Sicilian cart). Since neither of us had seen the famous Passion Play at Oberammergau in Germany, we decided we should see this one.

If we had known what the drive was going to be like, we would never have ventured forth. Aci San Antonio was a thousand feet above sea-level. We kept climbing and climbing tortuous, steep and narrow mountain roads. Afraid to miss the right directional signs and thus lose our way, we were constantly vigilant. The drive seemed endless.

But the Passion Play was worth the effort. That a small town on the roof of the world, with a population of about 12,000, could have staged a drama of such magnitude depicting the suffering, death and resurrection of Jesus Christ was incredible. The production would have pleased the residents of Oberammergau in the Bavarian Alps. When the procession moved up a long narrow street, a car blocked the way. Four young men, exhibiting the same ingenuity as the rest of the townspeople, simply picked the car up and deposited it elsewhere. The entire spectacle staged on the courtyard of the Church of Sant'Antonio Abbate lasted until one a.m. By this time I was shivering with cold and running a fever. But I insisted we stay until the very end. I had to preserve the performance on film. I don't know how Rita managed to descend the mountain, but we arrived safely at our hotel in Acireale.

Since Acireale stood on an Etna lava bed, it was not surprising that the volcano was a popular topic of conversation. Even during this Holy Week, Mt. Etna was spewing lava. While we were there, a French woman and her young son got too close to the crater and were killed.

Along the road to Syracuse, which followed the coastline, we saw beautiful groves of lemon, orange, fig and almond trees. Older than Rome, Syracuse was, for centuries, second only to Athens in its cultural radiance. Archimedes, the greatest mathematician of the Ancient World, and the poet, Theocritus, lived here. The Apostle

Paul preached here. In its port, the Athenian navy perished in one of the great sea battles of antiquity.

Syracuse's ancient glories survived in its ruins. Its Greek theatre (467 B.C.) overlooking the sea is the largest and best preserved of its kind. I was overwhelmed. In the golden days of Greek drama, Aeschylus braved the sea voyage from Greece to see his plays performed here. Pindar, the poet, and Sappho came too.

It was in Syracuse where we saw the gaily coloured Sicilian carts drawn by plumed donkeys. Descended from the Roman chariot with its two wooden wheels, the *carrettas*, identical in size and shape, were found all over the island. Traditional paintings on the wooden back, sides, and even the spokes and rims of the wheels, depicted incidents from the times of Charlemagne and his paladins fighting the infidels. (Charlemagne was a legendary character in Southern Italy from the times when the troubadours sang his epics and the Arthurian cycle.)

From Syracuse we pushed into the interior of Sicily to Agrigento. The drive across the mountains was hectic. Finally, we made our descent down the mountains covered with vineyards, almond and olive trees, to Agrigento.

Egypt has its Valley of the Kings, Agrigento, its Valley of the Temples dating from the fifth and sixth centuries B.C.. The so-called Temple of Concord, with thirty-four Doric columns, is the best preserved in the world. Even though I had seen Athens and Delphi, I was still amazed by this graceful Greek structure. It was an absolute gem, intact and majestic, surrounded by olive trees. I gazed in wonderment at its perfect beauty. So ended our wonderful round trip of Sicily, a land saturated with mythology.

We could not linger because we didn't want to arrive in Palermo too late in the night, because Palermo was the legendary hub of the Mafia bosses. As it was, we arrived very late and had difficulty finding a hotel. Rita left very early the next morning to drive to Rome.

I remained in Palermo for a few days before beginning my lecture tour at the University of Messina. To my shock, I discovered that my hotel was kitty corner to an apartment building that was being watched by a twenty-four hour police guard on an elevated platform who were protecting a judge living in the building. (A number of anti-Mafia magistrates who had orchestrated Italy's crusade against that secret criminal organization had recently been murdered.)

In my walking tours, I was surprised to find a sophisticated metropolis with a remarkable past. Wave upon wave of civilizations, Greek, Roman, Saracen, Norman, Spanish and French had left their marks. No fewer than three kings and an Empress were buried in the cathedral. But I was too tired to absorb much. Consequently, I cannot recall the historical sights that I saw.

However, I do recall that I was introduced to the artichoke, a Sicilian delicacy, at the home of Ada Giardino. I marvelled at the way she pulled the upright green flower apart, petal by petal and then dipped each petal in melted butter and drew it sharply between her teeth. After the petals were piled in a heap by her plate, she carefully scraped the flower's centre and ate the heart with knife and fork. My initiation was a failure. I have never eaten an artichoke since. However, I did enjoy Ada's stories about the German troops in Palermo when she was a young woman during the Second World War.

Stromboli

Since the time when Ingrid Bergman and Roberto Rosselini made Stromboli internationally famous, I had wished to visit this romantic isle. And so I did, when I concluded my 1956 summer trip here, before going to my new posting in France. I was shocked.

I don't know what I had expected: a beautiful green emerald isle on the blue waters of the Ionian Sea? Instead, what I saw was a black island with no streets, no electricity, no running water; (water was brought in weekly on a ship from Messina).

Black was the predominant colour. The soil was black; the lava was even black; the sand on the beaches was black. Very little grew other than a few stunted cacti and tomatoes smaller than grapes. I saw no animals, just a few thin chickens. The food was the worst I had ever tasted in Italy.

The island was jammed with university students, German, French and English (I met one lone Canadian, a graduate of the University of Toronto). Most of them were staying at the youth centre, a gift of Rosselini. I had to admire their curiosity and their stamina. All of them were roughing it, tenting or camping through Europe on one dollar or two a day. But Stromboli had only convinced me just how much conveniences and comforts meant to me.

However, my Stromboli visit was worth it because of the sight that I witnessed one night when a French couple and myself ascended Stromboli's mountain as far as the observatory. From here we saw the crater of the most active volcano in Europe erupting in outbursts of red-hot lava at regular twenty minute intervals, accompanied by a low, muffled rumbling. The spectacle was awesome. Even frightening. Who was to know when Stromboli would burst out again?

However, the next day, I couldn't wait to leave. The many black grottoes, the coves along the rocky coast, and the winding narrow paths failed to hold my interest. Stromboli, with its abandoned houses in ruin, with its few faithful inhabitants stubbornly struggling to survive, was a ghost island.

And yet, on this God-forsaken island, I received a telegram from a young, tall Sicilian journalist, Salvatore, whom I had met in Messina. Although I was flattered by his persistence, his seriousness frightened me. His ardour was so great he wrote a poem for me and had it printed in his newspaper. I had refused to give him the name of the pension where I was staying at Stromboli. But he was relentless in his chase. The little delivery boy was told to check every pension on the island. He finally found me in the last pension on his list, the San Domenico. I ignored my persistent admirer's telegram because I wasn't interested in a courtship with an Italian man. Penny was ashamed to associate herself with Serafina who was still caged and anonymous. In retrospect, when I read his poem I regret having been so insensitive.

France, 1956-1958

I arrived in Metz, the headquarters for Canada's #1 Air Division on 31 August 1956, after my fun-filled summer holiday. I was driven by staff car to my posting at Gros-Tenquin, #2 Fighter Wing in the Alsace-Lorraine region of France. It was one of four Canadian Air Force bases that operated in Europe as part of Canada's NATO commitment: #1 Wing at Marville, and #2 at Gros-Ten-

quin, both in France; #3 at Zweibrücken; and #4 at
Baden-Soëlingen in Germany. All bases flew the same
aircraft, single-seater F86 Mark 6 Sabre jets, which were
day fighters. Later in 1958 each wing converted one
squadron to the CF 100's two-seater, all weather night
interceptors for defence and reconnaissance. There were
also DC3s for transport and T-33 Silver Stars (T-Bird),
which were two-seater trainer jets. In a letter to me
Jeanette Arthurs wrote: "There was a great deal of
rivalry between the Mark 6 Sabre jets and the CF100
pilots, and even today the Sabre pilots speak disparag-
ingly of the CF100 pilots and aircraft."

I had no idea where I was being driven. But I noticed
that the landscape was pastoral. Farmers were still
broadcasting seeds by hand following traditional agricultural work patterns. Horses pulled ploughs guided by
peasant women. Cobs of corn were drying on eaves.
Honey wagons lumbered by us. Chickens, cows and
ducks kept crossing the road. Apple trees lined the
highways. Curves and corners of buildings had large
white patches painted on them, to guide drivers when
dense fog, which was common, made visibility difficult.

The homes were newly built with beautiful red
geraniums in every window. But I was surprised to see
huge stacks of manure gracing front yards; under German occupation farmers were ordered to put manure
piles in backyards. But as soon as the Germans left, the
farmers put piles once again in the front. The larger the
stack, the richer the farmer.

I kept seeing grim scars of the fierce fighting that
took place in the region during World War II: many
pock marked houses, tangled wires and concrete slabs of
the bunkers of the Maginot Line, pill-boxes which
proved useless in World War II, and ruins of bombed

buildings. But I also noticed an energetic building boom that was replacing the war's destruction. I kept seeing signs in German; before World War I Alsace-Lorraine had been part of Germany. And suddenly I recalled the tears I had shed in high school over Alphonse Daudet's *La Dernière Classe* set in this very region which told how one rural classroom mourned when Alsace-Lorraine was to be ceded to Germany.

Although #2 Fighter Wing was located in a swamp in the middle of nowhere, the base was a great place to live. We were accommodated in officers' quarters and a house cleaning staff looked after our rooms. Mess life was fun.

Our school was located at St. Avold, fifteen kilometres from the base, where a French-built housing project accommodated both the Canadian dependents of Two (Fighter) Wing, and the French families of a local mining community. Both Canadian and French students were housed in opposite ends of the same school. The French school authorities barred the door separating the two sections.

A few organized attempts were made to reduce the barriers which existed between the French and us. In May and June of 1957, a group of fifteen nine-and ten-year-old Canadian and French students met to study simple sentences, poetry and popular songs in both languages. And in the Primary School on 6 December, Knecht Rupprecht (Black Peter), with wicker basket, bell and chain, and a sack of switches, whipped, ever so gently, one student from each school for being bad. And St. Nicholas, dressed in bishop's robes and carrying a staff, distributed gingerbread cookies in the shape of himself.

A few of us made an effort to meet French teachers who introduced us to escargot, an unfamiliar treat I have enjoyed ever since.

The school was most unattractive and inferior compared to the one which I had left in Germany. Our staff room was small, narrow and dingy. The room where I taught Gr. XI Ancient History and English was a converted closet, so tiny and flimsy that Marion Burt, another high school teacher in the adjoining staff room, could hear every word I said.

June Knudsen, a talented, and cheerful music teacher from Toronto, remembers the freedom that female teachers had at the base compared to the Victorian behaviour code expected in Toronto in the mid 1950s:

> Not that we completely forgot proper conduct, but it was fun to be able to join the officers in the Mess for dinner every night, have fascinating conversations, (politics and sex were topics that were discouraged, but they were the most interesting), skating and bowling in the base recreation centre, playing darts, singing in the Mess lounge on Friday nights, and the Mess parties.

I remember one Hallowe'en Party when the teachers dressed in cancan costumes, danced to Offenbach's music, and won bottles of champagne.

I'll never forget the mess party where I overwore my contact lenses. The pain was excruciating. I spent the night putting cold face cloths over my eyes. I couldn't sleep. I couldn't see. The next morning, the doctor was so concerned he sent me to the huge American Military Hospital in Wiesbaden, Germany, in a staff car that was going there from Air Force Headquarters in Metz. It was a cold overcast morning in February and I was wearing my muskrat coat. I was so afraid that I hardly spoke to

the Air Vice-Marshall in the car. The American ophthalmologist told me that my blindness was temporary. I had
abused my eyes by wearing my contacts too long and had
deprived them of precious oxygen. He warned me never
to do it again.

June also remembers the fantastic bargains:

> We were given the privilege to shop at the large Ameri-
> can Post Exchanges — the PX. Our Canadian dollar
> was at a premium over the American. And there was no
> tax on many items like liquor, cigarettes and camera
> film, so we stocked up. I recall one friend buying ten
> pairs of shoes at the PX in Kaiserslautern because she
> could not get her 10½ AAA size on the economy [the
> local stores] since most European women who walk a
> great deal have wide feet. Life was wonderful. Two
> years of complete freedom!

Proximity of #2 Fighter Wing to Belgium, Holland,
Luxembourg, Germany and Switzerland made it possible to travel practically every weekend. A number of the
teachers bought German and French cars and three or
four of us would get together and travel to historic
towns and cities for special festivals, concerts, theatre
and opera. Like Germany, France, too, celebrated a large
number of religious feasts. The seamstresses of Paris, for
example, enjoyed a holiday on the feast day of St.
Catherine in November. St. Catherine's day cards were
even sold to commemorate this special day for old
maids.

Because of the Suez Canal crisis which created a fuel
shortage in France, gas was rationed and we were forbidden to buy it on the French market. We thought it
would put a stop to our regular weekend travelling, but
somehow we managed because distances were so short.

If life on an air force base was fun, it was also fraught with danger and death. A few days before we were to leave #2 Fighter Wing to return to Canada, early one morning when I was still in bed, a terribly loud noise awakened me. We were used to the breaking of the sound barrier, but this deafening sound was different.

June remembers:

> As I ran to the front of our barracks, I saw one of the doctors from the hospital staggering to the phone. I watched him trying to dial when to my shock I noticed that the skin from his arms was hanging over his hands. "Let me dial," I volunteered. "Tell me what to say." In a quavering voice he said that two aircraft approaching the base landing strip had crashed in mid-air, exploded and dropped on the hospital. Still in my memory, I can see a pair of my metal folding scissors sticking in the wall to support the blood transfusion that was being given to the doctor.

This horrible accident is frozen in my memory too. I saw the dentist so burned that his wallet in his back pocket had turned into black tar, and his skin hung in shreds over bare bone. He was naked to the waist. His eyes were sightless. The crash had blinded him, killed one pilot and several people, including the hospital pharmacist.

Christmas Vacation, 1956

On Sunday, 16 December 1956, I met Alfred, my brother, at the Air France terminus, the Esplanade des Invalides in Paris. After Alfred was settled in a hotel, we walked to La Madeleine for Mass. As we were standing in front of the church deciding where we were going to lunch, an event happened which is scarred in my memory. I usually dressed to blend with crowds but this time I was wearing my fur jacket and dressed like an American socialite. A young Frenchman approached me asking me whether I wished to exchange my American currency. I thought it was a good opportunity for my brother to get a good rate of exchange. Alfred handed me a $500 bill and the Frenchman began peeling away the French notes. I asked him to stop and give me the notes after each count of one hundred dollars. He refused and gave me the wad of notes at the end of the count. When we got back to Alfred's hotel room, I counted the money and, to my horror, discovered the Frenchman had given me only $250.00 worth. My immediate reaction was to report him to the police. But my lawyer brother stopped me, convincing me it would have been futile. I apologized profusely, vowing never again to exchange money on the black market. Knowing how terrible I felt, Alfred, the gracious man he is, did not berate me.

John Stephenson, a friend from home, who was studying at the Sorbonne, joined Alfred and me on our Christmas trip to Munster to visit the Beckwermerts, my brother-in-law's family. Alberta (Comox, B.C.), a colleague of mine, drove us to Soest where I had taught the year before.

We drove along the Mosel River, which meandered past a string of storybook medieval villages, and saw steep terraced slopes covered with vineyards and turreted castles perched on rocky outcrops; the skinny church spires that pierced the sky reminded me of the Rhine Valley. And then suddenly a massive structure with two arches loomed up before us. It took my breath away and I asked Alberta to stop the car so that I could investigate. It was called the Porta Nigra (the black gate), built in the fourth century, the mightiest town gate the Romans ever built. I found out we were in Trier, once, one of the leading cities of the Roman Empire, a second Rome north of the Alps, adorned with all the civic buildings of a major Roman settlement. Emperors such as Diocletian and Constantine each lived in Trier for long periods of time. The city had aroused my curiosity. I promised myself I would return some day. I never have.

After staying overnight in Köln, and attending Mass early the next morning at the massive Gothic Cathedral which still showed signs of intense bombing, we drove to Soest. Here, Alfred was enjoying himself so much in the 4th Field Ambulance mess that we missed the train to Munster, and Alberta had to drive us to Hamm where we could catch the Munster-bound train.

We spent the three days of Christmas at the Beckwermerts. And what a wonderful time we had. Mrs. Beckwermert had prepared a lavish array of holiday food. There were cookies galore: *Speculatius Pfeffernuessen*, and *Lebkuchen*; each kind flavoured with its own special spices used only at Christmas — anise, cardamon, ginger and cloves — and moulded in the shapes of stars and angels, hearts and animals. There was a Hexenhaus, marzipan and apple strudel with heaps of whipping cream, which Mrs. Beckwermert knew I loved.

During the late afternoon on Christmas Eve we were called into the parlour. Mrs. Beckwermert opened the French doors, and there to our amazement stood a wonderful tree towering towards the ceiling, trimmed in silver with flickering white candles clipped to stout green branches. We joined hands around the tree to sing

Stille Nacht, heiligen nacht. I heard Mrs. Beckwermert's wonderful soprano voice and Dr. Beckwermert's deep bass. Little gifts were laid out in small piles on tables, and on the chesterfield and chairs. I was impressed by an envelope decorated with a sprig of balsam stuck with wax. We partook of a splendid buffet with trays of open-face sandwiches, assorted breads — rich dark pumpernickel, light rye and white rolls — salami, salmon in chives, Westphalia ham, sardines and other cold cuts, cheese trays and fruit, nuts and chocolate. On Christmas Day, a succulent goose was given the place of honour at the table.

On 26 December Alfred and John left for Frankfurt and I left the next day for Hanover where I met Rita Bennett (Trenton) from #2 Fighter Wing.

We were on our way to Copenhagen because neither one of us had ever visited Northern Europe's largest city. It was cold, cloudy and humid; we left after only two days. However, I did take back two memories. I remember the bronze statue of the winsome Little Mermaid, a character from Hans Christian Anderson's fairy tale, keeping close watch over the ships in the harbour, and the innumerable twinkling lights that shone at night from Copenhagen's world famous amusement park, the Tivoli.

On our way back to Hanover we stopped at Hamburg. It was shrouded in fog and so we stayed only a day giving ourselves just enough time to walk through the notorious Ruperbahn, praised by the airmen at the base. We were not impressed. Rather than go to any of the night spots there, we chose to hear Donizetti's *Don Pasquale* at the new and modern State Opera House.

We had to be back in Hanover where we were to be the guests of a Royal Air Force Squadron at a New Year's Eve ball in the nearby, beautiful old town of Celle.

To our surprise we were told it was a costume ball. We were not prepared for this news. But we were not deterred. We put together a few bed sheets and pieces of jewellery and went as two Canadian Cleopatras. We danced until dawn. There were grand marches, Paul Jones, Gay Gordons, the Charleston and chicken dances. There were the Conga lines. One, two, three kick! We were giddy with delight.

Easter Vacation, 1957

I spent the Easter holidays of 1957 (17 April-29 April) with Jeanette Rigg Arthurs (Dunville, Ontario) my classy teaching colleague at #2 Fighter Wing. I felt honoured to be travelling with her in her new dark gold, sporty Karmann-Ghia, a curiosity wherever we went. We left Gros-Tenquin to tour the Loire chateaux country, Brittany, Normandy, the bulbfields of Holland and the World War I battlefields of Belgium and France, a distance of 2,200 miles. In between Brittany and Normandy we flew to the Isle of Jersey. Of this trip I wrote:

> The chateaux on the Loire are simply magnificent. We visited only a few of them: Chambord, Chenonceau, Angers and Chinon. They were all so alike and yet so different. Each told the same story of opulence, extravagance and luxurious living in the days of French kings and chatelaines. Each, too, had its own particular tragic tale to tell. Unfortunately there are few furnishings because much was stolen or destroyed during the French Revolution.

Chambord, in the middle of a royal game forest, the largest of the Loire chateaux, with its enormous staircase and conglomeration of turrets, cupolas, chimneys and gables, was described by the nineteenth century novelist, Henry James, as "more like the spires of a city than the salient points of a single building." It was the castle of King Francis I. On one of the window panes he wrote the celebrated lines translated into English as "woman is fickle; he is stupid who trusts her." The *son et lumière* was impressive: the courtyard glowed again with the flames into which the mob threw the castle's priceless tapestries and furnishings.

No other town in France captures the atmosphere of the Middle Ages like Chinon. We loitered along the narrow, twisting, cobblestone streets, along La Rue Voltaire with its ancient houses, and paused longingly at the Grand Carroi, the busy intersection of the Middle Ages, where Joan of Arc alighted from her horse to enter an inn. We climbed the steep ascent to the castle and wandered about, reflecting on the incongruity of a sleek American car parked against an old timeworn stone wall. I couldn't help respect the American's driving skill as he successfully manoeuvred the oversized Cadillac around the tight corners.

Brittany

We drove from town to town in this old province tucked in the northwestern corner of France, which has been little touched by modern development. Twentieth century technology had not intruded into the green meadows with their pasturing small black and white Breton cows. The odd architecture of the churches, and the fishing boats standing on their stilts in the harbour mud when the tide was out spoke of a distant time. Life continued in its peaceful and contented fashion as it did hundreds of years ago. We saw the women still wearing their traditional black velvet and satin costumes with tall, stiffly starched lace bonnets on their heads. As we drove through various districts the headdresses changed. In the market place at Quimper, I remember counting eight different shapes and styles. Many still wore wooden shoes.

I'll never forget Easter Sunday at Pont L'Abbaye. We waited outside the church to watch the congregation leave, and saw women, with high, white, cylindrical-shaped lace headdresses towering as much as fifteen inches above the wearer's head. As well, they were wearing black opossum capes or black lace shawls, and long black dresses. The men in their black velvet vests and wide, upturned-brim black hats with six to eight streamers hanging from the back made a picture that contrasted with the younger men and women in modern garb. I couldn't help wonder how much longer tradition and custom could last.

Even the churches of Brittany were different. They have a rough-hewn quality about them. When I saw the queer little lopsided church at Perros-Guirec with its midget dome and toy-like spire, I couldn't suppress my chuckles.

This rough-hewn architecture was best exemplified in the old "parish enclosures." Nowhere in our travels had we seen anything like them. No wonder we lingered in Pleyben and St. Thegonnec. A parish enclosure consists of a church, an ossuary, an ornate calvary (burial chapel) embellished with dozens of stone figures, and to one side, an arch of triumph leading to an adjoining cemetery. Each one we saw possessed incredible originality. Although the calvaries were crudely made, weatherbeaten and covered with green moss, they were interesting.

The scenic beauty of Brittany was a joy to me: the apple, peach and cherry trees all in bloom; the pink almonds and pink and white chestnuts, the yellow gorse which lined the highways; the wisteria falling along the walls of the houses; the lush green meadows and trickling streams; the calla lilies, the largest we had ever seen; and the rose-coloured rhododendrons. Coming from a place that has virtually no spring, I was enthralled by all this glow of colour and spring freshness.

We visited St. Malo, the ancient walled town on the coast, for its Canadian ties. In a land of memorial loving peoples cognizant of heroic deeds and valour, I knew that Jacques Cartier, who set sail from St. Malo in 1535 to discover the St. Lawrence River and found Quebec, would not be forgotten. In vain, we looked for a statue, but were relieved when we saw *Rue Jacques Cartier*. My faith in the French people was restored. Once an ancient pirates' stronghold, St. Malo was completely destroyed during World War II. Its massive mediaeval ramparts overlooking the whole seafront and the wide sandy beaches luckily survived.

I loved Dinan on the Breton coast, charmed, as I was, by the old cobblestone streets, the churches, the castle and the old black and white timbered houses on stilts with their overhanging balconies.

Channel Islands

We left our car in Dinan and we flew to the Isle of Jersey. We made a complete circuit of the island. The panoramic beauty of the sea, the fine sand beaches, secluded coves, and sheltered bays, the steeply rugged coastline, and the spring flowers, in full bloom, were a pleasure to behold.

The famous thoroughbred Jersey cows grazed in the pastures. We learned, however, that these cows were gradually losing their ground to tourism.

I was delighted by the natural beauty of Jersey, but I was even more interested in learning about life in Jersey under German occupation during World War II. I was surprised to hear that the Germans used Russian forced labour for their building projects, deported non-Jersey residents to Germany, and forbade radio listening. But German fortifications and observation towers were now being utilized. A German bunker, for instance, formed part of a tea room.

Normandy

I found the landscape of Normandy, much like that of Brittany and Jersey, beautiful: succulent green pasture lands, streams of gentle waters, beautiful spring flowers and fruit trees all in bloom, the unpretentious manor, the long seacoast with its high cliffs, sandy beaches, and the quiet peace.

However, I found myself, once again, more attracted to the cities of Normandy because of their World War II history. Allied forces landed in Normandy in 1944 and most of the heaviest fighting took place there. As a result, Normandy suffered more than any other part of the country during World War II. And for the first time in France — in Le Havre, Caen, Rouen and Falaise — I felt the same horror that I had experienced in the demolished cities of Germany. I saw the same devastation: jagged fragments of walls, empty shells of buildings, blocks and blocks of wasteland. I remembered how I had marvelled at German vitality and industry. I had somehow attributed an indifference and inertia to the French. But I found them here emerging from the ruins, rebuilding their shattered towns and homes with vigour.

Jeanette and I drove to Rouen to see the exact spot of the pyre on the Place du Vieux-Marché where Joan of Arc was burned alive on 30 May 1431. The king she had helped to crown at the Cathedral at Rheims did not offer to save her. I spent a few minutes recalling her fate: how she was able to convince the king that she was inspired by God to help save France; how, dressed like a soldier, she led the French army and broke the eight month English siege of Orleans; how she escorted the unseated Charles VII to be crowned King of France; how, in 1430, she tried to help recapture Paris, but was captured by the English who sold her to the Catholic Church to be tried by an international ecclesiastical court; and how she was tricked into admitting she was a witch after months of questioning. We visited the bomb-damaged Cathedral of Notre-Dame whose stained glass windows and spires dominate the city. I was spell-bound.

The giant thirteenth century Benedictine Abbey of Mont St. Michel, perched on a 264 foot mound of rock, is said to be the greatest wonder in France. On our approach it was enveloped in mist and barely visible, silhouetted against the gray skies. But gradually the mist disappeared and the monastery stood impregnable before us in all its grandeur. The abbey is cut off from the mainland at high tide. The sea that separates the rock from the mainland is extremely dangerous because the tidal movements produce a difference of up to forty-five feet between high and low tides.

But it was low tide and it was Easter Monday. The French were out picnicking; hundreds of cars were parked on the dried mud beaches and sheep were grazing on the flats among the rich seaweed.

Jeanette remained in the car while I visited this marvel. Elbowing my way through hundreds of sightseers who crowded the long, single narrow street, the Grand Rue — at first, a steep ramp, and later a stairway lined on both sides with souvenir shops and eating places — I finally arrived at the abbey church to discover that the tour lasted an hour and I didn't have the time. I was disappointed because I had looked forward to seeing the Lace Staircase inside.

We visited Dunkirk, best known as the scene of the heroic retreat of the British in 1940, when anything that could float evacuated 350,000 men who were completely surrounded by German forces. The wind was cold; the skies were gray. I ran out on the fine sandy beach and stood silent and pensive recalling that miraculous evacuation in the blessed fog and calm over the chilly waters of the English Channel.

Belgium

We stopped at several sites where so many horrors of the First World War were committed. At Ypres we remembered Canada's fighting men whose courage in the face of poison gas, a new weapon used by the Germans, won them recognition as first-rate troops. They suffered over 6,000 casualties here and the city was literally wiped off the face of the earth. We saw directional signs to Paaschendaele and Mons, to more World War I battle sites where Canadians distinguished themselves.

We stopped at several of the many military cemeteries, and the words of John McCrae's *Flanders Fields* kept coming back to me as we walked solemnly "between the crosses row on row" :

> We are the Dead. Short days ago
> We lived, felt dawn, saw sunset glow,
> Loved and were loved, and now we
> Lie in Flanders Fields.

And I saw the bright red fields of poppies stretching as far as the eye could see. They have become my favourite flower.

I loved to recite Byron's poem *Waterloo* which presents the famous ball before the decisive battle (15 June 1815) where the Duke of Wellington defeated Napoleon. It begins:

> There was a sound of revelry by night,
> And Belgium's capital had gathered then
> Her Beauty and her chivalry, and bright
> The lamps shone o'er fair women and brave men;
> A thousand hearts beat happily; and when
> Music arose with its voluptuous swell,
> Soft eyes looked love to eyes which spoke again,
> And all went merry as a marriage bell.

I don't know why the poem appealed to me so much, but I told Jeanette I had to visit the actual battlefield. We didn't take any of the tours because we were in a hurry to start our drive home.

When my eyes caught the direction sign for Ghent, I suddenly recalled teaching Browning's "How they brought the Good News from Ghent to Aix." I remembered that my students and I traced the horse-back ride

on a map of Belgium, and that the rhythm of the lines
had entranced us:

> I sprang to the stirrup, and Joris, and he;
> I galloped, Dirck galloped, we galloped all three;
> "God speed!" cried the watch, as the gate bolts undrew;
> "Speed!" echoed the wall to us galloping through.

The Keukenhof Gardens, Holland

We drove through Belgium to Lisse, in Holland to see
the famous Keukenhof Gardens. A spectacle met our
eyes. 27 April weekend must have been the peak of the
tulip season because Holland — between Haarlem and
Leiden, an area of light, sandy soils which is ideal for
growing bulbs — was a border to border carpet of
colour. Even the cars were bedecked with garlands of
flowers (a custom in Europe with the first spring flowers).

Words are hopelessly inadequate to describe the
celebrated bulbfields of the Keukenhof. The Dutch
bulbgrowers have converted an old estate of one hundred acres into a showplace of beauty. There were huge
orange, and black tulips; hyacinths of the purest blue,
and pink and white; narcissi and jonquils; forget-me-
nots in pink and white and blue. There were tulips in
formal beds and daffodils in wild settings. There were
winding paths and little lakes, statues and fountains. But
everywhere the tulip reigned in its cultivated beauty and
perfection.

Flanders

We saw the First World War killing fields of Artois on the flat Flemish plains of the Western front. We visited the Allied graveyards. The endless rows on rows on rows of stark white crosses shocked me. As we slowly walked between the rows, reading the names of the slaughtered, I was appalled at the many nameless graves "known only unto God." And suffused with a sadness I cannot describe.

The battle at Vimy Ridge marked the first time Canadians served together as one group forming the Canadian Corps. We saw the maze of trenches and tunnels and remembered the bravery of Canadian soldiers during the fierce eighteen-month battle (1916-1917) waged between the Allies and the Germans. When it was over there were 700,000 dead and nine villages wiped out. I gazed at the undulating terrain and stunted vegetation of the earth that refuses to yield fruit, and I listened to cuckoo birds singing. For Jeanette, catching the huge Canadian War monument at Vimy rising out of the fog was "one of the most moving experiences" of her life.

I kept noticing the contrast between the monuments dedicated to the dead of World War I and the unpretentious memorials of World War II: a modest plaque on an abandoned pill box; a small slab of stone commemorating the spot where a few soldiers perished at the hands of the enemy, or where a partisan was shot; or a simple stone paying homage to those deported to Germany never to be heard from again; or perhaps just a line reference added to an old World War I monument.

Each Sunday is a minor celebration when the brass bands (practically every hamlet has one) and male choirs come out of church to herald the day of relaxation. On

Sunday, 28 April, we saw a parade with four bands. It was Kermis (carnival time) and everyone was celebrating the arrival of summer. Early the next morning at 7:30 a.m. when we were leaving Lille, we saw another parade with a brass band, and men in high hats.

We passed through Armenteers and Jeanette and I sang the words of the World War I British army song:

> Mademoiselle from Armenteers
> Parlez-vous?
> Mademoiselle from Armenteers,
> Parlez-vous?
> Mademoiselle from Armenteers
> She hasn't been seen for forty years
> Inky-pinky parley-vous.

Germany, May 20, 1957, Weekend

Jeanette and I, once again in her Karmann-Ghia, drove to Rothenburg-ob-der Tauber, a jewel of the German Middle Ages, the "best preserved medieval town in Europe."

We drove to Heidleberg and then followed the Neckar on either side of which unfolds a landscape of high wooded hills, vineyards, and hidden valleys. It was fun to drive under old town gates, to come suddenly upon hills crested with castles in ruin, and castles well preserved, to watch little streams lazily lingering along, and narrow canals slowly flowing in front of old houses, to discover "secret" towers.

We enjoyed stopping at quaint old towns like Dinkelsbühl, a medieval city preserved intact, its walls still standing, complete with moat, gates, towers and bastions where we saw the women and little girls wearing dresses with square necklines filled with ruffled lace, puffed sleeves and aprons. And we saw Michelstadt, with its remarkable Town Hall and its three cross-braced gables supported by oak pillars, and Würzburg, with its bridge over the Main River protected by its stone saints (reminding me of the bridge across the Tiber in Rome), and its beautiful Romanesque cathedral with its pure white and gold Rococo interior.

Of course, the highlight of our trip was Rothenburg; beautifully situated on the steep banks of the Tauber. A *bürgermeister* (mayor) who, in 1631, during the Thirty Years' War, met the challenge of a conquering Catholic general by drinking 3¼ quarts of wine "bottoms up" saved the Protestant village from annihilation. (The tankard was on display at the Reichsstadt museum.) In World War II, an assistant secretary of war was able to spare the town once again, this time from an artillery barrage. As a result, the village has preserved its pure medieval appearance completely. Most medieval cities which we had seen had expanded beyond the walls with new industries. But Rothenburg was still cloistered inside its walls with the tourist industry, its main source of revenue, conducted with dignity and subtlety.

We were reduced to admiring silence as we wandered along narrow cobblestone streets flanked by timbered houses with picturesque high gables. The many towers and turrets, gray and darkened by the patina of ages; the heavy wooden doors and gates to the city; the sturdy walls; the massive fortresses; the many old fountains brilliant with scarlet geraniums; even the proverbs in German script on the outside walls of buildings; the wrought iron ornate brackets displaying the trade symbol of the shops; beautiful ancient wood carved doorways with their old-fashioned lanterns; and in a corner niche of many old homes, small statues of the Virgin (the city's patron saint), or a shepherd or a knight in armour, all combined to evoke in us a dreamy, peaceful atmosphere. I was transported back to the Middle Ages in a lovely fairytale.

At St. Jacobkirche we admired the Blood Altar carved in wood by the Renaissance sculptor Tilman Riemenschneider. It is truly a work of art. Above the altar a crystal capsule is said to contain drops of Christ's blood.

On our way back to Gros-Tenquin we passed through the ancient city of Worms (devastated in World War II). In 1521, the Diet of Worms issued its edict against Martin Luther who had appeared before the Holy Roman Emperor to defend his reforms against the corruption of the church. I saw the church door where Luther nailed his declarations.

Le printemps in France and Germany is a wonderful season. *Les cigoynes sont de retour. Les arbres sont tour en fleur.* Spring flowers in inconceivable variety — buttercups, marsh marigolds, forsythia, snowballs, magnolias, hepaticas and daffodils — bloom everywhere.

And there were numerous flower festivals. On 20 April 1958, at Gerardmeer, the Pearl of the Vosges, I witnessed the *Fête des Jonquils*. I counted twenty-six floats in different shapes — a Sputnik, a huge perfume bottle, an old carriage — entirely covered with wild daffodils. 2 May is the *Fête de Muguets*, when friends and lovers give each other a nosegay of lilies of the valley, and it was on this day that I saw lilies of the valley being sold along the road ways. In Alsace cars are covered with flowers and their occupants throw flowers to passers-by.

Spring was also the time for bicycle and motorcycle races, and for parades celebrating religious feasts and national events. The German and French people love a parade. I do too. On 1 May, the parade at Vahl Eberseng in Alsace has been held every year for two hundred years to thank the Blessed Virgin Mary for saving the town from the cholera plague. The merrymaking at these religious feasts never failed to amaze me. There was nothing like it back home. Church bells rang: brass bands played. A motley group of marchers — altar boys, priests in rich vestments, villagers, and men in red uniforms and steel helmets — marched and sang and prayed. It was a happy time.

On 21 May, in Sarreguimines, we saw a parade of nineteen-year old boys in fancy hats and boutonnieres with a huge French flag and brass band celebrating their last year of freedom before their compulsory military training.

Summer 1957 Trip: Europe and the British Isles

Gwen Chapman, another colleague at #2 Fighter Wing, Frances Kozystko, who had flown over from Canada, and I left by train from St. Avold, on Saturday morning, 29 June, on the first lap of our journey to Spain. We spent our first night in Dijon and left the next morning, stopping for a few hours in Lyons.

We spent our second night at Avignon, staying long enough for us to see the Pont Saint-Benezet (The Pont d'Avignon of the popular song which I loved to play on the piano as a child). I used to imagine the laughter and dancing in celebration of many a feast day when the Popes lived in Avignon five hundred years or more ago.

We got off the train to explore Marseilles, France's bustling port on the Mediterranean where we counted four British destroyers. We walked along the Canebière, Marseilles' Champs Élysées, where we saw people, some in their native costumes, from all over the world. But what I remember best is the garlic market in one of the main squares where long strings of garlic cloves were sold by the kilogram, and the steep steps, lined on each side with statues, that we had to climb to reach the railroad platform.

It was twilight when we first saw the flood-lit citadel of Carcassonne, silhouetted against the dusk, perched on its hill looking like a drawing from a fairy story of knights of old. We stayed overnight at the Cité with its medieval decor within the walls of the fortified city. The next morning we took a tour of this greatest surviving medieval fortress and marvelled at the genius of fourteenth century French military architecture. Our train passed through Toulouse which our guide books said was "the greatest unknown city" of France. We decided to get off to see for ourselves. But with only two hours at our disposal we saw only the Romanesque Basilica of St. Sernin, begun in 1060, with its wealth of relics, including a thorn from the Crown of Thorns, and the head of St. Thomas Aquinas.

Lourdes

We arrived in Lourdes at nine p.m. We could see the floodlit basilica and hundreds of candle-carrying pilgrims waiting for the procession to start. But we wanted to make certain we had a room for the night before going to the procession. There were no vacancies in the first hotel where we stopped. I rushed to another across the street, where, luckily, there was a room available. After we had made quick verbal agreements, Gwen and I ran to the basilica grounds which were nearby because we didn't want to miss the procession. Frances stayed behind to make sure we had the room. Experience had taught her not to take any chances. She didn't join us until hotel forms were filled and the luggage was safely in the room.

We stood speechless on the lower ground as we watched the scene before us: the three spires of the grey basilica high on the crest of the hill, the tall trees flanking it on either side, the crescent moon behind in the charcoal grey sky, and the pilgrims carrying their torches descending the hill on either side of the basilica. A chill ran down my spine when I heard the familiar strains of *Ave, Ave Maria*.

As the pilgrims slowly passed by us, one in particular caught my attention: a beautiful, raven-haired young woman, looking so pert in her red beret and red sweater, in a black hooded wheel chair so common around the grottos. She was singing the hymn with such fervour that I was ashamed of myself for every time I had grumbled or complained.

The procession slowly descended the slopes of the hill to the lighted statue of the Blessed Virgin which stands in the centre of a circular, fenced-in plot. Hundreds of fresh flower bouquets, offerings to the Immaculate Conception, were lying on the fence.

We were dumbfounded at this mammoth demonstration of an intense faith that had brought 6,000 pilgrims all the way from Italy, Spain, Denmark, Ireland, and the United States. An Irish priest told us that there would be six times that number the following week.

After the procession was over, we just wandered speechless throughout the whole area, visiting the Basilica and the grotto. We didn't want to leave.

It wasn't until the next morning in the bright sunlight that the full significance of the shrine struck me. I was standing on the very spot where Bernadette Doubirous, a frail girl of fourteen years, had the first of eighteen visions in 1858. The ninth time the Virgin appeared, a tiny stream of water started trickling in the grotto. Today, the spring flows abundantly, and large numbers of sick people flock to the site for the miraculous waters. At home I had heard so much about Lourdes; I had seen the movie version. And now I was actually there. How lucky I was!

I kept going to the fountains next to the grotto where pilgrims were filling their plastic bottles and slapping the water on their faces to refresh not only the spirit, but also the body on that sizzling hot day.

Towards one p.m. 800 invalids congregated before the grotto for a service. I just sat on one of the benches and watched: little boys in sailor suits, dressed immaculately as only French mothers can dress them, with braces on loose, limp legs; adorable little girls in pigtails and ribbons; mothers and fathers carrying babies; old men and old women; young boys and girls; priests and nuns. Some were in wheelchairs, and some in stretchers; sickness has no respect for age, gender or rank. They were there because they believed and hoped. I'll never forget one little girl in a short white pleated skirt, one tiny leg in a brace, and the other loose and dangling, pushing her own baby carriage. As the priests preached to the sick, gentle nurses cooled feverish brows and held small tin cups filled with water to parched lips. The heat was unbearable. "Not my will but thine" the preacher said. And I couldn't help but admire the resignation, the fortitude of the sick. I didn't bother Our Lord with my own material wants because they were so insignificant compared to the others. I just prayed for the salvation of my soul.

While the congregation was singing *Nous sommes Chrétiens* my ears caught the sound of a beautiful tenor voice. It came from a tall, stocky man bronzed by the sun, with a bushy, black, curly beard. He was standing by the altar rail, fingering his beads. He looked bedraggled in a tattered and torn coat that was too tight and short for him, a black wool scarf, shoes with loose soles, and a dirty undershirt. But his piety and concentration fascinated me. His eyes were constantly fixed on the statue of the Blessed Virgin Mary before him. He must have been a walking pilgrim from Spanish Morocco (the special benediction service was being given in Spanish). And I admired him for his steadfast faith.

What impressed me most was the silence that shrouded the whole area. Thousands of people were coming and going. There were no moans and groans from the sick. They suffered in silence and silently prayed; the healthy moved in silence and silently prayed.

When I went to the baths, I found hundreds of invalids, wearing their pilgrimage tags, with their nurses, waiting in queues for their turn to bathe in the miraculous waters. Finally it was my turn to be ushered into a cubicle with four Spanish pilgrims. One, especially, won our sympathy because she was young and beautiful with expressive eyes, but totally unable to do anything for herself. I remember that all of us held back our tears as two gentle nurses tried to move her from her stretcher into the bath compartment. It was a struggle handled with utmost care. I recall how hard we prayed that God, in His mercy, would help her.

Then came my turn to go behind the curtain where two nurses stripped me and put a wet, white cloak on me while I said an act of contrition. I was then asked to descend the two steps into the bath. I was shocked to see human feces floating in the water, but I was not squeamish. Reciting the "Our Father," I walked into the fairly large pool, where there stood a small statue of the Blessed Virgin Mary which I was asked to kiss. Then I was asked to sit down while two nurses recited a prayer. And before I knew it the ritual was over. An inner peace had flooded my soul.

We visited Bernadette's home and the museum where many of her relics are found. But I kept returning to the grotto where hundreds of the crutches, symbolic ears, eyes and artificial limbs of the cured were displayed in recognition of the miraculous healing power of the Saint. I drank the holy water from the fountains and filled a large bottle to send home to my mother. I kept going back to the little side chapel where I meditated on the gold mosaic inscription on the altar, the very message which Our Lady gave to Bernadette: *Je ne vous promets pas de vous rendre heureuse dans ce monde mais dans l'autre.*

I prayed that the pain in my knees would go away. My prayers were answered.

Biarritz

After our solemn spiritual retreat in Lourdes, we decided that we needed some fun and relaxation on the ultra-chic Biarritz beaches, that were so popular with the international set. They were all that the brochures said.

We spent several days just basking in the sun, lolling on the fine sandy beaches, and dipping in the high waves. But we cut short our restful sojourn in order to be in Pamplona, Spain, for the annual Saint Fermin celebrations, which featured the running of the bulls.

Spain

Irun and the Spanish border! Gwen and Frances had to change their travellers' cheques and buy their train tickets to Madrid at Biarritz. I had bought my "Kilometric" at a 30 per cent discount, a green book covering 3,000 kilometres which contained detachable five kilometre coupons, which would have to be exchanged for rail tickets. Fortunately, I did not foresee the many frustrations my "Kilometric" would bring.

We were immediately impressed by the courteousness of the Spanish police who even held the fast Madrid express for us. To our surprise, it was clean and roomy, a striking contrast to the French train we had just left. And everyone had a seat too! I enjoyed gazing at the landscape — a patchwork of green and yellow fields — as we travelled through the countryside. The red, red poppies along the tracks reminded me of Spring at Gros-Tenquin. As we stopped at the various stations the local attendant would ring a bell suspended from one of the roof beams, to announce the arrival of the train.

Pamplona

At length we reached Pamplona for its annual week long fiesta in honour of St. Fermin, the patron saint of the city.

We hired a taxi to the Spanish Tourist Office that was crammed with visitors only to discover that all hotels were filled; in fact, they had been booked a year in advance. It was only then that I learned how famous the Pamplona Fair really was, attracting thousands of people from all over the world. We were apologetically told that rooms in private homes were all that was available.

We proceeded by taxi to the addresses which the Tourist Office gave us. Each one was already rented. At our third attempt, a neighbour who had overheard our plight offered us her daughter's bedroom. It was a very small room up six flights of stairs. The three of us had to share the same bed. The bathroom was large enough, but it was bare, with only a small basin and no racks or hooks of any kind. It did have a cork stoppered tub which was streaked with black and grey where the porcelain had worn off. We were grateful, however, because we knew that we couldn't afford to be fussy at this late date. We could speak no Spanish at this point and our landlady no English, but sign language and mental telepathy seemed to work.

Once we had our lodgings settled, we strolled to the main square, which was alive with merry-makers. Everyone was wearing a red kerchief tied around the neck and red sandals. The *caballeros* were dashing in their white trousers and red cummerbunds, dancing in the streets to the music of scores of small bands consisting of three or four accordions, tambourines and guitars.

The outdoor restaurants were jammed and we had difficulty finding a place to eat. I recall now how astonished we were at the low prices. A full course meal cost only one dollar. I had my first taste of a Spanish speciality, *paella valenciana*, a rice dish with chicken, shell fish, lobster, saffron, pimento, and kidney beans. It's as pretty as it is delicious.

At lunch time the next day, we met three Spanish cavaliers who "took over." We toured the countryside in their convertible and saw the penned bulls that were going to be used in the bull fights. That evening they escorted us to all the local festivities. The town was floodlit and a riot of colour. Sidewalk cafés were packed. Streets were jammed with policemen vainly trying to keep order. Noisy young people whirled wildly in the street. We sat sipping native wines, and munching langostinas (large shrimp) and other crustaceans dipped in a batter. We watched the splendid fireworks display.

Spanish dinners are eaten very late at night. It wasn't until eleven p.m. when we went for dinner in the upstairs dining room of one of the many restaurants which lined the main square. Dinner lasted nearly two hours, and then we ambled through the midway, which was not unlike the ones back home. I was surprised to see small children hopping about and skipping until the wee small hours of the morning. The festivities are round the clock and we marvelled at the tireless energy of the young people. We were exhausted. When we got back to our room, we didn't have the energy to discuss the cluttered, small bedroom, nor the sagging bed.

Sunday morning was the feast day of St. Fermin. High mass and a procession took place in his honour. The procession included soldiers of the church in colourful mediaeval garb, priests in rich vestments, high ranking military officers, dignitaries in top hats, bands in various costumes, and soldiers with rifles. Clowns called *Cabezudos* (bigheads), favourites of Pamplona youngsters, carried large thick rubber •balloons with which they spanked children, and even some adults who attracted their attention. My camera must have made me conspicuous because they spanked me. Grotesque figures, twelve feet high allegorical figures called *gigantis* (giants), which are actually old pagan symbols dating back to the Middle Ages, bobbed their heads as they passed by.

The streets along the procession route were decorated with streamers and banners. The statue of St. Fermin, in all its bejewelled splendour, was mounted on a platform and carried by six costumed bearers. As the statue entered the cathedral, a gun salute, a roll of drums, and a blare of trumpets were sounded. The crowds cheered and shouted their approval, jostled and pushed to catch a glimpse of their patron saint. And even we, who were standing precariously on a wall which separated the high road and the low road in front of the cathedral, felt a tingling sensation up our spines.

Sunday was spent again in revelry, with more bands, more dancers, and more noise. On this day, however, young people were wearing wreaths of garlic and carrying skin gourds of wine from which they refreshed themselves and toasted each other after their hot, wild gyrations.

Pamplona is the only city in Spain where the bulls are let loose in the streets and are chased by or chase any of the Spanish youths courageous enough to match their speed and skill against them. At seven a.m. Monday morning, six bulls were released from their pens outside town to charge through the streets to the bull ring with thousands of young amateur matadors who brandished old newspapers and sweaters instead of scarlet capes and gleaming swords. Carnival merrymakers cheered them on.

We got up at six a.m. to be sure to see them, but when we arrived downtown we found crowds so thick that it was utterly impossible to even get near the barricades, no matter where we went or how hard we tried. People had stayed up all night to make sure of a good viewing spot to watch Pamplona's celebrated "running of the bulls".

Unfortunately, by this time, I was suffering from an annoying rash. My whole body was aflame. I diagnosed it as bedbug bites, but I was advised to seek medical help. I decided to wait until we got to Madrid, hoping that the fiery rash would disappear by then.

Madrid

But the rash persisted after we arrived in Madrid. The doctors at the Anglo-American Hospital were sure it was neither smallpox nor German measles. They didn't know if it was food poisoning or insect bites, but they prescribed penicillin and calcium shots, and gave me conflicting advice on what not to eat and what to eat. After five days of semi-starvation, lots of sleep and numerous sizzling hot showers which, alone, relieved my body's itch, the doctors considered me well enough to leave Madrid despite large red sores all over my body.

My painful rash had stopped me from exploring Madrid as much as I had hoped. But I still saw most of the popular tourist sights in the highest capital in Europe, now a bustling twentieth century boom town, especially since the Americans have arrived. I also managed to squeeze, between guided tours and hospital visits, a few private strolls to see Madrid's quietly dreaming seventeenth century heart.

Madrid, the capital of Spain since 1561, like any other capital city, boasts many magnificent public buildings. Its Post Office, which the Spaniards call "The Madonna of the Mail", was the most beautiful I had ever seen. Next to Rome, Madrid is the only other city whose lovely fountains have impressed me. Its wide tree-lined boulevards and modern skyscrapers give it a futuristic look which London couldn't claim. Like Berlin, it was in the midst of much construction and large scale improvements to repair damage from its fierce Civil War. In spite of this modern look, there were many peaceful old squares and streets, old houses, palaces and churches, gates and doors. Only the recently constructed arches of triumph spoiled the harmony of old and new.

In spite of these arches, Madrid is a strikingly beautiful city. Its lovely El Retiro Park alone is a refreshing retreat from the scorching heat of the city. I enjoyed strolling along the wide formal avenues towards the lake in the park where boats can be rented. It was fun to sit in a shady corner and watch the small Spanish children, immaculately dressed, looked after by their uniformed nursemaids. I enjoyed just sitting on a bench, contemplating the beauty of the surroundings, the gardens, the trees, the lakes, and statues. The weigh scales which I had also seen in French parks made me chuckle.

The palatial Prado Museum, with its priceless art treasures by Italian and Flemish masters, Titian, Fra Angelico, Andrea del Sarto and Rembrandt, and by the Spanish masters, Velasquez, Goya, Ribera, and Murillo, is one of the most spectacular art galleries in the world. But it was the religious paintings of El Greco (1548-1625), the Roman-trained Cretan, which held my undivided attention. To me, his ascetic, convoluted style symbolized the spiritual mysticism that is such a part of a Spaniard's life.

I wanted to be in Fatima, Portugal by 13 July in order to visit the sanctuary of Our Lady of Fatima. But I needed a Portugese visa. I had my kilometric which I had to exchange for tickets at RENFE (Spanish state controlled railroad company offices) in order to reserve my seat in advance. When I arrived at the office I did not expect hundreds of people in lopsided queues at a maze of wickets. I elbowed my way to the nearest queue, only to be directed to another. After a quarter of an hour, I reached a wicket to discover yet again that I was in the wrong queue. This time I was sent downstairs where more queues crowded the room. At long last my turn came. The thought of not being able to get on a train when I wanted had just never occurred to me so that when I was told that there were no seats for the twelfth, I was stunned. Mechanically, my legs took me away and I just stood at the bottom of the stairs realizing that I had wasted nearly two hours. This was the first of many frustrations that I would have with RENFE.

By chance there was an English girl living in Madrid who had noticed my frustration. She told me about professional standers who could be hired to wait in queues for rail tickets. Tourist travel in Spain had increased so much that Spain did not have the facilities to cope. I scoffed at the idea of having to hire someone to buy my tickets. However, I was to cast aside this notion in my later travels. She suggested I return the next day when RENFE might be coaxed into finding a space for me.

Meanwhile, I thought it best to get my Portugese visa. When I was told I couldn't have it for several days I was annoyed. One set back after another! Using what little Spanish I knew, I tried to explain how absolutely imperative it was for me to have a Portugese visa. "Come back tomorrow," was the cool, calm response. I was beginning to see that mañana was a national affliction. The next day I visited the RENFE office again. The same long tedious wait, the same answer: "Come back tomorrow. Today, there's no room on the twelfth."

Friends had told me to use tears as a last resort. They said that they always worked. I knew that I couldn't turn them off and on at will, but I was so upset when the attendant told me that there was no room on the twelfth that tears did trickle down my cheeks. The man at the wicket was startled. He stumbled through an explanation, and after several pretences of examining his books, he silently handed me a reservation to the frontier town of Badajoz.

Spain's heat had been so oppressive for Frances that she decided to return to Canada, and Gwen, too, would leave after our visit to Avila and Toledo to visit her relatives in England.

Avila

Gwen and I took an all-day tour to Avila and the medieval imperial capital of Toledo. Seeing metalworkers, still practising the black and gold inlay work known as damascene, was not shocking; seeing two eight-year-old boys, producing the fine-tooled damascene daggers and swords, was. But what I like to recall is Toledo, standing grim, proud, and fortress-like on a granite promontory, with the River Tagus encircling it below, and the sombre beauty of the delicate greens of the olive-clad hills, the brilliant blue of the sky, the stark whiteness of the homes, and the silence. We climbed the steep and narrow cobblestone alleys to the highest point of the city where the sixteenth century turreted fortress of Alcazar stood. The decisive battle of the last Civil War was fought there. What I found gratifying was learning that in 1085, when the Christian army conquered Toledo, the conquerors were shocked to find Jews, Moors and Christians living together in peaceful co-existence. As capital of the country until 1561, Toledo was a centre of learning and the arts that fused Moorish, Jewish and Christian cultures. In fact, Toledo had developed a great school of translators and a centre of philosophic studies. Thus, the work of Aristotle, for example, was rendered into Arabic by Moslems and thence into Latin by Christians. Between them the two civilizations generated a climate of learning that was to take Europe out of the Dark Ages.

I had wanted to go to Avila because it was the birthplace of St. Theresa, one of the Roman Catholic Church's greatest mystics. I was enthralled to find a perfectly preserved walled and turreted city, the best Spanish example of a fortified town of the Middle Ages. The landscape was barren and treeless. Everything was a searing ochre which gave the city a foreboding appearance.

Within the walls, this was relieved by the early morning activity we saw when we strolled along narrow, winding cobblestone streets. The baker was delivering round loaves of bread from two wicker panniers, one on each side of his donkey. And wine and olive oil were being delivered on tap from huge jugs strapped on the donkeys. The City is dedicated to St. Theresa (1515-1582). Bakery shops sold St. Theresa cakes packaged in small gift boxes. We visited her birthplace, now the baroque Carmelite Church of St. Theresa, built from the sixteenth to eighteenth centuries on the site of her parents' home. We visited the Convent of the Incarnation where Theresa had made her professional vows, where she saw her visions, and from where she left to promote the Reform of the Carmelite Order. I saw the wooden pillow on which she slept, and contemplated the intensity of a faith that enabled her to experience the divine ecstasy which, in her writings, she expressed in erotic imagery.

On our return trip to Madrid from Avila we stopped at a roadside inn for refreshments. At a table near us was a group of well-dressed Spaniards. I was surprised that they asked us whether we were South or North Americans. It was a question I would be continually asked throughout Spain. But I suppose South Americans visit their mother country just as Canadians visit England. When we got up to pay, however, our bill had been paid. This kind of generosity would occur again and again.

I wanted to see El Escorial, the largest Renaissance residence in the world built by Philip II, about 50 kilometres from Madrid. I managed to reach the right train station, but discovered I was in the wrong depot. I had only a few minutes left to descend a flight of about fifty steps a few hundred yards away and to buy my ticket which I knew would be a frustrating experience. I had just enough time to dash into a coach just as the train was pulling out.

I sat in fear that I would miss my stop because Spanish conductors do not announce the names of towns, and trains stop only a few minutes at stations. However, Spaniards are very helpful and those in the coach assured me that they would inform me in plenty of time.

The railroad station at El Escorial was bare and forbidding. I had no idea how to reach the palace and felt helplessly lost until I spotted a Spanish policeman: he was wearing one of the funny black metal hats with the stiff visors in the back, giving him the appearance that his hat had been put on backwards. He directed me to a bus that took me directly to the monastery palace.

My first reaction to El Escorial (1563-1584) was one of disappointment. It was just a massive, austere structure. But once inside, the guide's wonderful commentary transformed it into a fascinating place. Here lived His Most Catholic Majesty, King Philip II of Spain, the mightiest potentate in Europe who lived an ascetic life-style and spent most of his time in a little spartan suite inside the huge fortress-cum-monastery. But his galleons were bringing the treasures of the Indies and the richest spoils of the Aztecs and Incas from his new found empire in the Americas. Every Canadian school child learned about how that great English seadog, Sir Francis Drake, whose name became a symbol of terror and fear all over Spain, had "singed the King of Spain's beard." Determined to stamp out heresy, Philip planned to strike down the heretic Queen of England who rewarded pirates like Sir Francis Drake and supported the Dutch in their struggle for independence from Spain.

Here Philip planned his 1508 invasion of Protestant England under the reign of Elizabeth I with his invincible Great Armada. Every Canadian school child learned about the Defeat of the Spanish Armada, about how the small and nimble English boats were able to fight off the clumsy Spanish galleons. My ten-year old mind had imagined the daring sea fight and the defeat of the mighty Armada. The Elizabethan Age of British History had intrigued me since I first learned about English buccaneers, the slave ships, and the Spanish Menace. Now I recalled those exciting days, years later, in the very building where the Spanish King lived. I was thrilled. As I left, I turned to gaze at El Escorial once more.

Since there was still an hour before the bus to the railroad station would arrive, I decided to walk. It was a bright sunny day and I was enjoying the downhill stroll, observing the lush green fields, and the flowers, when I suddenly realized I was on the wrong road. There was no car or person in sight. I didn't want to retrace my steps because I thought there would surely be branching roads. But there were none. I was frightened, more from the prospects of missing my train (Spanish trains do not run regularly) than anything else.

Finally, I noticed a man with a large straw hat working in the fields. I went to him and asked where the railroad station was. He informed me that it was a long way off. I was disappointed. But he added that he would show me a short cut. He escorted me up a steep bank to the railroad tracks and told me to walk along the tracks to the station. Once I was on the tracks I could see the station in the distance. Before I was able to head in that direction, however, he tried to kiss me.

Luckily, I managed to break away. I don't think I've ever walked so fast in my life. I didn't want to run for fear he would sense my fright. Once out of his sight, however, I literally ran to the station and into the ticket office. It was closed, and would open only fifteen minutes before departure time. I was frustrated. I wanted to detach myself from that unpleasant incident. I wanted to feel the ticket, the means of a safe exit, in my hand. But that couldn't be. I went, instead, to the café in the station and sipped lemonade until the wicket opened. When the train pulled in, I wasted no time in boarding it.

Portugal

Six of us — Zoe, her two boys and her Portugese maid, as well as a Spaniard and myself — shared a compartment. We turned out the lights, but after we had each settled into a position we thought might induce sleep, suddenly the light was turned on. A tall figure who displayed his shining badge of office appeared in the compartment. He was the passport detective, a well known official on all Spanish trains. We resented his intrusion.

We could not get back to sleep, but the night passed quickly because Zoe was an interesting woman. She had known luxurious living as the wife of a Romanian in the Consular Department in Lisbon during the war. But rather than return to a Communist satellite country, she and her husband had chosen to remain in free Europe.

It had been a struggle for her family. Her husband, a university professor, had difficulty obtaining a position. However, their luck had changed when the year before her husband had obtained a teaching position at the University in Saarbrucken, and she herself got an executive position in Madrid. They were miles apart, but when two young boys have to be fed, clothed, and educated, economics take top priority.

Zoe spoke English beautifully. She had majored in languages at the Sorbonne. Maria, her devoted Portugese maid from the bygone days of prosperity, was a bastion of strength and courage in the lean years. She spoke Portugese, Spanish, and French, but she could neither write nor read any of them. She must have been only in her thirties, but Zoe reminded me that Portugal had no compulsory education.

The day brought its scorching heat. We were covered with soot; the mosquitoes and flies kept pestering us; the train kept crawling at a snail's speed. The delicious cherries, and lemonade couldn't distract us from the heat and soot.

A border incident, however, broke our lethargy: Maria was taking home presents for her relatives and friends, just remnants of yard goods and pieces of cloth which she had collected and accumulated for the day when, after twelve long years, she would be able to visit her family. She had carefully stored them in pockets and sleeves and among the various clothes in the suitcases. The Portugese customs officials asked Maria to open her bags. None of us was aware of what Maria had done, not even Zoe. To our surprise a yard of pyjama material left over from the pajamas she had made for Zoe's husband was pulled out and displayed dramatically. Then other bits in rapid succession were plucked out: silk, cotton and wool fragments. Poor Maria! She was trying to explain but the customs men, completely ignoring her, kept exhibiting the evidence. We just sat and watched the drama unfold. After the inspection, which must have lasted a quarter of an hour, Maria and the inspector, with heaps of material in their arms left for the Customs office accompanied by Zoe. I felt sorry for Maria. She had been diligently salvaging this material for twelve years, yet she had to return to her folks empty-handed. She was heartbroken.

The incident delayed the train half an hour but the officials never hurried. At last our dawdling train carried us over the border. Portugal was green compared to the dry, beige landscape of Spain, and the houses gave the impression of being newly white-washed. But soon, not even the change of scenery, the cork trees, eucalyptus, and rice fields, which first excited me, could make us forget the baking heat.

Smudged with dust, smoke, soot and grime, we entered Lisbon's station, and it was such a black and foreboding place that I was glad to be with Zoe. Her friend's chauffeur met us at the station. Thoroughly exhausted, I finally got settled in at the Tivoli Hotel. A cool, refreshing bath soon gave me renewed energy and I decided to arrange excursions for the next day. I headed out into the beautiful streets with their many outdoor cafés and parks and found my way to Cook's, where I managed to book a tour to Fatima the next morning.

On our way to Fatima we passed through Vila Franca de Xira, a small town that was celebrating The Festivities of the Red Waistcoats during the full moon in July in honour of the *campino* (cowboy). The big civic celebration marks the opening of the bullfight season. The town was decorated with flags, banners, and blue and white steamers strung across the road. The gleaming, whitewashed homes in one single strip on both sides of the street were garlanded with huge rosaries of olives, beads, holy pictures of Our Lady of Fatima, palm leaves, and large flower rosettas. There were flowers everywhere. Huge wicker baskets filled with fresh flowers (I especially recall the large mauve daisies) hung from the sides of houses. Embroidered bedspreads and tapestries hung from windows and over balconies.

We saw the *campinos*, dressed in their short red boleros, green stocking caps bordered with red, embroidered white shirts and hose, bright red waistcoats trimmed with glass buttons, and short knee green breeches, astride their horses, carrying the *pampilho*. This is a long wooden pole with a sharp metal tip with which they guide the black bulls from the pasture to the bull ring. It is interesting to note that in Portugal, the *corridas* is waged on horseback and the bull is spared, whereas in Spain it is waged on foot and the bull is killed.

Fatima

It was a three hour drive from Lisbon to the little village of Fatima. As we alighted from the bus, the bare white landscape before me was impressive. The same question was on all our lips: "Where did the Blessed Virgin appear to the three little children minding sheep on 13 May 1917?" Our guide pointed to the spot. I was surprised to see only a simple wooden shack open on three sides with a statue of the Blessed Virgin in the centre. Very long candles were burning on racks. White marble plaques with golden inscriptions of thanksgiving covered one wall. I noticed a Canadian inscription. To the right was the olive tree under which the children knelt, when six times they saw the vision of the radiant Virgin Mary appear in a cloud. Despite being imprisoned for three days by the local administrators, the children stuck to their story, quoting the Virgin Mary's prophecies. Within weeks, the site of the apparition had attracted thousands of pilgrims. I saw barefoot pilgrims, many of whom sheltered themselves from the scorching sun under black umbrellas, travelling on their knees on the long path leading to the basilica.

We heard Sunday mass at the Basilica of Our Lady of the Rosary which stands a few hundred feet from the shrine. It looked so starkly white, so new, so clean, so bare, so simple in design compared to some of the dark, cluttered, and overly ornate, churches of Spain, France and Italy. As I entered, the organ strains of O *Sanctissima*, one of my favourite hymns, were filling the church, and I felt very much at home. A wedding ceremony was being conducted in one of the side chapels.

The Basilica faced a huge square and was flanked on each side by a hospital. There were no souvenir shops, no organized rituals. Behind the shrine was one small shop where religious articles were sold. Silence reigned in spite of the hundreds of pilgrims. "How different from Lourdes," I mused. We lit candles, washed ourselves at the fountain, and prayed.

We had lunch at the convent of the Dominican Sisters who operate a restaurant. I was very much astounded when a nun who spoke "American" greeted us. Our lunch was wonderful with wine, lobster, and shrimp. My two companions were Belgian teachers from the Congo. I was surprised to learn that the Belgian Government not only gave their teachers in the Congo an annual paid vacation but they were also allowed to enter most European museums and art galleries free of charge.

On our way back to Lisbon we passed terraced slopes of olive trees which reminded me of the vineyards of the Rhine Valley. We visited the famous monastery at Alcobaca where the twelfth century kitchen is so large that six oxen could be roasted at one time. We saw the musty dining room where Queen Elizabeth was feted the month previous and the Tomb of the Unknown Soldier where she laid a wreath. It was a Sunday and the Portugese themselves were visiting their national monuments. The square in front of the monastery was alive with singing and brightened by the red clay earthenware of Estremadura spread out in front of the shops.

We were also taken to Batalha, the great Dominican Abbey, the most magnificent architectural monument in Portugal. It is a rare treasure of the highly ornate Manueline style of architecture which fuses Arab and Christian details to create a style native only to Portugal. Images and symbols reminiscent of Portugal's voyages of discovery — waves, seaweed, corals, ropes, exotic fruits and animals, chains, anchors, and sails — are placed side by side with Christian symbols to produce a fabulously flamboyant and robust decoration.

Although I found the Manueline style impressive, I was more interested in our guide's talk on Portugal's age of glory: how Portugese seamen ignored stories of monsters and bottomless pits in the oceans and explored the globe; how their exploits were inspired by one man, Prince Henry, known as The Navigator (1394-1460). It was Henry's inspiration that led Bartolomeu Dias to round the Cape of Good Hope (1488), Vasco da Gama to India (1497-1499) and Pedro Alvares Cabral across the Atlantic to Brazil (1500). For over one hundred years the conquistadors of Portugal brought back gold and precious stones, silks and spices, and exotic Oriental products to make Portugal one of the wealthiest countries in the world. But dynasties come and go. Portugal had her "one fierce hour and sweet." The sixteenth century was Portugal's golden age. There were now only proud guides to remind us of Portugal's glorious past.

Nazaré

Ninety miles north of Lisbon, on the Atlantic coast, we stopped at Nazaré one of the most picturesque fishing

DND SCHOOL - 2(F)WING RCAF FRANCE
TEACHING STAFF - 1958

villages I have ever seen. It was Sunday and yet it seemed
that the whole community was working on the shore.
The fishermen were wearing costumes characteristic of
centuries ago: baggy trousers of coarse wool, tartan
shirts, and long, black stocking caps in the tassels of
which they banked their money and tobacco. They were
repairing their nets and working on their brightly
painted, heavy, high- prowed boats styled after Phoeni-
cian galleys with flat bottoms and broad beams to fit
them for riding the heavy ground swells and turbulent
seas offshore. Hundreds of these boats were cradled in
the sand. All was activity. Boats were coming in and the
air smelled of fish. The old women wore their long black
fringed shawls and flat pot-shaped black felt hats. Fisher
girls, wearing wide skirts in big check patterns, inflated
by layers of pleated petticoats, seven if unmarried, two
if married, carrying flat boards covered with silvery
sardines on their heads, trudged barefoot through the
sand. Others were putting the fish to dry on racks set up
on the beach. All was alive at the water's edge on the
wide sandy beach.

Lisbon

We arrived in Lisbon in time for a few of us to go on a
tour of a typical Portugese restaurant to hear the *fado*,
the folk songs of yearning, intimately associated with
seafaring, that are sung to a melancholy guitar accompaniment.

The next morning I arose early to explore the city
on my own. The sky was cloudless and the heat even
bearable. Stubby cable cars were climbing Lisbon's
steepest hills, and in the old quarters, labyrinths of
narrow streets were clinging to hillsides. I loitered along

the animated river front. There were ships, barges, an incongruous mixture of barefoot fishwives carrying flat-bottomed baskets of dripping fish on their heads, sailors, stevedores, and trucks loading and unloading fresh vegetables and fruits. The harbour was cluttered like any other quay of a great port. Bars and warehouses lined the streets. There was a lot of poverty, and I tried to look as inconspicuous as possible in a faded black dirndl skirt, white cotton blouse and sandals. (My movie camera revealed me as a tourist.) I was surprised to see workmen still using pick-axes to repair the streets.

There was little that was very old in Lisbon because of the disastrous earthquake of 1755. The riches of its many palaces, churches, libraries and convents — the treasures looted from Africa, India and Brazil — had vanished . However, on the rubble of the fallen city rose a metropolis, large and beautiful, with wide, tree-lined avenues, parks, beautiful squares of black and white mosaics, miles of mosaic walks, and houses adorned with beautiful ceramic tiles.

One building reminiscent of Portugal's glorious past, the Aviz Hotel, known throughout the world, enthralled me. A former castle of only twenty-six rooms, it is richly furnished with authentic antiques and tapestries. The bar, with its beautiful wood panels, was a jewel.

The train for Seville was leaving at eleven p.m. I was being wined and dined by a Portugese gentleman proceeding to Angola, the largest of Portugal's overseas provinces. The time had passed so quickly that I had only about twenty minutes to get to the train station. We had to take a fast cab and then find a porter. We searched the station in vain for my train. After we had boarded and unboarded several trains, the seconds flying and the "time of departure" sneaking up, in the midst of thick crowds scurrying to and fro, the porter finally dumped my heavy suitcase and me in a compartment. I sensed that I wasn't in the right coach.

It was one of those individual compartments which sit ten to twelve people facing each other. The only communication among the compartments is by the outer doors which are on either side of the train, and I was the only occupant in my compartment. I was afraid. Every time the train stopped I wished someone, preferably a woman, would enter.

After several stops, a conductor checked my ticket and informed me I wasn't in the right place. I was on the wrong train! But I was lucky. He escorted me to a compartment that was occupied by a clean-cut young sailor in a new train that was waiting on the tracks. After a few awkward moments of silence, a Spanish-Portuguese sort of conversation ensued. He told me he had witnessed the drama at the station and had informed the conductor that I was on the wrong coach. A Portuguese man, unlike a Spaniard, does not talk to unknown women, especially if she is unaccompanied; he had broken tradition.

I tried to catch a few winks, but my sailor considered it his duty to amuse and feed me until four a.m. when he got off. About a quarter of an hour later the conductor told me that I had to get my passport checked. During the five minute stop I had to rush to the Portuguese passport control and get back on the train again. In my chase I met Jim, a young American soldier stationed in Germany whom I had previously met on the Madrid-Lisbon run. I was pleased to see him again, because although it was fun to be with local people, I felt more comfortable with North Americans.

At the Spanish border we got off to board another train. No one had told us about border crossing regulations. While Jim looked after the luggage I proceeded to look for someone who could enlighten us. After running back and forth across the tracks for anyone in any manner official, I discovered we had a two-hour stop in which bags and passports had to be checked and tickets bought. The ticket wicket was closed, but after an intensive search I found someone who would sell us tickets.

It was early in the morning and yet it was baking hot. I wasn't looking forward to the train trip to Seville. From past experience I knew it would be slow, hot, and uncomfortable. The trip to Seville took sixteen hours. A map showed that the distance was practically negligible, but there were no direct train routes.

Seville

Thoroughly worn out, Jim and I arrived in Seville. There was no air, just sticky heat! Jim planned on taking the next train to Madrid where it would be cooler. I took a cab to the Hotel Christina. I was too restless to take a siesta. Instead, I tackled the fierce heat, sauntering along the bleached streets. Everything was closed tight. Nothing stirred! It reminded me of the deathlike stillness of Athens from two to five p.m. At five o'clock, doors were unbolted, gates unlocked, shutters flung aside, shades raised, and life began to move again. But I was too tired and went to bed.

The next morning I arose early and took the city walking tour. Seville's colossal cathedral was overwhelming. Built in the fifteenth century, it is the world's largest Gothic structure and third largest cathedral. But it wasn't its size that dazzled me, it was its wealth: statues

dressed in capes of satin or damask encrusted with pearls
and strands of gold and diadems glittering with precious
stones; silver and gold lamps; bronze candelabra; ornately embroidered clerical vestments decorated with
precious rubies, emeralds and diamonds; gleaming gold
monstrances and chalices; and ecclesiastical furniture
rich in precious jewels. Nearby stood the Giralda,
world-famous landmark and symbol of Seville, formerly
a twelfth century Arab minaret, built to be the most
beautiful tower on earth. Church spires have always
fascinated me, but Giralda was unique. I just stayed in a
corner admiring its delicate beauty before the guide
broke my reverie.

We sauntered through the orange-scented streets of
the Barrio de Santa Cruz, Seville's old Jewish Quarter. I
was captivated by its twisting and cobbled squares, its
narrow lanes and white-washed houses with green shutters, flower filled balconies, and pot-bellied iron-grilled
windows overflowing with roses. When we peeked
through open doors we saw the invitingly cool shade of
patios enlivened by fountains and brightened with pot-
ted plants and copper vessels. We were reluctant to leave
the trim and clean, perfumed sweetness of Santa Cruz's
quiet residential streets. I returned later that day.

The Alcázar, built by Pedro I (1350-1369) on the
site of the former Moorish fortress, the finest example
of Mudéjar architecture in Spain, was stupendous. Its
most grand room was the Hall of Ambassadors. The
magnificent, delicate Moorish dome was simply awesome. We stopped in the gardens where we relished the
fragrance of jasmine and myrtle. My guide plucked a
jasmine for me. It was my delight for the whole afternoon.

After the tour, as I was returning to the hotel, a woman stopped me to ask if I were Canadian. Conversation started and I met Mary Boley, (Toronto) a Department of National Defence teacher at Soest where I had taught two years before. Her friend, Agnes Cheyne from Scotland, had seen me posting a letter to Canada at the hotel the night before and had recognized me. We made arrangements to have dinner that night at the hotel.

In the meantime, I strolled through the parks, scented with tangerine trees, and along the palm-shaded walks until I thought it was time I should get my rail ticket to Algeciras. How I dreaded going to the RENFE! I was not the least surprised to find a long queue of sitters, squatters, and standers. It was four p.m., and the office would not open until five. All was locked and barred. I went to the end of the line and waited.

At five o'clock the iron gates opened. Nobody moved. I decided to enter. No sooner had I reached the wicket than I heard shouts and screams, a cacophony of sound. The office staff tried to control the stampeding mob. Several policemen appeared and pushed the mob back into the street. Fingers were pointing at me and I realized that they thought that I was going to be served before the ones who had been in front of me.

The policemen didn't know what to do with me. They tried to calm the crowd, especially the two ringleaders who were stirring the mob. Finally, peace was restored and people flowed to the various wickets in an orderly fashion when a policeman escorted me to a wicket for "internal travellers." He remained by my side until I had bought my ticket. I liked his protective bulk hovering over me. I had been overcharged for my reservation, but I didn't dare make an issue of it. I had already inadvertently caused a riot. I wanted to vanish. I left as fast as my legs could carry me, occasionally sneaking a glance behind.

Mary, Agnes, and I thoroughly enjoyed the night of Andalusian dancing on the Roof Gardens of our hotel. Spanish dance held an inexplicable attraction for me: the man, in his high-waisted trousers and clicking heels, and the black-haired woman with her swirling colourful flounced skirts and flashing eyes dancing passionately to the beat of castanets and the snapping of fingers! What captivated most were the hands and wrists of the women dancers. Graceful arms caressed the air in sinuous gestures, and hands moved sensuously.

The next morning I arrived very early at the station. Spanish stations were very shabby, unpainted, with no caféterias, and no waiting rooms to speak of! They had none of the amenities I had found in Italy, Germany or France.

When I presented my ticket, the collector made me understand I could not take my heavy suitcase on the train. I had never had any particular love for that bulky suitcase of mine. I hated its size, its shape, its tawny canvas cover, but most of all I hated its heavy weight.

But here I found myself refusing to part with my suitcase. This was my opportunity to discard my detested burden, but I knew Spanish railroads only too well, and so I refused, and just sat on it. Its strength had served me well on French trains and in stations when no other seating accommodation could be found. Suddenly I began to appreciate that suitcase of mine. Could a suitcase, not as formidable, have provided a comfortable bench for me? How many times had I lugged it, dragged it, and pushed it? My suitcase was now part of me. I loved it and wanted it. No one was going to take it away from me.

In the midst of these good intentions, a policeman, tall and strong, came to inform me that I must part with the suitcase. I pretended not to understand. Feigning ignorance had worked so many times before! But this policeman wasn't going to yield so easily. He left, and just as I was basking in my new-won victory, he returned with another man who explained, in perfect English, that I could not board the train with the suitcase.

I protested, explaining why I could not part with my suitcase. How did I know whether it would ever reach my destination? In the midst of my questioning I noticed my suitcase being carried off by a policeman to the checking room. I knew now that all was in vain. At least I had not consented to abandon it! My suitcase could not accuse me of disloyalty. The Spanish way of doing things had come out on top again. I kept good watch of my suitcase until I saw it heaved on the train at the mercy of RENFE. I honestly believed I would never see it again.

The local people called the run from Seville to Algeciras "the horse back ride." It was aptly named, because the train just chopped its way on short rails. With the intolerable heat, the intolerable slowness, and the intolerable congestion with hand luggage of all shapes and sizes, and anxiety over my suitcase, I should have been utterly miserable, but I wasn't. The camaraderie among the passengers made me soon forget my frustrations.

Everyone in hearing distance joined in a conversation which was a mixture of as many tongues as could be understood, French, German, Italian, English, Spanish. Everyone also joined in a train meal. There were no dining cars on these southern runs; everyone brought his brief case or wicker basket lunch. Cloth serviettes (never paper ones) were spread out. Bocadillos (delicious miniature loaves of bread), always unbuttered, were eaten with smoked ham, cheese, salami or hard boiled eggs. Wine, beer, or mineral water was always drunk, and fresh fruit ended each meal. Every time the train stopped, there was a mad rush of passengers getting off to fill their red or beige clay jugs with drinking water from a fountain which was invariably found at every station. I enjoyed watching the bocadillos being cut with jackknives, and then stuffed. They were eaten with such gusto that I became hungry. My train companions insisted that I join them so much that I had to accept.

I forgot about my suitcase. At one transfer point where we had to walk a long underground passage, I was even happy I didn't have to bother with it.

The "horseback ride" was long considering the distance, but as I have mentioned before, there were no direct routes. Spanish trains always crawled at a snail's pace. Oddly enough, they arrived "on time." Spanish time that is. We crept into Algeciras. With my suitcase surprisingly safe and sound, I passed through customs quickly and boarded the ferry to the rock fortress of Gibraltar, the gateway to the Mediterranean Sea, in British hands since 1704.

Gibraltar

The crossing from Algeciras took less than an hour. On board I met two young, attractive wives of British naval officers stationed at Gibraltar, who had gone to Algeciras to shop. But it was a holiday and all the shops were closed. When I met them they were concocting the various alibis they would give their husbands who would have accused them of just wanting to take a trip.

When I told them I was on my way to Tangier and Casablanca they flooded me with horrible tales of Moorish atrocities against whites. They warned me profusely not to go. They succeeded in frightening me to such an extent that I gave up the idea of visiting Casablanca. By this time we were nearing "The Rock" as Gibraltar is known in those parts.

There was no delay in landing. I was a Canadian, a British subject. There were no formalities. The taxi we shared took me to The Rock Hotel. A fashionable wedding party was in progress and the management had no time to take care of me. I left my suitcase in the rotunda and went outside to begin my exploration of the rock fortress. The first thing I did was buy a Cadbury's chocolate bar which I had not seen for over a month. It tasted so good!

It was five p.m., and the streets were teeming with Spaniards going home after work, British soldiers, sailors and their wives, and tourists. The streets were cramped with small, well-stocked shops displaying foreign goods: Swiss and German cameras, French perfume, Spanish mantillas, fans, pottery, ivory and curiosities from the East, all free of purchase tax. Several modern hotels, and many saloons and bars featuring American jazz lined the narrow streets. I noticed signs which read "Do not feed the Apes" and "Apes might bite." When I inquired about the apes I was told that the Rock Apes of Gibraltar were the only native apes in Europe. And there was a superstition that if the apes disappeared from the island, Gibraltar would cease to be British.

I found a small cemetery with graves from the Battle of Trafalgar dead, once grey tombs, now green with the patina of age, the inscriptions scarcely discernible. And I contemplated the dead, who under the great sea captain Horatio Nelson, defeated the mighty French and Spanish fleets on 21 October 1805.

I experienced a sample of British hospitality when, after inquiring for the way to the American Express Office for information on Tangier, a British naval officer in short white pants and white knee hose took me there in his car.

By seven p.m., I felt I had exhausted the famous fortress whose area is only two and one-half square miles. Its strategic location had impressed me, and its size had surprised me. I returned to the hotel, ready to leave the following morning by air to Tangier.

Tangier

I flew Gibraltar to Tangier in twenty minutes. The Tangier airport was a very modern structure, but passing passport control was a long, tedious process. During the slow way up to passport control I met a group of English tourists who asked me to join them. I was relieved because after all I had heard, I did feel a bit of trepidation in this Moroccan city. At the airlines downtown office we hired a guide and three cars for the sixteen of us.

We toured the old town — the Medina — with its old, narrow, sloping, winding streets filled with shops where Moroccan craftsmen sold leather goods and gold embroidered slippers. As we dawdled along, taking pictures, we had one guide leading, and his assistant bringing up the rear; the guide was taking no chances, considering Arab hostility at being photographed.

To Westerners, the Casbah of a North African city is the red-light district evoking an oriental mystique. We were anxiously looking forward to a real adventure. But we discovered that the Casbah was only a walled fortress built on the steep sides of a hill in the oldest area of the city. As we wandered through the various rooms, the bridal chamber and the courtyard, I imagined sultans and their harems, pirates, spies, and political and sexual intrigue. But, to my disappointment, we merely entered a café, where we sipped some bitter mint tea and listened to Oriental music played by a group of Arabs squatted in circle formation. It was a weird drone to me because I find Arab music, with its endless repetition, monotonous to my western ear. I chuckled when I saw that the musicians had neatly placed their white, upturned-toed open-heeled sandals side by side next to themselves.

The Casbah was closely guarded, and we were told to hurry because it was noon time, the Islam hour of prayer. The flag was hoisted and all non-believers had to leave. The Casbah had been neither exotic nor mysterious. We all felt let down.

We took a sight-seeing tour around the city. From one of the steep promontories we witnessed a magnificent panoramic view of the blue Mediterranean and the Atlantic. We stopped to watch a snake charmer perform to the beat of drums. We wandered to the market by the waterfront which was teeming with Arabs and fresh fruit on display. The smallest of stalls were overflowing with bright yellow melons and green watermelons as well as other fruit and vegetables. I felt very uneasy taking pictures because the Arabs protested violently. I was grateful I wasn't alone and relieved only when we left the bazaar.

My tour companions left about four p.m. for the airport to return to Spain. I sat in one of the many outdoor cafés watching the people go by; the tall, slender Moorish women in their long hooded gowns and veils of red, yellow, or green chiffon walking so gracefully, were lovely to look at. A few wore sun glasses and even red nail polish. Some pushed Western-style baby carriages and held small children in western garb by the hand. Many looked prosperous; their garments were of the finest material, beautifully pressed and spotless. Most of the men were in western dress although I did see some draped in white. As I sat, fascinated by the exoticism of the East, I was constantly pestered by hordes of Arab shoeshine boys, and vendors who plied the café route along the main thoroughfare offering all kinds of Moroccan arts and craft.

About six a.m. the next morning I hailed a taxi for the pier at the foot of the hill from my hotel. The driver charged me an exorbitant sum. I had noticed that he hadn't engaged his metre, but when I drew this to his attention he explained that his metre was out of order. There were hundreds of people pushing, pulling and squeezing into queues at various wickets for tickets, boarding cards, Moroccan police passport clearances, customs, and baggage inspection. I hired a porter to look after my suitcase before I penetrated the noisy mob. After about three-quarters of an hour the Moroccan police declared me eligible to go aboard. Another haphazard queue bulging in the middle was slowly moving on board. Queues in these hot lands were not like our orderly queues. They moved very slowly. This slow pace, however, gave me an opportunity to look for American,

British, or Canadian passports. I felt safer when I knew these people were also present. In this queue I spotted two American passports which belonged to a charming school teacher from Pennsylvania, Louisette Logan, and her daughter Dinny, who for the past year, had attended a private school at Nancy, located not too far from #2 Fighter Wing. I had visited Nancy several times to admire Nancy's jewel, the celebrated Place Stanislas. We became deeply interested in each others' travels. By the time we reached Algeciras after a two-hour ferry ride, we made plans to meet in Majorca.

Algeciras, Spain

We arrived at Algeciras. I wondered why so few got off with me. I entered the station and inquired about trains to Granada. By this time I knew something was wrong. I was in the Port of Algeciras; I should have waited until the next station. Lugging my heavy suitcase, I ran to the platform. Luckily, the train was still there, but only long enough for me to mount the steps. I was still in the vestibule when we squealed to a halt in Algeciras proper.

The station was a dirty, small, untidy, unpainted, barn-like room jammed with baggage and overstuffed wicker baskets. To my surprise, there was only one wicket and in front of it a long queue at a standstill. I went to the end. But it was the Seville queue, the wrong queue. There were no schedules posted anywhere. However, I soon learned that the Granada queue would begin an hour before departure time at two p.m. Resigning myself to a three-hour wait, I just sat on my suitcase. There was no waiting room, no benches, no food. It was sweltering hot and sticky. There was no ventilation. But I soon had Spanish swains clustering around me, fanning me with newspapers, and a Spanish woman would, occasionally, offer me her fan.

In the midst of all this attention I noticed the Belgian honeymoon couple who had been on the Seville - Algeciras "horseback run." They had been to Tangier and had just cleared customs. The bride was limp with the heat and I remember wondering whether I looked as exhausted as she did. I saw the groom being approached by a Spaniard. (It was uncanny how foreigners were spotted.)

I was hot, sticky, and hungry; I hadn't had anything to eat all day. The Belgian told me he had just hired a "stander-upper" for himself and was going to get something to eat. I didn't want to have to pay someone to get a ticket for me. But hunger was getting the better part of me, and so against my principles, I, too, hired the "stander-upper." And into the burning heat I went to search for a restaurant. When I returned to the station, my "stander-upper" was still in the queue. When he was finally finished, I noticed he had bought tickets for at least half a dozen people.

I knew it would be an exciting trip to Granada when I discovered my travelling companions included a youthful grandmother, and her ten-year-old grandson from Tangier, as well as Philippe, a nineteen-year-old Spanish soldier who proudly showed me snapshots of his wife and baby. I spoke enough Spanish to make superficial conversation possible. I learned that Spanish privates earn only about twenty-five cents a month. But they wear white gloves! The heat was oppressive. My rash was becoming painfully itchy. My companions kept fanning and trying to entertain me. As a tourist in Spain I was the centre of attraction!

Granada

It was nearly midnight when we arrived in Granada.
Philippe came with me to make sure I had a room in The
Alhambra, a former Moorish palace. The next morning
I took a tour through the city and met a charming
American, Mary Staudt, and a South African barrister,
Julia Boyd Harvey. The Generalife Gardens, surrounding the Palacio del Generalife, was built in the fourteenth century by the Moorish rulers as a summer retreat. Here was a green magic carpet. After the bleached
countryside, and the muggy heat, the gardens were a
refreshing paradise. In its many nooks there were
scented gardens, an incredible perfection of roses, jasmine, myrtle, pomegranates, marigolds, custard-apple,
and orange trees. The slender fountains dripping crystal
drops refreshed me like a cool hand on a feverish cheek.

If I could go to only one place in Spain, I would
choose Granada's Alhambra, the massive fourteenth
century ochre-red Arab fortress-castle of brick and
stucco which stands high on a spur of mountain under
the Sierra Nevada, the highest mountain range of mainland Spain, hiding its beauty behind forbidding walls
and towers. It is said that of all the buildings the Moors
left behind them in Spain after seven centuries of occupation, none can rival the Alhambra for beauty. Inside,
intricate lacy walls, sweet cedar wood inlaid ceilings,
fragile relief work in stucco, intriguing Arabic script, a
brilliant mixture of tilework and plasterwork, elegant
balconies and galleries and cool tiled patios, left me
speechless. Each new chamber left me dazzled, like the
loggia of 124 slender and graceful columns surrounding
the fountain in the Court of Lions, and the amazing
honeycomb dome in the Hall of the Two Sisters.

To think that 700 years ago at a time when the Western world was semi-barbaric, the Moors were capable of producing such astounding beauty. It was unbelievable! I imagined the life of the Arab court with all its pomp and splendour, its conspiracy and intrigue, its sultans, spies, and harems, its gracious elegant living in this oriental castle which must be one of the world's most important architectural treasures.

If I felt I had had enough of beauty for one morning — admiration can be exhausting — I had a surprise waiting for me. Our guide had told us that the climb up to the Tower of Charles V's Palace would be worth our pains. We forgot the heat the instant we saw the green tropical vegetation of the foreground, the golden Andalusian sun, and in the distance, the snow-capped peaks of the purple Sierra Nevadas shrouded in grey mist. After the Generalife in its perfect proportions, the Alhambra in all its oriental loveliness, and then this beautiful mosaic of colour, I understood the Arab proverb that "God gives to those he loves a means of living in Granada."

By this time, Mary and Julia, like myself, were not only physically and mentally tired, but hungry as well. We had lunch at a *parador* (a State run hotel) nearby. I discovered gazpacho there. It hit the spot. I make the refreshingly cool soup myself now on a hot day. The girls introduced me to sangria, a cooling drink made of orange and lemon juice, peach pulp, and red wine over ice. It became my drink for the rest of the trip.

No sooner had we mounted the stiff grade back to our hotel, than we were off again on our afternoon tour. The Cathedral surprised me because it was so clean and white and brightly lit. In the sacristy of the Carthusian Monastery I saw the most florid baroque imaginable. We hurried on to the gypsy caves of the Sacromonte which are scooped out of the soft clay of the hills. The cave which we visited was comfortable with its electric lights and gleaming copper utensils, its walls covered with photographs of family members and pictures of the Blessed Virgin all cluttered with artificial flowers. A family of gypsies performed a flamenco-style song and dance routine called Zambra. A single, long drawn out cry, a sultry handclapping beat, and the Flamenco began. With their flounced skirts and their ebony black hair adorned with a single flower, clicking their fingers and crackling their castanets, the gypsy women danced dramatically. In their high-waisted trousers and heeled shoes, stamping their heels and sinuously moving hands and body, the slender gypsy men danced fiercely. It was not Flamenco at its best because mama's dancing had seen better days. By the end of the performance, I was tired of Gypsy Flamenco. My mind kept going back to the throbbing rhythms of *Habanera* sung by the gypsy girl, Carmen, in Bizet's opera, which I had seen at Nancy in France with Alberta (Comox, B.C.) in the spring.

It had been fun to share the Spanish sights with Mary and Julia. But we had to part, and the next morning I took the train bound for Barcelona and Majorca. I was not looking forward to the trip because I knew only too well the sluggish pace of Spanish trains and the monochromatic tawny countryside dotted here and there with a handful of houses or groups of cattle gathered round fountains by the dusty wayside. Spain was not a beautiful country like France or Italy. The countryside was arid; there was scarcely any grass, only unbroken expanses of stony, treeless, desolate sierras. An almost eerie silence filled the transparent atmosphere and the pale yellow desert, but the immensity of space, the nothingness, was awe inspiring.

If the train's pace was woefully slow, and the scenery desolate, the camaraderie on the train was animated. Our compartment passengers consisted of two American soldiers; a Belgian university student, Égide Lanphendries, two young Italian sisters, Luisa Criscovolo, a doctor, and Gianna, a university professor; two Dutch university students; a Spanish law student; and a Spanish soccer player. All were polyglots in varying degrees except the Spanish soccer player. We kept up spirited discussions ranging from Franco and his inability to cope with Spain's major problems of education and social reform to Égide's wonderful impressions of Canada. He visited Canada during the Boy Scout Jamboree of 1955, and we discussed large grocery stores, Chinese restaurants, baby sitting, the large breakfasts, and the large number of factory workers who owned cars.

It was fun because each of us had something special to contribute. We learned that the Dutch girl had her purse stolen and that the Spanish soccer player was going to a clinic in Barcelona to have his injured knee looked after. Soccer, next to bullfighting, was Spain's most popular sport. Spanish soccer players were heroes! He insisted on giving me a lovely key ring to remember him by. Spaniards loved to give souvenirs and so my protests were always in vain.

I soon forgot the pace of Spanish trains, the lack of food, and the empty countryside. Before I knew it, we pulled into Valencia. Égide and the Italian girls had finally convinced me to stop over in Valencia with them and then go to Majorca, rather than go to Barcelona directly, as I had originally planned.

Valencia

Valencia was in the throes of a month-long fair. Égide, the two Italian girls and myself decided to stay together. Never have I had so much trouble finding accommodation. It was past midnight. Gianna and Luisa eventually found a room in a pension.

But Égide and I couldn't find accommodation because I insisted on two rooms. A single room was available, but not two single rooms. By two a.m., I was desperate. I finally settled for one single, making Égide promise he would keep his distance. I drew an invisible vertical line running along the middle of a large bed across which he could not trespass. I put my money under my pillow. It was the first time in my life I had shared my bed with a man. I was nervous. Even though this tall, blonde, rugged Belgian was lying next to me, somehow I must have fallen asleep. When I woke up, I discovered Égide had been as good as his word.

We remained in Valencia three days because we were unable to procure any sailings for Majorca. Valencia, once a royal capital, had a fine collection of ancient buildings and claimed possession of the Holy Grail, which I saw in a thirteenth century cathedral. Each day we went bathing on the nearby beaches, and lay on sands not as fine or clean as those of Biarritz or Majorca. We listened to bands and symphony orchestras. We ate orange after orange which we bought for less than two cents each and drank glass after glass of *haschalga*, a cool milky almond drink. We watched an explosion of fireworks. But the night of folk dancing and my first bull fight impressed me the most. I had travelled nearly 3,000 kilometres in Spain. But I had missed bull fights in Madrid and in Seville. In Valencia I finally saw my first *corrida de toros*.

A Spanish bull fight opens with pageantry, a parade across the ring of all the participants except the bull. This entrance itself is reminiscent of the symbolic religious drama with its blood sacrifice that goes back to ancient times. A bugle fanfare! The great door swung open; the procession entered the area; the bull was released. At first I was dazzled by the colour: the young matadors wore white skin-tight silken hose; black knee-length pants; stiff, gold encrusted pink satin bolero jackets; rose coloured fighting capes; and the red, white, blue, yellow and pink ribbon darts (the *banderillas*). Then, the intricate, precise footwork of the matador and his beautifully executed cape passes intrigued me. I realized that the grace, skill, and courage of the matador was pure art.

If the grace and skill of the matador fascinated me, his courage and daring awed me. I thrilled each time he taunted the bull to tire or confuse him with his carefully controlled cape passes. I thrilled each time he ran to take refuge behind the wooden post. The bull stood in the centre, still for a moment, and then looked around, and the matador, running in a circle, poked it. The matador then raised a pair of gaily decorated darts, jumped into the air, and then plunged them into the bull's shoulder. I gasped when the swords dangled from the side of the bull and his thick blood dropped from the wound. I felt nauseous.

But the *aficionados*, waving white handerkerchiefs, whistled and shouted *Ole*.

I could not understand why one fight was stopped by the judge, thus saving the life of a fighting black bull that left the ring only after two white cows lured him out.

The bullfight had been interesting, but the folk dancing I saw in the roofless bull ring that same evening was more enjoyable. Égide, Luisa, Gianna and I sat on folding chairs for twenty-five cents to watch a four hour programme of dances typical of the various districts of Spain. Again, as in Seville and Granada, the hand movements attracted me. The snapping of fingers, clicking of heels and castanets, and the throbbing guitar to syncopated rhythms captivated me. In one of the dances, to my surprise, a statue of the Blessed Virgin was used as a prop. The costumes were lovely, especially the various head ornaments: huge tiaras studded with shining sequins and rhinestones, and the sparkling pins, clips and combs.

The four of us could get only deck accommodation from Valencia to Majorca. It was an experience I don't want to have to undergo ever again. We pulled out at about nine p.m. and didn't dock at Palma until eight a.m. the next morning. It was the longest night I have ever passed. At first, we watched the twinkling lights of Valencia fade in the distance. Then pitch blackness enfolded us and we tried to sit still in our assigned seats on deck to try and induce sleep. But no sleep came. I hadn't brought any extra clothes and a bitterly cold breeze made me shiver. I had never dreamed it could get so cold on the Mediterranean in the middle of summer. Égide kindly gave me his blazer and I wound my skirt around my legs. But we couldn't remain still. We kept wandering along the deck and up and down stairways, groping our way in the blackness. We climbed over baskets, suitcases, fishing and dining equipment, and gingerly stepped over men, women and children who were enjoying blessed sleep, lying on blankets, using their suitcases as pillows or propped against the ship's fittings. Égide decided to lie down on the deck floor to coax sleep. Finally, Luisa did too. Gianna and I were restless. Our only recourse was to keep wandering. We weren't totally alone. We carried on whispered conversations with those who, like us, couldn't fall asleep. We ate tasty Spanish sardines and bocadillos and chocolate which several young Spanish boys insisted on giving us

Majorca

At long last, and faintly, slowly, night broke into day. The dazzling sun soon rose and brought its warmth. But we were too exhausted to enjoy the sunrise or the postcard view of Palma, the Majorcan capital, as we entered its harbour. No sooner had we set foot on terra firma than we were besieged by hotel agents. We finally settled for rooms in a clean pension for sixty cents a night. We should have gone to bed, but thoughts of blue waters, wide beaches and brilliant sunshine were too much. Inquiring for a beach nearby, we were shocked to learn that Palma had no beaches. Majorcan beaches were outside the town. We could go by car: old wobbly, street cars; modern buses, or a small two-seater, open-air silver coloured Spanish car peculiar to Majorca alone. The girls decided to rest. Égide and I were planning to hire the small two seater, when a kind Spaniard overheard us and offered us a ride to the beach. The beach had a number of dress restrictions. Two piece bathing suits were not allowed. A fine was imposed on violators. We saw two American girls in two piece bathing suits who were asked by a policeman to leave. No one could dress or undress on the beaches. I remarked to Égide, "What a contrast to French beaches!"

As we deliberated on Spanish morality neither one of us could remember seeing young women throughout our travels in this hot country wearing bareback or strapless dresses, shorts, or slacks, or even men in shorts. I even recalled a woman pinning two long sleeves onto her short blouse before she entered a church. I recalled, too, the many daily manifestations of religious faith as the faithful took time to visit churches during the day, whether on their way to work, or on their way home, or during their shopping.

Because my friends could spend only three days in Majorca we decided to hire a private car to see the island in order to save time. We prepared our lunch of *bocadillos*, cheese, ham, Majorcan *ensaimadas* (delicious turbans of fluffy pastry), and two bottles of mineral water. We set out in our 1948 Plymouth. It was late July and the farmers were haying. The sky was bright blue, crossed with the Aeolian sails of scores of windmills.

We visited the famous underground grottoes of Drach and Els Hams. The stalactites and stalagmites were illuminated, and our imagination gave them shapes of palaces, Madonnas, and temples. In the Cuevas del Drah we came to the bottom of the Abyss and found a clear aquamarine pool. An illuminated boat was waiting for us and I enjoyed the coolness, a refreshing change from the scorching heat outside.

We were on our way to Valldemosa of Chopin and George Sand fame when our guide, who felt it was too late, began making excuses not to go. But it was only three-thirty in the afternoon. And Gianna and Luisa reminded him of our bargain. Finally it happened: the car broke down. Steam was gushing out of the radiator.

We stopped. Égide and the driver went into the fields where a few peasants were working and returned with a pail of water. We hadn't gone 500 yards when again the car stopped. We flagged another car which happened to be a taxi. He agreed to take us to Valldemosa. But when we wanted to pay our original driver a sum less the amount our new cab driver wanted, he wouldn't hear of it. He was going to report us to the Police claiming the breakdown was not his fault. We boarded his broken down car, which had miraculously recovered, and we proceeded to the police station. We explained our story in Spanish verbs and nouns. Our taxi driver told his. The Spanish police listened attentively and calmly. Finally, they phoned to find out the cost of the fare to Vallde-mosa. Our driver had to settle on the bargained price less the fare.

Our way to Valldemosa wound up steep mountains and precipices. The bold hairpin turns afforded scenery of magnificent beauty: terraced slopes of olive vineyards and green valleys, and the bluest water in the world. The serpentine drive reminded me very much of Capri. We finally reached the Carthusian monastery where Chopin and George Sand lived as lovers from November, 1838 to February, 1839. But the resort, in the middle of winter, was exceptionally cold, and the rain poured. Chopin started coughing and spitting blood. The rooms have been kept as they were in 1839. There were even flowers on Chopin's Pleyel.

Égide, Luisa and Gianna had to leave. I was sorry to see them go. I was alone once again and decided to look for more luxurious accommodation. I booked myself into the Bahia Palace with its private swimming pool, and looked forward to exploring the night life in Majorca. I heard *Granada* sung as I had never heard it before. I watched Spanish dancing, acrobatic acts, puppet shows and sleight of hand tricks. Orchestras played tangos and rhumbas as well as western dance tunes.

I had associated Majorca with only sunbathing, beaches and fun. No wonder I was surprised to learn about the antiquity of the island when I came across a Gothic cathedral, ancient castles and fortresses and Moorish horseshoe arches.

I met Louisette Logan and Dinny who were taking university courses in Palma, and joined them for a lecture in Spanish on Majorcan folk song and dance. Using a tape recorder for the music and skilful drawings on the blackboard, the professor drew rounds of applause from the students who had come from all over Europe.

My most enjoyable evening pastime, however, was to stroll along the beautiful corniche with its swank, flood-lit hotels and night clubs on the side of the hill over-looking the bay. The view was magical in the blackness of the night. The air was warm and scented with rosemary, mint, sweet basil and thyme. The lights twinkled on dancing waters.

Barcelona

After five days, which was all I could spare, I flew from Palma to Barcelona, Spain's ancient Mediterranean seaport city. On the plane my companion was a sophisticated, and fashionably dressed blonde Italian radio announcer. We spoke French because I was ashamed of my grammatically poor Italian. Once again I had difficulty finding a hotel. Finally, after an hour's search, I found one.

That night the Italian radio announcer took me to *Los Carocoles,* world renowned for its sea food. I have never eaten so much fish at one sitting in my life. Our first course was escargots which didn't have as strong a garlic flavour as the French. The main course included a variety of fish: huge shrimp, lobster, and crustaceans ad infinitum covered with a most tasty tomato sauce. I was stuffed.

We moved a few doors away to a typical night club which featured Flamenco dancing. Here we saw it at its fiery best. Later we took a cab to a fashionable outdoor restaurant where Barcelona's élite usually stopped for coffee during their Sunday morning walks. Having coffee at another restaurant to end a meal is popular in Spain.

The next morning, with guide book in hand, I wandered along Barcelona's beautiful wide avenues. I discovered an exciting city with 2,000 years of history, Roman ruins and medieval buildings. At the waterfront, busy and bustling like any huge port, stood an impressive statue of Christopher Columbus, perhaps on the very spot where in 1493 he was received by Ferdinand and Isabella on his return from America.

I admired the beautifully carved fourteenth and fifteenth century choir stalls in the Barcelona cathedral. Here, too, for the first time in Spain, I noticed scores of plastic models of legs, lungs, hearts, and hands scattered throughout the various chapels dedicated to various saints. These were symbols of various cures received by the faithful. I had seen thanksgiving plaques but never representations of the source of the physical ailment.

I visited the unique church of the Sagrada Familia, designed by Antonio Gaudi. Although it was begun in 1881, work still continues on its unfinished shell. I was fascinated by the four enormously high, honeycomb pinnacles. During siesta time I enjoyed sitting on a bench in the beautiful Paseo de Gracia to watch the trees being watered. The water flows from hoses into narrow irrigation ditches cut into the side of the concrete sidewalk, which followed the whole length of this long, lovely avenue.

Since I had heard how difficult it was to get out of Barcelona, I decided to fly rather than take the long train ride from Barcelona to the western border town of Irun. But all flights were booked for weeks ahead. I had to go by train and to the dreaded RENFE. The huge letters looked down in sheer mockery at me as if they had won a victory. Defiantly, I walked in. The office was crowded with swarms of people in zig-zag lines before an assortment of wickets and counters. Recalling previous experiences at RENFE I was glad to see several policemen patrolling. I was hoping to be approached by a professional "stander-upper," but none came. After a two-hour wait I learned there were no daily trains to the border and that the one for the next day was all booked up. After much convincing, however, I found a seat for the next night. Finally, the kilometric coupons were all used up! Hallelujah! I kept the book as a grim reminder of the frustrations it gave me, and of the heat and grime, the sweat and obnoxious odours, the cramped space, the absence of dining cars, and the snail-like pace of Spanish trains.

How I dreaded the long trip from Barcelona cross country to Irun. I was the only woman in a compartment with seven men. Probably because we were in the North of Spain, the train was cool, and, surprisingly enough, the first comfortable one since the Pamplona-Madrid run. The night passed quickly and we arrived at the border early the next morning. We had a two hour wait before we could cross.

I was inquiring whether the train, which had just pulled in, was the one to France when the conductor asked, offhandedly, if I had been cleared to board. I had passed customs but I had not passed police control. An Englishman whom I had met during the two hour wait was in the same predicament. We had fewer than five minutes to go underground to the other side of the tracks to pass police control. He took my passport. I watched our luggage, expecting to see the train pull away any moment. But the Englishman returned in no time. I don't know how he did it. But like me, he had no desire to be stranded in a desolate, frontier town. We rushed to the train and squeezed into the mob that was trying to climb in. We couldn't elbow our way beyond the vestibule. With about ten others and assorted luggage and boxes, we stood.

St. Jean De Luz

We stood all the way to St. Jean de Luz. I wasn't too surprised when I had difficulty finding a hotel in this quaint resort and fishing town. After I was finally settled into a hotel, I walked to the wide, sandy *plage,* which was completely deserted because it was siesta time. At five p.m. people started trickling in and by six, the whole beach was teeming with bathers; the scene reminded me of pictures I had seen of Coney Island. But lying on the sizzling hot sands was unbearable. I got dressed on the beach as the French do and decided to take a walk.

It was very windy as I strolled along the crowded beach which was filled with outdoor kindergarten schools: four and five year olds in recreation activities organized by their teachers. I finally arrived at the animated port where sky blue fishing boats were returning and unloading their day's catch on the quays. It was fun watching the fishermen in their yellow oilskin trousers.

The next morning I heard Sunday mass in Saint-Jean Church, the strangest church I've ever visited. It was typically Basque in architecture with its aisleless nave, gilded altar screen and three-tiered wooden galleries reserved for men. Models of ships hung from the ceiling.

Since it was raining steadily, I decided to leave St. Jean de Luz and go to Biarritz to collect luggage that I had left there. When I checked out, the owner of the hotel immediately asked me to open my suitcase. I knew I was caught. The proof was sitting right on the top: the most beautiful blue and white bath towel I had ever seen. No words were spoken. My life of crime began and ended at that moment.

On the bus trip from St. Jean de Luz to Biarritz we passed through the beautiful Basque countryside, but it was raining in Biarritz too. I quickly decided to go to the British Isles. Since I was in France, I knew I could rely on regular and fast train service. I planned to stop at various places for several hours in the same way I had done on my way to Spain. My first stop was Bordeaux, Poitiers next, and then Paris, where I stayed only long enough to arrange for my flight to London.

London

From London Airport I rode on the upper deck of a red double-decker bus to Victoria Station, and was not surprised to find everything the same as I had left it two years previously. It felt good to be able to read the posters and signs and to hear English once again. I hired a cab to the Regent Palace Hotel where I was surprised to find accommodation because I had made no reservations. Prepayment was requested. The lobby was teeming with people milling about. But the next morning when I was in a queue, nearly an hour, for breakfast I knew that I was going to look for another place. Luckily, I found a bed and breakfast near Marble Arch, central enough to establish it as headquarters for my walking tour of London. Although I had been in London twice before, I still felt I didn't know her. This time I was going to spend enough time to come to grips with her, to feel her pulse. I was going to discover her secrets on foot, to savour her beauties and her treasures.

She was all that I expected: exciting, fascinating, inspiring, alive. I delighted sauntering along Regent St., and Oxford Circus, peering through sophisticated shop windows, and being jostled by the crowds. I loved sitting in Trafalgar Square just to watch the pigeons and the people and the fountains. I loved to sit on top in the buses passing by familiar places: Piccadilly Circus, Bond Street, Grosvenor Square, Marble Arch, and Hyde Park. I loved visiting the art galleries and museums to view the treasures of an empire. I loved going to places I knew from years of English Literature studies. I walked along the quiet streets of Bloomsbury's residential area and wondered where Virginia Wolf, who became the focal figure in the "Bloomsbury Group," had lived. In stark contrast to the quiet residential dignity of Bloomsbury were the belching smoke stacks of the industrial working-class district of Whitechapel in London's East end, which I had difficulty finding, but had to see because of a poem entitled *Whitechapel* I had taught for Dr. Diltz at the Ontario College of Education. The last two lines of Aldington's poem accurately summarized what I saw: "Noise, iron, smoke;/Iron, iron, iron."

In spite of the tension caused by a strike that was in progress, I enjoyed sauntering through Covent Garden's fruit, vegetable and flower market to read the labels on the hundreds of crates and boxes which were being loaded and unloaded on the huge trucks by a skeleton staff patrolled by bobbies. I saw lemons and oranges from Cyprus, grapes from Spain, radishes from Italy, flowers from Guernsey, oranges from the Union of South Africa, apples from New Zealand, and pears from Australia.

Even under cloudy skies in the warm soft rain as I ambled around the Law Courts, Fleet Street, and the Strand, I loved being in London. I loved to watch the men of London striding to work in their black Hamburgs and tailored suits, carrying their tightly rolled black umbrellas.

There was a soft loveliness to the Thames and the Parliament buildings cloaked in mist and fog. I didn't even mind continually ducking for shelter and exploring in the London mist the narrow back streets, the mews, and the lanes near the Middle Temple.

London at night, bedecked in bright lights, in all her brilliance and radiance, enthralled me. *Fanny*, a musical comedy about life on the Marseilles waterfront, was disappointing. But Noel Coward's comedy *Nude with Violin*, a humourous take-off on modern art, was interesting.

An ear infection and the reappearance of my Spanish rash made me appreciate the kindness and efficiency of the staff at Charing Cross Hospital.

I fully expected to see somebody I knew in London. London isn't London unless you do. I wasn't disappointed. I met Isabel Ward from Soest, and Liz Brauer,

June Knutsen, Marion Burt, Carol Whelton, and Gwen Chapman from #2 Fighter Wing.

Everyday, and all day, London seduced me from the morning business rush for trams and buses, the afternoon shopping frenzy, the five o'clock underground rush, to the night magic of strolling entertainment seekers. To know London was to love her.

After five days of intensive sight-seeing, which I conducted with the same rigour that I study for examinations, I decided that I needed a rest. Basking in the sun on the beaches of Torquay, which travel folders call the "Queen of the English Riviera," was tempting. I read with anticipation about the "sea-bathing, the flower-filled gardens, the acres of public parks, the fine beaches, and the Mediterranean, blue skies." This English sun-drenched paradise would be my destination!

Torquay, Plymouth, Penzance, Lands' End, the Scilly Islands

I arrived in Torquay and met a rain drenched hamlet with steel gray skies. I moved on to Paignton where lead black skies and pouring rain welcomed me. I proceeded to Plymouth, one of England's choice seaside resorts, where I trudged in the rain and wind to *The Hoe,* where Sir Francis Drake was playing "bowls" when he received news that the Spanish Armada was in sight. It must have been a rare fine day when he made the observation because I couldn't see anything through dense fog and mist. I kept on walking until I arrived at the steps where the Pilgrim Fathers set out in 1620 for America and I listened to a Salvation Army band playing in the rain on the dock. I left Plymouth in the rain and decided to move on to Penzance and Land's End. More rain!. More rain in Land's End and the Scilly Islands. By this time I was thoroughly disgusted. My dreams of basking in the English sun were shattered. I left the rain-drenched "English Riviera" and struck out into the interior to Stratford-on-Avon.

Stratford-on-Avon

It was pouring rain in Stratford! An avenging rain only the English Riviera could rival! I took comfort in the fact that I wouldn't be dependent on the wet beaches for amusement. This was Shakespeare's town.

I was fortunate to find a room in the sixteenth century Shakespeare Hotel, one of the most beautiful timbered houses in the town, with each room named after one of Shakespeare's plays.

I went straightaway to the Stratford Memorial Theatre where scores of young people were scattered about the lobby with blankets and camping equipment, seeking shelter from the heavy rain. There was no performance that night because it was the night before the première of *The Tempest*. When I was told that all tickets were sold for the première, I was truly dejected. I would have to wait until the next morning for standing room seats.

I took my place in the queue very early the next morning. The students who had stayed up all night were at the head. I was excited because I especially wanted to see Sir John Gielgud as Prospero. After an hour's wait, there was only one person in front of me. When I reached the box office wicket, a voice told me there was no more standing room. I wanted to cry. I saw the manager, but to no avail. There was no use moping. I decided to see the attractions that made Stratford-on-

Avon a favourite haunt for tourists. After I had exhausted the Shakespearean attractions, I decided it was useless to try to amuse myself in the rain.

Blenheim

I bought a ticket to Blenheim to see Blenheim Palace, the residence of the Marlborough family where my wartime hero, Winston Churchill, was born. I was still numb from disbelief at his 1950 defeat at the polls. Reverentially, I gazed at a number of Churchill relics and marvelled at the grounds, among the finest to be found in England. I was now ready to return to London. But no public transportation to London was available at the time. I hitch-hiked instead and got a ride to Oxford.

Oxford

Ancient and beautiful Oxford had always enchanted me. I strolled down the famous High with colleges on either side. I was in love with the old buildings, their grey stone walls covered with creepers in glorious colours, and the great quadrangle of Christ Church. From the top of the bell tower of Magdalen College I gazed at the spires of Oxford immortalized in verse. I contacted a friend who invited me to one of the college refectories. I felt honoured. I could have stayed forever, but I knew I had to get to Canterbury to see the site of Thomas à Becket's martyrdom.

Canterbury

Ever since grade school when I studied British History I was attracted to Beckett's tragic life. But I learned that transport to Canterbury wasn't available for several days, and so I went to the end of the bus line from where I hitch-hiked a ride in the pouring rain. Since my English driver had never seen Canterbury Cathedral, he came along too. We stood before the altar steps where King Henry II's knights on 29 December 1170, killed Thomas à Becket who, like a later chancellor of the realm, Thomas More, became a martyr and a saint. I recalled the question which the king had asked of his courtiers in a fit of rage: "Will no one rid me of this meddlesome priest?" And the reaction of Thomas, who was the king's best friend: "If I had served my God half as well as I served my King . . ."

The rains kept pounding! I decided to go to London to catch a flight to Dublin.

Ireland: Dublin

On our way from the modern Dublin airport to the airlines office, I was immediately struck by Dublin's cold and wind especially after Spain's ferocious heat. But at least it wasn't raining! The public signs in Gaelic caught my attention.

I installed myself in the Four Courts Hotel, an historic building where Dean Swift and Daniel O'Connell had stayed in their time, and I set out on foot to explore the Irish capital. So many horses and drays on Dublin's cobblestone streets, and so many Irish in St. Stephen's Green, Dublin's oldest public pleasure garden, relaxing in the middle of the morning on park benches or feeding the ducks that paddled in the artificial lake shocked me.

But I enjoyed strolling along busy O'Connell Street crowded with statues of Ireland's greatest statesmen such as Charles Stewart Parnell, who vigorously championed Home Rule and land reform for Ireland and Daniel O'Connell, one of the greatest of all Irish patriots. A statue of England's famous sea captain, Horatio Nelson, was also there. "A single street," wrote William Butler Yeats, "commemorating three of history's best known adulterers."

O'Connell Street is dominated by the grand and imposing General Post Office with its huge Ionic portico and six fluted pillars completed in 1818. It was virtually destroyed in the Easter Uprising of 1916 when shells from an English gunboat on the Liffey River inflicted heavy damage. The bullet scars were still there. Fifteen Irishmen, including the seven signatories of the Proclamation of the Republic of Ireland, were executed by firing squad. Columns on the portico of the massive beautiful Georgian Four Courts, too, still bore the battle scars inflicted in 1922 when fighting broke out again between Britain and Ireland. For more than 700 years Ireland was ruled by England. Not until 1921 did the Republic of Ireland gain independence from England.

I toured Dublin Castle, which dates from 1208, built on grounds where the Danes had erected an earth and timber fortress. It had stood for almost seven centuries as the symbol of England's fierce, unbelievable tyranny. Its magnificent State Apartments didn't interest me as much as its carpeted chapel, the Catholic "Church of the Most Holy Trinity," formerly the Chapel Royal, which was being kept as it was received after the Irish Rebellion.

I attended the four o'clock service at the ancient Cathedral of St. Patrick, Ireland's largest church, founded in 1191, where the ghost of Jonathan Swift lingers. I heard "The Apostle's Creed" and the "Our Father" chanted, to my delight, by boy sopranos. I was shocked when a parishioner told me that Oliver Cromwell had stabled his horses in St. Patrick's during his appallingly cruel 1653 campaign throughout Ireland.

As I strolled in the vicinity of St. Patrick's, the streets were deserted. But as I wound my way back towards O'Connell St. there was more life. I saw scores of shabbily dressed children playing in the streets and in the crypt, a ghostly cavern of huge foundation stones and arches stretching the entire length of the Protestant Christ Church Cathedral. So much dirt, poverty and neglect saddened me.

Of all Dublin's landmarks it was the celebrated Book of Kells, completed around A.D. 800 when Ireland was known throughout Europe for its scholars and saints, in the library of Trinity College, which most impressed me. Monks laboured a lifetime in St. Columba's Monastery to complete this Latin copy of the Gospels. The skins of a hundred and fifty calves were used to produce the vellum pages and the colours were pressed from local plants and flowers. Its imaginative ornamentation, its floral and geometric motifs that included birds, dragons, animal and human figures, and its microscopic tracery have created "one of the world's most beautiful illuminated manuscripts."

While admiring this work of art — a different page of the book is turned each day for visitors to see — I met a seventy-year-old priest. We talked for over an hour until we found ourselves outside where he had parked his bicycle tied with his "mac" in a string bag. He told me about Ireland's seven-hundred-year struggle for freedom from England: the cruel English laws against Roman Catholics; the Cromwellian scourges and the Battle of the Boyne when King Billy, the Dutch Protestant William of Orange, defeated the Irish in July, 1690. He also told me about the Potato Famine in the 1840s when millions of people had absolutely nothing to eat and more than a million had fled Ireland for the Americas and that Dublin during the eighteenth century was considered one of the most glittering of contemporary European capitals (I had noticed many beautiful Georgian mansions in various stages of neglect and decay). Garrick and Mrs. Siddons had acted there and Handel had conducted, from his harpsichord, the world première of his *Messiah* with the choirs of both Christ Church and St. Patrick's, taking part. By the time he was finished, I, too, would have joined the ranks of the patriots.

Ireland: Cork

On the slow train to Cork I had ample opportunity to witness the Irish weakness for sweets where both adults and children gorged on candies during the whole trip. As I ambled about the port city of Cork, I came upon St. Anne's Church where the world famous Bells of Shandon were ringing, and dirty little bedraggled children were playing with cardboard boxes on the streets, hitching themselves to the back of wagons, or swarming around me to have their pictures taken. The old women gathered at street corners wore large black shawls over their heads. As I descended to the riverfront, waves of bicycles whizzed by me. As in Dublin, the smell of horses filled the air.

Old-fashioned shop windows displayed the widest assortment of merchandise I have ever seen. In one small shop window with wires strung across the top, I saw a vast array of articles: sunglasses, several tomatoes, a few apples, a package of jelly powder, a can of Bird's Custard, big jars of candles, dolls, a can of beans, birthday cards, soap, shoe polish, postcards, panties, shoes, aprons, towels, handkerchiefs, socks, plates, bowls, comic books, a book, *The Female of the Species*, tea, a newspaper, holy pictures, a jar of jam, a can of fruit, and cigarettes. To my Canadian eyes, the conglomeration looked junky, but I saw many such motley window displays in other Irish cities.

If I thought the shop windows junky, the Coal Quay Market, an open air fleamarket, was worse. Everything from bits and pieces of old furniture, fresh fruit, second hand clothes, and old books, to pots and pans and sweets and fish were offered for sale. These goods were scattered about in such haphazard fashion on the streets and on stall counters that I thought it looked like a rummage sale at its worst.

I kissed the Blarney Stone set in the battlements of the ruins of fifteenth century Blarney Castle, Cork's most famous landmark. I climbed the 120 steps up the tower by a narrow winding stone staircase. Hanging head down over the parapet, clutching a railing, while a fellow tourist held down my feet, I stretched my head to reach the stone for the gift of eloquence that legend claims is conferred on all who kiss the Blarney Stone.

On the Bus to Killarney

After experiencing Spain's slow trains, I wasn't too annoyed at the slow bus ride from Cork to Killarney along the southern coast. In spite of scattered showers and cool breezes, I enjoyed the breathtaking rugged coastline. The warm Gulf Stream caresses the land and exotic plants and shrubs flourish: palm trees, bamboo, arbutus, holly and other sub-tropical plants bloom in wild profusion among the peaks and rocks.

Glengarriff

We stopped at Glengarriff on lovely Bantry Bay, in County Cork, where G. B. Shaw wrote most of his play *Saint Joan*, and went on to visit the island of Ilmacullin, which had been painstakingly transformed from a desolate rock into a wonderland of dwarfed Japanese trees, lily ponds, rock gardens and all sorts of subtropical plants and flowers.

At Glengarriff I noticed a large station wagon with a Canadian licence. Two charming Irish sisters and their Welsh friend informed me that a Canadian mining company was working nearby. Their Irish stories and Welsh humour kept me amused on the bus trip to Killarney. Along the way we kept seeing women in their long, black hooded cloaks, and donkeys carrying huge wicker baskets filled with peat from the bogs. It was the first time I had seen peat not yet cut into blocks and bricks. In several villages, we passed large concrete squares on the ground which my Irish friends called "patterns." These were village dance floors.

It was pouring rain when, after nine hours on the bus, we arrived in Killarney. I had been complaining to my friends about the rain but their answer was typically Irish: "Won't it be greener afterwards!"

Killarney

The next morning I joined a group of tourists who had hired a horse drawn jaunting car to see the famous Lakes of Killarney in County Kerry. It was misty and cloudy; a soft quiet rain was falling, but I was assured it was only a "wee shower." We rode through the magnificent National Park at Muckross. I have neither seen lawns look so much like green velvet nor ancient oaks so magnificent. We passed holly and arbutus on our way to the ruins of the fifteenth century Franciscan Muckross Abbey, left vandalized and roofless by Cromwell's troops in 1652. We followed the lakes until we reached the sixty-six foot high Toro Waterfall which spills over Toro Mountain. We climbed up the mountain to see the magnificent scenic beauty above the falls.

There was no sun in the sky, but the haze and mist cast a spell of soft magic: the round mauve mountains and the three sleeping lakes merging into one long, delicate, silvery sheet of water. No wonder the setting inspired Wordsworth, Sir Walter Scott and Thackeray to sing its praises. Tennyson, too, under the spell of Muckross Abbey, wrote:

> The splendour falls on castle walls
> And snowy summits old in story
> The long light shakes across the lakes,
> And the wild cataract leaps in glory . . .

The Irish resented the Americans for "having bought Ireland out." Since I had seen, on poster after poster, "unemployed protest marches" and "emigrate, starve or fight," I kept reminding them that industry could bring prosperity to Ireland. They wouldn't admit there was any poverty: "We're only lazy. We don't want any American, British or German industry to spoil our beautiful Emerald Isle. Papa may drink too much Guinness or Jamieson but we like Ireland the way it is."

Limerick

I tried to leave Killarney for Limerick on Sunday and was shocked to find out that Irish trains (except probably those going or leaving Dublin) do not run on Sundays. I had to take a bus which took four hours to cover the sixty-eight miles from Killarney to Limerick. Spanish trains are slow; they have their counterpart in Irish buses. I first saw Limerick's lovely Shannon in the mist of a quiet early morning with a squadron of swans drifting across the shadow of the thirteenth century King John's Castle and the spires of ancient churches. I strolled along its banks and streets in a light drizzle. The large number of deserted and damaged buildings surprised me, and I asked whether the buildings were grim reminders of the rebellion. I was told only that the city was tearing them down in a rebuilding programme.

While strolling through Limerick, I stumbled upon a partly legible inscription on a stone plinth commemorating World War II dead. The plinth must have formed the base of a statue. I was fascinated. What had happened to the statue? When I returned to the hotel I learned that the statue had been blown up a fortnight before. The IRA disclaimed any part. And nobody, after two weeks, was still the wiser.

"The nail," on which merchants used to hang the names of those who owed them money — a custom that became known as "paying on the nail" — piqued my curiosity.

Galway

I left Limerick in the drizzle and arrived in Galway in a torrential downpour. I knew only too well how long these showers lasted. However, by the time I had my information about trains to Dublin, the rain had subsided into soft sprinkling, so that I could still see the sights of Galway. I got as far as Woolworth's, which is across Eyre Square, near the railroad station, when strains of a sweet and soft melody caught my ear. It came from a young beggar boy about ten years old who was singing Gaelic tunes in the rain. I stopped and listened, wanting to linger, but I had only the afternoon to soak up as much as I could of Galway's port atmosphere.

When her merchant princes carried on an extensive trade with Spain, Galway was prosperous. But England made her weak and powerless by destroying her woollen trade which competed with her own. The Irish are convincing story tellers. I began sympathizing with them and I, too, hated the English Black and Tans. "We have hundreds of years to catch up on, but we'll do it," they assured me. I left Galway wishing them the luck of the Irish.

Manchester

I took the train from Galway to Dublin where I stopped overnight, taking a plane to Manchester the next morning.

I shall never forget Manchester because one hundred years of industrial smoke had coloured it black. Its great cotton factories had helped make England prosperous, but had polluted the city. Buildings were covered with the black patina of smoke, dust and grime; even the few trees I saw were black. Manchester is not a tourist city. No wonder the bobby smiled when I asked him for directions to the tourist bureau.

Scotland: Edinburgh

It was a slow train trip to Edinburgh. I was surprised that the very country which gave the world the train was still using antiquated ones. Luckily, an interesting English-woman in my compartment explained the various sights along the way: the sheep that stay in their own fells, and the dry stone walls separating the fields. And if the Irish had waxed voluble about the English, she told me as much about the Irish. What impressed me most was the unending line of brick I saw. Everything — walls, fences, row houses, garages, business blocks — was made of brick of all colours: yellow, red, charcoal grey and brown. There was nothing to relieve the dull, drab brick homes with their narrow walled backyards. My friend's only comment was, "Where there's muck there's money."

I arrived in Edinburgh late at night and after taxiing for nearly an hour to find a hotel, I had to settle for the swank Caledonian where, to my shock, I had to queue for a washroom at an additional 55s a night (six dollars). The next day I took a room in a private residence suggested by the festival board.

Maria Callas, the tempestuous Metropolitan Opera prima donna, was starring in Bellini's *La Sonnambula* that evening. I stood in line for hours only to discover that there were no seats. I was extremely disappointed. But the attendant encouraged me to return that evening about five o'clock for cancellations. I consoled myself with the fact that she had given me more encouragement than the manager had at Stratford-on-Avon. In the meantime, I hurried frantically from one queue to another to get tickets for other events.

I was at the theatre at five. I stood and I stood. Finally two minutes after curtain time I got a cancellation. I was thrilled. Callas, as Amina, dominated the entire performance. To this day I have not forgotten the famous sleep-walking scene where Callas gingerly picked her way along a tightrope. No one in the audience dared whisper or cross their legs lest the disturbance should cause her to lose her balance and fall.

Il Matrimonio Segreto, a wonderful example of eighteenth century Italian opera buffa by Domenico Cimarosa, staged by the Piccola Scala, was delightful in its frothy, amusing episodes.

I enjoyed *Nekrassov,* a political comedy by the French philosopher and playwright Jean Paul Sartre. The play demonstrated the difficulty of maintaining personal freedom in a society obsessed by the threat of Communism. It also poked fun at the flippant way newspapers handled potentially explosive international situations. But the play was attacked for its caustic, anti-capitalist satire.

The world première of Jonathan Griffin's verse drama, *The Hidden King,* was interesting. Reviews were mostly unfavourable: the message was obscure, the huge cast unwieldy, and the four hour show too heavy and boring. But I enjoyed the spectacular pageantry of the court scenes of Renaissance Florence and Venice, and eighteenth century Portugal.

I thoroughly enjoyed the two 'fringe' plays probably because I knew them so well: Shakespeare's *Hamlet* and Thornton Wilder's Pulitzer prize winning play *The Skin of our Teeth. Hamlet* was staged by the Players of Leyton with an all boy cast. By unanimous consent Ophelia's acting was even better than in the film version.

I was looking forward to the military Tattoo staged by floodlight on the huge esplanade of Edinburgh Castle because Canada's RCMP were to perform their Musical Ride. But a bitterly cold wind and intermittent rain marred the evening's entertainment. To make matters worse, I could get standing room only. Luckily, we were shoulder to shoulder, and I managed some protection gained from the heat of the people around me and from their large umbrellas. In spite of my physical discomfort, I enjoyed the pageantry of massed bands and military exercises, but I thought the African dancing was out of place. I liked the Turkish soldiers dressed in authentic thirteenth and fourteenth century costumes, marching in their traditional, peculiar fashion. The highlight of the Tattoo was the RCMP's spectacular Musical ride which ended the show. My pride in Canada overflowed.

It was the last week in August. School was about to start in a few days. I booked a flight to London. On my flight back my itchy rash had erupted once again. The skin on my legs and feet was on fire. I rubbed on calamine lotion but to no avail. I made an unscheduled stop in Birmingham to receive medical attention. Once again I had nothing but praise for the British Hospitalization System. Since I had some time before my next flight, I took a side trip to Nottingham to visit Sherwood Forest, where Robin Hood defied the laws of the Norman overlords. The trip included a visit to Newstead Abbey, for many years the home of one of my favourite English poets, Lord Byron. From Birmingham I flew to London and then to Paris, and before I knew it, I was back at #2 Fighter Wing.

I was back at Gross-Tenquin for another year. My two-year-stay had been so full of adventure and opportunities to travel that I wanted more, and requested an extension of one year which was granted.

Europe had given me an exhilarating sense of freedom, an escape from the restrictions of my little home town in the northern Ontario wilderness of Canada. I had seen the great cosmopolitan cities of Europe and the Middle East. I had been able to pay a pilgrimage to a number of holy sites. I had made friends with other Canadians who remain close to me to this day.

But best of all, Europe was changing my attitude towards myself.

Natzweiler-Struthof Concentration Camp

On 3 November 1957, I made a pilgrimage, along with a group of teachers from #2 Wing, to the concentration camp at Natzweiler-Struthof, fifty kilometres south-west of Strasburg, the only Nazi extermination camp on French soil.

In 1957, twelve years after the end of World War II, it was a national monument. The black wooden barracks-like structures surrounded by an electrified barbed wire fence and guarded by watch dogs had been built in an idyllic setting in the Vosges mountains that commanded a beautiful view of the valley. A cold wind was blowing and I could imagine how winters at such a high altitude were unbearably cold for men and women in sabots and no socks.

I walked through the empty rooms in silence, staring in disbelief at the ovens in the crematorium, and the tables in the laboratory where inmates were skinned to provide lamp shades, and their teeth extracted for gold.

I saw the tiled walls of the gas chamber which was called the *Abstellraum* (switch-off-closet), and the tiers of bunks in the prison cells. I was appalled. I stopped at the scaffolding used for hangings and broke into sobs. I knew I was going to be sick.

The 25,000 dead of Natzweiler — Jews, gypsies, political opponents, homosexuals, disabled people — were a small number compared to the millions in Auschwitz. But their suffering was no less. No less was the unthinkable evil that perpetrated such a crime. The thought kept me awake for weeks.

Christmas Holidays, 1957

On 20 December 1957, I left #2 Fighter Wing for Luxembourg from where I would then take the Luxembourg-Munster train to spend five days of Christmas at the Beckwermerts, proceeding first to Amsterdam, and then to London for the rest of the festive season.

I was looking forward to celebrating Christmas once again with the Beckwermerts in Munster. Mrs. Beckwermert had made her special Christmas cookies and apple strudel. Everything was as I had remembered it from the year before except that this year a rabbit instead of a goose was given the place of honour at the Christmas Day table. We attended a performance of Wagner's *Die Meistersinger von Nürnberg* in Munster's splendid modern opera house where a wall from the old World War II bombed-out ruin was beautifully incorporated into the new modern structure.

On 27 December, I left for Amsterdam. The next day was my birthday and I remember waking up and sort of feeling sorry for myself. But when I walked down the stairs and the attendant at the hotel desk wished me a happy birthday, his cheerful greeting lifted my spirits. I have never forgotten it.

Several times I had visited Holland which, truly, is like no other country in the world. I went to its famous cheese market at Alkmaar, where the men still wore the traditional dress of the guild; Madurodam, near The Hague, a miniature city containing replicas of more than a hundred of the best known buildings in Holland; and Marken, where the inhabitants dressed in their distinctive traditional dress. But it was Rotterdam, the largest port in the world, that fascinated me. The city was completely rebuilt after World War II when it was heavily bombed; rebuilding had turned the centre into a pedestrian area replete with little statues and sitting areas. I had never seen anything so lovely. On this trip to Amsterdam I visited the Rijk museum to see Rembrandt's *The Nightwatch*.

London

I arrived in London on 29 December 1957, and the weather was beautiful. London was at its wondrous best. Shop windows on Regent and Oxford Streets glittered with holly, mistletoe, tinsel, red and green streamers, animated figures of Santa Claus and his reindeer, angels, and Christmas trees. Mirth and music filled the air. I walked for miles revisiting familiar places.

I saw the pantomime which I was told was a "must see" at the Palladium. To my surprise, it was not a pantomime at all, but an elaborate musical show. Margaret Lockwood played Peter Pan, the boy who refuses to grow up. I had never read James Barrie's dramatic fantasy, and so when Peter Pan flew into the air, I was delighted. Besides *Peter Pan*, circus acts were mixed with songs and dances. Since I could get only standing room tickets, I stood for three hours, completely engrossed in the afternoon's entertainment.

London's revellers thronged into Trafalgar Square on New Year's Eve wearing funny hats and carrying helium filled balloons that kept soaring up into the sky. I was surprised to see Eros barricaded with a high fence and the police arranged in a human chain to hold back anyone who was thinking of climbing to the top of the statue. A band, in front of Canada House, was playing Christmas carols — "Jingle Bells," "White Christmas" and "Joy to the World."

A gigantic, gaily decorated Christmas tree, ablaze with light, an annual presentation by the city of Oslo to commemorate Anglo-American cooperation during World War II, stood in the centre of the square. We were squeezed in so tightly that no one could move. I enjoyed my little space, and like the others, awaited the stroke of midnight. All of a sudden, it was 1958, and the new year was born. I was amazed at how quickly the police dispersed the crowds. After being so disappointed the previous summer in Stratford-on-Avon when I could not get tickets, I was thrilled to see Sir John Gielgud and the Shakespeare Memorial Theatre Company in *The Tempest* at Drury Lane. *The Tempest* is my favourite Shakespearean play. The opening shipwreck scene was amazing as were the dancers, silhouetted in fire, floating in the air. I wrote in my diary that "Gielgud spoke Shakespeare's blank verse with such an appreciation for the sense and music of the lines."

I had acquired a passion for the arts and I packed my week in London with theatre, ballet, art galleries and museums. I saw Verdi's *Rigoletto* sung in English, Sir Laurence Olivier in *The Entertainer*, and *The Nutcracker*

Suite at Royal Festival Hall. I visited the National Gallery, the Tate Gallery, and the Victoria and Albert Museum.

At the Victoria and Albert Museum I saw the handwritten manuscript of Charles Dickens' *Bleak House*: his small script and intricately reworked manuscripts interested me. A sixteenth century small harpsichord, decorated with the Tudor coat of arms and a raven with a sceptre, the emblem of Anne Boleyn, also caught my attention because it was, in all likelihood, played by Queen Elizabeth I.

I had learned from my earlier trips to art galleries that it was impossible for me to absorb too much. I like religious paintings and paintings of historical scenes and famous people whom I have studied. And I like the Impressionists. In the National Gallery, I lingered at Van Dyck's equestrian portrait of Charles I, Paul Delacroix's "The Execution of Lady Jane Grey"; El Greco's "Christ driving the Traders from the Temple"; and J. M. W. Turner's "The Fighting *Téméraire*," whose crew distinguished themselves at the Battle of Trafalgar.

Even though I had copies on wood of Antonello de Messina's fifteenth century self-portrait and Van der Weyden's "Portrait of a Lady" hanging on my dining room wall, I still enjoyed looking at the originals housed in the National Gallery. Also, I enjoyed admiring other favourites like Andrea del Sarto's "Portrait of a Young Man," Van Gogh's "Sunflowers," Van Eyk's "The Arnolfini Marriage," and Claude Monet's "Bathers at La Grenouillère."

And London Again and Again

At home I had the highest regard for British craftsmanship and always looked for the trademark "made in
England" as a guarantee of the highest quality. In London I was drawn to shops designated "by appointment
to Her Majesty, the Queen." As a result, London was my
favourite city for shopping. I knew I could trust names
like Jaeger, Pringle, Burberry, and Wedgewood. I loved
the great department stores — Harrods in
Knightsbridge, Selfridges on Oxford Street, Fortnum
and Mason in Piccadilly and Liberty's of Regent Street.
My Christmas, birthday and even wedding presents
were bought in London. And I bought lengths of British
woollen suiting which I had made into tailored suits for
my parents when I got home. My mother wore hers for
years and my father was buried in his.

There are three visits that are grounded in my memory. On one visit, after I attended a performance of *My
Fair Lady*, word spread that Lady and Winston Churchill
were leaving from a side entrance. I rushed to see them
just as Lady Churchill, hatless, and dressed in black with
a diamond pin on her coat, was getting into their limousine. Winston Churchill looked pale, old and frail,
compared to his statuesque wife. As the car started up,
the lights went on, and Lady Churchill smiled and
waved, while Winston took off his hat and looked so
gentle and beatific. A woman next to me shouted, "God
bless you."

On this same visit, I invited my friends, Gill Don-
mall and Barry Taylor, to afternoon tea at the Ritz in
Picccadilly where we were told Princess Margaret had
held one of her engagement parties. While we partook
from a menu which read, "selection of Finger Sand-

wiches: Smoked Salmon, Ham Cucumber, Cheddar Cheese, Cream Cheese and Chives, Egg Mayonnaise/Scones with Strawberry Jam and thick cream/and/a Choice of Pastries/or/Cream Cakes/Indian or China Tea," the Palace Court orchestra played nostalgic melodies. I enjoyed the elegant and sophisticated atmosphere. On Sunday afternoons there was tea dancing from 4 to 6:30 p.m. (I had gone to several Sunday afternoon tea dances in Germany and loved them.) I couldn't help thinking, "what a civilized way to live."

On another visit I rode around London on a motorcycle driven by a doctor friend from #2 Fighter Wing. At first I was afraid. But then I enjoyed the freedom and the wind blowing through my hair. It was a fun weekend with such artistic personalities as a poet, novelist and sculptor and their English girlfriends. We enjoyed a Chinese dinner and a cruise down the Thames to Richmond. But it was the hilarious London barn party that ended the weekend which shocked me.

And in the Spring of 1958, I was in my ophthalmologist's Harley Street office being fitted with newly improved contact lenses — a hard lens with a hole at the bottom that covered the whole eye — when suddenly, the nurse called me to the phone. I couldn't imagine who it could be because I knew nobody in London.

To my shock, it was my mother phoning from Italy, worried because she hadn't heard from me. How she ever managed to find me was a miracle. She had phoned #2 Fighter Wing and the teacher who answered the phone could tell her only that I had an eye appointment in London, England. My mother was one resourceful lady. Despite several fittings, I could never tolerate my new contacts.

Nevertheless, I felt at home in Britain. English was my language. I had a respectable knowledge of the history, geography and literature of Britain. British culture was my inheritance. I related to what I saw in Britain. I celebrated British achievement.

I identified with my British education, or at least Penny did. But I was still running away from my Italian inheritance, not quite ready to accept the fact that Serafina also had traditions and cultures to which she belonged. As Penny, I felt English, but as Serafina I knew that I would never feel truly at home in the English culture I had grown to love.

Paris, 1956-1958

I returned to Paris many times during 1956-1958 when I lived in France. Each time I meticulously explored a new *quartier* on foot with my Michélin guide in tow. But my best memories are those times I spent with my friend John Stephenson, who had taken a year's leave from his teaching post at the Fort William Collegiate Institute to study French at the Sorbonne. (We had first met in the Fall of 1952 when I returned home to teach at Hillcrest High School and he became a wonderful friend to both my family and me. When he died prematurely in 1989, I lost one of my best friends.)

John and I saw Paris in the springtime when the horse chestnuts were in bloom, and Paris in the autumn when the plane trees brought to my mind the first paragraph of Dickens' *A Tale of Two Cities*. We never went to the girlie-girlie shows, to the Folies-Bergère or the Moulin Rouge. We went to the Opéra and the theatre. We saw matinee performances of Puccini's *La Bohème* and *Tosca*, and Wagner's *Tannhauser*. We saw

Rossini's *The Barber of Seville* and Gounod's *Faust*. We saw *Tea and Sympathy* with Ingrid Bergman, and T. S. Eliot's *The Cocktail Party*.

We made a pilgrimage to the *Académie Française* because it was charged with safeguarding the purity of the French language. We visited the Pantheon to pay tribute to Voltaire, Jean-Jacques Rousseau and Émile Zola, who were buried there. We visited the Père-Lachaise cemetery to pay homage to Héloise and Abelard, Balzac, Sarah Bernhardt and Oscar Wilde.

We sat at sidewalk cafés, sipping apertifs with John's Sorbonne friends, and we talked about the French people, lesbians and aphrodisiacs (two words I had never heard before). It was here where I first heard the French expression, *Ce que femme veut, Dieu le veut* and the Latin, *Tempus, edax rerum*.

We would sit sipping Pernod at a sidewalk table at the celebrated Café de la Paix in the Place de l'Opéra, watching the crowds stream by, and then we would go to the large corner café called Aux Deux Magots, the Left Bank's hangout for the intelligentsia, hoping to see Jean-Paul Sartre and Simone Beauvoir.

Once we went to the Caveau des Oubliettes, a popular, dimly-lit underground cellar. As we sat on hard wooden benches, I caught sight of large metal artifacts sitting on a shelf. I don't know whether John knew, but his Sorbonne colleagues told me they were chastity belts. I was horrified. We discussed medieval times, the *lettres de cachet* of the French Revolution, and dabbled in metaphysical topics. I have forgotten the names of the old French folk tunes which were sung, but not the chastity belts that sat on the shelf.

World's Fair at Brussels, 1958

On a lovely June weekend Eric A. an N.C.O. from #2
Fighter Wing, and I drove to Brussels to see the World's
Fair of 1958, the first World's Fair I had ever seen. Each
of the world's nations tried to display their achievements
of the last half century in the fields of science, culture,
technology, and commerce. It was stupendous. The
cherry and chestnut trees were in full bloom. And flamingoes stood on one leg and lifted the other like prima
ballerinas. I was overwhelmed by the ultra-modern, and
strikingly original designs of the pavilions set against a
background of flowers and fountains, artificial lakes and
waterfalls, parks, birds and animals as well as natural
woodlands. They were awesome.

Dominating the fairgrounds were the two large
pavilions of the Soviet Union and the United States,
competing with each other: the Soviets tried to stun the
visitor with the sheer size and weight of their industrial
might in a heavy-looking, grandiose exhibition palace
while the Americans tried to woo the visitor with their
charm and casualness, displaying pretty girls in beach
attire in a light and airy circular palace. In the American
pavilion we saw *South Pacific* in a new medium called
Circorama. It was wonderful.

I remember being disappointed in the Canadian
Pavilion. The St. Lawrence Seaway was poorly represented. There was no mention of Alberta's oil industry.
There were no food concessions. Although the story of
the influence of climate, geography and Canada's great
natural resources on a small and diverse population was
well told, the story of Canada's agriculture industry was
not. However, I did feel that the displays featuring the
Eaton's catalogue, our motels, our sports, and our

schools on wheels were good. The Royal Canadian Mounted Police, who were strolling about, were particularly popular with the women visitors.

I was attracted, however, to the Czech pavilion that boasted a scale model of a real hop orchard with wonderful marionettes.

We rode high over the main thoroughfares of the exposition on a Swiss cable railway, a funicular type system, consisting of two-seat shells which provided not only transportation for our foot-sore bodies, but also afforded a spectacular panoramic view of the 500 acre fairgrounds.

But the feature that impressed me most was the Atomium, the symbol of the Fair, 360 feet high, consisting of nine huge gleaming silver spheres arranged in the structural shape of an atom proclaiming man's entry into the atomic age and the peaceful uses of atomic energy. At night the atomium shimmered silver, fountains danced with orange, white and green waters, and animated tube lighting darted back and forth across the darkness. The Brussels World's Fair of 1958 was a marvel to behold.

On this trip, as on others which I have made to Brussels, I had to pay a visit to its most famous citizen, and oldest inhabitant, Manneken Pis, and to the Grand Place. The Mannekin Pis is a small bronze statue of a chubby boy peeing into a fountain. He has such a long history that he owns an extensive wardrobe of costumes donated to him. He was wearing a GI uniform this time.

On this 1958 trip, I made sure we saw the Grand Place at night when we could experience the full theatrical effect of the illuminated burnished facades of the ornate Baroque guild houses, rich with gilt and fancy carvings in the finest flood-lit medieval square in Europe. It was a magnificent and unforgettable sight.

Italy with Mom and Dad, July, 1958

My parents arrived in Paris from Canada on 3 April 1958, six hours late. We spent three days admiring everything foreigners admire about Paris and then the three of us flew to Rome. On Easter Sunday we attended Mass in St. Peter's sung by the jovial John XXIII. My mother was ecstatic. She and I also ascended, on our knees, the twenty-eight steps of the Scala Santa (Holy Stairs) brought to Rome by the Empress Helena. According to tradition it is the same flight of marble steps which Jesus ascended in the house of Pilate. Dad met his brother whom he hadn't seen in nearly fifty years.

Mom and Dad remained in Italy until Elizabeth Brauer (Coaldale, Alberta) a colleague from #2 Fighter Wing and I drove to Rome in our rented Deux Chevaux, to pick them up. We then drove through northern Italy to Germany to visit the Beckwermerts and then to the airport in Paris where they flew back to Canada.

When my mother saw the sign to Verona she wanted to see Juliet's tomb. How could we tell her that the authenticity of Shakespeare's drama about youthful passion and family feuds was tenuous at best? But Elizabeth dutifully took her and we saw all the sites devoted to the memory of the star-crossed lovers: Juliet's house with the marble balcony that Romeo climbed "with love's light wings" at 23 Via Cappello; Juliet's tomb in a former Capuchin monastery in the Campo di Fiera, a brickwork crypt which contains a rough medieval stone trough in which Juliet is said to have been laid to rest;

and Romeo's house along the Via delle Arche Scaligere near the Church of Santa Maria Antica.

I was always anxious to see monuments of Dante, Italy's greatest poet. As an exile from Florence, Dante first found refuge in Verona. A monument to him sits in the middle of the Piazza dei Signori. We sat at an outdoor coffeehouse, the "Caffé Dante," and looked at the elegant Renaissance loggia and the two towers, and I meditated on the brief quotation from the speech of a damned soul in Dante's *Inferno*, which T. S. Eliot uses to introduce "The Love Song of J. Alfred Prufrock." To my surprise, we saw streets littered with disposable syringes and needles and concluded that Verona must have a serious drug problem.

Ever since I can remember, my mother has had a special devotion to Saint Anthony of Padua. The *Messagerio di San Antonio* regularly came to our house until my mother died in 1979. My sister, Mary, now gives me a subscription to an international edition published in English. For the past twenty-five years each 13 June an outdoor procession is held in honour of the saint after whom my local church has been named. And so it was, as pilgrims, that we visited Padua. My mother was elated.

Padua's Basilica of San Antonio was a huge oriental-looking edifice which enclosed the tomb of St. Anthony in the Chapel of the Saint whose altar, in black and white marble, was terribly congested with votive tablets and testimonials from numerous devotees. I did not find the dim and cluttered Basilica beautiful.

A monument by Donatello, of a figure riding haughtily on a giant horse like a Roman Caesar, near the left side of the church's facade, however, appealed to me. It was of the fifteenth century *condottiere* Erasmo da

Narni, called *Gattamelata* (Tigercat), who served the Republic of Venice as commander-in-chief of its army for a few years. The name, *Gattamelata*, intrigued me because my cousins' address in Rome was Via Erasmo Gattamelata.

Elizabeth, a tall, strong, very capable woman whom I admired greatly, deserved a medal for her driving skill and patience. And my parents deserved another for their grace under pressure, as well as their sense of humour during all the little crises that arose because our French car had only two horse power. They never uttered a complaint about their cramped quarters in the little car. Dad's observation that it could only pass tractors and donkeys soon became a continuing joke. Heavy with passengers and luggage, the Deux Chevaux could not even crawl up steep hills. Invariably it had to be relieved of our weight before Elizabeth could coax it to the crests of the hills. Once, in Assisi, it had to be lifted up by four young Italian men before it could negotiate a sharp narrow turn in a street. It always insisted on being put on trains through the long tunnels in the mountains. American tourists, who were unfamiliar with the French car, would hover around it, asking questions and exclaiming, "what a cute car!"

And yet it harboured delusions of grandeur. Only at a Mercedes-Benz dealership would it get serviced.

Behind the Iron Curtain, 1958

After Elizabeth and I saw my parents off, I embarked on a trip that took me behind the Iron Curtain. It was in the late summer of 1958, over thirty years before *glasnost* and *perestroika*, the fall of Communism, and the collapse of the Soviet Union in 1991.

The Cold War was raging. The admiration and respect that the West had for the heroism of the Soviets had ended. The USSR was enjoying superstar status; it had surpassed the United Sates in space age exploration with the launching of the first satellite, Sputnik I, in October, 1957. We were all afraid of what the USSR might do. I was terribly frightened. The politics of fear had created horror in the western world. In the U.S.A., Senator Joseph McCarthy's witch hunts for communists had created a reign of terror. Canadian military personnel were forbidden to go behind the Iron Curtain. I was associated with them, and I suspected that if I asked for permission to go, I would be refused. As a result, I stealthily made plans with a British company to join a motorcoach tour through East Germany and Poland into Russia and then through Czechoslovakia. I was plagued with guilt, and I feared being caught or disappearing without a trace in Russia. Russia, herself, feared the enemy without (spies, saboteurs, and suspected western contacts) and within (Jews and intellectuals). There was the Secret Police; there were the show trials.

Although I was glad that I was on a package tour, I was still very frightened. To make matters worse, when the day arrived for me to leave, I still did not have my Czech visa. Nevertheless, I did not give way to my fears and bravely boarded a train for Hanover, Germany where I met my tour which had started in Bournemouth, England.

On the night of 28 July 1958, at the Hotel Waterloo in Hanover, terribly anxious and worried, I met Jack, the driver of the bus that was going to take us through the Iron Curtain into Russia. My first question was, "Do you have my Czech visa?"

Jack replied, "The Czech visa is a collective."

I immediately asked, "Is my name on it?" When Jack said he didn't know, I was in a state of disbelief.

I retorted incredulously, "You don't know."

His response was casual: "because I don't have the Czech collective visa. I'll receive it at the Polish-Czech frontier from the Czech guide. The Czech embassy in London did not have it ready for the tour departure date."

I was like one obsessed. Anger was welling up inside of me. My heart was pounding.

I fired, "Well I simply can't go on the trip. What if we go to the Czech frontier and discover my name is not on the collective visa. What will happen then? How can I go through East Germany and Poland alone?" There was reason for my anxiety. The last time Jack had taken the tour through the Czech border, officials would not allow an English parson and his wife to enter the country. They had to leave the tour and take the train through Poland and East Germany.

After many reassurances, Jack convinced me that the company would have sent me word if the visa had not been secured. Nevertheless, I couldn't sleep that night.

Words of warning from friends kept haunting me. Never go out alone. Never stand with your back to descending steps or a pit. Always read carefully what you sign. Don't be too curious. Be as inconspicuous as possible. Don't mix with the other passengers; they might be Communists. My parents' parting words at Orly Airport, Paris, kept haunting me: "They'll send you to Siberia. We'll never see you again."

The next morning I announced to the driver that I'd like to send a wire or make a phone call to the tour company's office to enquire about the visa. He again tried to reassure me that he was certain everything must be in order. Reluctantly, I boarded the coach. I was assigned a seat next to a bespectacled, balding young man in a brown tweed jacket which he would wear throughout the whole tour.

I was heeding the advice of my friends. I was still uncomfortable, and I spoke only when I was spoken to. Contradictory thoughts kept flooding my mind. You still have time to leave. Why do you have to endanger your life just because you want to see the contemporary scene in Russia? Go and relax on the Riviera. Forget about this desire for knowledge. I wanted to see how the Russians really lived. And what if you can't get out? You can't ask the Air Force for help. What will you do then? I reproached myself for my misgivings, and I tried to console myself. What could happen anyway? Look at all these people. I gazed at each of the twenty-six passengers, all seated in their proper places before me. They're not afraid. They're enjoying the scenery. But they're probably all Communists. They don't have to be afraid. I've been working for the Department of National Defence overseas. My passport says so. I looked at each person again. I never expected so many women. And here there were sixteen of assorted ages and sizes. I wondered why they were taking such a trip.

Suddenly, a soft Irish lilt, broke my reverie: "We're coming to the border." "He's an Irishman, and I think he's not feeling too secure, either," I mused.

We had arrived at Helmstedt, the border town separating East and West Germany. Here was our first experience with border formalities, the first of many instances where we were forced to wait silently and patiently. Here we learned our first lesson in border photography. A French bus, "*La Tourisme Française*," was standing still. Most of the passengers were milling about outside. Suddenly we saw a small, wiry, middle-aged woman dash into the bus and quickly duck into her seat. She was trying to hide her camera. Then we saw an officer board the bus and usher her out to the border house.

Naturally, this incident frightened us. We all agreed that we would not break barrier photography rules because it wasn't fair to jeopardize the safety of the other passengers. It was here, therefore, that I realized that everyone else was just as afraid as I was. And I was more convinced of it when a passenger counselled that we should remain quietly seated in the bus, and that no one should appear too curious when border officials entered and took our passports.

During our wait, I discovered my companion's name was Walter, a high school teacher and freelance writer from Belfast. He wondered why I was so quiet. I told him why I was preoccupied. Somehow, right then, I knew I had discovered a friend. Walter proved to be a true friend throughout the whole trip. He had that sense of humour God gave only to the Irish, and the art of story-telling with which He favoured them too.

I considered myself lucky to be his seat companion because he knew Russian history. And since we didn't have a guide, his history lessons were not only informative, but also delightful because they were enlivened with his own perspective.

After about an hour's wait, we entered the Deutsche Democratische Republik on the Hanover-Berlin autobahn built by Hitler. Suddenly it became deserted. The familiar autobahn signs that I knew so well were there, but the heavy fast traffic of West Germany's autobahns was no more. Even though we stopped for teas and "trees", we were able to cover the 172 kilometres from Helmstedt to Berlin in record time.

I was new to these teas and tree stops. There were no toilet facilities on board. Jack had to listen to twenty-seven individual opinions as to where to stop. In the end, he made the decision, in spite of "bushes too low," "not enough trees," "trees too thin," "ground too wet," "incline too steep," "land too open," "peasants working," or "men looking."

But my greatest source of amusement were the teas. Passengers were advised to bring their own tea, sugar, sweets and cups because there were no restaurants along the highways of Iron Curtain countries. Everyone had brought their little stores with them except me. I didn't want any tea. I thought surely we're not going to waste time stopping for tea every day. I underestimated the English love for tea, because we stopped not only every day, but twice each morning and twice each afternoon.

Tea drinking for the English was like a religious ritual to be executed at a certain time each day like the Moslem time for prayer. My fellow passengers seemed to receive some sort of physical rejuvenation by indulging in this beverage. I would sit back in the coach, amused, as I watched them drink of this fount of life while they sat along the roadside or wandered around the environs, or reclined on the grass and weeds, or straddled the ditches. After the ritual, faces would glow, tempers would moderate and good humour would reign. Philosophically, I thought, *Chacun à son gout* and I resigned myself to wait behind the Iron Curtain for the English and their teas.

In East Berlin I had Jack wire the tour company for information regarding the Czech collective visa. I knew that if I were to leave the tour, this was the logical place where I could easily fly out. I waited and waited for a reply. Both Jack and Walter assured me that no news was good news. There were two now to share my anxiety. It wasn't until we got to Moscow that Jack announced that he had received word from London that I was included in the collective visa.

Poland

We crossed the Oder River, between Poland and Germany, the new frontier since World War II, guarded by two very young Polish soldiers with fixed bayonets. I sensed a brooding silence and an uneasy stillness. The countryside was a picture of loneliness with only the border house and a makeshift tent to break the monotony. I don't know why, but the silence was contagious. During the one and one-half hour wait for border formalities, the two uniformed border officials were especially fussy about our passport pictures and visas, not a word was spoken by the twenty-eight seated in the bus. Now, whether this silence was borne of a fear of the unknown, uncertainty as to whether we'd ever return alive, or anxiety as to whether all our passports were in order so that we could even enter Poland, I can't say. But I do know that when the "all is well" salute was given, we sighed with relief. Pent up vocal chords lustily released, "we're off."

What we saw on our way to Warsaw was a catalogue of misery, oppression and suffering. Buildings in shambles, mostly devastated by war, thatched cottages, unkempt dirt roads, no cars. Farmers trailed behind ox carts laden with cut hay. The harvest was bountiful, and yet the fields were untidy. The countryside had a sloppy appearance. Even the many wooden shrines weren't the well-kept shrines of France and Germany. Everything seemed to be in decline or deteriorating. Poland, sandwiched between Germany and Russia, with almost no natural defences, has endured a stormy and checkered history of fierce and heavy fighting, occupations, invasions, partitions, mass evacuations and repatriations.

I felt better when a friend of mine, who had visited Poland during the summer of 1939, assured me that although things looked a little worse, the Poles are traditionally very casual, and that, although by our standards of living, they live poorly, they have plenty to eat. The smiling faces of little fair-headed children running out barefoot in the warm dust to wave enthusiastically at us cheered me. Even a pink ribbon in a little girl's hair and a red babushka on a hard working peasant woman, after the dull and drab clothes of the East Germans, was a welcome sight.

If rural Poland was shocking, Warsaw was staggering. It was practically all in ruins; 92 per cent of it was destroyed during the war. But the city was being rebuilt, as far as possible, as a replica of its former self. I was surprised, however, that new buildings were being constructed along uniform straight lines, unlike the strikingly original buildings I had seen in the newly reconstructed cities of Germany: Cologne, Essen, Dusseldorf, Hamburg, and Berlin's "City of Tomorrow." Many were erected in rough brick held together by mortar, still without their plaster faces and still un-painted.

Stalin's gift to Warsaw, the mammoth Palace of Culture and Rest stood in the middle of Warsaw in all its pure, white, box-like Russian style — unimpressive to the eyes of a western sophisticate. It was an exact copy of Moscow's "multi-storeyed" buildings. The sensitive Russians wouldn't dare stain the purity of the language of communism by referring to them by the imperialistic word "skyscrapers."

Life continued amid the scars of the past, the empty gaps, the broken fragments of walls, the vacant shells, the lean-tos, and the lower storeys. Window displays showed a flair for design, and the sophistication of pre-war Warsaw. We sat at fashionable sidewalk cafés, unknown in Russia, and watched the leisurely life of a Sunday afternoon with promenading stylishly dressed women and men.

Warsaw's women showed their traditional sense of style and taste in clothes. They were much better dressed than the women we would see in Russia, where no attempt at all was made toward glamour and attractive-ness. In the store windows of Warsaw, I saw pictures of girls in bikinis and bathing suits. Such cheesecake pic-tures were taboo in the puritanical USSR. The Russians were concentrating on essentials first. Fashionable clothes would come in the future paradise of the worker.

Warsaw was regaining its old metropolitan gaiety through the revitalized cabarets, cocktail bars and night clubs. Moscow would have none of these. The Soviet

Union was working hard, first on technical advances, scientific research and industrialization.

And yet in the Polish night clubs, even in the best hotels, an informal air prevailed, a touch of the proletariat-Russian style. The waiters wore shirts with open collars and no ties. They accepted no tips, though Willie, our Polish guide, told us he always slipped the headwaiter extra *zlotes* to encourage him to give good service. Members of the band played in their shirt sleeves, wore no ties, and no uniforms. Western tunes were popular. I remember that "I'm Dreaming of a White Christmas" was played everywhere we went, at the Crocodile Night Club where I met Adlai Stevenson, and at the swanky Palace Hotel where Mr. Hanki, ex-President of the Polish Government in London during the war, was dancing.

The gallantry of Polish men impressed me. Before and after each dance, my Polish partner clicked his heels and kissed my hand. I loved it. When we were leaving Poznan, a city just inside the Polish boundary, where we spent our first night in Poland, two local swains with whom I had been chatting and dancing the previous night greeted me with bouquets of carnations in the hotel lobby at seven a.m.

Although most of us enjoyed our Polish school-boy breakfasts of cheese and ham, rolls, jam, butter, eggs, all the pop we wanted (coca-cola, lemonade or orangeade), plus coffee or tea and lemon, we found our meals rich and heavy. We were served five eggs a day, and we ate weiner schnitzel topped with fried eggs noon and night. Mineral or soda water was served at all meals. We were never served fresh fruit.

I saw no bananas, oranges, grapefruit, or peaches anywhere. Only wormy, tiny, green apples and pears were sold in the small outdoor stalls. I saw few cars in Warsaw, and hence little traffic and few policemen. I did notice cars of Polish manufacture that looked like our 1947 Fords. Buses were imported French Chaussons. There were few tourist cars, although I would see many in Czechoslovakia from Bulgaria, Holland, and France. I also noticed two Volkswagens, and one Karmann Ghia, but they were parked near the various Embassies so they probably belonged to foreigners.

Most businesses in Poland were state-owned except for a few small tailor shops, hairdressers and shoemakers. Private ownership wasn't forbidden in Poland or Czechoslovakia, but it was made so difficult through very high taxes that private owners were usually forced out of business.

Salaries were poor. A lawyer earned about $150 a month; a teacher about sixty dollars. Willie, our guide, who was still a student in International Law at the University, received a tuition grant of about twenty dollars a month; four dollars a month of which went for room, and four dollars for board in the University caféteria.

Books and newspapers were cheap. In the book stores we noticed translations of Conrad, LaFontaine, Socrates, Sartre, Balzak, Dickens and Wells, and English papers, such as the *Manchester Guardian,* and *The Times,* as well as French and German papers could be bought in our Warsaw hotel. In Russia, where a monolithic unity of thought prevailed, the only English paper available was the *Daily Worker.*

There was complete freedom of worship in Poland since Gomulko had scored his political triumph. Poland was about 90 per cent Catholic. Religion was taught in the schools. I saw no red stars. Church spires and crosses dominated the skyline.

I was surprised to learn that not everyone belonged to the Communist party. (Out of a population of twenty-five million only 1.5 million were members of the Polish Communist Party.) It was a very exclusive, carefully screened group. Membership was a privilege. Paradoxically, party membership meant "total submission to discipline, hard and thankless work, as well as grave risks and dangers." (But the advantages must have been many.)

Our tour took us to Wroclaw, the Polish name for Breslau, which had been an old, highly industrialized German town before the war. It was now desolate in its heaps of rubble and incredible destruction. Hundreds of brick skeletons, rent and tortured, outlined against the sky, reminded me of East Berlin as we explored the dark and deserted streets.

Contrary to general belief we were free to discover the city for ourselves. Willie's duties were to get us settled in hotels, to arrange for our meals, and to act as our interpreter. We spent most of our time wandering through the streets of Lodz, Poznan, Warsaw, and Wroclaw, talking to the people in any language, mostly German. While I was filming a street scene on Roosevelt Street in Poznan, we noticed, in the trolley car queue, a young man kiss his girl on the cheek. Anne, my roommate and I waited for a repeat performance to capture on film. They noticed us, and before we knew it, a conversation began. She could speak only Polish, but he was an opera singer, and thus we managed to communicate in German and English. They insisted we join them for a drink at a restaurant across the street. It was crowded, but we found a place, and we ordered the bottles of pop. A fat lady was playing, "Smoke Gets in Your Eyes" and "Begin the Beguine" on the piano. I remembered the first question the young man asked: "Has everyone in your country a car, a refrigerator?" He was sincerely interested in my country and the Canadian way of life. We discovered that his wife's family had owned a ceramic factory and had been wealthy at one time. We spent a delightful hour with them. They insisted on paying the bill. We insisted they take our packages of cigarettes.

We left Poland with a feeling of hope for this once proud country, because Polish youth was searching and probing. Gomulka insisted on socialism his way. But I noted that God was still the measure of all things.

Russia

When we arrived at the Polish-Russian border, we discovered that Sir John Hunt and his party were there waiting for clearance. Everyone in the tour group tried to squeeze into elbow room position on the unpainted wooden barrier to talk to or get a good look at Hunt, the leader of the successful Mt. Everest climbing expedition and his party of eight men in three brand-new white Vanguard station wagons. They were on their way home after climbing the Caucasus Mountains, the first foreigners to do so in twenty-one years. We may have been foolhardy, but we paid no attention to the warnings from the guards not to lean against the railing. We were excited at meeting a group of famous people who spoke our language. The guards realized this, and didn't press their warnings.

We discovered that the Hunt party had to leave their station wagons at the border during their six-week stay, because they weren't registered in the visas. Not even telephone calls to the Kremlin could remedy this clerical blunder! We all thought it was a big joke, not realizing, of course, that in a few minutes we would be in a similar predicament. We enjoyed listening to their experiences. But all too soon the barrier was lifted, and waving and shouting goodbye to them, we left Poland to enter the USSR. We didn't get very far, about one hundred feet, when a jovial, Russian border official entered our bus, collected our passports, and introduced us to Larissa, our Russian guide, a plump, pretty twenty-two-year old brunette. She wore a smart blue rayon print dress, white gloves, sandals, purse, white earrings, but no stockings. With her cheerful "Good Morning" in perfect American English and her winsome smile, she made a crash landing with the men of the group. The women were more cautious of their first encounter with this Russian "secret weapon."

Larissa explained that we would have to wait about fifteen minutes for border formalities. It was eleven a.m. We were all in good spirits. However, the fifteen minutes began to drag on and on. Several hours passed. There was no restaurant, no place where we could get anything to eat. The waiting room was cool, however, and a primitive outhouse was available. The place was a hive of activity, with several English parties, one Italian, and many French people who were waiting for their exit permission. I was kept amused by the stories they told of their Russian experiences, and I even took a spin in an ultra-modern French Citroen. (During my two-year stay in France, my one desire had been to ride in one.) Here I was, at the Russian border, riding down the highway, expecting any moment to be shot at by the many patrols wandering about because we hadn't yet received our clearance. However, after driving several thousand feet, my driver turned back. Soon, time became heavy. We were famished, exhausted from the heat and idleness, and worried about our fate. Everyone kept asking the same question — why this delay? Finally, we were told that two visas were incomplete because they didn't include the word "autobus." We were waiting for permission from Moscow to allow these two persons to continue. There was no deviating from orders from the Kremlin. Reminders of Sir John Hunt's calamity!

Larissa, our guide, was very upset by this unforeseen delay. She had made plans to meet her boyfriend, who was leaving for his Black Sea holiday, the next day in Moscow. And now, if we followed the itinerary, she would never make it. Finally, at six p.m., after a seven-hour wait with nothing to eat, word came through from Moscow. The two could continue with the bus and so we were off. Just four kilometres to Brest-Litovsk, a Polish town before World War II, and we would have our dinner.

We had no sooner parked in front of our restaurant when a huge crowd began to gather around the coach, curiously inspecting the writing on it, the licence plate and the tires. This was just a preview of later receptions because crowds swarmed around us everywhere we stopped, pushing and pulling, eager to talk, proud to recite their whole stock of English. One Russian told me that all they wanted was peace and friendship with the West. Every time we left, they would wave and blow kisses. At first, I was reluctant to talk because I had been given so many warnings not to appear too curious, and to be as inconspicuous as possible, but now I realized that I was missing a lot of fun. How I regretted not having learned any Russian words. (We couldn't even read signs, because, although Russian is completely phonetic, the letters are derived from the Greek.) I did pick up many words, and with sign language, and that mental telepathic sense that seems to work with strangers and nationals, plus a smattering of German and French, I got along.

In Moscow, where Anne, and I were covered with insect bites, we broke through the language barrier. We found a drug store, but we couldn't follow the routine of going to the cashier, getting a credit slip for the amount to be spent, and then exchanging it for the desired article, because we could not explain what we wanted. We made buzzing noises; we showed our large swollen bites; we gesticulated swooping flights of mosquitoes. Nothing worked. Then Anne drew a bee. It worked.

Little boys, especially, flocked about us, always wanting to exchange their badges for chewing gum, post cards, coins, and pencils. Cigarettes had no exchange value whatsoever, and we soon discovered that our pence had lost their exchange value too. One afternoon in Red Square while we were waiting for a policeman, who was in no hurry to hail a cab for us because he wanted to chat, a huge crowd, as usual, gathered around us with the little boys again wanting to swap. Anne produced all sorts of Belgian, German, French and English coins which she wanted to get rid of. Accidentally, a shilling dropped on the pavement. As soon as one of the boys noticed it, all was lost. He insisted on the shilling. Nothing else would do. Business shrewdness displayed at such an early age, and yet not to be utilized in a society where there was no private enterprise!

We travelled the whole night. The next morning we took a sightseeing tour of Minsk, the capital of the newly independent republic now known as Belarus, the site of the Chernobyl nuclear disaster of 1986. Minsk, devastated by the Nazi invasion of Russia, had been rebuilt according to original plans.

We left Minsk after lunch joining the new highway which followed the road taken by Napoleon's retreating armies in the cruel winter of 1812. The Pripyet marshes, eerie in their isolated death-like silence, were an immense natural, geographic barrier. For the first time I was aware of the empty vastness of the USSR.

We drove all night across the White Russian plains, a lonely almost treeless flat land with increasingly isolated brown wooden villages. We covered 800 kilometres in ten hours. The road was almost devoid of wheeled traffic except for the occasional grey collective farm truck, numbered in large white figures, trundling slowly along with a party of workers in the back.

Exhausted, we arrived at our hotel in Smolensk, on the Dnieper River early the next morning. Queuing up for our rooms, we were doled out small sheets of waxed paper. It became a standard joke that we judged a Russian hotel's category by the quality of the toilet paper. The plumbing facilities of all the Russian hotels we stayed in were absolutely deplorable (except for the Hotel Ukraine in Moscow). Our rooms were over-furnished in heavy Victorian style. Heavy wine-coloured velvet drapes covered the windows, and a heavy white material covered all the chairs and chesterfields. But our rooms were clean and comfortable.

Smolensk, on the medieval Amber Road from the Baltic to the Black Sea, was practically levelled during World War II. The efficient local guide who took us on a sight-seeing tour kept reminding us of Russian bravery and sacrifice during the war against the Germans. She

showed us the grave of a Russian heroine whose husband had been killed by the Germans early in World War
II. Wanting to avenge his death, she wrote Comrade
Stalin for permission to buy a tank with her savings.
Stalin granted the permission. She drove her tank in the
front lines and was killed. Her tank was the first Russian
tank to enter Berlin. I had seen this tank in the Russian
memorial just inside the Bradenburg Gate. The guide,
who had a fanatical hatred for Nazism and Fascism,
couldn't understand why we were now helping our
former enemies.

We visited the local Park of Culture and Rest. (All
parks in Russia are known by that name.) There were the
usual children's amusements — swings, merry-go-
rounds, and ferris wheels — but I also noticed men
playing chess and table tennis. There were also little
theatres, and concert and lecture halls, closely controlled by the government. I found the many statues of
modern youth in various activities of work and play
scattered throughout the park, pleasing in their modern
simplicity and freedom of movement.

Our local guide referred to everyone as Tavarisch.
Even Lenin was Tavarisch Lenin, Comrade Lenin. "We
have no titles, no degrees, no letters after a name," she
said. "We make no distinctions. A factory engineer is no
better than a good factory worker. In fact, they make the
same wage."

We were taken to the Orthodox Church of the
Assumption since several of us had expressed the wish
to see a church. For nearly forty years churches had been
left empty and uncared for. As a result, the church was
badly in need of repair. A service was being conducted
by a priest robed in a faded yellow cloak of tawdry
material that looked like a cheap curtain. I couldn't help

thinking of this poor priest who, I was told, had attended the Lambeth Conference of Churches in England the previous spring, when I later saw the fabulously rich church vestments, chalices, crosses, and icons in the Kremlin's museum. However, I was moved and inspired by the devotion and piety of the 200 or so parishioners — mainly shabbily dressed little children and old women (as Larissa pointed out to me). I'll always remember how one playful little baby, about two years old, dirty and bedraggled, played with two of the tiniest, dirtiest, most grimy teddy bears I had ever seen.

Everyone was standing: there were no prayer books, but lips were silently moving. I felt the presence of a deep religious fervour. It was the first time that Larissa had ever been inside a church. She sneered and ridiculed the various parts of the service: the kneeling, the making of the sign of the cross, the tabernacle door opening and closing. She wanted to know what purpose that "thing" (the censer) served. She told me, "Russia's youth is educated now. We don't need God. We believe in science and nature. There is no other world; there is just this world." Soviet philosophy was purely materialistic. Religion was considered a refuge for the poor illiterate who needed protection. I think it was Karl Marx who stated that religion is the opiate of the masses. Youth didn't need that protection. They relied on themselves: "reasonable egoism" was the term Larissa used.

From Smolensk to Moscow, a distance of 400 kilometres, I noticed only one gas station. Our driver used the Russian mineral water, which was always included in our box lunches, to fill the radiator of the coach. As we drove into Moscow, huge blocks of new apartments topped with TV antennae (TV sets were very cheap, about eighty dollars) immediately attracted our attention. Our hotel, the Hotel Ukraine, the largest in the country and probably the best in Moscow, was one of those seven "multi-storeyed" buildings that the Russians had recently built to show the Americans that they too could build skyscrapers. Anyway, the Russians did not believe in very tall buildings, so the construction of "multi-storeyed" buildings was stopped. The hotel was formidable rather than luxurious. The lobby was spacious, with a high ceiling covered with a mural depicting Russians at work and play. I noticed that Soviet paintings depicted social scenes with fanatic detail. I saw no abstract paintings. The corridors were dull and drab, the floors unwaxed, unpolished. There were no stairs. But our rooms had private baths! The hotel was filled with about 1,500 guests, because there were delegates from all over the world attending a number of conventions. I noticed many Indians and Chinese in their national attire, and, of course, the scores of Americans were easily recognized too.

Moscow, the fifth largest city in the world, was unlike any other city I had seen. It had no glamour like Paris, no beauty like Rome, no excitement like London. It gave me no spiritual uplift, and yet it cast a spell over me. Perhaps it was the mighty, saw-toothed fortress walls of the Kremlin, in the heart of Moscow, topped with massive medieval towers, or perhaps it was the Russian architecture of the Kremlin's oddly shaped palaces, cathedrals, and gilded, onion-shaped cupolas that intrigued me. Or perhaps it was the dazzlingly beautiful St. Basil Cathedral built by Italian architects in the fifteenth century. It has nine towers, surmounted by nine cupolas, each different from the others, breathtaking in their spiralled, twisted, and chequered designs in brilliant shades of red, green, yellow and turquoise looking like the turbans of some fantastic sultan. I stood awestruck at this architectural splendour. Ivan the Terrible, who ordered its construction, must have also been struck mad by its overpowering beauty, because he had the eyes of the architect plucked out so that he could never duplicate the cathedral's unique beauty.

We were never allowed to enter Ivan's shrine. I tried many times to get in, but there was always a different excuse. "Oh, there's nothing in there now; reconstruction work is being carried on; the museum inside is closed." We heard it was being used as a storehouse.

I was also intrigued by the curious paradox of the gilded crosses and the ruby stars silhouetted against the sky, Moscow's silence, and the panoramic view I beheld standing on the Lenin Hills beside Picasso's huge Dove of Peace, erected for the International Youth Conference of 1957. But perhaps it was also the serene purity of the white lights of Moscow and the stillness of the night which captivated me. There was none of the flashing coloured lights of the western world to razzle-dazzle me.

Whatever it was, Moscow fascinated me. It was a spacious city. Its avenues and boulevards that fanned out in all directions from Red Square, like the spokes of a wheel, were very wide with eight lanes of traffic, wider than Paris' Champs Élysées. Of course, Moscow has its narrow, winding cobblestone blind alleys too, because she is over 800 years old. We poked along these streets — streets that the typical tourist doesn't see. Contrary to general belief, we were free to travel anywhere by ourselves. Of course, there were no public places to go to, and no signs. Because we could not speak the language our forays were few. We strolled along a few back streets, and noticed old wooden hovels, some adorned with intricate carvings. "These are being gradually torn down," our guide explained. They had already demolished 69 per cent of them, and were replacing them with huge apartment blocks.

Red Square was the greatest open space I had ever seen in the centre of any city. I found it both frightening and interesting, since it was the scene of many momentous events in Russian history, and because it was here that the great public demonstrations were held on May Day.

Across from it stood the huge G.U.M. Department store, which operated on three floors linked by footbridges over arcades. The store gave the Muscovites a glimpse of the lovely consumer goods in store for them in the future paradise of the workers, but even here, window displays were unimaginative.

The smoothly polished dark red Lenin Mausoleum stood along the Kremlin Wall in Red Square. It contained the mummified bodies of Stalin and Lenin, the man who ordered the execution of Czar Nicholas II, and was the symbol of the Bolshevik Revolution. Thousands were lined up in the angular queues winding slowly all day across the cobbled width of Red Square. In our queue there were hundreds of young Pioneers, Soviet tourists and foreigners, many carrying wreaths and bouquets of fresh flowers. A large Korean delegation was bringing a gigantic wreath. I was surprised at the huge numbers waiting in an orderly and quiet manner to pay homage to the two revolutionary heroes.

When our guide noticed the length of the queue, she had us ushered to the front of the line. In single file we descended inside the crypt. I gazed at the waxen faces and hands of the two resting in their glass coffins. Lenin's jaw had a determined hardness; Stalin had a smug look on his face, and a faint trace of a smile. I was so engrossed in their facial expressions that I almost desecrated the austere solemnity by tripping over a step. An alert guide rescued me. Before I knew it, I was outside.

Moscow was a clean — immaculately clean — city. There was absolutely no litter in the streets; a change from the dirt in London and Brussels. I saw women cleaning the streets with their dust pans and brooms as late as nine p.m. The Russians were proud of their clean cities. The elevator boy in our hotel stopped the elevator just to dispose of his butt in an ash receptacle in the lobby of one of the floors. There was even a puritanical morality in entertainment and dress. There were no cabarets, no cocktail bars, no night life in Moscow. I remember being told I would see many drunks in the street. But the whole time we were there, we noticed only two. (Our guide told us the Government just raised the price of liquor.) There were no risqué advertisements. In fact, there were no advertisements at all; no neon lighting. No emphasis was placed on sex in their movies. Dress was very modest. No shorts were allowed on the streets. I saw no *décolleté*, no bare backs or strapless dresses. Russian clothing, to the eyes of a western sophisticate, was dull, drab, badly cut, of cheap quality and expensive.

Most of the women were encouraged to make their own clothing. They bought pre-cut packaged dresses, available in three different patterns which they assembled and sewed. The favourite pattern must have been a loose fitted dress with a bottom circular panel of pleats, because practically every woman I saw was wearing one. Some of our women who witnessed a fashion show, a promise of what the future would bring in Russian couture, told me the clothes looked miserably shabby.

Clothes must be practical anyway, since women all work. I saw them driving trucks, trolley cars and buses, and working on tram lines. I saw them tarring the roads, working in manholes, and unloading gravel. Across from my hotel window, I saw women laying bricks for a new apartment building at eleven p.m. by floodlight. During our university tour, I saw a woman electrician repairing wires in one of the gyms.

I considered Larissa, a Russian Jewess, well dressed compared to the other women I saw. She told me that she modified the patterns. I could see she had a flair for style. And yet Russian women were acutely conscious of the clothes foreigners were wearing, especially shoes. In one restaurant a waitress wanted to buy a pair of Italian sandals I was wearing. They realized their clothes were shabby, but they were willing to sacrifice their own personal wants for the achievement of the state. The state had to concentrate on essentials first, technical progress, and scientific research. Emphasis was placed on industrialization. I couldn't help but admire these tough, patient, hard-working women for their discipline and self-sacrifice.

But they made no attempt to be attractive. Hair-dressing shops were extremely old-fashioned. Hair styles had an outdated, tightly-permed look. Nail polish was just out of the question, because it was so expensive. One of the Russian women in the British Embassy wanted to buy a bottle of any shade from us.

The prices of normal consumer goods (including souvenirs and luxury articles) were exorbitantly high, even with the favourable rate for tourists of ten rubles to one dollar. Yet TV sets, radios and records, were cheap. I bought five 33 1/3 long-play records of Verdi's *Rigoletto* for one dollar each. Books were cheap. We saw outdoor book stalls every few hundred feet in the shopping areas.

My travelling companions bought cans of caviar, little dolls in national costumes, and small lacquered boxes. But I felt the workmanship and finish were poor. Actually, there wasn't really much I wanted to buy. I was surprised that there were no Sputnik items for sale. I searched for miniature Sputniks in the huge, attractive, modern, well-stocked children's stores which boasted escalators. But no luck. (I finally got a Sputnik miniature in exchange for a ballpoint pen.) I later found some for sale in the toy shops of West Germany's Cologne. I recall now that in the Russian pavilion at the Brussels World Fair, the musical Sputniks had been made in Switzerland.

Consumer goods were bought on a cash basis. There was no credit, although Larissa informed us that buying on the instalment plan would soon be introduced. I hastened to tell her it had many faults. The Russians were encouraged to save and they were paid 6 per cent interest on savings. They could own their own car and furniture. Most people lived in State-owned apartments, but they could own their country home if they built it themselves. There was no property tax. Public utilities were very cheap. Holidays were cheap. Income tax was negligible, twenty rubles a month on an income of 850 rubles a month. People earning less than 500 rubles a month paid no income tax. Scientists, writers, musicians, inventors, and university professors earned large salaries. I met a professor at the University of Moscow at the only gas station between Moscow and Smolensk who was sporting a camera worth $300. The best paid people were the intellectuals.

Russian restaurant service lacked the polish, the finesse and refined touch of Western cuisine. Dirty dishes weren't removed. Used serviettes were left on the table. Heaping dishes were set before us, and bottles of mineral water, beer, and lemonade, were opened at the table and passed back and forth. The waitresses wore fancy high, white starched Victorian head pieces, shabby brown uniforms (brown seemed to be the favourite colour for waitress uniforms, even in the Hotel Ukraine in Moscow) — and a motley assortment of sandals and ankle socks. They were very friendly and tried to be helpful while smiling through their stainless steel teeth. But their service was as unrefined as the sugar and salt that were on the table. Russian food was heavy and rich. There was no fresh fruit available. I saw no bananas, oranges, grapefruit, or any tropical fruit of any kind anywhere in Russia, although our guide told us that bananas could be bought for twelve rubles each, about $1.10. In fact, we were all so starved for fresh fruit by the time we left that as soon as we landed in West Germany, we all dashed to buy dozens of oranges. I made my first western meal after Russia a feast of bananas, oranges, and grapefruit. We subsisted on the first course, which was usually a good *hors d'oeuvre* of smoked fish, rolls, cheese and tea (the coffee was terrible). But I enjoyed the sliced tomatoes soaked in sour cream, the sour bread, the sour cream cabbage soup, and the tumbler full of yogurt. I loved Russian ice cream which was served for dessert at every meal. There was one Russian dish, that, by unanimous consent, we considered delicious — chicken kiev. We had it at our farewell dinner along with Russian champagne.

Muscovites were proud of their underground railway. It was fabulous. The total length of all operating lines was only sixty-five kilometres with forty-seven stations. But the stations were lavish, spacious, flood-lit, air conditioned, spotless and magnificently decorated. They were veritable works of art. Each station had a distinctive theme such as the history of Moscow, the Russian theatre, or the Great Patriotic War against Hitler, and motifs inspired by the various republics. I especially liked the one dedicated to the memory of Russians who fought and died in World War I. It was very modern in stainless steel, blue glazed tile, and the murals depicted actions of the three services. All were palatial, rich, and ornate in their polished marble or glazed tile floors and walls, porcelain bas reliefs, paintings, sculptures, mosaic murals, stained glass decorations, and beautiful huge cut-glass chandeliers in bronze settings. This type of lighting was so different from strip flourescent lighting, that it never failed to impress a member of our party. I saw no advertisements, no graffiti. A long steep escalator descended deep into the underground where grey and green subway trains thundered to a standstill every 30 seconds. They were clean and fast, so fast that a few of our party missed their stop. Luckily, they got off at the next station and were able to take the next train back to where we were. What I liked best was that the name of each station would be pre-announced over a PA system. Three million passengers used the lines daily. The crowds were so thick that a friend of mine and I, straggling behind taking pictures, lost the others of our group. However, tourist parties were easily recognized, and just after we had asked an attendant, who was going to provide a helpful young man to look after us, our guide found us.

Muscovites were also very proud of their university. It was a colossal, sprawling architectural complex, the central building towering 700 feet high (thirty-two stories), had a clock on one of its side steeples larger than

Big Ben. When Larissa made this startling announcement
to our English group, a lively and challenging discussion
ensued. The university accommodated 25,000 students.
We visited the well-equipped classrooms, laboratories
(the science block alone had 700 laboratories), and
special reading rooms, where I noticed that each large
desk was fitted with map and newspaper racks. An
examination was in progress in one of the rooms. The
candidates were seated one beside the other on long
benches in elevated bleachers before long tables. "It
would be easy to copy," I exclaimed. Smiling, Larissa
informed us, "Sure, I did."

Russia spares no money on the education and training of its youth. There was an elite of specialists and
experts. But in our several days' search for the only
Roman Catholic Church in Moscow, Intourist officials
kept shunting us back and forth because there just
weren't any "experts on churches."

Nurseries were provided for infants as young as two
months. In the cities, education was compulsory from
seven to sixteen, in the country seven to seventeen.
Music, ballet, and art instruction was free. Promising
students were paid a monthly stipend. The Russians
believed that education could transform the whole of
human nature. This was the supreme aim of Communist
ideology.

We acquired Sasha in Moscow when Larissa felt that
our group was too large to handle on her own. I honestly
think that some of us were giving her a hard time. Larissa
was very temperamental and emotional, and when questions would get too tough, her throat was always too
sore to answer. She was exasperating at times. When we
used the phrases "must you," and "are you allowed to,"
she was hot in her denunciations, and would retort, "We

don't have to do anything; we are free." She was touchy and sensitive when Anne and I wanted to give her a pair of lovely nylons. She would not accept them. We wanted to thank her for getting the address of the only Roman Catholic Church in Moscow (there were no telephone directories). After several days, we discovered why. She thought that we were giving her the nylons because we thought she was poor. We finally convinced her otherwise. Sasha proved to be a Godsend. Twenty-four years old, speaking perfect English and Chinese, he could have passed for any young Westerner with his crew cut, imported shoes from Czechoslovakia, and imported Italian sun glasses. We had so many interesting chats that I came to regard him as a pet. True, he had all the answers. I accused him of memorizing the Russian catechism on the one hundred Favourite Questions of Tourists. He admitted all guides studied International Law. I found him serious, intelligent, absolutely certain that his system was the right one to the point of stating that it didn't have any flaws. Dedicated, he had a missionary zeal for the Communist system. I couldn't help respecting his intense loyalty and patriotism.

Naturally, Sasha and I disagreed on many things. Sasha claimed that the regime, only in its forty-first year, had made significant industrial progress. I agreed, especially in relation to space exploration. After all, they had produced Sputnik. "But then, we can't always be the champ," I jokingly stated. "Perhaps," I naively asked, "these achievements have been secured by time rather than by socialism?" In all fairness none of the guides ever flaunted this Russian "first," and their new superiority. They kept stressing they wanted peace.

The topic of religion was always a controversial one. Even though his mother was Russian Orthodox, and had

icons around the house and prayed, Sasha didn't believe
in God, claiming that religious belief was a form of
oppression, that it interfered with progress, and that it
preserved the old order and status quo. Religion was not
taught in the schools. In fact, the whole history surrounding Christ was completely left out of Russian
history books.

We exchanged views on the political and economic
scene. "We have a socialist system now," he claimed,
"but we are striving for a classless society." I admired this
striving for perfection. And yet, how could I admire it
when it was being achieved through force and a monolithic unity of thought that was repugnant to me.

At first he asked no questions about my country, but
once his curiosity was peeked, he asked many questions:
"You have many political parties but they have the same
platform? You can criticize your government, but can
you change your system? Our economy is steadily going
up, yours goes up and down. Why does yours go down?
Why do you have so much unemployment?"

He argued that Russia had no unemployment problem such as we had because the nation's energies were
controlled by a systematized, planned economy. Consumer goods, the standard of living, public ownership,
and the one-party system were our favourite topics of
conversation. Sasha always insisted his way of life was
best. In fact, he never would concede that it had any
flaws. I tried to remind him that our system had produced a better standard of living, and that capitalist
economic theories were creeping into their system. He
claimed that the war caused a great setback in their
planning. "We will surpass the industrial and agricultural production level of the U.S.A., if there is no war
and if the capitalist countries don't interfere in our

business. Come back to Russia in ten years, and then you will see for yourself what a one-party-system can achieve. Then I can prove to you which system is better."

I looked forward to seeing this future paradise of the worker, this proletarian Utopia, this Kingdom of Heaven on earth.

Czechoslovakia

As soon as we entered Czechoslovakia, a "people's democracy," as our guide, Lottie, a charming young woman, called it, I was impressed by the prosperity I saw. For the first time since we left Berlin I noticed that the homes were painted and the farms well kept. Of course, I kept reminding myself that there was little or no war damage here.

And yet as we passed through many small towns, I noticed innumerable abandoned shops, especially restaurants, the owner's names still faintly visible, relics of the passing age of private enterprise, for everything, as in Poland, was state owned and operated. We passed several factory towns with blocks and blocks of workers' flats, all topped with TV antennae, because, as in Russia, TV sets were very inexpensive.

I hadn't seen one red star in Poland, but along the way to Prague, the capital, I kept seeing huge red stars: red stars encircling hammers and sickles on the front of trains, trolley cars, and buses, mounted on factory roofs, on the roofs of public buildings, and even on private homes. Prague itself was covered with slogans on red banners such as "Friendship with the Soviet Union," "The Soviet Union our example," and "Peace With the Soviet Union Forever."

Czechoslovakia, like the model democratic republic it was after the First World War, was now the model satellite, since its takeover by the Communists. I recalled the views of a few Poles whom I had met: the Czechs were too conformist, too docile. They had conformed to the Germans, and now they were conforming to the Russians. But, as Lottie explained, the Czechs had attempted an underground partisan movement many times, but there were too many traitors: "And so we wear our mask-like expressions and resign ourselves to the contemporary scene with that eternal hope that a system based on fear, hate and force will eventually crumble."

Lottie was a Pole by birth, but during the war she lived in England, a Polish refugee. While there, she married a Czech and, after the war, went to live in Prague where her husband deserted her soon after their arrival. Stranded, and with no knowledge of the language, she was forced to earn her own living. Energetic, resourceful and aggressive, she luckily was given a permit to work as a dressmaker. She remarried, and when Czechoslovakia began promoting tourism, she became a guide. But she was soon fired because she had too many Western contacts (a sister in England). However, after three months, through the influence of her mother-in-law, who was the secretary of the local Communist committee, she got her job back.

We had many interesting conversations, and she confessed she lived in constant fear. She wouldn't dare speak her mind with her in-laws or friends, because she couldn't know whether or not there was an informer among them. There were many secret police, she said, especially in hotels, and many political prisoners. (In Poland, if there were this sort of police terror, I certainly wasn't aware of it.) As in Russia, the Czech government used education from the time of birth to indoctrinate Communist ideology. Lottie then told this story to illustrate the government's attempt to distort and warp the truth in the minds of the young:

> the Ministry of Education told the primary pupils in my daughter's school that they were fortunate to have a lovely school, because schools in England were white-washed stables. My little daughter, who had attended an English school, stood up and exclaimed: "No, no, that's not true — we even had free lunches and free milk."

Naturally, Lottie had much explaining to do when her daughter came home. "I had to warn her," she said, "that she must never do that again or even talk about England for the safety of the family."

"Why don't you try to leave?" I asked.

"My husband has an artificial leg. We can't flee, I've tried many times through the various embassies. It's impossible. I know you just can't understand it," she said. "You'd have to live here."

I was glad that I didn't.

Religion was not encouraged, but tolerated. Churches and church property were owned by the State. Priests were paid by the state. Religious instruction was given outside of school hours. I saw no monks or nuns in Prague. But we were allowed to visit the world-famous shrine to the Infant Jesus of Prague. I recall expressing my desire to buy a few religious articles. To Lottie's surprise, and my disappointment, the shop was closed. But on the morning that we were leaving Prague, Lottie handed me a little package. To my amazement and delight, it was a small statue of the Infant Jesus of

Prague. She had not forgotten. Nor will I ever forget her little deed of kindness.

Prague, the city of 1,000 spires, was a charming composite of past and present. Old picturesque Prague, the city of Good King Wenceslaus and the church reformer, John Huss, delighted me. There was practically no war destruction. Ancient monuments and memorials were still standing. Modern Prague looked prosperous with its bustling life on wide streets.

"More prosperous than last summer even," observed an English head school mistress who had visited Prague the year before. In fact, it looked like any Western European city except for the innumerable slogans and the many military men looking extremely smart and well-groomed. The shops had gorgeous window arrangements with all the glamour and sophistication of the west. I would even compare them favourably to the ones on the exclusive Königs Allee of Dusseldorf, the Paris of Germany. I suppose the memory of a once highly competitive society can't be entirely stamped out even in a totalitarian state.

Western touches were everywhere: girls in slacks and shorts, forbidden in the streets of Russia; men wearing suede shoes; telephone directories, unknown in Russia; waiters with ties; food served with the refined touch of western cuisine. I saw huge silver platters being used for the first time since we had left Berlin. In fact, the people were very conscious of the west. Our local guide who told me that she had been the Girl Guide Commissioner for Prague, was looking forward to being Adlai Stevenson's private guide in a few days' time, and that she became a tourist guide in order to meet western people. She was starved for western contact: "Unfortunately there are not enough tourists from the west."

To crown our last day's stay behind the Iron Curtain, the manager of our Prague hotel presented the ladies in our group at our farewell dinner with half a dozen carnations, and the men with an extra dessert of meringue topped with whipped cream. I breathed a sigh of relief when we crossed the Czech-German frontier with its electric barbed wire curtain.

And miraculously my period ended. Instead of having a normal period throughout my trip behind the Iron Curtain, I continued to bleed weeks after it should have stopped. This unusual bleeding increased my anxiety and discomfort. I was afraid that I had a serious illness and was going to bleed to death. But Anne reassured me that my body was simply reacting to the emotional stress and that she had experienced the same problem when her mother died. But I continued to worry, and lived in terror of my Kotex bleeding through. (I never thought I could write those words.) It was rumoured that Russian women used wads of cotton rather than sanitary napkins. In desperation Anne and I would tear up bathroom towels and I would sit on layers of newspapers while on the tour bus and dash out into the forest whenever we stopped for tea.

My trip in the Eastern bloc countries had been a personally harrowing experience but I had witnessed a great modern power that had survived the horrors of a revolution and two world wars.

U.S.S.R., 1982

In 1982, twenty-four years after my first trip to the U.S.S.R. I revisited the Soviet Union with a group of Canadians to find out whether socialist philosophy and the power of the people had been able to produce "the future paradise of the worker." By this time the Soviets had launched the first man into space (Yuri Gagarin), the first woman (Valentina Tereshkova), the first man to walk in space (Alexsi Leonov) and Earth's first soft landing on the moon, thus maintaining their commanding lead in space exploration.

We departed from Montreal's Mirabel Airport on an Ilyushin-62 jet of Aeroflot Soviet Airlines on 12 August 1982 at 18:10. The plane was run down. I could see water trickling down by my side and the service was poor. We arrived at Sheremetyevo Airport the next day at 11:50.

The following day we flew from Moscow to Irkutsk, the capital of Siberia, a distance of 3,223 miles. I had always thought of Sibera as an empty wasteland, a hostile land of forced labour camps for Soviet dissidents. I was surprised to find a flourishing urban centre of nearly 500,000 people, founded more than three hundred years ago as the starting point for the first Russian trade caravan routes to China.

It was a beautiful day when we arrived, and during our city tour I was intrigued by the intricate designs of the sculptured woodwork on the facias and shutters of the wooden houses which stood in stark contrast to the huge, bold concrete structures of the major cities.

Touring the Siberian countryside, I noted a world no different from the boreal forest of Northwestern Ontario. Nor was the terrain any more forbidding and inhospitable.

As we drove to Lake Baikal (Russia's sacred sea) our guide expounded on its uniqueness: it was over three million years old; the abundance and variety of its life forms were found nowhere else in the world (e.g. a freshwater seal; its hot springs percolated in its waters and on its sides; its setting in a rift valley surrounded by mountains made it over a mile deep. I was impressed. But when he told us that it was the largest fresh water lake in the world I had to disagree.

Having grown up on Lake Superior's shores, I knew that my lake was. And when he told us that the waves on Baikal could rise as high as fifteen feet, I explained that in 1975, the *Edmund Fitzgerald* was sunk in waves of over forty feet. Our discussion on the two great lakes ended with our agreeing that although Lake Baikal was deeper, Lake Superior was larger. And although I could respect Baikal's age and uniqueness, my heart belonged to Superior.

From Irkutsk we flew to Alma-Ata, the capital of Kazakhstan and to our amazement, saw a gigantic skating rink where Olympic speed skaters practised.

And then we toured the three legendary Asian towns on the fabled ancient silk route to China: Tashkent, Samarkand, and Bakhara, which, despite their turbulent history, preserve their former grandeur and the matchless beauty of their shrines.

In Samarkand, one such shrine was the Registan ensemble comprising three monumental *madrasahs* (Islamic Colleges). The Soviet authorities were in the process of restoring them, but even in their deteriorated condition they were simply awe-inspiring. Their towering minarets, elegant columns, and vast domes faced in flawless multi-coloured glazed mosaic tile with floral motifs, calligraphy and geometric patterns were a wonder to behold. I was reminded of the Islamic artistic beauty I had seen in Izfehan (Iran) years ago. Today I have forgotten the names of the Islamic mosques and *madrasahs*, but the blue mosaic radiance of huge majestic domes and tall and slender minarets is rivetted in memory.

From the ancient architectural splendour of the Islamic world we went to Sochi on the Russian Riviera on the Black Sea, the largest and most popular resort and health spa in the Soviet Union. It was hot and muggy. After the beauty of the three cities we had left, Sochi was downright ugly. I couldn't wait to leave.

If I had been unprepared for the beauty of Islamic architecture, I was even more unprepared for the beauty I witnessed in Leningrad (now St. Petersburg). It was the city that Peter the Great had built on the River Neva in the eighteenth century to rival Venice. In 1917 this imperial city of the Romanovs fell to the revolutionaries. It is one of the ironies of the Revolution that the Bolsheviks did not destroy the buildings of the royal family they so abhorred. In World War II, one and one-half million people died defending the city during the nine hundred day siege when Hitler's troops tried to capture it. (Half of Leningrad's population starved to death.)

The city has been restored to its original architectural grandeur and beauty. It was absolutely stunning with its colourful onion-shaped domes, spires, cupolas and the magnificent ornate imperial palaces of green and blue, pink, yellow and white which were reflected in the waters of the canals. We visited the celebrated Hermitage Museum in the Winter Palace, which is one of the world's treasure chests of art. As I followed our Intourist guide from one gallery to the other, my amazement grew. There were so many masterpieces: Italian, Dutch, Spanish, English. So many French impressionists — Renoir, Degas, Cezanne, Gauguin — whom I love. I paused to admire Rousseau's "Tropical Forest," El Greco's "St. Peter and St. Paul," Joshua Reynold's "Cupid untying the zone of Venus," and da Vinci's "Madonna with a Flower." Each time the guide had to pull me away.

On the twenty-first day of our tour we returned to Moscow. Sasha, our Moscow guide of twenty-five years ago, had told me to return in ten years "to see what a one-party-system could achieve." After a quarter of a century I did not see much improvement. Moscow had spread out to the suburbs and had built blocks of tenements in the Stalinist neo-classical style. Television masts still crowded the roofs. There was still an extreme housing shortage. The women still looked dowdy in their simple flowered frocks. I still saw no fresh fruit and vegetables. There was still a total absence of the style and opulence visible in the streets of any western city of comparable size. It seemed that the Soviet citizen was no better off than he was twenty-five years ago. His ideal state, the proletarian Utopia, was still only a dream.

THE ORIENT AND MIDDLE EAST, 1959

After three wonderful years of teaching in the Department of National Defence schools in Germany and France, I returned to my teaching job at Hillcrest High School. But I still wanted to travel. I had been infected by wanderlust. The thought of circling the globe lured me. Miss Rutledge, who was the long-time Head of the Commercial Department at Hillcrest, caught my travel bug and decided to come with me around the world the very next summer. We were to meet Miss Marjorie Copping, a French teacher at the Fort William Collegiate Institute, in Singapore. Except for a few missionaries in India whom Miss Rutledge knew, and Miss Copping, who had already been in the South Pacific, we knew nobody else who had visited Asia. Miss Rutledge and I agreed not to nail ourselves to a firm itinerary. We made few preparations and harboured no expectations. I relied on what I had learned in my childhood Geography and History classes. I wanted my trip to be full of surprises. The wonder engendered by just being in strange places is an attraction in itself.

Before 1959, Europe was the preferred destination. Today, Asia has become trendy. Television and motion pictures have brought Asia into our very living rooms. We watched the Vietnam War on television. We can see "Ghandi" and "Seven Years in Tibet" on video. But my companions and I were there before anybody heard of the Vietcong, the Khmer Rouge and the Killing Fields. We were there before karma and mantra and guru be-

came household words. We were there before the beat-
niks and the hippies discovered India, Nepal and
Afghanistan. We were there before Asians found their
own voices, before Salmon Rushdie, Vikram Seth,
Bharati Mukherjee, Rohinton Mistry and Kazuo
Ishiguro began writing their post-colonial literature.

Our trip did not start with a bang. Our flight from
Thunder Bay to Winnipeg was grounded because of
poor weather. The C.P.R. agent, Mr. Little, fortunately
found us places on a freight train bound for Winnipeg
where we had to go to get our cholera, yellow fever and
typhus shots. Paradoxically, we would be flying west to
get to the Far East.

Hawaii

On 28 June 1959, after a non-stop flight from Vancou-
ver to Honolulu, we arrived in Hawaii.

Hawaii was a girl's hair adorned with hibiscus. It
was walking down Waikiki's famous Kalakaua Avenue in
bare feet, shorts, and a gaudy aloha shirt and feeling
right at home. It was sensing a little of the mystery of the
East, knowing you were some place different, and then
walking into a shiny drugstore and having a hamburger
and a malted. It was clear skies, white sands, balmy
breezes. It was just lying on Waikiki Beach.

Hawaii was a tourist in a silly hat of green leaves. It
was a tourist wearing a lei, the scented flower garland of
carnations or orchids. It was complete freedom. Wear
what you like — pedal pushers, a lace shirt, a *muumuu*
(cotton print nightgown) or *holoku* (a long loose princess style dress). Our slim and lovely hostess at a dinner
party wore a cherry red *holoku,* and she looked stunning.

Hawaii was a paradise for the nature lover. Exotic tropical flora in the most gorgeous colours thrived: orchids and birds of paradise, breadfruit and flame trees. Huge trees like the banyan flourished there. High mountains, extinct and active volcanoes, sheltered bays, and lush valleys blended to constitute vistas beautiful to see. And thanks to a public-spirited ladies' organization that had fought to preserve the beautiful scenery, there were no billboards to blemish the purity of the natural surroundings.

Hawaii was a history of kings and queens with such fascinating Polynesian musical names, like Kamehameha and Liliuopalani. Memories of Hawaiian monarchs still lived because parliament met in the former throne room of the Iolani Palace, the only royal palace in the United States. We visited Kawaisho Church, the Westminster Abbey of former Hawaiian kings, and saw the statue of King Kamehameha who had conquered all the islands.

Hawaii was Pearl Harbour, where more than 1,000 crew members are still trapped in the sunken hold of the "Arizona." This left me numb. Lost in reverie, I recalled the tragic history on that awful day of 7 December 1941 when the American naval-military complex came under a fierce surprise Japanese aerial attack. Even more poignant was the Pacific War Memorial cemetery in Punchbowl Crater with its 14,000 small, plain white stone slabs in neat and tidy rows.

Hawaii was Japanese, Chinese, Korean, Hawaiian, Filipino and American, all living harmoniously together. It was this sight that induced in me a hope for the future, that perhaps the stone slabs did not stand in vain. Hawaii was Robert Louis Stevenson's grass hut where he wrote his adventure stories. It was now situated on the grounds of the Waioli tea room operated by The Salvation Army.

The tea room staff were going on a holiday to Canada the following week, through the generosity of Calgary's mayor.

Hawaii was pineapple and sugarcane. At the Dole pineapple cannery, I don't know how many pineapple rings I consumed, nor how many paper cups of pineapple juice I drained.

Hawaii was fascination. It was lovelier than I dreamed; and more industrialized than I had thought. Its magic wove a spell on this *malihini* (foreigner) so that I cannot rest until I hear the trade winds whisper again, the surf murmur, the palm trees sway, and the hula dancers chant, *Aloha*!

Japan

Except for American GIs, very few tourists visited Japan in 1959. In the west, sushi and tofu were not popular foods; the haiku was not a recognized verse form, and sumo wrestling, growing bonsai trees, and calligraphy were not widely known.

We left Honolulu, the capital of Hawaii, on Thursday, 2 July at ten p.m. After a flight of twenty hours, including a brief stopover on Wake Island, we arrived in Japan on Saturday morning at noon, having crossed the International Date Line somewhere in the Pacific and losing one day.

My first impression was disappointment. I was expecting a land ablaze in sunshine and flowers. But it was raining and no flowers lined the highway to the hotel as we had seen in Hawaii. Cherry blossom time had passed. We would have intermittent pouring rain, drizzle, fog and mist during our whole visit. Despite the terrible weather, travelling in Japan was a joy. We stayed on the main island of Honshu, exploring it from fast and punctual electric trains and on foot, unafraid and confident. We could not blend into the homogeneous scene, and we felt strange going out in a city where we could not speak the language, but there wasn't a predicament from which we could not extricate ourselves.

Travelling by train was interesting. I liked the three musical note gong which preceded announcements. The Japanese trains were very crowded. Passengers must sit close to each other, and because the trains run so smoothly and quietly, it was very easy to doze off. On several occasions, I found Japanese men sleeping on my lap.

We had to keep constant watch for our desired stops because the trains stop briefly and their automatic doors open and close quickly. Once we got off two stations too soon. Fortunately, trains run very often, and in twenty minutes we were able to board another, and continue to our destination.

On the trains, watching the Japanese fascinated me. I watched them eat their lunch with chopsticks out of wooden boxes, called *bentoh*, divided into neat compartments for their boiled rice, fish and seaweed.

Watching them drink their tea was fun too. The Japanese love their tea. And just as the western newsie used to shout, "soft drinks, sandwiches and coffee," the girl vendors on Japanese trains shout, "tea, fruit, box lunches." There is one difference, however. The Japanese vendor is a well-groomed young girl in a spotless blue uniform and white gloves who carries individual small pottery teapots with wire handles and ceramic lids that also serve as cups, plus a kettle of boiling water. Miss Rutledge would have her cup of tea on the train while I ate oranges.

Japanese are obsessively clean and hygiene conscious. The saluting railroad station masters, drawn up stiffly at attention in immaculate navy blue uniforms always wore spotless white gloves. Japanese men wore beautifully laundered white shirts and carried fans in their back pockets as well as damp towels in their briefcases, which they would wrap around their necks and wipe their hands and faces with. We even saw a few wearing smog masks.

I also enjoyed watching well-behaved Japanese school children in their uniforms, with blue pleated skirts and white middies, white running shoes, and ankle socks, and with school bags strapped to their backs, chewing gum and eating candy and ice cream.

As we watched from our train windows, the countryside fascinated us. Except for a few flowers such as hydrangeas and dahlias, the countryside was spread with a beautiful, magnificent carpet of various shades of lush green. The lush green rice paddies which we passed were dotted with pure white herons, and were meticulously nursed and cared for by hundreds of women in blue and white polka-dot baggy trousers and large straw hats. My astonishment grew daily as I watched them at their back-breaking work, bent over from the waist, with water up to their knees, working in the pelting rain with only a plastic sheet or a bamboo mat on their backs to protect them. The rice, which would be harvested in November, was about one month old. After the rice harvest, wheat would be planted, but hemp was being harvested now.

Besides paddy fields there were tea plantations and vegetable gardens. Every inch of land was cultivated. The Japanese must be the best gardeners in the world because the neat and tiny farms which we passed were simply a delight to see.

We visited a number of Buddhist temples and Shinto shrines in Kyoto, Kamakura, Nara and Nikko and admired the simplicity and purity of their architecture, and the Zen restraint associated with Japanese aesthetics. I contemplated the mind that created them and the religion that inspired them. These historic monuments attested to the glory and splendour of bygone civilizations. But, as mysterious and alluring as they were, they did not overwhelm me, as did the Alhambra at Granada in Spain and the Parthenon of Athens. If their temples and shrines could not overawe me, however, the exquisitely designed gardens which surround them revealed a Zen aesthetic of excellence and refinement. The Kasuga Shinto Shrine in Nara and the 3,000 bronze and stone lanterns that line the avenue leading to it stand in perfect harmony with its natural setting. Patterned on classical lines with some shrubbery, water and rockery, the gardens were an escape into a world of beauty and art. In their natural settings of tall pines and streams, I found refreshing repose.

In spite of the West's invasion of Japan, traditional religions survived. I saw hundreds of pilgrims and young white-robed Shinto priests wearing wooden sandals milling about their shrines. Even though the Emperor had publicly renounced his divinity (a renunciation forced on him by the Americans), most of the rural Japanese believed he was divine. As Shintoists, they believed that there were gods everywhere. Mountains, rivers, trees, and rocks were gods who took care of them while they were alive. They also deified their great men; their heroes became gods. All over Japan were *torii*, gateways made of wood that served as entrances to the

Shinto spiritual world. And every home had a small shrine to the memory of the family's ancestors, and services were held every morning and night to venerate them, because old age was considered an honour, not a disgrace. We watched a procession during a Festival of Lanterns celebration that honoured their ancestors. The Japanese believed that the spirits of their dead relatives visited them every year for four days in July. So they celebrated the happy return of the spirits. At the same time, some Japanese are Buddhists. It is interesting to note that funerals are held in Buddhist temples, and weddings in Shinto shrines.

Fortune tellers in the shrines practised a booming trade. They had hundreds of gimmicks from crystal gazers to lucky numbers. If your fortune was a bad one, you hung it up on a tree near a pagoda and the bad luck would disappear. The trees around the shrines were covered with numerous pieces of paper, knotted and tied to the branches. Anyone could pray to the Shinto gods for good health, business success, or a marriage partner.

With a payment of one hundred yen, Miss Rutledge asked for happiness and was rewarded. She and I, more-over, were assured life for one hundred years because we successfully climbed and descended the highly slippery Shinkyo Sacred Bridge, a crimson-red lacquered bridge in Nikko.

The devout made a variety of offerings such as food, rice, melons, tea, candy, fruit, flowers. In front of the colossal sitting Buddha, at Kamakura, cast in bronze in 1252, I saw a large bowl of pomelos (like our grape-fruit).

In their flower arranging and tea ceremonies, the Japanese had achieved the height of refinement. I was so enchanted by the green tea ceremony that I saw it performed twice. The art of making and drinking tea followed traditional ritual. Movements were slow, quiet and deliberate, and every detail counted. Where so much behaviour was ceremonial, all gestures were important. Our hostess, sitting on the floor with legs tucked respectfully behind her, and feet covered with spotless *tabi* (Japanese socks), made a number of low bows throughout the ceremony. First, she passed cocktail tidbits, then she served pink, green and black serrated gum drop sticks which I enjoyed. The most important guest, usually the oldest (in this case Miss Rutledge) received her tea first. The hostess, who assumed the proper decorum kept her eyes cast downwards as she turned the tea cup counter clockwise several times with her fingers placed precisely around the rim of the cup. The cup's design faced the guests. A low lacquer cabinet housed all the ingredients for the ceremony and rested beside her. Although I sat enthralled, I couldn't drink the bitter green tea, but good manners dictated that I take a sip and make an audible sound.

A geisha house showed the same Japanese love for beauty, harmony and tranquillity. When you entered, you first took off your shoes. Then you were provided with a pair of slippers that were too big for you. You then dragged your feet to a typical Japanese room where small low tables were arranged in a "U" fashion. You sat cross-legged and shifted through various contortions until you found relief. I didn't find relief because I was not accustomed to sitting on a cushion on the floor for very long. However, you tried to forget the pain in your back because on the small table in front of you was a plate of *hors d'oeuvres* of cheese, ham, hard-boiled egg, and soy beans. A geisha, pretty in her colourful kimono costume, elaborate hairdo, and white painted face, gave you a hot wash cloth to wipe your hands and face.

A geisha's training took from three to five years, and the profession usually stayed within the same families. She learned to entertain: to sing, to dance, and to make conversation. At our geisha party, our geisha danced barefoot to a chant, a drum and a *koto*, a three-stringed plucked instrument. The dances were more like pantomimes, each movement symbolic of a season, tea picking, or an umbrella. We played baseball in pantomime. It was fun to hear the geishas give the commands: "Throw the ball, hit the ball, change bases — You win — I lose." Baseball is a favourite Japanese sport, although tennis is running a close second since the royal heir met his commoner wife on a tennis court and the romance was the talk of the country. Then we played a "Christian" game, as our geisha called "musical chairs," except that pillows took the place of chairs. The girls couldn't exhaust their repertoire of games: we picked up kewpie dolls with chop sticks, and we "dug coal." The girls were young and pretty, but I felt that the games were childish.

Traditional Japanese theatre had long enjoyed fame, and I could now understand why. On the largest stage I have ever seen, I saw *The Tale of Genji* a classic Kabuki drama, where all the characters are played by males in traditional make-up. It was a glorious spectacle, stylized like opera. Although I didn't understand the language, I admired the ravishing costumes, the fabulous settings and the calibre of acting. And I witnessed again that flair for harmony and desire for perfection. I was truly disappointed when our guide let us stay for only one-half hour because he thought we would be bored by a play lasting nearly five hours.

I also enjoyed Japanese modern theatre. In the Kokusai theatre of Tokyo, over 300 young women in costumes ranging from beautiful flowered kimonos and wooden *getas* to glittering scanty western dress staged a modern dance revue. The sets were a feast for my eyes. And I wasn't surprised when one of the acts was baseball. Surprisingly, however, there were no intermissions. One act followed the other in rapid succession until twenty of them were completed in one solid sweep.

A Japanese restaurant also revealed an aesthetic of simplicity and refinement. We had sukiyaki at a typical inn. It was pouring rain and so a porter, holding a large umbrella, protected us from the car to the door of the inn. We took our shoes off in the small vestibule (everything in Japan is small). Our waitress in kimono met us and we see-sawed the usual courtesies. The Japanese take their time in their greetings and farewells; they consider handshaking and kissing unsanitary (only in public, I'm sure). We raised our feet to have our slippers pushed on while we were supported by the porter. Then we were ushered in through a small, narrow corridor past several small rooms to our special room. There were no windows of glass but windows of translucent paper, probably mulberry or rice paper. There were no curtains. There were screens, sliding doors and the *takanoma*, an alcove in the room where a vase of flowers is kept and a scroll is placed on the wall. Our *takanoma* also boasted an incense burner. The *takanoma* is the focal point of the room, and the most important person always sits with his back to the high point. In the centre of the room was a low table with two cushions. The floor was covered with a wall to wall woven rice straw matting called *tatami*. We managed to sit on our pillows.

Our waitress entered and closed the sliding doors. Quietly, but pleasantly, she began to prepare our sukiyaki before us. She served us each a beaten raw egg in a bowl, and I immediately recalled the raw egg of my first restaurant meal in Germany. However, we soon discovered its role. The very, very thin slices of beef that she deep fried in a pan on top of a portable gas stove were dipped in the raw egg. They were absolutely delicious. Naturally, there was a bowl of steamed rice and a variety of Japanese vegetables on a large platter. We sipped hot saki which I didn't like, and our waitress served each of us one at a time. I appreciated the waitress's graciousness, the delicious food and the relaxed serenity in the room. When I left, I noticed that my shoes, which I had left haphazardly the way they came off, were neatly placed side by side, ready for me to slip into. Again our waitress came to say goodbye with the little obeisances, and the umbrella man protected us to the taxi.

While we were left alone in our private room to finish our meal at our leisure, I visited the bathroom, because I wanted to see what a Japanese bathroom was like. All fixtures were smaller and closer to the floor than ours. In fact, the toilet was just a hole in the floor, with a porcelain rim and two raised, corrugated porcelain foot-shaped imprints.

My curiosity got the better of me in Miyonashita too, when we asked two American gentlemen who were staying in a traditional Japanese inn if we could see their bedroom. Slippers were provided, of course, at the street level of the hotels, and a *yukata* (housecoat) in each bedroom. There were no bedsteads, but mattresses were placed on the floor. There was no dining room. All meals were taken in your room. Your waitress served you and even fanned you while you ate, and looked after you in a quiet way.

Of course, Western ideas had taken over in many ways. There was a "brown hair" craze. Many of the girls had dyed their glossy black hair brown. At a very swish Tokyo night club, I noticed that most of the hostesses did not wear kimonos but gorgeous, long gowns, mostly strapless and bare back. Many of the floor shows were poor Western copies. I was disappointed that there were no acts with a pure Japanese flavour.

The Japanese are a formal and proper people. Only once do I recall spontaneous laughter, and as soon as it was over, the well-ordered and proper behaviour resumed. Curiously, it happened on our second attempt to see Mt. Fuji, Japan's most famous sacred mountain. The first attempt had been a complete fiasco because the whole country was completely cloaked in the thickest fog I have ever tried to see through. Consequently, because our time was limited, we wanted to make certain our second attempt would not fail. The tourist guide at the Fujiyama Hotel in Miyanoshita (one of the most charming hotels I have ever stayed at), with its mountain setting and many private mineral baths, recommended a bus route that served the local people in out-of-the way places. She warned us that it was not for fussy tourists. We were the only westerners on the bus, but we didn't mind, accustomed as we were to this, many times on the trains.

The road to Mt. Fuji was a narrow trail, newly blazed, with huge rocks and deep holes, winding its way up and up. The driver was skilful, however. I was enjoying the scenery, when, all of a sudden, my head hit the luggage rack and the Japanese roared. Then it suddenly dawned on us why they were all at the front of the bus;

and we two foreigners were the only ones at the back. By the time we moved all our belongings to the front, the outburst of laughter had subsided and the passengers had resumed their dignity and silence. It was also comical watching the young ticket girls jump off the bus, run to the back and whistle directions to the driver. And when the bus was about to cross rail tracks, the girls jumped off, ran across the tracks, and blew their whistles to indicate that the tracks were clear.

Incidentally, we did see the snow-covered cone of Mt. Fuji dominating the landscape just as billowing white clouds magically hung back.

The Japanese had made a spectacular economic post-war recovery. Tokyo was Asia's most westernized city with its modern skyscrapers, new construction, its bustling crowds and entertaining nightlife. Its nine million people made Tokyo, in 1959, the largest city in the world.

As a result, there was an extreme housing shortage. We could see the congested, cramped living conditions. Small, black, unpainted wooden houses that looked like packing boxes were stacked one on top of the other and left exposed to the weather. There were no chimneys and no clothes lines. Washing was hung on bamboo poles (no clothes pins were used; the items of clothing were pulled through the poles). Wages were still low. An elementary school teacher earned about forty-five dollars a month; a high school teacher, one hundred dollars; an interpreter about $140.

Tokyo was a neon world at night. I was dazzled by the numerous flashing neon lights and beautiful illuminations that lit up Ginza Street, Tokyo's most famous shopping district. Tokyo's taxis, however, could be frightening. Drivers shouted their way through, weaving

in and out of traffic, on crowded streets, suddenly rico-
cheting us to our destination.

The American presence was still strongly felt. Our
hotel in Tokyo, the Imperial, specially designed by Frank
Lloyd Wright to withstand the earthquakes that frequently erupt in Japan, was filled with American
businessmen.

American regulations were still in force. In the ancient city of Kamakura, I noticed an English sign, "No
smoking while walking." And at the statue of the Great
Buddha a sign in English said, "Don't climb on the statue
as it is considered sacred."

Although western aid had certainly been a large
factor in Japan's economic recovery, the Japanese character also played an important role. The Japanese
worked hard. In a Tokyo park I did not see power lawn
mowers, but groups of crouching women cutting grass
with small scythes. I saw men and women crushing rocks
by hand and carrying them in two baskets attached to a
pole over their shoulders. They were thrifty. Even in our
luxury hotel in Tokyo, I saw the desk staff using recycled
paper for memo pads. I also saw them using bags made
of pasted newspapers. Their desire for perfection made
them also pay attention to minute details. This pursuit
of excellence was revealed in Japanese craft and lacquer
ware, damascene work, silks, wood-block prints, porcelain, pottery, dolls, and fans. This desire for accuracy
struck me when a Japanese man on a train asked me
whether the "t" in *often* was pronounced and whether
the accent fell on "of" or "course" in the expression "of
course."

Hong Kong

We were ready to leave Japan for Hong Kong. Just before take-off time, Pan-Am told us we were "bumped off" the flight. They offered us two choices: stay another day (Sunday) in Tokyo, or fly later in the evening on Air India. Miss Rutledge didn't want to stay another day. I wasn't particularly interested in either option. After a spirited discussion we finally decided to fly Air India.

After the fuss in Japan and the overnight flight we arrived next morning in Hong Kong, grimy, greasy and tired. To our disappointment our hotel room was not ready and we grudgingly took a guided tour of Hong Kong to fill in the time. Surprisingly, I enjoyed the private car tour. A striking, tall, middle-aged Italian artist with long gray hair and a wonderful mustache entertained us. He was living in Paris, and had exhibitions in New York from time to time. Now on a Far Eastern tour, he was sketching its exotic peoples and sights.

He would give money lavishly to the countless little street urchins carrying baby brothers or sisters on their hips or backs. He was never confronted with the problem most tourists face about "professional" begging. My friend gave willy-nilly. To see pathetic little waifs smile in glee as prospects of ice cream or candy danced in their eyes gladdened his heart. His generosity impressed me, and I kept reminding myself of this whenever he became impatient with our picture-taking. He carried no camera. I sympathized with his anger because I knew what it was like being without a camera in a group of enthusiastic shutter-bugs.

Hong Kong was fascinating. We stayed longer than we had expected. Pat Pang, a former Hillcrest pupil, was visiting Hong Kong with his family, and introduced us to the charming Kan family, a cultured and refined family with roots for generations in Hong Kong shipbuilding. They completely took charge, not in any obtrusive manner, but whenever we were free, they were. Consequently, we saw many more native sights, heard many more native noises and smelled many more native odours than we ever could have on our own.

Traditional Chinese culture survives in Hong Kong amidst the most modern Western amenities. We were fortunate that our friends showed us the Chinese side of Hong Kong: Chinese food in floating restaurants, Chinese opera, circus, theatre and movies, Chinese tea houses, plays, and dances.

The Chinese meal I remember best was at a Buddhist monastery. About twelve of us, seated around a circular table enjoyed a nine-course vegetarian delight from soya beans and rice, to mushrooms and almonds, to seaweed and cashews. I appreciated the hot, wet face cloths provided before and after meals.

At the Po Hing (All is Joy) Opera House in Kowloon we sat for a five-hour-long performance of a Chinese opera. I don't know whether I would choose to hear one again. It was a lavish spectacle of dialogue, music, song and dance. The orchestra was very noisy and loud because of the harsh wail of horns, the bashing of drums and the clashing of cymbals, the piercing notes of two-stringed fiddles, the chiming of bells, and the ringing of gongs that accompanied the action on stage. The singing, to my Western ears, was discordant, because the arias were astonishingly high pitched. Whether it was a ribbon dance, or a monkey or sword dance, the dancing was acrobatic and spectacular. The antic movements of the masked drama on the Ramayana theme (a great

Sanskrit epic, one of the holy books of the Hindus) were especially funny to a Western observer. Costumes were fabulous and much more elaborate and ornate than we were accustomed to. Shimmering and sparkling with coloured stones and gold and silver threads, they dazzled me completely.

As we shuttled on *The Star* ferry that links Kowloon on the mainland and Victoria on Hong Kong Island, we picked our way through an assortment of water vehicles, sampans, tugs, fishing boats, motorboat taxies and tall junks, and became very much aware of the seething crowds, the noise, and the frantic tempo of the two thriving cities. On shore, we elbowed our way through a sea of people, feeling the hectic vitality: men doubled-over, pushed mobile hardware shops; skinny running men in tattered brown shorts pulled rickshaws; women, yoked to wicker baskets, trotted with babies on their backs; women in coolie hats carried large cans on bamboo poles; men pushed bicycles loaded with hay bales and firewood; people rode in horse drawn vehicles, or scooters; children carried baby brothers and sisters on their backs; shoeshine boys and joss stick pedlars shouted their wares and diaperless toddlers in slit open pants relieved themselves whenever and wherever they chose. The streets were a maze of narrow alleyways jammed with open-fronted small stalls, displaying a closely packed profusion of their wares in open sacks, baskets, trays, strung on wires, hung from pegs, dangling from rafters, piled on counters, draped from bamboo poles, spread out on the pavement, stacked in doorways, and thrown into boxes, all crowded into incredible confusion. In the doorway of a tiny cubbyhole I saw a tailor sitting in front of a foot pedal sewing machine. In another, a shoemaker. And in another a cooked food stall.

We visited the floating fishing village of Aberdeen where sampans and junks were closely packed together and scores of people were packed like sardines in their small boats. These boat people live their entire lives on the water with their floating shops and restaurants and customs that go back hundreds of years. Small children with ropes around their waists to stop them from falling over the side, play on the tiny decks and learn to row, sail and swim, for neither they nor their parents go ashore often. For centuries they have been a people apart, forbidden by Chinese law to live ashore or marry landowners. While we were eating in one of the floating restaurants, I saw several children in a boat holding up large coolie hats to catch coins tourists were throwing down to them. I was struck by their seriousness and agility.

As we climbed up to Mt. Victoria we saw the luxurious mansions of the rich in jarring contrast to the poverty below. From Victoria's peak, the panoramic view of one of the world's great harbours nestled amidst the towering hills and mountains of Kowloon and the islands of the South China Sea was breathtaking. But then in Chinese, Hong Kong means 'fragrant harbour'. Especially at night, the harbour view with all its lights was a romantic fairyland.

This brave little British colony has had to grapple with serious refugee problems. In 1948 its population was 80,000, and now it is 3,000,000. Refugees from Communist China have arrived in phenomenal numbers after their perilous boat or land journeys from Red China. They squatted on rooftops and in congested, refugee apartments, if they were lucky. A family of twelve might occupy a small cubicle ten feet square. They crammed sampans and junks. They lived in ramshackle tar paper, cardboard, scrap wood or burlap huts in shanty towns or smoke-filled, opium-infested cells.

When there was no room, they lived on the pavements. Here, I saw them eating their meals of boiled rice and taking a bath. I saw mothers ironing or breastfeeding their babies, children curled up in corners, or playing and scavenging and sleeping, with no attention paid to hygiene or sanitation.

To find jobs for them all was inconceivable. Consequently, as an intelligent Chinese (a refugee himself and a former Chinese government official) told me: "You're always too old when you apply for a job. Companies prefer to hire a younger man for lower pay." He also told me, to my surprise, that many of the businesses — banks, movie houses, import-export offices — in Hong Kong were owned by Red China. "It is ridiculous not to recognize Red China. There is no sense to boycotting its goods. The Chinese have lost faith in Chang Kai Shek."

Our Chinese friends drove us to see the hinterland, known as the New Territories, which looked to me like a vast patchwork of green rice paddies. Hong Kong's border with Red China was at the north of the New Territories, twenty-two miles from Kowloon. Through this opening in the Bamboo Curtain, many refugees passed daily into Hong Kong. They told us that the Territories would be handed back to Red China in 1997. At the time I did not appreciate fully their fearful concern for the fate of Hong Kong Island and the Kowloon Peninsula. On 1 July 1997, Britain handed back Hong Kong to the People's Republic of China on the condition that Hong Kong's free-enterprise economy would be maintained for at least fifty years. An intriguing anomaly, it is now a tiny enclave of capitalism within the largest Communist country in the world.

Hong Kong was a shopper's heaven, a paradise for the bargain hunter because it was a duty free port. Some of the world's great temptations — Swiss watches, German cameras, British tweeds, silks from India and Thailand — were for sale. Competition was keen; stores were open ten to fifteen hours a day. There were no large department stores, but I was overwhelmed by the countless number and variety of small specialty shops, hotel shopping arcades, chic boutiques, emporiums, and open-air markets. Miss Rutledge and I could not resist. Custom-made clothing was a Hong Kong specialty. I had a lovely *cheongsam* made from pure silk printed with large scarlet hibiscus flowers. I just loved myself in it. I bought table linens, yards and yards of fabrics and two pairs of prescription eyeglasses. Today Hong Kong is not the shopping paradise it was in 1959 because it has become too expensive.

It was time to go to Singapore. We had already cancelled our reservations and stayed in Hong Kong two days longer than we had expected. Our Chinese friends brought us gift boxes of ginger and other sweets to the airport. They had been so generous, so caring. I was moved.

On my second visit to Hong Kong en route to China twenty years later, I felt trapped by the noise and pollution, the bumper to bumper traffic and the shoulder to shoulder pedestrians. I couldn't wait to leave the city which I had remembered with such fondness.

Singapore

Singapore is a tiny island republic on the southern tip of the Malay Peninsula which gained independence from Britain in 1965, six years after our visit. We met Marjorie Copping at the Raffles Hotel, the legendary symbol of Singapore since 1887, named after Sir Stamford Raffles who, in 1819, landed on Singapore Island and established a British colonial outpost. I had not heard about this luxury hotel, the most spectacular in the Orient. But both Miss Rutledge and Marjorie had read about it in Somerset Maugham's stories. A luxury hotel it truly was with its fourteen-foot moulded ceilings, grand arches, tiled teak and marble floorings. We toasted our meeting with the world famous "Singapore Sling" which was concocted in the hotel's Long Bar in 1915. And we enjoyed high tea in the beautiful Palm Court which was probably named after an exotic kind of palm tree shaped like a Chinese fan that grew in front of the hotel.

The port of Singapore was one of the world's ten most important ports. Traffic in the crowded harbour was busy. I could see ships from all over the world: four American destroyers, massive container ships and several huge British ocean liners. As we drove in our private car or walked along the empty streets, it was like any quiet Sunday in any big city. The Indian stores and others of different faiths that don't observe the Christian Sabbath were open, because Singapore has many races, colours and creeds. We remarked on the large number of Christian churches and the open water channels running along the main streets. But very little moved or disturbed me greatly.

Singapore lacked the character and colour of Hong Kong, with its breathtaking harbour views and towering hills and mountains. But it was clean and orderly. I saw no litter, no beggars, no one poorly dressed. (Under the recent leadership of Lee Kwan Yew, it has become the most affluent country in Asia after Japan, and the cleanest, safest and most orderly city in the world. Spitting, littering, jay-walking, gum chewing and smoking are prohibited on the streets. Drug dealers are hanged.)

I saw modern office blocks and well-kept high-rise apartment buildings with the whitest laundry hung from bamboo poles on all the balconies. I found the well-dressed men and women in various national outfits interesting to watch. I admired the irresistibly beautiful Chinese women with jet black hair pushed back and clean, glowing burnished complexions walking with elegance and grace in their side-slit *cheongsams* which just asked for male attention. And Indian women, wearing rather heavy eye-makeup, round red spots in between the eyebrows and red stripes down the middle part of their hair in their lovely saris which must be one of the most flattering garments a woman can wear. I admired the graceful carriage of Malay women in their ankle-length straight blue skirts with long white tunics and the whitest long scarves draped about their heads. As well as young girls with long black braids hanging down their backs. One young woman puffing a thick green cheroot posed for me. Her poise gave her a look of self-possession, even haughtiness.

Several more scenes have left their memories. We visited the famous Tiger Balm Jade House, with its unique collection of over 1,000 pieces. And there, in one of the rooms, I saw a young boy sprawled on a chesterfield, reading and listening to Western hit tunes blaring away from a record player, while on the dressing table in front of him was a large portrait of the Tiger Balm's widow who had just died. Flanking the picture were two burning candles. In front of it was a dish of oranges sliced in quarters, two dishes of boiled rice and water, and a pot of tea. Jossticks were also propped up. The incongruity of a centuries-old tradition of ancestor worship and the infiltration of the western way of life amused me.

We stopped to watch a Chinese funeral procession. Scores of mourners carrying lighted tapers walked behind the corpse. Some wore white hoods over their heads, because the Chinese consider white the colour of sadness, and red the colour of happiness. Immediately before the flower-covered catafalque crossed a bridge, the sons of the deceased knelt on the road and threw chopsticks and money on the road in front of the bridge. Six chartered buses which would later carry the walking mourners ended the long procession.

As we drove from Johore Bahru to Singapore we stopped to watch a strange religious ceremony involving a rooster. Marjorie was just frantic with concern for the poor animal. Positive its fate was sealed, she cornered a few of the worshippers to inquire about the rooster. No one understood her! While the ritual was in progress and Marjorie was fluttering about to save the rooster from its destiny, a group of little children played hopscotch, oblivious to the rooster's sentence and Marjorie's fury. Poor Marjorie, alone in her private "Be Kind to Animals" campaign, so vigorously conducted wherever she went.

By the way, the rooster was set free at the end of the service and when Marjorie saw it, it was strutting away, the cock o' the roost.

Thailand

We concentrated our visit in Thailand to Bangkok and more specifically the city's oldest section where the major temples, palaces and historic monuments are located. Despite the traditional respect for monarchy and religion, Western commerce and trade had taken over. (Bangkok now suffers from some of the worst traffic jams in Asia, as well as pollution, noise and prostitution.)

After 800 years of Buddhist influence, Thailand may have more images of Buddha than human inhabitants (90 per cent of Thais are Buddhists). We saw scores of Buddhas created in bronze, marble, jade, crystal, stucco and solid gold, sitting, standing or reclining. We saw the most famous, the Emerald Buddha, carved from a solid piece of green jade, housed in the main chapel of its temple in the Grand Palace. Stolen from Laos in 1780 when Thailand was still Siam, it sits high on a gilded altar with a royal, nine-tiered ceremonial umbrella behind and crystal balls representing the sun and moon on either side.

We were fortunate to be visiting the Temple of the Emerald Buddha Thailand's most sacred Buddhist shrine, on the day the King of Thailand visited to launch the Buddhist Lent (20 July). Dressed in a white uniform, he looked young, gentle and gracious as he walked under a large umbrella held for him, bowing and nodding to his silent people as they sat cross-legged on the ground. Protocol demanded that no one stand higher than he. The ceremony was dignified and orderly. An orchestra was playing, and a choir of small boys chanted. I saw offerings of flowers, paper money, jossticks and candles in large beehive shapes. I saw a woman presenting lotus flowers to an aide walking beside the King as he was leaving the Temple to get into his yellow limousine. Traditionally given to monks and royalty, the lotus symbolizes enlightenment because it rises from mud, just as Buddhism rises above earthly corruption. Young, barefoot, saffron-robed priests with shaved heads hugging black lacquer begging bowls mingled among the crowds. When I offered souvenir Canada match boxes to several who had posed for a picture I had sneaked, they refused to take them. I later discovered that they cannot directly accept anything from the hands of a woman because a woman was considered unclean.

I was disappointed when I was forbidden to take movies of the King and the ceremony. But the next day I made a special trip to the Marble Buddha where the King was expected and where movies were allowed. After standing in a light drizzle for an hour and one-half, I got my movies.

It rained every day we were in Bangkok. But we didn't let it interfere with our activities. Monsoon downpours don't last very long. We got drenched but we would be dry in fifteen minutes. The streets glistened and steamed in the hot sun. I liked the intense greenness which the tropical, glossy foliage would acquire after a rain. And I enjoyed the wonderful earthy smell of rain-soaked vegetation unique to tropical lands.

Of Bangkok's nearly 400 *wats* or Buddhist temple-monasteries, we visited five: Wat Po, the temple of the colossal Reclining Buddha; Wat Traimit, the Temple of the Golden Buddha made of 5.5 tons of solid gold; Wat Benchomobophit, the Marble Temple; and Wat Arun, the Temple of the Dawn. At Wat Phra Keo, the temple of the Emerald Buddha, bronze statues of royal white elephants stand guard at a monument that shelters a king's crown. Huge statues of scowling Chinese warriors

equipped with swords, staves and javelins kept evil spirits away from Wat Po. Dancing monkey warriors
supported a section of facade at Wat Arun. Here the
moon god Pra Chan, astride a white horse, surveyed his
mortal subjects from a niche lavishly decorated with
porcelain mosaic. This temple was decorated with mosaic composed of tens of thousands of fragments of
porcelain, truly a marvellous sight to behold. The tem-
ple-dominated skyline gleamed with the red and green
porcelain tiles of the roofs rising tier upon tier.

Hundreds of miles of canals, called *klongs* in Thai,
radiated from the Chao-Phya River. Despite the rain we
took a tour on one of these canals, whose banks were
lined with low wooden houses raised on stilts to guard
against monsoon floods. A flight of steps led down to the
water where we saw Thai children bathing and swimming, and women washing dishes and laundry. We saw
a postman in a boat delivering mail and a butcher weighing meat. We saw sampans that were floating markets,
laden with fruit of every kind, bananas, mangoes, pineapple, as well as rice, cocoanut and bamboo and
vegetables. We saw sampans with live chickens. We saw
floating kitchens preparing lunch while hungry patrons
waited on their steps.

We saw, perched on a slim pillar, a new, elaborately
carved and gilded spirit house with two vases of fresh
flowers. These expensive miniature temples are status
symbols and provide shelter for the guardian deity of the
home. The klong was alive with all sorts of boats:
longboats, flat-bottom boat, roofed boats, and some that
looked very much like our canoes and kayaks. A few
were paddled by agile children, or poled by women in
large lampshade hats. In spite of the unbelievable traffic,
people stopped to have a visit and chat.

Mr. Dingwell, a Hillcrest colleague, had asked us to contact Mr. Thavil Osathanugroh who owned a chain of dispensaries. They had met while Mr. Dingwell was working for the Colombo Plan in Malaya. Mr. Drug Store, as Miss Rutledge called him, because we could not pronounce his name properly, was very kind, driving us in his iron car throughout the city, but with a speed that made Miss Rutledge frantic with fear. Responding to our request, Mr. Drug Store arranged a visit to Pana-Bhandhu, a private boarding school operated by friends of his. We were respectfully greeted with a prayer-like clasping of the palms, a gesture known as *wai*, and then we were shown around the school. Pana-Bhandhu was a large, new, two-storey building with clean, bright, but bare classrooms and very little blackboard space. All the classrooms faced a long outside corridor, an ideal way to save space and money, but probably not feasible in our cold climate. There were 3,000 students and ninety teachers. Non-specialists taught half-time — fifteen hours a week — with the other half for marking and checking pupils' work. Specialists taught nine hours with twenty-one hours devoted to marking and correcting assignments. I liked this arrangement because I consider meeting with students about their assignments of major importance in the learning process. Incidentally, corrections were made in red ink in immaculately tidy notebooks.

There were forty to forty-five students in a class. All students wore the navy blue and white school uniform. At each desk hung a plastic water bottle. Watching a French class of fourteen year olds studying noun clauses and the passive voice impressed me. Reverence for teachers was very strong. I saw a female student kneeling beside a teacher's desk when her paper was being dis-

cussed. Schoolteachers were addressed as *khru* (guru).
During a ceremony held once a year, the student body
assembled to offer incense and flowers to the teachers
and to formally ask for their blessing. At the end of the
tour our hosts served us Coca-Cola, as popular in the Far
East as Pepsi is in the Middle East. I shall hold the staff's
spontaneous warmth and dignified decorum in my
memory for a long time.

We spent an enjoyable evening watching displays of
Thai classical dancing. The dancers wore lavishly bro-
caded and sequined costumes, and richly ornamented
headdresses sparkled and glittered. As they danced with
stately footwork and the most delicate hints of facial
expression, I was mesmerized by the rhythmic, intricate
play of hands, arms and torsos. I'll never forget how the
fingers were curved back to the uttermost! I did not
understand the religious significance and symbolism of
the complex choreography, but the skill of the ritualistic
gestures fascinated me.

Nor will I forget the hundreds of dressed and undressed Buddhas carved out of all kinds of substances, in
all sorts of positions and sizes from the beautiful, priceless Buddha being sketched by art students in the
National Museum to the tiny "homespun" Buddha in
the dormitory of the private boarding school.

Cambodia (Kampuchia)

We went to Cambodia to visit the temples of Angkor Wat
in Cambodia, the greatest archeological find in South-
east Asia. Surrounded by dense jungle, they were only
152 kilometres from the Thai border. We were warned,
however, that the trip could be dangerous because of
Communist rebels in ambush, raiding cars, and the ter-

rible conditions of jungle roads. Our taxi driver reassured us that he could get us there and back safely. No problem. We decided to risk the journey. I was looking forward to exciting adventures en route.

We left Bangkok for Siem Reap, the gateway to the ruins, well supplied with box lunches, visas and protection money for watchmen and border officials to ensure safe and quick passages across bridges and frontiers.

The countryside was fascinating. We passed green flat paddy fields of rice and thatched roof cottages on stilts, stuck into pools of water. We stopped at colourful markets bulging with bright tropical fruits and vegetables we had never seen or heard about: the dreadful smelling durian, which is supposed to have aphrodisiac properties; rambutan, looking like huge spiked strawberries; pomelos like giant grapefruit; pure white mangosteen; mangoes; pawpaw; lichees; and star fruit. We passed betel nut vendors with only a tooth black as ebony still left here and there in the mouth. A woman wrinkled with sun and age and a solitary cracked tooth stained with betel juice was happy to pose for me. We passed women in their typical reed-woven large lampshade sun hats varnished against the rain, roasting corn on the cob on their charcoal braziers. We passed shaven-headed Buddhist monks wearing saffron-robes and carrying black lacquered begging bowls. We passed the lush, thick jungle on both sides of us, and we passed willowy bamboo and mammoth ant hills. We passed epic herds of water buffalo (over one hundred in one), and carts drawn by white oxen with painted horns. How Miss Rutledge envied them cooling off, submerged in the water of the swollen ditches. We passed bullock carts with huge wooden wheels. We passed washed-out bridges and buses stuck tire deep in muck. We passed women repairing roads and floating paddy-fields with teams of black buffaloes ploughing through them. We stopped in villages where we saw naked little boys holding their mother's hands and little wailing girls, terrified on seeing us, clinging to their mother's legs. I saw a little girl looking at us bewildered as she clutched a little white doll in her arms. We bounced on the rough jungle roads over rocks and lurched into potholes and ruts, our heads banging frequently against the car's roof. To my disappointment, we arrived without adventure in Siem Reap, having experienced no mishap whatsoever.

Of the hundred temples that lie scattered in the jungle surrounding Siem Reap, we concentrated on Angkor Wat and Angkor Thom, the two most fabled of the Cambodian monuments built between the seventh and eleventh centuries. The reconstructed structures were miraculous when I saw how the gigantic and powerful roots of enormous trees had interwoven themselves among the blocks of the stone walls so that over the centuries this vast compound of structures was completely covered by dense jungle vegetation. Mighty monuments of past civilizations were ruined by the tenacious roots, branches and trunks as well as the intertwining, entangling and interlacing undergrowth which crumbled, split and crushed the stone in some places; in others, tightened and cemented it. Our guide, a handsome, blonde, athletic Frenchman, who was in the import-export business in Phnom Penh (the capital of Cambodia) tried to show us how tough the long branches were, hanging down like bell-ropes, by swinging on them like Tarzan. I was duly impressed. Freeing and clearing this tangled jungle growth and vicious root networks was a Herculean task.

Angkor Wat is one of the largest temple complexes in the world, covering an area about 1.5 by 1.3 kilometres. What fascinated me was the 800 metre long bas-reliefs that encircle the galleries of the first terrace of the temple. The figures depict scenes from Hindu classics such as the "Ramayana," or a vast array of Hindu deities, Vishnu and Krishna and Shiva, and elephant gods, holy vultures, hooded cobras, lions, lionmen, bulls, buffalo, mythical bird-men and serpent deities. Or they celebrate the greatness of King Suryavargman II . But what held my awe were the soft feminine shapes of the celestial waiting women and divine dancing maidens, exquisitely and delicately outlined in stone. I thought of the geniuses who had sculpted them.

Historians believe Angkor Thom, five miles south of Ankor Wat, to have been a city of more than a million people. From 802 until its capture by the Thai in 1431, it was the capital of the Khmer Empire. It is a walled city protected by a moat. What left me dumbfounded here was the Bayon.

The Bayon is set within the vast walls of Angkor Thom. Built in the exact centre of the five square mile city, this temple was connected to four city gates by roads for elephants and people. It is pyramidal in construction, with fifty towers and nearly 200 giant four-faced heads chiselled on stone walls. Giant faces oblivous to change and turmoil met my gaze everywhere I turned — faces hideous and beautiful, faces grinning and sombre, faces serene and tormented, and faces inscrutable. It was a breathtaking sight.

The Bayon's bas-reliefs were also truly amazing. They stretched for twelve hundred metres and incorporated over eleven thousand figures. They show both Hindu and Buddhist influences but most show scenes of everyday life in the twelfth century kingdom. The incomprehensible magnitude of the grandeur around me left me speechless.

French archeologists had painstakingly reclaimed, from the tentacles of the jungle and the erosion of time, something approaching the original grandeur. But there was still much more reconstruction work to be done. Numerous structures were in poor condition. Broken fragments of statuary, chunks of friezes and massive carved-stone building blocks in various stages of ruin were scattered everywhere in the galleries and on stairways, on massive towers, in courtyards and on terraces. Many were weathered to unrecognizable knobs and indentations. I silently mused on the unimaginable sweep of history these stones had witnessed. Shelley's poem "Ozymandias" and the temporality of worldly things came to my mind. I was brought back to reality when I noticed a young Cambodian family enjoying a picnic among the ruins and the jungle's towering trees. I greeted them in French and they responded.

Our guide told us that the ruins were accidentally discovered during World War I when a bolt of lightning broke open the green roof of the jungle, revealing the presence of the ruins to a French plane that was flying overhead. However, I have since read that references to a lost city overgrown by jungle were made by European missionaries as early as the sixteenth century. But it was not until 1863 that the French naturalist, Henri Mouhot, told the world about his incredible find. I like my guide's story best.

To this day I regret not being able to poke about the rubble and rummage among the ruins further and learn more about the architectural and sculptural genius of Khmer art. But, unfortunately, I became ghastly ill and spent one whole day on the bathroom floor of our hotel, beside the toilet, feverish and nauseated. The humid heat was oppressive. The mosquitoes were unbearable. We drank gallons of water. Poor Miss Rutledge was drenched with perspiration. How she dripped and dripped and dripped!

We had allotted four days for this side trip to Siem Reap. Weak as I was , we left as scheduled. I was grateful that I had taken my elephant ride before I got sick. I still have the photo of me sitting in the decorated howdah. But I was disappointed that we didn't get to see Phnom Penh, considered to be the most beautiful of the French cities in Asia.

The drive back to Bangkok was just a blur on my memory. According to a Bangkok female doctor I was suffering from amoebic dysentery. I remembered having accepted an invitation from a well-known French journalist for a drink in our hotel bar. He had ordered a scotch and water. Wishing to appear sophisticated, I ordered one too not realizing that the water was tap water. The doctor prescribed some medicine which soon revived me and my spirits. Life was worth living once more.

We had travelled by car from Thailand into Cambodia in the southwest of the Indochinese peninsula. Today the only way is by air since tourists are advised not to travel by bus, train or car.

Present day Cambodia is the successor state of the mighty Khmer Empire which from the ninth to fourteenth centuries ruled much of what is now Vietnam, Laos and Thailand. For ninety years from 1863 to 1953 when independence was declared, the French controlled Cambodia. For fifteen years King (later Prince, Prime Minister and Chief-of-State and then King again), Noro-

dom Sihanouk dominated Cambodian politics. In 1970
he was overthrown by the army and fled to China. From
1969 Cambodia was drawn into the Vietnam war.
American and South Vietnamese troops invaded the
country to root out North Vietnamese Communist
forces. They failed. In his determination to radically
restructure Cambodian society along rigid Maoist lines
the Khymer Rouge leader, Pol Pot, conducted a reign of
terror for four years (1975-1979): relocating people
into the countryside, torturing to death or executing
intellectuals, or anyone who had any artistic talent, or
who wore glasses, who spoke a foreign language or who
looked as if he/she had soft hands. Along with hundreds
of thousands more who died of mistreatment, malnutrition and disease, at least one million Cambodians died
during the Pol Pot regime. They also destroyed virtually
all of the country's *wats*.

At the end of 1977 Vietnam invaded Cambodia and
overthrew the Khmer Rouge who fled into the jungles.
During the 1970s and 80s they fought a guerilla war
against the Vietnamese-backed government.

In mid-1993, under the United Nations, a super-
vised cease-fire, large-scale demobilization, repatriation
of Cambodian refugees from Thailand, and the resettle-
ment of displaced people within Cambodia have taken
place. It is an uneasy peace. The civil war continues in
varius forms. Forty years of savage fighting, bombing,
land mines and booby traps have left their horrible scars.
Cambodia is one of the poorest nations on earth.

Burma (Myanmar)

Throughout the 1960s and 1970s no tourists were allowed into Burma. Under the repressive military regime

that was in power it had virtually sealed itself off from the rest of the world. A socialist country, it follows Communist precepts. A black market economy continues to boom. According to U.N. standards Myanmar is one of the ten poorest countries in the world. During the popular uprising of 1988, 5,000 people were killed and since then daily life has been overshadowed by fear.

Going to Burma, now called Myanmar, was a last minute decision. Ever since I became fascinated with the melody and words of Kipling's marching song, "On the Road to Mandalay" I had wanted to visit Mandalay, Burma's last capital before the 1805 British takeover. But my main reason this time was to purchase a star sapphire, the stone for my birthday month, December, because an English businessman in Bangkok had told me I could get better and cheaper ones in Rangoon. He had lived there while it was under British rule, and he knew what he was talking about. He also told me that if I bought my Burmese currency in Bangkok where it could be obtained ten to one, I would certainly get a bargain. Consequently, I bought enough Burmese currency to buy a very good star sapphire. And with a letter of introduction to the manager of Rangoon's best hotel, (whom he knew very well) I was all set.

Our visit in Rangoon (now called Yangon) proved interesting right from the start. In Bangkok I had made the acquaintance of two girls who were English correspondents for a British news agency. They were on their way home after a year's work in Laos and wanted to go into the Burmese hinterland for stories about Communist raids. At the airport in Rangoon they discovered that their Burmese visas were not in order. Their special press cards, even their tears, proved futile with the Burmese officials, one of whom was wearing his dead mother's tooth set in a ring. There was a very sick stretcher patient on board the S.A.S. plane, and the girls had caused an unscheduled two hour delay in their unsuccessful attempt for entry into Burma. The event made the headlines in one of the morning's papers.

We waited at the airport in Rangoon for over an hour for a bus to take us into the city while torrential rains pounded the ground. Officials smiled benignly. No one seemed to worry about the time lost. No one seemed to "know" anything. Their cavalier attitude towards punctuality began to upset us. Once again, Oriental bureaucracy was trying our patience.

Intermittent showers or outright downpours limited our explorations on foot in Rangoon. However, Johnny Hope, a charming young Burmese Air Lines official who spoke English well was very attentive and made my visit enjoyable. He had gone to English schools and had even visited Sweden as an S.A.S. employee. He had also served his time as a Buddhist monk for which his parents had received much merit. (A Buddhist concept that links good works in this life to rewards in the next. Even a spell of a few weeks or months as a monk-in-training in a *wat* is believed to confer great personal merit particularly on the mother.) Johnny took me sightseeing and to dinner in a hired war surplus jeep. I was being very cautious about the food I ate now. But I did try some cocoanut rice, chicken curry, pickled mango, saltfish and hot chilies.

Johnny was a patriotic nationalist, anxious for his country's economic and social reforms. He sadly admitted that in their vast, rich arable land, butter had to be imported. He feared the Communist infiltration of his country. As I listened to him, so serious and enthusiastic,

I felt that Burma would somehow make the difficult upgrade to prosperity.

I was too sick to notice very much in Rangoon. But I was told that since the British left in 1948 little had been built or renovated. However, I do recall the vast bell-shaped Schwedagon. The most sacred Buddhist temple in Burma, it dominates the entire city from its hilltop site. There were over 8,000 gold plates covering the pagoda; the top of the gold spire was encrusted with more than 5,000 diamonds and 2,000 other precious or semi-precious stones. The compound around the pagoda had eighty-two other buildings with equally resplendent shrines and towers. As usual, we had to remove our shoes and wander about barefoot. But the dirt and filth surprised me. (I had not seen the Hindu temples of Calcutta and Benares yet.) Devout worshippers were bobbing in prayer. One woman with a tightly rolled and oiled paper umbrella sitting on her head was taking a bouquet of flowers to a favourite deity.

I remember a native girl in the typical sarong and transparent white blouse with gold clasps (Kabaya). Since the Burmese have little confidence in their inflated currency, they prefer to buy gold in the form of wearable ornaments. I also recall a luxury hotel in construction, a gift of the Russians, and monkeys on the streets eating roasted corn on the cob.

With my letter of introduction to the hotel manager, which the Englishman in Bangkok had given me, I started my search for the star sapphire. He proved congenial and helpful enough, supplying me with a taxi to visit the various jewellers. None of them could show me star sapphires set in rings. There were many small stones which I could have bought, but they weren't half as nice as those I had seen in Bangkok.

The hotel manager had warned me that things had changed since the British left in 1948. Consumer wants had changed. There were so few tourists that it didn't warrant stocking rings of precious gems.

I was disappointed. I decided to change my money into Indian currency which I would be needing soon. I discovered that I could not convert my money into any currency because it had not been registered on a currency form. I was in illegal possession of my Burmese money.

I went to the hotel manager and told him of my predicament. He introduced me to the hotel jeweller. He had no star sapphires. It was nearing closing time. We were to leave the next morning, and I was saddled with seventy dollars worth of useless paper! Finally the jeweller showed me a gold ring with six pigeon bloodred rubies in a gorgeous setting. I liked it immediately. But this time I didn't have enough money. I told him I would be back, hoping that he would reduce his price since he could see I was in no hurry to buy. He didn't. Of course, I hadn't revealed my real reason for my delay. Miss Rutledge and Marjorie were nowhere about. I tried to phone another acquaintance at another hotel. She was out. I was between Scylla and Charybdis. I couldn't legally buy any Burmese currency except at a bank, and they were closed. I wouldn't dare ask the jeweller to take American currency because the hotel manager had warned me that the government was taking all sorts of measures to curb black market practices. I had visions of myself behind bars! Well, this would teach me a lesson, my self-critical voice told me. But as luck would have it, in the hotel lobby I noticed an American woman whom I knew had also bought Burmese currency in Bangkok. I asked her if she knew about the government's anti-inflationary tightening policies. In soft whispers I told her all I knew. She was only too happy to get rid of the Burmese currency she thought she wouldn't need. It was just the amount I needed to enable me to buy the ring with the pigeon bloodred rubies. How I enjoyed wearing it! Its attractive setting later tantalized many an Indian jeweller who wanted to copy it.

Once again we had departure problems. The airport bus never did arrive at our hotel to pick us up as scheduled. I ran an Olympic race to the Air Lines office which was nearby to investigate. No official was around. I saw the bus in front of the office, but no one was in charge. I was worried until I saw Miss Rutledge and Marjorie with several of the hotel porters carrying our bags to the bus.

India

We were whisked ahead of the other passengers to the customs officials who filled out our forms, only to be ushered to a waiting room where we were to remain until everyone on board had been processed. The wait seemed interminable. Because Indians travelled with an assortment of many bags — soft bulky suitcases tied with rope, flimsy cardboard suitcases, burlap bundles, bed rolls, cans of all sizes and shapes, coal-oil lamps, bird cages, large cooking pots, hampers, food baskets, water jugs — the inspection was time-consuming. Initially, I waited patiently, absorbing the scene before me, a mixture of East and West in colour and dress. But I became restless as time dragged on. There was no snack bar or caféteria. I was hot, tired, sticky and hungry. After a three-hour-wait, we were all finally huddled into a bus heading for the Indian Air Lines office in the heart of Calcutta, India's largest city.

The office was small and drab, but the staff checked our tickets immediately and called a taxi to take us to the Red Shield Hotel, operated by the Salvation Army, where Miss Rutledge's friend, Miss Ann Munro, a long-time Baptist missionary and former M.L.A. in India had arranged our reservations. Miss Munro proved to be a wealth of information as we taxied Calcutta in pouring rain, light drizzle and glaring sun. She told us that since 1947 when India was granted independence after 150 years of British rule, the face of Calcutta had been gradually changing. The huge department stores on the principal street had gone. Monuments and memorials to English heroes had been removed from public view.

The monument to the prisoners of the Black Hole of Calcutta, which had been moved for safekeeping into an Anglican churchyard by a group of loyal Englishmen, reminded me of the sadness I felt when, as a young student, I studied about the horrible event. One hundred and forty-six British were imprisoned in a tiny under-ground cellar during a hot summer night in 1756, but only twenty-three "haggard and half-insane" people sur-vived. I recalled, too, that Robert Clive, who had avenged the tragedy and helped to found Britain's em-pire in India, became my hero. I felt a lump in my throat as I mused on the monument's ignominious end.

But other institutions of British India were still visible, testifying to the commercial vitality that fuelled British imperialism: the mission schools, the banks, the many massive Victorian public buildings, the 1930s dou-ble decker buses and the railroads. The lingua franca was still English and Indians still drove on the left.

I had read about India's poverty and misery, but I was not prepared for what I saw on Calcutta's streets and sidewalks: small children in brown tatters of rags; naked little boys who looked like solemn old men; young girls who looked like toothless old hags; blind and limbless beggars, who, we were told, were a professional class whose bodies were deliberately mutilated to appeal to tourists' sympathy. I found this reality overwhelming.

At the main railway station we saw homeless people lying, sitting or squatting in their makeshift shelters assembled from anything that the poor could get their hands on: bits of old cardboard, packing cases, and corrugated iron, sacks, and pieces of wood and metal. The stench of human excrement was difficult to bear. While we were photographing this appalling destitution, a police officer appeared and ordered us to go to the police station with him. We tried to protest, but he maintained that we had broken the law by taking pictures of the "refugees." It didn't matter to him that we were just tourists ignorant of local regulations. And so with the police officer in "our" taxi, "our" taxi driver took us to the police station.

We were sat down on a long wooden bench in front of the police chief prosecutor who asked for our passports. After the policeman explained why he had apprehended the culprits sitting on the bench, he left. Our remonstrations to the effect that there were no visible notices forbidding photography at the train station proved to no avail. Just exactly what the penalty was going to be, I didn't dare guess. I was truly frightened.

When Miss Munro produced her card as a former Member of the Lower House in India, the attitude and voice tone of officialdom immediately changed. Our pompous prosecutor had turned into a fatherly advisor, benign and gentle. He would let us off this time; he would not confiscate our film nor take our cameras away if we would just fill out the card he handed us. "But please, no more pictures of refugees," he pleaded.

We couldn't leave the police station quickly enough. Thanks to Miss Munro, we were safe; our cameras and film were untouched. Our taxi driver had finally got rid of us and was nowhere to be seen. We had taxed his patience and his reputation twice that morning, and he would have no more of us for all the love of tourist dollars. We had made him park in a zone where he claimed he had no right to be, even after a policeman had said it was alright to park there, and to top it all, he had to drive his passengers to a police station. As soon as we had been seated on our wooden bench, he brought in Miss Munro's umbrella that she had left in the car, and made a hurried departure.

We now had to look for another taxi. No one would stop. It was as if all of Calcutta's taxi drivers knew of the offence we had just committed. It became a joke among us, when, in the afternoon, we were being privately escorted, like distinguished guests, through the spacious and elegant rooms of the Governor's palace.

In between our sight-seeing tours, we were constantly trying to get plane reservations to Benares (now called Varanasi), the sacred city to which every Hindu, at least once in his or her life, tries to make a pilgrimage. But the self-important officials at the tourist office showed no interest. For the first time on our trip I saw Miss Rutledge lose her patience and react angrily at their breezy indifference and casual attitude. Utterly frustrated, we finally decided to go to Benares by train.

But we nearly never got to the railroad station. We just could not find a taxi. Everyone at the Red Shield scattered in four directions trying to hail a cab for us, but to no avail. We were exasperated. The scene soon put me in a laughing jag — in the twilight of an Indian night, the two streets of the hotel were lined with people waving, screaming and jumping on cabs to make them stop. At last, a taxi stopped. Our Red Shield friends actually formed a posse to be sure that the driver could not escape.

Our driver was a Sikh. Even though he knew that we had only fifteen minutes to get to the train station he refused to help with our luggage. We were to experience several such incidents of caste, abolished by law, but still in practice and jealously guarded.

In spite of the heavy traffic, we made the train in the nick of time. We breathed a sigh of relief when we entered our large private car with two long wooden benches on each side and a white enamel washbasin at one end. Throughout the night we kept shifting positions on the hard narrow wooden benches, unable to seduce sleep.

At last day broke, and we could see the brown earth and the brown mud huts that might not be there tomorrow if the heavy torrential monsoons poured. The whole countryside was empty of agricultural machinery of any kind; land was tilled in the manner of their ancestors and life in the villages essentially unchanged from past generations.

We were met at Benares by a welcoming committee from the Clark's Hotel. Again we encountered the Hindu caste system when the guides refused to help the porters put the luggage on their heads. Keeping them on the head, I thought, was an accomplishment in itself. But

I soon saw that getting them there was an even greater feat. After several attempts, aided by all of us, except the guides who just stood and watched, all the luggage was lifted on to the heads of the porters.

If I was appalled by the poverty and misery of Calcutta, I was more distressed by what I saw in Benares. The city sits on the banks of the Ganges, which Hindus believe is the goddess Ganga; thus it is venerated as the most sacred city of the Hindus. Every Hindu at least once in his or her life tries to make a pilgrimage here. Thousands of pilgrims from all walks of life, every caste and every part of the country arrive each day to bathe in or drink from the sacred river in order to be purified of all sin.

We hired a sturdy little rowboat to observe the masses of humanity in the sacred river and on the *ghats*, landings with wide stone steps leading down the banks to the river's edge. Worshippers were bathing, praying, doing their laundry, polishing brass pots, diving, floating, wading, brushing teeth, sudsing hair, blowing their noses and spitting, drinking the holy waters and sprinkling them on their foreheads with no regard for sanitation.

We watched the thin blue smoke twisting up to the sky from the burning pyres on the *ghats*. It is the lifelong hope of all Hindus to die in old age on the banks; to be cremated there and have their ashes sprinkled across the holy waters.

Once back on shore we walked among the people on the *ghats* and we watched men getting their heads shaved as a symbol of their renunciation of worldly pleasures. We watched Brahmin priests, sitting cross-legged in the motionless lotus position, eyes closed in deep meditation under large umbrellas. We watched professional letter writers composing declarations of romantic love, Indian women in their colourful saris selling aromatic garlands of orange marigolds and roses, and a father dab coloured powders on his child's forehead.

A carnival atmosphere prevailed, noisy, loud and gay with radio music and the shouts of street sellers advertising their wares. Car horns constantly honked at goats, cattle and people. Hawkers hounded us and postcard vendors, shoe-shine boys and purveyors of trinkets constantly assailed us. The profusion of this street life exhausted me. I found the congestion and lack of privacy unbearably claustrophobic. The pungent scents of sandalwood, jasmine, tamarind, oleander and oriental spices combined with the stench of diesel fuel, and excrement from humans and animals nauseated me. I usually sought direct contact with the local people. But this time I was squeamish. At the same time, I was ashamed at my own disgust. It was only when I was told that Gandhi himself visited Benares just once because he could not take it (and he had even lived with the untouchables) that I accepted my own repugnance as a natural reaction.

It is difficult to write about my feelings without appearing callous or insensitive or guilty. But I found the Hindu temples in Benares, as in Calcutta, filthy and garish. They were cluttered with numerous images to the many gods and goddesses which Hindus worship: gods of protection and preservation, goddesses of mercy and prosperity, some with thousands of hands and others with scores of heads, as well as images of an array of animals both mythological and real: cows, elephants, monkeys, dogs, and peacocks, with the most gruesome of faces.

However, I did visit one clean temple. It belonged to the Jains, an offshoot Hindu sect. The ascetic Jains were a revelation to me. I was told there were only 250,000. I saw them wearing masks over their mouths to prevent them swallowing insects, and watching where they walked in order not to step on bugs because they respect all life as sacred.

In Benares, as in Calcutta, we heard about the changes wrought by Indian independence. I met a French-Canadian Capuchin priest in the Catholic mission at Benares, who told us: "Since the English troops have gone, my congregation has diminished to a mere handful — a few of the Clark's Hotel people. All lessons in the Catholic mission school that served 500 students are given in Hindi. We are not allowed to teach the Catholic religion."

He showed us the priests' study room and refectory: "We have a refrigerator, but the Indians don't know or perhaps don't want to learn how to use it. We have to check and supervise the most menial tasks to be sure they are done, for example, the tea towels washed occasionally at least."

Since we were not committed to any fixed schedule, we now had to decide whether to visit Kashmir or Nepal, a unique Himalayan mountain kingdom landlocked between India and China from where we could see Mount Everest. We knew that we would never climb Mt. Everest, but we felt that even a glimpse of it would be worth our while. But we had to get to Patna from where we could book a flight to Kathmandu, the capital of Nepal.

We decided to go to Patna by train. We made no reservations hoping we could just board the Patna bound train. We could not get on the first train, although

I truly felt that if our porter had asserted himself we could have. We sat on our suitcases and waited on the station platform for the next train. I found the life around me both fascinating and disturbing. I kept watching a wealthy Indian with a western taste for clothes accompanied by his own holy man, a dirty, shaggy-looking individual with tangled hair and ragged orange robe. My gaze kept being interrupted by the requests of the ubiquitous beggars. In spite of warnings, I could muster no resistance to their misery, especially to the blind. I gave them money and was glad.

Our porter soon assured us that we could get on the next train. He could arrange it with some train official, for a price. This news upset me and I found myself making comparisons to my own country. I was the holder of the purse. We had to get on the next train. It was very late at night and we had no hotel reservations in Patna. I relented. The railway cars were packed. Passengers were crowding the doors. They were climbing on top of the train to ride on the roof. Others were even diving headfirst through the train windows. It was a mob scene. A wild and frantic rush of passengers carried us along in the crush of the elbowing, pushing and pulling crowd who were screaming to our porter who, in turn, was yelling at various railroad officials. At last we managed to burst into a car occupied by a dignified, educated young Indian who gave us permission to stay. This necessitated his rearranging his numerous bags, parcels, bed rolls, cans of food, and water jugs.

No one slept. At train stops, the young Brahmin would hurry to another car where the ladies of his party, one of whom (his wife, presumably) he finally brought to our coach, so that she could get to sleep.

He confessed: "My mother still will not accept food from servants belonging to the untouchable caste whose touch is considered impure. But the younger generation is more broad-minded." And yet I could not reconcile his statement with the fact that he himself kept his porter standing throughout the whole journey, even though he was the only occupant on the long bench.

The young Brahmin and I had interesting talks between train stops. I told him that I was surprised and confused by the way India worked. When he tried to explain Hindu religious practices I soon discovered my abysmal ignorance of Hindu spirituality. The India I had read about was Kipling's jingoistic "lesser breeds without the law." I just could not fathom the complexities of a philosophy of life where poverty is holy and not judged as a failure. I soon realized it is impossible to understand India without gaining some understanding of Hinduism because Hindus constitute 85 per cent of the population. This religion with its caste system played a major role in almost every aspect of Indian national life. He recommended that I read the Bhagavad Gita, which he told me had influenced American thinkers like Ralph Waldo Emerson and Henry Thoreau.

We arrived in Patna at two a.m. The platform of the railroad station was full of sleepers lying curled up, or on their backs, stomachs or sides on filthy brown rags or pieces of cardboard. I had to pick my way gingerly over and around them. There was no sign anywhere of possessions. I was appalled. The next morning, while I was riding in a pedicab (bicycle driven taxi), I actually saw a man scoop up and eat some fresh moist dung which a cow had just excreted. I gagged. I later learned that he may have belonged to a sect known as Aghori dung-eat-ers who have no prohibited food, although, it is said, they have an aversion to horse meat.

In Patna, Miss Rutledge wanted to get her hair done, but she was told she would have to go to Calcutta because Patna had no hairdressers. However, we did find a Bata shoe store where Miss Rutledge delivered yards of nylon and men's nylon shirts to Mr. Jain, manager of the Bata store in Patna, for a former pupil's husband who started the store there. Mr. Jain's father was a Member of Parliament, the Minister of Food and Agriculture. When we expressed a wish to see a session of parliament, Mr. Jain was certain that through his father's influence we could.

We were ready to leave for Nepal, but once again, Indian bureaucracy infuriated us thoroughly. We didn't think we were ever going to get on the plane for Kathmandu, the capital of Nepal. In spite of our many telephone calls to the Indian Air Lines' office, the officials could not tell us the precise time of the plane's departure or when they would pick us up. Nor did my three-hundred-yard-dash from the hotel to the airlines office produce any new information. The unruffled officials showed absolutely no sympathy for our anxiety. It seemed as if they were always the source of our endless frustration. After what seemed like an eternity we were finally picked up. India has its own pace. And high-strung Westerners who expect instant attention and crisp efficiency are infuriated.

Nepal

The ancient kingdom of Nepal lies between China and India. In the Western World, it is known as the home of the Sherpas, the tough Himalayan climbers; the home of the fighting Gurkha soldiers; the land of the Yeti, a mythical abominable snowman; and Shangrila a mystical kingdom hidden beyond the Himalayas.

At the airport in Kathmandu (now called Patan) a smiling, clean-cut lad of about eighteen, dressed in tight white jodhpurs, long-tailed white shirt, and a Western jacket, greeted us and inquired whether we would like a hotel. We soon learned that he was from the Snow View Hotel, the hotel owned by an Indian and his Canadian-born wife. Since an Englishman I had met in the Red Shield in Calcutta had suggested the Snow View, we decided we would stay there. Mr. Mendies, the Snow View's proprietor, soon came to meet us.

Mr. Mendies looked after everything including our passports, visas, and bags. We were soon packed into his American car, a luxury in Nepal, en route to his hotel. I saw very few cars, although there were quite a few green jeeps, the Indian "Land Rovers."

The Snow View wasn't a former royal palace like the Grand, the only other hotel in Kathmandu. But my Calcutta informant had told me that the Snow View's plainness was more than made up for by its homey, cozy atmosphere. I wasn't disappointed. Mr. and Mrs. Mendies were very friendly and pleasant. (Mr. Mendies, who had had a variety of jobs in India, met his Canadian wife at a Salvation Army prayer meeting in Calcutta.)

We were not afraid to eat at Snow View. Its water was boiled "under personal supervision," the milk was imported, and its vegetables were grown in the hotel garden. It was a relief not having to worry about the food.

Mr. Mendies gave us Krishnu, the smiling chap who had met us at the airport, to be our guide for our walking tours. We soon learned that Kathmandu, the capital city of a country of 8.2 million, provided no hairdressers, and no bakeries. Its narrow, twisting streets were stony and muddy, worse than our back lanes. I was shocked.

Shut off from the rest of the planet by the highest mountains in the world, and politically isolated by royal decree, Kathmandu had been a forbidden city. Before 1950 entry into this remote and mysterious kingdom, the birthplace of Buddha and the land of Everest, was by invitation only. Since 1951 tourists had been trickling in. (It was to become the hippie capital of Asia in the 1960s.) Nepal still had no rail connections and offered only a jeep road which was constructed as late as 1950. It was no place for a tourist who liked night-clubbing and stylishly served food. Mr. Mendies trained the first waiters a few years before we arrived. When the Americans came, his students went to them for more money. But Mr. Mendies was still training waiters.

Since I know woefully little of Nepalese religion, I found their animal statues of sacred monkeys, dogs, cows and mythical animals grotesque, their carvings of humans gruesome. I found their erotic temple art simply obscene. I was told that Nepalese wood carvers were renowned for their depiction of sex scenes — ranging from the romantic to the raunchy — that decorate so many of their temples. But somehow I just couldn't appreciate the craftsmanship. I soon just refused to look at the erotic carvings. As a young Roman Catholic woman, I wasn't very tolerant of what I saw. Nothing could have prepared me for it. And I can tell you there is nothing like it to be seen in the Western World.

The Nepalese had one of the oldest and most complex cultures in Asia. They still clung to ancient customs like their worship of Kumari, Nepal's living virgin goddess, believed to be an incarnation of Kali, the wrathful consort of Shiva, the God of destruction and terror. The lady-in-waiting of the Kumari waved to us from an upstairs window of the beautiful home with its over-hanging balconies and intricately carved latticed windows where the Kumari lives an isolated life. (When the Kumari begins menstruating, a sign that she is human after all, she has to retire and return to her home. She is replaced by another specially chosen young girl.)

Religion, an exotic mixture of Hinduism and Bud-dhism, was a powerful force. It governed the daily lives of the deeply spiritual Nepalese. It was a public affair. I saw women carrying trays of coloured powders, rice, and flower petals to stone images of their gods. I saw a woman applying vermilion paste to the forehead of a deity and pasting a food offering across its mouth. I saw a man saluting an image carved on stone. I saw another woman who pressed her forehead against an image of Kali, the goggle-eyed, black goddess of destruction hold-ing a sword in one hand, a dagger in another and holding in two other hands severed heads dripping blood. Her protruding tongue was as bright as a red raspberry. This statue stands in the centre of Kathmandu and it is said that anyone who tells a lie in front of it will die. I saw still another woman who left offerings at a small shrine of an elephant-headed God of good luck.

One religious rite which intrigued me was when about a dozen worshippers, men and women, lined up against a temple wall, cross-legged, and placed flowers into geometric patterns on large squares of coloured cloth. Little oil-filled *puja* lamps flickered by their sides. They would move the petals or put their palms together, prayer-like, according to instructions incanted by a person sitting on the temple wall. I had the impression that they were making a mandela.

Although I felt honoured when we were invited to visit the China Lama, the alleged representative of the Dalai Lama, I was not spiritually moved. Dressed in a red satin coat, and spinning a hand-held prayer wheel, he welcomed us into his home. His flawless English, spoken as he sat lotus-fashion in a large chair impressed me, but his business acumen shocked me. As a sideline to his religious profession, he was in the carpet business, selling Tibetan rugs. We did not buy, but a young American couple, whom we kept bumping into, did make a purchase.

We spent our time walking about Durbar Square, the busy heart of Kathmandu. A bronze statue of an early eighteenth century king sat atop a tall stone pillar. The king rests beneath a cobra with a flared hood and on the cobra's head there is a small bird. According to legend, the king will not die until the bird flies away. I was intrigued by the Nepalese tiered pagoda-style temple architecture, especially Nepal's oldest *stupa*, the Swayambhunath, with its beautiful gold-coloured towers and the staring eyes of the all-seeing Buddha, painted on each of its four sides. It was called the Monkey Temple because of the hordes of monkeys who roamed around the temple living on the offerings of food which the people left there. I soon began to resent them because they were constantly hopping, chattering, climbing up my legs and milling about us. Everywhere we went, there were monkeys, even monkey twins. I would gladly have exterminated them.

Street scenes were at times depressing. Since there were few roads, goods had to be transported by human carriers and animals. I saw short, brown, bandy-legged

men bent double under heavy loads of wood on their
backs. I saw spindle-shanked men run with bamboos
which had heavy earthenware pots suspended at either
end slung across their shoulders. I saw old barefoot
women with tump lines on their foreheads supporting
unbelievable burdens. But once, to my delight, I heard
two wandering minstrels playing the *saranghi*, a stringed
instrument that looks like a violin. I saw people with *tika*
marks of red paste and rice on their foreheads. They
were offerings to the family deity for protection.

As everywhere else in the world, I noticed the love
and affection of parents for their children. Babies were
always pampered. I learned that children marry at seven
and eight years of age, and smoke at five. Like most
children, they were lively, responsive and curious as they
clustered excitedly around us, eager to touch us and to
hold our hands.

Even adults found us curiosities. Mrs. Mendies told
us that the children used to like to pinch her "elastic
skin." She was sure the Nepalese thought that white
people had elastic legs.

I especially enjoyed being invited to the official
opening of the American Consulate in Kathmandu on 6
August. We arrived in time, but the important Nepalese
dignitaries were late. No one was surprised. We knew
only too well just how casual was the oriental attitude to
time. The guests included several young, tall and slim
Indian women stunning in their saris, several slender
American women in sleeveless dresses and sunglasses,
and a number of American naval personnel, photogra-
phers and journalists. While they sweltered under the
scorching heat, I was enjoying the delay, listening to the
Royal Nepalese Army Band, taking movies, and sipping

the cool tall drinks that were being served by waiters dressed in typical Nepalese attire.

The ceremony took place on the roof, a vantage point which offered a spectacular view of Mt. Everest, the highest peak in the world. Unfortunately, it was the monsoon season, and the snow capped peak was hidden under fog and mist. However, I was able to admire the incredible ingenuity of the Nepalese farmers who tamed the mountains into beautifully terraced gardens.

Even as a Canadian, I was moved by the formal part of the ceremony, the raising of the American flag, while a Navy sergeant stood stiffly in a salute and the American national anthem was played.

The long delay had given me a chance however to chat with a number of American officials who explained Nepal's history and current reforms. I learned that the United States were involved in an economic, educational and medical assistance program since 1951. I met a few of the doctors who had given up lucrative practices to pioneer in the most unbelievably "primitive" conditions in a country so backward that Mrs. Mendies collected a few empty bottles and empty cold cream jars we were discarding. She told us the hospitals were so short of supplies that she would salvage the bottles that tourists threw away and cut off the sleeves from men's white shirts to serve as bed clothes.

The Indian Embassy, until 1950, was Nepal's only link with the outside world, and it wasn't until 1959 that Nepal joined the International Postage Union. Prior to this time, all letters passed through the Indian Embassy in Nepal, and were then carried by runners with spears through the mountain passes into India.

Three days in Nepal was enough for me. The sight of several women suffering with elephantitis haunted

and tormented me. I was covered with large mosquito
bites myself and lived in constant fear of picking up
meningitis.

India

We flew Indian Air Lines from Kathmandu to Agra. The
Agra airport was shabby. I later discovered it had been
built by the Americans during World War II. We came to
Agra to see the Taj. Its story has been handed down in
history as one of the world's most beloved love stories.
As I stood before this gleaming white marble marvel, I
was lost in wonder and enchantment. For the first time
in India I stood in awe of the sheer beauty of a building.
Built by the grief-stricken Moghal emperor Shah Jahan,
as a tomb to a beloved wife to perpetuate her memory,
it took an army of 20,000 men, and more then twenty-
one years to complete it in 1653. It still stands today,
majestic and beautiful in its simplicity, the greatest example of Moghul architecture. The essential design of the
building is simple: a giant dome surrounded by four
smaller domes rises above a square marble terrace, and
at each corner of the terrace there is a slender graceful
minaret. But the intricacies of the structure are endless.
The corridors and facades are lined with exquisite
screens of hand-carved marble as delicate as white lace,
and the entire structure is decorated with flower inlays
made of lapis-lacquer, mother-of-pearl, jade, agate and
carnelian. All of these elements are combined to create
a masterpiece with nothing to blemish its harmonious
unity. I could not take my eyes away.

Not only was the Taj in itself a white rhapsody in
stone, but its perfectly groomed green gardens and calm
reflecting pools were also a delight. The harmony in

colour and design pleased the eye, but it was the tranquillity and calmness of the whole scene that
overwhelmed my senses. Miss Rutledge and I spent
several hours just strolling about. I sat on a white marble
bench in front of it, too overawed to speak. Nearly forty
years later a widely circulated photograph showed the
late Princess of Wales sitting alone on the same white
marble bench, admiring the Taj.

Whatever else we saw in Agra was overshadowed by
this precious jewel. All that day, I travelled in a trance,
mesmerized by the Taj's magic. But the old master crafts-
man, sitting cross-legged, fashioning a marble plate with
a design I had noticed on the walls of the Taj, in one of
the many wonderful handicraft stores we were led into,
captured my attention. I marvelled as I watched him
place the thinnest red stone petal on a rose. He could
create only two marble plates a month, which were
selling for only two dollars each. I succumbed to the
beautiful crafts before me, dazzled by the gorgeous
Benares silks and ornate brocades with silver and gold
threads, the ivory carvings, the copper and brass inlay
with exquisite designs in red, green and blue enamel,
filigreed silver and tortoise shell.

We were assailed by vendors selling garlands of
jasmine blossoms associated with good luck, and fortune
tellers, palm readers and astrologers. One astrologer
kept pestering me, insisting that he could give me the
name of the man I was going to marry. I half-heartedly
gave in. To my utter shock, he spoke the name,
"Stephenson" in his heavily accented English. John and
I were close platonic friends until he died in 1989.

We made arrangements to travel to Jaipur, the capital of the desert state of Rajasthan by private car since
once again we were having difficulties with air reserva-

tions. En route, we visited Fatehpur Sikri, built by a
Moghul Emperor who constructed the city by flattening
a ridge of hills. It had to be abandoned after fourteen
years for lack of adequate water supply. However, the
city's palaces, its mosque, its fort, and its carvings and
paintings survived, silent relics of the Moghuls who
created an architecture dramatic and yet elegant. It was
this Moslem simplicity of design, achieved by good taste
and imagination, that never failed to fascinate me, to
make my nerve endings just tingle. The Hindu art and
architecture of India, on the other hand, never failed to
repulse me. For the sake of fairness, however, I was told
that the part of India I visited did not contain examples
of pure Hindu art, occupied and invaded as it was by
conquering nations. For Hindu art and architecture at
its best, where the Moslems did not penetrate, I was told
that I must visit Southern India.

I'll never forget how ashamed I felt after a young
Indian, bursting with pride came up to me, beaming,
"It's beautiful, isn't it?" He was referring to the enormous, modern Hindu temple in New Delhi newly built
by Birla, the Indian car manufacturer millionaire. Just as
he spoke, I had been trying to muster an appreciation for
the temple, searching myself for appropriate expressions
of awe and humility. But I could not help thinking how
garish it seemed to me. His reaction had staggered me.
Yet the religion that had inspired it, and had perpetuated
the poverty I saw in Benares and Calcutta must have
possessed powers of strength-giving vigour, and peace of
mind to its followers. For how could it have held such a
man as Gandhi? How could it hold such a man as
Nehru? That was part of the mystery of the East which
baffled me.

Our driver to Jaipur had been the American Colonel Siemen's chauffeur during World War II. He was a good driver. One had to be a good driver on India's terrible highways, which were worse than our back lanes in the 1940s.

If I forgot that I was whizzing by in a twentieth century vehicle (I couldn't because we were being jerked, bumped, and hurtled) I easily imagined myself in a world of centuries ago, for rural India is still as it must have been hundreds of years ago — barefoot peasants were tilling the tired beige soil with wooden ploughs. I didn't see any farm machinery of any sort. I did see women washing clothes, women with huge brass vessels at wells, one with a brass water jug on top of another perched on her head, water buffalos wallowing in green pools, mud villages, ragged children, bullock carts, a menagerie of queer looking birds of beautiful colours and hues (parrots, peacocks, minah birds), and monkeys by the score, all squealing and screaming. Monkeys were regarded with special affection. Hanuman, the monkey king, was a favourite figure in Hindu religious rites. Oxen, elephants, camels and cows were also considered sacred because their milk is symbolic of the spirit of divine motherhood.

Our driver was in a hurry to get to Jaipur before dark because he had heard that several bridges and roads were washed over by the monsoons. Consequently, he wasn't wasting time even to stop so that we could take pictures. Of course this annoyed us and really frustrated Marjorie. I can still hear her say: "Oh, wouldn't that make a wonderful picture. Oh, there's so much picture material here." Thank goodness Marjorie was with us. I'm sure I wouldn't have half my pictures if she hadn't reminded me: "You'll regret it when you get home.

You'll be sorry that you didn't get more pictures." But it was hot and my camera was heavy! It was so much bother to stop the car and wriggle ourselves out. The driver was in a hurry and the many animals were restricting his speed. Dozens of white cows were just strolling or lying in the middle of the road. Once, in order to avoid a cow our driver swerved so quickly and sharply I suddenly found myself on Miss Rutledge's lap. The peacocks, India's national bird, also kept strutting to the middle of the road to have a wide stage for the exhibition of their tails. In Rajusthan, peacocks were very tame and wandered through the villages in large flocks, helping themselves to grain, seeds and grass. There were scores of them on the way. Indian birds, unaccustomed to cars, kept hitting the grill and windshield. Poor Marjorie kept lecturing our driver on cruelty to animals. Evelyn and I kept silent. Our driver had to be in Jaipur before dark.

We did find a bridge washed out. We had to get out of the car and detour across mud and water. I still don't know how our driver managed to get the car over the detour. Workmen repairing the bridge told us that the car in front of us sank deep into the mud, ruining the suitcases in the trunk. But slowly and carefully our driver jolted his car to safety on the road. Not one of the workmen had volunteered to help. We shot into Jaipur at sunset. Our driver was pleased. We had arrived on schedule in spite of many obstacles and hazards. He was wonderful.

Driving through Jaipur to our hotel was exciting. It was sunset, and the city, encircled by rugged mountains, glowed a brilliant orange and rose pink. (Jaipur is known as the pink city because its magnificent palaces are constructed from a pink-coloured sandstone.)

Hundreds of people in gay colourful garb were milling about. Jaipur was in a festive spirit. The farmers were in town celebrating. The rains had come; the harvest would be plentiful. It was 19 August, and another age-old custom (Rakhi) was being celebrated when, from ancient warrior days, brothers assumed a protective responsibility towards sisters. Sister would place a coloured thread on brother's wrist and brother would pledge his everlasting aid in all things. Even Alexander the Great became an Indian queen's brother on this day, and having to comply with the conditions of the ritual, he was forced to liberate his enemy, the Indian king, because his "sister" had asked for her husband's release. I wanted to get out of our taxi and have fun too, but we drove on to our hotel, a former Maharajah's palace.

The next day we visited the local points of interest, but it was the people who fascinated me most. The women wore bright, long, very wide cotton skirts, blouses and head shawls of bright crimson, iridescent pink, aquamarine, fiery orange and yellow. The *tilak*, a round spot of coloured powder on the middle of their foreheads, the mark of the third eye, symbolized wisdom. Tiers of silver bracelets adorned wrists and upper arms; gold adorned ears, noses and toes and heavy silver, ankles. The women were a riot of colour as they surged forth barefoot in groups, dressed in their colourful finery and family fortunes. Even the men were colourful in their immense bright turbans, twisted in all sorts of ways. The men of Jaipur were famous for wearing the biggest and brightest turbans in the whole of India.

The crowds were boisterous. Outdoor booths with all sorts of native sweets and cakes heaped high like yellow or pink mountains were everywhere. Refriger-

ated, ice cold water, buttermilk, and sandalwood sherbet
stalls, each with its stock of about ten glasses, were
scattered every few hundred feet. It was frying hot, and
these stalls were doing a booming business. Who cared
about hygiene and sanitary precautions? People were
thirsty. A glass was rinsed now and then during a lull in
business. We didn't eat street food and avoided fresh
green salads and raw vegetables because we were warned
that dysentery was endemic. The hodgepodge of vendors, of bangles, balloons, and souvenirs were all
hawking their wares. The farmers had lots of money to
spend. The crowd was scattered in groups: some
watched a band of musicians, others a juggling performance, still others a wrestling match. Some socialized,
squatting on their haunches on the grass under huge
black umbrellas.

I was having so much fun that I didn't want to go
back to the hotel. Consequently, I enjoyed the half-hour
taxi drive to relocate the display of pottery Marjorie had
seen at the start of our tour. The driver was exasperated.
The crowds were a menace. But it gave me another
opportunity to enjoy them. At last we found the pottery
display: row on row of black and red earthenware vessels. Marjorie took a picture.

We visited the Maharajah of Jaipur's palace, a fantasy
in pink. It comprised several buildings, all gorgeously
furnished with plush carpets, crystal chandeliers, huge
portraits, and gilded chairs decorated with precious
stones. The panels of carved alabaster, intricate inlay
work, and mirrored mosaics left me breathless.

The Maharajah was in England at the time. As I
gazed at his portrait while the palace guards recited their
commentary, I noticed the English medals and decorations on his breast and wondered what he thought of the

change in India. I felt a pang of pity for him, but just for an instant, because I quickly recalled the misery and squalor outside the palace walls.

Camels are the most practical beasts of burden in the desert regions of India. Rajasthan is arid, little more than a desert. It was not surprising to see a caravan of twelve camels superciliously file by in front of the palace. Later I saw more camels parked in front of the beautiful Palace of the Winds that housed the Maharajah's harem, who could observe the main street without being seen. I photographed a rider sitting on his camel holding a large black umbrella to shield him from the sun.

The rain fell in torrents on our way to the airport. I had never heard rain pelting and hammering the good earth with such force. But by the time we reached the airport the rain had stopped, and we were able to fly to New Delhi.

New Delhi was fast becoming like any other thriving modern capital city. The new city built by the British as their capital, boasted parks, enormous modern public buildings, and vaulted arcades and wide thoroughfares. There was only one difference — no traffic jams. It contrasted sharply with the narrow streets and slums of the crowded walled city of Old Delhi which was the capital of the Moghul emperors who ruled between 1526 and 1857.

Mahatma Gandhi had always fascinated me: the man who called for civil disobedience and massed organized non-violence; who preached the sanctity of all living things, who encouraged cottage industries with the spinning wheel as the symbol of his program; and who wore the homespun *khadi*. He was the master teacher, the apostle of peace.

No wonder I was delighted when our guide took us to Raj Ghat, the hallowed spot where Gandhi was cremated on 31 January 1948. We had to remove our shoes before walking into the garden area. Some of the members of our group laid flower garlands on his plain *samadhi* (place of cremation), as simple and bare as the life he led; others prayed at each of the four corners. All of us respectfully paid our respects. I felt comforted because they were honouring him, a man whose sole interest in life was his motherland. Our guide proudly articulated India's history when I asked him questions about Gandhi and his horrible assassination, about the English, about the Indian mutiny which he insisted on calling the "First War of Independence," and about India's present problems. He had that zeal and spirit of high purpose that pioneers all have.

Every day that I spent in India made me wonder just what the English had done during their rule of 200 years. During the nineteenth and the first half of the twentieth century, India was regarded as the "brightest jewel in the British crown." But the village people (80 per cent of the Indian population) were still living as they did 200 years ago. Our guide told us that in the whole of India there was only one small fertilizer plant. The squalor, and illiteracy, the poverty and disease were still there. As one educated Indian told me, under the British Raj, the Indians could not even manufacture their own needles! I could sympathize with his anger. But most educated Indians were not bitter towards the British. They didn't want to be reminded of past pain; they looked ahead, and were working towards a better future now that the yoke was off. If the British did not bother to improve the economic and social conditions of India, they did establish the principles of democracy and parliamentary government. Because of them, the world's largest bastion of democracy is India.

Through the good offices of Mr. A. P. Jain, we were fortunate to witness Indian Parliamentary government at work! Three visitors' permits had arrived at our hotel, too late for us to break prior commitments. But we had difficulty replacing them, having to go to one of the government buildings where we encountered strict entrance regulations. Hundreds of men were hanging around the lobbies and entrances, waiting for appointments, all desirous of political favouritism and patronage. A. P. Jain, M.P., was out of town; his secretary, his under-secretary, under-under-secretary, under-under-under-secretary, as well as a few really submerged clerks were in his office to meet us. All were extremely courteous as they pressed the palms of their hands together and greeted us with the Hindu salutation *Nameste*, which is Sanskrit for "I bow my head to you," with heads slightly bowed as a mark of respect. Then came the logical question, in heavily accented English: "Why do you want another visitor's card?" We had difficulty in convincing them why.

However, everything was soon arranged, and the next day we were provided with a special guide. We were taken through the President's house. The huge portraits of former English viceroys and their wives still hung on the walls. The huge spacious ballroom, which held many a splendid fashionable ball in the days of the Raj was scarcely used now, because, we were told, western-style dancing had not caught on in India.

On Wednesday, 12 August at eleven a.m., after having been liberated of our cameras and purses, we entered the public gallery of Lok Sabha, the lower house, or house of the people. It was a solemn moment

for me. I had never attended a session of parliament
before in my life. We tiptoed quietly to the first row, not
to miss anything. I noticed a number of women members. I was glad. But the continuous exits and entrances
of the honourable members annoyed me. Apart from
this annoyance, I found the discussion about the Communist demonstration at the Indian chancery in Ceylon,
and Nehru's answers to opposition members' questions
most interesting. In his soft voice and in his flawless
English, Nehru hoped that at least the members were
mature and would not lose their heads. There were no
hot denunciations, no retaliative reprisals but a quiet
proposal that the matter would be investigated further.
Time would simmer down tempers. Tolerance was a
blessing! And the Hindus had lots of it.

A dull debate on the possibility of the nationaliza-
tion of India's banks took place. Unfortunately for
Marjorie, we missed a debate on the "Prevention of
Cruelty to Animals" Bill. But she does have the newspaper describing the debate to prove that some interest was
being shown towards her pet concern.

We were delighted when an M.P. stopped to drive
us to our hotel, while we were waiting to hail a cab in
front of the round and red Parliament Buildings, which
in their spacious surroundings were very impressive.
This was the second instance when an Indian M.P.
picked us up. (At the Afghanistan Embassy, where we got
our visas free of charge much to our surprise, we were
taken back to our hotel by another Indian M.P. No
wonder we thought India's M.P.s were "prima!")

On the Sunday evening of 9 August we attended a
wonderful dance recital in the Fine Arts Theatre. There
was only one performer, Yamini Krishnamuti. Although
I didn't understand the significance of her movements, I

appreciated her technical skill and aesthetic sensitivity. Classical Indian dancing was centuries old. It was an art jealously guarded and carefully preserved. I liked what I saw of its gestures, movements, and poses. I even enjoyed the interlude of instrumental music. The musicians with their strange looking instruments were squatted on the floor of the stage at one end. The vocal accompaniments, some invocatory chants, others more recitative than melodious, fascinated me. For most Westerners, the music would probably have been considered discordant.

If India's elected representatives impressed us favourably, her airlines people thoroughly disgusted us. We were volleyballed around from one airlines office to another because we had an OPEN ticket. No one wanted to take responsibility. Indian Air Lines were supposed to be the Indian agents for T.C.A., K.L.M., S.A.S., Pan American and B.O.A.C., but they refused to carry us, claiming that it was illegal not to have a carrier company marked on our tickets. Our tickets had been purposely left open, in order to give us flexibility of time and route. Several days of rushing to air lines offices, only to be shunted back and forth, completely infuriated Miss Rutledge. At first, I accepted the see-sawing as part of the game. But I soon became just as impatient and frustrated. I phoned the Canadian Embassy and told them of our plight. They suggested that we try B.O.A.C. with whom they conducted their business. B.O.A.C. got us out of India. At the outset of our trip, we had no intention of visiting Afghanistan. In Nepal, however, an English lad who was staying at the Snow View told us we should, at all costs, visit this country, where the *purdah* still existed. He talked Marjorie and me into it. Miss Rutledge had no desire to visit any more hot coun-

tries she could otherwise avoid. However she yielded.
Afghanistan lying on the back doorstep of the Soviet
Union between Pakistan and Iran, was an ancient country of Asia. For thousands of years long caravans
carrying silk from China to the Middle East moved
along the narrow trails through the hills and valleys of
Afghanistan. On his way to India because it alone afforded access through the Khyber Pass, three hundred
years before the birth of Christ, Alexander the Great had
led his Macedonian Greeks through its mountains. I
wanted to go by bus from Peshawar to Kabul, the capital
of Afghanistan because I wanted to see the Khyber Pass.
But the reports of bad roads, crowded buses, uncertain
timetables, robbers, and brigands, deterred my companions. We eventually decided to fly from New Delhi to
Kabul.

But I was lucky to get out of New Delhi. While we
were going through customs, one of the officials casually
asked me how much cash I was carrying. Since I had the
night previous taken stock of my cash on hand, I inno-
cently told him the right amount. Then he asked to see
the currency declaration form I had filled out in Calcutta. (Indians love forms) The cash figures didn't
match. I had committed a grave crime. Once again I
could see I was going to have difficulties with Indian
bureaucracy. How could I have more cash now that I was
leaving the country than what I had when I entered the
country? I argued that the amount declared in Calcutta
was an approximate figure. The exacting officials
opened my suitcases and dumped out the contents. They
felt, poked, squeezed and rummaged to the bottom,
over and under and across to the sides, into the linings
and compartments of my suitcases. When they saw my
many films in their yellow boxes they suspected I was

selling them at black market prices, because it was practically impossible to buy film in India. I had visions of
their confiscating all my priceless film and all my money.
I could see myself branded as a smuggler and a perjurer.
Even though India offered the British legal system and
the writ of *habeas corpus*, I knew that I would not get a
fair trial because of the political abuse, bribery and
corruption that existed. I was innocent, but they could
make me look guilty. I wanted to cry.

Suddenly, I was ushered into a waiting room, where
an officer of the Indian Tourist Office wanted me to
answer a questionnaire. He had saved the day! I did not
dare give him any suggestions for improvements. I just
wanted to get out of that airport, away, far away, right
away!

Afghanistan

On 13 August, we landed at Kabul, the capital city of the
small landlocked mountain kingdom of Afghanistan.
Located 6,000 feet above sea level, Kabul is nestled on a
well-sheltered plateau at the foot of rocky and barren
mountain ranges. The simple small shack greeting us at
the airport looked lonely in its bleak, barren, dusty
brown surroundings. But I was so grateful to be out of
the airport of New Delhi. There were no hotel representatives meeting us here. There was no one at the
airport except a few American and Indian embassy people who were meeting compatriots. Nobody seemed to
notice us. We waited uneasily on the hard wooden
benches in the spartan reception room. Finally, we were
ushered into the tiny customs room. A small station
wagon was soon provided for us and we were driven to
the Kabul Hotel, the best in the city. On the well-paved

highway I noted the absence of overhead wires (thanks to Russian aid), something uncommon in my own hometown even today. Except for two wandering pedlars who carried brightly coloured rugs slung over their shoulders, Kabul's streets were practically empty.

Kabul Hotel, too, was a shock. What a gloomy place! It was a sprawling compound of dingy bare rooms. But when the pleasant and courteous manager informed us that there was no vacancy in the hotel we were stunned. He explained that the country was preparing for the Afghan Independence celebration, and that there were a number of visitors in town. (I did notice several Red Chinese guests.) However, finally, after much deliberation, he gave us a huge bedroom plus a sitting room. We were relieved.

If the hotel and the initial news of "no vacancy" stunned us, the dining room completely dumbfounded us. To get to it, we had to cross a wooden bridge that joined the two upper parts of the building, go down stairs, pass through several rooms, down a corridor, cross a courtyard, and climb stairs. The dining room was as dull and dingy as the rest of the rooms, and swarming with flies. We tried to find a table with a clean tablecloth, but there was none. After waiting about one-half hour, a waiter in a brown, soiled tunic arrived. He was pleasant enough, but not a trained waiter. Marjorie's serviette was soiled and stained and definitely needing a good wash. Miss Rutledge's was as bad. The waiter took them, but returned with two just as bad. The same ritual occurred at every meal time. But the roast beef was the best we had tasted on our whole tour. Miss Rutledge and Marjorie ordered it for every meal. I just couldn't eat in the fly-infested dining room! I survived on the most delicious fruit I have ever tasted in my life: melons, grapes, peaches and apples. I read recently that in the thirteenth century, en route to the Peking court of Kublai Khan, Marco Polo, travelling overland along the ancient trade route of Central Asia, had praised Afghanistan's melons as "the best melons in the world."

But our manager, in his gray caracul hat, a permanent fixture, did try to please. He sent us a representative from the Afghan Tours who, he said, would plan our activities for us. And so it was that Mohammed Seddiq Haider, dressed in a western gray pin-striped suit and the typical grey caracul hat, took charge. It wasn't surprising that he spoke fluent English because he had spent several years in the United States at the Afghanistan Embassy.

Mr. Haider drove us around Kabul and into the surrounding rural countryside. The wheat was a beautiful golden yellow. The harvest must have been just as it was in Biblical times: a young man riding a donkey guided two oxen that were dragging a heavy raft around the perimeter of a large stack of wheat, and another young man using a long stick guided a team of eight oxen, yoked together, as they trampled the wheat round and round a central post. Two young men wearing beautifully embroidered vests watched. Because the landscape in Afghanistan was predominantly drab expanses of rock and sand, the Afghans loved decoration. On the road we saw a few gaily decorated trucks spilling over with people clinging to them with such agility they seemed magnetized. We also saw a few horses with brightly coloured saddle bags and one horse-drawn carriage sporting pompoms and tinkling bells. But the ugly donkey was still the beast of burden. They slowly plodded forward carrying unbelievably heavy loads from sacks of grain to exceedingly long poles. I was reminded of G.K. Chesterton's "The Donkey":

> When fishes flew and forests walked
> And figs grew upon thorn,
> Some moment when the moon was blood
> Then surely I was born;
> With monstrous head and sickening cry
> And ears like errant wings,
> The devil's walking parody
> On all four-footed things.

We passed a group of men enjoying their tea under the shade of a tree. There were no women about. Mr. Haider told us that men and women did not mix in public.

Mr. Haider not only looked after us in the afternoon, but he was also an attentive host in the evenings. He had a wide circle of friends among various Embassies, and so we visited their homes. Here I saw a different picture of life in this underdeveloped country of 7,000,000 sandwiched between the U.S.S.R. and Pakistan: beautiful modern homes with walls 30 inches thick set inside high courtyard walls, up-to-date amenities of the west such as western plumbing and western attention to hygiene and sanitation! The foreign service was well looked after. At an American Embassy party I even met a chap who had gone to Assumption College, my *alma mater*.

I didn't see the squalor and poverty that I saw in India. The tribesmen from the hills wore beautifully lined multi-coloured cloaks reminiscent of Biblical times over a wide assortment of long-tailed shirts and wide baggy trousers. Men's heads were always covered in a variety of headgear from a coloured turban with a sheath of cloth hanging down the back to caracul or embroidered cloth hats. Children wore sandals. I didn't see one barefoot lad or an undressed child.

Mr. Haider took us to the Women's Co-operative School, operated by a group of high-class, educated Afghani women. Six hundred women, a great many of them in their thirties and forties, were learning for the first time to read and write. Most of them were married and their children attended classes in the same school.

As we visited the plain and bare classrooms, I noticed only one panel of blackboard space in each room. Nasser's picture, along with the King of Afghanistan's, were displayed on the front wall. The kindergarten room had pictures taken out of American magazines displayed on its walls.

The students stood up to greet us when we entered a room. Their eagerness and seriousness impressed me. And I'm sure we pleased them by our complimentary remarks on their knitting, exquisite embroidery work, cross stitching and beautifully executed *pishtu*.

All the students were dressed in pale blue, calf-length dresses and long stockings. Some even wore cuban-heeled shoes. Their drab dull brown or green *chadri* hung on hooks on the back walls of the class-rooms. These they would have to put on as soon as they left the building because their faces had to be completely covered when in public.

How the women hated the *chadri* (the ankle-length tent-like hooded cloaks worn over the women's clothes and faces when outside their homes), especially our young, twenty-two-year-old guide, tiny and pert Laily Waheed, one of the school's directors. She hated having to view the outside world through an embroidered lattice work. Since she had spent several years in England

where her husband served in the Afghan Consular service she spoke beautiful English. And having been
exposed to women in the western world, she envied
their freedom and their independence. But as she escorted us to the various classrooms, she proudly beamed
that the women of Afghanistan were slowly but surely
winning their emancipation too. The wearing of the
chadri would soon be relaxed, and the women would be
allowed to go out in long-sleeved, high-necked dresses.
Mrs. Waheed proudly told me:

> For a year now unveiled girls have been allowed to
> work as telephone operators. For the first time this
> spring about ten women of high-ranking Kabul families
> started work as receptionists and stewardesses for Ari-
> ana Afghan Airlines. Women are now working in the
> hospitals and soon they will be working in the factories.

I didn't see any women working in Kabul's bank, however, where we had to wait over an hour to get two
twenty-dollar American Express traveller's cheques
cashed, while we filled out countless forms.

I noticed that much attention was being paid to the
study of health. An American woman whose husband
was working on an American aid project was giving her
services free of charge, teaching courses in first aid,
hygiene and better living. It seemed strange to see
women of forty learning about personal cleanliness and
grooming for the first time. They were taught "to use
soap every time you wash and then rub dry with a
towel." Face soap was unheard of and towels were a
precious commodity. A picture taken from an American
magazine showing a little girl brushing her teeth with
one hand and holding a tube of Kolynos toothpaste in
another was being utilized to stress the importance of

brushing one's teeth. Realizing that toothpaste and brushes were luxury items in Afghanistan, I asked Mrs. Waheed how she managed to use the illustration. She explained that they actually brushed their teeth with a *miswak*, a twig about six inches long, taken from the *keeke* or *neem* tree. The end of the twig is chewed and juice that is thus worked up acts as a toothpaste. This juice, rich in chlorophyll and Vitamin C, had a detergent effect and whitened the teeth.

To Afghani women the study of the importance of milk in the diet was a new revelation. (There are no cows in the country. Milk is taken from goats, sheep and camels.) With another attractive illustration taken from an American magazine showing a ballerina tying the shoelaces of her slippers with a glass of milk on the floor beside her, Afghan women were learning that ballerinas drink milk to keep up their strength because the work of a ballerina is strenuous and tiring. So they, too, required milk for strength in their daily strenuous work. The ladies were told that milk was a perfect food essential to growing children and pregnant women. They were also taught how they could use milk in a variety of ways to produce all sorts of appetizing dishes from rice pudding (*kheer*) to a creamy fudge (*Gulqand*).

"Of course you, in your country take all these things for granted," Mrs. Waheed continued, "but to these women such basic fundamentals of good health are new discoveries. They are the rays of hope for a better life."

In a country where many women die in childbirth because of ignorance, because custom forbids male doctors to attend female diseases (there are no women doctors) something must be done. And Afghani women were finally doing something about it. Their task was gargantuan. The cooperation of the government was essential. In a country where women must obtain permission from their husbands to go even to the market, the cooperation and consent of all males in the cause of women's education was essential. And the women, bound by taboos centuries old, had to be willing themselves to break with custom and accept the new freedoms. This they would be encouraged to do only if the wives and daughters of tribal chieftains set the example.

Mrs. Waheed's enthusiasm, and her evangelical dedication to the improvement of women's lot in her country made me happy. I left the Women's Co-Operative School feeling certain that with vigorous zealots like Mrs. Waheed, the women of Afghanistan would not fail in their struggle against illiteracy, ignorance and bondage.

Afghanistan has a harsh desert climate. Neither the dry, dusty Afghan winds hammering sand mercilessly against my face, nor the danger of sliding off the slippery seat of my *gadee* (a two-wheeled horse-drawn taxi) could irritate me this time as I bounced along back to my hotel. I was lost, soaked in thought recalling words of the brave young suffragettes of the Women's Co-Operative school who would never yield in their fight for equality: "The beauty of the face is not complete without an educated mind. For the proper and harmonious working of a family, the education of the fair sex is essential."

(Afghanistan is now struggling to recover from the Soviet invasion of the 1980s and years of civil war which have left a decimated population, a devastated countryside and great political uncertainty. Fundamentalists are in control and do not permit women to wear western dress, makeup or being seen alone in the streets.

Mrs. Waheed's bright new world for Afghan women has been shattered.)

Ariana was the only airline that could fly us direct to our next destination, Teheran, the capital of Iran. I harboured misgivings about flying on it, but I didn't dare express them to my companions. Ariana's Kabul office was shabby and small, musty with a small town informality. Nothing like the elegant and spacious Air Line offices of the West. Our reservations were registered on a large sheet of paper in the most unbusinesslike manner. The airlines didn't even adhere to a definite schedule. I wondered whether we would ever reach our destination. But Ariana landed us safely in the very modern airport at Teheran.

Iran

It was like being thrown into a hot oven when we opened the door of the airplane at Teheran airport. It was the first time during the whole trip that I found the heat unbearable. On the way to the hotel I was struck with the silence of the city. Streets were still and vacant. Even dogs and cats were nowhere to be seen. I had read a great deal about the glamorous life of the Shah and the royal family, and their parties for the rich and the famous, and had always envisaged Teheran as a bustling, noisy, commercial city influenced by the west, especially by Germany and the United States. To see it completely deserted was a shock, but I soon realized it was Friday, the Moslem Sabbath.

I can't remember why we just didn't relax in our hotel rooms, but we didn't. We couldn't stay very long in Teheran and we knew that we had to get as much information about sightseeing tours as quickly as possible. That was easier said than done. Even the American offices weren't much help. The local government tourist office was indifferent and their rates terribly high.

However, once back at the hotel, I stumbled into a big burly man who looked like a boxer. He seemed to be familiar with the office staff, and I told him of our plight. Immediately he volunteered to give us a comprehensive tour of the city at half the price of the government office. We accepted!

Because of the Moslem Sabbath we were going to miss the Golestan Palace. But he assured us he could get us in, even though the palace was closed to tourists that day. We didn't question his "know-how" because we realized that this would be our only chance.

The Golestan Palace was fabulous. The huge spacious room that held the Peacock Throne was breathtakingly beautiful with its dazzling mirrored mosaics, its rugs and paintings. The jewel-encrusted throne glittered with precious emeralds and diamonds. But what impressed me most were the most beautiful chandeliers and Persian rugs I had ever seen. As I read the reports of the Shah's recent wedding reception at the Palace, I could imagine the Palace gleaming and shimmering in glamorous regal splendour. (In 1979, the Ayotollah Khomeini, a Shiite religious leader, led a revolution that overthrew the Shah.)

The rugs at the Palace had so overwhelmed us that we wanted to visit a rug factory. Our opportunity came at Isfahan. There I witnessed a sight that disgusted me. Seated on a high scaffold was a row of tiny little girls with quick nimble fingers working away at a wall of thousands of coloured threads. Following the intricate sketches before them, they were weaving the most beautiful patterns on a huge rug commissioned by a wealthy

Persian. The little girls were four and one-half years old. I can still see them with kerchiefs tied around their small heads, with solemn little faces and big black inquiring eyes, eyes that would be blind by the time they were twenty. They earned from twenty to forty cents a day. Our guide was quick to add that lunch was provided *gratis* for them. He explained that since it took four years for the little girls to finish some rugs, there wasn't much profit left.

The attention span and the intent concentration of the little girls had amazed me. I couldn't help but wonder why our children were so different, why they became so restless so quickly! That is one feature of the Eastern way of life that has never failed to impress me — this complete concentration of youngsters, whether it was a little Indian boy weaving beautiful brocade in Benares, or a young Persian in a bazaar carving a design on a copper vase, or a young Japanese apprentice concentrating on minute details on a lacquered bowl, or a small Indian apprentice never lifting his eyes from hammering a huge brass tray. I should love to know the secret of how to train youngsters to concentrate in the oriental manner.

Iran was rich in historical interest, and thus we found it difficult to select places we could visit during our limited stay. Miss Rutledge wanted to leave as quickly as possible to get relief from the stifling heat. For the first time on the trip, the heat was wearing me out too, but I wouldn't give in. Luckily, there was Marjorie, whom I'm sure controlled a private automatic temperature switch. She seemed to have the temperature controlled all the time. After much discussion as to where we should go we finally agreed that we would go to Isfahan (Marjorie's choice) and the Caspian Sea (my choice). Miss Rutledge reluctantly submitted. Solomon, the hotel manager convinced us that we should let him take us to the Caspian Sea because he was willing to guarantee our safe arrival. Since we thought we had better be cautious in a strange country, we hired him.

Iran is one of the highest countries in the world. Most of the country, except for narrow strips along the coast, lies on a high plateau with an average height of four to five thousand feet above sea level. The rough gravel mountain roads were not like the sleek, blue, paved Swiss or Italian. If I thought the hairpin turns of the serpentine ribbons that kept dizzyingly mounting on the island of Capri had been dangerous, the mountain roads of Iran were simply terrifying. And the fierce winds that blew the harsh sand from the beige parched mountain slopes mercilessly lashed both road and vehicles. I didn't know which was worse — the dust that choked me and parched my lips to such a dry corrugated texture that they crackled when they parted, or the thoughts of crashing down perpendicular bare rock to certain death. As we kept surging higher and higher, we noticed several car crashes. These didn't help to dispel my horrible fears. I prayed to God as we kept nearing his domain, to preserve us from such an end. After what I thought was a final summit there was always another peak, just a little steeper and higher, just around another blind corner. I was sorry I had suggested this terrifying trip.

At last a change of scenery. We finally reached flat lands, flat green lands: the emerald green of an oasis, with orange groves and palm trees. Oh, how good that green looked! And just as the nomad blesses an oasis as it looms in sight, I blessed this pleasant greenness. Solomon said we were nearing the Caspian Sea. Located between Iran and the U.S.S.R., it is the largest land-locked body of water in the world. We passed fishing villages decked out in rugs to celebrate the Norad Celebrations. We passed fertile fields under a clear and dazzling sky. When we finally reached the sea, the dust had vanished and cool fresh breezes blew. I was glad that Miss Rutledge could cool off. We passed several empty seaside resorts. There were miles and miles of beach but no one there. There were a few modern buildings in the process of construction, mostly restaurants and hotels. We had tea in one of these new unfinished restaurants. A group of schoolboys were eating heaping bowls of steamed rice.

Finally, we reached our hotel (a former palace) at Ramsar, standing elegantly in the middle of lovely terraced gardens and tree-lined walks with a green mountain as a backdrop and the blue sea. It looked like an Italian Renaissance palazzo plopped down in this out-of-the way place. I was surprised to find such opulence, such beauty.

But the interior of our Iranian hideaway wasn't as opulently furnished as the exterior had suggested. The glassed-in-showcases in the large main rotunda displayed cans, cartons and jars of imported British and American foods: baby foods, corn flakes and jams. In Russia I had judged the category of our hotels by the quality of the toilet paper ranging from newspaper of various "tear" resistance and sizes to sheets of sandpaper or waxed paper. Here in the Far East I judged the category by showcases ranging from the rummage sale variety of odds and ends, to the elegant "haute couture" of glittering ball attire.

We enjoyed our quiet interlude at Ramsar, the pearl of the Caspian Sea. Solomon and I enjoyed the high warm waves splashing over us. Miss Rutledge and Marjorie enjoyed their walks. The beach was rough with tufts of weeds scattered about, not the smooth powdery soft white sands which I had expected, but the sound and the smell of the water and the fresh breezes were pleasant, certainly more agreeable than the scorching heat and the fierce sands further south.

The women bathers looked like a select, swanky, sophisticated group such as I saw at the internationally famous Biarritz Beach. Most of them, whether in bathing suits, or lovely western dresses, looked as if they had stepped out of a page in Vogue. They must have belonged to Iran's westernized high society. I didn't see any women wearing the *chador*. Nor did I see any men wearing the long flowing robes and turbans that form part of traditional Islamic dress.

The return drive was a nightmare I shudder to recollect. Solomon deserved a gold medal for his driving skills. Even Miss Rutledge, who looked upon him as a shrewd exploiter of tourists, condescended to pay tribute to him. I honestly don't know how he was able to manoeuvre the hairpin turns of the circuitous mountain roads as he sliced the thick fog that completely shrouded both mountains and roads. We passed a number of parked cars that did not dare to tackle the fog. I secretly wished we could stop too. I tried to keep my eyes closed so that I couldn't see what the driver couldn't see. And yet he seemed to guide the car as if by some sort of radar supplied by an unseen hand. I felt as if I were on a merry-go-round being elevated and lowered, going round and round.

Finally, we crawled into a small village where Solomon stopped at a café that was still open. Miss Rutledge and Marjorie got out. I stayed in my sanctuary to observe my surroundings. We were on the main street of a village, a muddy washboard road peppered with rough jagged boulders. Even an army jeep would have regarded the road with distaste, but Solomon crawled over it as lightly as he could, to spare his car and his passengers.

Solomon had looked after us well. We arrived at our hotel exhausted and grimy, but Solomon deserved all the credit. It had been a gruelling experience for him. I couldn't help comparing him to Roland in Browning's "How they Brought the Good News," except that no friends flocked round to pour a last measure of wine down Solomon's dry throat. I wanted to kiss him, just to show him my appreciation, but there was not even a cup of hot tea to refresh him!

We had only a few hours rest before our plane flight to Isfahan. The city possessed the most beautiful mosques imaginable. The Koran forbids Moslems to create human and animal images. Consequently, the magnificent mosques of Iran were decorated with geometric designs, floral motifs and texts from the Koran in Arabic. The mosaic tile work of the turquoise dome of the Masjid-i-shah Mosque was simply breathtaking. I was so entranced that my eyes just kept being uplifted to behold its bewitching beauty. The effect on me was incredible, like a conversion. I felt I was being lifted up to God.

No two domes in the whole of Iran were exactly alike. They were similar in style, but their details differed. The cream-coloured tile work of the dome of the Sheikh Lutfullah Mosque looked as if it had just been polished it gleamed so in the sun.

Our sightseeing in Isfahan was hectic. The streets were jam-packed with honking cars, screeching brakes, noisy scooters, motor bikes, and buses. The jostling, raucous crowds were a constant nuisance. Our driver kept being stopped by policemen who were trying to hold back the surging crowds, and to designate certain streets as "one way" or as "no entry." Our driver did his best, squeezing in and out of the heavy traffic.

The town was decorated with flags and banners, coloured lights and rugs to celebrate both Norad and the Shah's return. Huge beautiful rugs covered victory arches in a square where a victory rally was held. Rugs covered buses and store fronts, and photographs of the Shah were everywhere: photographs of the Shah's face in right profile, and in left profile, and photographs of the Shah in full royal regalia, in military uniform, and in street clothes. They were posted on bus, car and shop windows, as well as truck windshields. There were big photographs in big stores, small photographs in small shops, medium-sized photographs in medium sized stores, and huge portraits in prosperous establishments. (Twenty years later in 1979, the Shah would be overthrown, and the world's most ancient monarchy become the Islamic Republic of Iran.) In the parade there were army trucks, tanks (some American), Iranian soldiers, earning about fifteen cents a month and civilians. The crowds were excited, in anticipation of the rally that evening. I was sorry we couldn't stay.

Dayoni, our Teheran guide, was not unlike most Eastern men who were fascinated with North American women. He took a special interest in me above and beyond his call of duty, inviting me to dinner and taking me to the Djafari Sport Club in Teheran to witness a gymnastics class which he said I had never seen the likes of. (In Iran, women were not seen with men in public. Of course, I didn't know this.)

The Djafari Sport Club was no western-style stadium. Hexagonal in shape and domed, the ten-year-old
structure looked more like a monument with its beautiful mosaics and bas-reliefs. I felt like visiting royalty as
we were ushered to an elevated private observation
room. I noticed that there were three such rooms for
visiting dignitaries while the ordinary people sat below
on bleachers. Our private viewing room held five box
seats and a small table with a vase of gladiolas in the
centre. No sooner had we sat down than bottles of
Pepsi-cola and a tray loaded with cookies were brought
in. Everyone seemed to know Dayoni and paid defer-
ence to him.

Spectators were trickling in and finally the stadium
was filled. I noticed that I was the only woman present.
I mentioned it to Dayoni and he said it was perfectly "in
order." At first I felt squeamish, but then I rationalized
that surely Dayoni would not jeopardize his own prestige by violating some sacred rule stating that no women
were allowed. Or would he? He was such a dare-devil
that the Iranian women in semi *chadri* probably dared
him to invite me.

Just as I was immersed in this thought, drums began
to roll, a strange music began and eighteen of the biggest, burliest, brownest, barefoot men appeared. To the
accompaniment of drums and the chanting of a religious
invocation — "God help us" — they began to do
pushups, feet astride, and jumping exercises. They
would begin very slowly, and then with the crescendo
and accelerando of the music their incantations followed and movements gained momentum until they
worked themselves up to a feverish pitch. They dripped
with perspiration which they wiped off with red towels.

They performed all sorts of strong men acts, such as lifting a chain weighing forty kilograms and thrusting it back and forth over their heads. They threw wooden clubs weighing fifteen to twenty-five kilograms, twenty-five feet high and caught them in perfect time to their litany-like chanting. They performed as a group and as individuals in a pit, each, with very little space. One act I can still remember was circling on the spot on one foot with arms outstretched. One gymnast worked himself up to such a wild frenzy that he lost control and had to be caught by a colleague. They walked on their hands; they rolled on carpets on the ground level and then jumped into the pit. They danced what appeared to me an African tribal dance. They flexed powerful muscles; they did head exercises all to drum, cymbal music and chants.

I detected a locker room camaraderie among the performers. In fact, the relationship among them appeared affectionate. Wrapping themselves in blankets, they dismissed themselves in ceremonial fashion for a well-earned steam bath. For me, the show had been an interesting novelty, not so much the exercises themselves, but the whole demonstration with its religious overtones and musical accompaniments.

If our entrance had been exciting, our exit was sensational. We were ushered into the office of the "boss," a giant of a man who had just returned after a series of wrestling victories. The victory arch covered with gorgeous carpets in front of the stadium had been erected in his honour. As we left the club, all the spectators stood still and watched us leave, and I again felt like visiting royalty.

Unfortunately, Dayoni became very jealous when I had made a dinner date with an Iranian guest at the hotel. He kept insisting that I had to spend my last evening in Teheran with him. Consequently, from six p.m. to twelve a.m. he kept pestering me. He told me he was going to box the other fellow out. He kept phoning my hotel room. They were both phoning me. I decided I would go out with neither. Poor Miss Rutledge! She couldn't get to sleep and I went to bed hungry because I could not go down to the hotel dining room for fear of meeting my two friends whom I knew were there. I just wanted morning to come in a hurry so that we could fly away.

Ever since my first trip to the Middle East in 1956, I had wanted to visit Baghdad, the capital of Iraq, in the fertile valley of the Tigris and Euphrates Rivers in the area known as Mesopotamia. About five thousand years ago, between 3,500 and 2,500 B.C., the first civilization developed here.

In every capital city I had made inquiries about obtaining an Iraqi visa. Each time I was told that it was difficult to obtain but that Teheran would be the best place to get it. I made three trips before I was given an audience with the Iraqi counsel. Each time I noticed the anteroom of his suite of offices filled with men waiting for appointments. Each time I was made to feel it was a singular honour and privilege to see the great potentate himself. On the third attempt I was ushered into his large office. I had to submit to a cross-examination. Then an indoctrination course followed on the merits of his government's policies. Did I know what his government was doing for the children, for family life? Do we in the West, celebrate a "Children's Day"? He showed me a copy of the *Iraq Times* and pointed to a special section devoted to the children of Iraq. He gave me the newspaper. Then in solemn, sinister tones he told me that "the west is paying the price of Israel," and that we became their enemies when his country overthrew imperialism. His fanaticism was frightening me. I was too afraid to protest. All I wanted was a quick exit. When he smiled that he could not grant me a visa unless I waited two weeks, I told him I was no longer interested in visiting Iraq and darted out of the door.

Our plane was due to leave Teheran at six a.m., but when we arrived at the airport we were told our plane wouldn't leave until eleven a.m. We finally boarded a plane chartered by a group of American university people en route to the American Oil Company at Abadan. We were taking the long way to Beirut, but we were able to participate in lectures the group was hearing as we passed over a sea of sand, camel trails, the Tigris and Euphrates and the Persian Gulf.

Kuwait

Our group disembarked at Kuwait airport. If leaving the airport at Teheran was like being thrust into a hot oven, crossing the tarmac at Kuwait was like plunging into a red-hot blast furnace. The sitting room was swarming with men in long white ankle length shirts; a few wore western style tweed or checkered suit coats over them. But all wore a head covering of flowing thin white material held down to fit the head with two black twisted cords. The veiled Moslem women were completely covered in black *chowdahs*. A steamy, smelly heat was pervasive. Everyone was gulping pop. Pepsi rather than Coke. (The printed proclamation in Arabic and English on the bottle read "non-alcoholic") By the time we inched our way to the counter to use the complementary chits, the ice-cold pop had been sold out.

There was standing room only, and I leaned against a post watching the crowd. The veiled women were having difficulty drinking their pop or coffee. Parents were showering their love on their pampered children. As I was enjoying watching the crowd, the "all aboard" signal came.

On the plane, Miss Rutledge and I, and a male passenger, were the only ones aboard to enjoy the private services of two stewardesses. I reluctantly smuggled some cartons of cigarettes for one of them.

En Route to Israel

We stopped at Beirut the capital of Lebanon. I saw very little change from my visit in 1956 three years earlier.

In Jerusalem the small and crowded airport that had greeted me in 1956 had been transformed into a new large roomy one. Gone was the casual and chatty atmosphere of the old. Tourism at the airport was now big business with uniformed female receptionists and many officials.

I soon realized that only at the airport had conditions changed. Old Jerusalem was as I had left it three years before.

Israel

From our elegant American Colony Hotel, a former Turkish palace, we took a taxi for a three minute ride to the Mandelbaun Gate, located in the Jordanian section of Jerusalem. Our driver stopped at the Gate and took our bags out of the car. There were signs that read, "Danger No Man's Land Keep Out." A porter from the

Jordanian passport control office came running to the
gate for our bags and the three of us walked to the
control office. Here we had to wait until a group of
American ladies and two young German boys had been
cleared. In very short order our own exit visas were
endorsed. And once again we walked another short
distance, about 300 feet, to the Israeli passport control
office. We were asked to wait outside on a bench until
called for. A sign read "Israel Frontier Halt." (Since
Israel has fought many wars against neighbouring countries its exact borders have changed several times. In
1967, after the "The Six-Day War," it acquired East
Jerusalem and the West Bank with its historical and
religious towns such as Bethlehem and Jericho from
Jordan, the Gaza strip and the Sinai Peninsula from
Egypt and the Golan Heights from Syria. The occupied
territories included an Arab population of about 1.5
million.)

I felt strange as we waited on the wooden bench. It
was a bright cloudless day with a cool, refreshing breeze.
A thin slice of white moon was visible in the clear blue
sky. Sand bags and empty oil drums, serving as flower
pots for red begonias, were stacked against a wall of the
building. In front and behind me I noticed several damaged and deserted homes that must have once been
spacious and beautiful. Traces of their former beauty still
survived in their exquisitely sculptured wrought iron
balconies and fine scroll work on arched doorways and
windows. If stones could speak, what tragic stories these
stones could tell!

As I mused thus in the silence that was broken only
by an occasional American car with its familiar black and
white UN license plate or an UNRRA truck loaded with
bags of flour, I recalled the events in history that had

caused this "No Man's Land." I recalled that summer in 1956 when the Sinai campaign against Egypt was in full swing and how I had been afraid to cross this strip because of all the stories I had heard about the indiscriminate gunfire and border raids. And now three years later I had crossed it, but this time it was the silence that was disconcerting. Here and there tall green cypresses pierced the horizon line. Cacti and other hardy plants that defy arid soil emerged from the land. I noticed all around me coils of barbed wire and concrete dragon's teeth.

"Welcome to Israel" was boldly outlined on the frontier structure, but not everyone was welcome. Arabs living on the Jordanian side could see their homes now occupied by Jews, but they could not enter them. I recalled the many sad stories the Arabs had to tell, Arabs now living in Jordan who had once been wealthy, with roots in Israel dating back hundreds of years, now reduced to ignominious impoverishment. Their money was being returned to them in bits after having been frozen in Israeli banks for seven years! There was the Israeli custodian of enemy property who was keeping the rent money. But this was no compensation for broken homes and broken hearts.

Border formalities were quick. The officials even filled out our forms for us. In no time we were being whisked away in a taxi through the streets of the New Jerusalem to the YMCA.

The "Y" that met my eyes was completely unexpected. Jerusalem's "Y" was a magnificent edifice, and the most imposing "Y" I have ever seen. The new, modern YMCA in Athens in 1956 had impressed me, but this one possessed a dignity that ultra modern buildings don't usually evoke in me. With its lofty central tower, pleasing proportions, and well-kept gardens, it was beautiful. Hundreds of children from teenagers to small youngsters were milling about. And I felt right at home when I saw a chart displaying the amount of contributions from Canadian "Ys" to a current campaign that the Jerusalem "Y" was undertaking.

We took a private car tour of the historical and biblical sites in and around the New Jerusalem. We visited the Memorial Chamber of Jewish martyrs, where exhibits of Nazi atrocities and brutalities were displayed: bars of soap made from "pure Jewish fat," labelled and numbered; the sacred tora desecrated into all sorts of worldly uses, from handbags to wallets, men's vests and shoe pads. I knew about the incredibly horrific treatment the Jews had received from the Nazis, but the memorial chamber rekindled a shuddering horror within me.

We visited Mt. Zion and the traditional tomb of the House of David where hundreds of thin white candles were burning. Atop Mt. Zion we visited the Church of the Dormition where the Blessed Virgin rested prior to her Assumption. We visited the Coenaculum (the Room of the Last Supper). The bare empty room disappointed me, but I tried hard to visualize the Last Supper in the surprisingly empty and windowless room.

The Church of the Visitation, presumably built on the site of the summerhouse of Zachariah and Elizabeth, whom Mary visited, provided a better praying place for me than did the Church of St. John, built over an ancient cave, the birthplace of St. John the Baptist. Only a few Franciscan monks were about in these relatively new churches.

As we drove about the Judean hills where Christ lived and preached and suffered, I felt a serenity that neither twentieth century traffic nor the uneasy tensions of the times could destroy. *Terra sancta* it truly was.

In spite of her venerable millennia, New Jerusalem was a bustling modern city. Our guide, manifesting an intense national pride, a pride that I was soon to discover is a trade mark of all the people of Israel, wanted to show me this business activity. He took me to an Espresso restaurant. Here for the first time during my trip I saw women wearing western-style hats. Everyone was in modern western garb, and I was shocked to see a Middle Eastern country so western.

Our guide, Belabel Katz, was a patriot, Israel must have been proud of. His life had been a nightmare as were most of the lives of the Jews who had finally found sanctuary in Israel, but he didn't dwell on his past very much. It was the future that he spoke about, not only his own future or that of his children, but the future of his children's children and that of Israel. And, as he spoke in evangelical tones about his country, he made me envy the youth that was creating Israel with a fierce loyalty and force unequalled in modern times. He made me wish I were a Jewess helping to rejuvenate this tired old land with new vigorous blood. In only one other country had I found that same intense national pride, that same missionary dedication, that same consciousness of tremendous achievement. And that was in the Soviet Union. But Sasha and Larrissa did not evoke any desire on my part to live in the Soviet Union.

Mr. Katz told me how his country had to cope with the problem of language. How Jewish immigrants from seventy-five lands — from India, from Persia, Poland, Arabia, even America — had to communicate with each other in a common tongue. Seventy-eight languages were spoken, but Hebrew was the official language. In

1948, after World War II, almost 2000 years after the Romans had expelled the Jews from Israel, Palestine, on the Sinai Peninsula, was divided into two nations, Jewish and Arab and the state of Israel was born. Jews from all over the world came to settle in their independent Jewish homeland. (But others, including Arabs, Christians, Druze and Bedouins live here also.)

I asked Mr. Katz how his country had been able to integrate immigrants from Oriental countries with customs, habits, and traditions so different from the west. He confessed it was a colossal problem. Immigrants from the same countries tended to collect in the same settlements. "Parents cannot transcend the social barriers, but their children can," he told me. "Can you imagine an aristocratic Dutch Jew inviting a Yemenite Jew for a fourth in a game of bridge?" he asked me. "It can't be done now, but it will with the children. The children are the hope of Israel."

Mr. Katz continued: "We are a normal country like any other country. We must have our crooks, our farmers, our murderers, our traffic violators — we must be just normal."

On the train from Jerusalem to Haifa I saw men in work clothes and in shorts, girls in slim jims, and women in cheap print dresses. Some were munching away at apples and peaches; others were biting into thick chunks of bread and jam. Some were reading and others were dozing off. We were comfortably seated on our reserved seats, but some who were standing were swaying and falling into our laps. It was like any other train in any place else. There were two exceptions: the concentration camp numbers tattooed on so very many wrists, and the ear locks dangling from the black, wide brimmed hats of the young orthodox Jews. And then I knew I wasn't in just another ordinary country even though Mr. Katz's words kept ringing in my ears.

I have nothing but praise for Israel's Government Tourist Offices. After the haphazard tourist service we had experienced in Asia, tourist service in Israel was like manna from heaven. Here, at last, were schedules, brochures, booklets and maps that we hungered for in so many other countries. Assistance in finding accommodation and in planning sightseeing tours and all sorts of schedules were available everywhere. Never before had we met such thorough and efficient organization.

The tourist office in Haifa deserves special mention. It was through their tireless efforts that a package containing my notes and diary from my trip was returned to me. In my concern over a taxi to take us to Jerusalem's train station, I had left the precious package on a bench at the "Y." I was devastated. My parcel had to travel from the "Y" to the Jerusalem tourist office, to Haifa and to me.

Haifa was an interesting city. First of all, it was beautiful. The vista from the top of Mount Carmel overlooking the Mediterranean so pleased me I had to revisit the spot just to crystallize the beauty in my mind. The panorama from the exotic Persian garden of the golden-domed Temple of the Bab, world centre of the Baha'i faith, was also a feast for the eye. The Baha'ists are an interesting religious sect. They have neither religious rites, nor preachers, nor creed. Their religion preaches the unity of all faiths, all races and all people. I had never known of their existence until I visited Haifa.

Haifa's industry and commerce, and its cultural and technical institutions made it Israel's fastest growing city, a testament to Israel's astonishing economic and cultural development. The building noises from cranes, bulldozers and diesel engines were everywhere.

And yet it wasn't this thriving cosmopolitan modern port city which impressed me. It was the surrounding countryside! It was here that we saw the heart that gave Israel its very life. For without land that was fruitful, there could be no Israel. Land that hadn't been cultivated for thousands of years was now being worked. In the blistering sun, I saw strong men driving tractors, working in the banana plantations, vineyards and rice paddies. With strong backs and strong hands, they were clearing the land that was polka-dotted with thousands of huge rocks and boulders. Land that had been barren was now being tilled and made to bear fruit.

Shortage of water had been the chief concern, but the fertile brains of the Jewish people soon remedied this problem. Everywhere we drove, we saw irrigation ditches, giant water pipelines, and thousands of feet of sprinkling water hoses. Never before had I been made so aware of the need for water, the water needed to turn the desert into a green oasis. As I drove through newly-cultivated green lands, I couldn't help but admire the energy, perseverance, enthusiasm, and ingenuity responsible for this remarkable transformation. I rejoiced in Jewish triumphs while Mr. Katz's words kept floating in memory:

> We must return to the soil. Our ancestors were shepherds and farmers. We have established a reputation in the business, commercial and financial fields only through necessity, when governments prevented us from being farmers. Here in the new Israel, if we are going to survive, we must return to the soil.

In a world-renowned social experiment in communal living, Jews were returning to the soil, reclaiming and enriching it, to produce an abundance it had once upon a time.

Since stony dry hills and marshy plains are problems too Homeric for individual farming, a pattern of settlement — the kibbutz — developed. The kibbutz is a communal settlement where everything is shared. It is more than an economic unit. It is also a unique social experiment that, up to now, has functioned successfully. We visited the Deganya Kibbutz, the oldest kibbutz in Israel, founded in 1909 on the shores of Lake Tiberias where Ben Gurion and other Russian Jews had settled approximately fifty years ago. New larger homes and larger common dining rooms had replaced log cabin style buildings. We could see that conditions had improved. We saw heavy machinery for the first time in our trip and the fresh green lawns were a pleasant shock.

I asked Mr. Katz whether the present generation remained on the kibbutz where there must be rigid regulations. He reluctantly admitted that many of the youth refused to endure the hardships, suffering, and toil of their pioneering parents. He was quick to add, however, that living in a kibbutz was on a voluntary basis, but volunteers were becoming more scarce.

Israel was being transformed into a paradise on earth through modern science, chemistry and technology. But, regardless of what modern science was achieving, Israel was still *terra sancta*. Ancient historical and biblical shrines were preserved. I visited places that had been only sacred names, but now they had more meaning for me: the Place of Elijah's sacrifice on Mount Carmel, where the great prophet defied the priests of

Baal; the monastery of Our Lady of Mount Carmel, to whom my maternal grandfather had special devotion.

In the hollow of the Jezreel valley in Nazareth I saw the grotto where the Archangel Gabriel appeared before the Virgin Mary and announced the Immaculate Conception. A young Franciscan monk, with his head leaning against the Angel's column marking the spot where Gabriel stood, praying in complete contemplation, was oblivious to the milling crowd. Near St. Joseph's Church, built above the grotto where the Holy Family lived on the northern side of Lake Tiberias, were the Roman ruins of Capernaum, where Jesus preached. A little further north at Tabgha, Jesus had performed the miracle of the loaves and fishes. On a hill behind Tabgha I saw The Mount of Beatitudes, where Jesus preached the Sermon on the Mount: "Blessed are the poor in spirit for theirs is the Kingdom of heaven." On the main Tiberias road, barely twelve kilometres from Nazareth (the largest Arab city in Israel) lies Kafr Cana stretching out in the shade of olive, fig and pomegranate trees where Jesus transformed water into wine at the wedding feast of Cana. Our guide refused to stop here, however, because of Arab hostility to tourists. A little further east, Mount Tabor dominates the plain of Jezreel where the Transfiguration of Christ took place.

Many sacred places looked as they must have in Christ's time. Men were still riding donkeys along the narrow winding streets of Nazareth, the city of Joseph and Mary. Women in long flowing robes still carried brass vessels on their heads. Sheep and lambs were grazing along the banks of the Sea of Galilee, the only fresh water lake in Israel. These holy places comprised a spiritual journey to cherish for a lifetime.

We were told we should visit the historic city of Acre, besieged repeatedly over the centuries by Romans, Arabs, Crusaders, Turks, Napoleon and the British. I finally convinced Miss Rutledge that we should explore Acre on our own. We took a *sherut* from Haifa north to the walled Crusaders' capital city of Acre. A *sherut* is a taxi that waits around bus stops. It scoops up prospective bus passengers who get tired of waiting for a bus or who are in too much of a hurry to care about extra *prutots*. We fell into both categories. We were tired of waiting and we didn't care about paying a little extra. We were already saving pounds! But you can't dilly dally when you see a *sherut* standing still. You dive in. I got stuck in the middle seat where the two adjoining seats meet at such a sharp angle that sitting there was quite a torture. It is this seat that makes the *sherut* a taxi for seven. Miss Rutledge got left outside. It was only after I tried getting out of the taxi that a kind passenger left to give Miss Rutledge his seat.

After our cramped, painful ride of fourteen miles, we welcomed an opportunity to stretch our legs. We decided to walk about the old Arab town where more Arabs than Jews live. We poked through the bazaars, peered into courtyards, and visited the Museum with its fine collection of Crusader pottery. We toured the astonishing excavations of the Crypt of St. John of the Knights Hospitallers with its elegant ribbed vaulting. Our guide drew our attention to a fleur de lis carved in the stonework. And then we enjoyed a glass of *gazoz* (a soft drink) at a restaurant overlooking the old port with the remains of an old Crusader tower in sight. I couldn't help recall this brave strategic stronghold's conquered history from the days of Crusader knights and Turkish *pashas*. Even the great Napoleon had laid an unsuccessful siege! As we wandered along Saladin Street, named after the man who drove the Crusaders out of Jerusalem, I was pleased to see the antiquity of the old city within the walls contrasting with the new Acre outside the walls, spanking clean, and modern.

If it hadn't been for the silence of the Sabbath that reigned over Tel Aviv, I would have thought I was in any metropolis of wide avenues and ultra-modern apartment buildings. But on Fridays at sundown all activity ceases in Israel. I wanted to cancel my plane reservations in order to remain a day longer in Israel, but all offices were closed, and I couldn't send a telegram.

In the harbour at Tel Aviv I could see a huge liner standing off shore. It couldn't dock. Saturday was Sabbath! And if there were children on board who, for twenty-five years, hadn't seen their anxious parents at the dock, they couldn't rush to meet them. It was Sabbath! No cyclists were allowed. Some Israelites didn't even smoke on the Sabbath.

Since Israel is absorbing an immigrant society of Jewish exiles, nearly every immigrant has a story stranger than fiction to tell. Joseph, our guide in Haifa, escaped Poland during the Nazi atrocities and went through Russia to Japan. During the latter part of World War II he was deported from Japan and landed in Israel. Katz, our Jerusalem guide, made his way to Israel from Austria. Both have never heard from any members of their families. On our Haifa tour a honeymoon couple were speaking in Italian. The groom had escaped Rumania through Hungary and Austria. A patient in a local hospital discovered after three weeks that his nurse was his daughter whom he hadn't seen in twenty years.

And yet Israelis didn't dwell on the past. The future belongs to them. It might still continue to be a shaky one in this tiny Jewish state born out of war and growing up in an atmosphere of a cold war. But they had the best trained army in the world. Two-year military service was compulsory for girls as well as boys with certain exceptions based on religious grounds or marriage.

Israelis worked hard but they also played. Consequently, the beach at Tel Aviv could compete with America's Coney Island. Tel Aviv's night life, and its sparkling, swank cafés could rival New York's. Prosperity seemed to reign. Prices were higher than in Jerusalem, or in Jordan, but as one Arab explained to me as I was buying Christmas cards at one of the shrines: "If I lived in Jordan I would have to pay only five cents for a card. But I wouldn't have the five cents. Here it costs fifteen cents, but at least I have the fifteen cents."

The Tropics and the New World, 1961

It was the summer of 1961. From 1955-1958 I had lived three years in the Old World. During the summer of 1959, I had travelled around the globe. It was time for me to get to know the other New World, the Caribbean, and South and Central America.

The Caribbean Islands: Jamaica

On 3 July 1961, I arrived in Kingston, Jamaica, booking in at Courtleigh Manor. My sinuses were bothering me and I was looking forward to heading straight for the ocean, hoping that the salty water would help. Instead, I contacted my brother-in-law's relative who insisted that I attend a Canadian community picnic celebrating Dominion Day.

It took four hours each way by diesel railway, "The Cornwall Express." The countryside, with its sugar-cane and banana plantations, groves of oranges and cocoanut palms, and its tropical agriculture — coffee, bamboo, even rice — was lush and varied. But it was the profusion of colour that overwhelmed me: violet, orange and pink bougainvillea; coral, yellow and deep red hibiscus; white oleander; purple-blue jacaranda; claret- coloured passionflower and pastel orchids of every shade. I could not stop photographing them.

Jamaica is the world's largest bauxite producer. I noticed much open-cast mining of bauxite. A Canadian mining firm refines the bauxite into alumina which probably accounts for many of the 180 Canadians working in Jamaica. It was fun meeting a number of them on foreign soil, especially Mr. Walter Buchan, whose family home was on Carrie Street in Port Arthur which is very close to my own home.

Our main topic of conversation was West Indian Federation. It was regarded as a liability by some and a boon by others. Some of the whites I spoke to didn't want to see any change in the status quo. (West Indian Federation never matierialized. The movement, however, generated a demand for political independence from Great Britain. In 1962, Jamaica, and Trinidad and Tobago were granted independence; Barbados in 1966.)

In the summer of 1961, Jamaica was still carefree and safe. I was able to walk and visit the beach without fear. Swimming in the salty waters cleared up my sinuses.

Antigua

I don't know why I stopped over in Antigua. It was very dry and windy, so windy that I did not enjoy lying on the white sandy beach.

English sugar cane planters settled Antigua in 1623 and it is still British in many of its traditions. I remained only one day in St. Johns, the capital of Antigua. But I had the fortunate opportunity to listen to a steel band called *Brute Force*. The sweet sounds the Antiguans could get out of empty and tall oil drums cut to different sizes, then hammered into various depressions and elevations, was remarkable. Since this was a relatively new innovation, there was no music written for these home made instruments, and they played numbers like "Mashed Potatoes" by ear.

On 6 July I left Antigua for Martinique and then on 8 July I flew from Martinique to Barbados.

Martinique

Martinique is a little piece of old France in the Caribbean. So committed were the French to their West Indies colonies (Martinique and Guadeloupe) that in 1763 they surrendered their political rights to Quebec in order to remain on their islands unchallenged by the British. Since 1947 Martinique's citizens have been citizens of France.

I stayed at the Hotel Impératrice on a tree-lined boulevard in Martinique's capital, Fort-de-France, named in honour of the Empress Josephine, the beloved wife of Napoleon Bonaparte, who had been born to a French planter in Martinique in 1763. The white marble statue depicting her wearing a Regency gown with the grace of a Greek goddess stands in the middle of the grand square in the capital.

The Gallic charm of the city reminded me of my two years spent in France. I ate freshly baked croissants for breakfast. The French flag flew everywhere; French cars outnumbered American and German. Pepsi-Cola was still *la boisson de l'amitié*. Grey-haired French ladies put a bluish tint in their beautifully coiffed hair. Meals were served in the polished French manner. I saw the words *Liberté*, *Egalité*, *Fraternité* carved in the wall of one of the public buildings. And monuments to war heroes were inscribed, *Martinique a ses enfants morts pour la France*.

I visited a kindergarten of five year olds at an *école maternelle*. I was amazed to see their copy books so beautifully kept and *l'écriture* and *dictée* written in ink.

Little pictures were painted with water colours. The teacher proudly showed me a hooked rug and demi-point the children were making. A little French flag with the date and a story of two sentences about a duck were written on the blackboard. There was an aquarium. Several drawings as well as *un horaire* were posted on one of the walls. The room was very small, poorly lit, with very little blackboard space. In spite of the dark and shabby room, the children were enthusiastic, serious, and spanking clean. The teacher had studied in France and returned every five years for professional improvement at Government expense. I noticed a *tableau de service* for playground duty. The playground was a very small rectangular inner courtyard.

Fort-de-France looked prosperous despite the deep open gutters. I found the creole women wearing their traditional turbans and massive earrings attractive. It seemed that only the black women carried large wicker baskets on their heads. I saw people writing their letters in the post office where tables and chairs were especially provided. "Jamais le Dimanche," which I loved, was the rage.

Compared with Antigua, Martinique had lush vegetation. The rain forests were bursting with bamboo and breadfruit trees. It rained daily, but the showers didn't last very long; nevertheless, everyone carried an umbrella at all times.

I was overwhelmed by all the beautiful flowers that I saw: hibiscus, bougainvillea, jacaranda and poinsettias. The iron grillwork balconies on the homes overflowed with flowers. And yet vegetables like carrots, radishes, lettuce, beans, asparagus and celery had to be imported, and these were very expensive. But the tropical fruit I loved to eat was plentiful: pineapple, avocado, guava, bananas, papaya, custard apples, mangoes and cocoanut.

Barbados

Barbados was flat, a complete coral island with a thick layer of topsoil. Roads wound through coral rock cuts. The Bajans, as the natives are called, hued this coral for foundations for their small shacks. I saw where Hurricane Janet had hit and the government housing scheme that replaced dull brown shacks with attractive, brightly coloured homes of cement.

Whereas Martinique was decidedly French in language, style and charm, Barbados was English. In Bridgetown, the capital, Nelson's statue sat in Trafalgar Square, and the public buildings on the square were gray Victorian Gothic. St. Michael's Anglican Cathedral, originally built in 1655, faced the main square. I visited the square again during my Caribbean Cruise on the Queen Elizabeth II (Christmas 1997) and the square was exactly as I saw it over thirty years ago. I watched a cricket match for a little while, and enjoyed high tea at my hotel served with English decorum. There didn't seem to be much poverty in Barbados. When I went to Mass the natives in the congregation were well-dressed.

I was entranced by the "limbo," a fantastic dance where the dancer has to bend backwards under a horizontal bar without dislodging it. It is lowered, and the dancer gyrates underneath it until the lowest rung is reached which is usually not an inch more than his pelvic axis. I saw the fire limbo performed by two Bajans wearing red scarves tied around their heads and a red cloth decorated with sequins and crystal beads over their shorts. One wriggled under the bar with a glass of water on his forehead. Bent backwards, he propelled himself by the sides of his feet. A piece of material soaked in kerosene was tied around the middle of the crossbar and lit. The dancers thrust feet or arms or chest into the flames.

The band played calypso music too. I was beguiled. How I love to listen to "Island in the Sun," "Banana Boat Song" and "Yellow Bird," all popularized by Harry Belafonte. It was impossible not to fall under the spell of the beat. I danced all night.

Calypso lyrics are rich in satire and innuendo. But the ones the tourists hear, I am told, are sanitized versions of the folksongs the African-West Indian peoples sung of an evening long ago, expressing their feelings on all sorts of subjects from social injustices to sex. The Bajans spoke a distinctive English which I found interesting to listen to.

I found Barbados, as I did Antigua, exceedingly windy. Christopher Columbus might have blessed these steady trade winds, but I did not appreciate them. I am told, however, that no one could stand the heat, if these cooling breezes didn't blow. On my way to Farley Hill, where *Island in the Sun* starring Harry Belafonte was filmed, I found a shore where winds don't howl. The Farley mansion displayed the elegant extravagance and luxury of 200 years ago. This giant estate was surrounded by sugar cane fields. The family had scattered long ago and the mansion was now abandoned, left to the ravages of time and nature. The royal palm-lined boulevard refused to accept such an ignominious end. In spite of the tropical growth trying to take over, the mansion still stood as a proud witness to the life that once belonged to the Farley family.

Trinidad

The immigration officials were surprised at seeing a young woman alone, arriving at one a.m., at the airport in Port-of-Spain, Trinidad. I didn't want to appear helpless, but I didn't want to be aggressive either. I explained that I hadn't planned to arrive at such an hour, but that the plane was late. I also explained that I didn't want to stay in Trinidad because I wanted to go to Tobago, the legendary home of Alexander Selkirk and to lie on the wide sandy beaches there. They informed me, however, that it was impossible to get there at that time of the night. When they discovered that I didn't have a hotel reservation, they were worried. Finally, Cecil, one of the officials suggested that if I waited about fifteen minutes, he would be off duty and would help me find a hotel. It was pouring rain as it can only in the tropics. I accepted his offer gratefully.

After several attempts we finally found a vacancy. Cecil had so impressed me as a gentle and caring man that I was looking forward to getting to know him. We made arrangements to meet the next day. That night the heavy, dense, tropical rain battered the corrugated tin roof of my room. I was frightened. I couldn't wait for the sunlight of the morning. I didn't like being alone in a cottage of a hotel, and so I moved to the Bretton Hall Hotel.

The next day I explored the city centre on foot. Cecil picked me up in the late afternoon to take me to the Civil Service Association Club. I was the only white woman there. And I was unashamed. In fact, I felt a tinge of pride, for this was a foreshadowing of the future I felt was coming.

We talked chiefly about West Indian Federation and all of its implications. In terms of education, Cecil felt Trinidad was ready. He pointed out that in the club room we were in, there were at least five BScs, six BAs and one MA. He also insisted that there was no colour distinction, but that there was a class distinction on the islands. Many of the whites were against West Indian Federation because they feared reprisals. They claimed that the blacks didn't know how to handle money, and that they had no culture, and no background. "After all, what do you expect," one white told me, "they've just come out of the cane fields like swarms of ants." Cecil was against federation for a different reason:

Trinidad doesn't have the money to be independent. There is much jealousy and rivalry among the islands themselves. The small islands fear being gobbled up by the larger ones like Trinidad and Jamaica. Jamaica feels it should have the capital by right of its size and economic activity. The small islands claim they should have the capital in order to improve their economies. There are some in Trinidad who want to put the parliament buildings on the present U.S. Naval Base which the Americans say has been leased to them for ninety-nine years.

We talked about the violence that I had heard existed in Trinidad. Cecil discounted it as the work of a few gangs of juveniles who become bellicose after night-clubbing and getting charged up with the sensuous calypso dancing. He continued:

Trinidad is different from the other islands because it has a polyglot population. There are blacks and whites, East Indians and Chinese. When the slaves won their freedom they didn't want to work in the sugar fields and so the planters imported Chinese and East Indian labour.

Cecil did not mention the original inhabitants, whom we know as the Arawaks and Caribs.

I had thoroughly enjoyed my evening with Cecil. I respected his opinions and admired his courage. We were only together hours really. But I was attracted to him, even tempted to stay in Trinidad longer. West Indian speech patterns still seduce my ear.

Cecil had arranged a meeting for me with Miss McShine, a friend of his. Miss McShine was the principal of a girls' school. She took me on a thorough tour of her large school, which was spilling over with 1200 students. I had never seen a school so cramped and congested, classes back to back and facing each other and yet there wasn't a sound. I heard the pupils sing. I inspected their neat notebooks. There was neither time nor space for fancy introductions to lessons. The students were self-motivated. They came to school to learn. I was very impressed.

Miss McShine invited me to her lovely home decorated in a musical motif. She played a few of her own compositions on her grand piano. I sat entranced. What had that horrible white said? Here was a highly intelligent and educated black woman. Like Cecil, she was thoughtful, and kind too, taking a stranger in. I was ashamed I was white. She served a delicious lunch with the quiet elegance and dignity of a people who had been accustomed to the art of gracious living: Trinidadian salmon in a wine sauce with sultana raisins and bananas, and Trinidadian fruitcake with homemade passion fruit ice cream for dessert. My words were too inadequate to express my gratitude.

I stayed in Port au-Prince so long that I had to give up my plan to go to Tobago.

British Guiana (Now Guyana)

From Trinidad I flew to Georgetown, the capital of British Guiana. To my surprise, the person seated next to me was Cheddi Jagan. To his surprise, I knew who he was. In 1953 The People's Progressive Party, headed by Jagan, an East Indian dentist and a Marxist, won an overwhelming victory, and he became the country's first popularly elected Prime Minister. The British authorities deposed him, however, for alleged Communist connections. He gave me his card and asked me to contact him if I needed any help. On the other side of me sat a gentleman whose name I have forgotten, who was promoting an association called "The European Common Market." It was 1960 and the term was new to me. I recall, however, telling him that I didn't think it would work in Europe, given national loyalties and human nature. A united Europe, a new Europe, was a fantasy. The concept was unrealistic. Today, of course, European union is a reality. How wrong I was!

After exploring Georgetown's town centre on foot on my first day, I spent the rest of my days at the hotel's swimming pool and my evenings dancing. There were a number of attractive American servicemen on leave staying at my hotel. We sunbathed and went swimming. We spent hours wrapped up in the intriguing conversations that took place around the hotel's pool. I was having so much fun; everyone was in high spirits. At night I danced with Eric to such romantic tunes as "Are You Lonesome Tonight?," "I've Got You under My Skin," and "Strang-

ers in the Night." Before we parted, we stayed awake all
night. I drank Brandy Alexanders. We did nothing more
than cuddle and kiss. He cut a two dollar shinplaster into
halves, the only sentimental thing he had with him. He
kept half and gave me the other half as a memento of
our time together. We promised to write, but we never
did. I recently found my half of the shinplaster.

Needless to say, I was not looking forward to going
to Paramaribo, the capital of Surinam. Nor did I like the
fact that I was going to be stuck there for four days. But
I had no other options.

Surinam

Once again, I lucked out on the hotel I picked. The
morning after I arrived, the hotel manager informed me
that Hollywood was filming a movie and the cast was
staying in the hotel. The two actresses in the film whose
names I can't remember had left the day before. And
only two stars — Rock Hudson and Burl Ives — were
left. He asked me whether I'd like to meet them and
whether I would like to visit the set. I couldn't believe
my good fortune.

The film was called *The Spiral Road,* and when it
came to Thunder Bay, I must have been the first patron.
It was about the experiences of a young physician, an
atheist, in the wilds of the Netherlands East Indies.
Instead of filming the picture there, they filmed it in
Dutch Guyana because it was cheaper. Rock Hudson
played the role of Dr. Anton Draper, and Burl Ives, Dr.
Brits Jansen, a veteran jungle doctor. For three days
running the manager drove me to the set built as a native
village in the tropical rain forest not far from
Paramaribo. I must have taken hundreds of feet of film.

When, in the Hollywood movie, I saw the burning of the village which I had captured in my own movies, I was delighted. I was introduced to Rock Hudson and Burl Ives, both of whom were very friendly. Burl Ives even sang "A Little Bitty Tear" for me. During the making of the movie the two stars were usually too busy to chat with me, but we had a wonderful time in the evenings at the hotel.

I enjoyed the tropical fruits and spices, fruits that had once been only names: guava, papaya, mango. Cocoanut, nutmeg and cashew, cacao and the vanilla bay leaf. The variety and abundance of the flora and fauna amazed me. There were 200 varieties of orchids in Surinam. There were interesting plants like the kapok, and a sensitive plant that bows its stems like a shy school girl as well as a powdered fern that leaves its white imprint on your arm if pressed against it; birds' nests that hung down like long string bags, cannon ball trees, huge nuts that dropped their lids when ripe, and seeds encased in fan-like enclosures. Nature is so amazing! Before I knew it, the four days which I had dreaded to spend in Paramaribo flew by quickly, and the day I had to leave for Brazil had arrived too soon.

South America: Brazil (Belem)

I wanted to see the Amazon, the biggest river in the world, and so I flew from Paramaribo to Belem, which is the largest port on the Amazon, one hundred and twenty kilometres from the Atlantic.

My memories of Belem are few. I was so exhausted that I slept for two days and did not leave the hotel. I even had my meals sent to my room. But I left myself a day to explore the town which I found run-down. I noticed remnants of its opulent past in its statues and parks; in faded colonial buildings and the patches of fine blue tile work on sidewalks, homes and bridges. I was reminded of my visit to Portugal. (Around the turn of the century a rubber boom had made Belem a city of luxury and culture, a tropical Paris. The town had electricity, telephones, streetcars and a distinctly European ambience in the midst of the tropical forest. In the 1920s the rubber boom ended.) I spent most of my time wandering around the Mercado Ver-o Peso which covered several blocks along the waterfront. It was busy with boats loading and unloading bananas and pineapples, and vendors and buyers coming and going. There was a large array of waterfront stalls selling medicinal herbs and roots, bark and leaves, dead snakes, teeth amulets, potions and spices, vanilla, cacao pods, cassia, and cinnamon for cooking and seasoning meat, rice and beans. I felt uneasy the whole time. The crowds eyed me suspiciously when I was filming. As a young woman travelling alone, I knew I had to be cautious.

The two days I spent in my hotel room to rest had given me time to write letters. On my way to the airport I gave three letters plus postage and tip money to the concierge. The letters were never mailed. This loss of the narrative of my escapades in British Guiana and Surinam upset me because I had no other record.

Brasilia

I was lured to Brasilia because the media had celebrated it as the world's greatest planned city of the twentieth century. Brasilia became the capital of Brazil on 12 April 1960, when Brazil discarded its old capital, Rio de Janeiro and moved it inland. Brasilia was like no other city in the world. It was in the middle of nowhere, miraculously sprouting out of the red desert earth of the central plateau. It was spectacular with its shining, spanking new government and apartment blocks, boldly innovative and modern buildings of concrete, chrome and glass in ultra-modern shapes like a cup and saucer upside down, an aquarium, and even an airplane. (I was reminded of West Berlin's pregnant oyster.) A red dust covered everything because the soil was so red and dry. Sod had to be imported as did all food stuffs. The people who worked in the construction and service industries lived in *favelas*, unpainted wooden shacks in a ramshackle shanty town called Free City thirty kilometres from the centre, a Dawson City of the tropics. They could not afford to live in town. No one — politicians and bureaucrats alike — wanted to live there anyway. Although a road connected Rio and Brasilia, the airport was the busiest spot in town. Members of Parliament and public servants flocked to Rio for the weekends. Absenteeism at meetings of parliament was a chronic problem.

Brasilia was one place in the universe where men outnumbered women. A young Brazilian invited me to the nightclub at the Brasilia Palace Hotel and there must have been about fifty handsome men and only a handful of women. No wonder that night clubs had opened and closed down. After the claustrophobic closeness of Belem's streets, the wide boulevards and open spaces of Brasilia were a welcome relief. But distances were enormous. No one walked because the sun sizzled, and there were no trees for shelter.

It was interesting to talk to Brazilians about Brasilia. Most of them thought that Brasilia was a mistake, a colossal waste of money, time and effort. They felt that the money could have been better utilized in the development of the interior rather than creating a showpiece of non-productiveness. They claimed that President Kubitschek had made himself a millionaire out of the deal, buying land and then selling it at inflated prices.

Rio de Janeiro

The first place I wanted to see when I arrived in Rio was Copacabana, the most famous of Rio's many beaches. There were few tourists because it was winter time (although it was much warmer than our summer). The leaves had turned colour and were falling. I rustled through the mottled and speckled leaves and enjoyed watching life on the beach. Young and old were swimming and bronzing their skins. Young men exercised and played volleyball, and barefoot boys dribbled soccer balls on the sand. Scantily dressed young girls displayed their bodies with style and confidence. The beach was a ritual, a way of life for Brazilians. For me, one beach was the same as another, but for Brazilians, different times brought different people, and the beaches, themselves, had their different groups of regulars. In fact, even different parts of one beach attracted different crowds.

I also had to climb Po de Açûcar (Sugar Loaf). I didn't go to the top because I was too frightened to get into the cable car when I saw it suspended in mid-air between the two levels. I contented myself with the panoramic view of the first level. Even at this stage, the view from Sugar Loaf was stupendous. Rio's physical setting jammed between ocean and escarpment, with miles and miles of soft white sand and beautiful curving beaches was stupendous. The skyline in the light haze against green and bald mountains with different shaped peaks and heights was breathtakingly beautiful. At night, with the twinkling lights of the City framing the bays and lining the lake down below, the sight was spectacular.

There was so much haze and mist hanging over the city that I was unable to photograph Corcovado (the Hunchback) as well as the massive statue of Cristo Rendentor (Christ the Redeemer) with its welcoming outstretched arms, that stood on top of the lofty mountain. Twice I tried and both times I was disappointed.

Rio belonged to the new world of skyscrapers and perpetual motion. I had never, in any other city, been hesitant to cross a street. There was never a traffic policeman during peak hours, and it was a standard joke that even the police, were afraid. As a result, there was absolute confusion on the main arteries. But Rio had the drama, the elegance, and the joie de vivre of the Mediterranean. It lived out-of-doors. I loved it.

Rio, nevertheless, belonged to the old world too. The downtown area had its charming old houses and buildings compressed here and there between the new apartment buildings.

Urologists from all over the world were attending a urology conference in Rio. In Brasilia I had met the Australian delegate, Dr. Keith Kirkland, who invited me to the social events of the conference in Rio. I felt honoured. There were cocktails at the famous Copacabana Palace Hotel, and dinner at a country club where scores of bottles of Chivas Regal and Glenfedich were placed on the tables. I sat next to Sir Eric Riches, one of Great Britain's leading urologists and his wife at a dinner party given by one of Rio's chief urologists, Dr. Paula Alberquerque, at a most fashionable Country Club with restricted membership. I felt privileged. I was sorry I had to refuse an invitation to a dinner party at the Rio doctor's home, but I felt that if I didn't leave Rio, I would never finish my trip.

I hated to leave, even though walking on Rio's black and white mosaic pavements was like negotiating an obstacle course. They were made of tiny black and white stones set in beautiful symmetrical and floral patterns. But time was destroying them. There were patches of broken pieces, empty holes, sagging spots, areas that heaved, dipped and dived, and occasionally, areas under repair. Even the parts that had been repaired were dangerous, since the craft of mosaic sidewalks had been lost. In spite of this lost art, Rio's citizens were energetic. They cut down a mountain to solve a traffic jam and used the gravel to fill in the harbour to solve another area congested with traffic. There were many more problems to solve, but the people of Rio were proud, and their city was growing even though they would sadly say that it was going down in prestige because their capital had been taken away from them. However, they seemed to have faith in President Quadros, whom they felt was an honest man anxious to make Brazil an important third power. I had spent three glorious days in Rio, but it was time to go to Sao Paolo.

Sao Paolo

I never dreamed there were such thriving, huge, and modern cities in South America such as Rio de Janeiro and Sao Paolo. Although they had their grand high-rise office complexes and apartment buildings in glass, concrete, and steel, they also had charming old buildings that reflected a European charm. They still preserved their numerous statues honouring their great, and their fountains and monuments gave these western metropolises an old world appeal.

I had seen more new construction, especially in the Sao Paolo region, than I had seen anywhere in Canada. Brazil's manufacturing, industrial and commercial interests seemed to be concentrated here. As I explored the city, so masculine, strong, and vigorous, I kept recalling Sandburg's "Chicago. " The traffic was incredible. The hustle and bustle had a North American type of vitality, but the orderliness of the long queues for buses and elevators reminded me of London.

When I drove to Santos, the largest and busiest port in South America, along a four-lane highway which wound down a 2,500 foot cliff, I was reminded of the Golden Mile outside of Toronto. I saw the sign *Nova Fabrica* everywhere. Everywhere I turned I saw the names of American companies: Goodyear, Caterpillar, Frigidaire, and Firestone. The dockside activity was fascinating. The port was huge with hundreds of towering cranes, derricks and dock houses. I saw scores of trucks loading and unloading sacks of coffee beans on the various ships. I'm sure 90 per cent of the cars on the road were Volkswagen and 99 per cent of the diesel buses that belched dense black fumes were Mercedes Benz. Despite this frantic modernization, most of the road construction was still done by men shovelling and swinging picks.

It was winter, but people were swimming, picnicking, or strolling. I thought that the beach at Santos was far prettier than Copacabana in Rio. There were wide boulevards with flower beds, statues, and sidewalks stretching along the beach which was miles and miles long and yards and yards wide. Mosaic walkways in black and white were everywhere. Beautiful poinsettias in full bloom, covered with dust, lined the highways.

Brazil was a Roman Catholic country. I saw statues to the early missionaries of the Church everywhere. During Holy Year all civil servants were even given a paid-two-month-vacation to go to Vatican City. However, I was told that Brazilians had just inherited their religion. It was a habit and very few really understood it. I did notice very few people at Sunday masses reading prayer books.

The fruit stands were heaped with fresh fruit such as watermelons, oranges, and bananas which I bought for less than one cent. I loved the fresh fruit so much that I practically survived on it. Coke was less than four cents a bottle. I didn't see much poverty in Sao Paolo, but the *favelas* in Rio were appalling.

I took time to visit Campinas, sixty-three miles west of Sao Paolo where I spent several hours at a coffee *fazenda*. Here I saw row upon row of coffee plants and learned how the coffee beans were picked, dried and shipped. I also saw a banana plantation that was miles and miles long.

Uruguay: Montevideo

Montevideo, the capital of Uruguay, the smallest of the South American republics, is the country's largest city. Its inhabitants are predominantly white, most of them descendants of immigrants from Spain and Italy.

Founded in 1726 by the Spaniards, who wanted to discourage Portugese incursions from Brazil into Uruguayan territory, Montevideo was a city of wide boulevards and public squares, beautiful parks, glittering beaches and lovely residential areas. Narrow, twisted streets of the colonial sections surrounded the harbour.

What attracted me most, however, were the many monuments scattered about the parks, especially La Carreta (the ox-cart), honouring the country's early settlers in the Parque Batille y Ordonez, and the bronze stage coach monument in El Prado Park. Both were of such heroic splendour that I kept visiting them, each time admiring their rhythms and the story of toil and hardship they told.

But my most exciting experience was meeting Howard, an American Lieutenant-Colonel, who took me to a swanky night club where three Uruguayans sang folk tunes, and a chanteuse sang in English, German and French. We were inseparable for two days. We played nine holes of golf on one of Montevideo's beautiful golf courses and discussed how Uruguay, Latin America's first welfare state, could afford such generous benefits. For example, a childless woman with twenty-five years of service could retire at fifty, and married women could get three months maternity leave. This type of generosity was unheard of in 1960!

And on my last night in the city we went dancing, even though I wasn't feeling very well. I have never forgotten the evening because we danced to my two favourite French songs, "Parlez-moi d'amour" and "J'attendrai." Our relationship was much like my others, brief yet memorable. In those days, I enjoyed the spontaneity of meeting attractive strangers. The immediate sense of intimacy that often emerged was exciting and provided pleasurable interludes to my otherwise solitary travels.

Argentina: Buenos Aires

No sooner had I checked in at Hotel Claridge in Buenos Aires that I had to call a doctor. When he told me that he was putting me in the hospital I was shocked. I left my bags in the hotel, and I left a message for Howard, whom I expected in the city later that afternoon. I then hired a taxi to take me to the American Hospital.

I spent a week in the hospital. According to my doctors at home, the doctor had prescribed every antibiotic known to the medical profession. Even when I was discharged from the hospital I did not know what I had. One of the antibiotics must have worked, however, because my fever went down, the rash around my nose subsided, and I felt better. Howard visited me the first evening. Unfortunately, he had to leave the next day, but he ordered his bat-man, a young Lieutenant, to visit me. The young Lieutenant came each afternoon until he, also, had to leave Buenos Aires. The hospital did not provide laundry facilities for its patients, but I was fortunate that the English patient in the bed next to me had her mother do my washing. Telephone service in the hospital was frustrating. Two of three pay telephones, were forever out of order. The third was on the top floor. One of two elevators was usually not working, but when I could get to the top floor, no telephone line was ever available.

As soon as I was discharged, I began my exploration of the city. Buenos Aires was a cosmopolitan capital. I marvelled at its wide, tree-shaded boulevards lined with stately mansions, the flower beds, arcades, elegant shops, beautiful parks, fountains, sidewalk cafés, and splendid monuments. It reminded me of Paris.

But the city was becoming rundown. Although its streets were bustling, the walkways were heaving and filled with potholes. A few were being repaired; others should have been. Many were torn up but there were no workmen repairing them. Its beautiful old buildings were crumbling away. For example, the Teatro Colon, one of the world's greatest opera houses, was sadly in need of much repair. I felt that the city was like a well-groomed grande dame who had not completely resigned herself to a slow decline. She still powdered her face and painted her nails, yet her face had deep furrows and her nails were hard. Over thirty years later I revisited Buenos Aires on my way to Antarctica. I could see no change. The Teatro Colon was still badly in need of a facelift, as were the city's walkways and streets.

At one time, foreign capital had poured into Buenos Aires to develop railroads, industry and agriculture; the railways and public utilities had been all English owned, managed and operated. Since the eighteenth century, the English, who dealt in much contraband, had enjoyed considerable prestige. They never condescended to learn Spanish. Today, the English speak Spanish, and the railways are government-owned. The English are no longer held in awe, but I sensed an English flavour. Argentinian men dressed in that English style I like so much.

Two highlights in Buenos Aires were my lunch at the British Consul's home, which was arranged by his wife's mother, whom I had met in Trinidad, and my full day *estancia* tour. When I told the British Consul that I was going on an *estancia* tour he told me that he was sorry to see the ranches declining and shifting to tea and cotton cultivation. On my way to the *estancia*, we travelled across the pampas, Argentina's fertile grazing lands for cattle and sheep raising. Here we saw the gauchos, wearing their handkerchiefs loosely wound around their necks and black felt hats with upturned rims, breaking horses and herding cattle. But it was the barbecue and the evening's entertainment which fascinated me. Meat, especially beef and pork, was bountiful. I never saw such huge steaks as those that were being barbecued. For the evening performance the gauchos donned their classic costume: an embroidered bolero style jacket, knotted scarf, baggy pants, wide leather belt bejewelled with silver coins, and short spurred boots. The rhythms of old Spain danced from guitars, concertinas and combos. I was fascinated.

Chile: Santiago

Crossing the Andes was a spectacular sight. The sun shone brightly; the numerous snow-capped peaks, each the same and yet so different, looked like foam icing crowning bald and barren mountain ranges. On board our Comet to Santiago was a soccer team from Spain. Chileans, like all South Americans, are enthusiastic sports fans. They love horse racing, soccer, and polo. Each city has huge sports stadiums and dozens of elite Jockey Clubs. At the airport, the press and radio were waiting for the Spanish team. There were microphones, cameras, and tape recorders.

Santiago was a beautiful city surrounded by mountains with wide and long tree-lined avenues, impressive homes and many parks, so typical of South American cities. Like Paris, Santiago was planned to be lovely. San Cristobel and Santa Lucia, two imposing rocky hills in the middle of the city, were beautifully landscaped with magnificent gardens, paths, ornamental pools, medieval towers and porticoes. Since Spanish conquistadors did not discover gold and silver in Chile, there are no colonial palaces such as those found in Peru.

I didn't find the skyscrapers of Brazil here. Law required buildings of reinforced steel, concrete and low height because of the earthquake peril. There wasn't the traffic chaos of Rio either. Drivers seemed to follow some sort of driving code, and they obeyed traffic lights and policemen. Nor was there the new construction frenzy of Brazil's Santos.

It was winter. There was snow, but the more hardy flowers were in bloom. I was entertained by a Chilean veterinarian. We ate local scallops and listened to Chilean music.

I couldn't believe the degree of resentment against the Americans who are called *gringos*. I could not count the number of times I saw *Yanqui outside* and *Viva Cuba* splashed over walls.

Peru: Machu Pichu

Peru is famous as the land of the Incas. As soon as I landed in Lima, I headed for the lost city of Machu Pichu, the last refuge of the Incas, deep within the Andes mountains and forests. The physical setting was breathtaking because Machu Picchu is built on a saddle between jagged Andean mountain peaks twenty thousand feet high above the Urubamba Canyon. Some were snow packed and had glaciers, others were bare and barren, while still others were covered with thick forest growth.

So remote was the location of Machu Picchu that this spectacular city in the clouds was never found by the Spaniards. But why it was mysteriously abandoned no one knows. Legend claims that the Incas kept moving up the mountains to escape the Spaniards and finally

wound up in the Amazon jungles. Another legend claims
that when the Inca city of Cuzco was taken, the Virgins
of the Sun (like the Vestal Virgins of the Romans) took
refuge here in this most unlikely and inaccessible spot.
No one knew of Machu Picchu's existence until the
American historian, Hiram Bingham, stumbled upon the
ruins of this ancient city, almost by accident, in 1911. He
unearthed 174 skeletons in burial caves, 150 of them
female.

At first glance I saw a great flight of beautifully-con-
structed stone-faced terraces coiling their way skywards.
I marvelled at the engineering mastery over stone when
I saw the immense size of the stone blocks weighing a
hundred tons or more. And I marvelled at how they
were transported without the wheel, using only strong
draught animals like oxen, and how they were set without iron tools. As I got closer, I discovered the colossal
strength of the walls that made this majestic royal capital
an impregnable mountain fortress. Once I entered the
stronghold I wandered through a maze of ruins —
watchtowers, farmed terraces, temples, palaces, plazas,
aqueducts — to reach the giant sun-dial of the sun-wor-
shipping Incas. There were no carvings or statues (unless
they were all looted) such as I had seen at Anghor Wat
in Cambodia. Throngs of tourists were milling about the
ruins, but they held no interest for me because I was
wrapped up in awe over the mysteries of this Inca world.

Cuzco

When Colombus arrived in the Americas, Cuzco, nestled in the Andes Mountains, was the flourishing capital
of the Inca Empire that stretched 32,000 kilometres
from central Chile to southern Colombia and from the

Pacific coast to the fringes of the Amazon. The highly civilized Incas had even built stone surfaced roads throughout their huge empire!

When Francisco Pizarro and his small band of steel-clad conquistadores entered the capital in 1533, the city contained elaborate palaces and temples richly adorned with gold and silver, emeralds and other precious stones. The Spaniards were astonished. By the end of the 1500s, captured, looted and settled, Cuzco was a quiet colonial town with all its gold and silver looted.

Although many of the Inca buildings were torn down, nothing could destroy the superb foundations. The Spaniards kept the Inca foundations for their own colonial mansions. I marvelled at the stone masonry. The Incas used neither mortar, nor cement, nor metal tools, only stone hammer construction. Inca stone masons made such precise joints that even a razor's edge cannot be inserted between the stones that are chiselled to fit perfectly together. Such perfect joints boggled my mind.

Sight-seeing in Cuzco was fascinating. I saw what must be some of the narrowest stepped streets in the world. As always, in South America, the wealth of the churches astonished me. In the Baroque Cathedral the tabernacle was made of solid gold, containing 331 pearls, 263 diamonds, sixty-two rubies, 221 emeralds, eighty-nine amethysts and forty-three topazes. I could not believe my eyes.

Lima

The highly elaborate, imaginative interiors of Lima's churches, as in Cuzco, were unbelievably rich in gold and silver, precious stones and paintings, mahogany and cedar. I saw gold and silver altars, gold vessels adorned with precious stones, silver crosses, gold and silver jew-ellery, handsome wood carvings, and paintings on ceil-ings. The Church of Santo Domingo contained the re-mains of the western hemisphere's first saint, St. Rose de Lima. Blessed Martin de Porras (who had just been canonized) as well as the mummified body of Pizarro, assassinated in 1541, the archetype of the Spanish con-quistador who, in the name of the cross and sword, conquered Peru.

But I saw more begging in Lima than in any other South American city. I often wondered whether the rich, safe behind the high walls of their cool courtyards and elegant palaces, were aware of the other side of life. I saw Indian families hugging shaded walls with a handful of wares in front of them; Indian women surrounded by their many children always squatted on the pavements with a few oranges, bananas, trinkets or religious articles for sale. A priest told me that once he wanted to buy the whole heap of oranges a squatted Indian woman was selling. She refused to sell them all because she would then have to go home, to a dark, tiny, windowless and airless shack with a dirt floor.

This sad plight of the Indians bothered me terribly. I just stood and watched them for hours, ashamed of myself for staring. I remember watching them at Urubamba while we waited for our train to take us to Machu Picchu. While harsh chilly winds blew, the Indian women, in full skirts and shawls, sat on the cold, bare earth along the railway tracks trying to sell a few hand-fuls of beans or tiny bundles of herbs. There was no begging. But silent and reserved, they waited, some barefoot, some with shoes made from discarded auto tires. Perched on their heads were brown derbies or white panamas with black bands. There were young girls with old faces nursing babies, and babies tugging at their mothers' black braids or chewing away at the dirty blankets which confined them. Only an occasional sob from an unseen baby wrapped in a blanket tied around a young mother's shoulders broke the silence. I could feel the young mother colouring as she swayed from side to side to pacify her child and rock him back to the silence that is the Indian child's legacy. I admired the stoic dignity of these women.

In this wide chasm between rich and poor, it was not surprising to see growing unrest, hatred and suspicion. I should not have been so surprised when my guide in Cuzco showed me the pistol he carried in his pocket all the time. He claimed that since he was in the tourist business, the local communists had labelled him as a capitalist and an imperialist collaborator.

In Lima I saw Communist signs posted everywhere as well as a large picture of Fidel Castro with a poetic tribute to him on the bulletin board at the University of San Marcos, the oldest (1535) in South America. In fact, I kept seeing signs such as *Viva Cuba, Viva Fidel, Cuba nosa exemple*.

I spent a lot of time in Lima's museums. What I found most interesting were the pre-Columbian treasures in its Gold Museum such as the mummies and skulls, which showed the relatively advanced state of medical knowledge in these pre-Hispanic cultures. Inca doctors were especially skilled in performing head operations, since their weapons were designed to hit heads. Many of the skulls showed holes left by successful brain surgery. The Incas must have had dentists too, because casings for the teeth were on display as well. I even saw straight pins. The mummies were especially interesting because the Incas buried their dead in the pre-natal position. Mummification was practised in Peru thousands of years before the Egyptians. I saw well-preserved mummies in baskets and in little nests. I saw others sitting down, their elbows on their knees, and their hands with long fingernails on the sides of their faces. I saw a beautifully preserved seated mummy said to have been a sorceress 1,500 years ago. The richly decorated ancient pottery, ornate nose rings and intricately beautiful weaving in a variety of geometric patterns left me amazed. The colours were exceptionally well-preserved.

Pisac

I watched the Incas at mass in Pisac, famous for its weekly Sunday market, an hour's drive from Cuzco through the sacred Valley of the Incas. Pisac is an Indian world almost as it must have been, when the Spanish conquistadors founded it in the sixteenth century. Ancient Quechua traditions were mingled with Christian practices. There were no prayer books and no rosaries, but a wonderful chanting echoed throughout the church. After the Quechua mass, I witnessed a colourful procession of four mayors in their robes of office, silver staffs and chains, marching to the home of the priest, who is the most important person in these Andean villages, for his messages which they would take to their peoples.

Trial marriages were common. Couples married after the first child was born. Infant mortality was high. One child out of every five died before the age of four. If he lived to five, he most likely would live to fifty.

Tourists flocked to the weekly Sunday market in Pisac. After attending Mass I visited the market. Here I saw huge mounds of coca leaf for sale. The local priest told me the coca story. I found it incredible. Indian workers on the haciendas were given a daily ration of coca leaves. These dried green leaves killed the chewer's sense of fatigue and hunger and gave him a feeling of euphoria. Since chewing these leaves, which had a narcotic effect, became habit forming, there were regular fifteen minute breaks (like our coffee breaks) for *chaecha*, the Quechua word for chewing coca. Under the effect of this narcotic, the Indian worked harder under conditions which would kill most other people. This was exactly what the landowners wanted. Thousands of years ago the Incas themselves used the plant with the greatest of discretion. Its cultivation was severely restricted under their government and only the ruling caste was allowed to chew the leaf. They recognized the damaging effects of the drug and handled it with care. Its indiscriminate use has been one cause for the Indians' deterioration.

Ecuador: Quito

I stopped off in Ecuador because I wanted to see the Equatorial Monument. In my Grade VII Geography class I had learned that latitude was measured from here at 0° because Ecuador straddled the Equator. The Equatorial Monument was just like I remembered it in pictures. Like the typical tourist, I was photographed with one foot in the northern hemisphere and the other in the southern. I also mailed postcards marked "Equator."

I arrived in Quito, once the northern centre of the Inca Empire and the colonial capital of Ecuador, for the Feast of the Assumption on 15 August, an important day in the Roman Catholic liturgical calendar. Throngs of the faithful were praying in the churches where altars were laden with calla lilies. There were over one hundred churches, convents and monasteries. I visited one church after another — churches of the New World — where behind the main altars I discovered *retablos* (altar paintings), towering ornately carved and richly gilded screens depicting a mélange of devotional images. Never had I seen such rich interiors. Seven tons of gold were used to decorate one church. The churches looked like mammoth, lavish jewel boxes. Never in my travels, even in Spain, Italy or Portugal, had I seen such wealth. Here, as in the rest of South America, statues were dressed with rich clothing from crystals, beautifully embroidered satin, brocade and velvet, to net with sequins, and beading, and even crowns of precious gems and real hair. Christ on the Cross wore a real crown of thorns. Unknown sixteenth and seventeenth century Indian artists created church carvings and paintings in human rather than ethereal forms that were quite unlike anything in Europe.

I had not seen the begging in Quito that I saw in Lima. But there was oppressive poverty. Every few yards I saw Indian women squatted, breastfeeding their babies, usually in a shady corner with a few tubes of lipstick or a few candies for sale, surrounded by children sleeping or eating but never playing or screaming. The filth and tatters were incredible. The women wore no shoes but always a hat. Nowhere in my travels had I seen man as beast of burden as I saw in Quito. I saw a veritable moving hardware store with chairs, tables and brooms on his back.

Quito does not have the sophistication of Lima or Buenos Aires. Its fascination for me was its colonial, old world ambience. From 1535 to 1822 when Ecuador was liberated from Spanish rule, life in Ecuador, as in the other South American colonies, was pleasant for a few wealthy families who lived much as they would have in Spain.

Once a major Inca city-state, Quito was totally destroyed by an inter-tribal war shortly before the arrival of the Spanish conquistadores. The present capital was founded on top of the Inca ruins by a Spanish general. Many colonial buildings survive in Quito's old town, which was a treasure house of the best in Spanish colonial architecture, art and churches. I enjoyed just strolling about and photographing street scenes in spite of the fear that gripped me now and then. Indians do not like to have their pictures taken. But there were teams of policemen always about. And I am grateful to them because they seemed to show up whenever I was in a jam. How they reprimanded the natives! In the old Spanish section of the city, the narrow, steep, twisting cobblestone streets, overhung with pots of flowers on iron-grilled balconies, were lined with white and yellow houses roofed with red tile. They were a photographer's delight. However, orange and banana peelings were everywhere and the odours were unpleasant.

I was fortunate to hear a concert of Italian arias by an Italian opera company in the Coliseo. Even though we were sitting on the equator, I was wearing my fur jacket. In fact, I was terribly cold because Quito lies between two towering Andean mountain ranges at 9,000 feet above sea level.

Paradoxically, despite the wealth of the church in buildings and ornamentation, the Roman Catholic church was poor here. It had been persecuted for years, and every now and then the clergy was told to leave. There weren't enough priests, one for every 10,000 people, whereas in the United States the ratio was 1:500. Schools were few.

(In some Central American countries, Catholic schools were even forbidden.)

Colombia: Bogota

I stayed only two days in Bogota, the capital of Colombia. But I was able to visit its two most important sights: the Gold Museum and the Salt Cathedral. I also attended a wonderful performance of Tennessee Williams's *The Glass Menagerie* with Helen Hayes at the Teatro Colon. Bogota lay on a very extensive and flat plateau 8,000 feet high. It was extremely interesting to see tropical plants, palms and eucalyptus growing along with temperate plants. The mountains were completely covered with green vegetation. In the heart of a huge mountain of rock salt at Zipaquira, fifty kilometres north of Bogota, an underground cathedral had been carved out of the solid salt, capable of holding ten thousand people. On the tour to the Salt Cathedral I met an extremely wealthy Ecuadorian, a short, stocky, and cocky twenty-five year old, whose father owned huge banana plantations. We were engaged in wonderful conversation until I mentioned the poverty in his country. At this point he accused me of "being against him." "There is no poverty in my country: there is work for everyone who wants to work," he insisted. He added, "There is no need for anybody to be poor." And yet Ecuador was one of the poorest and least stable South American countries, with an annual income of $165 a year.

Once again, the churches — most of them dating from the seventeenth and eighteenth centuries — were treasures of fantastic beauty and wealth. The amount of gold I saw in Bogota's churches was absolutely staggering.

The most moving Christ I had ever seen was the Fallen Christ at the Church of Montserrat. He was carved so realistically that his eyes appeared to be shedding tears. Many miracles had been attributed to Him.

The Gold Museum contained an amazing display of over 30,000 gold pieces from all the major pre-Hispanic cultures in Colombia as well as jewelled crowns of thorns, gold tiaras, rosaries, and crosses encrusted with precious stones.

I had never fully appreciated the long and eventful history of the South American republics until this trip, especially of the history of their liberator, Simon Bolivar of Venezuela, part Indian, who had struggled against the Spaniards for years, spurred on by the ideals and successes of the American and French revolutions. His beds, swords, letters, even a lock of his hair as well as memorabilia of other famous generals who fought the Spaniards were all carefully preserved.

Central America

Every country of Central America except Costa Rica has had a history of violence, revolution and unstable governments. Earthquakes and volcanic eruptions have also caused great destruction.

I visited Panama and Costa Rica which has no army and is the most settled and successful of the Central American republics as well as Guatemala, the original home of the Mayan Indians, an advanced and thriving civilization who built elaborate temples, pyramids, palaces and city states. By the time the Spaniards arrived, the mysterious Mayan civilization was almost extinguished.

Panama City

From Bogota I flew to Panama City to see the Canal, one of the world's greatest engineering wonders finished in 1914. In the mid-twentieth century, conflicts arose between the United States who built the Canal and Panama over control of the Canal Zone and riots broke out in 1964. In 1977 the new Panama Canal treaty began transferring the Canal from American to Panamanian ownership. (When the treaty expires on 31 December 1999, Panama will have full charge of the Panama Canal for the first time in history.) I strolled around the Plaza de Francia with its poinciana trees and obelisk commemorating the early efforts of the French who had worked for twenty years to build the canal. A bust of Ferdinand-Marie-de Lesseps, the French engineering genius who had directed the construction of the Suez Canal, but who had failed with Panama because his company went bankrupt, surveyed the Plaza de Francia.

At the height of its importance Panama City had outclassed Lima in splendour and commercial interests. In 1671 it was sacked by the notorious English pirate Henry Morgan. I visited the ruined plaza which reflected the accuracy of his siege, and the ruins of the Catedral de Nuestra Senora as well as the old sea wall which was built to protect the colonial city from pirates. Luckily, the beautiful golden altar in San Jose Church was saved from Morgan's attack on the old city by a resourceful monk who painted it black to make it look like wood.

But the event in Panama which remains frozen in my memory happened when I was on my way back from seeing an unattractive statue of Balboa, carved of white marble overlooking the Bay. In 1513 Balboa was the first white man to see the Pacific despite what John Keats says in his poem, "On first Looking into Chapman's Homer":

Then felt I like some watcher of the skies
When a new planet swims into his ken;
Or like stout Cortez when with eagle eyes
He stared at the Pacific — and all his men
Looked at each other with a wild surmise —
Silent, upon a peak in Darien.

The event happened on a Sunday morning at ten-fifteen. Flanked by two burly American ex-Marines, I was walking in the middle of an empty street in a poor area inhabited by blacks living in unpainted ramshackle hovels and tenement houses with wooden balconies. Just no one — no one — was about. I remember commenting on the eerie silence. Suddenly my two companions noticed that their wrist watches and wallets which were in their back pockets had disappeared. Not one of us saw or heard anybody. We were absolutely dumbfounded. The three of us were walking side by side. The thieves did not steal my camera bag which I was carrying, nor my large brown alligator bag which one of the Americans had slung over his shoulder. We reported the incident at the nearest police station. The only police comment was that we were lucky we were not all stripped.

I was so horror stricken that I walked to the American Zone where I felt safe. Only Americans, who administered and operated the canal, could live in the

Panama Canal Zone. With its beautiful gardens and clean homes, it was a much-needed refuge for me. Even the air smelled sweet. Here I wandered through the Post Exchange and gorged myself on a banana split, a hot fudge sundae, and a hamburger in quick succession.

Costa Rica: San José

I decided to leave Panama immediately and flew to San José, the capital city of Costa Rica, one of the most modern Central American countries. After my traumatic experience in Panama I decided to stay in the elegant Gran Hotel on the Plaza. In Costa Rica, buildings were built low because of earthquakes. The houses were clean, tidy and were painted bright colours. Even their oxcarts were gaily painted. Local farmers took a tremendous pride in these beautifully painted wagons and they decorated each one individually. The mountains were cultivated to the very top. The countryside was lushly fertile, producing all the fruits and vegetables of the temperate zone along with tropical plants such as avocados, papayas, mangoes, pineapples oranges, bananas, coffee and cacao. Calla lilies bloomed everywhere.

I attended Sunday mass and thanked the Lord for protecting me in Panama City. It was not hard to find a Catholic Church because the overwhelming majority of Costa Ricans were Catholic. Seated next to me was a barefoot Indian woman. I noticed a clock hanging on one of the pillars exactly like the one we had in our dining room at home.

Sunday night I observed the famous Promenade when beautifully dressed young ladies, linked arm in arm, went strolling and were ogled by the young men, preened and varnished for the mating rite who sat in small cars that bordered the narrow streets. It was not considered proper for girls to go anywhere alone. Dating was unheard of. The promenade was a way for young men and women to be seen. I'm sure that many a shy glance had led to romance.

Hardly a building survived in Costa Rica from the colonial period, and there were few public historical monuments even though Christopher Colombus discovered Costa Rica in 1502. I was enchanted by the block-long, beautifully ornate Teatro Nacional located diagonally across from my hotel. Insulted after the touring prima donna, Adelina Patti, had cancelled a performance in 1890 for lack of a suitable hall, wealthy coffee merchants raised export taxes in order to pay for its construction. San José's National Symphony Orchestra was practising when I visited the theatre.

Cartago

Cartago, in the temperate uplands, was chosen by de Coronado, the Spanish governor, as the capital in 1564. But shortly after independence from Spain in 1823, the capital was moved to San José.

Despite its political decline, Cartago is still an important religious site because the shrine to Our Lady of the Angels, which housed a six inch high, black statue of the Virgin affectionately called "La Negrita" Costa Rica's patron saint. Annual pilgrimages on 1 August are made to her to celebrate the original appearance in 1635 of "La Negrita" at the spring which flows out behind the church. The interior of the church was made of beautiful wood and the pillars were painted with stencilled floral and geometric designs in the bright colours so typical of Costa Rica.

To my surprise, we were able to drive up to Irazu Crater. At 11,260 feet, Irazu is the highest volcano in Costa Rica and the most feared because it is one of the most active, continually boiling and dumping ash and mud over Cartago, practically destroying it on more than one occasion. While farmers who cultivated its slopes live in fear of it, they are also grateful for the soil's rich volcanic deposits.

I wanted to visit Guatemala to see the largest market in Central America at Chichicastinago, but I needed a visa. I did not anticipate the difficulty I would have in getting it. When I was just about to give up, I discovered that there was a Canadian Consul in San José, but he was not listed in the phone book. I found him, by accident, in the newly-built Hotel Europa where he had just established his office.

Guatemala: Chichicastinago

Getting to Chichicastanago was fascinating. It is situated in a high mountain valley about ninety miles west of Guatemala City. On my way, I often wondered why the corn seeds didn't tumble downhill because the corn grows on the steepest slopes without any terracing. We passed many coffee plantations. The waxy green coffee leaves were shimmering in the sun. Banana and other tall trees shaded the precious plants. Oxen were still used because machinery would be useless on mountain slopes cultivated almost to the very top. We zigzagged up paved roads that wound their way through the mountains. The green wooded slopes and cultivated patches were breathtaking. We passed cultivated fields of corn and wheat deep down in the valleys and villages of thatched roofed huts and colourful Indians, all wearing the distinctive dress of their villages.

My first glimpse of the famous market was a dazzling display of colour. The Indians wore the typical colourful dress of each highland village from the surrounding countryside. The brightly coloured handicrafts and wares for sale were in great abundance and large variety: jewellery, pottery, leather goods, fabrics, flowers, fruit, vegetables, spices, kitchen utensils and other domestic items. I was intrigued by two Indian women weaving the most intricate patterns on portable looms which were tied at one end around their waists and at the other end to a tree. I bought six beautifully woven colourful hand towels. After more than three decades the colours look as good as new.

The scores of tourists from the United States and Europe visiting this isolated and remote market town surprised me, but most surprising of all was seeing Ed Mazzucca whom I hadn't seen since Normal school days in North Bay over twenty years before. I first recognized his voice.

It wasn't the market, however, which intrigued me the most, it was the activity at the white-washed Santo Tomás Church (c.1540) located on the site of a Mayan temple on the main plaza, in the heart of the market. Before entering the church, the Indian worshippers performed a number of rituals. On the church steps fires were burning. Indians were kneeling in prayer, crossing themselves, swinging clay censors of copal incense to frighten off evil spirits, and speaking aloud to their ancient gods. In fact, the broad sweep of steps was engulfed in clouds of incense which emitted a sweet fragrance.

I could not enter through the massive front door. Instead, I had to enter the church through the right side entrance because permission to enter the front door must be obtained from the guardian spirits. The interior was a blaze of lights. Along the whole length of the church scores of white candles of all sizes burned in honour of the saints, ancestors, and Mayan deities. I saw an Indian lay-priest holding candles, blessing a couple for fertility purposes. I saw other Indians praying at the many dark altars. On the church floor, Indians spread out their flower petals, red for the living and white for the dead, to honour their forefathers in the traditional Mayan manner. I was told that, in springtime, the Indians put corn seeds on the altars. Scores of Indians moved about the church, praying and chanting their plaintive tunes. The whole sight was unforgettable and unbelievable. The blending of Roman Catholicism and ancient Mayan ceremonial ritual totally baffled me. When I expressed my shock to a local priest, he told me that traditional Indian ritual and languages had become an integral part of Catholic ceremonies.

In Peru as in Pisac, there wasn't the noise, the loud buzz of conversation, or the screaming and running children we usually associate with our fairs. The Indians spoke in very low whispers, and transactions were orderly and calm. I liked their serenity, their dignity and their poise. The children were extremely well behaved, probably because they stayed bundled inside their mother's shawls so long they didn't talk or walk as early as our children. I regretted not being able to converse with them.

My visit to a primary school was depressing. I entered two of the dingiest, gloomiest rooms I have ever seen. And yet what was going on impressed me. The teacher was using homemade, yet ingeniously concrete visual aids. Local fruits and seeds were on display. They taught me to say, *"Me gusta venir a la escuela temprano."*

Like other ancient highland towns founded during the conquest, Chichicastanego retained the unique culture that was born of the clash of two civilizations. Although the Indians had adopted some of the European customs forced upon their ancestors as far back as five centuries ago, shreds of their customs still survived, blended with those of the Spanish. Place names, folk legends, dances, and their languages preserved their Mayan ancestors who, between 2500 B.C. and 1000 A.D., built a complex civilization and remained in power until the Spanish conquistadors conquered them in 1523. In my fractured Spanish, I asked them about their legends and dances. After a long conversation about their culture, they agreed to perform a traditional dance for me. I had to wait about a quarter of an hour to give them time to go home for their masks and costumes. They performed the Dance of the Conquest, the most popular performance at fiestas. Recreating the story of the conquistadors who came and took their land, the participants represented personages like Indian chiefs, conquistadors, medicine men and bulls. The actors spoke a ritualized, satirical script which mimicked the appearance and behaviour of the Spaniards. Although I didn't understand the language, I knew the message they were trying to communicate. The conquistador wore a wonderful hand-carved wooden mask, with cheeks painted the brightest and most gruesome pink, eyes pale blue, and hair and beard vivid red. The mouth was twisted into a sneer.

Mexico City

Surrounded on three sides by rugged mountain peaks, Mexico City sat on a soft lake bed that was slowly sinking. Our plane flew between the volcanoes, Popocotepetl (smoking mountain) and Iztaccihuatl (sleeping woman), whose snow-capped peaks rose about 17,000 feet. The sight was breathtaking.

Unfortunately, I was able to spend only two days in this great metropolis because my rash had returned with a vengeance. Nevertheless, I took a guided tour to Teotihaucan to see the massive ruins of the ancient city located about thirty miles north of Mexico City. By 500 A.D. it had a population of 250,000 and covered twelve square miles with pyramids, temples, marketplaces, and dwellings, one of the largest cities of the world at the time. Teotihuacan was mysteriously deserted about 650 A.D.. When the Aztecs arrived, the city was a vast flat field of amazing ruins.

I stood awestruck in front of the great Pyramid of the Sun which rises over 200 feet (or over 250 steps), the third largest pyramid in the world. Unlike the great pyramids of Egypt, Mexico's pyramids were used as worship centres, not gravesites.

The University of Mexico (1551), the oldest University in the Western Hemisphere, also left me awestruck. It was a showpiece. The most dramatic murals were displayed on every available wall surface. A huge iridescent mosaic of Mexico's past covered the entire exterior surface of the eight storey, windowless tower of the library. And a three-dimensional mural portraying the history of sports in Mexico from the pre-conquest to the present covered the Olympic Stadium. I had never seen anything like it anywhere in my travels.

I hunted high and low for a statue or memorial to the celebrated Spanish conquistador, Hernan Cortes, (1485-1547). Once he defeated the Aztecs, he chose the capital of the Aztec kingdom of Mexico as the site of his administrative capital of New Spain in 1521 rebuilding Mexico City, and reviving its shattered economy. I mentioned my search to a guide who told me that there was no monument to him because his name was synonymous with greed, cruelty and trickery. He also told me that Cortes was a hunchback, cross-eyed, bow-legged and extremely short. Diego Rivera, the Mexican painter, caricatured him as a pig on the mural of the President's palace. If only teachers could make History real with details like those. But alas!

I did find a bronze monument to Columbus and to Cuauhtémoc, a beautiful figure of the last of the Aztec Montezumas.

At the end of my summer travels, the horrible, itchy rash that I had had in Spain erupted anew. Was it sunburn, bedbug bites or allergy? Who knew? I scratched and scratched. It was bothering me so much that I was actually looking forward to a cooler climate.

AFRICA, 1963-1964

Assignment: *Where Elephants Have the Right-of-Way*

I arrived at Entebbe International Airport in Uganda on 30 August 1963. Bounded on the west by Congo, on the east by Kenya, and on the south by Rwanda, Uganda straddles the equator in the heart of Africa. Canada's Department of External Aid in their Special Commonwealth Africa Aid Programme had assigned me to teach at Bishop Willis Teacher Training College in Iganga, Uganda.

During the seventy-mile drive from Entebbe to Iganga, I soon realized that I had entered a new world. In glorious sunshine, we drove past well-cultivated tea, sugar, coffee, cotton, pineapple and banana plantations, and beautifully lush, dark green vegetation. At one point the good tarmac road suddenly filled with a family of baboons and we had to stop to let them scurry across. After several hours we arrived at Iganga, located in a tropical swamp twenty-five miles northeast of the industrial town of Jinja where I got my first glimpse of Lake Victoria, the world's second largest lake and the source of the White Nile. The village of Iganga seemed to be a mere section of the main highway to Kenya which was lined with two rows of *dukas* (small shops) owned by East Indians. I was truly disappointed. But when we drove into the college compound that was exploding with colour and fragrance — red and white bougainvillea, crimson-red poinsettia, orange red flame trees, coral creepers, hibiscus, white oleander, yellow acacia, red-hot poker trees and white frangipani — and I saw well-groomed lawns, neat modern white stucco and stone buildings, and lovely winding red *murram* paths, my disappointment disappeared.

I would never have suspected that the college was located in a highly malarial swamp that was once reputed to have been the end of the world. Although Uganda sat on a plateau 3,000 feet and more above sea level, one-fifth of it was lake and swamp. Malaria, trachoma, sleeping sickness, hookworm, amoebic dysentery, polio and meningitis were endemic. Although the heat during the day was debilitating, the nights were refreshingly cool. I always slept with at least one blanket.

The College was operated in the British residential school tradition by the Anglican Church of Uganda, but grant-aided by the central government that was in the process of taking over the country's denominational colleges and making them non-denominational. A long and bitter conflict had raged in Uganda between the Roman Catholic and Anglican Churches. A Roman Catholic like myself on an Anglican mission station was unheard of. This new ecumenicism was interesting.

My student, Stephen James, was to write: "My father being illiterate and a pagan, he let some children [out of twenty-four] join different religions and as such we children argue against some other religious beliefs. So we get conflicts there between ourselves." I soon discovered that the "pagans" were, in reality, a deeply spiritual people.

The college was also an experiment in co-educational Primary Teaching Training, with its forty-five girls and ninety boys ranging in age from eighteen to forty.

On the first night of my arrival, the Vice-Principal took me on a tour of the college grounds. At one point, she stood stark-still when she heard a rustling noise and then went to investigate. On finding nobody, she became very annoyed. I queried her annoyance.

She replied: "They're making love."

I asked, "who?"

She answered, "our students."

I suggested that they were probably just necking.

She curtly answered: "There's no such preamble here."

She proceeded to tell me that in traditional African society, the primary function of a woman is to bear children, not to become educated. I had just learned what I was going to find out later, that my students were caught between two worlds.

My female students were beginning to question traditional taboos. Naomi told me: "Women do not eat chicken or eggs (based on ideas of infertility) except now, a few educated ones."

There were many courageous girls like Perpetua who openly protested and defied old customs, even if it meant undermining parental authority:

Once you are born a woman, you have to suffer more than any other person. A woman must not whistle on any account. A woman is interested in all sorts of singing and yet she isn't allowed whistling! A woman is not allowed to sit on a chair except when she is at school. Is there any special way of sitting that God commanded?

I personally find these restrictions very offensive, and as I have had some education do not agree with them. I ignore them completely. Though old people do not very much allow young people to stay together yet in our village Bukonde there are many young ladies as I am who thought it wise to form a sort of association to discuss these matters.

But there was always a sense of frustration and insecurity in their attempts to adjust to the changing expectations. Education had liberated them from the deadly conservatism of the tribe, but education had also imposed a new set of taboos, different concepts of morality, and different conceptions of propriety.

A girl who became pregnant while a student at the college was immediately expelled, but her boyfriend was not. Traditionally, it was not a woman's right to say "no." (At the neighbouring Roman Catholic School, a girl would be expelled only after three pregnancies.) Expulsion meant the end of a girl's education and a life of drudgery bearing children, working in the *shambas* (fields), and carrying water and firewood back to the village. Women were used as cheap vehicles of transportation. I was told they didn't need spare parts. The home was ruled by the man of the house whose authority was vested in him by the clan. A woman's husband had absolute authority over her. He could beat and punish her in any way he chose and he had absolute rights over her children.

The girls were not entirely independent of the inherited social habits they once thought to be good and correct. While I was at the college, several girls were expelled because they became pregnant to the distress of the other girls who thought the rule of expulsion after one pregnancy was draconian. In this regard, a delegation of girls came to me for advice: "White women have ways to prevent pregnancy. Will you please help us?" I pleaded with the principal, the Reverend Philip Tidmarsh, M.A., on their behalf, even mentioning the

Roman Catholic leniency, but he would not break the college rules. Old traditions, however, were breaking down. A European cigarette factory in Jinja employed women, and many African girls were becoming nuns.

In the many lively debates we had in our English classes, I soon discovered that even the men (they objected strongly to my calling them boys) struggled between the old and new. Although they would take the negative in "Polygamy should be abolished," a few would, in the end, concede reluctantly to the new economics of life which forced them into monogamy. Most of my students' fathers had three or four wives. Each wife in a polygamous marriage lived in her own small hut, had her own food supplies, cooking pots and children. And yet my male students would take the affirmative in "The Bride Price should be abolished." There was no credit, no "buy now — pay later" plan. If at any time the goods proved unsatisfactory, the price was refundable.

An exacting code of ethics governed their lives. Wilson wrote: "children are not allowed to sleep in the same house with their parents when they are of ten years of age. A mother or a father is forbidden entry into a son-in-laws's house." Such customs of avoidance of certain situations might seem foolish to a Western sophisticate, but they were probably based on need for the common good and implemented to avoid tension or the possibility of incest. Failure to comply was punishable. Important events had their special rituals. Male circumcision was an important rite of passage. Aaron wrote: "one is considered to be a man when he is circumcised and not until his circumcision is he allowed to marry or to associate with the elders."

There is the correct procedure to follow at a burial.

Sally wrote an essay on "Death" for me:

When a person dies whether old or young, important or not, he is regarded as a very important dead body. The people in neighbourhood contribute money for buying bark cloths, blankets and coffin if the finance is quite sufficient. The women and girls, cry loudly most of the time. Meanwhile men dig up the grave pit, and make huts out of twigs and banana leaves.

When the grave pit has been dug, the nephew and niece of the dead person, take water in bowls to wash the whole body of the dead lastly. While they do that, men arrange barkcloths and bands to wrap the body, and band it tightly. When the dead body has been well tied, six strong men volunteer to take the body to the pit. On their way, all people cry and shout loudly and they throng the way.

The most sorrowful time occurs when the people see dimly through their tears, the descending of the dear friend. The impulsive women crawl to the border of the pit and are about to fall at the bottom of the pit and be buried alive. This give an irksome work of seizing and banding them for a moment. Bold men cover the pit and stamp the earth tightly.

The death of a member of the family causes anger and hunger, no food is cooked when the dead person hasn't been buried. Smoking is nowadays allowed. As a sign of bitter grief, people wear old ragged clothes and shoes are not worn at all.

Gradually after a few days, the sorrow relapses until the rule for crying every dawn is forgotten and turned into joy. A week after the burial, women demand and receive a musical drum. They play it all night, they dance, and they warm themselves with blazing fire in intervals.

The president of the clan, holds a meeting and agree upon the day for people to go back to their families. He arranges for the final meal which is heavy. He invites many friends to come and see the heir. When it strikes twelve noon, the heir is announced by the president. The heir promises to be kind, social, obedient as his predecessor was.

The last night, is quite entertaining, all attendants sing, drink much beer, after which they dance and forget the recent bitterness of their anger.

Although both men and women students were seeking a way of life other than the one they had inherited, there was much about the traditional life that I admired.

Social customs possessed their own graces. Greetings were ceremonial and had their own correct gestures and responses. I'll cherish forever the sight of Phoebe lowering herself to the ground on her knees when she met her mother with a baby on her back, hoeing in the field. She extended this courtesy, so full of dignity and feeling, when she greeted each of her father's three other wives balancing hoes on their heads and babies on their backs.

Visitors were accorded gracious hospitality. Guests meant conversation and conversation was the main source of recreation. Luckily, I learned a few standard phrases of Lusoga, the local language, and we were able to conduct a conversation, limited as it was. The rumour would usually spread, "this woman speaks our language," and they were thrilled.

Guests were joyful trouble. Children were given quick cold scrubbings and had clean dresses thrust over dirty ones before being presented. Mothers washed and changed into their best *busuti* (dress) to look elegant; all this was done without conveniences, and with little water at their disposal.

Food had a social value. It was regarded as a method of keeping on good terms. I felt at ease squatting on the floor of a mud and wattle hut, eating *matooke* (steamed plantain) with my fingers. The Ugandan starchy staple of *matooke* or cassava is almost entirely carbohydrate and deficient in protein. Some tribes eat field termites or ants because they are a good source of protein. I remember that a popular topic of conversation among the African members of our staff was whether white ants, that are considered a delicacy, tasted better pan fried or raw. Because the college grew its own groundnuts, beans, maize, sweet potatoes, bananas, pineapple and sugar cane, the students were served a varied diet: *matooke*, with a sauce of ground nuts or meat; *posho*, a cornmeal porridge with sauce; boiled sweet potatoes or cabbage; rice and bean sauce.

Gifts of food constituted an integral part of traditional hospitality. Wherever I visited, I received gifts of food — several cobs of corn, or a few bananas — always offered with two hands extended, for, as was explained to me, they give and take with their whole selves. A gift-giving event which has stayed in my memory was when I gave Father Slot a sum of money to build a new church that would be named after my father, who had died while I was in Africa. The Reverend organized a celebration on the site after the foundation had been erected, during which a group of his women parishioners performed a ritual dance in a circle and presented me with a cock.

I don't know where I got the notion that the whites had introduced education into Africa. But in harbouring this view, I was ignoring the tremendous influence of the African home. Suffice it to say that many of the numerous clan regulations and tribal taboos that were taught were pure superstitions; such as, "when a sister and a brother together make sexual satisfactions they die" and "when a boy sleeps with a woman on her parent's bed, the parents die."

But I marvelled how African parents were able to educate their children in their tribal lore with a success that would be envied by any Canadian teacher. My pupils could relate, with amazing detail, the past history of their tribes and family, even though, as Joshua wrote: "Our father died when I am told, I was of a height under one's knees."

"In Uganda, there were great dynasties with long and honourable histories," my students informed me. When in 1856, the two British explorers, Speke and Burton, set off to find the headwaters of the world's longest river, they were, six years later, the first Europeans to appear at the court of the Kabaka, Mutesa I, of Buganda, one of the five kingdoms of Uganda. They found themselves among an advanced political organization and a royal line that went back without interruption for at least 400 years.

I was astounded by my students' knowledge of their geography, and the names of their lakes and rivers before the white people came and changed them. For example, the River Nile, in Lusoga, was called *Kiira* because of its many waterfalls.

But it was the history of their surnames which intrigued me most. I soon discovered that brothers and sisters did not necessarily have the same surname. Each possessed a clan name which could be different from another family member, but in addition to the clan name each was given another name to commemorate a special event at birth. One student wrote an essay entitled, "Why I Am Called Keeya by Name."

Keeya is one of the few names which comes from English words. The sound of the name is more or less of the K.A.R. In July of 1943 my mother allowed me to enter into this miserable world. As she was giving birth to a child, the District Commissioner of Busoga was touring in his country. On the very day when I was happily brought out of my mother's womb, the District Commissioner of Busoga was in our village. When I had just spent only two hours on this earth, he (the D.C.) came to our home. He was met very happily by my father as my mother was laying under a banana tree painfully and happily too. The D.C., Gombolola Chief, Saza Chief, Muluka Chief, the dog of the D.C. and many other people who followed him, were taken to the latrine, and the shamba of cotton and the D.C. gave a credit to the work being done by my family. He came home again from the shamba and he saw a child covered in a barkcloth and a mother laying rather painfully and happily also he saw some marks of blood on the ground and he pitied her.

"Why did you not take this woman to the hospital?" the D.C. asked my father. And the father answered that because the hospital was very far from there. Then the Bwana (D.C.) promised to build one for that Gombolola. He came nearer to where I was and opened the cloth which was covering my face. He looked into my face and I smiled, as I was told, and he did the same! Then he said, "This child is very brave from his appearance and bold, too. The people around laughed and clapped hands. He went on, "the second world war killed many of our men in K.A.R. and I hope this will join to replace the dead ones." And after that he went. Then from there, my father named me two names, one for the family and one for the D.C. For the family I was named Kabiredi and for the D.C. Keeya which sounds moreless the same as K.A.R. (K.A.R.) the name given to the present Uganda Rifles.

Although there was, until about seventy years ago, no written language in Uganda, the African parent had also successfully handed down a tribal literature that abounded in stories, songs and proverbs which illustrated tribal morality. I recall Zikusooka who wrote that his name "is a short wise saying whose approximate interpretation is, Patience is bitter, but its fruits are sweet."

I always found the students' vernacular songs enchanting. In fact, the work songs they sang in the very early mornings while they hoed during the community work period made my supervising them a more pleasant chore.

The African home gave the child his or her language, not through instructions in formal grammar, but through language use. This was done so well that Africans were loquacious, so loquacious that at first I found my students' constant chatter annoying. But then in Uganda, silence was not golden. Silence was a matter for reproach, because a silent person was an object of deep suspicion. In class, my students loved to debate.

Although the education which the African home offers was valuable, it was limited and limiting. My pupils' total orbit was their tribal society. Their background of experience was narrow. Over half of my students saw their first elephant on a school excursion at the Nile Centenary Celebrations in Jinja the year before. And yet in Uganda's two huge game parks, the elephant is such a common sight that signs read "Elephants have the right of way." These great grey giants may appear remarkably calm and dignified, but they are wild and unpredictable, so that I was only too happy to give them the right of way.

Not one of my one hundred and twenty-eight students had ever seen a violin or even a picture of it. Few had ever seen an electric stove or a lampshade. As a result, they especially enjoyed the North American magazines I brought over with me. They loved to look at the beautifully coloured pictures and the large advertisements, especially the food advertisements because our foods were also unknown.

There was a frantic rush for book learning because there was supposed to be a special magic in learning to read and write. Consequently, anyone who was in the process of learning to read and write was held in great esteem. A student of mine, Alice Joy, told me, "I am never expected to do such dirty works as cleaning the latrines or sweeping out the courtyard when I go home on holidays." Aaron , another student, wrote that his fellow workers in the cotton ginnery where he was employed at holiday time: "respected me as though they are subordinate to me and I am always called upon to say the blessing when eating. I being the only one child of my father's children educated, that leads me to be loved more than I expect."

Literacy was equated with the status of white men. The notion prevailed that an educated African didn't get his hands dirty, held a white collar job, punched a typewriter and wore a tie. This attitude towards manual labour was a serious impediment to agriculture and industry. To counteract this attitude, each student at the college had to participate in community work. Families, and even a whole village, would often make tremendous sacrifices to have even one child finish school: acquiring the school fees was a struggle of the greatest magnitude. Ground nuts, bananas, sugar cane, maize, yams and cow peas were used to pay for school fees, but cotton was usually the cash crop most often used to pay them. The child, however, was expected to recompense his family. The financial burden of the educated African towards his extended family of assorted relatives was incredible! And yet not once did I hear any complaint. One of my students wrote: "I always supplicate God so that I finish up my course successfully so that I can in return help my parents as they always help me."

Competition for entrance was stiff. One year there were 700 applications to Bishop Willis Teacher Training College for only thirty-two first-year places. During the first year, content subjects — Religion, English, Nature Study, Health, History and Geography — were stressed. The following three years stressed professional work-method instructions and teaching practice. Graduation from the college entitled the successful school graduate to be a Primary Teacher of grades one to six. I taught academic English and Music as well as Reading and Music Methodology. There were no courses of study, no curriculum. I gave diagnostic tests which determined my subject content. Since the language of instruction in the Primary School was in Luganda, I had to translate my demonstration reading lessons into the vernacular. Hence a word recognition lesson on "dog" became a lesson on *embwa*.

I discovered that poetry appreciation and verse composition were new experiences. Choral reading was new. Play-acting in English was a new experience too. It was while directing *The Iroko-Man* and *The Incorruptible Judge*, both written by the West African playwright, D. Olu Olagoke, that I soon learned what born actors they were. Their capacity to create skits spontaneously based on their folk tales never failed to impress me.

During choral reading, I noticed that students confused our "l" for "r." "Prease" for "please," for example. Once, when I was visiting the Headmaster of the Demonstration School in his small, dingy, cluttered office, I spotted a binder labelled *Stork Book*. I asked him whether he kept lists of newborn babies in it. He replied that he kept a list of all the school supplies and equipment in it. I checked to see whether perhaps I had confused "stork" for "stock". It was "stork."

My students did not know the tonic sol-fah system, but they learned very quickly and soon their own rhythms and harmonies invariably took over. One of my students wrote: "My ten brothers and sisters can at this time sing "Home on the Range" quite nicely. Once I even concluded that they sang more beautifully than my classmates."

Books were scarce and primary school supplies which I took for granted — crayons, coloured paper, reading charts, games and toys — were unknown. The pupils had no means of duplication except by carbon. Even the old-fashioned jelly-pad, which I had used years ago, was unknown. It was no wonder that they just devoured the teaching materials that Canadian publishers and my teacher friends gave me: film strips, flash cards, picture dictionaries, word games, Pre-Reading activities, and colouring books. I also brought several jelly pads and one-half-dozen pitch pipes for which the African teachers were also grateful. We improvised with local materials: stones and seed pods for arithmetic counters and balls, ropes and hoops made of banana fibre for the physical education classes.

I had expected poverty, but I was totally unprepared for the lack of material possessions. Very few of my students had any personal belongings. Knicker inspection invariably proved that most of the girls owned only one pair or none. When I learned that many of the primary students from the model school walked from four to five miles to school without breakfast or anything to eat until they returned home, I gave the school enough money to provide lunches for all the students for the rest of the year. I recall my shock when one of our cook's wives gave birth to a baby boy. She had no diapers, no blankets, no toilet paper, no bottle, nothing except an old discarded woollen sweater and banana leaves.

I also recall the excitement my students expressed on the morning of their first independence anniversary, when, for breakfast, they were given a slice of plain bread instead of the usual cornmeal porridge, with a cup of tea as a special treat. Tea was considered a luxury. One of my students wrote: "On Christmas Day people in my village enjoy themselves by taking much of the native beer and eating a lot of meat and sincerely speaking, this is the day many houses including mine take tea in the whole year."

I went to Uganda thinking that I was going to educate the Africans, but they had educated me. They shattered all the stereotypical notions — that they were backward, uncivilized and pagan — I had brought with me.

I may have been paralysed by the cobra I met in the W.C., and by the news that the Reverend Ledger's baby had narrowly missed being bitten by a puff adder, and by the grunting hippo that visited me while I was directing a play out-of-doors, but a few scary memories such as these are overshadowed by numerous pleasant memories. I recall Deborah's reaction to a taffeta and net dress I gave her: "Oh, Miss Pet, it's too beautiful to wear even for Sundays. I just like to sit and look at it and touch it sometimes."

I recall the magic moment I felt when I saw my first lion, when I marvelled at the pygmies' exquisite sense of balance, when, on my first visit to the college library, I spotted Sheila Burnford's *The Incredible Journey*, when I saw Victoria Falls and a dense flock of flamingoes suddenly take to the air in Nakuro National Park, when I listened to the wonderful Gregorian chant sung by the barefoot Roman Catholic choir next door to our mission station. And Solomon's letter on my departure for Canada in the idiom of his ancestors: "Miss Pet will never be out of my memory for she is now a scar on my face."

Christmas trip in Africa, 7 December 1963 to 25 January 1964

I was looking forward to my Christmas trip to South Africa. On my way I would be attending the *Uhuru* (freedom) festivities on 11 December when Kenya would gain its independence from Britain.

At five thirty a.m. on 7 December Fathers Boss and Kiyana and I set off from Iganga in my white Volkswagen Beetle for Nairobi on the first stage of my summer holiday to South Africa. We kept climbing up the steep rocky escarpment of the great Rift Valley, crossing the equator, winding our way across the highlands where the land rises to ten thousand feet. Rain was pouring ferociously as only tropical rainstorms can. Even with my overcoat on, I shivered with cold.

Kenya

We passed the huge beautiful tea estates of Kericho, the tea capital of Kenya, where we stopped at the Tea Hotel for lunch. A fashionable wedding reception with top hats and morning coats was in progress. We passed coffee plantations, pyrtheum fields, fields of wheat, and pasture land. We gradually descended into the Rift Valley, that mysterious geological fault in the earth's surface. The view, as I stood on the 8,000 foot ridge, was breathtaking. The Kenya highlands are fertile, the best farming and cattle ranching in the country. So unlike the steaming impenetrable jungles I had associated with Africa. It was a farmer's country. I am not a farmer. I do not like barnyard odours. But as we passed the well-kept farms, the vast expanse of rolling plains, and the wandering herds of well-shaped cattle, I felt a freedom that attracted me. I wished I were a Kenyan farmer. Father Slot reminded me of the blood, sweat, tears and toil of the early settlers and of the tough veterans of two World Wars who had worked with their bare hands and had braved such dangers as hostile natives, disease and wild animals to bring the land to its present beauty and prosperity.

We reached Nairobi that evening. The priests drove me to the Convent of the Italian Consolata Missionary Sisters. Out of their anxiety for me since they were afraid of the mayhem that Kenya's *Uhuru* might bring, my friends had billeted me there for the week of festivities. To my surprise, the Sisters did not share their fears. I was free to wander at will. I gave Father Slot the use of my Volkswagen Beetle for the seven weeks I was going to be away, and bade him farewell until 25 January 1964, when he would pick me up in Nairobi.

Since I had arrived four days prior to the momentous day, I spent the time getting to know Nairobi, a wonderful city of streets shaded with violet jacarandas and brilliant purple bougainvillea and visiting Nairobi National Park, which was only five miles from downtown Nairobi. The park had no elephants, but the high concentration of other animals so near to Nairobi downtown traffic was remarkable. On one day a pride of seven lions thrilled me. They reminded me of Landseer's couchant lions that guard Nelson in Trafalgar Square. We sat and watched for over an hour as they sat motionless in two little groups. Then one would roll over and exercise his paws in the air. They would play together. They would yawn. Then one would get up gracefully. I loved to watch the suppleness of their bodies. The lion is truly magnificently made. They were so affectionate, so relaxed. Playing there or just sitting or lying, they looked so serenely peaceful, so harmless, until dusk gradually descended and one by one each got up and slowly paced away to take up their positions, determined, and alert, eyes and ears wide open for the kill.

"The Birth of a Nation"

It was a minute before midnight. The huge *Uhuru* stadium, built especially for the occasion, was plunged into total darkness. The British National Anthem was played. His Royal Highness, the Duke of Edinburgh, stood at attention. And for the last time the Union Jack was lowered. Sixty-eight years of colonial rule had ended. Kenya, "Colony and Protectorate," was no more.

On the stroke of midnight, the lights burst out. The new Kenya National Anthem was played, and the new black, red, green and white flag of Kenya was slowly raised to the top of the forty foot flagpole. A moment of stunned silence followed, and then a roar of applause echoed throughout the stadium. A moment of history had been written.

The ceremony was especially historic since Kenya's long struggle for independence by its freedom fighters, the Mau Mau, had been a violent one, with numerous raids and burnings, tortures and murders.

Prior to this symbolic flag raising ceremony, twelve hundred African dancers from Kenya's main tribes, in their beads and bangles, spears and shields, feathers and skins, thrilled the assembled guests for several hours with their dazzling displays of traditional tribal dances. The colours, sounds and vigorous movements overwhelmed me. I heard only the haunting war chants, saw only the fascinating tribal costumes and felt the rhythmic beat of drums, gongs, rattles and hand-clapping. I soon forgot the steaming radiators, the abandoned cars, the snail's pace of traffic, the long trek through soggy ground and sticky mud, the light drizzle, and the long wait for the dignitaries.

The Prime Minister of Kenya, the Hon. Jomo Kenyatta, the leader of the Mau Mau movement, whom the British had jailed, drove around the arena in his white Lincoln convertible, a gift from the American business community in Kenya, jauntily swishing his familiar zebra-tail fly whisk, with his latest African wife in a tweed coat at his side. (His white English wife was flown to Kenya for the event). Cries of *Uhuru* and *Harambee* (the Swahili equivalent for "all together, heave") Kenyatta's clarion call for national unity filled the air.

As the entire arena throbbed with jubilation, a nostalgic feeling surged within me, when I heard the familiar tune of "Auld Lang Syne," and the men of the King's African Rifles, in a starkly solemn ritual, handed over the regimental and Queen's colours to the newly-born Kenya Rifles who marched and counter marched smartly and slowly past the saluting base. The hushed arena watched, awe struck at the precision and stirred by the familiar strains played by the colourful massed bands. With pomp and ceremony, the crowd was being prepared for the solemn midnight hour. Tension mounted and emotions burst loose with deafening applause as midnight brought its dramatic climax. With a burst of fireworks, the most spectacular display I have ever seen, a new state was born. I walked back alone in the early hours of the morning to the convent, filled with the joy of the birth of a new nation.

Kenya

The evening's programme had culminated weeks full of *Uhuru* festivity. I felt the exciting anticipation, a wonderful unrest, as I strolled through the gaily decorated streets of Nairobi, Kenya's attractive modern capital, alive with the kind of holiday spirit that one feels at home on Christmas Eve. I jostled with the friendly and happy crowds carrying small Kenyan flags in the national colours of red, black, green and white. Men, women and children wore lapel badges and garments — dresses, shirts, hats and ties — printed with the word "*Uhuru*, 1963" all over them. Indian women, elegant and graceful in their colourful long flowing saris, and tribal elders in their monkey skin capes, as well as barefoot tribal people from up country in their distinctive dress, had all come to the big city to celebrate. Sikh policemen in their beards and tightly wound turbans, khaki shorts and olive putters were friendly. Family groups gazed at colourful and imaginative shop-window decorations. One, which I thought was very misleading, showed Africans "Before *Uhuru*" covered with grime, grease, and sweat, lifting a car out of the mud with wrenches, their women folk toting heavy loads on their backs and heads climbing up a hill. "After *Uhuru*" showed a happy, clean family group of Africans with straightened hair riding merrily in a white convertible.

Flags of all nations adorned the broad Kenyatta Avenue, formerly Delamere Avenue, lined with flowering trees and shrubs. The modern, very attractive business blocks along Government Road, and the public buildings of Coronation Avenue were decorated with bunting, flags, huge shields, drums and spears. Roundabouts and fountains were decorated with Kenya's armorial bearings and coats of arms. Kenyatta's picture was everywhere. The father of the Nation, in his beaded hat, in his western suit, and in his tribal costumes stared at me where ever I turned. The Sisters at the convent where I stayed had his picture prominently displayed over the front porch.

My fellow boarders at the convent had tried hard to dissuade me from strolling along Nairobi's main streets alone. The Goan airline stewardess even put me on house arrest on her day off. The Goan switchboard operators were horrified that I was walking alone from the downtown area to the convent several miles away. The Italian secretary, whose father had been a POW in Kenya during World War II and had settled there after the War, told me about the horrors of the Mau Mau massacres in the 1950s. She told me hair-raising tales of having to sleep with a pistol under her pillow, of chopped heads, slashed wrists, bolted doors, locked windows, lowered shades, and the "trusted servants."

None of their stories could stop me. One day's imprisonment on holy ground was enough. I broke out and enjoyed the festivities which took place with a kind of dignity and order that friends in Uganda, who had disapproved of my visiting Nairobi for *Uhuru*, could have never imagined. I had even talked to one of my favourite singers, Harry Belafonte, who had given a wonderful concert to honour the event.

*

On 12 December, I met Keith Andrew, a young Austra-
lian manager for a pharmaceutical company in East
Africa, stationed in Nairobi. I had been introduced to
Keith in Uganda several weeks after I arrived in Africa.
And I was looking forward to this trip we had planned
because he was much fun to be with. We drove to
Malindi and Mombasa, spent Christmas Eve in Zanzibar
and then went to Dar-es-Salaam where Keith left me to
return to Nairobi, and I continued my trip to South
Africa alone.

   We started off on our motor tour descending gradually from the vast stretches of scrub land on the Kenyan
plateau. We spent the night at Kilaguni Lodge in the
rugged and wild Royal Tsavo Park in Southeastern
Kenya , the largest game park of its kind in the world,
halfway between Nairobi and Mombasa, traditionally
famous for its over twenty thousand elephants. I learned
that their prodigious appetite needed several hundred
pounds of vegetation per day. Unfortunately, they open
the trunks of the baobab, one of East Africa's most
remarkable trees, to get at the pithy fibre lying underneath, causing the trees, hundreds of years old, to die.
The next day we went searching for animals. But it had
rained heavily for a week and animals don't come out in
the open when it is too wet. Several travellers told us
they had seen a herd of almost forty elephants. But by
the time we got close to them, we saw only two covered
with red mud. Disappointed, we started our drive for
Malindi.

   The vegetation began to change to the tropical flora
of cocoanut, palm, and banana trees. It got more humid,
and even hotter. From Mombasa to Malindi we passed

great sisal estates, row after row of large sharp-leaved bushes. The beaches were not as clean as I had expected because the recent heavy rains and winds had brought up much debris on the beach and it would be some time before it could be cleaned. As a result, we spent a lot of time in the pool at our hotel, The Eden Roc.

I now shudder in disbelief when my memory goes back to the Eden Roc pool. I was lying on the pool's concrete pavement sunning myself when I lifted my head and noticed that everyone in the pool and at poolside was silently leaving. I sat up to reconnoitre the situation. There was no one in sight. Turning my head, I saw, to my surprise, a snake less than five feet away from me. I looked at it, face to face admiring its long, coiled, slender body; its narrow head and large eyes. It looked so elegant. I wasn't frightened. To this day I don't know why I didn't panic and rush away. Instead, I reached for my camera to take a movie of him. There was a deadly silence. I could hear the whirring of the motor in my camera. As if he knew he was being photographed, he lifted his neck, jerked his head, opened his mouth, and extended and retracted his tongue. When I finished, I put my camera down and continued to sun myself. Twice I sat up to photograph him. I don't know how long it remained there beside me. After a while I raised my head and noticed that it had slithered away into the tangled bushes and foliage behind me.

Sixteen years later when I met Keith in Australia where he was living, he reminded me of the event. He told me that the snake had been a black mamba, the largest poisonous snake in Africa and that every time he remembers, he recoils in shivers. When I read recently that no snake in Africa is more dreaded than the black mamba, that it is the world's fastest snake, and that two drops of its venom can kill a grown person within ten minutes, I know that my guardian angel and my ignorance had protected me.

It was fun jumping into the surf of the warm Indian waters or just sitting in the warm puddles when the tide was out, or lying on the powder soft sands, sparkling with gold coloured specks, which Keith claimed were valuable minerals. The sun was glorious. It was so relaxing to sit beneath palms rustling in the refreshing trade winds, sipping tall cool drinks. We beach-combed and looked at all sorts of marine life that Keith identified. We picked driftwood, scoured clean from the tide, and all sorts of shells. Keith snorkelled in the Blue Lagoon; we viewed multicoloured fish through a glass- bottomed boat, and watched the three cornered sails of the Arab *dhows* swell gently in the soft breeze and slowly sink below the horizon.

Malindi, one of the greatest of the medieval city states along the Kenyan coast, was an interesting resort town with its narrow streets, and its Arabian and Portugese relics. There was a modern monument commemorating Vasco da Gama's 1498 landing. I found the African women here fascinating. Some wore ropes of many coloured beads which formed a high collar around the neck. Some had ears, wrists, neck and ankles encircled with wire coils and spiral brass bracelets. Most were decorated with scars on forehead, chest and stomach. All carried heavy babies in a sling tied tightly across bare breasts. Many were disfigured from carrying so many babies in this fashion. Barefoot, with babies on backs and heavy loads on heads like pack animals, these women could still walk with an ease and grace which I envied. With the forty yards of fringe they were wearing as skirts, covered with a length of cloth tied tightly at the waist, their walk was most sensuous. I had great difficulty photographing them. They were sullen, indignant and even defiant. But when I offered them a few shillings they would giggle or smile and I would get my pictures. At Sunday Mass I was surprised to see a few barefoot African nuns.

Ten miles south from Malindi, we explored the ruins of Gedi, which are preserved today as a national park. Gedi was an Arab port town that flourished between the thirteenth and seventeenth centuries. Its demise remains a mystery. The forest has invaded the town and magnificent trees tower over the walls and arches. The excavated portion of the town reveals a great mosque, a palace, and a number of wealthy merchants' houses, all built of coral stone. I enjoyed trying to locate them, named according to their interesting finds: House of the Ivory Box, House of Venetian Beads, House of Scissors.

In the small local museum I saw blue and white porcelain bowls from China, Venetian glass beads and glazed earthenware from Persia. The displays showed that the town must have had active overseas trade connections. The pillar tomb, a kind of tomb that is utterly alien to the rest of the Islamic world, fascinated me. The enigma which is Gedi intrigued me.

We spent only a few hours in Mombasa, Kenya's principal port on the Indian Ocean, before boarding our plane for Zanzibar. But before we left, we visited Fort Jesus, built by the Portugese in the late sixteenth century, now used as a museum, its soaring stone walls rising from a coral ridge above the harbour. It was four days before Christmas Day.

Zanzibar

Zanzibar, the island of cloves, was a joy. I grew to love
this quiet, sleepy Arab town with its narrow twisting
streets like Jerusalem's labyrinth of alleyways. It's hard
to believe that less than a month after my visit, a bloody
and bitter revolt that deposed a sultan raged in these
very quiet alleys. (But violent events can erupt suddenly
in Africa, the non-native population apparently unaware
of the native turmoil that often lay beneath the surface.)

It was the Christmas season, and yet there were no
signs of Christmas, no holly or tinsel or mistletoe, none
of the smells associated with Christmas. A decorated
Christmas tree stood incongruously out of place in the
lobby of the Zanzibar hotel where we stayed, as well as
the few dusty Christmas cards scattered among station-
ery in the cribs or boxes of the crowded Asian shops.
Christmas Eve was like any other day on this clove-
scented isle. By ten p.m., the hotel doors were closed, as
is usual, and no one stirred. I went to Midnight Mass in
the Roman Catholic Cathedral which was attended
mostly by smartly attired Goan women. There was only
a handful of Europeans, and a few native women wearing their colourful *khangas* (large squares of cloth in
brilliant colours and fantastic designs), some, as always,
still breastfeeding their enormous babies at two years of
age. A thin little Goan priest sang mass. I missed such
Christmas carols as "O Holy Night" and "What Child Is
This?" A small tropical manger scene sat to the right of
the main altar, and I thought of the more impressive one
back home with its snow and spruce trees. When Mass
was over the parishioners dispersed quickly. There was
no exchange of Christmas greetings. The streets were
empty as I walked alone to my hotel.

However, I enjoyed the glorious sunshine, the warm waters, and gentle breezes. I shuddered to think what the weather was like at home: snow drifts, slippery icy roads, frosted windshields, stalled cars, skidding tires, and the awful ache of my freezing fingers. But I missed my mother's Christmas pastries, her *turdilli*, and *scalille*, her dark fruity Christmas cake, and Christmas dinner with egg-nog, turkey, cranberry sauce, hot mince pie à la mode.

Keith and I visited clove plantations. We saw the red flower buds spread out to dry under the tropical sun. We visited cocoanut palm estates where I learned that the white nutty matter was eaten fresh or dried and when it was sun-dried, it was called copra and makes cocoanut oil. The leaves were used to make roofing for village homes.

We strolled along the palm-fringed beaches; we swam in the warm waters of the Indian Ocean; we took pictures of the outrigger canoes, and old dug-outs that the lobster fishermen used. We sauntered along the narrow streets and peered into the small exciting shops. We marvelled at the well preserved and massive teak-wood Arab doors, handsome in their brass bosses and lotus, chain, and fish carvings. We watched the old Arab *dhow* harbour bustling with activity as strong-muscled Africans loaded and unloaded spices. We saw a cart filled with long ivory tusks. Passing centuries hadn't changed the scene.

At one time, Zanzibar was the most important slave market in the world. We crept into the dark slave caves on the Zanzibar beach where the Arabs hid those slaves who were not sold for work on the island itself, before transferring them onto *dhows*. We saw the square where the slaves were auctioned off, and the wall where they were hung. (Great Britain, France, Germany and the United States were involved in brisk slave-trading activities at Zanzibar by the beginning of the nineteenth century.) Today, the Africans still do the manual work; the Indians control the retail trade, and the Arabs, who own the clove estates, are the aristocrats of the island.

Zanzibar was a vital terminal for missionaries and explorers like Speke and Burton, both of whom were looking for the source of the Nile, and for Livingstone, the missionary abolitionist African explorer, and Stanley, whose words on finding Livingstone, "Doctor Livingstone, I presume" have become famous. It was here they hired their porters, few of whom ever came back. The house that Livingstone stayed in before his final voyage is still on the edge of the tidal backwater just to the north of the Shark Market. We visited the interesting museum filled with artifacts of the slave trade.

We attended a Moslem wedding where only women were present at its initial stages. I was amazed to see that under the hooded, drab, black coverall garment *bouiboui* (worn for modesty) the women were heavily ornamented in gold and precious gems. In the African bazaar I even detected slim jims showing under some cloaks.

The modern schools of the Aga Khan community were a pleasant surprise. Followers of the Aga Khan were very westernized and their hospitals, schools and community centres were modern and attractive.

I found photography difficult. An aristocratic Arab trader, his head swathed in yards of material, with a silver dagger at his waist, told me he became enraged when he had to pay to see his own picture at the movies of Zanzibar's *Uhuru* celebrations on 10 December. He complained: "They always tell you they'll send you the pictures. I never got mine yet."

We enjoyed the company of several Zanzibar natives: Ambrose, a smuggler; Mr. Villani, Keith's business associate, and his wife; John, who was in the lobster business; and Jumo, the movie star, who had appeared in many films such as *West of Zanzibar*. It was Jumo who woefully said to me one day, when I remarked that it was fun to be in Zanzibar, "Oh *memsahib* before it was fun. Now everyone talks politics."

There must have been many men talking politics right then because a revolution took place a month later, unseating the Sultan who had represented the traditionally powerful Arab minority on the island. Besides local politics, another popular topic of conversation was President Kennedy's assassination that had taken place a month before.

We left Zanzibar in the pouring rain early Christmas morning to fly to Mombasa where we would pick up our car to drive to Dar-Es-Salaam.

Tanzania

On our way to Dar-es-Salaam, Tanzania's capital, which means "haven of peace" in Arabic, we passed native villages with clusters of mud and thatched roof cottages, vast sisal hemp estates, streams of women in their *khangas*, men in their long white *kanzus*, and Arabs in their maroon fezzes. It didn't feel like Christmas Day. Except for "Winter Wonderland" and "White Christmas" that we heard on the car radio it was like any other day. We decided it was too far to try to get to Dar-es-Salaam that night so we started climbing up a circuitous road to the mountain resort of Lushoti, 4,500 feet above sea level.

The roadside paths were constantly in motion with groups of walking children waving and laughing, and people on well-laden bicycles. Lush green vegetation, fresh mountain springs and beautiful mountain scenery delighted us as we wound our way up the Usambara Mountains. Much to our surprise we were able to get down the muddy *murram* trails the next morning even though we feared that the night-long torrential rains had washed out bridges. Again, we passed streams of greased and ochred, slim-waisted, narrow-hipped, tall Masai warriors wearing lengths of cloth like togas knotted over one shoulder. And we passed columns of heavily over-laden women carrying cargoes of wire coils, beads, chain mail, and safety pins on garments of softened cattle hides.

Their appearance fascinated me. They converted animal horns, bones, shells, hair, feathers, and skins into dazzling headdresses, garments and body ornaments. I was always intrigued with their hair styles. Some had their hair greased with red ochre and plaited into a large number of short pigtails that looked like black ropes hanging down like a mop over their heads. Others had their hair parted in checkerboard fashion, and still others in fuzzy peppercorns. Some had the sides of the head shaved with patches of black rectangles or squares confined to a central ridge running from forehead to nape. The Aloket headdress — a loop of woven giraffe hair attached to a large cone-shaped mud-plastered chignon at the back of the wearer's head — of the Turkana tribesmen was especially fascinating. Turkana herdsmen carried carved wooden pillows designed to preserve their elaborate headdress. I bought one.

Many men had hugely pierced earlobes stretching to their shoulders, plugged with wood cylinders, or coils of wire. Others had their lobes distended by the circular wooden discs of their early adornment as warriors flapping limply. Still others put their distended lower lobes over the top of their ears. With their shining, satin-textured skins and their soft velvet eyes, I found their carefree, easy grace attractive whether they were herding or grazing their cattle, sheep and goats, or just passing by. Picture taking was always difficult. The women would scatter into the tall grasses and lie flat on the ground until we would leave.

Dar-es-Salaam was a disappointment. It had none of the sophistication of Nairobi. Its city centre was uninteresting, shabby and scrubby with sturdy heavy structures, a legacy from German colonial days. But the shady promenade fringing the harbour was beautiful and the buildings in the suburbs, the hospitals, schools and the most fantastic Roman Catholic church I have ever seen, were modern and attractive. The Asian and native quarters looked the same as the ones in Nairobi and Kampala. I had to have a police escort to photograph the native market. Once the tourist bureau explained to me why the natives were so belligerent and indignant, I appreciated the situation. It appeared that Tanzania's government, through the radio, press and posters, was telling the people that tourists brought money into the country, and thus they should be willing to have their pictures taken. The natives, however, thought that if the government was making money they should share in the wealth too.

We stayed at the Dar Club, once the bastion of British imperialism and colonialism, and the most exclusive club in Tanzania. As a deliberate rebuke to British rule, the government was now operating it with a policy of universal access.

A very modern museum attracted a lot of our attention. It displayed tribal weapons, musical instruments and masks, as well as Livingstone's note books, personal letters, clothing, British flag, surgical instruments, and faded photographs. Even a section of the tree where Stanley met Livingstone was on display.

We spent delightful moments at beautiful Oyster Bay when the tide was out, picking shells, exploring the depths of warm coral pools, jumping in the warm breakers, and walking barefoot on warm soft sands.

It was my historical interest in the slave trade that took us to Bagamoyo, once the hub of the slave trade, fifty miles north of Dar. Slaves seized by the Arabs from their villages all over Tanzania were shipped from this coastal port to Zanzibar and Arabia. But we had difficulty finding the house where Stanley made his preparations for his expedition into Central Africa. It seemed as if no one had heard of Stanley or Livingstone. Even the police officers appeared uninformed. They came with me to inspect some writing on a stone nearby. It was a plaque honouring some German dead. We discovered a house which a European woman said was the house we were looking for, but I wasn't sure. We did find the chapel where Livingstone's body was laid by his native porters after its final journey from the interior. A French-Canadian Roman Catholic priest was in charge. We visited a museum nearby, where we saw the chains of slave gangs, and all sorts of original documents of the slave era. I was appalled.

As we wandered about the old town we stumbled upon a stranded car with two Russian families and a month old baby. I couldn't understand why they were in this remote native village, so far from the main road. They claimed they were Nairobi bound. But we were very suspicious. The army mutinied in Dar soon after. In Dar, Keith and I separated. He returned to Nairobi and I continued my trip en route to South Africa.

Nyasaland (Malawi)

On 29 December I flew from Dar to Blantyre, Nyasaland where a wealthy, and well-educated Indian exporter importer in ground nuts and copra, Mr. Haji, whom I met on the flight, took an avuncular interest in me. Hence I saw more of Blantyre and its environs than I would otherwise have seen. It was an old colonial town with very few modern buildings.

It was the people whom I met that made Blantyre interesting. And because the Rhodesia-Nyasaland federation was breaking up in two days' time, on 31 December, conversation sparkled with intensity and enthusiasm. The Mayor, Mr. Satar Sacranie, an Indian, who had chambers at Lincoln's Inn in London, strongly favoured the dissolution. He could foresee a great future for Nyasaland which had a strictly agricultural economy based on cash crops of tea, tobacco, and maize, but virtually no other resources. In fact, the boss of Nyasaland's Malawi party, the brilliant and megalomaniac Dr. Hastings Banda, the Father and Founder of the nation, the "beloved Messiah, the Liberator," presided at a mock funeral of the ten-year-old federation and set fire to a coffin representing federation and threw the ashes into the Shire River. Most of Nyasaland's hospitals and schools were built during federation.

Under the federation, Dr. Sacranie's wife, a graduate of the University of Bombay, complained that Moslem women had no vote because they were polygamous. She however, could vote because she was a university graduate. She told me that, "the amount of money a woman had, could also grant her suffrage." Both she and her husband were very vocal in their denunciations of the white Rhodesians.

We visited the home of Mr. Haji's business associate, Mr. Mohammed Hussein, who was half-African and half-Indian. The living room was lined with four sofas and six armchairs. There were six radios in the room. Large pictures of Indian movie stars decorated the walls. A vase of artificial flowers sat on the table which was fringed with six metal collapsible chairs. We drove in Mr. Hussein's modern American car to Mozambinque where Mr. Haji wanted to buy pigeon peas from a trader Mr. Hussein knew. But Mr. Haji was stopped by border officials because he carried a Tanzania passport. I had asked him why he had surrendered his British passport. He told me that he was sure Nyerere would give the Indians a fair deal and that he had nothing to fear because he had always treated the African fairly. The border official would not recognize the Tanzania passport and so Mr. Haji had to remain at the border. I was allowed to pass because the official noticed that as a Canadian citizen I was also a British subject, but I had to leave my precious Bolex movie camera behind.

Mozambique

As soon as we crossed the border into Mozambique I saw a Roman Catholic chapel and a pillar surmounted by a cross built by the Portugese explorers to mark the discoveries they made for God and country. Mr. Hussein and I went to see the Portugese trader.

The Portugese trader owned a clean modern restaurant several miles from the border. When we told him what had happened, he went to the border himself and came back with Mr. Haji. We had a very appetizing lunch. Mr. Hussein did not eat because he was not sure whether the meat had been killed according to Muslim law. I admired him for this.

We drove the seventy miles to the trader's estate. The countryside looked scruffy; the tea estate was badly tended, and the maize fields were untidy. We didn't see the flowing files of walking or bicycle-riding natives that we were accustomed to seeing in East Africa. A few tattered children were eating salted dried mangoes. We passed no native villages, just the odd mud thatched hut. Mozambique's villagers were flocking into Nyasaland and to South Africa.

We finally arrived at the trader's elevators. He also owned the general store, which I could see was very well stocked. Four men were working on treadle sewing machines, and a number of women were buying coloured beads and lengths of cloth.

A group of women were squatted under the shade of a tree outside, with baskets of bright yellow corn kernels sitting in a row in front of them waiting to be ground at the trader's grist mill. Mr. Haji detected weevils in the pigeon peas so he did not buy. We drove the seventy miles back through a violent rainstorm.

Southern Rhodesia (Zimbabwe)

On New Year's Eve I flew to Salisbury, (Harare) capital of South Rhodesia, just in time to attend a black-tie New Year's Eve party to which Edward Somppi, formerly of my home town, invited me. I saw my first Santa Claus of this trip. Conversation naturally centred on the dissolution of the Central African Federation which was breaking up that very night. Most of the guests were very bitter towards Britain. "Betrayed us, that's what Macmillan and his girlfriend Macleod have done," I was told. In protest, a few of the guests had refused to buy British-made products. They complained bitterly:

> Our forefathers actually conquered this land. We have brought all that is modern and progressive. We have developed agriculture — the largest tobacco market in the world is here — we import auctioneers from the southern U.S.A. We have spread education. We have built the railroads, the roads. We provided the air transport. We have maintained a stable government. We do have the colour bar. Would you invite the street cleaner, window cleaner or porter to a party of yours?

A Norwegian paper company manager said: "I left South Africa because I disapproved of apartheid. But since I've been here, I don't know that South Africa might be right after all. Oil and water don't mix. I probably will go back."

An English insurance executive who, ironically enough, was dissuaded from migrating to Canada by a Toronto bishop who alleged that there was a difficult racial situation in Canada told me that he just "lived for the day" in Southern Rhodesia.

All expressed this same uncertainty and insecurity. As a result, they were really living it up. The standard of living the Europeans enjoyed amazed me: spacious homes with swimming pools all cared for by servants: cooks, houseboys, gardenboys, as well as nurses and nannies to take care of their children.

Salisbury was a bustling booming city of skyscrapers. Its expansion was staggering. In 1941 there were 18,000 whites; in 1962, 90,000. There were 200,000

Africans. I didn't know whether the whites or blacks would accept this minority position without a fight. I did know that there were intense feelings of resentment, frustration and discontent.

South Africa: Johannesburg

I enjoyed being part of the cosmopolitan crowds of Johannesburg in the Transvaal with its towering office blocks, busy department stores, and exclusive boutiques. Its growth from a gold rush camp of tents, shacks, and wagons in 1886 to the largest gold mining area in the world has been phenomenal. I felt the affluence in the chic, smartly dressed women, in the well dressed Africans, and in the bustle of the place. I was literally walking on gold when I walked on Joburg's streets. It's a long way beneath, but it's there. The towering mine dumps of yellow slag were constant reminders.

When I arrived in Durban, Natal, the city was splitting at the seams with thousands of white holiday makers jamming the hotels and beaches. Since most of the factories, building trades, and schools had shut down from 18 December to 13 January, South Africans flocked to popular seaside resorts (in spite of the shark hazard), and I had great difficulty finding a hotel. Christmas spirit was still in the air. Santa Claus still peered from windows, and a huge manger scene still stood in the main park.

Durban had an exotic flavour of contrasts. I saw beaded Zulu belles with elaborate headdresses, with hair that had been rubbed with fat, clay, and cow-dung so as to stiffen it into a kind of felt. Eventually this bun of felt reached remarkable proportions and it could then be worn in several styles. I saw some that looked like dunce caps and others, like that in Queen Nefertete's picture. Since such elaborate coiffures could easily be deranged in sleep, it wasn't surprising that, when I entered their bee hive huts, I saw wooden pillows used as cheek rests.

A Roman Catholic church sits smack in the centre of the Indian market, which was congested with flowing humanity. The Indian women were wearing silk trousers and tight tunics, and the Indian men wore trousers of a white soft cloth and western style jackets.

I took a five-day-motor coach tour from Durban to Capetown, following the famous Garden Route filled with South African history. The natural beauty of the landscape — coves, headlands, mountains, lakes, rivers, golden beaches, and mountain passes — was stupendous. We crossed the Transkei, one of the homelands, a fertile tract of soft rolling hills where the Zhoas and the Pondos had been granted self-government by the Nationalist government. The only whites allowed were missionaries, traders, (if they behaved themselves), and government officials. Fog, mist, and rain accompanied us throughout the entire Transkei, disappointing me terribly. An extract from my letter dated 10 January 1964 to my sister Rita, says:

> The huge waves are lashing against the shore; the spray rises high. The sea is rough and the strong cool winds are blowing hard. I've never before felt such high winds. As I walk along the shore, I wonder, whether if, on such a day as this, Diaz in 1487 landed on the shore and named it Algoa Bay.

Capetown

Capetown, the Republic's oldest city, known to fifteenth century mariners as Cape of Storms, is beautifully located between Table Mountain and the sea. Unfortunately, fog and mist blotted my view when I went up by cable car to Table Mountain to admire the harbour. Parliament was moving from Pretoria, the administrative capital of South Africa, to the Cape because Cape Town was the parliamentary capital six months of the year. There were many historic buildings. The Castle, built in 1666 as a fort for the protection of the early colonists, was now a museum housing period furniture such as beautiful stinkwood wardrobes. I also saw several well-kept homes in the Cape Dutch style of architecture. There was an impressive modern statue of Diaz looking vigorous and confident. He had been the first to round the Cape, in the good hope of eventually reaching the East by sea in 1487. It was my interest in apartheid that took me to South Africa. I wanted to compare the living conditions of the South African native to those of Uganda. And thus I spoke to as many people as I could about it. It was sacred to many, embarrassing to some, personal to everyone.

There was Ruby, whom I met on a tour of the Valley of the Thousand Hills, an Afrikaner, definitely convinced that the blacks were savages not ready for citizenship. She had a farm in the Transvaal, knew the Zulus well and spoke their language: "I like them but I wouldn't associate with them. They don't know how to drink from cups nor sit on chairs. A rare steak they wouldn't know what to do with it." Ruby was married to an Englishman after what she termed "a Dictionary courtship" during which she learned to speak English. She took me to see the African Follies. Most of the performers were Cape Coloureds with white or nearly white skins: "Oh, but they're black inside. Their insides are full of demons, darkness. They might look civilized on the outside. But we've just slapped a coat of paint on them and forgotten about the inside." Ruby referred to them as coons and kaffirs, two most derogatory terms.

There was Lil, a Jewess born in South Africa, who asked, "Do you think it's fair for disabled native ex-servicemen to receive half the pension just because their skins are black?"

It was strange to see Indian waiters and porters, doing the menial jobs that are reserved for them through the *Job Reservation Act*, when in Uganda and Kenya it was the Indian who drove the Mercedes Benz. I found it strange, too, that the Japanese were given white status recognition while the Chinese were not. It was deemed to be economically necessary, since Japan imported a lot of South Africa's products.

There was the dear seventy-nine year old lady who had clung to me on the Garden tour from Durban to Capetown, who told me:

> Why do they have to label it with that word. We had it when Gen. Smuts was here. They are getting cheeky now. We've always had it. We've got to have it. We've worked hard. We can't be driven into the sea. You people don't understand. Those of us who have been raised out here know just a bit more about the natives than the people who haven't been raised out here. We are just as much African as the Bantu. This is my country. Would you give your country back to the Indians?

A successful businessman, Mr. Sack, continued:

> One man one vote is out. The position of the white man must be maintained. We're outnumbered four to one, thirty-two million whites to 128 million Bantu. In the U.S.A. its nineteen million Negroes out of a population of 180 million whites. We want no interference in

South African domestic affairs. The UN has an Afro
Asiatic majority. It should be called 'disunited.' The US
is afraid of that majority. There won't be an internal
revolution. The Bantu are too disorganized. And anyway, they have never had it so good. There won't be
any sabotage. We'll fight to the death. We shall annex
Bastoland, Swaziland, Bechuanaland. South Rhodesia
will join us.

Immigrants were streaming into South Africa from Britain and Kenya. Pat was one of 1000 immigrants who
arrived in Durban from Britain in December, lured by
the attractions of a subsidized paid passage, and room
and board paid for three weeks. She was a song and
dance artist who had appeared in *My Fair Lady*. "Well if
I don't get a suitable job it will have been a holiday, a nice
respite from that horrible English weather." I thought of
the sub-zero weather back home, the high snow banks,
the abandoned cars and the snow shovelling and ice
storms. I agreed with her. The weather was certainly
better here.

Janet had invited coloureds and Bantus to her
twenty-first birthday party before apartheid had a name.
She belonged to the radical sect, the *avant garde*, the
underground at her university:

> But the guests all separated into groups — the col-
> oureds in one group, they are not accepted by the
> Bantu, the whites in another, etc. There was a natural
> separation. It's not really a question of colour — it's
> everything that goes with it. Tradition, customs, back-
> ground. They are hundreds of years behind. You can't
> absorb culture over night. You can't become educated
> overnight.

There was Elena, an Italian doctor married to a South
African during the war. She was realistic, without any
delusions:

> Apartheid is wrong. It's not a question of morality.
> Don't be so idealistic. Let's be practical. The whites
> have to survive. Let them fight for it. We still have a
> few more years to enjoy ourselves. England granted
> independence for fear of Russia. Morally whites have
> rights too. It's a case of economics. We are going to
> need them. We are going to lose our cheap labour, our
> nannies.
>
> Anything can be bought. Life is an effort. This is
> all part of the evolutionary process. You can't have full
> political equality. The Bantu voted for the candidate
> who bought them blankets. Their votes were finally
> taken away. I spoke to some house servants. They did
> not like the native locations where there is much rob-
> bery, violence and a high crime rate. There aren't
> enough police. The pass rule is one way the govern-
> ment is trying to keep down crime.

The Springbok Hotel manager in Joburg told me:

> They were still teething. In England the people who
> were removed from the slums in London kept their coal
> in the bathtub. It took them thirty years to realize what
> the contraption was for. You can't hurry this develop-
> ment. We've begun to remove the slum here. You have
> to treat them as not too bright children. I like them.
> They like me. They bring me peaches from their gar-
> dens. South African peaches are delicious. If they
> weren't happy, they could disrupt the country in ten
> minutes by flooding the mines.
>
> New industry is coming to South Africa. Cyril
> Lord, the Lancashire mill's magnet ,brought his skilled
> technicians and started a factory in East London. The
> Communist Suppression Act is good. Russia is training
> angry young men and they are returning here dedicated

Marxist, to take over positions of influence in the civil service.

Verwoerd's New Year's Radio message to the Bantu was interesting. He said the child cannot become independent without growing slowly under the care of a father. This is a gradual process. He warned them of the danger of wanting too much and then told them the story of the dog with the piece of meat in his mouth, who saw his reflection in the pool.

I left South Africa more confused than ever. The colour bar, as a government policy, revolted me. I shuddered at the sight of *"nie blankes* — white only." There were two official languages, English and Afrikans, a simplified form of Dutch. I was horrified to see "For Europeans only" on park benches, in the post office, and at railroad stations. And I cringed when I read, "for European children only."

To know what is fair to all the races is a complex problem. I do know, however, that a minority privileged oligarchy is not just. It is revealing that I could only speak to privileged, white South Africans, because the country was so noticeably segregated. However, the few native South Africans I did see were better dressed and seemed to enjoy a better standard of living than the Africans I knew in my town in Uganda. It seemed paradoxical that in such a brutally racist and oppressive country, there were a few Natives who were actually enjoying a good standard of living compared to Natives in most other African countries.

From Joburg, I flew to Livingstone. Surely those aren't the famous Victoria Falls, I kept telling myself as I stared at them through the plane window. They looked so puny. And the mighty Zambezi was a sluggish river, sprinkled with scores of green islands. I was disappointed.

Victoria Falls

I heard its rumbling thunder before I actually saw it. And then I saw it — the greatest river wonder in the world. I gazed greedily, speechless at the beauty before me — the foaming waters of the Eastern Cataract plunging over a perpendicular wall of rock into a deep chasm below. The roar was something, the like of which I had never heard before.

Wherever my vantage point, I was in awe of the Falls' spectacular ever-changing beauty: Rainbow Point, where the sun hit the spray to make gorgeous rainbows, and Main Falls, where the mighty waters (seventy-five million gallons a minute) hurled down into the 355 foot gorge with such force that thick opaque clouds of spray were pushed upwards. At Devil's Cataract, the spray was so thick at times that it was like a curtain hiding the falls from sight because the waters rushed down the slanting slopes into the deep gorge below.

Rosemary, an English nurse from Basutoland whom I had met in the hotel where I was staying, and I walked through the rain forest, drenched to the skin by the numinous spray that the falls worked up. It was an exhilarating, a spiritual experience. I liked soaking in the cool refreshing waters, feeling the wind blowing the water in my eyes and across my face. I liked squashing along the soggy trail, and creeping under dripping woods. I liked feeling the water seep through my shoes, and trickle through my toes in my hush puppies. I even liked the feel of my wet clothes clinging to my body. I liked the fresh taste of the water. And when I stood on

Danger Point directly over the gorge, I felt an over-whelming urge to leap into the tumbling white waters.

Whenever we stopped, a new beautiful sight presented itself along the one and one-half mile length: a boiling pot of churning white waters, molten grey tranquil waters, waters dripping slowly and serenely, waters sprinkling, waters descending with noble majesty, waters chasing, racing, short quick puffs of mist, long columns of mist, thick dense clouds of mist, mist quickly scattered by breezes, spray filling chasms, spray rising slowly up hundreds of feet, wide gorges, narrow gorges, wooded islands, lush green slopes of palm groves. All was a glorious spectacle. How could I not believe in God?

Livingstone's memorial held my attention. Wearing trousers caught up with string tied around his shins, a cap with flaps, a walking stick in one hand and a Bible and field glasses in the other, Livingstone gazed at the Falls. He looked the courageous explorer he was, with a strong physique and a manly stride. A look of quiet wonder filled his face. In my mind I could hear the words attributed to him: "Scenes so lovely must be gazed upon by angels in their flight." The longer I looked at him the more I wished I could have known him.

I spent over two hours in the Livingstone Museum. I was entranced by the missionary explorer's life. Many of Livingstone's personal belongings were on display: his sextant, thermometer, walking stick, his hippo hide whip, his chronometer, and his letters. He was a deeply religious man dead set against the slave trade, a peace loving man, who didn't want to use arms against the natives. While I was reading his letters, I heard local school boys who were also scanning them refer to Livingstone's poor handwriting. I had to chuckle. Learning that Livingstone had a brother in Canada also excited me.

The main topic of conversation at the Victoria Falls Hotel was the election of Northern Rhodesia's first Prime Minister. The outcome was a foregone conclusion, a landslide victory for Kaunda, another prison graduate of colonial rule, jailed by the British and later groomed by them to take over the copper rich protectorate. Zambia, as Northern Rhodesia was called after independence, is destined to be a multiracial society in which Kaunda promised that the rule of law would prevail and that no individual would be victimised because of his country of origin.

Kaunda's policy made economic sense, since European and South African know-how is essential to the booming mining industry. But there wasn't the same number of white settlers in Northern Rhodesia as there was in Kenya. Whether Kaunda can persuade his rank and file to accept in spirit and in letter the moderate and constitutional pace of reform, is another question. He has warned, "we shall crush ruthlessly any attempt to overthrow this government by unconstitutional means."

A mechanical engineer who had no use for a black nationalist government told me: "My men are afraid to take them to task because the Africans intimidate them. Wives and children are dear to my men. How can we maintain standards without discipline? You can't run a company without discipline. Things are going to pot."

But Moses, my African guide at the craft village proudly beamed: "Because we are so behind and we must catch up. We will have all the freedom now. We must work hard."

We were lucky in Livingstone National Park. We saw herds of zebra playing and running on the wide plains. One was so cheeky that he kept trying to poke his head through the front window of our car. We stayed; he stayed. He really looked like a horse with black and white striped pajamas. Two others were scratching themselves against a tree. A kudu calf wanted to get to know us too. He stuck his head into our car. I was afraid. An ugly warthog kept scratching the car, and having his dinner by the roadside. We saw many species of buck: sable, eland, waterbuck, and wildebeest. We watched two young impala playing and locking their beautiful horns. I was part of the natural world of Africa and I loved it.

From Livingstone I flew to Nairobi where I wanted to remain a few days. But Fathers Slot and Vester were anxious to get me back to Iganga.

"Mutiny at the Border"

"Everyone is warned to stay indoors. All traffic on the main Nairobi-Nakuru road is halted," announced the newscaster on the wireless early that morning, 25 January 1964, but Fathers Slot, Vester and I had not heard it. We had already left Thika on our way to Iganga. We got as far as Navaisha where a spiked road block and security police with rifles stopped us. We could go no further. The army at Lanet Barracks — the Kenya Rifles — had mutinied. They had raided the armoury and stolen arms and ammunition. "Gone on a sit-down strike," one security police informed me, "for more pay, promotion and better living conditions." Kenya's President, Jomo Kenyatta, had promised a better standard of living for all.

How long we would be delayed no one could hazard a guess. I counted sixteen buses and thirty cars. Tall thin Kikuyus with spindly legs, tall thin Kikuyus wearing castoff Army greatcoats, water soaked and filthy; tall thin Kikuyus wearing shapeless European hats, and patches and repatched patches; and tall Masai with ochred hair and shoulder length earlobes limply flapping as they hurried to the front of the queue; and tall Masai with their distended lobes tucked neatly over the top of the ears were tumbling out of packed buses. Fidgety Arab traders got out of their Mercedes-Benzes. Blonde burly Kenyan settlers with hairy legs slammed station wagon doors. Indian women in long flowing saris, and Sikh men in tightly wrapped turbans and net enclosed beards left their children-loaded Volkswagens. It was only 8:30 a.m.

"The scene must be recorded for posterity," I casually remarked to one of the Kenyan settlers with the hairy legs, as I proceeded to take pictures.

"Posthumously," he snapped back.

His cynical remark was food for thought. I photographed nervously. An hour passed. Father Vester was getting irritable.

"Is there another way we can go?" he asked.

The Sikh police inspector replied, "there is no other way."

We would have to wait. I was enjoying it all. Father Slot resigned himself to waiting. Father Vester was getting more edgy, more impatient. He wanted to be in Iganga that night. After an hour and a half, the Sikh policeman announced we could get through. Everyone jumped into cars. The road block was lifted. But we didn't get very far. We had to turn back. I could hear shots being fired.

"I've been here forty years. It's something bigger than an *askari* mutiny. The Commies are behind it. Look what happened in Zanzibar, and in Dar," commented a bulky settler. "I've had enough," complained a young white man."

> I've lived in Kenya all my life. My father was a D.C. [District Commissioner]. My young brother accidentally shot a tribesman two years ago. He was acquitted. But my mother was beaten up. I've been working on a tea estate for six years, was assistant manager. There was a series of strikes. The ring leaders wouldn't listen to union representatives. I couldn't sack anyone. But I was bodily thrown out. I'm fed up. I'm leaving, leaving a 2000£ paid year job. For a twenty-three year old, that's not bad. I'm going to England. Luckily my company has found me a job there. But I don't want to leave. I love Kenya. But I'm fed up.

He spoke in chopped sentences and his lips were dry. I could feel his intense resentment.

"Everything's going to pot," whispered an African in Western dress.

"Why," asked Father Slot.

" I don't know," was the calm reply.

They spoke in Swahili. But Father Slot remained silent. Europeans were very cautious now. Finally, we heard a commotion. Motors roared. Front cars were moving. We jumped into our car.

"Go quickly, sir," ordered a British officer in a camouflage jacket, standing beside an armoured car.

"Duck," ordered Father Slot, "We're going in front of the barracks."

Fear suddenly gripped me. I obeyed Father Slot's order but I raised my head high enough so that I could scan the surroundings. We shot past Lanet Barracks. I noticed British soldiers in steel helmets with rifles cocked on both sides of the road. They had taken up positions in ditches to cut off any mutineer, or sniper who had escaped camp and might be hiding in the long grass. I saw lorries, tanks, jeeps, Red Cross ambulances. Now, like Father Vester, I wanted to be in my mission station so safe and holy.

There had been a heavy exchange of fire. A Kenya Rifles private was killed and a passing African civilian was shot in the arm. Bullets had whizzed across the road. But by the time I had time to think about all this, we had passed the danger zone.

In Nakuru, all was quiet. The Indians had closed their *dukas*. We drove up the escarpment. The beautiful Rift Valley with its rich soil and prosperous farms was below us. At twelve-thirty p.m. we reached the Jolly Farmer Hotel at Molo 8,100 feet in elevation. It had taken us four hours to go 127 miles. The hotel was a charming English colonial style stone building. The spacious ladies' room was well appointed. It told me a story. The empty bar told me another. I felt sad.

"You made it," observed an Englishman in khaki shorts.

He, too, had been in the queue. Others who had made it, soon arrived.

"They're not letting any others through," he added.

We all sat down for a beer. The Englishman in khaki shorts continued:

> The soldiers wanted their own officers. The Tanganyika Rifles had English commanding officers, Uganda Rifles have only English training officers. Kenya Rifles have English Commanding officers. That's it. They go to Sandhurst and want accelerated promotions, private to a field marshal overnight.
>
> I've been here for forty-one years. In 1952 I could have sold my tea estate. I stayed on. Schools are multi-

racial. My children are going to Australia. I can't run the estate myself. They can't seem to guarantee law and order. I'm going to have to sell. What is going to happen to my Africans who have been twenty to thirty years in my employ? I don't know. They will be too old for the new owner. Who will buy my farm? A rich Indian from Uganda probably. No, the mutiny isn't Communist inspired. But they're pretty slick those Russians, like the snow ploughs they sent as aid to Guinea. They wouldn't know any better. They wouldn't be able to tell them from an ordinary plough.

An elderly American couple who missed their flight in Nairobi were stranded because of the mutiny. A tall, good looking Kenyan with a fractured leg on his way to Nairobi for an operation, was also stranded.

Over my coffee, taken in the lounge, as is usual in these parts, I read in the *Kenya Weekly News* that a number of farms at present owned by Europeans were in the process of being bought by the Central Land Board for compassionate reasons, and that, in the first instance, they would be offered for purchase to Africans with a loan of 90 per cent, repayable over twenty years, at 6.5 per cent interest.

The Englishman in the khaki shorts continued:

Boy, the old b — is taking a firm stand against the mutineers. He's not going to be a Nyerere. He's not going to give in to their demands. I cheered. I've since found out it took six hours of quiet persuasion on the part of his European advisors to convince him of the necessity of this firm stand.

Do you know he reminded the soldiers of the distinguished record the K.A.R. had in the war, how they fought bravely for a colonial power, and now how disloyal they have been to their own government. It's only those blasted youth wingers, raw recruits. It's essential the government have the army behind him. It's going to be like the South American republics. Whoever controls the army controls the country. Unemployment — now that will be a headache.

They're not reliable, honest. They are lazy; they steal; they drink pombe (a local alcoholic beverage).

My night watchman the other night drunk himself to sleep on the job, and several of the cows wandered off. I phoned the police who after a few hours rounded them up. I fired the bloke, who objected vehemently to his sacking. He thought that since the cows had been found he should not be fired.

"But everything seems to be operating smoothly today," I remarked. "O yes, because they think the *mzungi* (foreigners, the British) are in power again."

I found this conversation exciting. Father Vester was getting fidgety. He still wanted to be in Iganga by nightfall. But Father Slot suggested we stop at a farm in Eldoret owned by a Polish couple who were friends of his: "Thirteen years ago they were selling charcoal for a living, like the natives still do," Father Slot said. "Now they own a prosperous dairy and chicken farm."

We arrived in Iganga late that night only to find that the *askaris* of the Uganda Rifles at the Jinja Army Barracks had also mutineed.

The next day I heard that Kenyatta had punished his mutineers according to military law, thus taking a harsher line than either Nyerere, who disbanded both battalions of his Tanganyika Rifles and replaced the aberrant *askaris* with members of his party's militant Youth Wing, or Obote who arrested twenty ringleaders and then loaded 500 more Uganda Rifles aboard buses, and had them dropped off in the back country, where they had to make their way to their home villages.

Zaire (The Belgian Congo) Trip, 21 April–12 May 1964

In the early morning of 21 April, in my white Volkswagen Beetle, my redheaded American girlfriend, Sis, who was in charge of the Busoga Eye clinic at Jinja, and I, began our trip to Zaire to see my Belgian friend, Égide, whom I hadn't seen since 1957 when I first met him in Spain.

We passed the long elephant grass country of heavily populated Busoga with its luxuriant vegetation, its banana, maize, groundnut, cotton, and coffee shambas, and its rectangular mud and wattle huts with their corrugated tin roofs. We passed through beautiful Mbale, nestled in the fertile wooded foothills of Mt. Elgon, up-to-date and modern, Uganda's third largest city. We passed the cement works of Tororo, and its asbestos sheet factory. We stopped at the hospital at Soroti to inquire about a Canadian nursing sister, Blanche Snyder, who I thought was working there. After much effort, the two African filing clerks told us she had left on a dispensary safari. I wasn't so sure. We drove north-east to Moroto. As we neared Karamoja, the landscape began to change from lush green to bleached beige, from soft moist valleys to vast, dry open plains. We counted twenty-five giraffe browsing around the acacia bushes, commanding the plains with their disdainful air.

I had heard that the Karamajong tribesmen went about naked. But I really didn't believe my informers. I do now. At first, Sis and I started to count the number of naked men we saw, but we soon gave up because every man was naked. And after the first day, the naked novelty wore off. The men's elaborate hair styles became our centre of interest.

Night descends abruptly about 7:30 p.m., and there is no twilight in tropical Africa. It was dark when we reached Moroto, the administrative headquarters of Karamoja. We had no idea where we were going to stay. There were no hotels. The rest house was all booked up. But there was a couple from Mweri who recognized me and suggested the Moroto Club. They directed us there but no one could give us any information. The couple suggested we sleep in their room at the rest house. But I had a feeling Blanche Snyder was stationed in Moroto rather than in Soroti, and so we went to the hospital. One of the African nurses recognised the name. Miss Snyder was at home. We found Blanche after much difficulty and she kindly took us in.

Next morning we rose early to explore this district where civilization had not yet made any impact. The Karamojong are a proud, independent people averse to interference and content enough to be left alone to follow their traditional way of life and age old tribal customs. There was no electricity. Even the bicycle had not made any great inroads. But we did talk to an African dog-catcher swinging a rope noose, hunting for diseased dogs.

As we watched Moroto's early morning life between the two rows of *dukas* that comprise its shopping centre, I was impressed by its leisurely pace. There was none of the brisk vitality that characterizes a western town's morning trade. A drowsy sluggishness prevailed as natives slowly congregated to the shops. An Asian shopkeeper, who sold us the tobacco we were going to give the natives who would pose for pictures, told us that, if the Europeans left Moroto, he would have to close his shop.

I enjoyed watching the Karamajong: long lean herdsmen carrying their stools, head rests, and walking sticks. At one time, these warriors carried spears. But carrying spears was now forbidden by law. The Uganda Rifles conducted an all out search for spears, and Sis and I were able to buy them at the administrative office where they were collected and stored. Cattle-raiding, poaching, and spearing had to be prevented in the name of progress. But a man is scarcely a man if he doesn't raid, so one still reads of Karamajong raiding. How else can a man prove his manhood? And young men need cattle to get married, many cattle in a country where one can have as many as five or six wives.

The bride price in Karamoja was high, between sixty and one hundred head of cattle depending on the quality of the girl. One cow was usually worth thirty dollars so a Karamajong could pay $1800 to $3000 for a wife. The price was much higher here than any other district in Uganda. But then again, you could see what you were buying here. The girls wear a short goat skin skirt fastened round their hips, and a small leather apron decorated with cowrie shells. Their ears, necks, and wrists are heavily ornamented with iron coils, spiral brass ropes of beads, and chains that serve as adornments and status symbols.

Although most of the women were topless, a few sported brassieres as an outer garment. Believing that this western style undergarment would become fashionable, I wrote to my broker in Canada to buy me more shares of Maiden Form bras. The novelty soon wore off, and African sales had no influence on the stock.

We didn't see the single file processions of pedestrians, nor the hundreds of cyclists fringing the dusty road, that were a common sight in other provinces such as in Busoga or Buganda. Nor did we see as many babies. We did see the occasional warrior loping down the road, his body draped in a long black cloth, toga fashion. I found the men's coiffures always interesting. The Karamajong male is not concerned with clothes, but he does pay attention to his hairdo. Hair was woven with a mixture of clay or dung into a frontal, felt-like mat, into which wire coils were inserted as receptacles for ostrich plumes. Sometimes the chignon of felt reached remarkable proportions hanging out at the back of the head or rising up like a dunce's cap according to the wearer's taste. Sometimes this chignon was encased in a woven bag with a wire probe stuck into it to arrange the coiffure when necessary. With their decorative hair styles, their pierced ear lobes hanging in fleshy loops or sporting ear ornaments, and their neck and wrists encircled with wire, the men were always wonderful to look at.

The women's hair style was also interesting whether the clumps of hair had been allowed to grow until they could be twisted into black strings that form a mop-like cap over the top of the head or whether the sides of the head were shaved and the twisted black ropes of hair confined to a central ridge. Lip plugs were popular with both men and women. We asked a medical assistant dressed in western clothes, to whom we gave a ride, why he didn't wear a lip plug and the elaborate coiffure of his countrymen. He replied that he was a Christian and didn't play with his body.

The Karamajong are semi-nomadic, pastoral people. As hunters and nomads their movements were largely governed by the rains. During the dry season they took the cattle from one diminishing waterhole to another. The cattle were always tended by the men. Boys graduated to this duty by minding sheep and goats first. We saw little herdboys as young as four years old. Four or forty years of age, they were always naked except for the leather sandals which protected their feet from the small, stunted, white thorn bushes with their prickly white spines. We noticed many skin ulcers on legs. We noticed some cultivation, mostly by the women, but I did see a few naked men ploughing with metal ploughs and oxen.

I enjoyed the bargaining process we had to go through for picture taking. The farther we got away from Moroto the fewer *donari* we paid out. In fact, it was fun to see what the natives chose from our assortment of trade items. Tobacco was always popular, although some insisted it be packed in our empty Kodak boxes. Our candies, *tom-toms* as the children called them, always produced beams. A few bananas secured one beautifully muscled warrior, a veritable Atlas he was, perfectly proportioned. As I photographed him, he posed dramatically, peeling and deliberately munching his banana. He had that natural African flair for acting. Since the staple diet of these people was milk mixed with blood, the banana must have been a special treat.

Before drawing blood from a cow, these hunter-herdsmen first tied a ligature round the animal's neck to make the jugular vein swell up conspicuously. The operator then shot an arrow into the vein. When it was withdrawn, blood flowed freely from the wound and was collected in a calabash. The ligature was then loosened, and the puncture in the vein was stopped with a plug of cow-dung. The blood was later mixed with an equal quantity of milk.

Bargaining for the stools that the men carried about with them was fun. These three legged stools, six inches high and six inches in diameter, were carved from a single log. With their simple proportions, curved lines of the tripod, and the hollowed-out seat, they were fitted with a leather thong to slip over the finger, and were used as portable chairs. The men also carried their head rests, which were used as a cheek rest when they lay down, so that their elaborate coiffures were not deranged in sleep. With a bit of Swahili, gestures, smiles and shillings we were able to communicate.

Getting close to the Karamajong was not always so pleasant, however. We saw the effects of horrible hydroceles, hernia, eye diseases and deformities, which shocked us. The stench, even with young children out of doors, was nauseating. The dirt, grime and grease were appalling. And yet when it rained you should have seen them all scamper to shelter. A Karamajong just doesn't like getting wet.

We hated to leave this curiously fascinating region where the European was still cause for children to scream and to hug their mothers tightly.

We drove through the farmlands of Teso where grains, groundnuts, and cotton grew. Here, I saw, for the first time, a custom I had not seen before in Uganda: strapped to mothers' backs were babies wearing enormous half-gourds doubling as sun helmets. Later in West Nile, I would see woven weed sun shields.

Outside of Lira, sixty-five miles from our destination of Gulu, we encountered a tropical rain storm. The rain shot down like bullets, striking the car with vicious ferocity. We had to stop. Sis wanted to return to Lira for the night, but the storm began to abate, and I suggested we continue. A station wagon pulled up and informed us that the road was terrible but passable. We were cautioned to drive slowly.

Since coming to Africa I had acquired a passion for
game parks. In a letter to my mother I explained why I
loved them:

> It's thrilling to be driving through the vast open plains
> — the savannah land dotted with the euphorbia and
> thorn trees, a few clumps of low bushes here and there
> — and come across a herd of elephants grazing. In spite
> of their size these giants are graceful. I love their quiet
> dignity. They never seem to be flustered like the silly
> little wart hogs who scamper away with their tails rig-
> idly raised like aerials, or the buck who lope quickly
> away. But the buffalo which are very dangerous just
> stand and stare at you. Of course we stay at a respect-
> able distance because these animals are wild (I've been
> constantly warned) and many a foolhardy tourist has
> been gored and killed. And me who loves to get out of
> the car (we're warned not to) but I never venture far.
> The silence and serenity of the game parks never fail to
> impress me. I feel so very near God when I'm there, as
> we drive along and suddenly spot an impala, or a pack
> of buffalo. That's what's so thrilling. You're always ex-
> pecting to see something around the next bend. But
> that's the thrill of it. You never know what you're going
> to see.

Murchison Falls National Park was an absolute delight.
But it was different from the other game parks I had
visited. There was a wilder grandeur, a more rugged
splendour in its rocky, wooded hills. The waters of the
mighty Victoria Nile squeeze through a deep funnel-like
cleft in the escarpment, less than twenty feet across, and
plunge down 141 feet. Although the falls here could not
compare to Victoria Falls, they were still awesome. Since
the roads in the park were so abominable, we took the
launch trip up the Nile from Paraa to the foot of Murchison Falls. The cruise was fantastic. We saw elephant,

hippo, buffalo, waterbuck, giraffe and the Nile crocodile.

I enjoyed watching the park's multitude of hippos
with their small turreted eyes and mouse-like ears. They
remained submerged in the shallows all day. Occasionally they showed their ugly, massive, jowly faces above
the surface of the water. Or, suddenly, they would dart
into the water as we approached, the occasional one
daring to linger just a little longer to show his courage,
so that we would never know that a hippo was there,
until gradually, one of the more curious would poke his
head up to see what was going on. Now and then, a
brave one would emerge from the water, give a gigantic
yawn, displaying his vast fleshy-pink mouth to inform us
he had had enough of our presence.

The river was the last remaining stronghold in
Uganda of the enormous Nile crocodile that grows to
twenty feet or more in length. We saw scores of them
lying on the sandy banks sleeping with their mouths
open, but as soon as they felt we were too close, they
would slither into the river. I was disappointed that I
didn't see any with birds in their mouths. Since the croc
has no tongue, the birds eat the flies that pester them.

The sight of elephants always thrilled me. We were
lucky; we saw herd after herd. I never tired of watching
the bodies of these great, grey giants heave and pitch.
Whether they were eating or strolling, their movements
were so dignified. I have been told that though their gait
appears easy and leisurely, the distance they travel in a
short time is surprising.

We wanted to spend more time in Murchison, but
we had to be in Pakwatch, a small town on the banks of
the Albert Nile by dark, and we didn't know whether the
town was on our side of the Nile or not.

It was on the other side. When we reached the ferry site it was getting dark. I'll never forget the two elephants silhouetted against the dusk, at the water's edge. But Sis was worried. There was no ferry and no one in sight. I suggested we sleep in the car. We drove up to a line of shacks, where we could see some Africans, but they were drunk and sullen looking. I was a bit apprehensive now, too. Suddenly we sighted the ferry crossing and the river. We quickly left. I honestly think it had made a special trip to get us. The attendant was kind and concerned, wanting to know where we were going to stay the night. "At a mission station," I bravely replied. I had heard of a Verona Father mission station in Pakwatch. He told us how to get there.

It can get pitch black in Africa — so black that it has a physical presence you can feel and touch. We crept along in our car, afraid of missing the station. To our surprise, we passed an outdoor theatre where Africans were standing, watching a film on a small screen. I noticed a sign: "transient labour camp." We decided we had better move on fast. We finally found the mission station. A young, bearded priest in a white cassock greeted us in a very nervous fashion. He explained that they were all priests and could not give lodging to two women. But he suggested a convent which was only twenty miles away at Angel. We tried to follow his directions, but after about twenty-five miles we knew we had missed the turn. A lorry driver, who noticed that we were lost because we had passed him three times, showed us the right turn. The nuns cleared out their reception room and we set up our camp cots. As if the anxiety of finding a place wasn't enough that night, Sis couldn't remember where she had placed the car key. She searched everywhere — no key. We finally went to bed, waking up next morning to the refrain of *dominus vobiscum* coming from the small chapel next door. Sis finally found the key in a pail. And we were off for the Congo border.

The Congo Crossing, 25 April 1964

We arrived at the Congo border. Two women with no visas and no car registration papers! A car packed with things we shouldn't have! No wonder I was frightened to get out of the car. My fear gathered momentum as tales of Congo border crossings which I had heard — how the officials stripped and raped women, even nuns, how they extracted money and valuables — rushed to my mind. I dismissed my fears. The unknown would prove exciting. I got out of the car and walked resolutely into the border office!

There were four young African officials in an assorted array of uniforms seated at desks in a small cluttered room. One, who appeared to be the chief officer, wanted to know why I had taken so long to enter the office. He spoke to me in French. Did I think he was coming to me?

I immediately saw that the situation was going to require astute handling.

"Your visas," he demanded.

I handed him our passports. Sis's American one under mine. I kept stressing the fact that I was Canadian, hoping the information would distract him from the American passport.

"No visas?" he noted.

"We didn't have time. We had heard it took six months. If we waited that long we would not be able to visit my friend Égide whom I haven't seen in eight years.

He is coming from Bunia and will be meeting us at the mission station at Mahagi," I explained.

I was relying on their exposure to traditional Gallic chivalry to appreciate my situation, but the response was only cold silence and inscrutable faces.

Then I heard the young chief asking the officer inspecting my passport, for the year of my birth. I could feel the palms of my hands and my back beginning to perspire. Now they would know that I wasn't as young as I appeared to be. I was both terrified and flattered. I doubted whether he would want a woman close to twice his age.

"Well, it would serve me right," I thought.

A look of incredulity crossed the chief's face when he heard the answer. For the first time in my life I was grateful for being too old! They said nothing more about the visas!

"Your car registration forms."

I remembered the Africans' respect for any official looking stamp. I handed over the forms the Uganda border officials had given me for the car. I tried to appear casual and pleasant. I humoured them, apologized for my faulty French, praised them for their impeccable French, and congratulated them on their efficiency — all this while the officer was inspecting my "registration form," turning it over and over again.

Finally he began writing out a form in long hand. (They were out of printed forms.) I knew then that the official looking stamp had worked its magic!

"Is it dangerous for two women to be travelling in the Congo?," I asked coyly.

"Certainly not, everything is quiet. [In actual fact rebels were raiding villages.] It's only the Europeans who cause the trouble anyway," was his caustic retort.

"Have you any gifts?"

"No," I replied, "just a few supplies."

In actual fact, we had cheeses, tins of tuna and salmon, tubes of mustard, bottles of catsup which Égide had written were unobtainable in the Congo.

The chief kept turning the pages of his ledger. Then he finally asked me, "Do you have any malarial prophylactics."

I hastily gave him all we had, grateful for such a harmless request.

The authorized crossing charge, however, would be four hundred francs. Four hundred francs sounded like an awful lot. My heavy perspiration returned. We didn't have any Congolese money, only East African. The officer, however, was only too happy to exchange francs for shillings. Four hundred francs would cost eight East African shillings. I just couldn't believe it. His honesty touched me! I was suddenly ashamed of my own subterfuge.

"We must keep your passports here," he told me.

I protested but to no avail.

"What is the best way to get to Mahagi," I asked. Égide was to meet us at the Mahagi Mission station.

"There is only one road from the border to Mahagi," he informed me. "I will show you if you give me a lift there."

I was only too pleased and asked him to sit in the front seat while I quickly climbed into the back of the car and perched myself on top of provisions and forbidden gifts. My head was dizzy from a tense crossing that had taken over an hour.

But we were in the Congo at last.

Zaire

We waited for the border official while he went shopping in Mahagi; then we took him back to the border. I asked him how he liked the conditions of the country.

"Independence is fine, but it's the people at the head of the government, those directing government affairs who are no good," he told me.

Once again, at the border, we gave a lift to another official who would show us the way to the mission station. He had us stop at a memorial nearby. Since it seemed that the memorial was important to him, I asked if I could photograph it. He was extremely pleased with my request and asked us to wait a few moments. Before I realized what was happening, an official arrived with a key. Crowds of young people began congregating around us. The glass door of the memorial was opened. An information board was removed. Then to my amazement there stood a full length portrait of Patrice Lumumba in green suit and goatee. I knew that Lumumba had become the Belgian Congo's first Prime Minister when, in June, 1960, the country gained its independence from Belgium and was called Zaire. Lumumba was assassinated a year later but his supporters established a rival government. Fighting broke out between the opposing groups. For the next five years the new nation was rocked by civil war. United Nations troops were brought in to restore order. (The country is now called "Congo.") Two files of youths solemnly arranged themselves around the monument. As I photographed, I worried about the size of the growing crowd. One young man, modishly dressed, gave me his card because he wanted a copy of the picture. I noticed he was secretary of "La Jeunesse." The reverence and zeal with which he talked about Lumumba, their Messiah and Redeemer, was beginning to frighten me.

I apologized for the inconvenience I had caused. "I did not know taking a picture of the memorial would necessitate getting keys."

"Oh no," we are glad. "It has given us an opportunity to see Lumumba ourselves," they replied.

When I recounted these events to Égide later, he was horrified. During the Lumumba regime, Égide was condemned to death by a military tribunal, lost a huge coffee plantation, lorries and his car. He had paid his way out, and now at the age of thirty, he owned a small coffee plantation and supplemented his income by teaching high school. He explained to us that the Mahagi area was a Lumumbist stronghold and that "La Jeunesse" was responsible for all the violence and rioting. There was even an eight o'clock curfew in Mahagi. I kept seeing soldiers armed with rifles in the mission stations.

Once inside the Mahagi mission station, I felt relieved. The priests were kind; the African Sisters, delightful, as they ran in all directions to make us comfortable. The red brick mission church was large and formidable. It even had tall stained-glass windows. Seated on the kneelers that served for benches, several African mothers were breastfeeding. I heard a baby crying from the confessional.

I could hear the choral responses, so typical of rote learning here, coming from the Mission School's classrooms. Suddenly, I heard drums, and several hundred boys, marching as in a military tattoo, came to a halt. They saluted the flag as it was lowered, and sang "Le Congo, mon pays" to a martial beat. It was noon and time for lunch.

The bishop, a very charming African, insisted we lunch with him. No sooner had we finished than Égide arrived. Égide didn't like the idea of the immigration officer keeping our passports. We drove back to the border. But the immigration officer was neither in his office nor at home. I noticed that the eyes of one of the other officials were glazed and that his speech was slushy. We gave up and decided to leave.

It was about 160 miles from Mahagi to Irumu, Égide's home. Sis drove ahead in my car with Adolph, a Spaniard in exile, because he had protested against the Franco government (his mother had been imprisoned for three years and was ultimately poisoned). He was teaching Latin and Greek for UNESCO at the same high school as Égide. Égide and I drove behind in the big van. The roads were terrible and dusty. At Logo, where we stopped, several soldiers were on guard. It wasn't until I talked with several of the young Belgian teachers that I realized the seriousness of the riots. The priest cautioned us to leave immediately.

We stopped at another mission station to pick up two European children who were boarding there. The buildings of solid red brick were attractively arranged. A little statue of the Guardian Angel, guiding a little child, was in the fountain in the centre of the courtyard.

At Fataki, we stopped at a beautiful hotel that was now closed, to pick up Égide's houseboy. The houseboy was so drunk that Égide refused to take him.

The hotel, once a popular rendezvous, with an attractive dining room and bar, was deserted. The owner told me she had to close down because the Africans slept eight or nine to a room and urinated in bed. Business was poor. I felt a pang of regret for the passing of the old order, its elegance, and its gracious living.

About fifteen miles from Irumu, Égide's home, the van broke down. It was about eight p.m. We decided that Sis and I, and the two European children should go ahead in my car. The two children, eight and five, were adorable, but so old for their years. They explained that the Africans were *gentils* when sober but when they drank, they became *foux*. As we approached Irumu, the children became excited, even though a weekend home meant just a few hours, because they would have to leave the next day for school again.

At last we arrived at Égide's rambling cottage. That evening, Égide hosted a dinner party with antelope, carrots, brussel sprouts, green beans, strawberries, banana cake and wine. It was fun seeing Égide again after so many years and listening to the political pronouncement of one African: "The living standards of our people must improve within the shortest time possible. Public haranguing about communism or capitalism will not help our cause at all, but instead will make it harder." I remembered the old Kikuyu proverb, "When two elephants fight, it is the grass that suffers."

Égide and I spent the evening reminiscing affectionately about our travels in Spain during the summer of 1957. We laughed heartily when we recalled the incident when I drew an invisible line down the centre of the bed we were forced to share. Égide confessed that if he were in the same situation again, he would not be such a gentleman. I was flattered.

The next morning, we left early for Mt. Hoyo, twenty-seven miles away from Irumu, to see the BaMbuti pygmies of the Ituri forest that lies in the northeast-corner of the Congo. The steep road was appalling, covered with loose stones and boulders, and deeply scored with gullies made by the heavy rains that poured down the mountain side.

We stopped at a mountain resort, dramatically situated, overlooking the Ituri forest, where the BaMbuti pygmies have lived for perhaps 6,000 to 7,000 years. Before us spread the dense jungle, as I had pictured the real Africa to be. My mind wandered to Joseph Conrad's *Heart of Darkness* and the ivory agent, Kurtz, lonely and mad, living deep in this dark rain forest.

The resort, owned by a Belgian, Mr. Borckmanns, had once entertained royalty. Now his guests were UNESCO workers, Belgian teachers and a few tourists like Sis and me who dared to visit. Mr. Borckmanns was charming, personable with the ladies, and knowledgeable about the country, especially pygmy lore. He had known the famous American anthropologist, Patrick Putnam, who had established a dispensary and a leper colony in a village that became known as Camp Putnam in the Ituri forest, and the English social anthropologist, Colin Turnbull, who had spent several years living with the pygmies and who had written about them.

I had expected Mr. Borckmanns to be bitter about his change of fortune, but he wasn't. He accepted it with philosophical resignation: "It's a natural change in the evolutionary process. True, I can't run my establishment in the four star Michelin category. And I have to supplement my income by taking a teaching position in Irumu. (He was Égide's principal.) But I'm going to continue."

Mr. Borckmanns was one of a few white men who had heard the *molimo* ceremony. It is a haunting memorial honouring the dead, which according to one critic "is one of the most beautiful rituals ever developed by a people." The ceremony is both a band's farewell to a beloved elder and a song of praise to the life-giving forest for its benevolence and abundance.

Mr. Borckmanns arranged for our meeting with the pygmies which took place in a small clearing hacked out of the wilderness. The pot-bellied pygmies with their crooked legs and closely cropped heads were cheerful and carefree. Mr. Borckmanns joked with them, and there was much chattering, laughing, giggling and horseplay. The adults were totally unselfconscious in their little fibre belts. The children and babies were naked.

They performed one dance after another, shuffling and swaying in circle formation for several hours to the accompaniment of drumming, chanting and handclapping. Most of the dances imitated the hunting of animals.

During The Elephant Dance, the dancers enacted the stalking, the spearing and the slaughtering of an elephant. Single handed, armed only with a short handled spear, the pygmies get under the elephant for the kill. In the Monkey Dance, before I knew it, one pygmy was up my leg, and another had Sis's shoe. Like most Africans, the pygmies have a natural flair for pantomime and acting. Their exquisite sense of balance and the energy and agility of their extravagant leaps amazed me.

Mr. Borckmanns delighted in conducting us to the caves nearby, which were used in *King Solomon's Mines,* and to the famous waterfalls seen in most Tarzan movies.

The next afternoon we drove to Mambasa, fifty-nine miles away, to buy ivory and masks. We passed pygmy villages and the black impenetrable Ituri forest. The road was atrocious. Unfortunately, we killed five chickens and one goat during the trip.

On 29 April, we were on our way back to Uganda. At Logo where we stopped to have a snack of pineapple rings and bananas, we met several Belgian teachers who were on their way to the education office at Bunia to register a complaint. They were going to refuse to teach if the government could not maintain law and order. Two of their staff had been wounded during a raid of a nearby village. The students who wanted their teachers to stay also sent a delegation to protest.

I recalled the words of the White Father, "they are young; they can't and won't take it."

We arrived in Mahagi too late to cross the border which closed at 4:30 p.m. Consequently, we stayed at the mission house with the African sisters who were delighted to have us back. They couldn't do enough for us, running here and there to provide us with pails of warm water, basins, towels, and new bars of soap. After supper we found two glasses of water by our bedsides.

When I took their pictures, I had to wait until they put on their new, black, sturdy shoes which squeaked as they walked. One wanted a special picture taken with her friend who had tribal scars on her face. I chuckled when another threw a lovely clean dress to a little girl who was playing in the courtyard. The little girl just put it over her soiled one.

We had dinner with the African bishop. I enjoyed the French cuisine. One of the White Fathers brought out a special honey cake sent to him from Brussels and a box of cigars. I found it all so touching. The bishop gave me a beautiful picture of himself in his episcopal robes.

We crossed the border the next morning at a cost of a bottle of beer and a Fanta. Our passports, which I had thought we would never see again were returned. Sis and I had bought three magnificently-carved ivory tusks as well as many ivory figurines which we had hid under the car's hood.

We didn't breathe easily until we were safely across the border into Uganda.

Uganda

We headed for Arua in the West Nile to stay with Dr. Williams, who was in charge of the hospital there. It was still operated as a bush hospital where the patients were responsible for their own meals which relatives usually come and cook for them. "This reduces costs," Dr. Williams explained. We met a young missionary who had been recently deported from the Sudan, doing translation work at the mission hospital.

When I mentioned that I wanted to see the rare white rhino, the doctor kindly arranged to provide us with Joshua, his able foreman as a guide. We drove to the banks of the Albert Nile where the white rhino, rarest of Uganda's large mammals, was protected, since rhinoceros horn was much sought after by traders for export to Asia, where it was in much demand as an aphrodisiac.

At the game warden's camp we were provided with two *askaris* carrying rifles just in case we met a wounded buffalo, a very dangerous animal. Many a ranger had been killed by buffaloes. We tramped through the open plains looking for our rhino. I had a terrible cold and felt like quitting many times, but I persevered. After several hours and five miles, our *askaris* decided to quit. Luckily, Joshua was not ready to quit. On our way back, he touched my shoulder. He had spotted a white rhino. We got out of the car and followed him. There he was, standing still, ugly, with a massive head and a single huge tusk. Quietly and stealthily, we followed him until we were directly in front him. Joshua threw some rhino dung at him to cover the human smell. "Rhinos are very short-sighted," he whispered and encouraged me to get closer to him so that I could take a better picture. It was 6:30 p.m. and getting dark. I was too afraid. I was content photographing him from a little distance away. And he wasn't white as I had expected. He was grey like the other species I had seen. Joshua explained that the white rhino has a broad mouth and a square jaw more like that of a hippo. I looked again. Joshua was right.

The West Nile Region was sparsely populated so there wasn't the trachoma that one found in Busoga. Like Karamoja, the countryside is savannah. The people here ate manioc rather than *matooke*. The West Nile was Uganda's main tobacco growing area and I noticed that the East African Tobacco Co. had many tobacco plantations. I also noticed a number of young girls who were completely naked except for a clump of leaves fore and aft. They demanded five to ten shillings for their picture.

Arua was a clean, attractive little town. We visited the Roman Catholic cathedral which was a very imposing building. I was amazed at its furnishings: a marble altar, gold candlestick holders, beautiful statues, and paintings. To find such wealth in this remote part of Africa was incredible. We recrossed the Nile at Pakwatch. Two magnificent elephants were crossing the road to go to the river. I got out of the car and walked as close as I dared to take their pictures.

It was just one thrill after another on this homeward journey: more elephants so close that my hands on the steering wheel were wet, and Sis could touch them; beautiful Karume Falls; wide stretches of plain with scattered acacia and candelabra euphorbia with their green fluted columns; sausage trees with their large pendant fruit; demure caramel-coloured Uganda kob leaping in the air; wart hogs hurriedly trying to cross the road, with tails erect like antennae; and wild buffalo, black and menacing, grazing in the open euphorbia grasslands.

That night I retired early in the hotel at Masindi. It was in the process of changing hands that very evening. One of the porters was asleep in a chair. The receptionist woke him up and commented, "you'd think he was a paying guest." The next morning, shining new cutlery with the monogram of "Uganda Hotels" appeared on the tables. The manager complained about the inefficiency of the waiters, and remarked, "I really don't know whether they are waiters."

Sis had to go back to work. The first part of my circuit of Uganda was completed. I drove back to Iganga, and from 1-4 May, tried to get rid of my cold.

Uganda Trip 14 May weekend

On the long weekend of 14 May I set off on the three-hundred-mile drive from Iganga to the Queen Elizabeth National Park with three young people, Ruth, a volunteer worker from England, Gary, her Canadian boyfriend hitchhiking around the world, and Emmanuel, one of my students whose father had four wives and twenty-eight children.

We drove to Kampala in a tropical downpour and climbed up a twisty, *murram* road to Fort Portal. We stopped at Fort Portal, a charming colonial-looking outpost in the foothills of the Ruwenzori. When I saw the little thatched roof, mud-walled Roman Catholic church here with open gaps for windows and concrete slabs for pews at the mission hospital, I remembered the luxurious church I had seen in Arua. We then stopped at Butititi, where I had been originally assigned to a teacher training college operated by an order of American Brothers. It boasted a swimming pool and a beautiful chapel. We stayed at the Convent of the Ladies of Mary where I slept on Sister Francesca's bed, the second time I had slept in a nun's bed. The next morning, Ascension Thursday, I attended mass in the chapel.

We drove along scenic mountain roads among the fabled Mountains of the Moon to the copper mines of Kilembe. The peaks, unfortunately, were clouded in mist.

A letter from Don Treilhard, the Canadian smelter manager in Jinja, introduced us, and we were taken underground to the copper mine, which employed 4000 people, about 125 Europeans, one hundred Asians and the rest Africans.

From the beautifully terraced slopes, where the Mgambe tend their little farms in the Ruwenzori, we drove to the open parklands of the Queen Elizabeth Park. We took the launch trip along the Kazinga Channel which joins Lake Edward and Lake George. From the relative safety of our boat, we watched hundreds of hippo at close range as well as crocodiles idling on sandbars. The bird life was fabulous. The many fish in the channel attract waterbirds: pelicans, saddlebill, storks, cormorants, kingfishers and fish eagles. But, as usual, I found the elephants most interesting. I can watch them for hours, extending their huge ears like fans, tossing their heads, swinging their trunks, and now and then, plucking tufts of grass and flinging them into the air. We saw one with only one tusk.

The next day we witnessed a hippo shoot. The park has such a high concentration of hippos that Uganda's Makerere University, in conjunction with Cambridge University, was conducting research on them. Hunters shot about thirteen and slaughtered them. The stench was unbearable as the natives with pangas cut the bodies open. The Africans bought the meat. Chris, a Cambridge student conducting doctoral research on the feeding of the three largest grass eating animals — the hippo, wart hog, and topi — weighed and would study their organs, the adrenalin glands, the thyroid, and the stomachs, whose contents can weigh 400 pounds, the result of two nights' feeding. (An adult hippo can weigh three tons and a new born baby over one hundred pounds. Hippo steak isn't so bad if you can get it young enough.)

We drove to the extreme southwestern corner of the park to Ishasha to view the famous tree-climbing lions, a characteristic not commonly found in other lion populations. It was fun watching the lions, two beautiful females, with tawny, silky coats of fur, and splendid tails ending in black tufts. Both were just draped in the upper branches of an old fig tree. They uttered a few yawns. But it was their cubs that held our interest. Since our ranger spoke no English, I couldn't figure out whether the cubs were four days, four weeks, or four months old. They were delightful, snuggling up to each other, peeking out at us from in between the branches, and following us from branch to branch as we moved about in the car. For the first time, too, I saw huge herds of topi which, from a distance, appeared as dark specks. There must have been 1,000 grazing. It was incredible. At Ishasha, I could imagine what the Sudd must have been like before a channel was hacked through it. The lake was completely covered with Nile cabbage, and the

EMBRACING SERAFINA

channel was blocked on one side by a papyrus swamp, eight to fifteen foot plants topped with feathery green pompoms. It was a menace, however, because its jungle of stalks rose from an untidy, tangled, floating mass of roots and rotting vegetation.

For the first time in my life, I slept in a tent. I was afraid of the lions or elephants that might be too curious, but I enjoyed the night sounds of the animals.

From Ishasha we drove through green and folded hills and valleys, and magnificent mountain scenery. We got lost four times. We finally arrived in Kabale, the district headquarters of Kigezi, famed for its scenery. In fact, as we drove through the hills I noticed the prosperity of the farmers. The steep, striped hillsides demonstrated modern methods of resting land and combating erosion. Eucalyptus trees grew tall and shady along the road, with numerous barrel-shaped beehives hanging on them. From Kabale we drove to the kingdom of Ankole where the tall slim Bahima, dressed in robes of striped woven cloth, tend their herds of long-horned Ankola cattle.

At Mbarara, I stayed with the Rosses, Canadians who were on the same scheme as I, who took me to see the refugees from Rwanda-Burundi, about 10,000 of them. The Rosses told me that there is considerable controversy regarding them: they refuse to work even to maintain the roads. There is bribery and corruption; and the free food from America is mishandled. From Mbarara I drove through Masaka, Kampala and back to Iganga.

I remained at Iganga Teachers' College until September, 1964, the end of the term. My dad had died while I was there and my mother's health was not the best. I decided to return to Canada. I took the slow route home stopping at Nairobi, Addis Ababa, Khartoum, Lagos, Abidjan, Dakar, Paris and then home.

Uganda had achieved independence the year before I arrived there. Milton Obote was prime minister. Idi Amin was then a Captain in the Uganda Rifles. It was rumoured that he had only a primary school education, and that he rose through the ranks because of his gracious and amenable personality, but that he bore a grudge against the British because he had not been sent to Sandhurst Military College in England. I knew him as Don Treilhard's teammate on the Nile rugger team, and I socialized with him in the Treilhard home in Jinja. In fact, I even danced with him. In 1971, Amin overthrew Obote in a military coup and seized control of Uganda. In his "Africanization" program, Amin gave the entire Asian population ninety days to leave the country. Many of the Asians were descended from the Indian labourers, whom the British had imported over a century before to work in the building of the railway across Kenya to Uganda. Nearly two decades of slaughter, famine, corruption and chaos followed. Now, under the leadership of Yoweri Museveni, Uganda is slowly recovering from its nightmare.

My year had been truly a fascinating study. My firsthand experiences cast a whole new light on African cultures. I learned that culture is a way of life learned from one's social group. It is a way of coping with human needs. I read somewhere that a hungry cannibal lustily devouring a piece of leg of man is as cultured as Emily Post as she daintily nibbles on a piece of leg of lamb.

Full of fond memories, I reluctantly returned to Canada, firmly convinced that Canadian aid, whether in the form of teachers or fishing experts, hard rock miners

or surveyors was appreciated because the Africans themselves, told me so. I came home to a city anxious to hear
about my year in Africa. Wherever I was invited to
speak, I showed my movies to raise money for St. Francis
Leprosorium in Baluba, not far from where I taught in
Iganga. I distributed biographies of orphan children
from St. Philomena's Orphanage next door to my mission station which was operated by the Franciscan
Missionary Sisters of Africa in the hope that the children
would be adopted by my Canadian listeners.

Back at Lakehead Teachers' College, I was counselled by my superiors in the Ministry of Education to
start working on a post-graduate degree because Ontario's Teachers' Colleges would soon be amalgamating
into the universities. My travels for the next ten years
would be for research purposes.

CHINA, 1978

As soon as I received my Ph.D. degree I decided to visit China. In 1978 after thirty-two years of isolation, China finally opened its doors. We were the first non-speciality tourist group which a travel agency was allowed to bring into the country. This was a year before Coca-Cola arrived, and eleven years before the world watched in horror as Chinese tanks crushed the pro-democracy movement in Tiananmen Square.

On 23 May 1978 we had to cross the border between the New Territories (Hong Kong) and China at Lowu on foot. Today, one can fly direct from Canada to Beijing. Only a huge billboard notified us that we were entering a country whose life was based on Marxist-Leninist philosophy.

Our entry was so different from what I had expected — so quiet, even serene, such a contrast to the noise and frantic commercialism of Hong Kong. Official formalities were quick as Red Army men wearing red stars on their hats and rumpled green uniforms inspected our passports and customs forms. While we waited for our group of over one hundred to be processed, we were ushered into a huge room of upholstered sofas and chairs adorned with lace doilies. Huge murals depicted the union of the many nationalities in China.

When we were all processed, we boarded the train for Canton where we sat on comfortable seats and were served tea. The windows were wide and our seats swivelled so that we got good views of the countryside.

There were bare-legged peasants in broad straw hats digging and hoeing in the fields, an endless procession of carts, bicycles, old trucks and all sorts of beasts of burden hauling loads of cabbage, firewood, iron piping, old machinery, straw, pottery and sacking. The countryside was a mosaic of rich green fields, and we passed rice paddies and market gardens of beans, pumpkins and cucumbers. I saw very little machinery. We noticed a bleeding woman carried by jogging peasants who were rushing her to a first aid station.

In Canton, once beautiful buildings, with their sculptured balconies were crumbling. Mould covered their rundown exteriors. Sculptured figures were broken and names erased. Gigantic portraits of Mao and Lenin were posted everywhere.

China Before Coca-Cola

What can I say about my visit to The People's Republic of China? A country with the world's oldest living civilization and a recorded, written history that goes back nearly 4,000 years. A country that has survived feudal monarchs, imperialist warlords, colonial powers, foreign invasions, and civil wars in the timeless sweep of centuries. How well can a Western visitor really know this ancient land newly spawned by the Great Proletarian Revolution thirty-two years ago into an independent Communist state? A revolution which Chairman Mao Tse-tung, who, when seventy-two years of age, swam the great Yangtze River, undertook to modernize. In order to carry out this most ambitious and daring undertaking in history, Mao Tse-tung and his Red Guards purged China of anything that showed signs of being tainted with Western thought or privilege; condemned as Western decadence, anything viewed as personal, individual or self-centred, like playing the piano, keeping pets or even reading novels. He subjected to re-education the intelligentsia, anyone in an elite position, through humiliation, ingenious torture or exile into the countryside. And he eliminated between 32.25 and 61.7 million Chinese. Was this heavy cost worth it?

We saw only what official China wanted us to see — special showplaces with selected denizens giving carefully rehearsed speeches in the briefing sessions which invariably preceded our visit — no matter where we went — to communes, factories, hospitals, schools, museums. As we listened politely to the facts and figures on the progress that had been made in heavy machinery, shipbuilding, agriculture, and the chemical industry, which they delivered without notes and in a spirit of intense pride, we were given Panda cigarettes and cups of hot tea.

My notebook is filled with their statistics to show the improvements and achievements which they claim to have made in their living conditions — parks that had been extended one hundred times since liberation, lakes that had been dredged, temples and pagodas that had been restored, and production figures that had jumped four fold since those days when "paradise on earth was only for the rich." At the Chuhang People's Commune, for example, the leading member of the Revolutionary Committee recited a long list of figures to illustrate the great advances China had made since the revolution. Before the revolution, there had been only one primary school in the Kung Kiang Residential area in Shanghai, now there were nine primary, six kindergartens, six nurseries, and six middle schools.

And so, the achievements of Chinese communism were celebrated. House rent was only 3 to 5 per cent of the worker's wages, about $1.75 a month. Electricity cost fifty cents per month, water about forty cents. Men could retire at sixty, women at fifty; professors, male or female at fifty-five. The figures overwhelmed us.

Drastic and dramatic changes had taken place, but the Chinese still have a gargantuan task ahead of them. The government's goal was to achieve full modernization by the year 2000 in four areas: farming, industry, science-technology, and defence. The year 2000 appeared in bold figures on school chalkboards, posters in the streets, and on billboards in factory entrances. Workers and peasants were urged to labour harder and longer. Public loudspeakers in fields and factories exhorted the masses to surpass old production levels. Pace setters such as Danze and Tachia were household names. Advanced workers in factories were honoured with such awards of merit as badges, red flags on their work desks, and their names listed on charts. But how can they possibly achieve such an ambitious goal when their factories were thirty to forty years out-of-date, when their farms relied on human muscle rather than on machinery, when factories and farms evoked a sense of cottage-craft rather than modern industrial enterprises? One factory that we visited employed 350 people, mostly housewives, making flashbulbs — 1.4 million bulbs per month. I noticed a genuine effort to utilize the skills of women. When I mentioned this to our guide, she told me that Chairman Mao had said "since women make up half the human race, they must now be made equal so they can hold up their half of the sky." But the factory looked more like a backyard workshop with long sheets of paper hanging from the low ceilings displaying such didactic messages as: "It's an honour if you are honest." "It's a shame if you lie." "Pay attention to hygiene."

No wonder I kept wondering how they could possibly leap from such backwardness to advanced western production levels within twenty-two years?

Of course, I was impressed by the improvements already made by these hard working peoples. For above all else, China was a working society. Wherever I went, I saw the Chinese toiling in the fields, in the rice paddies, in the factories, in rain or shine, six days per week. Whereas Confucian philosophy had taught scholars to look down upon manual labour, Chairman Mao had made physical labour and hard work glorious. High School students must spend one afternoon or two or three hours per week doing some form of manual labour among ordinary people. With such a positive attitude towards work, it might be possible that they can catch up to the advanced technology of the west.

Our accommodations were disappointing both in comfort and cleanliness. Our rooms were shabby, grimy, and poorly lit with single forty-watt bulbs. Although the hardwood floors in our Shanghai hotel, The Shanghai Mansions, were highly waxed and polished, they were covered with scruffy carpets that were falling apart. Our bathroom floors and fixtures were dirty and unpolished. Used toothbrushes and hairbrushes were provided for our use! Bathtubs were stained yellow. Corridors were lined with brass spittoons. The Shanghai Mansions must have been a beautiful and stately specimen of British Victorian architecture, but it had now deteriorated, its wooden doors peeling and brick crumbling. In the pre-1949 days when Shanghai was called the Paris of the East, it was a graceful city of foreign concessions where expatriates lived in beautiful colonial mansions.

Our hotel in Beijing, the capital of China, was no better. It was part of an ugly, massive complex, grandiose, in the Soviet manner, built by the Russians about ten miles from Peking and recently reopened to meet the tourist trade. Many of our group reported bedbugs and cockroaches. So loudly did they protest that our tour company gave us a refund of thirty dollars. But when we heard that an American tour was politely asked to leave the country, after complaining too many times about poor hotel accommodation, the complaints from our group were not as loud.

My greatest shock was when I arrived for the Shanghai Opera performance of *The Women Generals* and was confronted with a sea of brown faces and muted blue unisex work suits transforming men and women into nearly identical units, tightly packed on hard bleachers. But my initial shock at the drab appearance of the audience soon vanished before the dazzling fairy-tale glitter of the stage. Although the music was discordant and cacophonous to my western ear, I soon became overwhelmed by the brilliant, vibrant colours, the richness of the fabrics, and the artistry of the performers. I could only gaze at the splendour and marvel of it all, as I silently mused at the contrast between the real world and the fantasy world on the stage.

Heavy-handed political propaganda was obvious everywhere. I did not see any letting up of the deification of Chairman Mao who had died two years before. In briefings and introductions, references to the Chairman were numerous. I saw his huge portrait everywhere. His quotations covered billboards. Chinese filed in large numbers to view his body in the mausoleum in Tiananmen Square in Beijing. And posters in English such as the following at the intersection in front of our hotel in Canton were not uncommon:

> Hold high the great banner of Chairman Mao. Adhere to the party basic line for the historical period of socialism. Grasp the key link of class struggle and bring about great order across the land. Persist in continuing the revolution under the dictatorship of the proletariat and strive to make China a great, powerful, and modern socialist country.

China's three most important historical sights — the Forbidden City, which covered an area of more than 250 acres and included 600 major palaces; the Great Wall, which stretched for more than 3,000 miles dating back to the fourth century B.C., the only man-made object, visible from the earth's orbit; and the Ming tombs, which lined both sides of the Avenue of Animals, once forbidden to all but an emperor's retinue — were a visual adventure and appealed to my intellectual curiosity. But remembering the Chinese whom I met brings back the fondest memories. I recall the zoo-keeper in Beijing who, when showing us the pandas in captivity, told us that the panda population was becoming extinct before Liberation, but since then, increasing by leaps and bounds.

I recall the courtesy and the attention of the English students and teachers at the University in Hangchow, while I sketched the development of literature in English Canada. I was nervous and perspiring heavily because the room was so crowded. In my excitement, I dropped the chalk and brush. A thousand hands were there to pick them up. Before I knew it, an electric fan was brought in to cool me. During the hour and a half lecture, my listeners took down copious notes. And when I finished I asked if there were any questions. A male student finally got up and said that he was puzzled as to the meanings of two words I had used — "robots" and "mores."

As a thank-you gift, the class presented me with a hand-embroidered silk tapestry of Hangchow, a beautiful vacation resort once favoured by the Emperors. According to Marco Polo, "so many pleasures may be found here that one fancies oneself to be in Paradise." The tapestry graces a wall in my recreation room.

I recall my little ten-year-old hostess who took my hand to guide me through the Children's Palace in Shanghai, a great sprawling building that had been, in pre-liberation days, a foreign embassy, and was now a centre for extra-curricular activities of children. She was in Grade four, and although she had been studying English for only one year, I had no trouble understanding her. Proudly she escorted me from one room to another where selected, talented children, all wearing red kerchiefs, were receiving after-school instruction free of charge in the arts, crafts and vocational skills.

In one room a group of children were playing Chinese instruments, ancient bamboo flute and recorder. In another, instruments of the modern orchestra. In still another, a choral group was practising. In another, a puppet show was in progress. Boys were repairing radios and working on model planes and model ships in other rooms. And in a huge room, a very large number of boys were reading comic books. In the gymnasium another very large group of boys were playing ping-pong.

The tour of the Children's Palace ended with a concert in the huge auditorium. A group of happy, healthy-looking school children, slowly raising a huge portrait of Mao, opened the show in a spectacular choral speaking number while dancing girls carried bouquets of flowers. Pantomimes focussed on boys day-dreaming about flying planes and exploring for crude oil for the motherland. The dance, music and song numbers were didactic in nature. Many had political titles such as "I love Chairman Mao in Bejing," "On the Golden Hill in Beijing," "Labour is Glorious" and "The East is Red," the common paean to Mao that one heard everywhere. A few like "Courage in Space," "The Spring of Science has Come" and "Presenting Red Flowers to Scientists" reflected the new stress on science and technology.

But what absolutely amazed me was the skill, precision, and aplomb of the performers. Not only did boys and girls of all ages from nursery school through high school sing and dance like confident professionals, they also performed acrobatics with a skill which will give the western world keen competition in the next Olympics. In fact, the talent and excellence of the performers were awesome.

I shall never forget the little kindergarten boy who volunteered to give me his drawing. After I had been watching a lesson where the children were asked to make a free hand drawing of an elephant, I asked the teacher whether I could have a few to take home to Canada because they were so good. Somehow, I had expected her to go around and just take the best to give me. Instead, she asked for volunteers. After an awkward pause, which embarrassed me, a brave little boy raised his hand. Needless to say, the whole class then followed his example.

Nor shall I forget the primary school children, all of whom seemed happy and healthy. And the affectionate rapport between them and the female teacher as they danced and sang to the beat of tambourines and the music of an accordion. The same was true of the junior kindergarten where the children had lots of fun playing a game called *Jumping the Yangtze*.

Nor shall I ever forget the sight of hundreds of Chinese exercising in a Shanghai Park at dawn, gracefully gliding through the slow ritual movements of *tai chi* to music broadcast over a large speaker. In fact, we would come across Chinese of all ages performing these ballet-like movements with the utmost grace and balance at any time during the day, solo or in groups, on the streets, in school yards, on balconies or in parks. While on the train from Shanghai to Hangchow, I even saw them exercising in the fields; on riverbanks, and on the railroad tracks because the Chinese took breaks for these exercises the way we take coffee breaks.

Next to France, perhaps, China has enjoyed a significant reputation for a great cuisine that is centuries old. While we were probably fed meals that few Chinese could afford, they were invariably served with no particular art. That is, until we were given our farewell banquet at the Pau Hsu Restaurant in Canton. It began with a cold plate followed by one-hundred- year old eggs which had been preserved in lime and buried in mud, a fish-eye and mushroom soup, and stewed dumplings with lobster filling. Then there was a fanfare! And waiters and waitresses brought us trays of roasted suckling pigs, held high above their heads, one for each table. They were visions of gastronomical delight. The skin called "crackle" was served with buttered wafers and sliced English cucumber. Then the pigs were taken away. And we were served broccoli with dove meat, chilled shrimp and broccoli, pig meat, and dove meat with vegetables and fried rice. We were then offered tea, or

warm light Chinese beer, watermelon, and finger bananas. The meal ended with four kinds of pastries. Then
a liqueur was served — *Mai t'ai*, a sorghum liquor which
smelled like lighter fuel. I chose orange pop which was
served at all meals including breakfast.

At another restaurant called the Red Door our
waiter was old enough to remember the gin and bitters
he used to mix for his English customers. Although we
would classify the Red Door as a shabby "greasy spoon,"
the soufflé à la gran marnier which he served was delicious, and his warm welcome, a treat.

Since English studies were compulsory and popular,
I asked to visit a class. My guide in Hangchow escorted
me through the middle school where students studied
such subjects as Farm Knowledge, Physical Culture, Hygiene, Fine Arts, Sports and English. In the English class,
my eye caught a story illustrating the exploitation of
poor Chinese peasants by a greedy, capitalist landlord.
My guide took the book quickly from me, and explained
that they were in the process of reforming their text
books. He wanted me to concentrate on the fact that the
English teacher had been a worker from a silk factory
who had taught herself English and was now allowed to
be a teacher.

There were about fifty students in the class quietly
working at desks arranged in rows, boys separate from
girls, in a minimally equipped classroom that was drab
except for the chalkboard which offered an impeccable
coloured chalk outline of production figures they hoped
to achieve by the year 2000.

I saw these students later at an outdoor class in a
light drizzle of rain among one hundred or so students,
not so quiet, obviously bored by the drone of a teacher
seated at the front of the class, giving a lecture on

politics. Politics is considered the most important subject of the curriculum because as Chairman Mao says, "Education must serve politics."

Chinese young people fascinated me. They seemed so unsophisticated: girls in straight shiny black hair cropped short, or in pigtails; in loose amply patched white blouses and shapeless dark pants; boys in crewcuts and white shirts and dark baggy pants. Girls and boys wore identical clothing, as an egalitarian measure. I saw no personal adornments: rings, brooches, makeup, and no professional hairstyling. But I did not see pimples, obesity, dull hair, or bad teeth.

I like to recall my little friend whose mother was a medical doctor, and father a journalist, telling me with great pride that during the Cultural Revolution when she was fourteen, she had left middle school and went to Northern China to look after sheep. She spent six years there in tough living conditions. Her shoulders still bore the scars from carrying heavy pails of water. "Water is hard to carry," she explained. Whether this dedication will continue I'm not so sure. She seemed very curious about my camera and the western world.

Mrs. Feng, another guide, on the other hand, who boasted that she had fed pigs and collected manure during the Cultural Revolution, was totally uninterested in material goods. It was she with whom I had long discussions about the Gang of Four, the Revolution, Chinese relations with Russia, socialism, and communism. The Gang of Four (blamed for everything today, even the suppression of true love) "rose to high power" during the Revolution and were at the height of their power in 1974 and 1975. She called their downfall in October, 1976, "a great event."

Although some thought the Cultural Revolution was a collective madness that lasted eleven years, Mrs. Feng defended it as being both good and bad. She explained that Mao tried to counteract the growth of an intellectual and bureaucratic élite, and tried to maintain the revolutionary fervour, believing that revolution never ended, that, like life, it was a continual struggle. A revolutionary must always be a learner; society, a factory; and the whole of society, a school.

To my question about the Russians, Mrs. Feng answered that in 1960 the Russians refused to give them any more aid, taking with them prints, designs and instructions relating to buildings and equipment in the process of construction. "Stalin made mistakes," she admitted, "but he was good because he helped us a lot during the liberation days and in the Japanese war. Nikita Khrushchev was trying to turn China into a Soviet satellite, and Chairman Mao and Premier Cho-en-lai could not have it."

The Chinese were genuinely afraid of a Russian attack. In fact, we were shown the entrance to an air raid shelter capable of housing 10,000 people. We also heard that there was an underground city under Beijing with factories, schools and hospitals.

According to Mrs. Feng, the purpose of the revolution was to create a new breed of human being, totally selfless, a self-critical New Society. But I suggested that surely this was impossible, given that human nature favoured individual instincts over social ones. I had been seeing top-level comrades riding in chauffeured limousines and dining in expensive restaurants. "Look at the responses of man throughout the course of history," I argued. She disagreed with me. She did confess, however, that China was still a hundred years away from pure communism, a classless society devoid of personal ambition, opportunism, careerism and selfishness, where the Marxist-Leninist philosophy — from each according to his abilities, to each according to his needs — would be strictly followed.

Mrs. Feng assured me that this New Society would be achieved through education, that a new-born child was a blank piece of paper, that it was their task to paint him the colour they wanted.

> The communist spirit will prevail. Chinese children are taught to love Mao and the Motherland, to live social-ism and not to forget the past and the sufferings of the Chinese people. They are educated not for self, but for service to others.

Although we disagreed on the basic nature of man, I could not help but admire this idealist, this Maoist puritan, who was so proud of the strides her country had already made and would make. After all, the masses were far better off than at any time in their long history. They might not be "free" in the Western sense, but they were free of the horrors of the opium trade, and the humiliation suffered by centuries of foreign and domestic exploitation. They might lead an organized, somewhat Orwellian existence; their employment might not be satisfying or meaningful on our terms; but they were employed; and despite rationing, they had more to eat than they had ever had. As well, they had health and medical services. No. 1 Department Store in Beijing might be poorly lit "to conserve electricity" and not very warm; it might look rundown and grubby; the fly-tox in its window display might be similar to models we had in our home forty years ago, but its counters were heavily stocked with a wide range of goods from age-old herbal remedies to cooking utensils and toys. They might have won these improvements at an enormous sacrifice which we would have labelled as a violation of human liberty and individuality, but the Chinese had cleaned Shanghai, which before liberation, had the highest prostitution, drug, and crime rate in the world. Nor did we see signs in Whangpu Park in Shanghai which read, *No Chinese or dogs allowed.*

Despite Mrs. Feng's rigidly spartan attitude towards materialism, her neighbours were demanding more consumer goods. China's pragmatic and realistic leaders knew this. The most popular counters in No. 1 Department Store were those selling electronics, radios, watches, televisions, camera equipment, and records. The goal of every Chinese was to own a bicycle, a watch, a sewing machine and a radio.

Beijing has come out of isolation, ironically reaching for the capital and technology of advanced western nations. American businessmen, eager for the largest potential market in the world today, were elated at the call. The Bamboo Curtain has lifted. Nearly two hundred years ago, Napoleon uttered a remarkable prophecy: "China? There lies a sleeping giant. Let him sleep, for when he wakes he will move the world." This sleeping giant no longer sleeps. Beijing has made an historic decision to seek western aid in order to propel itself into the twenty-first century.

Coca-Cola is the first American consumer product marketed on the mainland since the Communists took power in 1949. MacDonald's, Colonel Sanders, and Pierre Cardin have followed suit. Posters in Beijing are calling for debates on the issue of human rights. Whether this deviation from Chairman Mao's little red book can sustain his social and moral vision, or whether his vast human experiment that has changed the course of the lives of one-quarter of the human race can continue, no one is able to hazard a guess.

What is certain is that the United States has gone into China and that the country will never be the same China that I saw. Mrs. Feng knew what her China hoped to become. Whether the new emphasis on technological progress will be at the expense of her ideological purity, I cannot say. Whether conditions will go better with Coke, I cannot say.

In the summer of 1968 I visited Britain to do research for my M.A. thesis in the British Museum, the British and Foreign Bible Society, Westminster Abbey, Oxford and Cambridge Universities, Lincoln Cathedral, and Edinburgh University. Each library possessed its own imposing collections; each library had its own distinctive personality. Two have left lasting impressions: the British Museum and Oxford.

I was overwhelmed by the sheer size of The British Museum. Never had I seen anything like the great round reading room with its silent readers. Despite the formal and lengthy registration procedure, I felt privileged to be in this great repository of books, and to be allowed to hold books over four hundred years old, in my white-gloved hands. I handled my treasures lovingly. How well I appreciated Prospero's admission to Miranda that he had neglected state affairs because his priority was the "bettering of [his] mind."

In the Bodleian Library at Oxford, I refused to allow the tedious minutiae of obtaining the books upset me, but concentrated on the thrill of just being in this magnificent seat of learning where Erasmus and Sir Thomas More lectured, where, during the course of centuries, England's great minds had been nourished. England, that had recognized long, long ago the truth of Prince Hamlet's exclamation, "what a piece of work is man!

How noble in reason! how infinite in faculty! . . . in apprehension how like a god!"

I recall having difficulty tearing myself away from the university's grey walls and quadrangles, shining lawns, bridges and spires. The spires recalled to me *The Spires of Oxford* by Winifred M. Letts:

> I saw the spires of Oxford
> As I was passing by,
> The gray spires of Oxford
> Against the pearl-gray sky.
> My heart was with the Oxford men
> Who went abroad to die.

I thought of them when I read the words, "we few — we happy few," in a Chapel at Westminster Abbey dedicated to the Royal Air Force of World War I. I lingered a long while to pay tribute to them, when, just as I was leaving, a ray of sunlight shone, illuminating the words in a golden light.

Robert Burns had always been one of my favourite poets. I had taught many of his poems and songs, such as the tender melody of "Sweet Afton;" and the rousing "Scots, wha hae wi' Wallace bled," in which Burns pays tribute to two Scottish heroes, both of whom led the Scots against the English. I loved to quote fragments of his poems:

> The best laid schemes o' mice and men
> Gang aft a-gley . . .

> The rank is but the guinea's stamp;
> The man's the gowd for a' that . . .
> For a' that, an' a' that,
> It's coming yet, for a' that,
> That man to man, the warld o'er,

Shall brothers be for a' that

I even taught the dance steps to "Comin' thru' the Rye." It was right and fitting that, during the motor trip throughout Britain I took with Frank in the Summer of 1976, we stopped to pay homage to the Scottish poet we both loved.

We strolled along the pathways made sacred by him, immersing ourselves in his life and times, slowly admiring the monuments erected in his honour that dot the Ayrshire countryside: his cottage at Alloway, his home in Dumfries, the Auld Kirk where Burns was baptized, Kilmarnock, Maybole, Mauchline, and the banks of the Don.

We visited the haunts, museums, churchyards, taverns and memorials associated with his poems: "Tam o'Shanter," "Highland Mary," and "Holy Willie's Prayer." We heard Burns' cantata "The Jolly Beggars" for four voices and piano.

As a memento of our trip, Frank gave me *Poems and Songs of Robert Burns*. Dried rose petals still adorn this poem when I recently opened the book:

O, my luve's like a red red rose,
That's newly sprung in June.
O, my luve's like the melodie,
That's sweetly played in tune.

For a moment I allowed myself to indulge in reverie, and then I remembered another of Burns's songs that Frank used to recite: "Ae fond kiss, and then we sever!/Ae farewell, and then forever!"

The story of Scotland's Bonnie Prince Charlie had always appealed to me ever since I was in grade school. Consequently, we had to visit Culloden where Frank, a staunch Protestant, gloried in the defeat of the Roman Catholic Bonnie Prince Charlie by England's Duke of Cumberland, ever after known as The Butcher. Highlanders "lay dead in layers, three or four deep." And I, a staunch Roman Catholic, saddened by the cruel battle in April 1746, could only sympathize with the Highlanders who, for months, followed their Bonnie Prince, now a hunted fugitive, with a $30,000 reward on his head. Once he escaped by dressing as a female-servant. But his loyal followers refused to betray him. At last, the half-starved, ragged fugitive escaped to France from which he was eventually expelled, spending the remainder of his life in Italy where he died in 1788, the last of the Stuarts to fight for the throne. The battlefield reminded me of the rough terrain at Vimy Ridge where Canadian soldiers had covered themselves with glory against the Germans in the Spring of 1917.

On a Saturday on 17 July 1976 while Frank and I were driving up steep Highland roads on our way to John O'Groats, singing two Harry Lauder songs we both loved so well, "Roamen' in the Gloamin" and "Keep right on to the end of the road," we stumbled upon the Highland Games in the mountain village of Tomintoul.

We stopped and stayed the whole afternoon. The Pipes and Drums have fascinated me ever since I was a little girl . And so listening to such tunes as "Scotland the Brave," the "Skye Boat Song" and "Will ye no come back again" was a special treat.

But what interested me most were two of the heavy event competitions, because I had never seen them before: the hammer-throwing, and the tossing of the caber. As with all events, the hefty competitors, dressed in knee socks and tartan kilts, got three tries.

Another attraction of our trip was seeing Bronté country, immortalized by the famous sisters in two novels which I loved to teach, Emily's *Wuthering Heights* and Charlotte's *Jane Eyre*. I toiled up the steep main street of Haworth, a grey unlovely, west Yorkshire town to visit the hilltop church and the Museum that used to be the old parsonage. And I strolled in the moors, feeling the wind blowing through my hair and the brooding spirit of the bleak solitude from which the sisters drew their inspiration.

Our visit to the British House of Commons was interesting. The informality I saw amazed me: members were slouched in their seats; a few had their feet on tables. There was cheering, booing, and pounding on tables. Insults were hurled; members who were trying to speak were interrupted. When the noise became intolerable, the Speaker would call out, "Order, Order." The economic policies of the newly elected Labour Government of James Callaghan were being challenged by Sir Geoffrey Howe, Treasury Affairs critic for the Tory opposition under Margaret Thatcher. I couldn't believe the rowdiness I saw.

In 1986 I spent another summer in England at the Moravian Archives and the British Library in London, the Archives in Liverpool, as well as the Scott Polar Institute in Cambridge doing research for my book *Northen Voices: Inuit Writing in Canada*. I was also looking for material on John Ojijatekka Brant-Sero, probably, the most interesting Native author of the first decade of the twentieth century, who saw himself as the historian of the Six Nations Indians, and gave public concerts and lectures in Great Britain.

At the Scott Polar Institute, handling George Cartwright's *A Journal of Transactions and Events during a*

Residence of Nearly Sixteen Years on the Coast of Labrador, published in 1792, was a special treat. Cartwright had taken back to London five Inuit, one of whom was the shaman Attuiock, who in 1772, on seeing England's cultivated land observed that the land was all "made." Nearly two hundred years later I, too, had made the same observation.

In spite of the daily rain, I took a boat on the River Cam to see the "Backs" where the college grounds sloped down to the banks of the river, and strolled along the walkways where great scholars had trod. I listened to the King's College Evensongs. The strains of Psalms 56, 60 and 61 and the lovely "I Sing of a Maiden" celebrating the Blessed Virgin Mary, still ring gloriously in my ear. I looked forward every day to my afternoon tea of hot scones with strawberry jam and real Devonshire cream. It was on this trip, too, that Barry Taylor (now deceased), whom I had first met when he was head-master at the private boys' school in Uganda, and I saw the Russian prima ballerina, Natalia Makarova who was just wonderful.

It was on this trip that one hundred dollars in sterling was stolen from my room at the RP Hotel in London, a huge complex without private baths. Returning from my bath, I unlocked the door to my room, and to my shock, a clean cut young man walked out. I asked him what he was doing in my room. After replying that he was there to check the windows, he bolted away. I followed but lost track of him. I later noticed a message left by an earlier guest: "Do not leave money or Other Valuables in your room if you are going to take a bad, take your valuables with you — a guest whos been robt." In the cafeteria that evening I learned that a gang of thieves had keys to some of the rooms. I barricaded the

door of my room with all the furniture that was move-
able. The next morning I saw the thief being chased and
immediately looked for another hotel.

Despite this unpleasant experience, I still kept visiting England. And although I have been increasingly
drawn to the ancestral land of my parents, England is
still precious to me. I relish the memories of Stonehenge
and the early English Gothic Cathedral of Salisbury with
its 404 foot spire, the tallest in England; the White Cliffs
of Dover which Kate Smith immortalized in song during
World War II; and Hadrian's Wall built at the order of
the Emperor Hadrian himself about 120 A.D..

I still recall with fondness the ancient walled Roman city of Chester with its galleried shops and quaint
half-timbered Elizabethan buildings and beautiful Win-
chester Cathedral made famous in America by the 1966
hit tune of British rock groups like the Beatles and
Rolling Stones when they invaded the United States.
And because I saw the Cathedral with Gill Dommall,
whom I first met in Edmonton, Alberta when she was
staying at Pembina Hall, the Graduate Girls' Residence
where I was Assistant Dean of Women, the visit was even
more memorable.

I also like to recall a more recent motor-car trip with
Lee Treilhard from Winnipeg in October, 1995. We
concentrated our stay in East Anglia. Here I saw an
England which I had never seen before. There were no
mighty cities, but interesting towns and villages, each
with its own unique history to tell, each guarding all that
rural England holds dear, scattered throughout the pastoral countryside.

Lee and I enjoyed our quiet walks stopping to admire Abbey ruins, market squares and great houses with
massive stables. In Lavenham, Suffolk, Lee, a farm girl

at heart and a lover of horses, paused in front of a stable to look at a pair of beautiful horses. Just as I was about to join her, I felt a sudden sharp pain in my right ankle. The farm's border collie had bitten me. We went immediately to a private clinic where the doctor gave me a rabies shot. But two days later the bite was swollen and infected. We drove to the hospital in Bury St. Edmunds where once again I experienced the efficiency of British hospitals.

The highlight of the trip, of course, was the wedding of Gill Dommall and John Hicks which I attended on 14 October 1995 at St. Anne's, the parish church at Baslow. I loved the Anglican church service. The Latin hymns — *Gloria in Excelsis Deo, Jubilate Deo and Ave Verum* which the choir sang — made me feel at home. It was also fun to visit Gill and John's home in Eyam, Derbyshire. Late one afternoon, while we were trying to find a bed and breakfast which a Canadian couple operated, I entered an art gallery to ask for directions. I was so enthralled by *Autumn Reflection* a piece of machine embroidery by Verina Warren that I bought it. It now graces a wall of my living room where I can admire the Derbyshire landscape.

I don't know when I realized the truth that most of England's oldest abbeys, churches and cathedrals had been romanesque in substance and influence. But I remember being shocked that Westminster Abbey had once been a Roman Catholic church. None of my history teachers had ever mentioned this. At first, this insight caused me much anger. Perhaps Serafina was chastising me for naively believing that the British Empire was the apex of Western culture. But, in recent years, I was beginning to feel a real connection that made me feel at home in a land that I had idealized from afar since childhood. And now that I am writing this book from a place of self-acceptance, my image of self is healed, and Serafina and Penny have reconciled, Serafina can acknowledge, without shame, her connection to an incredibly rich and highly influential history and culture that is as equally important a facet of my life as my Italian-Canadian heritage.

Italy, Again and Again

After my trip around the world, my teaching stint in Africa and my visit to China, I realized how much of a stranger and intruder I had been in these distant lands. I had been curious concerning the lives and habits of other peoples, but discovered that they lived in totally different worlds than my own. I did not belong. The gap between our cultures — in religion, customs, traditions and ways of life — was enormous. The Orient was not my frame of reference. My Roman Catholic religion has always been vitally important to me and central to my life. European civilization is my heritage. I knew I would never travel to the Far East and Africa again.

I was middle-aged, still groping and tentative for something inside me which I could not yet express, something which was buried within me. I still felt the need to travel to faraway places. The glamour and excitement of these other worlds still seduced me. In 1980 I spent three months in Australia while on a sabbatical. I took a guided tour of Eastern Europe and the Balkans in 1981 and I travelled to Soviet Asia and Siberia in 1982. I was wandering the world in a kind of free-wheeling cocoon still trying to find myself, but not fully understanding my obsessive need to travel, nor fully aware of what I was trying to avoid, until it suddenly occurred to me that the only country in the world that I could embrace wholeheartedly was the land of my parents.

I relate to St. Peter's, to the Uffizi and the Pitti, to the Coliseum and the Pantheon, in a way that I cannot relate to the temples and shrines, the palaces and monuments, the art, sculpture and music of the Far and Middle East. Dante, Da Vinci, Michelangelo, Caravaggio, Aquinas, Petrarch and Giotti, Verdi and Palestrina say something to me. I finally began to realize that I would have to return to my ancestral homeland.

Rome

> Latin is a dead language
> as dead, as dead can be,
> it killed the ancient Romans
> and now it's killing me.

I used to chant in high school. The language of the ancient Romans might not be heard anymore, but I had discovered that the glorious imperial past of ancient Rome was not dead. I returned to Rome in the summer of 1984. On this trip, more than on any other, I methodically explored Rome's various districts. I discovered that it lives in the present in a most dynamic way. I watched children play hide and seek among decapitated statues while their nurses gossiped, perched on the remains of a rostrum. I saw cats, fed by a woman with dyed red hair, parade about the Porta Ostiense with the arrogant mien of possession, while I read plaques on the walls of the Gate, commemorating the liberation of Rome when Allied Forces breached its gates and secured the bridges over the Tiber; I caught young lovers stealing a kiss in the highest gallery of the Colosseum where countless gladiators and Christian martyrs were served up to the lions; I licked my *gelato* strolling about the fountain in the centre of Piazza Navona, once the stadium of Domitian that could seat 30,000 spectators. As I walked down the Via del Teatro di Marcello from the Capitoline, I saw the bulk of the theatre converted into an elegant collection of flats. I stood on the bridge of Sant' Angelo to peer down into the Tiber and recalled the lines:

> Oh Tiber, Father Tiber,
> To whom the Romans pray,
> A Roman's life, a Roman's arms
> Take thou in charge this day.

I gazed at the enormous round castle fortress of Castel Sant Angelo with its cylindrical tower and tremendously thick walls, begun in 139 A.D. by Emperor Hadrian as a mausoleum for himself and his family, atop of which the golden archangel, Michael, sheathes his sword. Just as I was wondering how Tosca, who threw herself over the parapet wall, could fall into the Tiber, a friend whom I had not seen in years tapped my shoulder.

Wherever I find myself, Catholic churches have always been my refuge. It is my practice to visit several every day to get away from the noisy crowds and the fierce heat outside, or just to sit and listen to the silence. Mostly, I like to chat with my Lord, to thank Him for my blessings, to make deals with Him or to plead forgiveness. I have always felt close to God in His house.

I welcome the spirit of joyful fellowship I see expressed in the modern church. At St. Agnes Church in Rome one Sunday, the priest may have said Mass with his back to the altar, but the outward happy manifestation of faith moved me. The hymns — one of which was *dai il mano a suo fratello* (Give your hand to your brother) — sung to an accompaniment of organ and guitars, were jubilant. Instead of a sermon, a number of parishioners gave their personal reflections on the Sunday's Gospel. During the recitation of the Lord's Prayer, we joined hands across the main aisle. I felt a wonderful sense of community.

At another Roman church, I watched a children's choir standing in front of the congregation clapping their hands and having fun while they swayed to and sang wonderful hymns of gladness. Each first-communion candidate went up to a microphone and announced his or her name. When the last child had finished, the candidates stood in a line to a burst of applause from the congregation. However, when I wanted to hear the traditional Gregorian chant, I could go to Sant Anselmo in the Aventine.

Of the dozen churches I frequent when I am in Rome, it is the Basilica of St. Peter's which draws me. My greatest thrill is to walk up the Via della Conciliazione, the broad thoroughfare that leads to Piazza San Pietro, and face the Basilica. Everything is the same as I have remembered it. I feel at home. But this time in 1984 I noticed more buses, and yellow cabs; more pilgrims from the third world; more people of colour, especially nuns; more food stalls with more visitors sipping cold drinks, licking ice cream cones and munching on pizzas and hot sandwiches; more small children and young people. A mobile post office had even been added. In my earlier visits, beadles kept men in shorts and women immodestly dressed in short sleeves and bare heads from entering the Basilica. Cameras were forbidden. All these regulations have now been removed.

St. Peter's is all magnificence and gigantic splendour. Each visit revealed a new column, new arch, statue, mosaic, altar or painting I had not noticed before.

During this visit I became enraptured by the golden sunlight radiating from Bernini's window, high above the main altar which bathes the Holy Ghost, in the shape of a dove, in a beautiful yellow light. The words of the hymn that I used to play on the organ of St. Anthony's Church promptly came to my mind:

Come Holy Ghost, Creator blest,
And in our hearts take up Thy rest.
Come with Thy grace and heavenly aid,
To fill the hearts which Thou hast made.

I also liked to stop and watch the young and handsome Swiss Guards in their brilliant red, yellow and blue striped uniforms with their black hats and red ribbons which were designed more than four hundred years ago by Michelangelo.

Ever since a madman put a hammer to the *Pietà*, my favourite statue, it sits behind bullet-proof plexiglass. Although I could no longer kiss my Lord's broken legs as I used to do, I could still gaze for hours at the heavenly grace and maternal love that are blended in the look of the immortally young Mother who grieves tenderly over the body of her son.

I have spent hours in the Vatican Palaces, which form a world in themselves — a group of elegant buildings with more than eleven thousand rooms — roaming through its museums, halls, galleries, libraries, chapels and corridors, admiring their innumerable artistic and historic treasures. On a fiercely hot day I visited deep inside the Vatican where I was looking for the College of the Propaganda in order to find a statue of the Ojibway Indian, William Blackbird, which according to his brother's *History of the Ottawa and Chippewa Indians of Michigan* (1887), was erected there. Just before his ordination as a priest William was mysteriously assassinated. No one was able to help me.

Among these incredible riches, a singular spectacle for me is the magnificent Sistine Chapel. In recent years, millions of dollars have been spent on its restoration. I have seen it twice since it has been restored, but I liked it better when the colours were tempered by the dust and candle smoke of centuries. I might be speaking in ignorance because I have never taken an art appreciation course in my life, but I found the restored colours too intense, overdone. Perhaps they suit the glare and blaze of sun drenched Italy!

I don't know how many times I have found myself in Piazza Barberini, but I had never entered the Capuchin Church of the Immaculate Conception near the Piazza at the foot of the once fashionable Via Veneto. This time I stopped to visit, and my attention was drawn to a cellar, an underground passage that exhibited skulls and bones of more than four thousand Capuchin monks who died between 1528 and 1870 arranged in Rococo floral and geometric designs. One chamber revealed whole skeletons cloaked in hooded brown Franciscan robes. Even the candelabra were made of Franciscan bones. When I visit cemeteries, such as the beautiful non-Catholic cemetery in Rome, where I lingered among the cypresses and pines, the wild rose bushes and the red camellias, to read the touching inscriptions on the tombs and to pause at the grave of Keats buried under a stone, engraved with a Grecian lyre, I am moved to reflect on my own mortality and recall these lines from James Shirley's "Death the Leveller":

Sceptre and Crown
Must tumble down
And in the dust be equal made

> With the poor crooked scythe and spade . . .
> Only the actions of the just
> Smell sweet and blossom in the dust.

Invariably, I also recite this prayer:

> Eternal rest give unto them, O Lord,
> And may perpetual light shine upon them. May they
> Rest in peace, *Requiescat in pace*, Amen.

On this occasion, however, I found the scene at the Capuchin church macabre. Perhaps its purpose was to mock the living, or to invite meditation on the corruption of the body. I did not linger, but left quickly. I stepped outside into the intensely bright light of a Roman afternoon.

On 19 August, I got up early in order to get to Castel Gandolfo for a public audience with Pope John Paul II. The courtyard was packed with people of all colours. But I was surprised to see so few priests and nuns. I noticed many excited Japanese and Third World groups waving their banners and cheering loudly. The magnitude of his presence was astonishing. A Korean choir of young people in long, red, white and gold dresses sang and jumped for joy when the Pope announced: "I see a group of Koreans not mentioned in my list." Young men were playing accordions and guitars. The Pope was relaxed and enjoyed himself as he listened to the choirs below. Then he repeated *bene, bene,* spoke first in English and then in Korean, Spanish, French, German, Polish and lastly, Italian.

The Pope's summer residence sits on a ledge above Lake Albano, the bluest lake I had ever seen. I went for lunch at a restaurant with a terrace overlooking the lake, choosing a table with a view. But the waiter refused to serve me there. I protested sweetly but to no avail. He moved me to a small table at the back by the kitchens. After all, I was a woman alone!

On this visit, as I had done so often before, I visited the fountains I love: "The Four Fountains" by Bernini in the famed seventeenth century Piazza Navona representing the rivers Tiber, Nile, Amazon, and Ganges; "The Fountain of the Triton" also by Bernini in Piazza Barberini; as well as his "Fountain of the Bees" on Via Veneto; the "Fountain of the Naiads" in Piazza Esedra, now called Piazza della Republica; "The Fountain of the Tortoises" in the small Piazza Mattei; and of course, "The Barcaccia" in the Piazza d' Espagna; as well as the "Fountain of Trevi," the most famous and spectacular of the Roman fountains featured in the film *La Dolce Vita*.

But the fountains I love best are in the Tivoli Gardens at Villa D'Este just outside Rome. I have made them my familiar place whenever I need to get away from Rome's blistering heat and want relief for my hot and sticky body. It is always cool and shady there. The fountains are not only a cooling blessing, they are also a visual and auditory feast as they gurgle, babble, and whisper, splash and crash, slither, slide and cascade over boulders from one terrace to another.

Some of the fountains have their own names. The "Oval Fountain," where slender maidens poured water from their jugs; the "Organ Fountain," where streams of water gushed from spouts and breasts; and The "Hundred Fountains" of *Roman Holiday* fame, where dancing waters sprouted from cabbages, lilies, lion's heads and boats. On one visit I was so bothered by the savage heat, I just flattened myself against a wall behind the Waterfall of Rometta. As always, I found peace and solitude along the wooded paths and amidst the sweet fragrance of the flowers. As always, I gasped with delight at some new treasure tucked away in a secluded spot. Refreshed, I return to the Eternal City contemplating the pleasure the alliance of man and nature can give.

Every time I am in Rome, I make sure I go to the Baths of Caracalla to see an opera. Among the imposing ruins where, in ancient times, sixteen hundred persons gathered to cleanse their bodies in tubs made of basalt, granite and alabaster and revel in the latest gossip, I witnessed a performance of Verdi's *Aida* with chariots, real camels, and all the pageantry and pomp which is always staged so well at Caracalla. On another occasion, I saw Bizet's *Carmen*, and on this trip, Verdi's *Nabucco*.

The audience was euphoric after *Va pensiero*, shouting *Bravo*, *Bravo*, cheering, whistling and stomping their feet. Their excitement was so infectious I began shouting, *Bravo*, too! The aria is sacred to Italians, second only to their national anthem. A journalist for the "New York Times" sitting next to me commented, "it wasn't sung well but the applause is magnificent."

The chorus sang the aria again to more wild applause.

It was fun to meet Louis F. I. Inturrisi who taught at John Cabot University in Rome, especially since I had read a number of his articles. We met several times afterwards for *tartufo* and *granita de caffé* at the trattoria Tre Scalini, in Piazza Navona, a rendezvous for the cinema crowd. But I'll never forget the lunch at the Giggeto in Trastevere where he recommended a specialty *fiori di zucca* (squash flowers). When they arrived, I was surprised. My mother had made the dish many times every summer — the yellow flowers of the pumpkin, in a batter and then deep fried. I didn't recognize the name in Italian and I've forgotten the Calabrese name for them. While researching *Embracing Serafina*, I read that Inturrisi's "lifeless body was found in his Rome apartment" on 7 August 1997. I was shocked.

It was on this trip that I spent much time with my cousins, Gino and Dino, who live in Rome. Today, I treasure the time we spent together because they had grown dear to me, and they are now both deceased. They would reminisce about the Second World War, telling me that their Dad fought in Yugoslavia, and escaped, only to be caught between the German and Allied armies. In hiding, he went months without food. They, themselves, fled Rome and lived in mountain caves. When the boys ate a biscuit given to them by an American soldier, they suffered the entire night because they had gone so long without food.

Born and raised in Rome they knew how to get around the chaotic traffic that clogs Rome's streets. Dino would drive me around back streets in the older quarters among seventeenth century palaces, churches, and musty old buildings not frequented by tourists. I recall our happiness together as he drove to the surrounding historical hill towns like Viterbo and Orvieto. One weekend, Gino drove us in his Mercedes-Benz to his wife Rosi's mountain retreat south of Rome, twenty kilometres from Cassino. It was an area of fierce fighting between the Germans and Allied forces, during World War II and the stories of rape and murder which Rosi told me were horrifying.

I ate the best food in Rome at Gino's in their beautifully furnished condo. Dinners were always sumptuous. I have never forgotten them. My refusal, which they taught me — *Io non voglio ingrassare* (I don't want to gain weight) was always met with *Alora, devo mangere finocchi e cetriolo.* (Then you have to eat fennel and cucumbers.) The feasts continued.

I remember one particularly wonderful dinner when Rosi served anchioves, black and green olives, cheese and ham slices; then gnocchi, eggplant in a fresh tomato sauce, swiss chard with onion, beef rolls, green peppers, cannelloni stuffed with spinach and ricotta, fried potatoes, veal cutlets, pumpkin flowers with mozzarella cheese, French bean salad, bananas, watermelon, cantaloupe, peaches, pears, an ice cream torte, coffee, wines and Sambuca (a licorice liqueur). Gino loved American musicals, especially *West Side Story* and *Oklahoma.* We listened to them again and again.

One of the highlights of my 1984 trip, however, was seeing Shakespeare's *The Tempest* since it is my favourite play to teach. It took place at the Parco dei Daini in the Borghese Gardens, Rome's largest public park begun by Cardinal Scipio Borghese at the beginning of the seventeenth century. But when I made enquiries regarding public transportation and available taxis since I was staying in the Aventine area, a distance away from the gardens, I discovered that there was no way to get back to my hotel after midnight. I was devastated. (There is even a sketch of the area drawn in my notebook which I remember memorizing because I didn't want to carry anything that would label me as a tourist.) It was unthinkable to miss this opportunity. I took a tram and arrived early, reconnoitring the area just in case I had to walk back. I sat in the front row, anxious and restless. When a young girl sat next to me, I was hopeful. After a decent time elapsed I struck up a conversation with her in my fractured Italian. (I am always painfully aware of the deficiencies of my Italian.) Giovanna confirmed the fact that there would be no taxis after midnight. I knew this but feigned ignorance. I told her my predicament. She offered to drive me back to my hotel. I breathed easily from that moment on. And, although the performance was in Italian, it was the best I have ever seen. It even surpassed that of a London performance with Sir John Gielgud, mainly because of the creative imagination of the Italians, which no other country has been able to match. "The storm scene was *stupendo*," my diary says. Sitting in the front row might also have helped, or perhaps it was its outdoor setting in the dark of night. After the performance, Giovanna insisted on taking me to Fassi in Piazza Fiume for a *gelato*.

I have walked miles exploring Rome's historic monuments and treasures and sat for hours on stone benches in her piazzas. Invariably, I am accosted by both young and old men. Roman males have an uncanny way of spotting "American" women. At times I enjoyed the chase, but it was often difficult to outfox or get rid of them. Once, by the Teatro Adriana, a young man was persistent. He finally got out of his white car and said: "Look, I'm alone, you're alone, all I want is company." For a second I was tempted. He seemed so sincere. But then my cautious self took over. Before I could even reflect on the incident, an older man in a large red car kept following me trying to pick me up. I decided it was time to return to my hotel.

Italy, 1987

I returned to Italy in the spring of 1987 to give lectures on Native Literature in Canada at the Universities of Messina, Catania, Pisa and Bologna. I was totally unprepared for the enthusiasm I found among Italy's academics and university students. My lectures even made headlines in local papers: *Conferenza del Capo degli indiani Ojibwa* and *e per raccontarci del Canada al dipartimento di storia arriva un "prof" che è . . . capo indiano.*

Not only was there interest in the Literature of Canada's Native peoples, but the Italian Association for Canadian Studies had been founded eight years earlier in 1979. I was surprised at the extent to which Italian academics were keeping abreast of Canadian cultural life. A seminar, "The Relationship with the Land in Canadian Culture" at the University of Messina in which I participated, attracted many Italian scholars. I was even more surprised at the large number of Canadian writers whom Italian scholars had translated into Italian. Professor Alfredo Rizzardi from the University of Bologna, for example, had translated Layton and Atwood. Northrop Frye's books and literary theories were familiar. In May, 1987, Frye was honoured in Rome at an international conference, *Ritratto di Northrop Frye,* which I was fortunate to attend. For three days, at Villa Mirafiori, Italian scholars read papers on such themes as "Frye and Blake" and "Frye and the Fable" in the presence of a silent Frye, listening patiently while I wondered just how much Italian he understood and what he was thinking. Ten years later in 1997, Carla Pizzini Plevano, who has translated Frye and McLuhan, would tell me that when Frye had stayed overnight at her home in Vicenza, her mother and he conversed in Latin, the only language they had in common.

There were many gala functions honouring Frye. Claude E. Charland, the Canadian Ambassador to Italy, gave a cocktail party at the Canadian Embassy in Rome on 25 May. I can't retrieve any details, but I do remember, however, the dinner in Frye's honour at the Hostaria Villa Massimo in Rome on 26 May, hosted by

Pierre Granger, Counsellor of Canada's Cultural Affairs in Rome. It was an informal affair. (I recall Robert Kroestch and Eli Mandel's wife being present.) I felt extremely honoured to be invited. The previous year, Professor Frye had won the Governor General's award for *Northrop Frye on Shakespeare*. I congratulated him saying that the award was long overdue. His response was an ironic reflection: "It was won for a collection of my essays for undergraduates." He immediately downed a shot glass of *grappa*.

After finishing my lecture tour, I stopped at Florence on my way to Rome. At the invitation of a member of the University Women's Club of Florence, I attended one of their meetings to learn that they too had problems attracting younger women members. On 5 May, a member invited me to a gala dinner in honour of Napoleon Bonaparte, hosted by the Rotary Club of Florence, and to my surprise, I was introduced to the assembly as a visiting professor from Canada. I have been an admirer of Napoleon and so I enjoyed the keynote address about one of my heroes. I had decided I was going to travel light on this trip. And so I brought only one party dress, a classic navy blue silk wrap around with huge white dots which I wore underneath a white blazer. Compared to the elegance and sophistication of the Italian women, I felt like a country bumpkin.

I enjoyed being in Florence, the birthplace of the Renaissance, and magnificent cradle of Italian art and civilization. I invariably gravitated to the city's largest square, the sculpture-studded Piazza della Signoria, the centre of ten centuries of Florentine life, where in 1498, the Dominican monk, Savonarola, was burned alive. I inevitably stopped, in the Loggia dei Lanzi to gaze at "Perseus" holding aloft the head of Medusa, Cellini's masterpiece in bronze, and at Giambologna's "Rape of the Sabines," a wonderful example of the sensuous interpretation of a classical theme, so typical of the Renaissance. After I feasted my eyes on these two statues, I stood in wonderment at a copy of Michelangelo's famous "David" nearby. I am never prepared for the Duomo, the largest church in the world after St. Peter's. Its huge bulk, out of proportion with the narrow streets that lead up to it, startles me. But once my astonishment faded, I admired its spectacular dark green, white and pink striped marble facade topped by a wondrous gigantic octagonal dome, the work of the great Florentine sculptor and artist Brunelleschi (1377-1446). I stood in awe of the three world-famous gilt bronze doors of the baptistry, carved by Lorenzo Ghiberti between 1425-1452, which depict biblical stories in relief. But it is the Byzantine mosaics of the Baptistry's cupola which simply enchanted me. Christ, the Universal Judge was in the foreground, and in the centre part of the cupola, a dazzling array of generations of Angels in the Byzantine style which boggled my mind. And then there were the wonders of Giotto's fourteenth century Campanile, the multi-coloured Bell Tower soaring almost three hundred feet above ground, regarded as the most beautiful bell tower in the world and one of the greatest creations of Gothic art.

I also made a pilgrimage to the house in Florence where Dante Alighieri (1265-1321), one of Italy's greatest poets, was born. Dante saw the divine and human nature of Christ reflected in Beatrice's eyes and taught us that human love leads us to love of God. It is no wonder that I love Florence. One of my favourite English poets, Robert Browning, eloped and fled to Florence in 1847 with Elizabeth Barrett, approaching forty, and six years his senior. They made Florence their home for fourteen years until Elizabeth died. Here they wrote the poems which I have taught time and time again: "My Last Duchess," "Andrea del Sarto" and "Fra Lippo Lippi." I cannot count the number of times I have quoted Pippa's line: "All's right with the world," or how many times I have read "How do I love thee?" from Sonnet 43 in *Sonnets from the Portugese*.

I had to leave Florence in order to get back to Rome where I was to meet my brother Franki and his twelve-year-old granddaughter Lisa. On the morning of 3 June, I met them at Fiumicino Airport. To my astonishment, my other brother Alfred, his wife Celina and their two-year-old daughter, Elysia, were on the same plane! I took them to the Hotel Anselmo where I had stayed three years earlier, a villa tucked away in luscious green gardens in the Aventine with its palaces and large villas.

We visited my favourite places: the Vatican, St. Peter in Chains, Michelangelo's "Moses," the fountains, and Bernini's little elephant supporting an ancient Egyptian obelisk in the Piazza Minerva. Lisa and I went to the portico of the eighth century San Maria in Casmedin, one of the gems of medieval Rome, which rises on the ruins of an ancient temple, where on a side wall is the Bocca della Verità (Mouth of Truth), a drain cover in the form of a great mask. According to legend, anyone who has told a lie and puts his hand into the stone mouth will be bitten by it. Lisa passed the test. Each time I am here, my eyes automatically soar to admire the twelfth century bell tower of Romanesque style, one of the loveliest of its kind in Rome.

We took a taxi to the Forum, the heart of ancient Rome, where, under a scorching sun, Elysia, in her mother's arms, cried inconsolably, as a guide droned on about the Temples of Vespasian and Vesta and the Arch of Titus. Amidst the ruins I let my imagination dwell on Cicero and Julius Caesar and Mark Antony's funeral oration in honour of Caesar, and meditated on the transitory nature of things.

On a blistering hot day, I ran an Olympic dash to find a glass of water for my brother, Franki, who was struck with severe chest pains while he was having his portrait sketched by an artist on the famed two hundred-year-old broad flight of Spanish Steps that were flanked by huge pots of azaleas and pedlars' carts loaded with flowers. None of us realized then how sick Franki was. He died less than a year after this trip. When I look at this portrait, I notice that the artist captured the look of a sick man. There is a grey pallor to Franki's skin and his face is bloated.

On another occasion when Alfred, with baby Elysia mounted on his shoulders, Celina, Franki, Lisa and I were descending the magnificent Spanish steps, Alfred thwarted a gypsy thief from pickpocketing a tourist's wallet on the steps below us by shouting at the top of his voice, "Thief, Thief."

We returned again and again to the Piazza Venezia which has grown dear to me. I know I will find an exquisitely tailored policeman in spotlessly white gloves on a podium in the centre of the busy square directing traffic with the grace of a conductor of a symphony orchestra. Just standing and watching him evokes the magic I felt when I first came to Rome. "And perhaps you'll be lucky enough to see Rome's sexy policewomen here," I told my brothers. They were — in high heels and painted toenails carrying walkie-talkies. They noticed the attractive blonde street-cleaners wearing green satin-laced-shoes and large green earrings.

A highlight for me was the outdoor midnight Mass on 6 June 1987 launching the Marian Year presided by Pope John Paul II. Franki, Lisa and I arrived early to be sure we would have chairs. It was a chilly breezy night. Franki and Lisa were restless and wanted to leave. But I so wanted to remain to hear the Latin and the Gregorian chant that they grudgingly stayed until the finish. The Mass ended with the joyful *Regina Coeli*, a Latin hymn of praise, which I have always loved, ever since I played it on the organ of St. Anthony's Church at home.

Italy, 1990

In the fall of 1990, I joined the one hundred and twenty member delegation from the National Organization of Italian American women to attend an International Conference of Women of Italian Ancestry in Italy. I had been reluctant to join the group because I had always been embarrassed by my Italianness. But my decision to go was, in retrospect, an important decision in my life. We were entertained lavishly at cocktail receptions, gala luncheons and dinners hosted by the regional and city councils of Friuli, Udine, San Daniele, Lignano, Ancona and Rome. We toured various industrial and commercial sites, such as furniture and pastry firms, a ham curing company, and a winery. We also attended a display of the Autumn/Winter 1990/91 haute couture collection of Cristina da Udine.

We met Francesco Cossiga, the President of the Italian Republic, as well as the Mayor of Rome who hosted a reception and luncheon at Villa Caffarelli. On 29 September, we had a private audience with Pope John Paul II. We climbed very long, steep, and tiring flights of stairs to a small room where we awaited his entrance.

Absolute silence suddenly descended when he appeared. He spoke briefly in English but I can no longer recall what he said. Our meeting was remarkable by its studied silence, in stark contrast to the boisterous response of his public audiences. I shook the hands of His Holiness.

The focus of the conference was business and entrepreneurship, two areas which didn't interest me too much, but several topics such as "Issues Facing Women of Italian Ancestry," "How Our Roles Are Influenced by Our Italian Culture," "Stresses Related to Career and Family Responsibilities," and "Are We Represented Politically?" were interesting. I can't recall many details, but I do remember the wonderful meals. For example, at the Green Hotel in Udine, we were served aperitivo Green, Prosciutto di San Daniele with figs, air-dried Beef and Rocket and Fruit tartlet, Risotto with mushrooms, Pumpkin Gnocchi with butter and sage, filet of beef Wellington, Parisienne potatoes, Zucchini Pascal, Apple Streudel with vanilla custard, coffee, Pinot bianco, Merlot, and Fragalino wines.

Sandra Banducci from Seattle, Washington, a member of the group with whom I still keep in contact, remembers the conference:

> My memories of the trip are sparse but what stands out vividly in my mind was the time you and I, Anna Amato and Louisa Napolitano, broke loose from the rest and took off for Assisi. We rented a car. I remember, as we approached the town from the road below, looking up at Assisi, backlit by the sun, and thinking what a jewel it was. The colour of that town perched upon its hilltop was an aged terra cotta apricot which I have tried to replicate on the walls of one of my bedrooms. It's not quite the same. Any way . . . our little adventure took us first to the Chapel of St. Francis (which I think was hit by an earthquake about five years ago when two

priests were killed). Then we headed down the hill along narrow paths to the village below. It started to pour buckets and all of us were getting drenched. At the bottom we found shelter in a doorway, which suddenly opened and the woman inside invited us to come in. She gave us towels to dry off, gave you a pretty silk umbrella which she didn't want returned, and helped me fashion a raincoat out of a huge, clear plastic bag. The food was consistently glorious. The banquet in Rome hosted by the Mayor was especially memorable. There were tables and tables *al fresco* laden with food: pastas, eggplant, salads, dessert, etc. each prepared in ten different ways.

In Rome the Canadian group was even invited to join the American delegation at a cocktail buffet by the Ambassador of the United States and Mrs. Secchia at Villa Taverna, an historic Roman villa first mentioned in tenth century papal documents by Popes Agapitus II and John XII.

But it was not the discussions nor the food that I valued most. It was the North American women who belonged to an association that was trying to counter the stereotypes of fat, fertile Italian women dressed in black and preoccupied with cooking pasta, who endeared themselves to me. They made my trip memorable because I discovered that I was not alone in my personal struggle with my ethnicity. We bonded. I was one of them. They encouraged my ethnic pride. They called me Penny. My Italian name was still a source of discomfort.

I continued my peripatetic life, still drifting, still on the run. I took Caribbean cruises. From Iqaluit on Baffin Island I sailed down the Labrador Coast to the French islands of Saint-Pierre and Miquelon in the Gulf of St. Lawrence and then visited Newfoundland. I flew to Tierra del Fuego. I took a motorcar tour of England. I participated in an historic expedition through the North West Passage.

Although these travels to distant places were full of adventure and culturally fascinating, I still felt an indescribable complex of tensions. My public persona was still so radically different from my private identity. It would take another visit to Italy for me to sort them out and rescue Serafina. This happened in the summer of 1997.

Italy, 1997

If I had been unprepared for the interest in Native Literature in Canada which Italy's scholars and university students showed in 1987, I was even more overwhelmed when I returned to lecture in the spring of 1997, the fifth centenary of Giovanni Caboto's explorations of Canada's North Atlantic Coast, to find how much that interest had grown in ten years. An ever-increasing number of students were now writing theses on Native Canadian writers like Maria Campbell, Jeannette Armstrong, Thomas King and Ruby Slipperjack. I was amazed to what lengths they went to get help. There was very little material available on Canada's Native people, and students relied on visiting Canadian professors or going abroad themselves. Sabina, a student at the University of Bologna, had flown to London but found virtually nothing. Late in August of 1997 she received a scholarship to come to Canada where she worked on my papers at Lakehead University. Paola also from the University of Bologna, went to Paris to buy books including my own *Native Literature in Canada*.

Wherever I lectured — Cosenza, Genoa, Bologna, Pisa, Turin, Perugia, Parma, Venice or Vicenza — I found

Italian students conscientious and eager. Their enthusiasm was so great that they would congregate around me after each lecture and would not let me go. In Venice they even found an empty room where I taught Pauline Johnson's "Lullaby of the Iroquois" and "As Red Men Die" and answered their many questions. In Bologna, a number of students, like Paola, who had a scholarship to study Francophone aboriginal literature in Quebec, had prepared a comprehensive fifteen point questionnaire for me to answer. Not only were Italian universities interested in the study of America's first peoples, there were also several associations committed to their study who sponsored several international conferences in which I participated.

Perugia was once the flourishing centre of Etruscan culture. Built on a hilltop dominating the Tiber Valley, it is an odd mixture of old and new. After settling down in my hotel, I climbed a steep hill to the city's main street, the Corso Vanucci, where, to my utter amazement, I saw literally thousands of students, shoulder to shoulder. I have never before or since seen so many students. At one end of the Corso, another throng of students was sitting on the broad steps of the Cathedral and the thirteenth century fountain. I was surprised to see it covered with green netting, still in the process of being restored from damage inflicted during the Second World War.

As everywhere else in Italy, with churches a few yards apart, one can always find a Mass. I stumbled upon one very near to my hotel on a Saturday evening where I was surprised to see the choir — men in formal black tie, and women in long black gowns holding their music in black folders — all looking so elegant.

At the international conference in Perugia, the majority of the papers were given in Spanish on topics

about the Indians of Mexico and South America, but
there was considerable interest in my paper, *Canadian
Indian stereotypes: myth and realty*, which I gave in
English.

I left Perugia with Naila Clerici, the editor of the
magazine, *Tepee*, whom I met at the Conference, and her
husband Beppe, for the seven hour drive to Turin. Beppe
had to carry my heavy bag up and down steep Perugian
hills to get to the longest escalator I have ever stood on,
which took us down to the new City and the parking lot.

I knew Turin to be an industrialized city, a Communist stronghold, the place where my Calabrese cousin
was sent to, and the location of the shroud in which the
body of the dead Christ was wrapped. But on this trip I
learned that, from a Longobard duchy and Frankish
earldom, Turin had passed finally to the House of Savoy.
It was truly a royal city. While Naila was teaching, I
strolled around the ancient city's historic centre. There
were wide avenues, crossing at right angles, spacious
arcaded porticoes, beautiful piazzas, palaces, and gal-
lerias that once sheltered the royals on their walks from
the Palazzo Reale (1658) down to the Po River.
Nietzsche and Dumas had lived in Turin. I walked in the
shade of the arcades which lined most of the downtown
streets and came upon a golden bull (Turin means bull),
imbedded in the wide marble pavement in front of a
famous old restaurant. Legend claims that if one wipes
his or her feet on its balls, one will have good luck. I
wiped mine.

The audiences at my lectures had always impressed
me, but I was overwhelmed in Turin. Naila had adver-
tised my lectures in two local papers; there was standing
room only. I was surprised at the extent of Indian knowledge which a few in my audience possessed. One

gentleman knew more about shamanism than I did. Another came up to tell me his great-grandmother had been a Lakota Sioux called "The woman who rides with the moon." He had visited her grave on a reservation in the States and would have liked to live there, "but unfortunately," he said, "my duties are here looking after my children."

The talent that Italian students have for foreign languages has never failed to amaze me either. The two student interpreters in Turin who translated my lectures instantaneously without having previously seen my notes were absolutely fantastic. Their knowledge about their own culture was also astounding. One of Naila's students, Tamara, invited me for a drive to the Palazzini di Caccia di Stupingi, to view an exhibition of paintings and artifacts belonging to the Napoleonic presence in Turin from 1808 to 1814. To my astonishment, she could identify a Caravaggio.

But what was even more startling was discovering just how much partisan activity took place in these parts during the Second World War. High in this mountain country, headquarters were established for Italian partisan groups that waged a ceaseless guerrilla warfare against German occupation troops. Naila Clerici told me her father was working in a factory in Genoa until the Germans took him to Dachau. He escaped and made his way back to Italy. When he appeared at his girlfriend's house, he was so emaciated she didn't recognize him. Vilma Ricci also told me that when her mother was fourteen years old she belonged to the Resistance and would cycle eighty kilometres from Bardi to Piacenza across mountain ranges, bringing messages to the partisans. Because she was so tiny, the Germans never suspected her of being a partisan. She was terrified, on one occasion, when several German soldiers came to inspect her home. Her two brothers' resistance uniforms were in the back yard. Luckily it was snowing and the snow covered the uniforms. Her uncle, however, was caught and sent to Buchenwald. Many Italians, she told me, were sent to concentration camps. To revenge Porta Lame, the most important battle inside Bologna of the Italian resistance against the Nazis, Hitler's troops shot one hundred incarcerated partisans. During the war, we had been "brainwashed" into believing the Italians were cowards. This knowledge, of course, had made me even more ashamed of my Italianness. On this trip, however, I was relieved to find out that the Italians had been fighting a war they didn't believe in, and that there were numerous individual acts of courage and heroism.

On the train trip from Turin to Parma, I enjoyed seeing the myriads of poppies growing along the railroad tracks and covering the spaces between the ties. At the station in Parma my eyes fell on a large sign with "Penny" printed in large bold letters held by Lois Clegg, an English girl, who was teaching Economics at the University in Parma. She was accompanied by Giovanni Grilli. I was relieved, when Lois invited me to stay with her.

At a dinner on the night of my arrival, I met many of the members of an association committed to the welfare of America's Indians who were very enthusiastic about all things related to North American Indians. Giovanni Grilli and his wife Vilma Ricci, and Michele Contini, another member of the Association, had visited many Indian reservations in the States. Michele had even spent his honeymoon visiting Indian reservations in the United States.

I explored the historic centre of Parma on foot, noticing scores of slim and fit women riding bicycles. I even noticed a poster advertising my lecture in a tourist agency's window next to another poster announcing a concert in memory of Maria Callas. In the Archeological Museum, my attention was drawn to a tombstone inscribed Petronio and Petronia.

My hosts, the Grillis and Lois Clegg took me to a concert to listen to readings of the Beat poets, Lawrence Ferlinghetti, Allen Ginsberg and Jack Kerouac, and writer Norman Mailer set against background music from a Celtic harp, a guitar, an Arabian lute and *tablo*. It was amazing.

But the event that truly surprised me was the wedding of Silvia and Vincenzo. When we arrived at the church, guests in a wide assortment of dress were milling about. I was surprised to see a variety of gaming tables in the porch at the front of the church, and the bride and groom standing at each side of the entrance handing out programmes for the service wrapped in a lilac ribbon. The bride stood radiant and pregnant, greeting each guest in a long, white, straight-cut, lace gown with a lilac shell underneath a long jacket, and shoes of lilac flowered cotton. A few white blossoms adorned the back of her beautiful, long, curly, blonde hair, and she carried a white shoulder bag. The groom was dressed simply in a black suit and no tie. As we entered the church, a choir of young people were singing to the accompaniment of a guitar. The church was very modern, bare except for a huge cross hanging over the main altar and a huge brown Madonna and child suspended over the left side of the altar. The service was to begin at 4:30. At five p.m. the bride and groom, hand in hand, rushed down the aisle, unaccompanied. Both bride and groom read from the Scriptures. Each member of the choir took turns reading the invocations to which the congregation responded, *Ascoltaci, o Signore.*

There were scores of lively little children, all beautifully dressed, ranging from infants, being breast-fed, to toddlers and young children running about, including the bride's one and one-half year old daughter in the arms of a friend. After the exchange of rings, a loud hosanna rang through the church. There were no traditional wedding marches. The Canto finale was the English song "This Little Light of Mine." I had never before been present at such a casual but interesting marriage service.

Since it was my first visit to Parma, Vilma and Giovanni drove me around the Po countryside, stopping in town after town, each proudly showing its ancient origins. The Grillis' knowledge of the cultural and historical past of this region astounded me. But the town I loved best was Mantua probably because I knew the name from Shakespeare's *The Merchant of Venice.* Mantua's history goes back to remote antiquity. It was an Etruscan town and later at the end of the third century B.C., Roman. Vilma and I licked a *gelato* in the Square of Broletto while we gazed at a thirteenth century statue of Virgil that sat in a niche of a wall of a building in front of us.

We stopped at the house of Rigoletto, where a statue to him stands in the garden, and I heard the melody of the famous aria *La Donna e mobile* (Woman is fickle) from Verdi's opera of intrigue, treachery and revenge, which my father used to sing so lustily in his wonderful tenor voice. I saw the outdoor cage at the Ducal Palace where prisoners had to sit, buffeted by the broiling sun of summer and the freezing cold of winter. But the jewel of our visit was hearing Mozart's *Divertimento in D* in the Academic Theatre. Its five tiers of balconies and wondrous ceiling appealed to me more than Milan's La Scala.

From Parma I took the train for the one hour ride to Bologna where Professor Rizzardi from the University of Bologna met me. Since 1979, when he helped found the Italian Association for Canadian Studies, the association has flourished, and more and more Italian scholars have become deeply committed. In a seminar entitled, "The Evolution of a Canadian Immigrant Woman in Canadian Society and Culture," Rizzardi's graduate students presented papers on Mazo de la Roche, Sara Jeannette Duncan, Emily Carr, Joy Kogawa and Margaret Lawrence. At another seminar, entitled *Terra Madre L'immaginario letterario e artistico della donna in Canada*, Barry Callaghan spoke on "The Shift from Male to Female Narrative Voice in Canadian Fiction," and his wife, the sculptor, Claire Wicks Weissman, showed slides of her drawings in a talk entitled "The Narrative Voices of Pain and Pleasures between Nudes." Carla Comellini read her paper *Ritratto di donna di Margaret Lawrence* and I discussed *Breaking the Mould.*

I was happy to be reunited with Carla Comellini, whom I remembered because of her work on the nineteenth century Canadian writer, Isabella Valancy Crawford, and because of her gracious hospitality which she had extended to me during my 1987 visit to Bologna. This time she took me on a walking tour of Bologna's historic centre. "Next to Venice," she told me, "Bologna has the best preserved historic centre in Europe. From the second half of the thirteenth century until 1859 it was the second most important town after Rome belonging to the Papal States." I noted a street called San Petronio Vecchio and commented, "Perhaps he's a distant relative of mine." "Could be," she replied, and she then proceeded to tell me that San Petronio was the patron saint of Bologna, a politician saint and bishop beloved by the city's inhabitants because of the civic work he carried out in the fifth century when barbarians were threatening and ruinous floods had devastated Bologna.

San Petronio's fourteenth century church (one of Italy's most superb Gothic structures and much admired by Michelangelo) symbolized local power; whereas the Cathedral of St. Peter, the Saint of Rome, represented the central power. Hence, St. Peter's had to be built longer than Petronio.

Michelangelo's Pietà in Rome had always been one of my favourite statues. But here in San Petronio I found it difficult to leave a terra cotta sculpture of another Pietà, "The Mourning of the dead Christ" with Joseph of Arimathea, John the Evangelist, the Blessed Virgin Mary and the three Mary's, including Mary Magdalen, gazing grief-stricken on the dead Christ resting so peacefully on a cushion, a gaping wound on his left breast.

Carla also took me to a launching of a book about London at the time of the Beatles. Bologna's litterati were there sipping champagne. I met an Englishwoman who had visited Bologna in the 1930s, fell in love with an Italian who, a few months after their marriage, became Mayor of Bologna. She was decrying the changes in the city's social life that had taken place in the past sixty years.

Bologna boasted hundreds of churches, monasteries, convents, and seminaries. In the nineteenth century many monasteries were converted into military barracks, schools, cemeteries, hospitals and prisons in what were called Napoleonic transformations. Professor Rizzardi booked me at the Erasmus, a hotel for visiting university professors that once had been a Jesuit motherhouse. Founded in 1088, the University of Bologna is the oldest university in the world, proudly counting Dante and Petrarch among its early scholars.

I could not count the number of churches I visited. Some just a few yards apart. All were adorned with calla lilies. In one, an American tourist told me how much he was impressed by the piety of Bolognese students because so many were lighting candles. I responded: "It's exam time and they're probably seeking divine help."

On 22 May, I had seen many women carrying bouquets of long stemmed roses to churches. Sabina's grandmother told me that it was the feast day of St. Rita of Cascia and the women were taking the roses to church to be blessed. An old tradition associates Rita with roses. Shortly before her death, she asked a friend to bring her a rose from her garden. It was not the season for roses to bloom, but to please the nun who was desperately ill, the friend went to her garden and was amazed to find a rose bush in full bloom.

Professor Rizzardi hosted an exquisite *pranzo* at his home and invited the Callaghans, Professor Carla Comellini and myself. His wife, Gabriella, whom he had first met in a bomb shelter during the War, was a perfect hostess and cook. I wrote in my diary that their condo was a "dream in white." There were even white gardenia plants. Before dinner we were served hot canapés and champagne. A Filipino girl served the meal on large platters: tortellini in broth; then pasta asciutta; tagliatelli in a mushroom, ham and pea sauce; roast beef sliced very thin; asparagus; stuffed tomatoes, a simply delectable chocolate torrone, a fruit torte; red and white wine, and grappa.

Italian railroad stations are a nightmare. My mammoth suitcase had become an albatross because distances were so long and there were so many flights of stairs to negotiate. I was thankful that this was not the case in Venice. The train stopped right on the station platform. I couldn't see anyone meeting me. And so I just walked to the baggage checkroom to store my albatross when I noticed a woman carrying a sign with my name on it. We walked to the Hotel Tivoli where I was booked. She left, having shown me on a map how to get to the Palazzo Zorzi, where I was to lecture that afternoon at three p.m. After I got myself settled, I made my way to the Vaporetto at San Toma Station on the Grand Canal, went six stops, got off at San Zaccoria, and then walked to the Palazzo.

In the lobby of the Palazzo, I noticed a poster announcing my lecture. But I had to climb several long flights of stairs to get to the right *aula* (classroom). Students soon began filtering in and I visited with them. I was amazed at the number of papers they were writing on different aspects of Native Canadian Studies from Native music and dance to philosophy. I was happy to find a chalkboard in the room because I always like to write key words.

After my lecture, a number of us walked to the Goldoni Book Store where Margaret Atwood was scheduled to sign her new Italian translation of *Alias Grace.*

Leon and Connie Rooke, Barry and Claire Callaghan as well as a large number of Italian-Canadianists were milling about waiting for the program to begin. The book shop was fiercely hot and crowded. Rosamaria

Plevano, who was working on a thesis on the Italian/Canadian poet, Antonino Mazza, suggested a stroll around Venice. She led me in and out of narrow passageways, up and down stone steps, across arched foot bridges, along streets looking more like alleys and called *calles,* and into empty spaces called *campas.* It was incredible. She told me that the canals were now clear of trash. But I was not interested in the water. The Grand Canal no longer fascinated me.

Never before had I realized that one could walk so far, so long, in this city of water. We walked into churches, each more crowded with art treasures than the other. We walked to the ruins of Teatro La Fenice (1790), which burnt in 1996. I asked Rosamaria how that could have happened with so much water around. She explained that the Canal was dry because it was being cleaned, and that the firemen had arrived late. Her mother had received wires of condolence from her many friends around the world when La Fenice burned.

I also took time to recall Shakespeare's *The Merchant of Venice* and *Othello*, and to appreciate Venice at the peak of her glorious past when, as a powerful maritime city republic, she had revelled in the splendour of her paintings, sculptures and architecture, and had stood firm against the Turks as a bastion of Christianity.

In Piazza San Marco, "the most beautiful drawing room in Europe," according to Napoleon, I noticed many more pigeons than I had remembered. Rosamaria told me that no matter what has been tried to get rid of them, nothing has worked. I also noticed more Japanese tourists than Americans. But musicians were still playing their nostalgic pieces at tea time in the cafés of St. Mark's Square, and the winged lions of St. Mark were still perched on their graceful high columns.

That night I was invited to a buffet supper at the Rooke's spacious apartment which they had rented for a month. It was a wonderful evening. I enjoyed my discussions with Atwood, Graeme Gibson, Branko Gorjup and the Rookes. The buffet, a combination of Italian and American dishes, was delicious: a variety of cold cuts, cheeses, breads, asparagus, tomatoes with basil and mozzarella cheese, potato salad, olives, tossed arugula, slices of apples and pears, champagne and wines. I had to leave early because Francesca, who was going to walk with me, part way to my hotel, had to get home. Connie Rooke was so thoughtful that when she noticed I would be cold once I got outside, she gave me her overcoat to wear. Francesca left me at some distance from my hotel. A surge of fear gripped me, but I draw strength from fear, and so I briskly walked back to the Tivoli on dimly lit narrow lanes that twisted and turned.

The next day, we picked up Atwood at the Hotel Sofital on the Grand Canal on the way to Palafenice to see Donizetti's *Lucia di Lammermoor*. The opera was staged in a huge comfortable outdoor tent which reminded me of the time I saw Stratford's first productions in a huge tent. Luciana Serra, who was about sixty years old, sang *Lucia* superbly. After all, opera is the willing suspension of disbelief. I remembered seeing Joan Sutherland, who was also around sixty at the time, when she sang *Lucia* at the Sydney Opera House in Australia in 1980. I marvelled at Atwood's knowledge of music. She told me that she had sung in her high school choir, and she sang a few of her favourite arias in the vaporetto .

In Vicenza, I was invited to stay at the home of Carla Pezzini Plevano. The villa, a former palace, had been heavily bombed during the war. Carla's father bought the one and one-half acres of land and an architect

designed the beautiful and spacious villa which incorporated walls of the ruined palace. The grounds were a
green paradise with tall trees: chestnut, poplar, acacia,
linden, pines, fir, Japanese willow, magnolia, weeping
willow, plum, apricot, cherry and apple. Rose bushes
lined the pathways.

Carla's ninety-two year old mother had her own
apartment in the villa. She had written a book about her
husband, a medical doctor who was a partisan during
World War II entitled *Il Capitano Mario* (Vicenza,
1994). She was sorting out old photographs at her desk
when we visited her. "We used to have parties for
twenty-five," she told me. "Now nobody comes here
anymore," she sighed as she took me through the elegant
library, parlour, and drawing room.

One afternoon, Carla and I climbed up a steep hill
near her villa to Monte Berico where, in the fifteenth
century, the Blessed Virgin Mary appeared to a farm girl
and told her that if a church were built in her honour,
the Black Plague that was raging would end. A Mass of
Thanksgiving was in progress in the Basilica of Monte
Berico with about seventy first communicants — girls, in
long white dresses and veils, and boys, in long white
robes. In one of the rooms of the Basilica we admired
Veronese's masterpiece, "The Banquet of San Gregorio
Magno," that lit up when we inserted a 3000 lire coin.

Vicenza presented a Renaissance look created
chiefly by Andrea Palladio. I had never heard of Palladio,
but I was told that he had influenced Indigo Jones in
England and Thomas Jefferson, who built his Mon-
ticello in the neo-classical Palladian style. Palladio's
beautiful Rotunda became the model for hundreds of
classical villas in France, England and America. But the
building that impressed me most was the classic elegance

of the Teatro Olimpico, designed by Palladio in 1580, the first covered theatre of modern times with a back-drop depicting a street scene in Thebes. It wasn't so much the theatre itself that impressed me, it was the fact that debates known as "the intellectual Olympics" took place there.

Casa Pigafetta also interested me, not because of a message carved in large letters on the outside wall: "There is no rose without a thorn," but because it had belonged to Antonio Pigafetta, who had sailed with Magellan around the world.

In Vicenza, I participated in a panel, "Canadian Writers in Conversation," along with Barry Callaghan, and Constance and Leon Rooke with moderator, Branko Gorjup. We all attended the launching of the Italian translation of Atwood's *Alias Grace*. Atwood is very popular in Italy — a celebrity. There were flash-bulbs, TV cameras and people milling about her, all anxious to say a word to her. Italian newspapers her-alded her arrival wherever she went. After the launching, Carla Pezzini Plevano hosted a buffet dinner in Atwood's honour, serving hot canapés and cham-pagne on her terrace overlooking Vicenza, and then, inside the villa, pasta and fagioli, turkey, meat loaf, ricotta, tossed salads, strawberry mousse, and wines.

I hated to leave Vicenza, because the Plevanos had been such generous hosts and Rosamaria such a wonder-ful companion. But I still had to go back to Rome and then Calabria. Rosamaria drove me to Padua where I had to catch my train. I had made pilgrimages to Padua several times but I always found the Basilica of St. Anthony so dark and cluttered that the last time I was there in 1987, along with Rita Ubriaco and Beatrice Calendino, we decided to visit the 650 year old Scrovogeni Chapel, a small Gothic church on the site of an ancient Roman amphitheatre, to view the earliest preserved frescoes by Giotto and his pupils. Painted some time between 1032 and 1306 the celebrated panels tell the history of the Redemption in thirty-four episodes from the Birth of Mary to the Last Judgment. Once again, there was no time to visit the Basilica. There was only enough time for a lunch near the railroad station. My mouth watered, when I noticed on the restaurant menu, my favourite Italian dish — gnocchi in tomato sauce. Not even peppering the dish with Parmesan cheese could camouflage the horrid taste of the sauce. It was the first terrible meal I had ever had in Italy.

Rome, 1997

My lecture tour of nine universities was over. Travelling from city to city had been exhausting because the Apeninne mountain ranges prevent east-west travel. As a result, I was forever changing trains and retracing my steps. Nevertheless, as in 1987, I had thoroughly enjoyed my lecture tour. I had delighted in the enthusiasm of the students and the generous hospitality of Italian academics and members of the Canadian Embassy in Rome: Marc Cousineau, Counsellor of Canada's Cultural Affairs, Nicoletta Barberito and Pauline Cadieux. I decided to wait in Rome for a week until Atwood's book launching on 3 June.

I was back in my favourite city. There were more tourists than I had ever seen before. As Nicoletta explained: "they are now coming in busloads from Eastern Europe." Nicoletta was helpful, a godsend. A beautiful woman with large expressive blue eyes, she spoke perfect English without a trace of an accent. With a Ph.D.

from Yale, she was intelligent and fun to be with. She took me to places I had never visited: the catacombs of San Agnese, where Nicoletta drew my attention to an ancient inscription of a loving husband which read "To my intelligent devoted wife" to the Church of Santa Costanza; the huge estate on Via Nomentina which Prince Giovanni Torlonia gave to Mussolini and his family. It was abandoned, but it was here that Mussolini had kept his young lions and eagle, and where his wife had tended her vegetable gardens and raised chickens. We were invited several times to the Palazzo dei Delfini, the home of Marc Cousineau, once, to a cocktail party honouring the Haida sculptor Jim Hart. Here, I met Max Ciferri, Pauline Cadieux's husband who had gone to university with Gavin Freitag of Thunder Bay. Pauline, who had been Pierre Trudeau's babysitter for two years told me some wonderful anecdotes about Shirley MacLaine's visits to Harrington Lake.

On 3 June, Nicoletta and I picked up Atwood and her husband Graeme Gibson at the Hotel Pantheon and then we walked to the Palazzo Canonici Mattei where the *Istituto della Enciclopedia Italiana con il patrocinio della Ambasciata del Canada* sponsored a reading and a reception in Atwood's honour. Vincenzo Cappelletti, the chairman, was most courtly in his introductory remarks, telling Atwood that she was better looking in person than her photographs portrayed her. I marvelled at the way Atwood fielded questions from the large audience.

My lecture tour had been successful, but then my professional life has always been a fount of security. I still had to tear away the shackles that were entrapping me on the deepest, most personal level. I did not know that they would be torn away so soon.

Since my first visit to Calabria in the summer of 1952 had been rushed, I determined this time to stay two weeks to give myself enough time to meet the Calabrese cousins I had never met before. My cousin, Leonardo Petrone, son of Alfonso, my father's youngest brother, invited me to stay at his home in Carolei a few miles away from Cosenza. I shall never forget his *gentilezza* and *cortesia*.

A widower, Leonardo lived in a modern stucco villa, kitty corner to a Capuchin monastery which had stood there for centuries. Set on a high hill, the villa was fenced, gated and guarded by Russ, a German Shepherd. His only child, Alfonso, lived with him and commuted each day to his law practice in Cosenza. Rosina, his cleaning woman, was washing the marble floors when I arrived.

During World War II, Leonardo had been captured in Sicily by the Americans. When Italy capitulated in 1943, he was sent to England where he spent three years. Because he spoke a little English — he had studied in England as a young boy — he was employed as an interpreter and given certain privileges. He was *finanzata* to Genna, the daughter of an English Major who was connected to the English Raj. He had little money and Genna would slip some money for a show or theatre ticket into his breast pocket. "Italian prisoners of war were very well treated in England," he told me. He had become a lover of everything English and bought only English cars. In 1997 he was driving an English Rover.

Prisoner of war stories fascinated me so much that I invariably insisted on details. On the train from Turin to Parma I sat next to an elderly man who had been captured by the Americans in Sicily and sent to the States as a prisoner-of-war. He was well-treated, he told me, even paid one dollar a day for working in a factory. But he didn't like American food: "Can you imagine, the Americans put milk in their tossed salads? After we Italians complained about this, we were served *pasta ascuitta*. Thank God!"

Leonardo's remarkable garden was his pride and joy: six apple trees of three varieties, four plum, several cherry and apricot, peach, olive, walnut, hazelnut, gooseberry, two persimmon, two pomegranate; a vine-yard of red and white grapes; rose bushes, bred for perfection and fragrance, blood red, pink, yellow, white and lavender; rows and rows of strawberries; and broad beans ready to be harvested. I marvelled at the fertility of the soil and the abundance of the harvest. His food cellar, too, was bountiful: huge vats of oil, cases of mineral water, sacks of apples, potatoes, onions, garlic and cans of olive oil.

Leonardo's mountain road, lined with shrubs of yellow-broom, descended sharply into a rough, stony and neglected path unfit for motor traffic. But the vista from its heights took my breath away. I would stand spellbound before the rural landscape, absorbing the beauty into myself until I could contain no more: soft, wooded, green, hills; richly cultivated fields dotted with round gold-yellow haystacks (some, covered with green plastic); distant mountain peaks; a medieval tower here and there; and ruins of castles jagged against the skyline.

I reflected on a line from Gerard Manley Hopkin's "God's Grandeur" "the world is charged with the grandeur of God." I sniffed the delicious aroma of freshly baked bread which was emanating from a small bakery next door to Leonardo's. My mouth watered. I plucked a marguerite. At the bottom of the trail an abandoned stone church which Leonardo told me was called the Madonna delle Stelle, to which the faithful made a pilgrimage once a year, caught my interest.

My relatives, children of my father's brothers and sisters who never left the land of their birth were all dead, but they had left many children. They were scattered throughout a number of small mountain towns of stone that dotted the Calabrian countryside: Casabona, Aprigliano, Rocca di Neto, Crotone, Cutro, Cetraro, and San Giovanni in Fiore.

These towns of stone are largely self-contained, self-governing and urban in character, each with its own *municipio* and town square. They are called *paese*, a word that means country, because the town was, in fact, the peasant's world, his country. Each *paese* possessed some features which made it unique, different from all other neighbouring towns, such as a shrine, or medieval tower. There were few green spaces to break the monotony of stone houses and stone steps. But flowers — geraniums, hibiscus, oleander, poppies, bougainvillea — bloomed everywhere — in large pots, window boxes, crannies, and along walls.

My relatives are mountain people: robust, energetic, hard working, strong. Their homes had large rooms with solid functional furniture and all the modern conveniences: freezers, microwave ovens, automatic washers and dryers, television sets and refrigerators. But the room that surprised me most was always the lavish bathroom. During my 1952 trip there had been no flush toilets. Now there were ultra modern toilets with matching coloured fixtures.

Leonardo put himself completely at my disposal for the two weeks I was staying in Calabria. Host, chauffeur, and fount of family lore, he was always accommodating. He was a skilful driver, negotiating his Rover on the steep and narrow stone alleys, lined with parked cars facing both directions, that dip and rise and turn sharply. I don't know how many times I held my breath and closed my eyes, refusing to watch his manoeuvring. Of all the sights he showed me, three remain locked in memory: the high and broad Sila plateau which I remember my mother describing, in rhapsodic tones, as a place of spectacular beauty where as a little boy, my father took the family's flocks of sheep to pasture. We drove under immaculate blue skies into an idyllic Alpine region through magnificent forests of birch, elm, oak, chestnut, fir and pine, jade-coloured mountain lakes and jagged mountain peaks. And I breathed the sharp Sila air.

Only a single towering Doric column, called Capo Colonna, remains of the first medical school in the world in Crotone. It left me spellbound as I pondered on past epochs and the erosion of time. Leonardo quoted Vico: "at the time when Rome was a shepherd's village, Pythagoras was teaching in Crotone."

If, at Delphi, I could not tear myself away from the charioteer, here, too, in the National Museum of Archeology at Reggio, Calabria, I stood breathless before two nude ancient warriors, standing more than six feet tall, with full beards, sensuous lips, the flowing hair of one tied with a broad ribbon, while the other wore an Attic helmet. I noted every beautiful feature. They are known to the world as *I bronzi di Riace*, two bronze statues discovered in 1972 in the Ionian Sea off the Calabrian coast near the town of Riace Marina where they had been for centuries.

On the first night of my arrival, Leonardo had cooked, among other courses, fave (broad beans). I was skeptical because fave are one of two vegetables I don't like. But I didn't want to repeat the fresh fig episode of over forty years earlier. I tasted the fave. To my surprise, I liked the way he had cooked them. Leonardo even ate them raw for dessert. I just couldn't go that far. I had some wonderful cantaloupe instead.

He told me that when his family entertained guests who didn't eat much, his father trotted out his refrain: *Grazie l'economia portato in casa mia* (Thank you for the savings which you have made in my home). And so each time I declined food, he would repeat his father's refrain.

The main pleasure of the Calabrese must be gastronomic. The beautiful word *pranzo* is the word for dinner. Food is talked about, looked forward to, and prepared with great care. Preparation is a social event. Every meal was a banquet. Not to eat well is equated with not eating a lot. Time after time I pleaded for smaller portions and fewer courses. I couldn't count the times when I would arrive to find my cousins making fresh pasta, cutting it into different shapes, ribbons, tagliatelli, covatelli or fusilli. Their tables overflowed with the sun-kissed flavours of the South, so unlike the bland monotonous flavours of store-bought fruit and vegetables at home. The variety and abundance of each course was mind-boggling. Prosciuto, mortadella cheese, artichoke hearts, olives, wild mushrooms, truffles, and peppers for appetizers and roast beef, lamb chops, roast kid, veal, chicken, sausages, and roast suckling pig for the main meat courses.

Fruit and vegetables tasted so much better in these sun-drenched lands. I had always been an indifferent eater, but here I actually loved the taste of the garden fresh vegetables: potatoes, zucchini, broccoli, eggplant, peas, beans, tomatoes, swiss chard, spinach, different varieties of lettuce, radicchio, and endive. And the vine-ripened fruit was wonderful: watermelon, peaches, apricots, cantaloupe, strawberries, cherries and grapes. I also remember enjoying the cookies and the cakes which Maria Pia, Natalina's daughter had baked. She had a reputation for "baking the best American cakes."

In Casabona I stayed three nights with Eugenia, Leonardo's sister, who had the bluest eyes. Eugenia distributed holy communion to shut-ins, and her deacon husband, Gigi, did volunteer work for the Bishop at Cotrone. Eugenia made several *pitta imbigliata*, my favourite Christmas pastry, for me to take home to Canada. I was so pleased. I also had an exquisite dinner with Antonio, Eugenia's brother, who had left the Jesuit seminary after he had studied for the priesthood for eight years.

On the weekend of June 7 Casabona was celebrating the *Festa di San Francesco di Paola*. As we walked from Eugenia's home to the main square, Eugenia stopped to talk to the old women who were sitting on rush stools and folding chairs outside their houses chatting and gossiping, watching the crowds go by. I found it amazing that the town, with a population of only 3,000, was so beautifully decorated with an elaborate network of white and green electric lights illuminating its centre. In the main cobbled square, so full of light, a local rock band was playing, and vendors were selling the stuff of daily living: panty hose, kitchenware, cigarettes, purses, watches, jewellery, shoes, everything from ice cream to car parts. Although the large throngs of young and old people as well as small children and babies in arms joyously participated in the festive mood that permeated the balmy air, I saw no rowdiness.

Gun shots heralding the *festa* woke me up on Sunday morning. Eugenia and I walked to the Church of San Nicola Bishop where the procession to the sanctuary of San Francesco di Paulo, a distance of three kilometres, was to begin. When the statue of St. Francesco appeared at the entrance of the church, there was loud applause and the town band started to play. Eugenia and I joined the procession on foot behind the statue. As it wound up and down the hills of Casabona to the sanctuary built on top of a high hill, I kept admiring the large and beautiful bedspreads that hung as decoration from the windows or balconies. Along the route we recited the rosary between musical selections from the walking band. Inside the packed sanctuary, I noticed a woman who had walked all the way in her bare feet. At the end of the service, when the statue of St. Francesco appeared at the front of the church door, there was another burst of applause. Luckily, we didn't have to walk back because Eugenia's husband picked us up in his car.

That night, from Rita Torchia's balcony (she is the daughter of Angelina, my father's sister), I witnessed the most spectacular fireworks I have ever seen. Rita was a statuesque woman who exuded serenity and dignity. Her father died when she was twelve, and she sewed and embroidered to support her mother and siblings. Her three children are doctors. One is a dentist, another a chiropractor, and another an oncologist doing breast cancer research in Rome.

I was taken to the grave sites of deceased relatives. Narrow passageways wove in and out of the rows of boxes stacked one on top of the another above ground. I gazed lovingly at the photographs in waterproof plastic ovals that adorned the marble slabs that sealed the boxes. I recognized only one, that of Zia Marietta, the Aunt I had met forty-five years earlier, who died of breast cancer.

A number of my Petrone relatives lived in farmhouses in the rural countryside. Since World War II, as part of an agrarian reform, the Italian government had been buying huge estates, dividing them and selling them to the people of the region. As a result, my relatives now own large plots of land, rear animals, and among other crops, grow oranges, lemons, grapes, olives, and grain.

Tutti stano bene, was the stock refrain. They expressed no interest in coming to America. Times had changed drastically since my father was lured to America's shores in 1912 when *la miseria* was the norm of life in Calabria, and every family's Columbus a hero. I, myself, saw a dramatic change since my first visit in 1952, when Calabria was still a poverty-stricken land. Now, forty-five years later, I was surprised to find so much comfort, prosperity, and even luxury. In the mountain town of Aprigliano, my relatives had a Yamaha baby grand piano as well as an upright grand, a computerized keyboard, and cellular phones. When I arrived, one of the children was playing the clarinet. In Cutro, Elvira's husband owned a huge factory which made pasta for dogs. Elvira and her husband built a huge apartment building in which each of their children had a beautifully appointed apartment in marble, ceramic tile, and the most modern furniture. This was not the Calabria I had first seen in 1952.

Leonardo's sister, Natalina, and I had been exchanging Christmas cards for years although I had never met her. Her energy, humour and warmth endeared her to me. She had married another cousin, Cicco, who had been left a widower with two daughters. Natalina inherited land from her father and along with Cicco's holdings, they had become successful farmers. Another cousin owned a wonderful orchard. His orange groves hung heavily with ripe fruit. He invited me to climb a tree and pluck a *partoghese*, as he called the blood-red oranges.

I also met a cousin called Serafina. I had never met anyone by that name before. It felt strange. Suddenly I felt less alone in the world. I was to meet many Serafinas in Calabria. And I began to appreciate the beauty of my name, and its etymology, its roots in the word Seraphim, the most elevated order of angels. Serafina was dressed in black because her sister Rita had died of breast cancer several years before and her son had died the previous year from cancer, a few months after he had graduated as a medical doctor. But she had a deep faith which enabled her to accept her "lot in life." At Cetraro-on-the-sea, we visited Yolanda, and I met another cousin called Serafina who, to my disappointment, died a year ago in her sleep. Yolanda was the tallest of the Petrone women. "And what gracious women they are," I wrote in my diary. They were making *tagliatelle* when we arrived. We dined on a sumptuous feast of roast beef, fish, sausages, beans and zucchini, tomatoes, and the tagtiatelle. For dessert, I tasted a wonderful macedonia of strawberries. Yolanda's daughter, Lauredania and I walked through the old historic town centre of Cetraro and entered a church where the Sacred Heart with open arms greeted me. I felt right at home. Serafina rented an apartment next door to Yolanda. She confided to me that she had married a railroad man with six children. "But he left me a *signora*," she said, and added proudly: "I will never have to wash dishes for my livelihood." Serafina kept our Zia Marietta's picture on her mantelpiece and told me that all her life Marietta had worked hard for her brothers. When I asked for more Petrone stories she told me that Marietta had bought a cassetta next door in Casabona. Because a German had been killed there during Word War II, she was able to buy it at a discounted price, but she died seven months later.

Serafina was raised in a region with an implicit history of caution, especially in relation to safeguarding family secrets, and so I appreciated her willingness to reveal family stories. She told me of the Petrone love for music and dance and coffee. She told me stories about our grandmother Serafina, about her daring and courage, and about her deep and abiding faith. She recounted the details of her death on 14 September 1944:

> All her life she was devoted to the Sacred Heart [I was not aware of this, but I am too]. She never missed going to Communion on the first Friday of every month in honour of the Sacred Heart. On her deathbed she had one favour only to ask of Him, knowledge of whether her son Giovanni had returned from the War, dead or alive. When she received a letter from him saying that he had survived the war she promptly thanked the Sacred Heart and said, My mission is ended." She turned on her side and drew her last breath. She was eighty-three years old.

I was beginning to feel proud in having been named after my grandmother. Eugenia told me an interesting anecdote about her father: "Dad had so much paper strewn about his studio — he even wrote down every time we kids were naughty — that we called him *caccacarte* (literally translated as shitting paper)."

Besides my Petrone cousins, I also met the Mauros, cousins on my mother's side who are scattered among the mountain towns of Calabria: Piane Crati, Figline and Rogliano. Three cousins are young intense and energetic school teachers who impressed me greatly. They extended the same courteous hospitality and spectacular feasts the Petrones had. I remember Maria Grazia, who speaks flawless English, taking me to the thirteenth century Duomo in Cosenza, to view the elaborate tomb of Isabel of Aragon, Queen of France who died in 1271 from a fall from her horse when she was six months pregnant. We also visited the Chiesa di San Giuseppe in Rogliano which has been converted into a museum of sacred artifacts. Gazing at beautifully ornate old vestments, gold chalices and monstrances, and priceless works of religious art made me feel at home.

I noticed that the Petrone and Mauro women, all southern Italian, were not stereotypical, "merely submissive" wives. Nor did they conform to the cliché of the highly emotional southern Italian peasant woman. They were cordial and intelligent. They were philosophical; they spoke in proverbs and in the idiom of their faith. They interpreted dreams. They reminded me of my mother. A combination of earthiness and spirituality, they exuded a restrained joy, in striking contrast to the dour and pessimistic outlook I remembered from my visit to Calabria in 1952. And yet vestiges of ancient superstitions still remained. Immediately after the ceremony in Piane Crati which made me an Honourary Citizen, I became ill and bed-bound in my hotel. A cousin and her husband visited me. She said that I was *affashinata*. I had been bewitched. I knew all about the *affascino*, the spell which a jealous person casts upon another. She asked me to give her a charm, anything that would counter it. I gave her husband a Canadian pen.

I revelled in the company of my relatives. I enjoyed being connected to family, to a past, to a culture, to roots. They were my kinfolk. It was strange hearing myself called Serafina. But I didn't seem to mind. It was a good feeling. I belonged.

Not only was I beginning to accept my name, but I was also becoming enamoured of southern Italy, a region maligned by the North as backward and primitive. There is even a political party whose mandate it is to separate from the South. Southerners even today have great difficulty finding accommodation in Turin. At home, too, wasn't Italianness associated with loudness and vulgarity? But I found respect and decorum, remarkable dignity and great courtesy everywhere. As well as the legacies of a 2500 year history: medieval castles and monasteries, ancient ruins, magnificent architecture, and important religious shrines. And even great art in obscure churches and museums. The past was everywhere, but the present possessed a vitality I had not seen in my first visit in 1952. This time I noticed new bridges and new roads, new industrial plants, hotels, and housing developments.

But it was the ceremony, sponsored by the *Amministrazione Communale di Piane Crati* in collaboration with the Università della Calabria which made me an honourary citizen of Piane Crati, my mother's birthplace in Calabria, that made me less ambivalent about my Italian identity and enabled me to accept the reality of my being Italian. The modern University of Calabria, an Italian rarity located in Rende, a suburb of Cosenza was

founded in the 1960s. It is the intellectual centre of
Calabria and intensely interested, through the efforts of
Professor Cesare Pitto, in Southern Italian emigration to
America.

I had boarded the train for Calabria in Rome. But at
a station near the outskirts of Naples it stopped for no
apparent reason. Rumours began circulating that Italy's
crack train had broken down inside the tunnel in front
of us. Passengers started jumping off. I didn't know what
to do. Nobody could help me. I decided to stay on the
train. Finally, after a delay of three hours, the train
started to move. We arrived in the coastal town of Paola
at 18:00 hours.

Professor Cesare Pitto of the University of Calabria,
and Dr. Walter Temelini from the University of Windsor,
who was lecturing at Calabria at the time, were waiting
for me. But we still had to drive twenty-two miles
northwest to Cosenza. Cold, fog and rain made the drive
from Paola to Cosenza dangerous.

We arrived at the Sala Consiliare di Piane Crati at
eight p.m., two hours late. A hundred people were
waiting for us on the wide steps. Cheers, reporters,
flashbulbs and T.V. cameras from RAI, Italy's national
T.V. network, and from the University of Calabria
greeted us. A little girl who had stayed outside for fear
of missing me, presented me with a huge bouquet of
flowers. I was overwhelmed.

Inside the *municipio* there was another large bouquet of flowers wrapped in cellophane. The head table
was lined with dignitaries. People were standing against
walls in the crowded room. Everyone rose when I entered. I was overcome with emotion. Professor
Francesca Citrigno presided. There were speeches from
Michele Scornaienchi, the Mayor of Piane Crati, from

mayors of neighbouring towns, university professors and government officials, both regional and provincial. The Mayor of Piane Crati presented me with a parchment declaring I was an honourary citizen of Piane Crati. He gave me gifts of books. The young local priest gave me a statue of St. Barbara who is the patron saint of Piane Crati. Telegrams from invited guests who could not be present were read. Then Professor Cesare Pitto introduced me. The room was suddenly quiet. I rose, deeply touched by the tributes and the outpouring of love around me. I was choked up and struggled to keep back tears. I read my prepared address in halting Italian. The entire room rose as one body, clapping and cheering. Relatives started to introduce themselves. I did not know how I was related to them. It didn't matter. They were Petrones from Aprighano, my father's home town, a few kilometres away from my mother's, who were giving me the gift of their love. And I was happy to give them mine. Embraces!

Citrigno opened the ceremony to the public for questions: "Why did you change your name to Penny? What is the significance of the title of your book, *Breaking the Mould?* Do you consider yourself Italian or Canadian?" I answered in English, thoroughly ashamed of myself because I could not speak Italian fluently. Professor Walter Temelini translated for me. The numerous questions provoked lively discussion. In the end, Flavio Giacomantonio a writer who had translated Shakespeare's *Julius Caesar*, declared that I may have broken the mould but that the mould was whole again with my return to my ancestral roots. "You are like the prodigal son," he said. There was a burst of applause. Never before had I felt so cherished. Never before had so much affection been lavished upon me. Tears welled in my eyes. Right then I was living the greatest moment of my life. They called me Serafina and I did not wince. For the first time in my life, I was proud of my Italian name. My personal odyssey had ended.

My life-long struggle with my name had been exorcised. I am now at peace with myself. Thus has my Italian heritage finally claimed me.

Acknowledgements

I feel I should give a word of explanation regarding my methodology in writing *Embracing Serafina*. "The Road to Now" as well as Chapters 9 to 11 in Part B were written exclusively for this book. The travelogues and essays from Chapters 2 to 8 were originally written for family and friends; the speeches were written and delivered for audiences of the day. They were, however, edited, honed and updated, but in no way were they tampered with as to places, people, personal reactions, reflections and opinions. I also wrote passages throughout the book to provide a determining frame to the narrative as well as thematic coherence. The passages focus on the gradual and growing influence my life of travel had in shaping me into the woman I am today. *Embracing Serafina* is not intended to be a travel guide but a book by a woman who was shaped by one culture and lived in another, a book of self-discovery.

I should like to thank the following people for sharing their memories: Jeanette and Bill Arthurs, Sandra Banducci, Joseph Beckwermert, Rita Bennett Bermell, Elizabeth Brauer, Shirley Matheson Cross, June Knudsen, Ruth Ratz Leblanc, Joan Lockwood, Louisa Napolitano-Carman, Vilma Ricci and Lee Treilhard. I also want to thank Willard Carmean, Joan Hoskinson and Celina Reitberger for reading my journals and encouraging me to continue with my project, as well as Elysia Petrone for her expertese with the Internet and Richard MacGillivray for his useful suggestions.

I am especially indebted to my typist, Colleen Tiboni, for her unfailing patience and good humour. To Lisa Stefaniuk, also, I owe a special debt of gratitude for her valuable criticial comments. For his interest in my manuscript and for his warm support, I am particularly grateful to Antonio D'Alfonso. And to the reference librarians at Lakehead University and Waverley Resource Library, I wish to extend my thanks. And special thanks go to the Senate Research Committee of Lakehead for their financial assistance.

List of Photographs

Printed in December 1999 by

VEILLEUX
ON DEMAND PRINTING INC.

in Longueuil, Quebec